The Myriasphere Origins The Darkness Rises

Daniel Cunningham

Published by Daniel Cunningham, 2022.

This is a work of fiction. Similarities to real people, places, or events are entirely coincidental.

THE MYRIASPHERE ORIGINS THE DARKNESS RISES

First edition. June 10, 2022.

ISBN: 979-8885673662

Written by Daniel Cunningham.

Table of Contents

I am dedicating this book to my mother, who died several years ago due to Cancer. She always encouraged me never to give up and to follow my passions. Even when I joined the Marines, she wasn't happy about thinking of me in a war zone, but she always was the person I could always go-to for anything. I wish she could be here to see my book come to life, and she will always be in my heart.

First Author

ond Author – Editor

Nathan Kurtis Cunningham

Third Author – Editor

Charles Albert Cunningham, MA

I have taken the feathers of two of my most faithful Archangels, and have created both you and your brother. Then I breathed My Breath of Life into both you and into your brother. Malon's purpose is to be my shield for all life that is created or born from my life. Soon the time of constant heavenly enlightenment will end. My faithful Archangels and all my faithful Angels will return to My Golden City. I made you each sleep a deep sleep and have taken your rib to make your wife, and your brother's rib and made his wife. I also breathed My Breath of Life into both of your wives. I have granted you and your brother and your wives very long lives so that you all may learn and grow together in order to defend all of my natural creation. Your brother is to faithfully serve as the High Priest of Malon and his wife as High Priestess. He is to be the first father of the Ignole people. You are to be the first father of the Cundo people and the High King of the planet Malon. Lead all Malon's peoples and creatures with honor and love. Be very fruitful and multiply for all My created Myriasphere depends on your people's knowledge, strength, and faithfulness.

- Last words God said to High King Thureos.

Chapter One
Prince Arthus: The Dream

Breathing heavily, I jolt awake. My blood is boiling. I try and look around, realizing I can only move my eyes. I try to speak, "What's going on?" But, I feel that my heart is pounding and beating against my chest. Again, I try to speak, "Where am I? How did I get here?" I move my eyes in all directions, and I still see nothing. I try and get up, but my muscles still aren't moving. I try to make a sound, any sound, but my throat feels clenched. As I gasp for air, I realize I can see the cloud of my breath, and yet it is very dark. I began to question, is there no one else here? In fact, I don't hear any sounds at all. I can't even smell anything. Why do I feel that there is this cold stone and metal ground beneath me?

I can't even let my mind escape. I've never felt like this before. My eyes are finally adjusting to the darkness. I now see the dark fog-like shadow that shrouds around me. Pushing against this sluggishness with all my energy, I lift my right hand. I manage to wave it, pushing the dark foggy air away from me. My eyes pointed to my right. I think I can see something, or someone there. Wrestling with my neck, I turn my head to get a better view.

There is a massive black translucent obsidian throne, which is trimmed in blackish-green gold and other types of metals. The throne has various skulls, ancient symbols, and various Demonic carvings on it. Sitting on the throne appears to be a large man, who fills the massive throne. He is wearing what looks like a suit of black and blackish-green gold metal armor. The armor is fashioned just like snake scales. There is also a giant multi-hooded snake-like shape-shifting black shadow overlooking the man and the throne. The faceplate of man on the throne's helmet has constant black flames coming out of it. He has dark and black-flamed-eyes. He turns his head and looks straight at me! Suddenly, several shadowy snake-like tails come out from where the man's legs were. The tails all grab and wrap themselves around my arms and legs. Instantly, I am lifted into the air and can feel my limbs being pulled away from each other. As the man stares at me, my silently screaming soul tries to tear itself away from my now writhing body. Just as suddenly, the shadow-like tails disappear and I am dropped down onto my hands and knees. The shadow like tails reappear, but now they are wrapped around my body and squeezing me. The attack now intensifying, I feel like my pupils are bursting out of my head. I start to lose consciousness, as any energy that I had left is now gone. Suddenly, the shadow like tails disappear again.

"Time to show you the future of your planet and people," says the man on the throne in a dark and very raspy deep hissing sounding voice.

Instantly I am back on Malon, standing in front of First God's Tree. It is no longer what it was. The same multi-hooded snake like shape-shifting shadow that I saw above the throne now overshadows the sky. First God's Tree, the main resource of all Life-energy, and fresh air on Malon, is consumed by dark flames. As my gaze circles around, I see everything I ever loved and once knew become just a mix of dust and ash. All the air on Malon is filled with smoke and a very dense dark fog. This thought overtakes my mind: How could the Archangels and my people let this happen?

"Now that you have seen your world, I will show you the fate of all of the universes," reveals the man.

I am suddenly overlooking the vastness of the universes. I watch in horror as dark flames, and the dark fog coming out from the man steadily destroy each and every universe; one after another.

I cry out in despair, "The universes I am supposed to protect are dying, and I can't do anything! I have failed!"

Chapter 2
Ariel Valley

"**W**ake up! Hey, Prince Arthus, you need to get up! Your grandfather, the High King is already ready and waiting for you!" Exclaims Arthus's caregiver.

(His palace caregiver, Sylla is an Ingole female who watches over him while his grandfather is always so busy. She makes sure the he is at all his appointments as well helps him with other task).

"HUH? WAS I ASLEEP? Where am I?" Asks Arthus, while rubbing his eyes and sitting up.

"You are at home. Did you have another nightmare?" His Caregiver, now concerned, asks.

"I must have. Oh, no, am I late waking up again, Sylla?" Arthus quizzes back frantically, looking for the time clock.

"I wouldn't say you are late just yet, but you better get dressed and get ready. Your grandfather wants to leave in fifteen minutes and directly asked me to come to make sure you get ready. I am not about to let the High King down. So get up and get dressed, my Prince." Sylla motions and commands to Arthus.

"Okay, I am up. I'll get ready and meet you in about ten minutes. Then we can go meet with my grandfather," replies Arthus. With that, Sylla leaves the room and walks down the hall where she is to wait on Arthus.

After ten minutes went by, Arthus finished getting ready. He left his bedroom suite and started walking down the hall. As Arthus walks up to where Sylla is standing, he says, "Alright, let's go find my grandfather."

"Oh, he's already grabbed your luggage and is loading up the Golden Griffin as we speak. Let's hurry and get to the Griffin loading dock," replies Sylla.

They start to walk up this grand root-tree looking staircase that twists up three stories. Once both reach the third story, they turn right and walk down the hall. Sylla turns and starts opening a large metal door with a symbol of a Griffin on it. Arthus can already feel the winds blowing as he walks out on the platform and sees his grandfather loading the Golden Griffin with his luggage.

As the two approach his grandfather, Arthus turns toward Sylla and says, "Thank you for waking me up out of that horrible nightmare. I appreciate everything you do for me."

Sylla, smiling, says, "Oh, it's nothing. I like working with you and your Grandfather. I wish I could have woke you up a little sooner. It seems like your grandfather could have used some help loading this luggage."

Arthus turns to his grandfather and asks, "Can I help you with those?"

His grandfather, laughing, responds, "No, it's all good. I can still load a few pieces of luggage behind my own royal hathi howdah, and I even ensured that the tacks were properly secured to all the loading straps of this Golden Griffin. You don't need to worry yourself about this old man!"

The High King turns to Sylla and says, "Thank you for getting Arthus up for me. It would have taken a lot longer, if I tried to do that. He is a stubborn prince to wake up."

Sylla, letting out a laugh, replies, "No thanks needed, my High King. I am here for you and my Prince anytime you need me."

"Okay, well, we will see you later, Sylla. We got a decent flight ahead of us, so we better mount up and take off," says the High King. He turns back to Arthus and tells him, "Make sure to say goodbye, it'll be a while before you see Sylla again."

"Oh, okay, goodbye, Sylla and thanks again!" Exclaims Arthus.

Sylla smiles and says, "Goodbye, Prince Arthus, I'll see you as soon as you are back here again."

With that, Prince Arthus and the High King, his grandfather, mount up into their royal hathi howdah, strapped onto the back of the giant golden-brown bird known as the Golden Griffin and take off into the sky towards Ariel Valley.

It is dawn. The wind outside their royal hathi howdah is blowing healthy and fresh as it whistles and dances around.

Raising his voice just enough to be heard above the sound of the wind, his grandfather says to Arthus, "As Prince of Malon, you need to experience and learn many things in order to understand your duties; especially how to best protect our planet. I am taking you to the head of Clan Ariel, one of the six clans of Malon. They are in charge of all agriculture and the ag-trade on our planet. Named after the Archangel Ariel, who taught them everything they need to know about how to best use our resources without causing any permanent damage to our world. He also taught them how to best hunt, gather, fish and farm, while utilizing the waters, lands, fish, animals, and the trees, without causing the extinction of any one species, or killing off the trees, and without destroying any of the other ecosystems of the planet around them. Thus allowing their clan to live on Malon in perfect harmonic balance with all of life."

At this distance and through the veil of their royal hathi howdah, Arthus can just barely make out Ariel Valley. Soon though, he can see the start of the fields, the ranches, and all of the farmlands that stretch out in front of them, filling the massive valley. As they approach closer, he starts noticing many clansmen out working, which surprises him. Thinking out loud he says, "The morning sun is not even peeking up over the mountains. Yet, here they are, working in the early dawn, just as if it was late in the afternoon."

"We are here!" Arthur's grandfather shouts to him as they swoop down onto an open area by a loading dock attached to large Grey barn.

It was obvious from all the noises and smells coming from inside the barn that it housed many Golden Griffins as well as other domesticated animals, many of which are native to Malon. Arthus sees a large Cundo man with short dark brown hair, chestnut brown eyes, and a full beard that reaches his chest. The large man walks up to his grandfather and immediately hugs him.

"Howdy! Welcome, my High King, to my humble home here in Ariel Valley!" Shouts the deep voice coming from the large man.

The High King shouts back, "Grag, my good friend! It seems like many years since I have seen you. How have you been?"

Smiling, Grag, answers, "It is great to see you, my High King! I have been well! Thanks for asking. How are you doing?"

The High King responds, "I am well. Time has been very generous to me. I am happy to hear that you are doing great as well, Grag."

The High King turns toward Arthus and says, "Grandson, this is the head of Clan Ariel, Grag. He is the one I mentioned that is in charge of agriculture and of course all of the ag-trades on the planet."

Arthus notices a young female Cundo around the same age as himself standing sort of behind and beside Grag. She has blazing red hair and deep green eyes. She seems to be a little shy as she is hiding behind her father. He can't quite make out too many details about her just yet.

"Yes, I see you brought your grandson, Prince Arthus." Grag turning and nodding toward Prince Arthus, declares, "It is good to meet you, Prince."

Prince Arthus nods back and says, "It is good to meet you as well, Grag."

Turning his head looking at Jade, Grag demands, "Jade, don't be shy. Come say howdy to the Prince and the High King."

Jade slightly and shyly walks around the edge her father, bows her head, and timidly says, "Howdy everyone."

High King and Arthus, nodding at the same time, respond, "Hello, Jade." Causing all of them to laugh.

Arthus notices that she is about the same height as himself and half the size of her father.

The High King turns toward Grag and says, "We have come to see how the harvest is going, Grag. I am also hoping to get your help to show my grandson what life is like outside of Harmony City."

"Ah... I see. So how long will you two be staying with us, my High King?" Asks Grag.

"I will only be here until dinner time, but I trust that I can leave Prince Arthus here to stay with you for one full year. I want him to learn everything he can about what life is like as a member of Clan Ariel. I believe a prince should know everything about the world at which he is gifted," declares the High King.

Grag, while looking at the sky and stroking his beard, says, "Ah... I see he's coming of age soon. You know, I do have a small building we can turn into Arthus's quarters for now. While we visit and get into all of that ag-business, here's a great idea: Jade, you go take Prince Arthus on the grand tour of the farming land and then go show him the lands and boarders around Ariel Valley."

With a whiny voice, Jade complains, "Ugh! ...Do I have to, Dad?"

Looking at her questioningly, Grag asks, "Oh... what... do you think Prince Arthus is cute or something?"

Using both her hands to cover the sides of her face, as she stomps her feet in protest, Jade screams, "NO, DAD, OH, HOW EMBARRASING!"

Arthus's face turns a bright red, almost the same color as Jade's hair. Both Grag and the High King burst out laughing.

Grag cuts his laugh short and says, "Get going now! The High King and I have much to discuss."

After Jade spends a couple of hours showing Arthus around the lands of Ariel Valley's farm fields, Jade turns to Arthus and tells him, "Now that I have shown you the main farm lands of the Ariel Valley. I will take you to see the lands and boarders around it."

"Sounds like fun, let's go!" Exclaims Arthus.

"Alright, but we gotta mount on Yaules if we want to cover ground quickly," says Jade.

"What are Yaules?" Arthus asks.

"What do you mean, what are Yaules?" Jade asks, confused.

"I mean, I have heard of rideable animals out here in the valley, but have never seen any," says Arthus.

"Well, that just means you're about to find out first hand!" Exclaims Jade as she grabs Arthus by the arm and just about drags him over to one of the large Grey barns that he noticed earlier in the day. When they reach the barn doors, Jade opens it and takes Arthus inside. Arthus sees a ton of stalls with these massive felines with long greyish-green fur that look almost like the ground inside of the barn.

"I have never seen any creatures that have greyish green fur! They look cool, actually!" exclaims Arthus.

"Yaules fur changes to the environment, similar to a chameleon, it's a defense against other predators," says Jade in a matter of fact tone. She looks at him while shaking her head, and questioningly asks, "Wow, you haven't seen much outside of Harmony City?"

Arthus, shrugging, responds, "No... I have not. I have never spent any time outside of the city."

"Ugh! You are the biggest city dweller I have ever met!" Exclaims Jade as she's laughing at him.

"I happen to have read holobooks and have seen something that resembles these in the holos of the library," says Arthus, trying to sound smart.

Rolling her eyes, Jade says, "I am sure you have." Jade then asks, "What has your oh-so-smart city books told you about them, then?"

"I mean... I had forgot what they were called, but I read something about them. I do remember I read that they live a very long life. I also read that they are one of the most intelligent creatures on our planet," responds Arthus.

"Well, at least you know something about them. Did the holobooks show you how to tame them, ride them, work with them, and how to treat them?" Asks Jade.

"No, they didn't even mention any of those things, just that they were wild felines that are large and predatory in nature," responds Arthus.

Sounding quite upset and stern Jade says, "Ugh!... T. Well, since I don't have time today, or even want to try to give you a crash course in how to ride one properly, you will have to do with riding one with me." Then she looks down and getting red in the face, sighs loudly while shaking her head and thinking aloud, "Dad, making me double-ride with the Prince of Malon, whom I just met... So embarrassing!"

Jade opens up one of the stalls and walks in. The large Yaule leans back as if it invites Jade to mount on its back. She grabs a small brush from a tray attached to the gate of the stall and then walks over and starts to brush the large Yaule with long slow gentle strokes. Jade hums with her voice as she strokes and it seemed as if she did this as a way to thank the feline for its loyalty to her. The Yaule purrs at Jade with each hum and stroke of the brush. After a couple of minutes of her humming and brushing the Yaule, it noticeably starts to relax more.

Jade, while getting on the Yaule and wrapping her hands around two larger fur areas on the back of its neck, looks back at Arthus and commands, "Now, come in here and gently pet the Yaule behind the ears, say hi to it, and then mount up behind me so that we can go on our ride!" With that same stern tone in her voice, she says, "You will just have to wrap your arms around my hips. Um. T."

Arthus did exactly as instructed and carefully climbed on behind Jade; timidly wrapping his arms around Jade's waist. As the Yaule starts moving forward, Arthus can feel the animal's hips and strength of its legs.

As soon as they get out of the barn, Jade says, "Lelelya." Arthus sees her push on the Yaule's fur with both hands. The Yaule speeds up as they travel westward away from the Grey Barns. As the Yaule speeds up, Arthus can feel the wind whistle through his hair and tickle his face and ears. The Yaule starts to leap forward as it grows in speed. Jade looks back toward Arthus and yells, "You have to hold on much tighter, or you will fall off!" He grabs her much tighter and even pulls himself closer to her. Jade shouts, "CAMPE," causing the Yaule to move faster as it leaps forward instead of just running. The leaps are far, and he can feel the strength of the mighty Yaule's legs, even more so now, as it leaping almost 10 feet with each jump. It's very fast in speed, and feels similar to bare-back riding a Golden Griffin, but on the ground. Arthus starts to make out a broad mountain range on the horizon as they come to the end of the valley. Jade yells, "LENCA," causing the Yaule to stop leaping and slow down. Jade says, "Putta," while she pulls back on its fur, causing the Yaule to stop completely. She then points to the mountains, turns to

Arthus, and says, "Those are the Golden Mountains! I love coming out here before the sun comes up because the sunrise turns the peaks gold. Hence the name, Golden Mountains," laughs Jade.

While loosening his tight grip on Jade's waist, Arthus exclaims, "I cannot wait to come back out here to check out this sight!"

"Alright, well let's head north!" Jade exclaims as she grabs the right side fur on the neck of the Yaule. She says, "Lelelya," the Yaule turns to the right to face north and starts to run again. She then yells, "CAMPE!" Arthus had forgot to hold on tight for a second as he gets jerked back, but grabs onto her just in time to not get blown off. Jade starts laughing at this, but her laugh is muffled quickly by the whistling wind. It feels like they have been riding for almost an hour as they start to see another mountain range on the horizon. Jade then yells, "LENCA!" The Yaule stops leaping and slows down. Jade again, pulls back on the hair and says, "Putta," causing the Yaule to stop. She turns to Arthus while pointing north at the mountains and says, "That is the Great Northern Peaks Mountain Range. They are still very far out there, but from here, you can just make out their peaks of snow and ice. I have never been there, but how I would love to go out there to meet the Cundos that live in Northern Peak City, and those that work in the Northern Peak Mines."

"I would also like to go there someday," says Arthus.

"Well, I would hope so since you are the 'Prince of Malon,'" says Jade as she laughs and quotes his high and mighty title playfully.

Out of nowhere, Jade says, "Lelelya." Again she grabs onto the right side of the fur on the back of the Yaule's neck. The Yaule turns eastward and starts running again. When she again yells, "CAMPE," Arthus is ready this time and already holding on for dear life. Riding for almost another hour, they both start to see the beginnings of a vast forest just beyond a barrier fence. Jade slows the Yaule down by yelling, "LENCA!" Once the Yaule slowed down enough, she stops the Yaule by pulling on its hair and saying, "Putta." Turning to Arthus and pointing to a vast forest, she asks, "Can you at least name that forest?"

Arthus laughs and says, "Of course, I live in Harmony City, which is around the heart of God's Forest!"

"Finally something you know," laughs Jade jokingly.

"Oh, hey look, there is a pack of wild Yaule's and their cubs!" Exclaims Arthus pointing to the pack of Yaules outside the fence.

"That pack looks familiar to me," says Jade as she quickly dismounts from her Yaule and goes up closer to the fence. "Oh wait, I do know that pack of Yaules! It is Fang's pack!" Exclaims Jade excitedly while jumping up in the air. "Let's go play with Fang and his Yaule friends and family, while she runs up and starts to climb up and over the fence.

Grabbing her leg just as she reaches the top of the fence, Arthus exclaims, "What are you serious? Have you not heard that wild Yaule's kill Cundos all the time?"

Shaking off his grasp, Jade replies, "Don't worry, I know this pack. I helped save Fang as a baby cub. He is one of my best friends. They love me. Come on it will be fun!"

"Alright, if you say so," says Arthus as he climbs the fence to follow her.

"Fang!" Exclaimed Jade as she is running up to the wild Yaule pack. Fang turns and sees Jade and lets out a growl as it runs toward Jade. Once Fang catches up to Jade, he starts to purr loudly and rub his side and back on her leg.

"Wow, Jade this Yaule really likes you." says Arthus as he puts his hand out for Fang to rub up against."

Fang, arching his back, baring his teeth and claws, swipes one of his large clawed paws at the air in front of Arthus hand.

Arthus quickly pulls his hand back and steps back a few meters.

"Oh, Fang, you overprotective cat. This is Arthus; he is the Prince of Malon," says Jade while petting him behind the ears.

Fang protectively growls at Arthus, and continues to make a low growl even as he was being gently petted by Jade. Inside Jade's mind she hears Fang complaining that she had brought Arthus with her. He does not know who Arthus is. He wants Arthus to go away. Jade does not yet understand that Fang is actually trying to communicate to her through his thoughts. She just feels like she can tell what Fang is feeling and thinking.

"I know, I know, but my Dad made me take him around and show him the area," says Jade. As Jade was petting Fang, he seems to calm down a little bit.

Arthus, preferring to live by keeping a safe distance says, "Fang, it's OK. I think we will become friends as well over time. I am glad you watch over Jade here." In more of a joking tone he exclaims, "She really needs someone to keep an eye out."

Jade gives Arthus a playful slap on the shoulder and says while laughing, "I don't think I am the one that needs someone to keep an eye out, Mr. Prince of Malon who doesn't even know how to ride a Yaule."

Seeing Jade's slap, Fang then rolls over, kicking his feet in the air, and allows Jade to pet his belly. He starts to purr and even seems to have a smile on his face.

After a while of watching Jade playing with Fang, and then even his pack of Yaule cubs, Arthus says, "Jade, I am certain that there is still more to see today."

Jade says, "Goodbye!" to her friends and watches as Fang takes off with the other Yaules back into God's Forest.

"Before we go back, let's take a short break from immediately riding the Yaules. Let's sit down for a bit on the hill over there by the fence line. Give me a chance to ask you more about yourself? And, what it's like growing up as Prince of Malon?" says Jade.

As they walk to the small hill by the fence line, Arthus asks, "What would you like to know?"

Jade leans in closer looking intently at his silver eyes, silver hair, and greenish skin tone. Noticing her gaze, Arthus blushes, and swallows hard as his heart races. A bead of sweat starts to trickle down his forehead. Jade asks, "Why do you have silver hair and eyes? I have never seen anything like this before."

"I am a half breed born of both Cundo and Ignole. My mother, Laella was Ignole, and as you know, my Father is Cundo," responds Arthus.

"Yeah, I like how your eyes look like twin silver moons," says Jade with a slight girlish smile. Then adds, "But, I did not think that Cundo and Ignole were able to mate and have kids together. I thought that is why they don't usually marry."

"You are correct, Ignole and Cundo do not usually marry or mate. It is challenging for Ignole or Cundo to procreate with someone of the opposite race as themselves and even more challenging when it is time to bare the child of mixed breeding. My mother, Laella however, chose to marry my father and knowingly and willingly sacrificed herself to give me life. It was the greatest gift of all. At least that is what my grandfather says. My father always says I am also of very rare bloodline breeding as was my mother, Laella was firstborn of the first family of the Ignole. My father is the only son to the royal family of the Cundo, being my grandfather, the High King, and my grandmother, Amethyst, the High Queen. May God rest her soul too, as she died of old age a while before I was born." says Arthus.

"So is this also why you have a greenish tone to your skin color?" asks Jade

"Yes, that would be correct. It comes from my Ignole mother, Laella" says Arthus as he sits down. Sadly looking up at the sky he says, "I do wish my mother, Laella was around. I have tons of questions I would love to ask her."

Jade lays down beside him, looking up at the sky as well, quickly changes the subject by saying, "You know you are pretty cool for a prince," causing herself to laugh slightly.

Arthus turns, smiles, and says, "You are not so bad for a country Cundo yourself. But, do you think I am a weird prince?"

Jade replies, "No... I think we can be friends." Jade sees that the sun is now starting to turn downwards slightly towards the east. "Alright, one more stop then back to the farmlands!" Exclaims Jade.

Arthus and Jade get up, walk over and jump the fence again and head toward the Yaule. After they mount the Yaule once again, Jade says, "Lelelya." She grabs onto the right side of the fur with her right hand on the back of the Yaules neck. This time the Yaule turns to the south and starts running.

Jade yells out, "CAMPE!" Arthus is ready for the sudden jolt of speed and is already holding onto Jade for dear life.

They were riding for one and a half hours when they finally can see another mountain range in the distance. Arthus notices that these mountains do not seem nearly as significant as the other two but still distinctive as they have a silver glow to them. He recalls seeing these mountains also in one of the holobooks he read.

Jade again slows the Yaule by yelling "LENCA!" and says "Putta" as soon as the Yaule has slowed down enough.

Arthus immediately exclaims, "I know those mountains are the Silver Peaks! I have read that they are famous for their silver-toned glow! Though, they are not as tall as they seemed in the holos, they are very wide in stature!"

"Yes and quite beautiful at night when the moon is above!" Exclaims Jade. They give off a glow like that of your eyes," says Jade, blushing slightly.

"Sounds amazing. I must come back to see this too some night," says Arthus. Noticing her blush, he smirks and asks, "Jade, will you be allowed to bring me back here one of these nights. You know, um, well, just so that we can see this together?"

Jade replies, "I'll have to think about that; maybe, but, ... only if you've learned to ride a Yaule by yourself. Anyway, we can't always have you riding a Yaule with me. You are the Prince of Malon after all. Alright? ... Well now, we really need to head back to the farmlands before the High King and my father start to worry that we've gotten eaten by some wild Yaules." With that, Jade promptly commands the Yaule and says, "Lelelya." This time Arthus notices she pulls onto the Yaules neck twice with her right hand. The Yaule quickly turns directly north. Jade yells out, "CAMPE!" Arthus, again is ready for the sudden jolt of speed by holding onto Jade very tightly.

After another hour of riding, they arrive back onto the main path that leads to the main farming fields.

Jade turns her head and yells, "JUST A BIT FURTHER! I DID HAVE FUN WITH YOU TODAY THOUGH!"

Arthus starts to laugh because of how her voice sounds in the wind, and yells back, "I DID TOO!" Arthus starts to see the Grey Barns up ahead. Only about five more minutes until they are finally back, he thinks to himself.

Jade yells, "LENCA!" causing the Yaule to slow down. Once they reach the barn, Jade says, Punta. Then Jade turns and asks Arthus, "Can you dismount and open the doors to the barn and stall for me?" Arthus dismounts and does as instructed.

Once the Yaule was back in the barn, Jade grabs the brush and starts to hum and brush the Yaule once again. She then looks at Arthus and says, "Alright, Prince Arthus, it's your turn to brush the Yaule." Arthus then starts to brush the Yaule, but Jade interrupts him exclaiming, "Ugh... you are doing it all wrong! Here let me show you." She grabs his hand and starts to show him how to stroke the brush on the Yaule. And says, "You also need to hum like I did too, as doing this seems to make the Yaule appreciate you more and it also bonds with your voice. When you begin to give it riding commands, you will appreciate that little tip of knowledge."

As Jade is holding Arthus's hand his heart starts to race, and he blushes. Jade notices him blushing and starts to blush herself. Arthus, however, does not see that Jade is blushing too. When they finish with the Yaule, they start to walk back to the farm fields. Upon arrival, they notice that High King Thureos already has a few Golden Griffins tacked and packed heavily with a variety of produce. He seems already ready to leave.

"Ah! Arthus, I thought I would have to leave without getting to say goodbye," says Arthus's grandfather picking him up in a great big hug. "I will return to get you during next year's Harvest Festival. That way you will get to witness and participate in the gift sacrifice."

"Goodbye, grandfather, I will see you in a year!" exclaims Arthus sadly. High King Thureos then climbed up into his royal hathi howdah on the back of his Golden Griffin. A big gust of wind followed as the small flock of Golden Griffins flew off. Arthus kept waving at him until he was out above and behind the sunset sky.

"Alright, Arthus let's all go wash up and then sit down to eat. At dinner, you must tell us how your first day of adventuring around the fields and valley went," says Grag.

Soon they were all seated around a big table where they eagerly awaited for Jade's mother to bring in the meal. As Jade's mother enters,

Arthus notices she also has red hair, almost the color of blood, and green eyes, a lot like Jades. She is a foot shorter than Grag. She is pushing in a cart with a large serving dish full of stew, several baskets with vegetables picked fresh from her garden that day, and a large basket filled with the most delicious smelling hot-cross buns; fresh from the oven.

Jade's mother looks over at Arthus and exclaims, "We are highly honored to have you as our guest, Prince Arthus! My name is Shelly. Welcome. How do you like the humble Ariel Valley, its farmlands, and all that it has to offer?" She asks.

"I really love everything I have already seen and heard of it. I am learning a lot. Jade showed me the Yaule and took me for a ride around to where we could see the mountains to the south, west, and north. Jade even introduced me to Fang and his pack of wild Yaules over by God's Forest," Arthus replies.

"Sounds like a lovely time! You can tell us all about it while we eat. First, we must give thanks to God for providing us with such a meal!" Exclaims Shelly as she turns to Grag and asks, "Would you like to lead us?"

"Alright, let's teach Arthus our common table prayer, shall we?" Asks Grag

"Yes... he needs to learn all our traditions. Isn't that right, Grag?" Shelly responds questioningly. Arthus nods in agreement.

"Agreed... bow your heads, and let's pray," instructs Grag. Everyone then bows their heads. At the same time, they all pray, "Come, God, be our guest. Let these gifts to us be blessed. May our souls be fed, ever on your living bread?" Trying to act like he knows this prayer, Arthus mumbles it along with them.

Shelly grabs the large dipper-style spoon, begins scooping up the stew and pouring it into her bowl first. Then she passes it around, saying, "Careful. It is very hot."

As Arthus pours the stew into his bowl, he notices that it has meat, potatoes, and some vegetables. He then asks, "What type of stew is this?"

"It is a potato and Dreg sausage stew, it is one of our most famous traditional dishes," responds Shelly.

"Well, it smells amazing," says Arthus as he grabs his spoon and takes a bite. Noticing right away that it is burning his tongue. He grabs his glass of ice water and takes a swig to cool down his mouth. "Wow, that was piping hot, but it really tastes amazing!" Exclaims Arthus. He puts more stew onto his spoon and then blows on it before he puts it into his mouth again.

"Well, thank you, Arthus!" Exclaims Shelly smiling.

Grag laughs at this and interjects and asks, "So... Prince Arthus, how was your first time riding on a Yaule?"

Arthus smiled and responded, "I had a lot of fun. They are so fast and strong. I very much enjoyed my ride with Jade, and I can't wait to learn to ride one by myself!"

"Yes, riding a Yaule is one of the best experiences a person can have here at the farmland, but did Jade tell you that Yaule is not native to Malon?" Asked Grag.

"No, I did not know that. I figured Yaule were native predators on Malon," Arthus replies, looking shocked. "I have read some holobooks about various animals, but never learned that."

"Yes, it's true. They were discovered on Creed, which is one of our twin moons. You should ask your grandfather how he gained the favor of the Yaule Matriarch. You know Creed was also where we met the Dwarven people. You will certainly get to meet most of them. Here on Malon they prefer to dwell in the North Peak City, which is a huge above ground and underground city that was built by both the Cundo and the Dwarves within the Northern Peaks Mountain Range. However, now that we are all substantially stuffed from this very fine meal, thanks to my lovely wife, Shelly, I am realizing that it is getting rather late. I will gladly share more stories about the Northern Peaks and surrounding areas another day. Let's get you out into your quarters where you will spend your nights during your visit here. Let's let the girls clean up. Follow me," says Grag.

"Okay," says Arthus, getting up from the table. Grag then opens the door, and they walk outside.

Grag takes Arthus around a couple of barns to a sizable looking tool shed style cabin. As Grag opens up the tool shed style cabin, Arthus notices that the inside actually looks in very good condition. Grag and Shelly have brought a hammock made out of Dreg leather, and a blanket made from its fur and hung it neatly in the shed. There also was a small desk, chair, and a small chest where he could keep the extra clothing he had brought.

"These quarters look very cozy," says Arthus admiring the shed.

"Thank you and goodnight," Grag says as he then heads back toward the house.

"Goodnight," says Arthus, feeling tired after a long day. After Grag left and Arthus showered and changed, he laid in bed, thinking about how his Father is doing. His Father is usually off training with God's Thorn, the elite soldiers of Malon's Guard, and the Knights. Arthus thought about how great it would be to join him someday. Arthus fell asleep thinking about this.

Chapter 3
Clan Ariel

Arthus stood up after helping Jade and Grag birth a new Yaule. They have been working for almost five hours straight. He wipes the sweat from his brow. He is wearing a dirty set of work pants and boots and a now dirty white tunic. He felt the fresh cold breeze on his hot, sweaty face, and it felt good.

"Arthus!" Yells Jade. "We are going to check on the Golden Griffin's eggs; then, I got a surprise to show you. Come with." She giggles as she ran off. Arthus watches her running off and follows after. Grag was already inspecting the machine in one of the barns that seemed to keep the eggs warm.

"This machine is amazing! You can see the handiwork put into every detail! I always thought the farmers here would be using mostly hand tools." Laughs Arthus.

"No, in fact, we use a ton of machinery here on the farmlands. All our machines were given to us by the clansmen of Clan Gearhead. They are the Dwarvens and Cundos that live in North Peak City and the Northern Peaks," explained Grag.

"Wow, I am astonished. I knew of machines and stuff we use in Harmony City but never thought they had created so many different things", says Arthus.

"Yeah, the Clan Gearhead is all of Malon's main source of all kinds of craft works. They are the best Engineers in all the galaxy. Well, that's what they tell us anyway," laughs Grag.

"Do you know how the clan got their name? All the other clans named after the Archangels, but they aren't," asks Arthus.

"Ah! Yes, their clan was awarded their name by your grandfather and the Archangels. They bestowed them with high honors for creating inventions that help all of Malon and advances in our technology. They are the only ones to have this honor granted to them. They are amazing with their handiwork. Be careful around that lot, though. They are a cheery crazy bunch and can get worked up over some of their inventions," laughs Grag.

"That is so cool! I hope I get to work with them someday. I would love to see them at work and see how they create all these different machines," says Arthus excitedly.

"Yes, the machines that the Clan Gearhead members design and create helps make things easier here on the farm, just as they do everywhere on Malon. I am so glad that all the clans live so harmoniously here on Malon. We do trade for anything we may want, or even might believe we need, which are beyond any of life's basic needs. While at the same time we are always giving to each other. Every clan has unique important responsibilities and tasks, which every clan member understands must be completed, and which all symbiotically complement the various strengths and solve any weaknesses of other clans. By faithfully completing each of our own responsibilities and tasks, and by giving to help each other, everyone can survive and grow on Malon. Even with us having six separate clans, we each watch out for and help one another, especially ensuring that all of life's basic needs are met for everyone. We really love to take care of each other. It's pretty amazing," says Grag with a smile on his face. Standing up and looking at Jade. Grag says, "Alright now that I am all good here, why don't we all head over and show Arthus the Pilgos.

"Wait, you have Pilgos here?" Arthus asks, surprised. Arthus read about Pilgos in the Library of Holograms in Harmony City. From the holograms, he knew that they were a massive domesticated animal that was known for their many uses. One is its meat. And the other is their creamy milk that is known even to have healing properties.

"Of course we do silly," smirks Jade. "What kind of stupid question is that?" She asks while shaking her head and laughing at Arthus.

Hearing and seeing that, Grag says, "Excuse us for a moment." Then he quickly grabs and pulls on his daughter, Jade's arm and walks her abruptly a reasonable distance away from Arthus. He then says in a stern voice, "Jade, you are being very improper with your words. Arthus is the Prince of Malon. Even if you are becoming the very best of friends, you must never ever speak so rudely. You must apologize to Prince Arthus immediately, and from now on you must remember to use proper etiquette in your words. In fact, no one, and I seriously mean no one, should ever hear you talk that sarcastically. Everyone deserves kindness in your words!"

Grag and Jade return as quickly to where Arthus was standing, where he is still thinking about the wonderful taste of Pilgos milk, and acting seemingly oblivious to what Jade had said to him.

Jade bowing her head in shame, says, "Prince Arthus, I am very sorry for being rude in my words to you. My father reminded me that I must use proper etiquette and not be sarcastic. Please forgive me for saying what I said to you."

Prince Arthus looks at Grag, smirked, and then shrugged his shoulders and replied, "It really was a stupid question!" Then he started laughing and patting Jade on the shoulders. He leaned in close to her ear and whispered, "But, if you had said that in court, you probably would have been locked in irons and thrown into the tower prison. It is a good thing that I see you as a close friend! You are forgiven! Standing upright and trying to look official, he says in a firm voice, "When you hear me say stupid things in the future, you are authorized to call me out on those. But, do be more careful of the tone of your voice, and especially of the words you choose to speak out loud. In the palace, I was always taught that speaking without thinking is very dangerous! Jade, I really do need to have a good advisor, and not one that I have to visit in prison! Ok?"

Keeping her head bowed, Jade timidly said, "Ok, thank you for forgiving me, and I will try to do my best to be a good advisor to you from now on."

Upon hearing that, Grag seemed satisfied that Jade was not in terrible trouble. He then says, "Well ok, then let's go see the Pilgos and get some very fresh warm milk."

When they arrive at the fenced area that houses the Pilgos, Arthus is still a bit reminiscing. He has had Pilgos meat many times before. It tastes amazing. It's been one of his favorite additions to meals. It makes sausage, bacon, steak, and a lot of other things. He remembers even taking some of the meat, frying it up and keeping it to snack on while he explored the palace. He continues thinking of all the great food he had back at the palace, and hoping that Shelly will make some of his favorite dishes.

As they walk up to the Pilgos, he notices that they are almost as large as a Yaule, and the females have udders that produce milk. The males had broader snouts and massive tusks. They didn't have any fur on them, but instead they have a thin slightly tough leathery hide. Their hides are used for many things, but sometimes they are cut up into small strips and deep fried into Pilgos rind chips. He enjoys eating Pilgos rind chips.

"Well, what do you think, Arthus? These are Pilgos, but knowing you, I bet you already probably read about them, am I right?" asked Jade a bit more carefully, while she still had a hint of a mocking smile on her face.

Ignoring her hint of a mocking smile, Arthus replied, "Yes, I have, and I have eaten a ton of Pilgos meat. I love the taste. I do hope to eat some soon here, and many-many times, while I am here. It is my very favorite meat, and I love it made so many different ways." Pausing barely for a breath he says, "Oh, and yes, a live Pilgos is very impressive to see up close. I do love the taste of their milk too..."

As Arthus continues rambling on about all the various ways he likes Pilgos meat prepared, Grag walked up to the female and attached some hoses with pumps to her nipples. He activated a machine that starts to pump the milk from her. Grag went over to another Cundo who was sitting outside the fence. Arthus noticed that they exchanged some words, and Grag motioned them all to follow. Soon Arthus and Jade and the Cundo are all following Grag into a big building that is freezing, and one hook is already holding up a skinned Pilgos. They kept following into another room, which was incredibly hot as it was lined with massive furnaces. There were also a great many barrels of tiny bits of crystalline salt.

"Salt?!" exclaims Arthus questioningly and asks, "Why are there so many barrels of salt?"

This question almost causes Grag to start bursting out laughing, but he immediately composes himself intentionally in front of Jade, and then says in a proper tone of voice, "Good question, my Prince. The salt is used within the big vats of brine where we soak the Pilgos meat. This keeps the meat fresh much longer than unsalted meat can last. By salting the meat, we can transport the meat to all of the different clans and cities here on Milon that need it. We even send some of the salted meat to Creed."

"Ah, I see," says Arthus. "That must be why all of the varieties of Pilgos meat tastes a little bit salty."

Jade walks outside and stays outside for a while during the time Arthus and Grag were inside messing with the raw Pilgos. She stands watching the milking machine until the machine causes the large milk container to get full. She turns off the milking machine, and continues waiting around outside for the guys to come out. Realizing they are not coming quickly, she starts to pick nearby vegetables and collects everything that they might need for dinner that night. After gathering what she needed, she just starts to head back towards her house, when she sees her father and Arthus finally come out.

Arthus walks out, covered in blood and salt. The sight causes Jade to burst out laughing while pointing at Arthus. He looks at himself and smiles. Arthus then decides he will have the last laugh and starts charging at Jade, trying to hug her.

Jade, screams and yells, "DON'T YOU EVEN DARE COME CLOSE TO ME LIKE THAT!"

Arthus replies with the question, "Oh, and what are you going to about it? You laughed at me now. I'm going to get you back!" He exclaims, still chasing after her.

As Arthus catches up with Jade, she says, "Ok, ok, I'm sorry, but now don't come any closer to me with that blood all over you. If you do, you can forget about me teaching you how to ride the Yaules."

Arthus looking at her questioningly, says, "Ok fine, but if you laugh at me next time that I have blood all over me, I will come after you and tackle you and share my bounty."

Still smirking at him, but trying her best to compose herself, Jade says, "Well, I can see that my father had you learn how to butcher and carve up your first Pilgos. We better get back to my dad before my mom gets angry that we are late."

As they get back to Grag, they both notice that he is hurriedly loading everything that Jade had gathered up. And, he is placing the meat that Arthus had butchered into a big pouch on the Yaule they had brought with them. Grag says to Arthus, "I thought you might appreciate this opportunity to eat some of your fresh unsalted Pilgos meat that you butchered yourself. It will taste even better than the salted meat you are used to eating in the palace, but when we get back, you really need to go to the bathhouse and clean up. By that time, we will have dinner almost done." "You go to the bathhouse too Jade, you both have been working hard all day. Hurry along now," commands Grag.

"Yes, father! It really does feel like it has been a while since I have been to the bathhouse," says Jade as she grabs and pulls Arthus with her.

Soon they were walking into a large building that had two entries and two completely separate sides—one for males and another for females. Jade looks at Arthus and points for him to go left through the door marked for males. Arthus nods and walks in. A Lot of other Cundo and Ignole men and even were already in there. Coming out from behind curtains in small private hot shower areas, they were wearing nothing but towels, ready to walk out into a massive steam-filled pool.

Thinking to himself, "He had read about these in the Library of Holos, they are called hot springs. Lava pockets heat the water. It feels even better than he could have imagined. All the aches and pains of the long weeks and months suddenly wash away. He regularly took showers, but this hot springs bathhouse was on a whole new level."

About an hour later, he is feeling refreshed, and dresses in clean work clothes. Then he adds a freshly washed tunic and goes outside where he waits on Jade, who came out from her side very soon after. He notices that she looks very refreshed, and her long red hair is smooth. Arthus, looking at Jade, starts to blush. She looks fantastic; he thinks to himself with a smile.

Looking at him questioningly, Jade asks, "You okay, Arthus? Without giving him a chance to respond, she says, "I bet you spent a little too long in there, your light green skin looks a bit red," she laughed. "Okay, let's go eat," she says as she grabs him by the arm and pulls him off toward her house.

"Alright... easy..." Arthus responds, trying not to fall, as Jade is dragging him.

Once they reach Jade's house, Jade opens the door, and they walk into the smell of grilled Pilgos steak, and some greens from the farm. As they get to the table, they both see Shelly pouring a nice glass of cold Pilgos milk.

Shelly seeing them both, says, "Hi Arthus... hi Jade. I am glad to see you both finally made it." Looking directly at Jade, she adds, "Well, at least this time, you are both just in time for dinner instead of making your father, and I wait on you."

Jade replies, "Yeah.... sorry about that, Mom. We are trying to make it on time more. The food does smell amazing. Thanks, Mom!"

Arthus nods, agreeing at Jade and Shelly, exclaims, "Yeah, the food smells delicious!"

Grag, smelling the food also, walks in and says, "Mmmm...I can't wait. I am starving after my hard day of farming and teaching Arthus how to butch a Pilgos."

Arthus turns toward Grag and replies, "Thank you for teaching me by the way. I am learning a lot and have learned a lot these past months."

"Don't even worry about it. I'm glad to help. Your grandfather and father both wanted me to work you hard while you are here. I have been thinking' about how well you have helped out around here. You are a speedy learner as well. I'll be sure to tell them how good you have been," responds Grag with a smile and an approving nod.

Shelly looks at Jade and says, "Jade, why don't you lead us in prayer this time?"

"Okay, everyone ready to say the prayer? Jade asks while looking at Arthus questioningly.

"Absolutely," Arthus responds.

They all bow their heads as Jade instructs them and leads them together, saying, "Come, God, be our guest. Let these gifts to us be blessed. May our souls be fed ever on your living bread."

With this, Shelly passes around the Pilgos steak, some smashed up potatoes, and the greens from the farm. They all grab some of each item and put it on their plate.

After eating, Arthus looks at Shelly and Grag and says, "Wow that was amazing! I don't think I have ever eaten Pilgos steak cooked so perfectly. And, Grag, thank you again so much as fresh unsalted Pilgos tastes incredible. I never had it that way before."

With a smile, Grag and Shelly exclaim at the same time, "Well, thank you, Arthus!"

Grag, looking at Arthus and Jade, says, "Better get this all cleaned up and off to bed. We have our bi-annual hunt game to get ready for. It only happens two times a year and helps us freeze up enough Dreg meat for all clans. The hunt is coming up in only another month. Although I have been training with both of you one day a week specifically for this hunt over the past two months, Arthus still must become one with his bow. So for the next month, all I want you two to focus on is the hunt and honing your skills. We will need those skills if we are going to get enough Dreg meat for the next six months."

After they all finish cleaning up, Arthus walks back to his cabin. Once inside, he sits on his small couch, looks up and thinks to himself, "I can't wait until this bi-annual hunt game! I have read everything written about this in the holos. The hunting team who kills the biggest Dregs and especially the most marked Dregs become the honored hunters of the bi-annual hunt —a great honor amongst Clan Ariel's people and amongst all of the other clans on Malon. Well, I better get ready for bed. I got a long month of training ahead of me." With this, Arthus got ready for bed and fell asleep.

Chapter 4
Preparing for the Great Hunt

That next morning while at breakfast, Grag explained to both Jade and Arthus, "Each clan chooses to send several hunting teams to help out in the bi-annual great hunt. This bi-annual hunt will be Jade's first time being old enough to join in the hunt. Arthus, you also are going to join in and we are allowing you to join as a Clan Arial team member, even though you are of Clan Arkwright. We are honoring you with this because you have faithfully spent this last year working very hard side-by-side with our clan. Our Clan Council members have made this decision to honor you in this way. They decided to place Arthus name alongside of Jade's name into this bi-annual hunting team drawing."

Grag continued, "God's Forest is a massive land area. In the center of the God's Forest, as you know is Harmony City. There is the ancient and very humongous God's Tree located in the massive circular holy sanctuary garden courtyard that sits on the south banks of the River of Life. As you know the palace is located up into that First God's Tree. The palaces many floors and walls are very much Life-Energy grown from God's Tree and is intrinsically and symbiotically part of that God's Tree. That God's Tree is known as First God's Tree on this entire planet. It was a seedling that God gave to the Alda Matriarch immediately after He created Malon and established the boundaries of the River of Life, and right after He created the Aldas as the guardian of God's Tree. They planted the seedling in the very center of where it still grows, well over 400,000 years ago. Immediately after it was planted, where it still remains, then God spoke and His WORD and Holy Spirit empowered the growth of God's Tree and it grew very speedily to such massive proportions. The very top of First God's Tree reaches past the stratosphere of our world, Malon. The top of First God's Tree is actually even into the ozone layer that surrounds Malon. Obviously the palace is not built up that high, because no one could breathe at that height. The palace however does have upper floors like where the High King's personal bedroom and training porch is located. On a clear day from the deck of his training porch one can actually see all the past the continent and out into the great ocean. The High Kings personal training porch is positioned higher than the tallest of the Great Southern Mountain Range and its Silver Peaks. God's Forest actually takes up a huge portion of the continent that we are living on. It is close to a thousand leagues at the shortest distance from Harmony City out to edge of God's Forest. On foot, it takes anyone attempting to hike through it several months to make it all the way to Harmony City, at its center. This continent, is the largest on the planet; around two thousand leagues from coast-to-coast going east and west at its center and about one thousand three hundred leagues going north and south along its center. And, it is not perfectly square. Well...you both have seen drawings of maps in your holo-maps, so I am not telling you anything you don't already know in your head. Anyway, just know it is a lot different actually being on the ground walking it out then anything you might have read or even heard about. God's Forest also has many dangers; several massive predators live among the underbrush, the trees, and especially near many of its waterways. And, you must be extremely careful and always ready to fight to the death with any of the wild predators lurking out there in God's Forest."

Grag then says, "The bi-annual great hunt will start at the very edge of God's Forest, which as you already know, is located over an hour's ride from the village by Yaule. Each team of two hunters are only allowed to actually hunt Dregs within a specific grid section of the forest. Each of these grid sections were called *hunting zones* and are each well mapped out. Scouts are on constant patrol. These scouts, as Arthus is aware, are special hunters known as the Rangers of the Silver Thorns. Silver Thorns are the most advanced military unit on Malon and are directly under the full authority of the High King and Prince Benroy, and governed by Clan Arkwright."

Then Grag says, "God's Forest is also the home of the Aldas. The Aldas are the guardians of Gods Forest. These creatures are massive walking living trees created by God to protect and keep healthy First God's Tree and God's Forest surrounding First God's Tree. The Aldas have never been a bother to any of the people of Malon. As long as we honor, uphold and show respect to them, to God's Forest, and to all of Gods natural laws, the Aldas have allowed the people of Malon to move freely through God's Forest and in all the nearby lands. By gaining the respect of the Matriarch of the Aldas over many centuries, many of the various clans on Malon have even been gifted by her with a seedling of the First God's Tree, which she herself has planted and nurtured near the various clan leader's homes and villages. There is one such God's Tree seedling growing near our home here. It is located in the very center the God's Tree Seedling Circle here in the farming village of Clan Arial. It is where we perform the Great Gifting on the first night of all of our Annual Harvest Festivals. We will hold this year's Annual Harvest Festival following this bi-annual hunt. It also serves as a holy place where local folks can go and pray and read and meditate from the ancient canonical books."

"For the past two months I have been training both of you how to survive and hunt, just as if you were out in God's Forest," said Grag. He continued, "At least one day per week, I specifically worked with both of you on different skills; showing you both how to properly use a bow and arrow, how to make fires using flint and steel, and how to find, cook and prepare various wild foods. I have even showed you the differences and similarities of various wild plants, in order to teach you what is edible, from what can harm you. I have went camping many times in the past with Jade, so I know that she knows how to setup fish traps and how to spear fish. I trust you will show that to Arthus when you are out together. There are other skills Jade knows already, that I know I did not need to repeat while training you both. I even showed you both exactly how to show respect to an Alda, just in case you ever find yourselves in front of one of these great tree folk. However much that I know and have tried to teach you, it is each of you that have been completely responsible to put into practice the skills that I have taught to you. Therefore, during this coming month, I will carefully observe each of you. I will be looking to see if you have actually followed through and carefully practiced the skills that I taught to you. I shouldn't need to pull either of you aside and go back over something that I know I already taught you. Why. Because, I won't be going with you into God's Forest. I won't be going with you into your hunting zones. I cannot do that, and so, I must be able to see over the next month that you truly were listening to me and practicing what I taught you. Next month, when you actually do go out towards your hunting zone, you must be aware of your surroundings and always be protecting each other at all times. Know that Shelly and I will be praying for you, that God will protect you and guide you. And, as ancient canonical book says, 'In the moment you need it, God will truly bring to your remembrance those things which you have learned.'"

"Soon it will be time for the bi-annual hunt," Arthus thought to himself. The season was starting to get cold again and the produce harvests were quickly being gathered from the farming fields. He smiled thinking back at helping Jade and Grag and many other Cundos out in the fields. He enjoyed using the curved blade tool with the long handle, which is called a *scythe*, to cut down some of the crops. He enjoyed helping to gather up all of the different kinds of crops. He sat up on a nearby hill and watched as several large farming machines were being used to spread out a special fertilizer made of liquid slurry from the human, animal and plant wastes that had been processed through a special bio-fuel processing plant located far downwind away from the Clan Arial farming village.

Arthus had accompanied one of his Cundo instructors and visited the bio-fuel plant and learned that this plant was built specifically for processing all of the human and animal excrement wastes. It also processed most of the plant waste materials. The bio-fuel plant completely eliminated all the odors, while creating excellent zero-emissions fuels, which are then used by one of the other clans for making various synthetic products. Some of the bio-fuels were highly pressurized and put into large metal bottles that had gauges and a knob attached to their tops. Those were used everywhere on Malon as a zero-emissions cooking fuel. Much of the zero-emissions fuels are also used for powering many of the various farming machines used by Clan Arial. Arthus learned that every bit of the waste products must be processed through a bio-fuel plant to prevent harm to all the waterways and all the water tables under the soil. Arthus also learned that the emissions in the air from all types of wastes must be captured to protect the ozone layer that God had created and which surrounds our planet and every other world planet where sentient life exists.

Arthus continued watching when several giant spinning blade machines turned the specially blended soils on the farmlands to prepare it for replanting early in next spring's season.

Arthus remembered that Grag had said to him, "Everything we need to grow any of the produce we grow here in Arial valley is found somewhere on Malon. God put it all here for our use, but God did not put it all in one place naturally. God expects us to work hard and gave us the wisdom to find those things, like sand from the shores along the ocean, blackened topsoil from various locations, clay from various places on the mountains, duff from the various leaves that are found on the ground in the woods, peat moss that naturally grows in swamplands, and the tiny bits of volcanic spongy white material. All of those various soil items were collected by hard work, and then through more hard work they were brought here. Again, through more hard work they were spread out on the lands. And then they get mixed together by the big spinning blade machines along with just the right amount of the liquid slurry fertilizer from the bio-fuel plant. Only then, are they ready to get planted, nurtured and cultivated by even more hard work. When we work hard and honor God in our working, this is just part of our reasonable service to God and to each other."

After that month of hard work and training, Arthus, sitting on the floor and meditating deeply in his cabin, with his shirt off, readying his mind for the bi-annual hunt game. He concentrates on his thoughts, trying desperately to calm his mind. His mind drifts with thoughts, "Very soon, it will be sunrise, when all the hunting teams would be showing their clan members, their families, and their friends just how much they learned." Excitedly, he thinks to himself, "I am hoping that Jade and I can be the ones to walk out of God's forest with the largest

Dreg. We are only going to be getting the official rules for the bi-annual hunt game exactly one hour before the hunt starts. Only after the sound of the shofar made from the ram's horn will they be allowing us to get started hiking out into our respective hunting zone areas. And, only after arriving in our zone, will we be able to actually look for any signs of the Dregs, track them, and hopefully find the largest Dregs in our zone. I heard from another team talking that they get points only if they kill the Dregs marked for specifically them on their holo-card devices, and extra bonus points for killing another team's marked dreg, but only if it ever is actually inside their own hunting zone that they received just before the hunt begins."

Arthus, making no headway with attempting to really do meditation, begins hearing a knock at the door of his cabin, stands up and exclaims, "Come on in!" As soon as he says this, Jade opens the door. She immediately turns around suddenly when she notices that Arthus didn't have his shirt or his tunic on and was standing there with the upper half of his body naked in the cabin.

Trying not to blush, Jade says, "I am sorry, I thought you were ready."

Slipping on his shirt quickly and then grabbing his tunic and walking to her, Arthus replies, "No worries, you can look. I am not naked. I just didn't have my upper body clothes on yet. It's not like I didn't already have my hunting pants on. Your Dad gave me these very nice Yaule fur pants. They are so warm and comfy. They are going to be perfect for the hunt today."

Jade, still somewhat embarrassed, turns around and asks, "Yes, I love these kind of pants. Did you also get your hooded cloak, made from the fur of fallen Yaules?"

"Oh my... I almost forgot all about the cloak. Thank you for reminding me as that would have been bad," replies Arthus.

"Ha, yeah, you will need them! Also, don't forget your Dreg scent gland spray and the soundless leather boots made from the skin of a Dreg. With those on you will get much closer to the Dreg without them noticing you are there!" Exclaims Jade.

"Yes, I packed my Dreg spray, and my Dreg leather boots are by the door over there," says Arthus pointing at his leather Dreg skinned boots.

Jade then asked, "Okay... how many arrows did you pack in your quiver by the way?"

"Oh... I think I got around thirty or so. It's packed full, but it's not a very large quiver," Arthus replies.

"Perfect. You don't want too large of a quiver anyway, especially when you are out in those woods, when you need to be moving swiftly. A larger quiver will only weigh you down and lessen your stamina, making you weak and tired much faster," Jade says in a matter of fact tone.

"I never thought of it that way. I am so excited about this hunt. I feel very prepared and ready. Don't you?" He asks.

"Definitely. I could barely sleep!" She exclaims.

"Tell me about it. I almost didn't get any sleep either tonight!" He exclaims back as he pulls his cloak on and pulls his hood up. He then grabs his tele-mask, *a mask that allows Jade and him to communicate and has an infrared technology enabling them to see heat sources through the forest better. It also has a tagging feature that helps in picking a unique color of heat signature for each of the team members. That tagging feature, when uplinked to the main satellite, allows them to directly see each other no matter where they are in the woods. It helps them to know where their team member is so that they are not accidently aiming their weapons directly at them when shooting at their Dreg.* He looks over at Jade after having all the gear ready and on and asks, "Well, what do you think?

"You look like a pro-hunter. Don't forget your handbag of snacks and supplies and your bi-annual hunt game holo-card", she replies.

"Oh yeah, I'll grab those too, thanks for reminding me again," he says, grabbing onto his satchel and checking to make sure he has his hunting game holo-card. "You also look like a pro-hunter yourself!" He exclaims.

"Okay... you ready to head to the hunter-gathering area?" She asks, looking at him excitedly.

"I thought you would never ask!" He exclaims back excitedly.

"Alright, let's go," she says, opening the door for him.

As they are walking up to the hunter-gathering area, they see five other teams, representing each of the clans, ready and waiting for the rules and instructions to start. They all turn and see Grag walking to his platform in front of them. He is waving to them all.

Trying to capture the attention of the crowd, Grag, let's out a loud whistle and announces, "Howdy y'all! Welcome to our second bi-annual hunting game of the year! It will be the last one of the year. As most of y'all know, this hunt is the most important one! It is the one that helps every clan get through the hardest months with the most amount of Dreg meat they can get. So each team needs to kill the largest Dregs you can find. As some of you may know, we also chose the two largest Dregs in each of your team's hunting zone areas. If you can hunt and successfully bring back these Dregs, you will be awarded high awards and make your clans proud! I wanna hear y'all cheer if y'all are ready for the hunt?"

The crowd erupts in a loud roar of various cheers.

Grag, laughing, puts his hand up, silencing the crowd, exclaims, "Alright... alright, y'all are gonna scare off all of the Dregs in God's Forest with that loud of a roar! Okay, let's get started! The number one rule this year is that y'all are going to have exactly one week from the start of the hunt to come back here with the largest Dregs you can find. The second rule, each team is only able to claim three Dregs. So even if you accidentally kill a smaller Dreg, you have to claim it as one of the three. Let me remind you that we can tell if you kill a Dreg because each of ya'alls arrows has special hit/kill trackers in them which allow us to see exactly what you hit, and if it died. If you hit it, but don't kill it you must do your best to track it quickly and kill it quickly. Your hunting game holo-card with your tele-masks will help you trace anything you hit and what you kill. You can see on the giant tele-monitor setup behind me that we observe what you see what you are looking through your tele-masks. Also, we have thousands of trail-cams hidden all over the place inside of God's Forest in each of the hunting zones, that uplink to the satellite and monitors. Rule number four is that you are to wear your tele-masks at all times with the exception of when you are sleeping and when you are eating. Do not under any circumstance turn them off while you are awake, and especially anytime while you are hunting. Rule number four is there is to be no hunting of Dregs outside of your own hunting zone. Your tele-mask will let you know if your targeted Dreg is outside of your hunting zone or not. Failing to follow these rules will disqualify your team from being able to receive any rewards outside of the three dregs your team needs to kill. Your clans are counting on each of you to show integrity and your skills while following the rules we have laid out! I am going to have each of your team line up and scan your hunting game holo-cards into the game scanner. Once you scan your holo-card, it will fully register you as a part of your team—each team, named after each of their representative clans. We will call you by your clan to come up and register your holo-cards. Okay, Clan Gearhead, please come register."

Arthus then sees two younger Dwarvens carrying two strange-looking bows that are sideways with smaller-looking arrows and something that looks like a trigger. Looking over at Jade, he quietly asks, "What are those weird looking sideways bows they are carrying?"

Jade, trying not to laugh at him, replies calmly, "Those are crossbows. They shoot out smaller arrows called bolts, but they are mighty and can certainly take down a target. Most Dwarvens carry these whenever they are hunting because they are compact and easier to use as Dwarvens have shorter arms, which prevents them from using any long bows and compound bows."

"Oh... that's kinda cool that the Dwarvens have something made specifically for them", Arthus says quietly.

"Well, it's not just for them, but if you want to learn more about them later, I would suggest looking them up in your Library of Holos back in Harmony City," responds Jade, trying to sound funny.

"Ha... that's very funny. I might just do that, though," answers Arthus.

"Shhh... quiet. I think my Dad is about to call the next clans," commands Jade.

"Next on the list is Clan Raphael. Please come up and sign in!" Grag exclaims.

Arthus and Jade then see two Ignoles carrying long bows and dressed a lot like themselves, except that their cloaks are designed with a special whole arm length healing pack that is sewed into the outside length of the left arm. They carried several emergency medical products in that along with their handbags. They also had their own special handheld holo devices, separate from the hunting game holo cards that everyone brought.

Turning toward Jade, quietly, Arthus asks, "I didn't know we were allowed any outside holo devices?"

"Oh yeah... well, those are members of the Raphael Clan. They are the researcher clan for all of Malon, so they always carry around special handheld holo-scanners. The images they scan gets uplinked to their research headquarters and there is where the images get converted into the holograms which everyone can see in the Library of Holos. They are crucial devices for ongoing research and that is why they are carried by most of their clan members everywhere they go", answers Jade quietly.

"Wow that's so cool, how do you know all this stuff, Jade?" He asks.

"My Father taught me many things about other clans during events like this," responds Jade back. "Now, shhh... pay attention. We don't want to miss our clan being called and look like fools," she commands.

With that, they both look back up as they see Grag call out, "Clan Urial, please come up and register."

Arthus and Jade then see two soldier Cundos wearing scout's armor. They seem to be more professional looking. Arthus, watching them both register their holo cards, thinks to himself, "I know that scout armor. They must be members of the royal scouts. They are some of the greatest scouts on Malon outside of Silver Thorn scouts."

After they walk off the platform, Grag announces, "The next clan to register is Clan Raziel! Please come and register. I hope this time you are ready for this hunt and try to get decently large Dregs", laughs Grag.

Arthus then sees two skinny, nerdy looking Ignoles wearing greenish lab coat cloaks, looking completely unprepared or ready, walk up on stage. They were wearing larger quivers than needed and didn't even seem equipped with the right arrows. He then turns to Jade questioningly with a half-smile and asks, "Who are they? They don't look like they are prepared or ready for this."

Jade, chuckling, answers, "Those are the members of the Raziel clan, and they never seem to come prepared for this event. They are not farmers, hunters, or even outdoorsy type of people. Their clan members are the librarians and historians of Malon. They do have to participate in the hunt because we must try and take part in order that all the clans on Malon can survive during the harder months. Last time they were in and out in less than two days and only managed to kill two smaller Dregs."

"Oh, so how do they make it through the harder months on that low of meat?" Questions Arthus.

"Well, they must participate, and just for participating, all the other clans chip in and send some meat their way. They are a very essential clan with their librarian and historical record keeping responsibilities and they really do assist Clan Raphael with their research. Plus we usually kill plenty enough Dreg meat between the other clans to help out," Jade responds.

"Hmm... well, that's cool. Malon really is an amazing place, isn't it?" Arthus asks.

"Yes. I love it here, but I do have dreams of what it would be like to travel outside this world. I just love adventure," answers Jade as she is looking up at the sky and looking as if she's daydreaming.

"Next to register is Clan Arkwright. Remember, everyone, and this is the clan you will want to beat if you are going to be known as the greatest hunters of the year! They have won for the past four years in a row. The only other clans to have beaten them are Clan Gearhead, which happened over ten years ago, and Clan Urial, which, as you have guessed, was five years ago."

Arthus then sees two members of the elite Silver Thorn scouts, one Cundo male, one Ignole female walk up on stage. They are both equipped with Life-energy Ruin forged bows and perfect hand-created quivers, handbags, and cloaks. They were indeed a sight to see.

Jade seeing this, also looks at Arthus and asks, "Aren't those members of the Silver Thorn scouts? I have never seen their armor before. Usually, Clan Arkwright only sends their Silver Thorn trainees. The High King must think these next several months are going to be harder than usual. Don't you think so too, Arthus?"

"Yes, they are members of the Silver Thorn scouts, and to the looks of it, they must be members of the elite blue team. See the seven blue stars on their scout armor? That means they are the top of the top scouts, just under the blue team Shield Scout Captain," Arthus observes, pointing at the shoulder of one of the scout's armor.

"I do, what do you think this means? Do you think it'll be a tough few months ahead?" Questions Jade, with a worried look on her face.

"I doubt it, and I bet my grandfather, the High King, and my Father, the King, decided to send some of their top scouts to see how I do during my first hunt. I would almost guarantee they are here to watch over my moves and report back to them", replies Arthus, looking a little annoyed.

"Well... if that is true. Do not let yourself get psyched out. We can beat those two. I have faith that we probably are the most prepared team here", says Jade, confidently. "We already know our hunting zone very well and we really know how to work together as a cohesive team. Many of the team members had their names put into their clan lottery just before they were given a month to prepare. Even though we to were given the same month to prepare for this hunt, we had been working great along-side each other in many ways for a few months."

"I'm glad you are confident. I feel confident too, but we will need to carefully pay attention to the perimeters of our hot zone. We don't want one of the teams hunting our marked Dregs," suggests Arthus, eying the six-star Silver Thorn scouts. "I am certain they wouldn't cheat by hunting inside our zone, but we don't want to accidently chase our Dregs into their hunting zone."

"You're right... I didn't even think about that. Once we make a camp, we will work on creating noise traps for around the perimeters of our hunting zone, which might help prevent our targeted Dregs from escaping into the other zones. At least we would hear if one ran into one of my noise traps. I also know how to add some extra heat sensor colors and tags that will allow our tele-masks to immediately see the other team member tele-masks. Just in case any of them might cross over into somewhere we might be aiming our arrows. If they are too close to the perimeters of our zone, I don't want to cause any hunting accidents," reveals Jade, smiling.

"Sweet, we will need to do that. Depending on the time we have left, we can hunt both our marks and go after another team's marked Dreg, if they are inside of our zone, which, as you know, would automatically make us the winners of the hunt," declares Arthus, now finding confidence in himself.

"Woah there... let's focus on claiming our hunting zone and ensure we hunt our marked Dregs first. There has only ever been one team in history to get three marked Dregs. If I am correct, that was your mother and your father. We do have a lot of tough competition," insists Jade.

Grag broadcasts, "Last but not least, Clan Ariel, please come register your hunting game holo-cards. This hunt we have a special guest joining in their first-ever hunt, I present Prince Arthus! My daughter, Jade, gets the honor of joining him in her first-ever hunt as well. Please welcome the newbies into our hunt games!"

The rest of the crowd starts to cheer as the two walk up on the platform and register their holo-cards. As they register their holo-cards, they notice that their two marked Dregs get added to the cards.

Grag, holding his hand up again to quiet the crowd, instructs loudly, "Okay, it seems that all clans have their representatives registered in the hunting game. Every team will start in the same area at the very edge of God's Forest. In exactly one hour, we will blow this shofar horn which means all of you hunters will make your way quietly inside of God's Forest and begin to head towards your assigned hunting zones. Once inside, you do have the option to roam as much as you want on your way into your hunting zones. I hope you all take this hour to figure out the best camp spots on your three-dimensional holo-maps. Choosing your campsites is the most important decision of the hunt. I hope you are all ready? Now, go to the edge of God's Forest and get any final preparations ready with your teammates!"

As they all reached the entrance of the forest, everyone split up amongst their clans to discuss their hunting strategies.

Chapter 5
The Hunt Begins.

Arthus and Jade pulled up their assigned hot zone area on their holo-map, and it seemed to be a three-day hike just to get there. Jade, knowing the area very well, picked out the two best possible camping spots on the way to their hunting zone.

Jade tells him, "Another important thing to do is never pick a specific spot to camp too far inside our actual hunting zone. Picking a wrong spot will disrupt the Dregs and chase them away from the campsite. We will need to find the Dregs eating, drinking, and resting areas. Once we have those and document when the Dregs use them, we can start hunting our specific Dreg targets. The hardest part is that these Dregs are amongst the oldest leaders of their pack. As such they are wiser than the young smaller Dregs and are rarely seen in the same areas over and over. They know exactly the looks, smells and sounds of the forest. They know how to hide themselves at the first signs of danger. Meaning that once we figure out their patterns, we will have to split up and communicate on when to take them out. Once we kill something in a certain area, other animals immediately tend to let out various warning calls. We gotta be very careful about this and kill them all simultaneously, or at least as quickly if possible. If not, our other marked Dreg will immediately disappear, possibly into someone else's hunting zone."

"Okay, I'll follow your lead once we enter the forest," Arthus responds.

After finalizing their strategies using the holo-maps and pinpointing the best and most likely drinking, sleeping, and feeding zones that the Dregs will use, they only have a few minutes left before the hunt begins.

Arthus then turns to see the two blue team Silver Thorn scouts walk up to where he and Jade are.

"Hello, my name is Aaron, and this is Lauren. We decided to come over and welcome you guys to your first hunt. I hope you guys do well. Don't forget this is also a competition, so if we get the chance to take out one of your marked Dregs inside our hunting zone, we won't hesitate to do so," says Aaron with a smirk on his face.

"Yes, welcome to the hunt, and remember, don't expect us to go easy on you newbies," insists Lauren with a confident tone.

"No worries, we are excited to go up against the very best during our first hunt. If nothing else, it'll teach us both a lot. But, don't be too quick to expect us to lose, just because it's our first time," replies Arthus, glaring with excitement at the two other challengers.

"Well, we won't keep you. We will see you all with the results in around a week. Don't try and keep up with us. We know with our training that we are much too fast for anyone else here. We know that Dregs aren't the easiest animals on Malon to hunt. There are several kinds of dangerous animals and reptiles. Be especially aware of any wild boars and bears. You even may want to steer clear of their tracks," adds Aaron as a matter of factually.

"Alright, we shall see you guys at the end of the week," says Arthus.

After the two Silver Thorn scouts walk away, Jade looks at Arthus and suggests, "I agree with you, I think your father and grandfather, sent them to keep an eye on you for your first hunt. We may really need to watch our shadows. Let's make sure they aren't just following us around too much and possibly making it more difficult for us to actually target our marked Dregs." With that Jade points her holo-card tagging at both of the Silver Thorn scouts, selects a heat sensing color and uplinks those into her holo-map. She then takes Arthus' holo-card and repeats the process. Then says, "Let's go around and get all of the other team members in this system too. If they ask, we will tell them we want to be sure we don't accidently aim our arrows at them while shooting at a Dreg. In fact, we will ask each of them to be sure they do the same thing for us. We really don't want any hunting accidents caused by a stray arrow."

Arthus nodding, replies, "I agree. Let's do that."

Barely finishing up on that task, they notice that Grag throws his hands in the air. He shouts, "Alright, everyone! Ready! In Five...four...three...two... one...", he then blows the horn. With that, the crowd sees the hunting teams running into the edge of God's Forest.

As Arthus enters the forest, he sees the two Silver Thorn scouts speeding up ahead he thinks to himself, "They are light jumpers! He has seen light jumpers before. They can make themselves pure light and jump to areas that have direct light from the sun. With the forest being so dense and having lots of shade, there aren't a lot of light sources to jump to, but it seems that there is just enough for them to jump from spot to spot silently and quickly. I am amazed and excited, because I know one day I'll be able to do that myself! I also know that light jumping is limited, and you can only travel at certain distances. I think it's only a few hundred feet at a time if I remember correctly."

Jade turns to Arthus and asks, "You going to follow me, or are we just going to stand here, stunned at seeing those Silver Thorn scouts move?"

Arthus, looking like he just got caught with his pants down, responds, "Uhh... yeah, I'm right behind you." He then observes Jade moving swiftly in the shadows. He has never seen her run at such a speed. He is running as fast as he can just to keep up. After a few hours of moving through the forest, trying to reach the first camp spot, they chose on their holo-map. Arthus signals Jade to slow down. He then asks, "You think we could take a break for just a little bit and grab a snack out of the satchel?"

"Sure, let's find a good spot and check for markings of wild animals, just to be sure we are in a safe area to stop," answers Jade. Looking around, she sees a beautiful area around some trees with a small stream. "Ok, let's stop here."

"Alright!" Exclaims Arthus, as he takes his satchel off and rummages through it trying to find some bread. After seeing the food, he sits down by the stream and stretches out. Jade sits beside him and grabs her loaf out.

"It is amazing here," says Jade looking around.

"I agree," responds Arthus.

After a few minutes of relaxing and eating some bread, they spot wild boar not that far downstream from them. Jade, somewhat nervously, turns toward Arthus and says, "Don't freak out, but there is a boar not that far away. We should get up and slowly get away from here. We need to move up the stream and then cross the stream, even if it starts coming after us, we will cover our tracks and smell through the water."

"Okay. I will follow your lead", responds Arthus quietly while slowly getting up and putting his satchel back on.

As they are getting up and starting to head upstream, they notice that the boar smelled the crumbs of the bread they just got done eating. It then started moving toward them. It then hears Arthus step on a couple of twigs, which causes it to spook and turn directly toward them. Seeing them, it starts to run at them. Seeing this, Jade grabs onto Arthus by the arm and pulls him in the opposite direction running upstream as fast as the two possibly could. Jade then jumps into the deeper part of the stream and starts scooping up water with her hands and showering herself. Arthus seeing this starts doing the same thing. Jade then points to the opposite end of the stream and exclaims, "We need to cross now!" They both start running across the stream, which is broader than they expected. Once they crossed, Jade again exclaims, "Don't stop, we need to keep going just in case the boar tried to follow us across the stream!"

After what seemed like twenty or so minutes, they finally stopped. Arthus looking at Jade, says, "Whew... that was a close one."

"Tell me about it. Those things are vicious predators and could easily tear us apart. We are not equipped with the best weapons to fight them at the moment," responds Jade.

"Alright, well, did that boar run us off our course for the first campsite?" Asks Arthus.

"Hmm... let's check our holo map", answers Jade opening the holo-map and pulling up the marker they created for the first campsite. "It looks like the boar ran us off course by only about ten minutes, luckily. We need to head east, but it's still about a four-hour hike from here to the camp."

"Okay, let's start heading that way," says Arthus looking a little tired from escaping the wild boar. After a couple more hours go by, the two decide that it's time for another break. Both sit their satchels down, grab their water skins, and realize that they have almost run out of water. Realizing this, Arthus, looking at Jade with worry on his face, asks, "Were we supposed to fill our water skins back at that stream we were at earlier?"

"Hmm... probably, but I don't think we were in the state of mind to think about that while we were being chased off by a boar. Let's check the holo-map and see if there is a stream or water source nearby," answers Jade, trying to ease Arthus's worry. She then pulls up the holo-map of the area they are at, while looking at it states, "Looks like there is a watering hole five miles to the northeast of here. Let's go there after we finish up here. As long as we move quickly, it should only take us about thirty or so minutes out of our way."

Determined to make it faster than that, Arthus confidently replies, "I bet you and I could make it there within twenty minutes."

Jade, smirking, says, "Oh... yeah. We definitely could, but we should also conserve energy so that we can get from there to our planned campsite and still have the energy to gather and setup our bivouacs."

"Yeah, that's true. It would be smarter for us to conserve our energy just in case we run into more boars roaming the forest", agrees Arthus.

"Alright, let's move to the watering hole. We can take a longer break once we get there and make sure that it's safe," says Jade reaching her hand out to help Arthus stand up. He takes her hand and, with her help, pulls himself up. They both then grab their satchels, throw it over their shoulders and start moving northeast.

Around thirty minutes later, they start hearing the splashes of a waterfall. As they get closer to the waterhole, Jade notices a ten-foot snakeskin laying by a tree not far from them. Motioning at Arthus, Jade points to a snakeskin, whispers, "That's called an ecdyses, or the shedding of a snakeskin. By the looks, though it is a little over two meters long and that may seem big, this snakeskin is from a young snake; no more than a year or so old." After picking up the snakeskin in her hands, she says, "We gotta be careful because that skin appears to be from one of the most dangerous kinds of snake. See here near the head end, and again in the middle of the length, how there are these strange feathers attached along the sides. This ecdyses is from a flying snake. There are a lot of historical stories about an ancient flying snake like Demonic creature known as Nagas, Quetzalcoatl, or Hydra by various clans here on Malon and even by the fallen humans on earth and by other sentient peoples on other planets. It has been known throughout history to almost magically appear and disappear, and can actually shape-shift very quickly too, so be extremely careful. I think that this skin is from one of its young. One of this size might not be a true-blood Demonic version, known as Nagas, Quetzalcoatl, or Hydra, but you might never know? Even a young flying snake of this size can kill a full-grown Cundo. They are known to grow to well over six meters long as adults. The true-blood Demonic ones that are written about in various historical records are said to be many-many times larger than that of its mixed-blood descendants and the Demonic ones can even shape shift into part human part snake forms. I really don't want to meet even one of its descendants, so please watch the sky; especially near the trees and along the top edge of the cliff up there. And, let's not get too close to the water. One good thing is that they cannot move fast when they are actually on the ground, but they do move very fast when in the water. They are known to climb up tall trees and then jumping off they drop and sort of float and fly down from the tops of trees. Pull out your long dagger and have it ready at all times. If we do see it and it tries to wrap itself around us, you must not hesitate to try and kill it. Seeing a snakeskin here, means that they probably live around here in the forest near this waterfall. I have been told that they are much more dangerous to outsiders, especially who are not aware of their habits. Just remember to be careful. Luckily I heard that they don't usually attack unless they feel threatened."

"Oh, well, that sounds like a fun reptile to deal with," says Arthus trying to be lighthearted, sarcastic, and funny.

"Yeah, that's not funny... let's just get our water skins filled and get out of this area," replies Jade looking around carefully, trying to make sure it's not right near them.

"Okay, I'll follow your lead since you seem to know a lot more about this reptile than I do," whispers Arthus back.

"I only know what I have read and what I have been told about them. But, seeing this two and half meter long snakeskin has easily brought all of that into my mind. I didn't mean to ramble on and on about this. I am just really, really scared right now," exclaimed Jade as she is looking around. Jade soon finds a long staff sized tree branch and picks it up. Then she starts walking carefully and slowly checking around the trunks of trees and larger grassy areas. She whacked the staff sized tree branch here and there. She continued to do this until they reached the watering hole. She then stuck the branch into the water and splashed it up and down and pushed as far as she could to make sure nothing moved around in the water. After a few minutes of pushing water around and checking the shallow ends of the water. Jade lets out a long sigh of relief, turns to Arthus, and states, "I think we are clear to fill our water skins directly from the waterfall here as it appears to be coming directly out of an underground spring, rather than from a creek above the cliff there. That water coming straight out from the cliff wall is much cleaner and safer to drink than the water that is gathered in this watering hole pond or in the creek below. Then let's get to our campsite. I think we should move straight there without stopping. We are only about two hours from there."

"Before we go, I think I do want to keep the snakeskin as a keepsake and to do more research once we get done with our hunting week" says Arthus as he carefully picks it up, rolls it up, and tucks it in between some clothing buried deep into his backpack. "I can hardly wait to get to the campsite tonight. I am ready for a good night's sleep," Arthus says while he noticeably starts relaxing his shoulders and becoming much less tense, almost as if the action of making a keepsake of this snakeskin seemed to give him some power over his fears.

After they filled their water skins, they made their way to the campsite. The two managed to get to their planned campsite without running into any other dangerous situations. Upon arriving at the area, they decided to gather branches and set up more comfortable bivouac style camp. Arthus told Jade, "I am going to go look for some stones, dry leaves, and sticks lying around the area. I want to set up a nice fire pit and get ourselves a fire going."

Jade agrees with Arthus and says, "That's a great idea. We also should create fishing spears and go to the stream nearby and try and catch a couple of fish. I will start to look for bait around the area and gather up a handful that we can toss into the stream and to try and lure them to a central area. I've been fishing with my Dad before, and I think I can recreate what he did. Last time we caught enough fish to eat on for three entire days. I do not think we can keep that many on us right now without the fish meat going bad. We will only need a couple of good-sized fish to eat for dinner tonight. And, tomorrow we can catch some for breakfast."

"Okay, I'll go ahead and gather the items we need while you are creating our fishing spears and gathering the bait," replies Arthus nodding at Jade approvingly.

"Sounds like a plan," let's meet up here in twenty minutes and get ready to go to the stream.

Twenty minutes later, Arthus has a small fire pit ready, for when they get back from fishing. Jade walks up to the campsite with the two fishing spears, and a small hollow log that has bugs and critters inside that she plans to use for bait to lure in the fish. She also put in some dead mince fish from the stream in order to attract any bigger fish. She also has a pile of sharpened sticks tied into a bundle, ready to use to build the fish trap in the stream. She is hoping that by building a small stream trap, then mixing together some dead mince fish with the small bugs and critters that will perhaps attract the smaller live mince, she can hopefully also attract some other bigger fish. Her goal is to spear the bigger fish when they swim into the fish trap when they try to eat the bait she prepared. She looks over at Arthus and asks, "Are you ready to go down to that larger stream and catch some fish? Cause I'm starving."

Replying with a nod, "Yep, I am ready and starving as well. Hopefully, we catch a couple of bigger fish."

Looking at Arthus questioningly, "You have never been spearfishing, have you?"

"No, I have never had the pleasure, but it sounds like a lot of fun!" He exclaims, with an excited expression.

"Okay, well help me carry that bundle of sharpened sticks and just make sure to stay quiet, relaxed, and be very patient."

"You got it, and I will be calm and relaxed. I'll even control my breathing as the bigger fish appear. Just give me a signal when you are ready to strike one, and I will aim at the other," he responds.

"Alright... I think we can make the signal a nod?"

"That's kind of a lame signal," he says while laughing.

Smiling, with a laugh, she replies, "Yeah... you are right that is a lame signal."

"I got one, how about we spin the spear above our heads one time. Then, exactly three seconds later, we strike," Arthus adds.

"Okay... we can use that as a signal for fishing. Maybe it will come in handy someday for a laugh, but only for fishing. Since we are going to be hunting far apart from each other and across from each other, two simple clicks made with our holo-reader and our tele-mask speakers is probably a better almost silent signal, and not one that would not spook the Dregs, when we are trying to hunt," Jade replies with a smile. "Alright... let's carry all this down to the stream and get ready for the fish to appear. It could take a long while."

Soon both arrived at the stream. The stream is about knee-deep and a little darker than Arthus and Jade hoped. Seeing that the water wasn't crystal clear, Jade says, "We should still be able to catch some fish. It does look like something disturbed at the bottom of the stream. Normally these streams are only cloudy when a storm, or an animal, or something has disturbed the dirt at the bottom of the stream and pushed it upward. I'll just toss the bait in over here," with that Jade tosses some bait into an area of the stream. She then starts to wade slowly into the stream, while trying not to scare the fish away. Arthus picks up the spear and starts to walk to the creek where Jade entered. Just before he comes into the stream, she raises a hand and waves for him to back away.

Stopping with a concerned look on his face, asks, "What is it, Jade?"

Jade, with an obvious fear look on her face, is shaking her head silently. She is looking frantically, yet slowly at the bottom of the stream. Arthus could sense something was wrong but wasn't quite sure what it was. Out of nowhere, she turns and starts to try to run for the bank, but a massive golden-green horned serpent's head with strange feathers on its head appears and with a lightning like spin it wrapped its large body around the lower part of Jade's legs. She yells out, "HELP; IT'S PULLING ME UND..." Just as she yells it out, he sees her disappear underneath the water. It causes her to lose her spear as she's frantically trying to use her arms to hold herself above the shallow water in the stream.

Arthus immediately pulls out a sizable jagged dagger that was in a sheath in the middle of his back. With the fish spear in one hand and knife in the other, he jumps in the water and in a throwing motion stabs the serpent's massive body with the spear. Arthus loses the spear in the process. The spear couldn't fully penetrate its slimy scaly skin. The spear only made a very tiny cut in between the snake scales. The giant Nagas released its grip just enough as it got mad at Arthus for stabbing it with a spear.

Jade quickly wiggled free, breathing hard and coughing up water, she rushed up and onto the shore. The Nagas immediately raised its head high up out of the water and at the same time swimming and slithering towards Arthus. When it then tries to wrap its slimy body around Arthus, reacting quickly, Arthus stabs the Nagas as hard as he can with his larger jagged dagger. The sharp jagged dagger penetrates through the Nagas' skin and gave it a large deep, painful cut. Like magic a second massive snake head grows out from where Arthus had cut the Nagas. This snakehead was much meaner looking than the first head. This new head had huge fangs and it could spread out the sides of this head like a cobra hood. The Nagas-Hydra Hybrid is now even angrier and full of adrenaline. Quickly it starts wrapping its body faster around him and starts constricting. Arthus began to get scared, but he suddenly felt a strange powerful Life-energy flowing out from his body. This powerful energy changed the color of the wind around him and electricity was in the wind, which actually pushed the two headed Nagas' coils apart and away from him.

As soon as the Nagas' coils gets pushed back and away from Arthus, Arthus also gets thrown out from where he was by the Life-energy and the force of the strange colored wind and electricity. Arthus lands abruptly about 5 meters away from the Nagas-Hydra Hybrid and up onto the shore of the creek. The strange Life-energy and strange colored wind with electricity seemed to take a hold of the Nagas-Hydra Hybrid, preventing it from attacking Arthus. Then there is a sudden roar coming out from the thick woods above the creek. The Nagas-Hydra Hybrid whips its two heads around to see what that roar is coming from. As it does so, a giant walking tree-looking creature, with a large root-like green beard, jumps from the hilltop overlooking the stream and starts to wrap it's a sizable root-like hand and fingers around the two heads of the Nagas-Hydra Hybrid. Gripping tightly the two faces and clamping shut both of the Nagas-Hydra Hybrid's jaws. The frantic Nagas-Hydra Hybrid tries to wrap its body around the huge tree-looking creature. Suddenly, though roots shoot out from the ground and catch the Nagas-Hydra Hybrid from every direction. The tree-like beast then raises yet another branch like arm and changes its finger like branches into large root-like spears which pierces the Nagas-Hydra Hybrid from every angle. The creature then crushes the Nagas-Hydra Hybrid's heads in one giant squeeze while picking up the Nagas-Hydra Hybrid and slamming it into the ground; killing it instantly. The huge tree creature turns toward Arthus and Jade and starts to study them. Although completely stunned, Arthus quickly bows his head low and raises his hands, signaling to the creature that they are not there to cause any harm to it or the forest. The tree-like beast nods back, turns, and starts walking away.

Still stunned watching the creature disappear into the thick of the forest, Jade turns to Arthus and asks, "Was that huge green and brown walking-tree looking creature an Alda? It almost looked like us. It had arms, two legs, ears, nose, mouth, and everything. Yet, its body, legs and arms looks to be made of tree roots, tree trunk, and branches."

"Oh... I would have thought with your familiarity with God's Forest like you are, you would have seen them here in God's Forest before? Well, anyway, yes. They are called Aldas. The Aldas are the guardians of First God's Tree. They are known to guard, protect and serve all things that live or that might come into God's Forest, such as us," explains Arthus.

"Yeah, I knew that they are the guardians of God's Tree. I just have never seen one up close before. I am happy it showed up when it did. Otherwise, we might be Nagas-Hydra Hybrid food. Oh dang, that reminds me, all that commotion probably scared off the fish", says Jade looking sad and annoyed.

"Hmm, well, that is true. But, we do have a very large dead Nagas-Hydra Hybrid now. We can cut it into sections, heat it over the campfire and eat that for dinner. I am so hungry now I could probably eat at least half that thing. I have heard snake meat is delicious. This Nagas-Hydra Hybrid is a type of snake, so let's try." replies Arthus.

"Uhg, I guess I'm okay with trying it out, and it better taste good like you say. I'm just starving, so let's get this thing and take it to our camp," agrees Jade.

"Okay, I'll grab the two headed end of the Nagas-Hydra Hybrid, you grab the tail end, and we will need to work together to drag it from here to our campsite," says Arthus.

"Alright... I can handle that. I'm glad I won't be anywhere near those heads," states Jade.

"Oh. I just figured once we get back, I can cut the heads off and cook those first for you to eat!" Exclaims Arthus jokingly. He continues, "What? You don't want to cook up some Naga-Hydra Hybrid eyeball soup?

"Ha... you are so hilarious," replies Jade as she's rolling her eyes.

The two then pick up the Nagas-Hydra Hybrid and start walking toward the camp. Arthus quickly notices that Jade is just barely guiding the tail end instead of actually lifting it. She is making him do most of the work on dragging the four meter long Nagas-Hydra Hybrid.

"You have to actually lift your end!" Commands Arthus.

After much effort, they are back at their campsite. Jade starts getting the fire going. Arthus then begins feeding the fire with wood and dead leaves to help it grow. Once the flames grow enough, Arthus stops and pulls out his jagged dagger, puts the blade over the fire, and starts heating it.

Jade, looking at him questioningly, asks, "What are you doing?"

Looking back at Jade, Arthus replies, "I'm heating the dagger to slice through the body of that large Nagas-Hydra Hybrid easier. It will also help with stopping it from bleeding everywhere as I am cutting it up. Also, cauterizing as I cut it up with my dagger seems like a great idea to me after seeing a second head grew like magic from the first wound I gave it with my dagger!"

"Hmm... I've never thought about doing that before," says Jade.

"Yeah, cauterizing works well. I have read about doing it in a survival holo-book. It said that it is useful to do, especially if you have to eat something poisonous. I think that Nagas snakes aren't poisonous, but still. I also asked my dad if it was good to do. He said, "Yes, it's one of the best survival techniques to use when you need to cut through an animal that is very large." So that's also why I am heating the dagger," replied Arthus.

"Oh, okay... well, that's pretty interesting to know," says Jade. Almost as if she's trying to make a mental note for herself.

Realizing something, Arthus asks, "How small should I cut up the Nagas-Hydra Hybrid?"

"Let's make it into Nagas jerky. Cut it into one-eighth inch thin slices. That will allow us to dehydrate the meat fast. You start working on that, and I'll get the fire area properly setup for making jerky," instructs Jade.

"Okay. I can do that," responds Arthus.

Jade gathers up the logs and puts them in the center of a small circle of stones. She picks up three long almost straight branches from somewhere on the ground. She then arranges them into a fairly tall teepee shape triangle above the fire pit. She then goes around gathering up a bunch of thatch branches. Upon bringing them back, arranges them onto the outside of the very top of the teepee to create a hut over the fire to catch and hold a lot of the heat and smoke. After doing that, she gathers three similar size smaller length branches from around the camp area. She sits down on a log and weaves together some of the thatch into a tough string material, which she then uses to tie the three smaller branches into a triangle. She then ties that triangle just below the very top inside of the hut onto the three outer teepee frames, thus creating a strong triangle on the teepee near the top. After doing this, she grabs slightly thicker branches and cuts notches in on each end, which she places like in a grid like fashion across the top of the triangle. She leaves a thumb thick sized gap between each one in order that the smoke can easily get past the meat she plans to hang on those. She then repeats this entire triangle grid like process about one foot below the other one. She uses some more of the thatch to create string again and ties up some more thatch and three long sticks with one shorter stick into a long obtuse rectangle, which she ties on one side only; creating an access door to cover one side of the teepee. She then makes two more similar door panels and ties them to the other teepee poles. They all work as access panels around where the meat will be going in.

"Okay... it's finally ready," says Jade.

"I've never seen anything built like that," responds Arthus.

"Once you have some meat ready, let me know, and I'll start hanging the strips of meat on all of the grid sticks that I created at the top of the teepee," replies Jade.

"Well, while I saw how busy you were building that smokehouse teepee, I made myself very busy cutting up plenty of meat strips ready to be hung," says Arthus handing a decent pile of meat strips to Jade.

"Make sure to leave a kilo or so of that Nagas-Hydra Hybrid meat in good sized roasts that we can cook on a tripod turnpike," adds Jade while grabbing the strips.

"Well don't worry. There is so much meat on this Nagas-Hydra Hybrid yet to process. I can easily cut several roasts like that," states Arthus.

Jade reaches in her handbag and pulls out a small metal container filled to its brim with a bunch of metal hooks. She starts hooking and hanging the slices of meat onto the two grids she had built.

As she is hanging the meat at the top of the teepee, Jade looks at Arthus and says, "Sweet. Let's take a few kilos of Nagas-Hydra Hybrid meat and stab it through with this longer branch that I cut from one of those fish spears we made earlier. Once we have the meat on there, we can place that spear closer to the fire on top of that tripod I created."

"Okay," responds Arthus as he grabs the three kilo sized roasts he had cut from the Nagas-Hydra Hybrid and takes them to Jade.

Jade is holding the spear she had made and stabs the meat in Arthus' hands. Arthus pushes the meat further until it's in the middle of the longer spear. Jade and Arthus pick up both ends of the spear and move it to the tripod set up over the fire. They carefully maneuver the spear into place, sliding it well under the smokehouse meat area of the teepee setup, which has a bunch of meat strips already hanging from the hooks on both of the grids up above. A little over an hour goes by, and the three meat roasts are fully cooked and ready to be eaten. The strips of Nagas meat hanging above, however still has at least five to six hours more too cook before they will be completely smoke dried into jerky. Arthus and Jade grab a hold of the spear and take it off the tripod. They carefully remove the meat from below as it is already scorching a bit black on the outside. They placed the three roasts on some large banana leaves that Arthus had found and cut and placed that onto their dinner tarp from their camping gear. The meat roasts are still very hot. Arthus and Jade wait around five minutes or so before she carves into one of the roasts and divides the meat between them. As they begin to eat, they quickly realize that Nagas-Hydra Hybrid meat has a uniquely bland and oily taste, yet it really is not a bad flavor. However, both of them wish that they had remembered to bring along some spices in their camping gear. And, with everything else happening, neither of them had thought to even look around in the woods to gather up any of the wild plant leaves, which are used for spices. Neither of them willing to say anything to each other about not having this already, as they both realized how crazy busy each of them were before dinner.

Jade looks at Arthus and exclaims, "What a day! Huh!"

"Yeah. We have had a full day of adventuring!" Declares Arthus back.

"How much more raw jerky meat do you think we have left?" Asks Jade while looking at the massive pile of sliced Nagas meat, ready to go on hooks."

"I don't know. I'd say we have at least two more times of putting the meat on the hooks. It will probably take us all throughout the night and into the morning to cook just what I already prepared. And, we haven't even cut into a third of the Nagas-Hydra Hybrid meat. I think I should drag the rest of his carcass far away from our campsite. The wild animals around here will surely find it and enjoy it," replies Arthus. He then adds, "I am certain that the smell of cooking meat has already got their attention. I don't think we will get much sleep tonight, as I am concerned that they might want to come into our campsite."

"Well, at least there will be plenty of Nagas-Hydra Hybrid jerky to eat for all of the rest of this week and maybe more; especially after we can gather up some natural herbs to eat with it," states Jade.

"Yeah, that is true. This situation actually worked out in our favor since we won't have to worry about fishing for the rest of our hunt; unless we just get tired of eating the jerky" adds Arthus while sitting back against the nearby tree.

Jade also slouches her back at a different nearby tree. She sets her holo-card timer to go off when she thinks that the meat will need to be switched out.

The two of them take turns. Only one sleeps, while the other one watches the meat, tends to their campfire and ensures the security of their campsite. Many hours go by and Jade's holo-card beeps, Arthus being awake for this first shift, gets up from where he is sitting, and then watching his step, walks over to the teepee and opens the three doors. He sees that the meat is finally ready and pulls each of the grid sections out which has the hooks tied to the meat and lays them carefully onto the dinner tarp. Then he takes all of the dried jerky off the hooks and puts them into an airtight container he took out from his handbag. He then loads up the raw meat back onto the hooks and places those wood grids back into the smokehouse teepee like they were before. After finishing, Arthus wakes up Jade for her shift and then climbs very exhausted into his hammock. Thinking once more about everything that happened already during this crazy adventure that day, he quickly drifts off to sleep.

Jade gets up and tends to the fires in both the smokehouse teepee and the campfire for her shift. When her holo-card beeps again, she quickly changes out the Nagas meat strips and places the dried Nagas jerky into her own airtight food container. Then she wakes up Arthus for the final shift of the morning and climbs back into her hammock to try to get some more sleep even though the sun had just started dawning for the day.

After just getting to sleep, she begins to feel the shuffle of something crawling around on top of her in her hammock. With half-opened-sleepy eyes, Jade notices that it is staring her directly in the face. She shakes and throws herself out of the hammock with a slam onto the ground. She pushes herself off the ground with a groan.

All this commotion caught the attention of Arthus. Bursting out laughing at the scene which happened in front of him. "Aww...look he's just a cute little fella," he says, still snickering.

"That was not funny. That squirrel was trying to eat me!" Exclaims Jade.

"Oh, don't be so dramatic! Look at the little squirrel, it's obviously just hungry. Hey, we should give it a little bit of Nagas jerky. I really do need to reward the little fella for scaring you!" Exclaims Arthus as he walks over to his satchel and pulls out some jerky from the container.

"Oh...alright. He is kinda cute. He just startled me, that's all," says Jade trying to compose herself.

"If that's what you want to tell yourself?" Questions Arthus with a smile while handing the jerky to the squirrel.

The squirrel lets out a happy sounding squeak while gnawing on the jerky. As the squirrel finishes eating, it scampers over to Arthus and starts crawling up his back and stops on top of his shoulder.

"Just look how friendly he is. I'm going to keep him. Let's name him!" Exclaims Arthus

"Well, it sure seems to like you. What are you gonna name him?" Questions Jade.

"How about Sparky! He sure gave you a jolt this morning!" Declares Arthus poking fun at Jade.

"Again, not funny. It's a unique name. I like it," replies Jade.

"Then it's decided, we will let Sparky travel with us until he decides to run away," says Arthus handing Sparky another small piece of jerky.

Sparky grabs onto the jerky squeaks again and shuffles around his neck to his right shoulder.

"Let's get our camp packed up and make sure we clean it up to appear as if we were never here. Then we really do need to start moving toward the next campsite location. We have around a day and a half journey to where the Dregs main roaming areas are located," commands Jade as she starts unhooking and rolling up her hammock.

"Hey, what if we did not stop tonight and try and get to the Dregs area. This could give us an advantage and an extra few hours of tracking," adds Arthus.

"Hmm... well, I'm not sure that would be the best idea. We could try, but if we get too tired, we may not be in the best area to camp," says Jade thinking out loud and looking at the map.

"I say we should at least try. Who knows, we might run into an excellent spot to camp that is closer to our hunting zone," conveys Arthus with a nod.

"Okay... I agree then. Let's hurry and get a move on," says Jade finishing up putting her hammock in her carrying bag. She grabs out some jerky and starts chewing on it. "Make sure you eat a piece of jerky now in order that that we don't need to stop for a long while," adds Jade with a mouthful.

Arthus tosses a larger piece of jerky into his mouth and puts his bag over his left shoulder. Sparky shuffles his way onto the strap and sits on top of the pack. "I think Sparky found his traveling spot," chuckles Arthus.

"Yeah, he looks comfy up there," says Jade smiling.

Arthus packs up all his own gear and then walks around, cleaning up and double-checking the entire campsite to make sure nothing is left that makes it obvious that someone used it as a camping site. He helped Jade dismantle the teepee smokehouse and hid all the parts of that up under the edges of some bushes where they would not be too obvious. Then he used his special camp-style folding shovel tool to dig up some of the wet soil from the creek shoreline, far outside the campsite area, and going back and forth carried that soil over to where the fire pits were located. He then completely buried both of the fire pit spaces with the wet soil to ensure that the fires were completely smothered. Using his shovel and being careful to avoid touching any of the heated rocks with his bare hands, he carried each of fire ring rocks over to the creek shoreline, to the same spot where he had removed all the wet soil, and dropped the rocks into the holes he made there. He then stomped around on the ground there to make that are also look as natural as possible. After ensuring the entire campsite was cleared and looked great, they both grabbed up their gear and start running towards the east again.

As the day goes by, they realize they are moving faster than they had expected due to not stopping and having food at the ready. Since they had already seen some of the dangers of the forest, they knew what not to do and where they should and shouldn't go. They had already passed where they were going to stop for the second night, and yet there was still a lot of daylight left. As they pushed eastward, they started to get closer to where their third camp would be. The day slowly escaped overhead, and they found a perfect stopping campsite.

Pulling out and looking at her holo-map Jade says, "I think we have cut at least five hours off our journey today. We were really pushing it. Tomorrow, it should be very easy, as long as we get up plenty early enough before dawn, to get all scented up in our Dreg scent and very quietly trek into our designated hunting zone. We really want to get all the way in our hunting positions before the sun comes up so that we are not disturbing the Dregs that live in the area."

"I agree. We really made good time today," replies Arthus setting down his bag and getting the camp stuff out, including his hammock. Thinking outloud he says, "I think there is still some time before dark to look around for some natural spices to eat with our Nagas jerky. I really hope we find something here to make this meat taste better."

"I don't think we should bother with a fire tonight. It's pretty warm out, and we don't want to bring any unnecessary attention to ourselves," suggests Jade as she starts setting up her hammock as well.

"I agree. Oh, we should let Sparky hang out in your hammock tonight since he enjoyed it so much the last time," adds Arthus jokingly.

"Haha. You are so hilarious. We should create a little bed for Sparky. I'll gather some thatch branches, and we can put them in a pile for him," states Jade while shaking her head at his attempt at joking.

"Okay, sounds like a plan to me. What do you think, Sparky?" Questions Arthus looking in Sparky's direction. Sparky just squeaks and shuffles over to the thatch that Jade is getting ready for him. "Yep, I think he's going to like the little bed you made for him," says Arthus.

After roaming around for a little bit looking carefully for any edible plants and spices that might help spice up the taste of the meat, Arthus notices that it is just getting too dark to see clearly. He gives up, and then goes to where his hammock is hanging. He climbs into his hammock and quickly drifts off to sleep from his very long day of running through the forest.

Chapter 6
The Hunting grounds.

"Arthus. Wake up! Exclaims Jade shaking him.

"Hmm... what is it, Dad?" Asks Arthus.

"Dad?... ARTHUS WAKE UP!" Yells Jade loudly into his ear.

"Huh? Oh, sorry, I'm awake. What happened?" Questions Arthus.

"Nothing, I just woke up and decided that it was alreay time to get a move on. We cut five hours off yesterday, and we must cut another four hours off our trek today as we really must be in our hunting positions before sunrise," says Jade proudly.

"You are correct, we really must do that," says Arthus as he starts climbing out of his hammock. As he packs up he says, "Might as well try and give ourselves the best possible chance at getting our two marked Dregs and hopefully even going after a third; one of our competition's marked Dregs would be awesome. I think we will be able to sneak into our hunting zones fairly easy with all this fog we have here today," with a determined look in his eye.

"Yeah, I agree. This fog is pretty heavy, but most of it seems to reach just above the trees. A fog this thick might actually hinder the vision we can see through our tele-masks a little bit, so we need to walk carefully too," adds Jade.

"Well, we will just have to be a little more careful today as we move quickly to our next camping area. I can feel that we are getting much deeper into the forest now," says Arthus spinning in a circle taking in the view around him.

"It's beautiful out here in the woods. So much life. It's one of the best feelings. I'm glad that we have more time to take in the scenery now that we are ahead of schedule," states Jade, also circling.

"One of my favorite things about being half Ignole is this," reveals Arthus as he walks to one of the trees, closes his eyes, and then projects his consciousness up through the tree and then above the tree absorbing all the feelings and sensations of the life of everything nearby. Once he did that, he begins to hear even the remotest sounds of the birds flying up in the sky above, and down through the tree all the bugs and critters on the ground, and even under the ground below his feet and out to the very edges of the roots of the tree that he is touching. Wherever the roots reach when they touch other tree roots and plant roots he can absorb the sensations of the next trees and plants. He can sense all of the life nearby flowing in and through his body. Arthus reaches out and grabs onto Jade's hand gently. Suddenly she is feeling everything the same as he is.

"Wow... that's incredible!" Exclaims Jade feeling all the life around her flow through her.

"It's a fantastic feeling, isn't it?" Questions Arthus.

"Absolutely!" Declares Jade. "I have never felt anything like that before" she adds as she seems to look right into Arthus' mind.

Arthus senses a bit of fear in Jade and immediately let go of her hand. As he lets go he quickly says with a concerned look, "Okay. Well, let's get a move on from here so that we can reach our destination before sunrise to get an early start on finding the Dregs," states Arthus.

Instantly feeling that incredible sensation leave her, Jade quickly looks away from Arthus and then says, "Yes, yes, let's go!"

They traveled quickly and actually made it to their hunting zone before sunrise. Arthus and Jade came to the spot where they had planned to set up their main campsite for the rest of their hunting week on the holo-map. It was a location high up on a hill, which has a small flat plateau area with a drop-off cliff on the side towards their hunting zone into almost a 100-degree drop to the valley below. The valley where the main hunt for the dreg would begin. On the rig, they tied to hammocks to a couple large trees that were almost to its top.

"Wow... we are probably one of the first teams to reach our main campsite!" Announces Arthus.

"I would have to agree," states Jade nodding her head.

"Let's quickly set up our campsite and then start looking for any signs of where the Dregs have any common feeding and drinking areas," adds Arthus.

"Already on it. We should also set up some barriers and traps around the campsite once we are finished," states Jade as she is gathering wood and setting up the campfire area.

"I agree. I think it would be smart just to alert us if there are animals nearby," says Arthus.

"I'll make some perimeter signal traps out of some of my clear plasti-thread, which I brought with me in my med-pack. I will attach a holo-signal alert to the trunks of trees at each end. That way, if anyone or any animal pushes against them, or especially breaks through them, we will know as we get an alert on our holo-cards," states Jade.

"Okay, I will work quietly gathering up the thatch, wood and rocks that we need for setting up our campsite and fire-pit, while you work on that. After I we finish with what we have to, we should separate and work our way towards our first planned hunting positions. While we are on our way we should both try to gather up as much intel on the Dregs as possible," insists Arthus.

"Alright... Yes, that sounds like a very good plan to me," replies Jade.

After gathering wood and getting rocks setup for the campfire, Arthus finishes setting up the campsite. Looking around at his handy work, he observes how he had neatly tied both of their hammocks to some of the trees nearest to the fire-pit he located in-between them. He notices that Sparky is resting peacefully on one of the hammocks. Arthus then sets up a small thatch bed area for Sparky up in a three large branch nook space of the tree behind the head of that hammock, then places several pieces of Nagas jerky in next to Sparky's thatch bed. He carefully picks up Sparky and lays him down gently onto his own thatch bed. Sparky moves around just a little bit to make himself more comfortable and then seemed to want to sleep.

After a quick bite to eat, Arthus follows Jade down from the top of the cliff area on a path that she had discovered that leads all the way down into the valley below. Once at the bottom, Jade went off in one direction along the valley Arthus went in the other. They both know that they are to carefully circle the outer valley areas looking for any signs of the Dregs movements. Whenever they found any signs of the Dregs, they entered a tag comment related to these in their holo-cards where both of them could understand what each other found.

Arthus soon came to a waterfall. He followed the river at the waterfall's base into the forest. It was the best place for the Dreg to get water from, and soon Arthus came upon several signs of the Dregs footprints. He scanned the prints with his tele-mask and into his holo-card. The scan allows Arthus to see how deep the prints go and about how large the Dreg that made it is. Arthus carefully follows the footprints farther into the forest valley. The trees here were much closer together. The underbrush is so thick at some points, and trees are stout, tall, and old. Arthus climbed up a tree and was actually able to run from the branches of one tree to the branches of other nearby trees. He seemed to make his way over the underbrush doing that. He quickly came to an open field amid the forest where there is a small patch of all kinds of flowers. They are a variety of the colors of green, red, and many others blended beautifully together. There were several Dregs hanging out in that small opening. They were a color of the forest; light green, having deep brown eyes. They were playing and resting. There was a small hill in the middle of the opening and at its top were two very large Dregs with great antlers that had leaves that grow out from their antlers. The leaves were the color of fall with a reddish hue; even its fur is starting to change color.

Arthus quietly sat down upon a large branch just inside the row of trees. He made sure that he was mostly out of line of sight of the Dregs. He was glad that the wind was blowing towards him; not the other way. He knew if the wind had been blowing away from him, they likely would have smelled him and ran away. He carefully watches the herd as they ate and played together. He thought to himself, "This seems like a large herd, with several young Dregs in the midst. I feel sympathy for the need to take the lives of such great creatures, but hunting is an important way of all of the clan's survival." As he sits leaning against the trunk of the tree, waiting and watching, feeling the cool breeze of the fall and the smell of the flowers, he actually starts getting a bit drowsy. But, he shook himself awake, as he knew the wind would soon change direction. He could sense the wind in his bones and did not want to be there when it changed. He made sure to alert Jade with his tele-mask and holo-card tagging system of what he had found. He noticed that Jade was almost to his location and would be there soon, but as Arthus doesn't want Jade to accidently spook the Dregs as she was coming from an up-wind position, so he notified her to stop approaching that area. He told her to instead meet him at the waterfall of the nearby river. He noticed that she immediately replied that she would instead head back the way she came and meet him at the campsite. Then he quietly stood up and made his way back along the branches toward the river. As Arthus approaches and follows the river back towards the waterfall, he uses a piece of fresh branch that he cut and covers up his own footprints in the soft ground. Then he headed back to where the steep trail lead back up the cliff to their campsite. He made sure as he walked that he did not leave his own footprints behind him. Soon he was walking back up the steep trail and arriving up on the top he sees several wild Yaules. He also sees that Jade is already back at their campsite, and with her is Fang.

"Look who I found," says Jade.

Fang growled a low growl at Arthus, while enjoying the feeling of Jade scratching him behind his ears.

"Where in heavens did you find them?" Asks Arthus.

"Oh, they were just inside the valley my way a bit. I followed my way all around my side of the valley towards where you said to turn back. On my towards you and on my way back I found nothing but one small grassy hill going up and out of our hunting zone area. Right by that grassy hill on my way back here is where I found Fang and his pack. They were laying out in the morning sun," replies Jade.

"I see, so they followed you back here," says Arthus.

"Yup, Fang recognized me at once and followed me here, then I thought, why not take Fang with us on our hunt tomorrow morning," adds Jade.

"Hmm, that actually might be a great idea," states Arthus. Then he adds, "As long as there are no rules against using any Yaules to help us hunt?"

"No, there are no rules against using any wild Yaules during the bi-annual hunting games, and Yaules are great at hunting. Fang may be young still, but he is old enough to hunt Dregs on his own already," says Jade.

"By the way, I do have great news. I found the herd, and both our targets were there," states Arthus. "I knew if I shot one, I would lose the other, so I just marked exactly where they were in my tele-mask and holo-card so that we can go back there to hunt together. I do hope that they will be there again tomorrow." he added.

"Sweet... I can't believe that both Dregs leaders were in one place!" Exclaims, Jade surprised.

Arthus pulls out his holo-map and shows Jade the waterfall, the river, and then shows her where the small open patch of ground with the beautiful colored flowers were. He explained how he got there running up above the ground from tree-to-tree. He told her about the hill and everything that he saw.

Jade smiles and says, "Okay... look," she pulls out her map and with her finger she follows several smaller trails that she had found on the side of the valley where she had circled. She shows Arthus the trail that she was following that led to where Arthus had sent her the message to stop. That trail she had followed also came to a very thick area of underbrush. It appeared that where she stopped was not too far from where Arthus had found the Dregs.

"Okay... if Fang and his pack head back my way around the valley and past that grassy hill. Then follow this path that I found which led towards where you were, and you head in the direction you took today again, then we should both come upon the flower patch around the same time. We have our tele-mask, so we will use that. If I can coach Fang and his pack to circle the open area you found and jump out into the open here," pointing a bit north of where they stage their ambush. "If Fang and his pack waits patiently there for us to get into position, and only then startles the herd from there, they should actually flee directly towards us. We can take aim and shoot our two big males with the leafy antlers, as those are our marked Dregs. I am sure one will try and lead the herd towards you, Arthus, and the other will lead the other half of the herd towards my position. The Dreg's tactics usually mean that they will have a couple strong older males take up their rear in order to attempt to face down Fang and his pack. They do that to attempt to keep the smallest members of their herd safe. I will take the marked Dreg that leads toward me. You take the marked Dreg that is leading towards you. Remember, we must time it right so we can hit these Dregs at the same time. So use your tele-mask and be ready. Also, make sure to check your aiming distance in order to lock onto your Dreg target for a kill shot. This will help you determine how best to shoot and time it just right," says Jade.

They both nod; finally, hoping that they have a good hunting plan.

"Are you sure Fang and his wild pack of Yaules will actually cooperate and come out only after we are in position?" Asked Arthus. "Also, once we kill the Dregs, how are we going to drag them all the way back here?" Asks Arthus.

"Hmm... good point, didn't think about that. But, I know that Fangs pack can help us though." Jade, still rubbing Fang's ears, looks directly into his eyes and says, "Fang, when we hunt tomorrow together, I will guide you to a spot. Then you must be patient for us to also get into our positions before you and your pack coming out of hiding and spook the herd of Dregs. Can you do that for me please?"

Fang gets up from where he is laying down. He makes several excited circular turns and suddenly his pack approaches up close to him. He motions with his front paws and one by one the members of his small pack each crouch down. He looks up at Jade and lets out a growl and motions again with his front paw. Jade, lifts her arm in the air. Then Fang also crouches down. Jade drops her arm and Fang pounces up into the air and all the other pack members suddenly pounce too.

Then Jade turns to Fang and his pack and asks, "Would you also be okay with helping us drag the Dregs back up here once we kill them?"

The Yaules all make a quick spinning motion and nod their heads and then let out a happy growl at the twin moons in the sky above.

Seeing that, Arthus seems satisfied that these wild Yaules will cooperate with the signals that Jade gives them says, "Alright! Well, I have a few kilos of raw Nagas roast that I placed in airtight container in my backpack. Do you think Fang and his pack will want to eat some of that?"

Jade responded, "Oh, wow, I didn't know you saved back any raw Nagas meat. But, yes, I do think they would like to eat that very much."

Arthus goes over to the tree where he had tied his backpack to a rope in the morning before they left, which he had pulled it way up into the tree for safekeeping. He loosens the rope and allows his pack to come dropping down. He opens his pack and pulls out the container with the raw meat. He takes his dagger and cuts two of the raw roasts into almost even sizes and hands them to Jade, who then gives them to Fang and each of the members of Fang's pack. After smelling the raw Nagas meat, Fang lets out a happy growl and starts gnawing on his piece. Each of the pack members then in turn start gnawing on their piece. After eating the raw Nagas meat Fang gets up, goes up to the tree where Arthus was standing, purring loudly reaches up with his paws onto the tree and without showing his claws he makes a scratching motion. Then he begins purring even louder and starts rubbing his head on Arthus' leg. Arthus, realizing that Fang was probably thanking him and wanting more to eat, reaches into his airtight container, pulls out another raw roast. This one he just gives to Fang whole, and says, "That is the last of the raw Nagas meat." Fang grabs the roast in his jaws and makes a circle motion around Arthus and the tree and then goes and lays down by Jade and starts gnawing on that roast. Arthus takes out his other container with the Nagas jerky, takes a handful of that and then puts both containers back into his backpack. He pulls the rope so that the backpack is pulled way up into the tree again. "Well, we better get into our hammocks and get to sleep early tonight, so we can be up way before dawn and get to where we are going to ambush those Dregs. Let's hope the Dregs use that same spot and stay together tonight!" Exclaims Arthus excitedly.

"Yep... I think that's a good idea," states Jade as eating some of her own Nagas jerky and then climbing into her hammock.

Sparky, hiding this whole time up on his thatch bed in the nook of the tree, jumps out from there and lands on Arthus's hammock, causing Fang to growl at it. Jade jumps out of her Hammock quickly and grabs onto Fang's ears. She holds onto Fang's neck and calms him down so that he doesn't pounce on Sparky or Arthus as Arthus is obviously trying to protect Sparky.

Sparky the squirrel is vividly shaking and chattering and trying to crawl underneath Arthus' blankets on his hammock.

Arthus quickly goes over to his hammock, says, "Its ok Sparky. It's ok!" Petting gently on Sparky's head. Arthus lifts Sparky up and holds him, while he climbs into his own hammock. Then he lays Sparky up on his chest near his chin and gently pets him while he covers him up under the edges of his blanket.

"Fang, this is our friend Sparky, he is with us. We found him stranded with no other squirrels in plain sight. He seemed hungry, so we fed him. Please be kind to our friendly squirrel!" Declares Jade.

Fang looks at both of them and then looks at the squirrel and puts its head down as if sad he can't chew up their newly found friend.

"OK! Then let's get some rest and check all out equipment again then later tonight. We will head down before the sun rises and be ready to mark our targets when sun rises. We might quickly finish our hunt and head out of this valley. One good hunting day should give us plenty enough time to get back out of God's Forest. Especially if we get both our targets at once." said Arthus

Arthus and Jade pulled out the holo map and zoomed into the place he had marked. The holo maps were incredible tech, and could not only mark a target, but zoom into the areas which they had highlighted. These were all pretty detailed map and terrain images. With those, they could plan out where they could approach and where to make their ambush and where the dreg would most likely flee once the hunt began.

"Ok Fang, you and your pack will need head to this way to that hill with me, and then you will need follow this path to here and then carefully spread out along the area around this way. Make sure you and your pack wait quietly before approaching the whole open area until you see that Arthus and I are in our hunting positions. Will you please do that for me, Fang? Can you convince your pack to work with us? Asked Jade as she scratched behind Fangs ears. He purred loudly and actually telepathically reassured Jade. Ok, good. "Then Arthus, you head in the other direction like you did earlier, and I will come to this position here. That way we should all come upon the flower patch around the same time. Once you are in position Arthus, contact me by signal by just pushing twice quickly, like I showed you on your holo-map-reader device. We don't want to make too much noise or motion. Then I will signal Fang. Then he and his pack will jump out here," Jade said as she pointed a spot on the map a bit north of where the flowered covered clearing. If Fang and his pack startles them there they should flee directly towards us. Then we can take our shots. When we get an opening aim for the two biggest males with the antlers that have the leaves growing out of them. Those are our two marks. I sure one will try and lead the herd towards you Arthus the other will stay behind to try and face down Fang and to keep the rear of its herd safe. I will take that one. They both nodded that they had their hunting plan and went off then laid their holo-map readers down to get to sleep, knowing that Fang would keep them safe.

The following morning Jade and Fang headed off to find the hill where they found each other the evening prior. Arthus once again headed down where the waterfall was, and then he slowly followed it downstream to where he once again climbed up onto the tall tree canopy. This time though he did go a bit more closer in the direction of where Jade's hill was, because he noticed the winds were coming from a different direction and did not want to spook the herd of Dregs from his scent. He was running as fast as one can from one sturdy branch to sturdy branch. Sun was starting to rise through the tree tops. Arthus already could smell the flowers; he made sure to stick where the wind was on his face so that he wouldn't alert the herd. He finally came alongside the flower patch. He could see from this high vantage point that the Dregs were all hanging out again near the little hill in the center of the flower patch area. Both of their Dreg Marks were there. He then carefully climbed down into the edge before the open field. He knew he needed to get a little closer, so he kept going until he wasn't too far from where the herd was located at the center. He could see the two leaders were still resting lazily on their knees the hill under the early morning sunlight. Wind was starting to chill more and more each morning, and laying in the open sun basking in its warmth and light must have felt nice. He heard two quick clicks in his tele-mask and he immediately sent two quick clicks back. Arthus watched and the Dregs did not seem to hear the clicks.

Arthus knew that Jade had agreed that she would be up on some of the larger branches that poked out over her edge of the flower bed. Arthus also knew that she would take the first shot, which was the signal that Fang and his pack of Yaules was waiting for.

Jade crawled out as far as she could, then sat down pulled out her bow and arrow. She gauged the herd's distance. She was just close enough to shoot at one of their Dreg Marks. She carefully aimed and fired her shot into the neck of the closest large male Dregs. That shot was Fang's signal.

Fang growled loudly and then he and all his pack members quickly leaped out from their hiding positions. The herd nearest to them burst into flight as the large Yaule came out in a flash, nipping at the heels of the younger smaller of the pack. The Dreg leader that Jade had shot with an arrow managed somehow to get up even though her arrow was embedded deep into its neck. It charged towards Fang as he quickly sprinted back to where Jade was ready. Jade was ready with her second Arrow and that arrow flew perfectly across the flower field and sunk directly into the oncoming Dreg's eye and buried itself into his brain, dropping it just on time as it was charging and preparing to stomp its hooved feet into Fang. It no longer felt any pain from her first arrow, it just toppled over and was dead.

The other Dreg leader sounded out a loud honk signal and was running full speed towards the tree line in Arthus's direction, attempting to lead the rest of the young Dregs towards safety. Arthus already had his first shoot ready, let it fly. and then instantly placed two arrows simultaneously on his bow string and as first arrow aimed screaming across just in front of the Dreg, which caused the Dreg to come to a halt hearing the arrow noise. Both of Arthus's second arrows he had already quickly fired off simultaneously buried themselves into the huge chest of the male Dreg. One of which had hit its heart, but not quite deep enough. The Dreg leader dropped forward, and there it lay still breathing but barely. Arthus winced as he had hoped to end the Dreg's life without the Dreg feeling any pain. He ran forward to the Dreg and took out his dagger and, with a quick stab and twist, ended the Dreg's suffering. Then Arthus knelt down by his killed Dreg. He called up the Life-energy within him and pushed it through the Dreg into the flowering field and out. He thanked the Dreg for giving its life to feed the people of Malon.

The herd fled, now leaderless, into multiple directions of the flower filled field towards the forest. Several of the smaller ones fell to some of Fangs pack that was still laying to ambush them from many of the sides. Fang also had killed a good sized Dreg. Afterwards he dragged it over towards Jade in his mouth, then having laid it down, and then placed a big paw on top of it. He then lifted his head and let out a loud growl, seeming quite proud of himself, while in fact he too, was thanking God for this hunt, and he thanked the Dreg for giving its life.

One of the older Yaule from Fang's pack came up to Arthus, with Jade and Fang not far off. It had somehow already placed Jade's kill laying over its back.

Jade smiled and said, "I think in my mind I can actually hear how they want to help us to carry our kills back with us, and they even want to travel with us on our way home." Then turning towards the Fang and the other Yaule, Jade said, "Ok, tonight we will sleep back at our campsite, and then tomorrow morning we will head back. We do have a couple of days left of the hunt, and we will need to bring back with these two large Dreg Marks with us."

Arthus nodded took out a bunch of rope from his pack on his back. He helped Jade to tie up her kill more securely onto the back of the Yaule that had it laid across her back. Then they tied his kill to another large female Yaule. The several younger Dregs and even the larger one that Fang had killed also needed to be brought back up to their campsite. Most were easily carried by the mouths of a Yaule, but as they were trying to travel together it is easier if they are tied on than dragged. Jade pulled a big rope out of her backpack too. They tied the kills onto the Yaules and then quickly headed for their campsite. While up at the camp, Arthus and Jade tied up two long ropes to a nearby tree and then they worked together and lifted the Dregs by their necks off of the ground. The then gutted and field cleaned their own two Dregs. Then they did the same thing to Fang's Dreg, while Fang sat curiously watching them. They quickly skinned and quartered and then cooked up about half of the medium sized Dreg that Fang had killed. The half they cooked they cut some meat off of to eat themselves. The other half they cut up farther and gave it raw to Fang to eat. Then they took the skin of Fang's Dreg and wrapped up the cooked meat leftover and tied it into a bundle. Then they helped clean and skin the rest of the five Dregs that Fangs pack had killed. Then they cut those up in ten even sized pieces so that Fang's fairly large pack could eat as much of those raw as they wanted. There was plenty more meat than eleven Yaule and Arthus and Jade could possibly eat in one meal. So they took up a bunch of leftover raw meat and wrapped it up in each of the smaller Dreg skins and also tied those into bundles. Then they cleaned up their knives, inspected their used arrows and then cleaned them off too. They took water from the tiny stream that bubbled out of the ground by some large rocks near their campsite and made sure all the blood was washed off of everything around their campsite.

There were a lot of bones that had been fairly picked clean by all the Yaules. Arthus and Jade watched as the Yaules then carried off most of the bones that had any meat on them which they had not chewed off, leaving them here and there out around the base of the cliff in the valley below, where other animals, birds and bugs would love to find them and eat any leftover meat on those. The bones that had been picked clean the Yaules actually buried away from the camp by several tall trees.

In the morning Arthus and Jade noticed that all the leftover bones were gone. The five meat filled Dreg skins were then tied onto the back of several of Fang's Yaule pack. They also tied their backpacks and hammocks and other camping equipment onto the Yaules along with their bundled meat packs. Two of the larger Yaule females helped Carry

Jade's and Arthus' kills. Jade climbed up on Fang's large back. Arthus rode up on top on a younger male Yaule, with Sparky in his favorite spot up top of Arthus's backpack, right behind Arthus' head. Then they headed down the cliff and out in the direction of the hill where Jade had met them before. They were making excellent time as Yaules can move almost as fast at the tops of trees leaping from one to another as they can on open ground. Suddenly Fang sensed something was wrong. All the Yaules stopped and crouched down. Sensing Fang's caution in her mind, Jade jumped off Fang's back and grabbed her bow and arrows and made ready. They had not yet crossed from their own hunting zone into the hunting zone of the one of the other hunting teams, but they were right at the edge. Arthus who was in the lead position had a strong feeling of caution too as then his young male Yaule stood up and slowly encroached upon the area into the other team's hunting zone. Back where Jade had jumped off of Fang, had carefully and crouching ready to spring at any second approached a fairly dense area of a thicket of briars and bushes and small trees. There just inside the edge of the thicket, Fang found that there were the two other hunters laying wounded. Fang growled and Jade ran up beside him. One of the two hunters was completely passed out and appeared wounded fairly severely. The other was awake, but he too had been hurt. She could tell that one of them dragged the other to where they were hiding in the thicket.

"What happened to you two?" asked Jade as she handed her water canteen to the hunter who was awake.

My team member had shot and killed one of the Dreg Marks, but then the other even larger Dreg Mark attacked him in anger. Then as I tried to shoot at him, my arrow missed and he picked up my team member by his huge rack of horns and threw him over. He is alive but barely. Then that huge Dreg leader also attacked me. I am wounded, but somehow I was able do drag my team member away from the clearing out there across the line in our zone to the only place thick enough to prevent that large Dreg from continuing his attack. Truly we were unprepared for the Dreg to have that reaction. We believed it would simply run away once the other Dreg was killed. We both let down our guards and this is the result of our failures.

Suddenly and seemingly out of nowhere a very large Dreg leader burst through the thick brush not far away from Jade. It was still very angry and had come to challenge them. Jade had already laid her bow and arrows on the ground while talking to the hurt hunter. She knew she did not have time to reach them and grab them so she pulled her two long hunting knives out of their sleeves. The Dreg had lowered its head towards her and began kicking the ground, which Jade recognized was a challenge stance that Male Dregs use when they are planning to fight one another, or when facing off against a beast that might be coming after the Dreg young.

Fang did not wait for the Dreg to come charging at Jade. He had quickly circled around to the side and using all of his power slammed into the side of the Dreg, who was already charging. The very large Dreg was knocked into a flip, but quickly recovered and was back on his feet then charging into the fight with Fang.

Jade, having grabbed her two long hunter's knives was not thinking of her own safety at all instantly ran and leaped into the air landing up onto the back of the Dreg and then sinking her two long hunting knives deep into both sides of the Dreg, just behind its two front legs. One of the two knives she hoped had successfully went deep enough to prick the heart of the Dreg. It howled in pain and anger as it then stumbled forward landing on the front of its neck and while throwing Jade off its back onto the ground. Jade feeling herself getting thrown quickly tucked and rolled on the ground and then just as quickly leaped back up onto her feet and ran off towards one side.

Fang did not wait to see if the Dreg was dead. He leaped in and grabbed its throat in his huge jaws and held it there on the ground until it breathed no more.

Arthus's smaller younger male Yaule meanwhile had circled back. When he arrived he saw Jade plunge her hunting knives deep into the sides of the Dreg, right behind its large front legs. And then how she had been flipped off the Dreg, and then how Fang grabbed and held the Dreg in his large fanged mouth. Before he even had a chance to get down off of his Yaule the battle was over. Jade had successfully, with just her two long hunting knives killed the rival hunting teams marked Dreg. Fang though holding it down by its neck, realized it really was her blade that had found the Dregs heart. Looking around where the battle took place Arthus realized that Jade had actually killed this other team's marked Dreg just inside of their own hunting zone.

Arthus jumped off of his young male Yaule and pulled off his backpack, which made Sparky have to move. Sparky wisely climbed up onto Arthus's shoulder. Arthus then found his med kit. Jade also pulled off her backpack and grabbed her own med kit. Then Arthus and Jade quickly did their best to try to help the two hunters.

Jade told Arthus, "Do not try to move the one hunter because of how badly he was injured."

The other hunter was also injured very badly too. Jade grabbed her small hatchet and chopped off some thick branches of a nearby bush. She used those and some ripped cloth from the shirts of the injured hunters to secure their broken arm and broken leg bones where they would not easily be moved. Jade worried that the one hunter had been thrown so badly that he may not even survive. She was afraid he might even have a broken neck. She told the one hunter who was still conscious and talking that he was not to try to move his friend anymore. She cut more thick branches into small sections and grabbed some rope and pieces of the dreg skins and made a brace to go all the way around the neck of the very injured hunter. She then looked at his upper body and could tell he had many broken ribs and possibly broken both of his collar bones too. His body is badly broken in many places. She chopped some long wooden poles from the smaller fast growing bushes. She laid them side by side right next to the unconscious injured hunter and carefully tied them together in four different places, turning it into a stable wooden bed. Then Arthus and Jade carefully slid that under his body to try and stabilize his body on a much stiffer and flatter surface. Then she tied ropes all the way around his body in several places starting with his forehead and working her way down towards his feet. Then they rolled some boulders over and under the makeshift platform at the injured man's feet to elevate his feet above his head.

Jade said, "This is to help keep him from going into shock."

Then she built one just like it for the less injured man and had his feet elevated like the other more seriously injured man. She tied him to that platform too, but only his one injured arm, chest and legs.

Jade warned him, "Do not try to untie yourself and move around. If you move too much your broken bones can sever an artery and you can bleed to death internally."

Arthus meanwhile pushed and pushed his Life-energy calming and healing pulses into the body of the more injured man. He was not trained enough in the healing arts to truly help them heal like the true healers were, but even what little that he did know how do, that actually did make a difference. The man's painful contorted face relaxed and his body also relaxed a lot. He was still very much unconscious but now he seemed to be sleeping more peacefully.

Once they had the conscious hunter on his own makeshift platform Arthus began doing the same thing where his broken bones were located, pushing his own Life-energy calming and healing pulses into his body.

Then they left some of the Nagas-Hydra Hybrid Jerky and some of the cooked Dreg with injured hunters. One of Fang's younger, but still quite large female Yaules was to stay at their side to protect them from any danger. They left her several large pieces of raw meat too. The conscious hunter told them where their own campsite was located. So Jade and Fang went there and quickly packed up their belongings and brought them to where the two injured hunters were laying down. Jade wrapped a blanket over the more seriously injured hunter and made sure that the other hunter could reach over and provide him water to sip on. Then Jade laid a blanket over the hunter that was still conscious.

Meanwhile Arthus located the Dreg that the severely injured hunter had killed before the other Dreg had attacked him. He had the Yaules help him drag the two large dregs over to two nearby taller trees and then used ropes to pull the Dregs bodies up so that he could gut them and field dress them too.

Jade had searched around and found some healing herbs which she made into a tea and then fed that to both of the injured men. The one that was unconscious she could only give him a tiny drip at a time into his mouth.

Once Fang assured Jade that the younger female Yaule would stay and protect the injured, then they added her second killed Dreg, which she had killed with her hunting knives, onto a third larger Yaule's back and tied that one down on its back.

Jade then assured the injured but conscious hunter, "I will only take the Dreg that I have killed with my own hunting knives with us on this trip to the edge of God's Forest. The kill that your unconscious friend had killed will remain field dressed and tied up on that tree nearby. The fairly large young female Yaule from Fang's pack will remain with you both protecting you. It won't take us long on Yaule back to reach the edge of God's Forest to send back real healers and other help. Arthus and I will go with the rest of Fang's pack now to get you help. Do your best to keep dripping a little of this tea into your injured friend's mouth. But only a tiny amount of drips at a time."

Arthus said, "If you have any healing skills with your own Life-energy, try your best to help yourself and your friend too. We will have help sent to you very quickly."

The injured but very conscious hunter thanked them both for their help and so Jade climbed up on her friend Fang's back and Arthus climbed back up on the young male Yaule's back he had been riding earlier, with Sparky again sitting in his favorite spot on top of Arthus' backpack right behind Arthus' head. Then they headed out towards the edge of God's Forest where they knew that they would be able to get the injured hunters some very fast help.

Chapter 7
The Harvest Festival

It did not take long at all when they came running on Youle back at full speed up to the edge of the forest, where they had started their hunt. This edge of God's Forest was still a few hours away from the farming village. Immediately they met Grag and several of the other villagers of Clan Arial, who appeared to be walking around gathering up herbs and such.

"Well, look at that," said Grag

He walked up and hugged his daughter.

"I don't think in all of history a team returned on wild Yaule back, and with three Dreg kills, my goodness, you two have really outdone yourselves. Well, lets us gather these burdens from our wild Yaule friends. I am sure they want to be free of them," he laughed.

"Before that father, we discovered two injured hunters. One of them very severely injured. And though we done the best that we know how for them, you need to send healers and some others to help them right away, said Jade quickly.

Oh, my said Grag, who quickly asked where Jade and Arthus had marked on the holo-map. Taking Arthus' holo-map, Grag quickly ran over to where several hunters were gathered together. He orders them to take one of their farm village healers and some Yaules and go back into God's forest to find and rescue the hunters at the location marked on Arthus' holo-map. Very quickly two of the hunters and one of their farm village healers with five of their own Yaules, were headed back out into God's Forest to rescue the two hunters. One of the older female Yaules from Fang's pack led them too.

Arthus ran up to them and said, "Oh Grag, they should also know that one of Fang's pack's fairly good sized wild female Yaules is there protecting the two injured and their Dreg kill is hanging on a nearby tree. We left them water and herbal tea and some meat. Fang's pack's wild Yaule was left with plenty of raw meat too.

Several of the adult town's folk, who had been there at the campsite just outside the edge of God's Forest throughout the whole hunting week, helped Jade untie and lift each of their large marked Dregs up onto their shoulders.

"Ah, Arthus, I almost forgot High King is back in our village helping make everything ready for the big festival tonight. I sure he'll be glad to see how you've grown and by your arrival today also with three kills," said Grag

Jade with a tear in her eye, petted and patted Fang, and watching as he then left to go join up with the rest of his pack to head back into God's Forest. Grag walks up to her and firmly placed a hand on her shoulder. Don't worry, my girl, I sure you see him again. That wild Yaule thinks of you as family, and if it ever wishes to become more domesticated, it knows that it can come stay with us in the village"

Jade responds immediately, "I know he doesn't want to become domesticated. What he wants, is for me to become wild; living out in God's Forest with him and his pack."

Grag shaking his head from side to side and then gently touching and lifting Jades chin with his big hand, looks her right in her eyes, and in a firm voice says, "Well that, is NEVER going to happen! Right?"

"Yes, dad, you are right, responds Jade with tears welling up in her eyes. And, then she looks down and away and says, "Fang knows that too. I don't know why I am just having this strong feeling that we might not get to see much of each other in the future. I hope it is not true."

"We never know all the future plans that God has planned for us. We simply have to trust that He has a plan! He would not have you become this attached to Fang, without having some special plan in mind for you both," said Grag.

At that Grag, along with several Cundos, who had all been camping near the edge of God's Forest during the hunting week, all mounted up on their already packed Yaules. Grag cheerfully orders, "It is time to head back home now." And with that, Arthus and Jade and the rest of the hunters all joined them and headed back towards their farm village.

Upon arriving at the farm village Arthus hears his name being called.

"Well, Arthus! Look at you my young man," said High King Thureos, as he was walking towards them. He then added, "How did your first hunt go?"

Upon seeing and hearing the High King, Grag quickly runs over and cheerfully claps the High King on the back of his shoulders. "Ha, ha! They got themselves three large Dregs! And, when they came out from God's Forest, they were even riding some wild Yaules," Grag yelled as he laughed. "This will be a hunting story told for generations!"

Jade blushed, and Arthus laughed.

"Well, I say you both need to go clean up and get dressed for tonight we will celebrate our Harvest Festival, and we can't have you both smelling like... well the way you do right now," said Grag.

Jade's face turned red; she smelled herself and winched.

All burst into laughter.

Arthus went to his small cabin and then got a hand carry bag with some fresh clean clothes ready for the bathhouse. Upon arriving at the bathhouse he discovered that Grag and his grandfather, High King Thureos was joining him. Jade was already there when they arrived. She smiled and waved and entered the female side of bathhouse.

Arthus, Grag, and High King Thureos all smiled and waved back. Then they walked into the male side. Grag and Arthus took a little longer than usual using the personal showers, as it had been a little over a week since either of them had been able to get clean. Coming out they both joined the High King, who was already sitting in the hot spring pool for a little while. Arthus noticed for the very first time in his life, how many scars his grandfather, High King Thureos had. His body was covered with them. Some look like they had to have been profound and nasty. High King Thureos notices Arthur looking at his scars and realizes what Arthus must be thinking.

"When you live as long as I have my grandson and you are responsible to protect and help bring all of Malon together, you gain a few scars here and there. Most of these scars are from various beasts and creatures all over Malon. Most of which, you haven't even dreamed of yet. Now tell me all about your hunting week. I want to know everything," says High King Thureos with a huge smile on his face.

Arthus sitting in the hot pool enjoying the feeling of the week's hunting trials all leaving his body, tells both Grag and High King Thureos all about the incident with the wild boar. Then he tells about finding the young Nagas' shed skin. And then he relates how they were attacked by a four meter long huge Nagas as they were going to fish near their campsite. He shared how when he stabbed the Nagas it magically grew a second head, just like in the ancient foreign stories about the Hydra. Then Arthus shared about the Alda who had helped save them and killed the Nagas-Hydra Hybrid. And, then he shared how they were then able to cook and eat some of that Nagas-Hydra Hybrid.

"I'll make sure to send a royal invitation for you to the Matriarch of the Alda, and when she comes we must then properly honor the Alda that saved you," said High King Thureos. "In fact you should join me, Arthus, when I present that royal thank you to her and hopefully to that younger Alda that you met in God's Forest."

After relating how he had discovered the beautiful flowering meadow with the little hill in the middle, where the Dregs were located, and how Jade had found Fang on a different grassy hill, and explaining how they planned out and carried out their planned hunt, where they killed the first two Dregs, and how Fang's pack had successfully killed five smaller Dregs, and how Jade and he had skinned all of those, and bundled up a bunch of raw meat in their skins. And then how Fang's pack had ate what they wanted from off of several bones and then carried them off to allow other animals, birds and bugs to find them, and buried the ones that the meats had been cleaned off of. Then on their way back right at the edge of their own hunting zone, finding the two wounded hunters. Then how Jade jumped up with her two long hunting knives onto the back of the other team's marked Dreg as it was facing off with Fang. He shared how she stabbed that Dreg just behind its front two legs on both sides deep into its chest. One of her hunting knives had found its heart. As the Dreg fell forward it flipped Jade off of its back and how

Jade tucked and rolled and came back up onto her feet only to find that Fang had jumped in and with his giant feline jaws held the Dreg down by its neck as it breathed its last breath. He told how Jade and he did their best to help the two hurt hunters. Jade seems to know a lot about how to stabilize someone when their body is badly broken up. And, he had used his Life-energy calming and healing push pulses like he had learned from his teachers in the Great Library. Those seemed to help the hurt hunters a little, even though he had not yet developed much skill with them. Then he was finally done telling his grandfather everything.

"You have grown a bit. I see that you faced some obstacles in your time here, but you need to know that tomorrow is the day that you will leave this place. Your year here is over, and now I will take you to Clan Gearhead in the Great Northern Peaks City, where you see and experience many new things. But I warn you, my grandson, the wild frozen tundra areas around the Great Northern Peaks Mountain Range are not even close to tamed land. Those wild lands are far more dangerous than even God's Forest. It will be bitter cold, and the wildlife there seems always hungry for a foolish wanderer to go into their territory without any knowledge of how to stay alive," said High King Thureos.

Seemingly all at the same time, they all said, "Oh, hot, hot, hot..." And that is when they all decided they been soaking in the hot springs water long enough and each climbed out of the pool. Quickly wrapping a towel around their naked bodies, they gathered up their clothing, entered the dressing area and got themselves dressed. Then they all headed out to where the Harvest Festival was setup.

Jade arrived at the Harvest Festival area just before they did. She was dressed in a special outfit for the festival, which was a bright green dress that matched her eyes. She had on a necklace of flowers and a smaller wreath like crown made of flowers wrapped around her head. She was standing up on the inside of a very fancy wrought iron gazebo that was also adorned with many beautiful flowers, feeling the wind blowing through her hair, and having her eyes closed. Seeing her there, Arthus stops and stares at her. Standing there his heart was racing; he didn't understand it, but she looked more beautiful than any of the things he saw in the forest or anywhere before. High King Thureos chuckled upon seeing his grandson standing there obviously staring at Jade. He shoves Arthus while laughing, which immediately made Arthus look away, blushing and come back to his senses.

Noticing Arthus, Jade says smiling, "Finally, you get back?"

"Ya. Sorry, grandfather wanted me to relate the whole tale of our hunting trip, and made me tell everything about it," said Arthus.

"That's cool... Well, now you really should go get yourself dressed up even more for this festival," said Jade smiling still.

Arthus nodded at Jade and then turns and runs back to his small cabin. Upon entering he notices that there is a package that his grandfather had left for him on his hammock. Inside the package he discovers a very nice pair of blue dress pants, which has a green-gold stripe trimming running down the outer seams. There is also a pair of super-shiny black leather dress buckle boots. There is a very fine dress white shirt that has a white and green-gold trimmed frill attached at the chest and at the cuffs of its long sleeves. Also, there is a fancy green-gold tunic with a matching blue striped trimming running down the outer seams of the tunic. The Crest of Clan Arkwright is embroidered onto the back of the tunic, and on its chest is a fine embroidered shield with the letter A on its outer face. In the background of the shield there is an embroidered image of First God's Tree. Arthus smiled happily as he put on the fancy outfit. He noticed quickly that the tunic fit his chest and waist exactly. It seems in fact just a bit tight. He recalled the last time he wore a similar dress outfit, when he was younger, and it too had fit him tight. He recalled that this kind of outfit forced him to always stand up perfectly straight and as tall as he possibly could. He recalls his father the Prince's words from when he was younger, when he had complained about how that dress outfit fit so tightly, "This is not an outfit meant for leisure and comfort, but for acting very proper and for looking ones very best!" He combed out his hair and then and tied up and back his long hair properly with his usual piece of bark. Then he carefully shaved off the few scraggly hairs that had grown from his chin and under his nose. Taking a damp cloth he cleaned the last of the soap from his face. Then there came a knock at his door, and he heard the sound of Jade's voice.

"Come in," he says loudly.

"I hope you are ready," she says quickly as she is opening the door. Suddenly she is smiling brightly upon seeing Arthus. "Wow, so this is what the Prince of Malon looks like, all dressed up fancy! Not bad! Not bad at all... I guess," said Jade as she was beginning to blush.

"Jade, you look like you could be queen of all Malon right now," said Arthus quickly without thinking, which caused Jade to blush very brightly. She then turn around quickly, and she walked outside. Stopping for a moment, waiting for Arthus to come out. Arthus steps out and then Arthus and Jade walked back to her home, not saying anything as both were still blushing. When they arrived at Jade's house, they discovered her father, Grag and High King Thureos were already standing outside the house with Jade's mother.

"Oh my, you two look so cute together," said Shelly.

High King Thureos laughed and slapped Grag on the back. "If they were just a little older, I'd say we're heading towards a wedding and not the Harvest Festival," remarked High King Thureos.

Jade and Arthus's faces immediately became bright red.

Grag grunted and frowned. "My daughter Jade is way too young for courting men and marriage!" Grag remarked.

Upon hearing that, High King Thureos began to laugh much harder. Shelly smiled with a twinkle in her eyes and also laughing at what Grag had said. She says, "I am not so sure that Jade is too young. I recall being almost her age when..." Before she could finish her comment, Jade huffed and stormed off by herself.

Arthus at the same time put his hand up over his eyes and forehead, lets out a big sigh, and then shakes his head. "Marriage..." Arthus mumbles, "No way, I am way too young for any of that stuff! Jade is beautiful, very – very beautiful. I really do like her a lot..."

Before Arthus could finish his thoughts a couple of Dwarvens ran up and interrupted everything. "High King, High King, the fireworks that ye ordered are all set up and ready for ye fine festival this evening," said one of the Dwarven people as they both bowed down deeply allowing their long beards to touch the ground.

High King Thureos waved for them to stop. "Thank you, my friends, but we have no need for anyone to bow here. This is not our High Court, but rather a celebration night for everyone's merriment and joy. It is Malon's Harvest Festival. In fact, let us save all of our bowing for only honoring God during the Great Gifting!" Commanded High King Thureos.

The two scruffy-looking dwarves stood up and smiled. They had black streaks smudged onto their faces and had very dirty hands. Their leather work aprons were worn loosely over their tunics. They had on very large well-worn leather boots and gloves. One had short hair and a long curly beard the other had a bald head. However, the Dwarven with the bald head had a huge blood-red color dyed mustache, which he wore pointed out like long spear tips well beyond his face. Both of them had large bushy eyebrows, so much so that they almost covered their Dwarven eyes. The bald Dwarven also had a very thick black beard that was very long, which he quickly grabbed up and tucked into his very dirty leather pants.

"We needs be heading out and gettin ready then," stated the bald Dwarven. Looking at the short haired Dwarven he says, "Come on let us go." They both started to bow again, but then stopped themselves having remembered the High Kings Command, and then turned and quickly ran back down the road the way that they had come.

Motioning with his hand to his wife Shelly, Grag says, "Well now, High King Thureos, we best get ourselves back to work to ensure that there are enough tables and chairs and place settings for everyone. All the food for the big feast should be fairly ready by now."

Arthus joined them as they were all walking around the village, making sure everything was ready for the Harvest Festival. They walked around to where there was a giant round circle edged with small shrub like bushes planted closely together and manicured like a fine hedge. Inside the very center of the giant circle, a fairly large seedling from First God's Tree had been planted, and from the looks of its size, it is at least several thousand years old. Surrounding this God's Tree Seedling there were several circles of many low natural stone altar like tables permanently placed there. These stone tables were beautifully covered with fine purple, blue and gold embroidered cloth. Many harvest gifts were laid upon those; crops mostly, but many types of killed animals were also laid there. The two Dregs Jade had killed, and the Dreg that Arthus had killed were also already laying out there on three of those stone tables. Arthus was surprised by this and wondered why all of this was laying out there on the natural stone altar tables surrounding this God's Tree Seedling. He observed several Cundos and Ignoles coming and bringing various gifts. Then he observed a small team of Dwarven people unload a heavily filled cart with various tools and various farming machines onto some of the larger stone altar tables.

With a smile on his face, High King Thureos was also standing nearby, observing Arthur's reactions and all the procession of the various local members of clans bringing their gifts. "These are all for the Great Giving, as we need to be thankful to God for everything; especially for the excellent crops that are grown during this season. We all bring various gifts from the land, from our hunting, and from our various skills that God has blessed us to learn, to understand and to use. Even those clans that design tools and machines also bring a tribute. Each year during Harvest Festival, at least a tenth of everything that is harvested, everything which we have hunted, and everything which each clan has either created, built, or discovered is brought, and as a gift being laid out here by this God's Tree Seedling, or to other similar God's Tree Seedlings in various places around Malon as a tribute. And, I saw the questioning look on your face as you discovered that yours' and Jade's first hunted Dregs, are laid right out over there on those stone altar tables. You need to be aware, always, any very first in their lifetime killed Dregs from any bi-annual hunt is a very important part of the Great Giving. Later tonight, you see a grand surprise," said High King Thureos.

Arthus hearing what his grandfather, High King Thureos had said about first kills, thinks to himself, "The Nagas-Hydra Hybrid was also a first kill on our hunt. I know it really wasn't my kill. It was rather the young Aldas that killed it. I actually still have a large airtight container filled with Nagas-Hydra Hybrid jerky left in my backpack, which I should bring and offer up also as a gift."

Leaving the God's Tree Seedling circle and arriving back at the main festival area people were already gathering in the town's center where the festivity would begin, they see a large crowd of various clans members beginning to gather. Arthus heads quickly back to his cabin, opens his backpack and pulls out the large air-tight container of Nagas-Hydra Hybrid jerky. Then he heads over to Jade's house to make sure Jade and Shelly didn't need any extra help. Jade wasn't in their kitchen. He learned from Shelly that she had locked herself in her room for a while already. Arthus knocked at Jade's door. "Jade, are you ok? Asked Arthus.

"Yes, I am ok. I will meet you over at the Harvest Festival area in a little bit, responds Jade through her closed door."

"Jade, if you have any Nagas-Hydra Hybrid jerky meat left please bring it with you. We need to be sure to gift it at the God's Tree Seedling Circle," Arthus said, still staring at Jade's closed door.

"Ok. Yes, I have a whole container still," Says Jade, who then opens her door slightly and holds her arm out of her door, with the rest of her body hiding behind her door. She is holding in her hand a container filled with Nagas-Hydra Hybrid jerky. "I am not ready yet. You take this with you and run it over to the God's Tree Seedling Circle and put them on one of those stone altars, and then please come back to help my mom while I finish getting ready," she says, still hiding her body behind her door.

Arthus thought to himself, "How could Jade get any more ready? She already dressed so beautiful in that bright green dress that matches her eyes."

"I will be right back, says Arthus to Shelly as he grabs Jade's container with his own and goes quickly out the door of their house. Arthus runs as quickly as possible back over to the God's Tree Circle and places the Nagas jerky one container on the stone table altar with Jade's two Dregs laid. And then one container onto the stone table altar where his Dreg was laid. Then he runs back to Jade's house to help Shelly.

Shelly smiled as Arthus carries several pies and other things, going and coming back and forth from the house to the festival area. After seeing Arthur make five quick trips back and forth, Shelli says, "Well, thank you very much for helping me with all of that. Now, you must head over and join your grandfather, the High King, as I am sure he is expecting you to be there with him right now. Jade and I will come along very soon." Then Shelly yells out over her shoulder, "Right Jade, you have to be ready for sure by now!"

"Coming very soon mother," echoes Jade through her closed bedroom door.

Arthus left the house and returned with the last load from Shelly to the festival grounds. The two Dwarven people he had seen earlier were nearby. Arthus noticed that they had actually washed up their face and hands and had changed clothing. Arthus walked over to where they were to see what they were up to. "Hello, sorry, I didn't get your names earlier when you both came to see my grandfather, the High King," Arthus said.

The two Dwarvens turned to him. They were sharply dressed now in a beautiful green tunics and had funny, tall hats on their heads. "Well, bit my beard, young Arthus," said the older looking Dwarven. "Name is Barg, and this is me son Targ of Clan Gearhead," said Barg.

"We be fireworks makers," said Targ.

"I see... When shall I get to see your craft displayed tonight?" asked Arthus with a smile.

"Ah, well that be after the Great Giving and only after all the Alda have come and gone away," said Targ.

"Alda?" Asked Arthus, looked confused.

Barg quickly elbowed Targ. "You wasn't supposed to ruin the surprise, you daft dolt. We sorry Prince Arthus forgive my blockhead of a child for ruining your surprise, but it as he said the Alda will come to collect all the gifts that people leave at First God's Tree and all of these God's Tree Seedling Circle Altars all over Malon. It is they that come each year to collect all up the Great Gift, and it is they that then go out and give it all back to the land and to various people and creatures in need. This act is what your people call the Great Giving, and it pleases God and brings blessing on Clan Arial and all of the other Clans. We Dwarvens even share some of our various tools and machines that we make each year. Even the crafting and displaying of our fireworks show is all part of giving thanks to the Ultimate Great Creator, the one you call God." said Barg.

"I like how we give to the Ultimate Great Creator by making the best creations we can," said Targ.

"I saw some Dwarvens unloading a wagon of tools and machines onto some of God's Tree altars earlier. I am so happy to know that even the Dwarvens join the Malon natives in giving to the Ultimate Great Creator, God. I know I will soon be spending time in the Northern Peaks with the Cundos and Dwarvens that live there. I hope to get to know you and your clan a lot better soon. Thank you for kindly informing me," said Arthus. He politely waved goodbye and walked away towards where his grandfather was. Thinking to himself, "Dwarvens. I wonder if those two are strange, or typical, like the rest of the Dwarvens people. He quickly reaches where his grandfather and Grag are seated along one of the largest tables.

"Join us! Soon the festival will begin," said High King Thureos. Arthus pulls up a chair next to his grandfather. Very soon Shelly and Jade came and sat down with them. The entire clan was here cheering, drinking, and talking. Soon a bell rang, and Grag got up and walked around to the center.

"Welcome, my fellow Clansmen and woman. Another long year has gone by and another year of plentiful harvest. Every clan thanks you for all your hard work every year as we grow and work to help provide food and subsistence to all of Malon. Now raise your glasses High to God and another year of bountiful crops," said Grag loudly for the clan to hear. The entire clan rose and shouted, then drank and cheered.

High King Thureos stood and walked around to join Grag. "Welcome, Clan Arial and to all the other clans of Malon that have joined with us here today, I, the High King of Malon, am extremely happy to be here with you this year. Thank you all personally for your hard work this whole year, and I especially want to thank Grag, Shelly, Jade and the other members of Clan Arial for helping Arthus to learn all that he could throughout this last year. He has grown up a lot in this past year. Jade and Arthus brought back their marked Dreg targets and brought back a bonus marked Dreg. We know that that Dreg entered their hunting zone, when it escaped out from its own hunting zone. Though I am certain that it is a felt loss to the other hunting team, in all fairness, making Jade and Arthus this bi-annual hunt grand champions. Let us please now give them a round of cheers and applause for proving they had truly gained many skills working and hunting together as a team, and for proving that they had the ability to use their knowledge and talents to come back safely after an entire week of facing and overcoming some of the dangers associated with surviving in the forest."

A loud cheer and stomping could be heard from the crowd.

Motioning for silence, "I want to thank all the other hunters from the different clans. You all have done well. Now with that done, let's eat, drink and be merry," said High King Thureos. Then both Grag and High King Thureos bowed courteously to the crowd and quickly went and sat back down.

The people of Clan Arial and their guests, laughed, danced, and sang well into the evening. As the sun just started to go down, everyone quickly headed over to the God's Tree Seedling Circle. Several Alda had already arrived at the God's Tree Seedling Circle.

High King Thureos immediately goes over and bows slightly holding his hands face up. He says something quietly to the Aldus' leader that looked noticeably older than the other Aldus. Then he turns and motions for all the crowd to bow. Everyone bows deeply including High King Thureos in the direction of First God's Tree. Grag blew on the Shofar that he was carrying and then he too bowed deeply.

High King Thureos says, "We thank You God for your bountiful gifts to all of us on Malon. We pray Your grace and mercy will keep us all together at peace with each other. We pray we keep helping each other as we have been doing these past many years. And, now we honor You and all that You give to us by giving back to You of Your blessings to us."

After the prayer, and before anyone stood up from bowing, Arthus notices that there were at least ten younger Aldas, each of them grabbing up several arms full of the crops and everything else that was given upon the stone altars. The Aldus even gathered up the purple and blue and gold embroidered cloths that were covering the stone altars. Nothing that was laid upon the altars was left. The eldest Aldus, motioned and then Grag and High King Thureos, stood up again before it. They bowed slightly again and held their hands palm upwards. The eldest Aldus, appeared as if he bowed back at them and then he moved two of its lower branches out towards Grag and the High King, twisting those two branches in order that its leaves had turned upwards where the bottoms of the leaves were facing the sky. Suddenly, all of those upturned leaves turned golden brown and fell off of their two branches. The eldest Aldus twisted its branches again, then lowered them again and stood upright. He then turned away from where Grag and the High King were standing. And then in moments was leading all of the younger Aldus back in the direction of God's Forest. Arthus noticed that the roots of the Aldus seemingly were walking almost effortlessly on the ground. The Aldus swiftly disappeared from sight on their way back to God's Forest. The sky by this time had become night and it was quite easy to see both moons and the many stars in the sky surrounding Malon.

High King Thureos then said in a loud voice, "Everyone needs to gather up very close together inside of this God's Tree Seedling Circle, but please remember, we are never to sit on any of these natural stone altars that surround any of the God's Trees on Malon. Only that which is permanently gifted ever goes upon these altars." Everyone did as he instructed. Then the High King said, my good friends Barg and Targ, please come forward right up next to me. When they were right next to the High King he said, "Thank you Barg and thank you Targ for providing the finale of this year's Harvest Festival. I know that everyone here is just as excited as I am to watch the fireworks show that you have prepared for this occasion. Now that the sky is sufficiently black with night other than the moon and the stars, and all the Aldus have gone safely away, you can begin.

With that, Barg and Targ then walked over to where they had several metal boxes all set up in a very wide ring like band almost completely encircling the God's Tree Circle. Each of the metal boxes had various sized length and width tubes aimed upwards at the sky. Outside of that ring band here and there around the circle were several very tall and wide metal rack-like displays. And, farther out again from those was another ring band of those metal boxes with the various length tubes aimed at the sky setup. Barg ignited the ends of a rather large strand of fuses, and suddenly there were many big bang, bang, bang, bang, bang... several fireworks shot skyward. Then there were many loud boom explosions going off in the sky. Several of the explosions created various colorful designs that burst forth like flowers, and then animal shapes. There was a grouping that when exploding began to sparkle and the sparkles were creating what appeared in the sky to look like the Clan Crest of Clan Arkwright. Then suddenly another set of explosions created what looked like Clan Arial. Following this there were other sets of explosions that each looked like other Clans Crests from all the various clans on Malon. After this then there were other sets of explosions and sparkles in shapes of Cundos and Ignoles using bows and shooting arrows across the sky. One grouping of several successive explosions looked like a wild Yaule was pouncing from one place in the sky to another. Another series of explosions looked like a flock of Golden Griffons were flying across the sky. Suddenly then the ring of the racks that were on the ground started going off simultaneously. There were spinning and whistling fireworks and then each rack sparkled simultaneously creating all the names of the various clans on Malon. As soon as these firework racks burned down, the third row of metal boxes started shooting up and lit up the sky with many loud bangs and hundreds of fireworks exploding in color one after the other in very fast succession. At the very end of that was another succession of explosions which then sparkled created a huge Clan Crest Symbol of the Clan Gearhead and immediately following that another series of explosions and sparkles happened which showed the words, *In Honor of the Ultimate Great Creator* lighting up the sky. That was the grand finale of the show. The entire fireworks show lasted just a little over half an hour.

With the fireworks show ended, everyone cheered loudly and then they all walked back towards the festival tent area. There was much cheering and drinking that continued on again.

It took around an hour for the smoke from the fireworks to clear the sky as it slowly drifted away in the wind. Once again the sky was clear and dark enough to see that the stars were filling the night sky. Both of Malon's moons were full and bright. Arthus rose up from his seat at the table and from there walked away from the party towards a hill not too far from the festival area. He lays down near a tree on his back, puts his hands up under his head, and begins looking up at the stars. Jade had noticed him leaving the main party group and decided to follow him. She sees him go up the hill and lay down. She walks up to where he is laying and then also lays herself down on the ground down with her hands placed behind her head like Arthus. She intentionally positioned herself on the ground fairly near to where Arthus was laying.

"I really do like this spot," she says to Arthus.

"Ya, me too. I can see all the stars from here," said Arthus sadly, but smiling.

"So... tomorrow you have to leave here and go to the Northern Peaks City. That is what I heard from my mother," said Jade sadly.

Arthus then sat up, scoots his butt over and leans his back up against the nearby tree. Then looking over at Jade as she is lying there, he slowly starts nodding with tears filling up in his eyes.

"Yes, tomorrow... my grandfather takes me away from here to go to the Northern Peaks City, where again I will stay and learn like I did here," Arthus responded, while obviously attempting not to completely start crying out loud.

Jade in the light of the moon clearly sees that he has tears running down on his cheeks, and hears the tears in his voice. She sits up quickly. She then moves herself over and puts her back right up against Arthus chest. And, then immediately lays her head back against his Arthus's shoulder, just below his chin. She then says, "Truth is... I don't want to see you go! You have become a very close friend to me." Tears were then welling up in Jade's eyes too.

Arthus, not exactly sure what to say, looked up to the stars and nodded. "You are a very - very dear friend to me too Jade," he said as he was crying.

With that, Jade smiled then turns her head a little so that her forehead actually touched Arthus' chin where her forehead became wet from his tears. Then she immediately hands Arthus a small gift that she was holding in her hands. "Here, I was going to give this to you later, but I know now that this is probably the very best moment to do so," she said, still smiling, yet having her own tears now also clearly rolling down her cheeks.

Arthus sits up suddenly, appearing a little awkward, and a bit worried, as his movement had actually forced Jade to sit up and move back a little. He quickly says, "But, I didn't get anything for you!"

"I did not expect you to give me anything. So, please, just open it," insisted Jade.

He opened the gift; inside was a nice set of leather wrist and forearm bracers made out of Dreg hide. There was a design beautifully handcrafted into their outside that looked very similar to the Clan Arkwright Crest complete with an image of First God's Tree. Around the edges were soft leather stitching tightly woven through tiny drilled holes. Around the upper forearm she had somehow embedded them with metal studs between the inner layer and the outer layer of the leathers which stood out from there to the outside. As he turned them and looked carefully at them, he then noticed that there is some more hand leather crafting designs on the insides too and writing which was also on the inside of each of the bracers that reads, *Jade and Arthus Friends Forever.*

Arthus smiled and said, "These bracers are so awesome thank you, Jade. I wear them always. Thinking more about what he said, he added, "Always, except when I am bathing, or working on something where they might get destroyed. I absolutely don't want to get them to get destroyed." And with that he puts his two wrists out and hands the gift back to her to have her help him tie them securely onto his two wrists.

Jade smiled, reaches out, takes the wrist bracers and ties them very tightly to his left and right wrists and forearms with the leather ties that she had secured to the bracers when she had made them. Then hearing music playing she stands up. She reaches a hand down toward him and motions him to get up too. Arthus smiling while taking her hand, also gets up. She then proceeded to coach him into dancing to the music with her there on that little hilltop for a while under the two moons and the stars.

The music changes from a fast tune to a slow dance tune. Arthus, cleverly following the tune, pulls her right up close to him, gently takes her head with his hand, lays it against his chest and shoulders and then continues to hold her gently, as they both slowly danced around in four-step circles. Both their hearts were racing. Arthus didn't want that night to ever end, but it soon did. The music died down, and everyone at the festival was heading toward their homes and guest quarters. Arthus, reluctantly ending their dance, but continuing to hold Jade's hand, begins slowly walking her back home, and yet not directly home. Rather decidedly, taking a longer route than necessary. No matter how slow they walked, even with that longer route, the walk was much shorter than he wished. Arriving at her home he knew he had to say good night.

"Goodnight Jade," Arthus says reluctantly.

"Goodnight Arthus, she replies. Then she gives him one last big hug, turns away and disappeared inside her house.

Arthus stood outside, with tears in his eyes watching her close the door behind her; knowing soon it be a very long time before they could ever spend any time together again. He slowly walked all the way around the entire village before running into Grag.

"I see you haven't retired yet, Prince Arthus," said Grag.

"You are right about that, I been just taking one last long walk around," said Arthus wiping the tears from his face.

"So she finally finished it. I see. She had been working on that for a while now," said Grag pointing to Arthus' new leather bracers. "Jade was afraid she wouldn't finish those in time. She wanted to make sure you didn't forget her during your travels," said Grag.

Arthus lifted his arms and looked again at the well-crafted bracers. "Ya, I really love them. I will wear them for sure! And, I will always wish I had thought of making something that I could have given to her," said Arthus.

Grag laughed and then sat down on a chair. "Sit here for a moment," says Grag pointing a second chair. As soon as Arthus was seated Grag looked him straight in the eyes and said, "Listen up now, because I am absolutely certain that you gave her the best thing she could ever want. You gave her yourself as a great friend. Ya, sure there are others around her age here, but most of the time we noticed that Jade was all alone. Her mom and I were always worried that she'd never have any really close friend. Then... here you came along to stay here this year with us, and now all she wants to do is spend all of her awake time with you. She was so excited to learn that you were going to be her team partner for the hunt. And, after this year of getting to know how responsible and respectful you are, her mom and I trusted that even though you were going to be out in God's Forest together alone for a whole week, that you would absolutely be honorable towards her and work to protect her. You have more than earned our trust and friendship too!"

"I guess we are both the same. I was mostly alone in the palace. There were the guards, all of the cooks, and all the cleaning staff. Then there were all my teachers and trainers. There were even other people that I happened to see every so often while studying in the Main Library. Yet, most of the people around me weren't anywhere near my age. Even those that did come around at all that were my age, seemed far too nervous in those circumstances to ever want to talk with me. It was clearly obvious that the youth living in the city around the palace did not especially ever want to hang out with a Prince. It was so incredibly awesome to get to come here and then to quickly have Jade become a real true friend to me. I know that would not have happened with anyone who really wasn't about my own age, but I know in my heart that Jade is very special. No one that I know even compares to her," said Arthus. Again tears welled up in his eyes and trying his best to wipe them dry. He added, "I am not even sure that I will find any real friend like her ever again." In his heart, he knew that she was more than that, but he didn't fully understand even his own heart yet. He knew he felt something far more profound about her, than anyone else, whenever she was around.

"We will certainly miss you around here, Arthus," said Grag. "Tomorrow, you head for the very wild cold northern tundra. And then on to the Northern Peaks City. It really is very different there than here, so I do hope you can truly prepare yourself." With that bit of last advice, Grag rose, stretched, and then headed towards his home.

Arthus stood up, took one last look around the festival area and then he too headed back to his small cabin. Inside he changed out of his fancy clothes into some much more comfortable nightwear and then immediately crawled into his hammock.

The last night Arthus would spend in his tool shed cabin was almost over. Arthus barely sleeps. He lays there imagining in his mind the cold dark wild tundra towards the north and the Great Northern Peaks Mountain Range, and what he might see when he gets to Northern Peaks City, where he knew he would soon be living. He knew that most of the villagers and guests were still resting after the big first night of the Harvest Festival that Clan Arial and their guests will continue to enjoy for about another week. He knew that every night for the next week the farm village would be filled with festivity and all kinds of merriment. Clan Arkwright regularly supplies extras for this kind of a festival to all the various clans on Malon. They do that to honor the various clan's hard working all throughout the year. Arthus realizing it is futile trying to sleep, gets up and dresses in work clothing. Then he packs up his trunk with the heavy blankets that were gifted to him. He unties his hammock and rolls it up and stows it and the rest of his bedding away in waterproof materials. He then decides to go one more time to the bathhouse to shower and try and relax in the hot springs pool. Jade was already up and was outside her house beside the small shower building that her family normally used. She was dressed in her nightgown and was wrapping up her freshly washed hair. Arthus noticed she was beginning to look more and more like that of a beautiful woman. His heart was racing. She smiled at him, glad seeing him walking up towards her.

"The showers are really nice and hot here, and I see that it looks like you are getting in one last good hot shower before you and the High King head across the tundra up into the Northern Peak Mountains," said Jade.

"Ya, I figured that would be a good plan, and I really don't know how soon I will get to enjoy any hot shower or baths. I'm sure they do have some once I get all the way up to the city, but I wanted to relax and at least start out feeling completely clean as I am on my way. I already finished getting everything packed up," said Arthus.

She nodded, and he could tell she was sad, knowing he is leaving soon. Changing his mind about going to the bathhouse, he smiles and then walks into the smaller shower building and turned on the shower. Feeling a bit more relaxed and cleaned off, he dries off quickly and heads back outside. He begins looking around hoping that Jade was still outside waiting, but she was not. Having a puzzled look on his face, he heads back to his tool shed cabin. Inside the cabin he quickly notices that on top of his trunk is sitting a new bundle of clothing that are tied up together with a ribbon. These clothes are far different from the clean work clothes that he is currently wearing. Untying the bundle he discovers, the pants are crafted of fairly thick leather. Even though the leather itself is fairly thick it is completely soft and pliable. The inside of the leather pants is lined with a very soft and very thick cashmere wool material. The outside of the pants has its legs completely covered with a heavy brownish fur. The buttocks area of the pants is also completely covered with that same heavy brownish color fur. The top area up front on the pants has been made of the thick soft leather. The pants opens and closes with a covered zipper and has a heavy leather strapping loop that pulls over a large oval shaped button. There are two fairly wide side slanting access pockets, one for each side of the front, which are each also lined on inside with the soft cashmere wool material. Halfway down the outside of the pants on each side there are two very big side pouch pockets. These are made to expand out a bit on each side when filled. There is a very fine chainmail liner inside of each of these side pouch pockets, which makes these pouches very strong. Arthus sees that there is a set of soft cashmere wool long underwear pants and long underwear shirt. There are also very thick wool socks. Then there is an extremely comfortable turtle-neck-style pull over shirt that again has been made with very soft and yet very thick cashmere wool. There is an oversized very thickly lined, thick but again soft pliable leather and again heavy fur covered hooded jacket. The inside of the jacket had some kind of soft, but tough white fur, which completely covered up the fact that the chest and back of the jacket had been made with a fine yet strong chainmail material hidden between that white fur and the pliable thick leather. The elbows of the arms and the top and backside of the hood also had a much tougher brownish color leather. There were also a pair of very thick leather boots that were covered in the heavy brownish fur and lined on the inside with the same white fur. Then there was a pair of oversized fur mitten style gloves, which also allowed for two fingers to be slipped into a larger first finger like area for allowing the ability for shooting a bow and arrow, while continuing to wear the mittens. Arthus put all of his new clothing on, except the mittens. Immediately after getting fully dressed up in these warm fur clothing, he actually felt fairly hot. He grabbed his long strapped satchel and placed his tele-mask inside of that. Then he hangs that over his head, neck and off his left shoulder, where it hangs loosely by his left hip. He then picked up the leather bracers that Jade had crafted for him, which had only removed to go to take a shower. He smiled as he looked at them carefully. Then he strapped them loosely to his wrists. He slips the mittens, one into each of the side pouches of the pant legs. He then buckled onto his waist his hammock carrier pouch in such a way that it is riding just above his butt. He lifts his backpack and slipped that over his shoulders. Then he grabs the end handle on his large wheeled trunk and heads out of the door of the cabin.

Arthus drags his wheeled trunk over to the loading and unloading platform where he knew his grandfather had tied their Golden Griffons. Leaving that trunk along with his backpack and hammock pack and tele-mask satchel on the platform, he then heads back to get the rest of his baggage from his cabin. Before he left the cabin this last time, he picks up the small dusting swish broom and quickly sweeps out the entire floor and then swept off the porch in front of the door of the cabin. He hangs the swish broom back onto its hook. Picking up the rest of his belongings and taking one last glance at the small cabin, he turned and walked once again towards the platform with the Golden Griffons. Arriving at the platform he discovers that the High King, Grag, Shelly, and Jade are gathered there with several Cundo assistants.

"Ah, good Arthus, I see you have already finished packing and bring over all your belongings. That is very good. We really do need to start heading over towards the Northern Peaks City before the sun gets any higher in the sky," said his grandfather, High King Thureos.

"Of course... I actually finished up a while ago... But, do we really have to leave so soon? I am definitely going to miss this place," said Arthus while staring deeply and smiling directly at Jade.

"Of course, remember why you are doing this. You must learn all about this world, not just a single part of it. The Great Northern Peaks Mountain Range is where you spend the next year learning about life in the bitter cold of the northern tundra, in the tall mountain peaks, and the Halls of Flames where Dwarvens and Cundos forge various metals, in the mines that are dug deep into the mountains, and in Northern Peaks City. There is a very large cold frontier fortress you will get to see when we get there," said High King Thureos.

"I do understand many of the reasons that you and my father need me to learn everything about Malon. But, please allow me a reasonable amount of time to properly give my thanks and give proper honor to these wonderful people here who have been so kind and generous to me this past year."

"Yes, you must properly give them all thanks for having provided your lodging and training as well as sustenance for this whole year. Please go quick and do hurry as you do that though."

Arthus walks towards the big agriculture processing barn from the platform where they would be departing from, and Jade ran after Arthus. She really didn't want to see him go. They had become good friends over the year, and both learned so much from one another. She couldn't even imagine or believe how much she would come to miss this Prince when he first arrived. She originally thought he would just be a pain to deal with, a sheltered prince, who be a burden, but he had truly shown himself as a great friend. Even more than that. Her heart had a deep ache and longing just thinking about him having to go.

Seeing her tagging along after him he says, "So Jade, you didn't tell me what you think of my new clothes?

"You look like a funny furry animal," she laughed.

"But, none of my new clothes are ever going to be as precious to me as much as this," Arthus pointing and showing her the two wrist and forearm bracers that she had given him the night before. Smirking he said, as he held his wrists out for her to inspect, "I do hope I tied them on correctly. I don't want these to fall off and fly away while I am up in the wind flying around. I do love them, and I will wear them always to remember you and my time here in Clan Arial," he said.

Hearing that Jade reaches out and unties and reties the bracers onto his wrists and forearms tightly and securely. Right as she had finished tying the bracelet, Arthus smiles at her and then grabs her in a big hug. He starts to cry and almost confesses, "You know, I really do love... I mean, like you a whole – whole lot Jade, and I will miss you so very – very much. I also need to thank you for this last year. I learned a lot from you, and I cannot wait to see you again."

Hearing the word love slipped from his mouth, Jade's face turned bright red, but she too had tears in her eyes, while smiling and hugging Arthus back. For a while, they embraced; neither one wanted to be the first one to let go of the other.

"HEY, WE ARE HERE WATCHING YOU TWO! Shouted Grag, which immediately caught their attentions. They stopped embracing. Arthus rubbed the back of his head and was just a little bit embarrassed.

Jade turned around and mumbled, "Looking the other way, face bright red, so embarrassing!" Then she adds louder, "You had better write me and even send me holo-messages soon," Then she continues mumbling, "Still not facing him, face is still blushing brightly... as she then starts walking away ahead of Arthus.

Arthus says, "Jade, wait up. I need to quickly go thank the Cundos who taught me about the farming and other skills. Jade slows down just enough for Arthus to catch up to her. He grabs her hand quickly and starts pulling her along faster towards the big barn areas where the Cundo farmers were preparing the harvest for the winter months. Arriving at the barns, Arthus lets go of Jade's hand, goes over, puts his hands together similar to how people often pray, *which is considered the proper way to greet various elders and leaders in Malon society.* "I greet and honor you in the Name of God, and in my own name for the way in which you have taught me, and took such great care of me this past year," he says over and over again to each of the Cundo farming leaders that has spent time teaching him anything.

"You are welcome, Prince Arthus. You have earned our respect and honor as well," relayed each of Cundo farming leaders."

"I also thank you in the name of the High King Thureos, my grandfather, and in the name of the Prince Benroy, my father, and in my own name, as you have been incredibly generous and kind to teach me your skills and provide me with an abundant sustenance. Your generosity and kindness will be kept in our hearts and well-remembered for the rest of our lives, Arthus proclaimed to each of the Cundo farming leaders."

"In the Name of God, and in the name of Grag our Clan Leader, and in our own name, we kindly thank you too for your personal attentiveness and for your following through with each of those things which we have taught you," responded the Cundo farming leaders.

Arthus puts his hands back down and then kindly hugs each of the Cundo farming leaders. Then he quickly grabs ahold of Jade's hand again, then hurries out of the harvest preparation barn. He pulls her along with him all of the way into the big barn where they butcher the meats. He then drops her hand and then goes and properly greets and thanks each of the Cundo butchers for teaching him the skills he had learned from them, using the exact same motions with his hands and phrases with his words as he had done in the farming harvest preparation barn. After he heard their responses as the butchers had blood on them, he smiles brightly and says, "I apologize for not showing up here prepared in my clothing to honor each of you with a hug, but know this, I am hugging you in my heart!" And, with that said, Arthus grabs ahold of Jade's hand again and heads back out of the butchering barn They then return quickly to the Golden Griffon platform.

Arriving at the Golden Griffon platform and still holding onto Jade's hand, he noticed how that Grag and High King Thureos were both laughing. He sees too that the High King had already changed his clothes and was also dressed up in an outfit that looked a lot like Arthus' with the exception that he had on a very long oversized fur coat. The High King's coat was also carefully dyed with the symbol of the Clan Arkwright on its back as well.

"You know that they really are very cute together. Grag, you actually might have to worry that my grandson has stolen Jade's heart," said High King Thureos slapping Grag on the shoulder.

Turning to Arthus Grag declares, "Well, Arthus, if you steal my daughter's heart, you had better own up to it!"

Both Arthus and Jade's faces were already bright red, and both didn't say anything.

"Ha, ha, ok, ok, well now we have officially caught them hugging, and blushing, and crying, and now again we find them holding hands. However, Arthus and Jade, it is time to say goodbye to each other. We really must leave here before the sun gets too high up in the sky or we will miss our ride. For this trip, we cannot take the Golden Griffons at all to go fly to up to North Peak City. That route is far too cold for them. Instead, we must go and meet up with the very next cargo shuttle heading across the wild tundra on the way to North Peak City," said High King Thureos.

Giving Jade one last hug, Arthus then turns to Grag and Shelly. He puts his hands together again like people do when they pray. He repeats, "I greet and honor you in the Name of God, for the way in which you have taught me, and took such great care of me this past year. I also thank you in the name of the High King Thureos, my grandfather, and in the name of Prince Benroy, my father, and in my own name, as you have been incredibly generous and kind to teach me your skills and provide me with an abundant sustenance. Your generosity and kindness will be kept in our hearts and well-remembered for the rest of our lives."

Grag and Shelly both start to have tears welling up in their eyes. Together they say, In the Name of God, and in our own names, we kindly thank you too for your personal attentiveness and for your following through with each of those things which we have taught you."

Grag then says, "Now bring yourselves in here for one very big farewell hug."

The High King, Arthus, Jade, Grag and Shelly all do one big group hug and then each of them hug each other. Arthus and Jade give each other another hug, and it was obvious to everyone that they did not want to stop hugging, but they do.

A giant cart being drawn by a giant Yaule is located along side of the Golden Griffon Platform. There are two other Yaules there too. One Yaule was out in front and one Yaule was in the back. Several Cundos were there already assisting High King Thureos and Prince Arthus. The Cundo assistants lifted and loaded everything Prince Arthus had placed earlier onto the platform onto the giant cart. Then some of them climbed up onto the High Kings' Griffon flock and unload everything he had brought along with him from each of their load carriers and trappings. Also, they unloaded the High King's personal baggage out from behind the High King's hathi howdah. The Cundo assistants quickly have everything both of them had brought with them all stacked and tacked very securely onto the giant cart. The Cundo assistants then bowed deeply and courteously to the High King and to Arthus.

Grag, looking at the Cundo assistants, smiling says loudly to them, "Alright thank you! Ya'all have other duties to attend to, so don't ya be dawdling around here!"

The High King spends a few minutes humming and brushing both his Yaule and the giant Yaule with the cart. After humming and brushing he takes the neck collar reigns from the Yaule with the cart and ties them over onto the Yaule he will be riding. He then checks once more that the Yaule's collars and all of the rest of the Yaule's tacking are buckled very tightly and properly on both sides of the Yaule. He then inspects the cart's wheel hubs. Seeming satisfied he climbs up onto his Yaule and looks back to see if Arthus is ready.

Arthus had also been humming and brushing the Yaule in the back that he was to ride. He too climbs onto his Yaule. Noticing that his grandfather, the High King is already mounted up onto his Yaule and looking directly at him, he quickly says to High King Thureos, "I know that I am taking too long. I know, I know, but... I am really ready now!"

"I will miss you so much! Don't you dare freeze to death up in the mountains! And stay safe," yells Jade as she bursts out crying very loudly.

Arthus's heart sank as he saw how hard Jade is crying. He had never seen her cry this hard before. He immediately had tears in his eyes again.

From the back of their Yaules, the High King and Arthus wave goodbye to Grag, Shelly and Jade. Then the High King begins leading them out away from the farming village heading towards the north where the cargo shuttle docking area is located.

Chapter 8
The Trip North

It takes them at least an hour just to reach the north/south cargo shuttle docks.

Arriving at the shuttle docks and climbing off his Yaule, the High King Thureos says to Arthus, "This is where all of the cargo supply shuttles come and go from. The cargo shuttles are very special mechanical machines made by Clan Gearhead, which can hover and fly out across the tundra. They built these specifically to get any supplies back and forth to and from Northern Peaks City. If you look out over there beyond the northern end of the docks you will see that there are two sets of cables mounted up on high poles leading away from each end of these two docks. Those cables are called, air tracks. Those air tracks have magnetic properties, which the cargo shuttles use to help guide them in each direction. The shuttle will land here between these two platforms and when everyone using the shuttles has finished loading their cargo onto or off of the shuttle, then the pilot of the shuttle will sound a warning before shutting all of the loading doors. Another alarm will go off fairly quickly. Then the shuttle will take off, turn around in the air track loops which you can see by looking the other way towards the south a little bit. Then it will come back through the other air tracks you see mounted on the poles going north again from the other two platforms you see over there to the east of this platform. They fly between those other air tracks going towards the north. And, they will stop at least once at the Great Northern Tundra loading and unloading point along the way through the tundra. These cargo shuttles are used to mostly carry various crops and meats from the Clan Arial here to the

Northern Peaks City. And, they do bring various tools and machines that Clan Gearhead has made down to these platforms here, where Clan Arial then transports those to and from the Golden Griffon platforms located back at their farm village. Clan Arial will either add those to their own storage and use, or they will send those by Golden Griffon flocks to all other clans on Malon along with much of the farming produce. Some of the shipments from here are even sent on a spacecraft up to Creed. Some traders on Hondargs also come here to these docks to pick up their orders they take over the Great Southern Mountain Range towards Blood Sands and the Ocean."

While waiting for their shuttle to arrive the High King and Arthus unload everything that was on the big cart onto the shuttle platform. Then they quickly get all of it stacked up and strapped down onto a large metal pallet. The High King then goes over and laid some Ruin rocks on the four corners of the large metal pallet holding all of their belongings. The whole metal pallet began to float in the air.

Soon a large multi-segmented shuttle arrived. and he then just walked it into the shuttle's storage section and then took the four Ruin stones off of the four corners and the pallet simply dropped into place. Then Arthus uses some special netting and the hooked end ratcheting strappings that were hanging inside the cargo shuttle to secure the pallet with their belongings to the floor of the cargo shuttle. He securely tightens the strapping by the ratcheting mechanism.

Then High King Thureos says to Arthus, "Good job! Now we will go ride in the forward shuttle compartment, where there is very comfortable seating." Then they both walked out of that shuttle segment and then towards the south end of long platform, where another shuttle segment was located, which also had opened doors.

As the High King and Arthus are going towards the open door, Arthus stops and looks more carefully towards the front of the shuttle. He notices that this segment of the cargo shuttle has more of a slightly rounded, but pointed shape. There is a large beautifully shaped see-through front window. The window perfectly fits on the inside of the metal that goes over and around the front pointier end of the shuttle. He could clearly see through the window that there was a Dwarven pilot sitting up on a tall seat. That section where the pilot sits appears to be very compact, but looks like a beautiful piloting compartment. Arthus noticed that there was a very shiny metal dashboard in front of the pilot with many round metal rings sticking out. Each of those round rings have glass facings on them and Arthus recognizes that these are in fact gauges. He sees that there are many rows of switches and many more rows of tiny lights of various colors. He sees many push/pull buttons here and there too. There is also a shiny sliding pull lever that appears attached to the arm of the pilot's seat. The ceiling above the pilot also has various switches and gauges. Arthus could tell that all of the switches, pull levers and push pull buttons were easily within reach of the Dwarven pilot.

Upon stepping inside of open door of this segment of the shuttle. Arthus immediately notices that it is very beautiful inside. It has been immaculately designed with ultra-fine but very thick black leather covering, which seemed like it almost covered everything. What wasn't made of that black leather was beautiful reddish brown, very highly polished natural wood trimmings. Arthus thought to himself, "The cargo bay segments, are nothing compared to this. They were very practical rectangle shape with only slightly rounded curved corners and completely made of metal. Each of the shuttle segments about two and a half meters wide, three meters tall and about 6 meters long."

Once they were seated in the front segment and had buckled themselves in with the straps and buckles that were hanging down from the top outside edges of the high-backed leather seating, into a metal loop that was sticking out a little bit, positioned between their legs. "This front segment is absolutely beautiful," says Arthus.

Still thinking about the shuttle design, Arthus remembered seeing just a little bit behind the very back segment of the shuttle has a weird-looking machine device that held a crystal in its center. Arthus had noticed that the crystal was almost as big as his hand. Arthus asked, "Grandfather, why is there a hand sized crystal located in the center of that machine in the far back end of these shuttles?"

"Ah, you noticed the Life-crystal... I see. Well, Arthus, Life-crystals are used all over Malon to power so many different things. I am certain that you have seen them before, but maybe not without any shielding covering them. Anyway, there are many of them around Harmony City. All of those ones are far – far larger than the one located on the back of this shuttle. You must have just never really noticed them before, as all of those that are indoors are kept highly shielded as they must be. I am sure you have seen the various tall and very thick light tubes that line the ceiling in the Main Library, and you also must have noticed similar light tubes located here and there all throughout the palace hallways. I am sure you also noticed the very well-lit pyramid shaped tops of the towers located on buildings around Harmony City. All of those also have these giant Life-crystals inside of them. The Life-crystals power almost everything in Harmony City. The one on the very back of this shuttle does not need to be completely shielded because it is located all the way on the outside of this shuttle. That Life-crystal is used to power this cargo shuttle" said High King Thureos.

"Oh wow, ok, I love it. I just learned something new," said Arthus smiling. "I remember seeing all of the massive towers around Harmony City. And, all of those towers have giant Life-crystals inside of their top pyramid sections, which glow brightly day and night. I know Harmony City is never dark anywhere. So, how long can one of the Life-crystals power the city? Arthus asked.

"Each of the life crystals easily lasts more than one hundred years," responded High King Thureos.

Arthus and the High King then notice that there is some commotion going on outside of the cargo shuttle farther down on the platform. Arthus unbuckled and unstraps himself and gets up and looks out the front cargo shuttle segment doorway and toward the north. There on the platform were several Cundos and Dwarvens working very quickly strapping down several large crates and other bundles to the metal pallets. They too used the four Ruin rocks to easily float the pallets from the platform into the cargo section of the shuttle. Upon seeing this Arthus returned to his seat, and once again straps himself back into the buckling system. A few minutes goes by and then two Cundos and four Dwarvens step into the front compartment and immediately realizing that the High King was in there, bowed deeply to the High King.

"We beg your pardon for not having properly greeted you before this, your Highness," said the oldest of the four Dwarvens, still bowing deeply. "So your Highness is heading with us up to North Peak City? He then asked.

"You may rise," said High King Thureos. "Yes, in fact we are. I am bringing Prince Arthus there to work with the leader of Clan Gearhead for the next year in order that he may learn as much as he can. Also, he will be living with a family there.

Looking out through the open doorway, Arthus notices that several Cundos were riding Yaules and going away with several of the large carts behind them. They appeared to be heading south back towards the Clan Arial farm village.

Soon there was a strange loud squawking sound coming from a round speaker grill located up in the black leather covered ceiling. Then the pilot's voice could be heard, "One minute to departure. Please quickly step away from all cargo shuttle bay doors and if you are on the platforms, get off those. If you are riding in the front passenger area, please be seated and buckle yourself in. If you are riding in any cargo bays, be sure to connect yourself to one of the security straps and hold on tightly. But please do make sure that all of your belongings are securely strapped down and tightened to the floor loops. This shuttle is headed to Northern Peaks City. The next stop will be in the wilds of the northern tundra. If you are not dressed for the extreme cold, I strongly suggest getting off here and changing your clothing and then start waiting on the next shuttle! All Aboard!"

As the shuttle bay doors closed, Arthus sadly turns and looks longingly out through the small side windows. Tears once again appearing in his eyes.

"Grandson, says High King Thureos. "Whenever you feel like crying because you are having to say goodbye to any dear friend, and especially whenever you might ever feel like that you lose someone forever due to their death...That is not what I meant to say, as I am not saying that anyone that you know is going to die on you soon... I'm saying this only because I can tell how much you already really do miss your dearest friend, Jade. Anyway... you should never allow yourself to feel ashamed of those kinds of feelings. And, don't even try to hold back your deepest feelings during times like this. There is no shame related to ever feeling this kind of way," Said High King Thureos in a very loving gentle voice.

Arthus sobs silently then breathes deeply in, allowing the feeling of loss to pass out from him through his breath.

"I really do hope I get to see Jade again soon," said Arthus.

"Ha, oh, you will for sure! Jade is around your age. You do realize that after your first One Hundred Years Life Day Celebration, you will be heading to the Malon Academy, where you will spend much time learning and growing along with everyone your age," said High King Thureos.

"The Malon Academy," questioned Arthus?

"Yes, but don't worry, you are only now just into your fifty first year. When we turn one hundred, is when we are considered as coming of age. After each person has their One Hundred Years Life Day Celebration, all of the clan members on Malon are then sent to the Malon Academy. Then for another nine hundred years you will meditate, study, train, and learn exactly what it means to be a clan member, and what your real purpose in life is. But, again, don't worry about that right now. Just look out the window; we almost at the first stop." said High King Thureos.

Arthus looked out where his grandfather had pointed. There beyond the deep snow of the tundra he saw just coming quickly into view were massive slanted metal walls, which Arthus guessed helped push the worst of the cold winds up and over the top of the small village within. The shuttle swoops down and enters a very long and dimly lit tunnel that goes all the way from the south end to the north end of this giant metal box like small city sized structure. The shuttle stopped deep inside the dimly lit tunnel in a larger platform area.

Suddenly that loud squawking noise comes through the speakers again. The Pilot's voice is then heard through the speakers, "Northern Tundra Village Stop. Please be sure to wait for the outer tunnel doors to be completely closed and wait for the all clear signal before attempting to unbuckle your seat strappings. The shuttle doors will open once I get the all clear signal. When exiting the shuttle onto the platform please watch your step. The ice and winds can make the platform here slippery.

Anyone helping with cargo loading and unloading here please use extra caution."

Outside the shuttle, but inside the tunnel there is a very loud alarm that goes off. Then the huge outer door behind the shuttle finally comes closed. The alarm continues, and very bright lights suddenly appear surrounding the cargo shuttle. Several Dwarvens appear out of side doorways with their crossbows armed and ready. They carefully inspect all around the perimeters of the shuttle and the surrounding platform area. Then as quickly as they appeared they disappeared behind those same doorways. Then the alarm is silenced.

Again that same squawking sound comes out of the speakers. The pilots voice is again heard coming from the speakers, "All clear, All clear. I am opening the shuttle bay doors now. Please watch your step."

The shuttle bay doors all slide open and instantly the air is freezing cold. Arthus quickly unbuckled his seat strappings and pokes his head out of the open shuttle door. He can already tell that this small tundra village was much different than the warm inviting Harmony City. In fact it was one giant metal box like structure with lots of dimly lit hallways leading into the various shops and living quarters of those who lived and worked there. There was absolutely no light coming through any windows as there was no windows. All the outer edges of this giant box like structure were slanted in at the top and out at the bottom. There were steep stairwells leading up higher into the structure and leading down into the ground below the structure. This was one of part of the larger underground mining that takes place from here and all the way up into the Northern Peaks Mountains. It was obviously not built for comfort, but for efficiency.

It wasn't long and again came the squawking sound from the speaker. The pilot's voice is heard again coming from the speakers, "One minute before I close the shuttle bay doors. One minute before I close the shuttle bay doors. Please watch your step. If you are in the passenger segment, please be seated and buckle into your seat strappings. If you are in the cargo area please be sure all loads are secure and strap yourself into the standing straps and hold on. If you are on the platform surrounding the shuttle leave immediately out the nearest exit." He then yells, ALL

ABOARD. ALL ABOARD. Then the doors on the shuttle are closed. And the really loud alarm began to sound again.

Upon hearing the announcement, Arthus quickly returned to his seat and strapped himself back in and buckled the bucklers.

With the very loud alarm sounding and the bright light blinking off and on three times, then staying off, the giant tunnel door at the northern end of the platform area slide open loudly. A series of flashing lights starts strobing in the tunnel ahead of the shuttle leading to out from this tundra stop. The shuttle pilot is talking again on the loud speaker: "Next Stop, Northern Peaks City. Next Stop, Northern Peaks City." The Shuttle then begins to lift up and moves quickly through the tunnel heading north out of the big metal tundra village.

The sky outside of Arthus's windows are very grey looking now. There are very massive evergreen trees which each seem to be far part from each other. So much so, that they each tree seems very much alone. The trees are mostly covered in heavy snow and ice. Everywhere he looks is snow and ice. Here and there he sees a giant rock sticking up sharply out of the ground. Even the rocks have snow and ice on their tops. It was no more than another hour and they were coming up to a very high mountainous area. Before the mountain there was another massive metal wall structure. The base of the massive brushed metal wall structure which appeared to start about five to possibly seven kilometers from the real base of the mountains. It too was set up where its base was angled about sixty degrees out from where the wall's top was located. At the very top of the wall structure Arthus could see that there was a matching metal roof material which appeared completely welded together to the wall. That roof reached completely over the entire five to seven kilometers of space going right up to and connecting with the face of the high mountains behind it. There ahead of them again was an entry tunnel going into the massive metal structure. Arthus could see that every so many meters apart there were what appeared to be heavy metal square access panels attached to the wall. All of these access panels were closed. He wonders if those are ever opened and what they might be used for. He makes a mental note to ask about these.

Again, the squawking speaker sound, and again the voice of the pilot is heard over the speakers. "Arriving at Northern Peaks City, Arriving at Northern Peaks City. Please wait until the outer tunnel door is fully shut, the alarms have finished sounding, and for me to give you the all clear message before attempting to unbuckle any of your personal strapping bucklers. All passengers are expected to depart from this shuttle at Northern Peaks City and report to the magistrate's office area before leaving the platform area. Be sure to collect all of your belongings from the cargo segments of the shuttle. Carefully unload any of your cargo onto the platform and secure them properly within the specifically marked areas of the platform. Make sure to have everything off of the shuttle before this shuttle is scheduled to depart again to the south in one hours' time from the moment we come to a stop. Again, please watch your step as the platform here can be wet and icy."

The pilot barely finished speaking when they entered the end of the tunnel with the strobing lights and the tunnel alarms blaring. The shuttle quickly came to a stop. The tunnel alarms continued blaring and an extremely bright light came on that exposed every centimeter of the shuttle and the surrounding platform. The outer tunnel door slammed shut. The alarm continued still as several Dwarvens appeared out of many doorways all around the platform. Each of the Dwarvens was armed with their crossbows locked and loaded. They came out and took aim at every nook and cranny all around cargo shuttle. Several of them inspected the tunnel behind the shuttle. Then they all quickly disappeared again behind the doors that they had come out of. That loud blaring alarm was turned off.

Again, the squawking of the speaker and the pilot's voice could be heard, "All clear! All clear! All passengers may now unbuckle their personal strapping bucklers. Please do be careful departing the cargo shuttle. Thank you for joining us today, and welcome to Northern Peaks City, the home of the Clan Gearhead, the honored makers of all the machines and tools on planet Malon and for Creed. Be sure to register your arrival at the Magistrates Office located at the center of the loading platform. Have a great day!

The High King and Arthus, the two Cundos and the four Dwarvens that were riding in the passenger segment all unlocked their personal strapping bucklers. Then they quickly but carefully departed from their and headed to the cargo segments of the cargo shuttle. The two Cundos quickly grabbed the hover jacks that were located on the platform and brought them to the cargo segments. As, there was a lot of cargo to unload, they waved over several other Cundo loading assistants that were waiting behind a gated area. The Cundos and these new Cundo loading assistants all quickly unloaded all of the farming crates and bundles that were loaded into the same shuttle segment that the High King and Arthus had used for their belongings.

Everything that is exported from the platform north of the Clan Areal Farms, and brought here onto this platform goes on the platform inside bright orange lines and under the huge sign that said, "Import Customs of the Northern Peaks City Cargo Shuttle Platform." All kinds of imports are moved from there through the large access doorway behind that space on the platform. Behind that door where the import customs department processing center is located. Then the Cundos started unloading the back cargo shuttle segment. There were several crates of live birds and other sorts of animals that were unloaded from the back cargo shuttle segment onto the platform. Those were moved down the platform, again inside bright orange lines, but this time under a large sign that said, "Live Animal Import Customs of Northern Peaks City Cargo Shuttle Platform."

Farther down the platform towards the way they had come in Arthus noticed several signs hanging over other spaces. Those were marked for exports, which would be taken from here to the Arial Valley platform.

Once the Cundos had finished unloading the normal cargo, the leader of that group came up to the High King and Arthus. Then putting his hands together in a prayer like fashion bowed his head slightly and said, "We greet and honor you in the Name of God, our High King Thureos, and also to you Prince Arthus. We humbly welcome you to our Northern Peaks City Cargo Loading Platform and ask to be of service in helping you unload your belongings.

The High King responded, "We thank you for your honored greetings and for your willingness to be of service, in the Name of God and in our own names."

Then the High King motioned to the Cundo that had greeted him to bring some of the Ruin rocks for the pallets. After successfully unstrapping it from the floor loops and hanging the tie-down strapping up on the inside wall of the cargo shuttle where it belonged, then the Cundo put the Ruin rocks on the four corners of the pallet, which lifted it slightly off the floor. Then the Cundo carefully pushed and followed the High King and Arthus out the bay door of the cargo shuttle and onto the platform. The High King and Arthus headed over to the Magistrate's Office located at the very center of the platform. You may place our pallet over there in that safety square please, while I report our arrival to the magistrate.

Then the High King motioned to Arthus, and both of them placed their hands together in a prayer like fashion. "We again thank you for your service to us in the name of God and in our own names," said both the High King and Arthus. "We trust that you will remain in faithful service throughout your lives here on Malon," they both concluded.

Arthus remained by the pallet with all of their belongings on it, while the High King entered the Magistrates Office to report their arrival.

Arthus looks around the large platform area and notices that it appears to have only a few exit options. The tunnel from which they came in on the cargo shuttle was the largest of the exits. But, there were basically only four exits on this side of the platform, even though there were many of those smaller guard shack doors that the armed Dwarvens had come out of earlier. When their doors happened to be open earlier he could tell that those were only a small enclosed well-lit and heated space with a chair and a couple of hooks from which the Dwarvens hang their crossbows. Those guard shacks did not lead anywhere else. There was the big door where the Live Animals were being moved off the platform into. That obviously led where the live animals were quarantined and then processed before being allowed to be anywhere else within Northern Peaks City. There was the big door which led directly into the Produce

Customs Department. There was the door of the magistrate's office. There were two doors that were obviously entries to the male and female latrines as they even had pictographs of a Dwarven male peeing into a stand-up urinal, and one of a Dwarven female seated behind a half sized door. The only other possibility which might be an exit appeared as if it was a much tunnel like hallway directly at the very end of the platform in front of where the nose of the shuttle currently was aimed. "That smaller tunnel there looks as if it literally goes directly into the face of the mountain," thought Arthus. From where Arthus was standing he could not see over the cargo shuttle to tell if there might be more platform there or other exits.

The High King comes back out of the magistrate's office.

A Dwarven female comes out of the magistrate's office wearing a heavy coat with chain mail stitch-sewed to its outsides. She is also wearing a fur lined Life-Ore Helmet with a fancy spear like spike sticking straight up in the air from its top She immediately commands two other Dwarvens, that were standing on each side of the Magistrates Office doorway, and each who heavy coats with chain mail stitch-sewed onto its outsides. Their helmets were fur lined like the Magistrates, but theirs each had a really sharp looking blade that started at their eyebrows and went straight up and over the tops to the back of their helmets. "Go to the Hall of Flames and announce that the High King, Thureos and Prince Arthus have arrived as scheduled.

At hearing that both Dwarvens ran as fast as their legs could carry them to the very northern end of the platform and disappeared into that tunnel that Arthus had noticed earlier. Within a few minutes about 30 Dwarvens, all with heavy coats that had the same kind of chain mail stitch sewed over the outsides, and all with came kind of helmets with the really sharp looking blade that ran from their eyebrows up and over the top and onto the back of them. They were all running as if in military formation again out from that tunnel that Arthus had noticed earlier. They were all in perfect step with each other, just like a military platoon would be.

The female Dwarven commanded, "Halt! All 30 of the Dwarvens immediately halted and stopped in perfect formation. The female

Dwarven then commanded, "Gather ye up all of the High King, Thureos' belongings and all of Prince Arthus's belongings and follow them to the Hall of Flames where they will be properly greeted as our guests of high honor.

Having heard that command all 30 of the quickly grabbed 15 long straps with loop handles on each end. Each of those straps was unrolled and speedily slipped through the bottom of the metal pallet. Each of the Dwarvens held onto one of the ends of the straps by the loop and lifted that up onto their shoulders, which lifted the entire metal pallet filled with all of the High King Thureos' and Prince Arthus' belongings.

The Dwarven female with heavy chain mail covered coat and the helmet with the fancy spear spike motioned to the High King and Prince Arthus and says, "Please honor me by allowing me to lead you over to the Hall of Flames.

The High King replied, "Certainly!"

And with that the High King Thureos and Arthus were led to the far northern end of the platform and then out through the smaller tunnel that leads to the Hall of Flames.

Arriving at the Hall of Flames, "Y'all can leave your stuff right over there, me High King. As I have had all of me men here ready to bring it right to where the Prince will be stay-en," yelled a broad-looking Dwarven Woman.

This Dwarven woman that had yelled from across the way appeared almost as tall as Arthus, maybe just a hint taller than Arthus, who wore an oversized fur coat much like both the High King and Prince Arthus were wearing. She did not even attempt to approach the High King, but remained standing far off by a fairly large fire.

"Ah Maddlynn... Clan Gearheads ingenious leader! I didn't expect you to meet me here yourself. You're mostly too busy for any of this kind of thing," said High King Thureos with a laugh.

"Ya... well, I had to make me a bit of time. Though, I'd much rather be down in my workshop working away, but them other Dwarven leaders thought it would be might rude of me not to come up here in person and greet ye and your young grandson Prince to our humble city," yelled Maddlynn. Clan Gearheads leader continued to stand way off by the open fire; warming her hands. Waiting Next to her was a larger Cundo man. He appeared to be trying to stay warm by the fire as well.

"Bout time you got here. Been freezing me wee rump off here. An me hair is almost frozen solid," yelled Maddlynn still not taking one step away from the fire.

Rather than standing off by the door, and having a shouting match, High King Thureos and Prince Arthus decidedly approach the two of them over by the fire.

"I am sorry it took a bit longer to get everything done today in Clan Arial, and of course Prince Arthus here didn't want to leave his little girlfriend," laughed High King Thureos.

"Jade is not my girlfriend, we are just really good friends," said Arthus as his face turned bright red.

"I'm just messing with ya," joked High King Thureos

Seeing the High King and Prince Arthus finally walked up to her, she turns "All righty then. This here tallish Cundo is Drake of Clan Gearhead," said Maddlynn pointing her thumb at the man next to her.

The Cundo man named Drake, bows his head and puts together both of his hands like in a prayer like fashion, and says, "I greet and honor you in the Name of God, our High King, Thureos, and also to you Prince Arthus. We humbly welcome you to Northern Peaks City." Then he unfolds his hands and extends them back out towards the fire and says in a more friendly way, "Hello, my High King, I am the one who has agreed to opening up our home to your grandson, Prince Arthus during his year stay with us. I truly felt that it was important that I should also come out here and properly greet you and honor you both. I knew you would want to meet before we head over to my humble home," said Drake continuously bowing his head towards the High King.

"Ah, I have heard of you, Drake. Your Ruin Crafting is the best I have ever seen," said High King Thureos.

"You praise me too much, but I do love my art and hope it helps make our world a better place," said Drake.

"Good, well, we better get out of this cold before her ingenious leader Maddlynn freezes her wee rumpus off and long before Prince

Arthus' wet tears for his lovely Jade freezes to his face," joked High King Thureos.

"Oh of course, yes, you are right your highness. Please, everyone, do follow me. You too Maddlynn, said Drake in a tone, meant to let her know she must obediently follow. Then in a gentler tone, he said, "I will show you all to my humble home," as he bowed his head again and again.

As they left that section of the Hall of Flames the thirty Dwarven men picked up their pallet and keeping in perfect step continued to follow them back out of the tunnel and into the freezing cold air of the city, but this time instead of turning towards the platform with the Magistrates Office, they turned the opposite direction and went around the back platform where the main city entrance was located.

Arthus paid close attention, observing everything as they were following Drake through the city. The completely enclosed city had several buildings all cramped together with no real spaces between them. As they walked through what appeared to be many mazes of fairly narrow streets and alleyways, noticing here and there sometimes were simple crafted ladders, and then here and there reasonably narrow staircases, each heading upwards to the multi-layered houses that are stacked one layer on top of the other. To Arthus it seems that there had been no building code rule of ensuring that any bottom outside support wall was actually continued all the way up and through to the very top by the city's main roof covering. The streets really were like a long winding maze. Some of the streets were reaching almost from one end of the city to the other without any alley way breaks between the houses. Then another street seemed that it had several alley way breaks between the rows of houses.

Without saying anything about this, Arthus thought to himself, "Why didn't they assign a really good city planner to lay out this city a little better before ever building it?"

Arthus observed how white and black smoke is pouring from all of the metal stove pipes sticking out of the sides every home and building, filling the air inside of the seemingly completely enclosed city with a heavy smog. Almost all of the fascia walls on the outsides of the houses were made from some variety of metal. There are obvious natural stone foundations under most of the rows of houses, and here and there were some partial stone columns, which appeared semi-attached to some of the houses. It was obvious that the builders used very little wood in the building of any of the homes within this city. Then as they wound around the maze of streets they came to one T in the road where they had to turn either to the east or to the west. The north side of the street was actually where the city walls met right up against the rock face of the mountain. Carved deep into the mountain were openings, and these openings almost always had big heavy metal gates. A similar deeply carved tunnel was where the High King and Arthus had met the Cundo named Drake in one of the Halls of Flames.

Silently Arthus wondered, "Do any of these large gates openings actually lead down into one or more of the underground mines? Or, do they actually lead farther inside the mountain to where houses might even be carved out of the actual rock of the mountain itself? Maybe both are true? Or, maybe not? More for me to discover and learn while I am here."

Drake led to the west on that street and continued walking on and on. But even though the street was very long that they took, not too much time past to reach Drake's house, as it was a larger house at the very end of that very long street with the back side built right into the western wall of one of the adjoining mountains, and the north side built right up against the face of the mountain they had been following. Drake's house was a well-built metal and natural stone faced building that appeared about three and a half stories tall. Again, there were no windows at all, just a grayish pale metal and stone house like many of the other buildings. It was a bit bigger than most of the houses that they had past getting up to here, and it appeared to be better built. They had been walking uphill coming up this very long street, and it was at the very farthest end of that street, tucked right up against this adjacent mountain fascia where the city roof becomes part of the house roof itself.

"We think that our home is one of the easiest ones to find in the city since it is tucked right in here in the very far northwest corner of the city. Please be kind and brush your boots clean using that there heavy grass rug out here on our porch. Then come right on in to the mud room and pull off your boots and gloves. My wife Crystal already has the fire going, and our son should be home already upstairs helping to get Prince Arthus's private room all prepared for his year's stay with us," said Drake.

"Ah, you have a son. That's good to hear. Prince Arthus will hopefully have another friend to learn from," said High King Thureos.

"Yes, and well actually we have more than one, but my other sons are much older now and already have their own places to be and things to do" said Drake a bit sadly. He then looked over and smiled at Prince Arthus and said, But, this son, he is about your Prince Arthus' age, though Prince Arthus actually may be just a little bit older.

"Ya, he is, an a bit of a ruffian, if I do say so," chimed in Maddlynn laughing.

Hearing Maddlynn say that, Drake just smiled.

"He spends most of his days in the hot forge room, or down in the mines. He is always helping us forge something, or helping out with the mining of various ore," said Maddlynn.

Just inside the front door there was a large shoe and boot shelving rack. Drake pulls off his boots, and says, "I hope you all don't mind following suit and pulling off your boots or shoes. My wife hates it when we track anything into any of the other parts of the house."

"My wife, Amethyst, the High Queen, God rest her soul, was very much like your wife in that regard," said High King Thureos as he pulls off his heavy fur covered boots. He then motions to Prince Arthus to do the same.

"I guess it would only be right to be obedient to your wife in this regard," says Maddlynn as she sits on the floor and pulls off her heavy gloves and her heavy boots, which she failed to clean before she walked inside.

After Drake, the High King, and Prince Arthus ensured that their boots were sufficiently clean to leave indoors, they carefully placed them onto the boot and shoe shelf rack. Then they walked into the main living room. Maddlynn, on the other hand just dropped her very dirty boots and gloves right by the front door on the floor-mat and follows them right out into the living room.

It was a fairly big circular room with a fire pit built right in the middle. There was a large metal flu that helped catch the smoke and heat which was built from the ceiling above down to a little bit higher above the flames of the fire pit. That large flu narrowed significantly at the very top, where an eight inch circular hole in the ceiling above had been cut. A double walled flu pipe went straight up from right there up through the other floors of the house and clear out through the city's main roof covering. It only ended about four feet above the city's main roof and had a really nice spinning rain cap attached to its top; ensuring that all the smoke from this fire escapes out into the sky, while most rain and snow stay out.

"It must be for the smoke to funnel all the way out and not bother the people living and working inside the house. Not at all a bad building idea," thought Arthus.

There was a rather thin long metal table that actually curved along the outer wall at one side of the living room. There were eight chairs on each side of the thin table. And, there was one chair at each end. The chairs all matched and were made of metal. Each chair had a beautiful hand-made embroidered seat pad tied neatly to them with a bow. There were no doors inside leading from this circular living room, just heavy hand-quilted blankets that were being used as doors wherever there was a doorway. There were huge hand quilted pillows that also had beautiful embroidery sewn into their tops all around the circular fire-pit where the people of the house often gathered together.

They all sat down around the fire; finally getting warm enough, Arthus takes off his fur coat. So did Maddlynn and Drake. After a little while the High King also pulled his own fur overcoat off.

Observing Madelyn up closely, Arthus noticed that she actually seemed a bit taller than all the Dwarvens he had met in his life, both in the palace and around Harmony City, and again while living with Clan Arial. She had brown hair tied into a braided ponytail, and she wore a brown heavy leather one-piece outfit. It was obviously leather pants which had been fused somehow at the top to the leather top she was wearing. The long sleeve leather top itself was front zippered from the neck all the way down and into the front of her pants. There was a leather

122

flap that was supposed to be snapped over the zipper, but Arthus noticed Maddlynn did not bother to snap any of the snap buttons closed. She also wore a heavy-looking leather apron over her outfit that normally should be tied around her body, but the ties to it too were left dangling down and dragging on the ground. Arthus noticed that these had left a tiny trail of soot wherever she walked. He recalled that she had very dirty heavy suede leather gloves that she had been wearing and her black boots, before she dumped those off in the mud room by the door at the front of the house. Now in the light of the room, he noticed that there were streaks of oil in her hair, as well as on her face. And, she had black soot smudged also onto her face and arms.

Observing Drake closely, Arthus notices that he has natural black hair that is kept rather short, way shorter than his own hair. Drake's hair is trimmed above his ears and off of his shirt collar. It is short, but not too short to comb, and it has a very neatly combed appearance. Drake also has a very well kept short beard. Arthus notices that Drake's face is a bit bonier in appearance then Grag's had been.

"Crystal, I am home! Zeck! Hey Zeck... Are you home Zeck?" Shouted Drake as he held his head looking away from everyone towards one of the blanket covered doorways.

"Yes dear, we are here," a very kind voice sounded from a woman who was walking down the stairs. A reasonably nice looking black-haired Cundo woman and a dark-haired boy right around Arthus age, but a bit taller, and obviously significantly more muscle toned than Arthus came out from behind one of the blanket covered doorways. Arthus observed the boy and was quite impressed by his muscle toned features.

Observing Crystal closely, Arthus notices that she was a fairly skinny woman, who wore a very clean white apron, which had a white lace frill attached all around its edges so that it added a little decoration beyond all the edges of the apron. The same frill lace material was turned the opposite direction all around her neck. There was a big front pocket on her apron with that same lace turned down at the top outside edge of the pocket. She had various sized sewing needles with short thin threads in their needle eyes poking out of her apron here and there. Crystal had her long black hair tied back neatly into kind of an oversized bun on the back and top of her head. And, she wore what Arthus thought might possibly be two knitting needles poking upwards out through the bun in the back of her head.

Observing Zeck closely, Arthus notices that he wears a rather clean coverall style leather work uniform. The style was not exactly like Maddlynn's, as his coveralls were rather pants which had a front flap with pockets on them which only partially covered his chest and which were connected to another x-shaped flap that partially covered his back. The back x-shape flap had what appeared to be tie down strapping material sewed at the top edge of each side of the leather flap x which went up over his shoulders and then clasped over onto metal buttons which were sewn onto his chest flap. The metal clasps appeared to have additional metal loops that had been sewn through front loops in each of the shoulder straps. Zeck is not currently wearing an additional leather apron like Maddlynn's. And, he isn't wearing any sleeves on his clean white cotton t-shirt. Arthus also noticed that Zeck's skin and hair is spotlessly clean. Zeck's hair is a little longer than Drakes. Zeck wears his hair over his ears and it appears to be cut all one length, which reaches down to the lower part of his neck. It was combed neatly back off of his face. And, Zeck has very sky blue eyes.

As soon as Crystal arrived in the living room she bowed her head and put her hands together in a prayer like fashion to the High King.

"I greet and honor you in the Name of God, our High King, Thureos, and also to you Prince Arthus. We humbly welcome you to Northern Peaks City. And, welcome also to our humble home. Please, if there's anything we can do to help our High King, Thureos or to help you Prince Arthus, just ask us anytime," said Crystal in her ever so kind voice, which really was soft and warming.

"Well, I won't be here long. I must go down into to the Halls of Flames in a short time with Maddlynn here. I also must go tonight to meet up with the northern guards. I have been invited to spend the night tonight with them at their barracks. Tomorrow morning, I will head off to see the chief of the Yelin in order to make sure that our trade deals and trade routes are all being well guarded," said High King Thureos.

Arthus remembered hearing word of the Yelin, had a questioning look on his face.

Seeing Arthus' questioning look, High King Thureos says to him, "A lot of people think of the Yelin as being a beast race, who live deep in the northern tundra. Though many city folks think of them that way, they really are mostly a peaceful race. The Yelin really do love living way out in the much harsher wilds of the northern tundra. I had once brokered a trade deal with them in order to help ensure peace between them and Clan Gearhead living and working in both Northern Tundra Village and in Northern Peak City."

"We do know you must have a lot to official work that keeps you very busy, our High King. Zeck... why don't you quickly show our guest, Prince Arthus, where his private room is and where he can store all of his belongings. Also, there are thirty Dwarvens freezing outside, waiting to help him move what he needs up into his room. Make sure that the ones that come inside to help carry anything take their boots and gloves off, or your mom's voice will not be as sweet and kind as we all love it to be. Our High King, my wife has prepared a lovely supper for you and for Arthus and for Maddlynn too. Please honor us for supper before you head away. She cooked up plenty of ram stew and desserts and such all for you all to join us tonight," said Drake

"That sounds lovely. I do enjoy ram stew," said High King Thureos.

"Oh, Crystal... homemade ram stew. Now yer talkin," added in Maddlynn with a big smile on her face.

"And, there is plenty of it, enough even for your thirty Dwarven helpers all freezing outside of our house. Prince Arthus and Zeck, when they finish helping get the prince's belongings carried upstairs, you be sure to invite half of them at a time to come inside to get warmed up by the fire pit and to eat some of my ram stew. Ok?"

"Ram, I have never had ram before; what does it taste like," asked Arthus?

"Ah yes, it is an animal that the Yelin that live out in the far northern wild tundra and up in the Northern Peak Mountain Range, and some of the people the of Northern Peak City raise as their main domesticated animal here. Their wool is what that soft woolen material on the inside your pants and even what your shirt is made out of. Their soft wool covered skin is that white softer material on the inside of your overcoat. And, the ram's meat is absolutely delicious, when it is slow cooked properly. It is not a meat that you will ever want to quick fry at all! Well... unless you love an extremely strong wild-tasting meat. There are many people that do like it that way too! Anyway, Arthus you really do need to understand how and why they trade ram meat and on some occasions they even trade some young live rams with other clans for different things they might need like the Clan Arial's farm produce. Trade is especially important everywhere on Malon, but even more so here. The northern tundra and Northern Peaks Mountains are seen as practically a wasteland of cold, snow and ice most of the year. Not very much to eat can grow around here. Sure there are trees and underbrush and several species of hardy wild grasses that the rams seem to love to eat. However, it is very difficult for people to eat tree bark, underbrush branches and hardy wild grasses. Even the wild berries found here and there are not producing enough to sustain the lives of people living here. Hence, clans, like Clan Arial, help the people here by growing almost all of the farm produce on the planet. The grains like oats, corn, barley, hops, and wheat grown in the south are traded with Clan Gearhead, who use a lot of that to help feed the rams and other animals living here. Some of Clan Arial's produce is even traded to the Yelin clans the Mammoth fur and other things only found out in the deep wilds of the northern tundra, which is also where many of the rams originate from. See Arthus, we on Malon try our best to help everyone the best we can. Each clan doing their very best with all of their own responsibilities and using their skills wisely then helps all of the other clans. Just like Malon is one planet and we all live on it in a symbiotic relationship to it, we also live in a great big symbiotic circle with all the peoples living on the planet. Several Clan Urial guards and several members of our own Clan Arkwright's Silver Thorns come up north here to help protect all of our trade routes from wild predators and such," said High King Thureos.

"Thank you so kindly my High King for offering your insights and wisdom to me," said Arthus as properly as he could. This is how he was always taught to speak to the royal family members whenever he was in the presence of anyone who was not in his immediate family. I really should hurry now as there are thirty Dwarvens still freezing and waiting outside," said Arthus. "I also see that I am getting quite hungry. I can't wait to try your cooking as it already smells delicious, Crystal," said Arthus bowing slightly.

"I see you have fine manners, young Prince. It is nice to have you here," said Crystal with a smile.

Zeck, standing by the same blanket covered doorway, then motioned for Arthus follow him up quickly up the stairs. On the second floor, there were four rooms. One was a bathroom with a strange-looking square wooden tub almost like Arthus saw in Clan Arial's bathhouses. The other three were bedrooms; one was Drake and Crystals, the other was Zecks, and the last room was small like a bigger closet. Coming down from an access hole in the ceiling was a steep set of stairs. Following Zeck into that room and up that stairs was a fairly large storage room. Along the far end was some shelving which had a lot of quilts and furs stacked neatly. Next to the shelving was many metal crates and metal trunks. A metal cable had been hung across the room out in front of all of that stuff. There against the wall Zeck grabs a big blanket quilt and hung it over the cable.

Zeck says as he is eyeing Arthus, "Prince Arthus, please excuse us for having to keep storage up here behind where we have set up your bedroom."

The space in front of the big blanket had been made into a fairly cozy third bedroom, with a large cot, a table with a chair, a tall lamp and there was a large space next to a wall where he could easily place all of his belongings.

"Continuing to eye the Arthus, Zeck says, "Kinda smaller than you're probably used to as the high and mighty Prince of Malon."

Arthus smiled. "My best friend in the world, named Jade, said something just about like that to me when she and I first met a year ago. However you might imagine the palace life of a royal, please throw all of those thoughts away! I do hope you will treat me just like you would anyone about your age here in Northern Peaks City. And, whenever we are alone together, drop the Prince of Malon from your vocabulary and your mind. I am just a normal, well almost normal, half-bred person about your age. I am half Cundo and half Ignole, thus my green toned skin and silver eyes. Otherwise I am completely normal. And, Zeck, we have the next year to become good friends. I know we will be busy as I must learn everything I can about life up here in the Northern Mountains," said Arthus.

"Of course you are a normal, almost normal, Prince of Malon...I mean person. I bet you don't even know what really hard work is, for being a Prince. I bet you are crying in a week to go home from the grinding work of the forge and of the mines," replied Zeck.

Arthus frowned and said, "No! I really do know what hard work is, and I will stay for a year, without complaining. And, I hope that I can prove to you and your parents, and even Maddlynn that I have earned your respect and trust. Hopefully by then even my muscles will grow out enough that I don't appear like some pampered prince from the palace, but a true son of Malon no matter what family I come from. I will show you that I am no different than you or anyone else. I really don't want any special treatment from the others here. I already work hard, just look at my calloused hands that I earned working hard in the fields of Clan Arial." Arthus showed Zeck his calloused hands. "Are these the hands of someone who had never seen work in his life? Asked Arthus.

"We will see; come on before my parents, or worse, Maddy comes up here to get us," smiled Zeck.

Arthus followed Zeck back downstairs and immediately goes into the mud room, puts his boots and gloves and overcoat back on. Then steps outside where standing there freezing in the cold are the thirty Dwarvens still in formation holding up the pallet of his and the High Kings belongings. Arthus quickly grabs off of the pallet his backpack, his hammock pack roll, his satchel with the tele-mask inside. And then places them inside on the floor of the mud room, and then closes the door from the outside. He then grabs his big trunk with the wheels on the one end. He pulls that off of the pallet and allows the wheels to drop off the end onto the ground with a thud. He again opens the house door and pulls the wheeled trunk in through the doorway. Then he goes back out and says, "Place that pallet down on the ground." The Dwarvens obey. Arthus then says, "All of you must come inside of the house, but please brush off your dirty boots there on the heavy grass footpad by the door. As soon as you enter. And you must remove your boots and gloves and place them neatly by the boot and shoe shelf rack in the mud room. Please, if I may get two of you to help me carry my large trunk all the way upstairs and up into the attic area where I have my bedroom. The rest of you please come in two by two at a time, removing your boots and gloves, then enter the living room and stand up close to the fire to get warm. There is room in there for at least half of you at a time, but do be polite and do try not to disrupt the High King and our honored hosts as you are all coming and going and warming yourselves by the fire."

Hearing that, the Dwarvens laid down the pallet. Two of the Dwarvens came up on the porch and cleaned off their boots as instructed. Those two Dwarvens then followed Arthus inside the house, After removing their heavy boots and gloves and laying them down on the floor neatly as instructed, they grabbed up Arthus' heavy trunk and followed him up the stairs and all the way up through the closet with the stairs leading up into the attic area. One Dwarven took the strapping that he was carrying and loop tied it around the handle of the trunk on the one end. He then climbed up to the top of those steep stairs and began lifting that end of the trunk up through the air. The other Dwarven lifting and holding onto the end with the wheels. Arthus' heavy trunk was quickly lifted all the way up and into Arthus' bedroom area. Then the Dwarvens descended the attic stairs. Arthus had carried his backpack up along with his hammock tube bag and his satchel. Then he came back down the stairs with the Dwarvens and motioned for them to come into the living room and join him by the fire.

The two Dwarvens went over and spoke with Maddlynn, and seeming to be reassured, came over and stood by the fire.

Arthus then went back to the front door of the house and motioned to the Dwarvens and said, "Hurry up now. It is freezing out here. Everyone on the left side of the Pallet, now come up here on the porch and clean off your boots here and step inside the mudd room. Take off your boots and gloves and neatly sit them there by the other boots and gloves. Then go in through the blanketed doorway into the living room and join your mates by the fire."

As soon as the 13 Dwarvens had all entered the living room and were standing up alongside of their mates by the fire, Crystal with a smile says kindly to them, "Here you are my friends," as she hands each of them a giant sized bowl filled with her ram stew and an oversized spoon. "When you are sufficiently filled and warmed up, will you please do be so kind as to go back out and relieve your other 15 Dwarven mates; allowing them to also come in to eat and get warmed up by our big fire-pit. I do surely wish I had a much bigger space here in my humble house, so none of you would ever have to be waiting out freezing in the cold."

Hearing Crystal say that, all the Dwarvens had a huge smile on their face as they started eating the hot ram stew from their bowls.

Maddlynn half yelled with a big smile on her face, "Don't ya fret yerself none, Crystal. None of the 'umble homes in Northern Peaks City are big 'nough ta hold an entire troop of me Dwarven welcoming guard. I am sure they all of me Dwarven welcoming guard greatly 'preciate yer very kind 'ospitality."

Prince Arthus and Zeck joined the High King, Thureos, Maddlynn, Drake and Chrystal at the long curved table.

Chrystal kindly says to Zeck and Prince Arthus, "We already said our prayers, before we started serving, while you were busy. Anyway, here are your bowls and I just filled them up so be careful as the ram stew in them is right out of that big cauldron there over the fire, and very, very hot."

Arthus bows his head and says a silent prayer. Zeck notices Arthus do that and respectfully bows his head and joined him. Then they both dug into their oversized bowls of ram stew.

After blowing on the large spoon filled with ram stew, Arthus takes a bite. "Wow, this is really, really good tasting," he says to Chrystal.

"Well there is plenty, so if you are still hungry after eating up that bowl, you can go help yourself to get another dipper full of the stew from that hot cauldron over there on the fire," replied Chrystal again in her very kind voice.

"Actually, when we done with Dinner, Prince Arthus, I have decided that you will follow me down to Halls of Flames, as I want you to see

130

where the smelting takes place, where all the forges lie, the kinds of tools and machines that are there. I also want you to see where and how the Dwarves that live here. You will be spending a lot of time between up here in the city and down below the city in the Halls of Flames. Also, I have decided that though you will come back here to sleep here tonight, I want you to accompany me first thing tomorrow to go meet with the Yelin Chieftain. We will have to travel on ice bear mounts to get there, and it won't be easy going. We should be back here in two days. After you come back, then you be staying every night here at Drake and Crystal and Zeck's," said High King Thureos.

Arthus replied, "Ok, I probably should bring along my backpack, and be sure that I have what I need in that. Will I also need to also bring my tele-mask?"

"Yes, I do think that will be a good idea. And, I should accompany you up to your room and help you decide what to pack in your backpack, from the items you already have. And, I have more items out on the pallet for you which I brought along with me. We will get into those items once we get down into the workshop and under Maddlynn's house. As this is your very first ground excursion into the wilds of the northern tundra, I want to be certain you are ready. And, believe me when I say, this is not going to be easy going. I too must ensure that I have everything that I need!"

The High King, Thureos then turns and looks at Zeck. "Zeck! I can see that you are not someone who wastes your youth. You are already a very strong young man. Therefore, why don't you join Prince Arthus and I for this trip to the Yelin Chieftain? That is, if it is ok with your parents?

At hearing that, Zeck smiled brightly and then with a questioning look on his face he looked directly at his dad, Drake.

Hearing the High King say this, Drake took in a deep breath, and then let out a deep sigh. "Alright, alright, Zeck. You can go, but you must promise to stay very close to the High King and Prince Arthus. And, you must be careful at all times, as all of the wild open tundra is no safe place. It is not even safe for fully trained knights!" Declared Drake with a bit of a worried look on his face.

After they ate their fill of ram stew and desserts, Arthus led his grandfather, High King Thureos, up the stairs to his bedroom. The High King and Arthus went through his backpack and pulled everything out of that, then went through his large trunk with the wheels. His grandfather helped him pick out exactly what to bring and what not to bring with him.

Drake was down in Zeck's room ensuring that Zeck also had his backpack filled with only the most important items for this two day journey.

After about twenty minutes they were all back in the living room, packed and ready.

High King Thureos says, Zeck you can leave your backpack here for now as Arthus and you will come back here tonight after we all go to the Halls of Flames. Arthus, you bring your backpack though because I do have some items that you will need packed in it from my belongings. I'll be sure to give those to you before you come back here tonight.

The Dwarven Welcoming Guard and Maddlynn were already outside patiently waiting. The High King, Thureos, Prince Arthus, and Zeck after getting back on their overcoats, heavy gloves, and heavy boots, all stepped outside. Arthus lays his backpack again onto the pallet. Then everyone followed Maddlynn and her Dwarven Welcoming Guard all the way back around the maze of streets. It took a while, but then they arrived at a tunnel entrance into the mountain. This tunnel leads to the Dwarven home area. There was a large sign attached to the rock face of the mountain above the tunnel entrance that read, "Halls of Flame." They entered the tunnel and the ground under them obviously descended downhill. As they descended it became hotter and hotter. In fact it became so hot that everyone stopped and removed their outer coats.

The High King walked up and laid his coat onto the pallet that already held the coats of the Dwarven Welcoming Guard and Maddlynn's coat. He was careful to ensure his coat was separated from theirs. He motions to Arthus and Zeck to do the same thing with their outer coats.

They soon came to an opening to a massive Cavern, where the walls were lined with stairs and many Dwarven sized doorway holes.

The High King says to Arthus, "Those are the Dwarvens' houses. These homes are hammered right out of the cavern walls into rock of the mountain surrounding the cavern. Most of these were built by the actual Dwarven family members that live inside them? A few of them were built by other hired crews of Dwarvens."

Many Dwarvens could be seen running here and there, always hard at work. Arthus could hear the clanging of hammers, and machine sounds. The sounds actually all came together like a musical tune in almost perfect rhythm. The forgers and miners' hammering combined into a harmonious way, and the Dwarvens were all humming along to themselves also as they worked. Thureos smiled, knowing what Arthus was thinking.

"It is music, grandson. You see, Arthus, the Dwarvens have a special belief that crafting and working is all a form of worship to God, which they call the Ultimate Great Creator. And, God is the Ultimate Great Creator, so it is right that they all call Him that! They call their work, *The Creation Song.* Dwarvens believe nothing favors God more than building something or creating something with all their heart and soul. So while they work, a Dwarven only thinks about the Great Creator's art. Then they pour out their heart and soul into everything they do. To them, God is the ultimate creator of all things, so any ideas or inventions that any of the Dwarvens might sign, ultimately they know that even those ideas for the inventions are coming directly from God into their mind. Therefore they are only joining in God's creative work. It is quite lovely to think about this the way that they do, and I believe that we too should believe and think exactly the same as we do what we do. Now you know a bit more of our slightly shorter hairy friends, the Dwarvens. Now, let's go down," said Thureos.

Maddlynn opened up a gate and stepped into a very large shiny metal box like contraption that had very ornate shiny fencing like materials on three sides and a shiny metal roofing that was about three meters tall. She motioned them to get inside of the box with her and said, "Now don't you go worrying none. This 'ere powered cable lift can easily carry all of ya'all's weight and then some."

As Arthus entered, he could see through the ornate fencing that there were some fairly large pulleys with heavily greased cables wrapped around them on the two sides of this.

After they were all inside, Maddlynn pushed a button. The powered cable lift moved down a long ways then came to a stop. Maddlynn stepped out of the lift and motioned for them to come out of it. Then she pushed a different button located outside of the lift and sent the lift back up to pick up her Dwarven Welcoming Guard along with the pallet holding their belongings. It did not take long for the lift to come back down. The Dwarven Welcoming Guard marched out still carrying the pallet. Then they all continued following Maddlynn along another winding cave-like tunnel until they reached another large cavern somewhat like the other one was above the cable lift, but this one seems much bigger.

Arthus thinks to himself, "This Cavern is massive and is even a bit hotter than the one located up above." He then notices that there is an enormous building built out of stone and metal in the very middle of this massive Cavern.

Maddlynn continues to lead everyone directly towards that enormous building.

"Ere we be at me 'umble house and workshop," said Maddlynn. Then she adds, "This is where I prefer to spend all of my time. I don't much like going up and out into the freezing cold, and I really do hate playing politics beyond managing all me Dwarvens duties!"

Hearing her admit that, High King Thureos said, "I hear you say that same thing every time I come here, but I will never believe that you would willingly give up being in charge of all the Dwarvens who live and work here. That one responsibility of yours always requires getting involved in the planet's politics too. You cannot enjoy the one, without also dealing with the other. There is a symbiotic relationship between them."

"Me know that," huffed Maddlynn. "But that don't mean me will ever find any way of enjoyin' it. But, don't ya be taken me wrong, me

High King. Me really do like ya me High King. And, me likes so many other peoples too. It be just all the constant complaining, bickering, and arguing that happens at them big political meetings. Sometimes political meetings even break out in fist-de-cuffs to settle a matter. That is what me hates so much. There has been a time or two that me was having to do the hitting and kicking to get them other peoples to settle down and work their problems out! Me really don't like it when me has to do that!"

"Well, I don't like it when that happens either. Many of my scars took place while trying to get all of the various clans and people's groups on Malon to finally come to an agreement. I learned to call that sort of thing, 'Negotiating with my dagger, or sword!' And, believe me when I say that there was plenty of that many years back."

Maddlynn says, "I bet ya have seen more than yer share of needing ta do that kind of politican! And, me is very proud of ya' being me High King of Malon. Me do pray often ta the Ultimate Great Creator fer' ya's wellbeing. Me hopes also that yer' kid, the Prince and yer' grandkid, this 'er scrawny looking Prince of Malon, continue ta be healthy and keep right on bein' such a blessin' ta everyone on Malon. Me knows how much a blessin' ya'all have been to all me Dwarvens on Creed. Now, ya'all hurry up and get ya inside me 'umble house and workshop! We's been dawdling around talking out here long 'nough."

As everyone entered the main floor of the giant building, Arthus looks around curiously. He thinks to himself, "Wow, this first main floor really is quite massive. It appears to have everything needed to build practically anything. It includes heavy anvils, several forges, smaller and larger smelter pots, a very large smelter, and even a large area for various types of engineering. There were metal lathes, giant drill presses, and metal tables here and there. Some were fitted with obviously well used grates on top and above those appeared to be mounted some sort of laser cutter machine.

Maddlynn points way up to the very back of building. Very high up a steel staircase and mounted on steel beams was what appeared to be a long rectangle metal box. There was an open doorway at the top of the staircase. And there were wide open window openings along this side, overlooking the entire workshop floor. That box contraption way up there be me 'umble house. Me can observe the whole workshop floor from up there in me house.

Arthus thought to himself, "That doesn't look like much of a house, but maybe enough for one or, maybe two Dwarvens."

Maddlynn then turns and looks at her Dwarven Welcoming Guard and commands, "Put the High King's Pallet way back over there below me house stairs on that platform. Then get your fur coats and gloves and take 'em to yer homes where they belong. Ya'll got plenty of other work ta do back here in me workshop. Thanks to Chrystal ye already ate yer' dinners, so don't ya be dawdling at yer homes." Then bowing her head slightly, "Let me go get what I need, me High King, and then we will head to the great forges," said Maddlynn.

Maddlynn climbed up her tall flight of stairs into her house and disappeared for a little bit. It did not take long and she came back out and climbed back down her stairs. Then Maddlynn led them back out of the large building and towards the back of the massive cavern. There were some other tunnels there in the back wall of the cavern. They went into the tunnel on the far right, which went even again on a downward slope. That tunnel emptied into a third massive cavern. There were rows and rows of very large forges—around five or so dwarves maned each one. Unique molten metal like lava streams are running in troughs throughout the room. Different types of metals were in each of the streams. Some of the streams came only a few feet apart from one another. Other streams were very far apart and much wider too. The wider streams had giant cranes with huge stone bowls hanging from them hanging over them. There were several mine ore carts on tracks going into the tunnels or out again to drop off their loads at the far end. A couple of Dwarvens and one Cundo were standing outside the mine shaft drinking water and holding their Pikes.

Maddlynn walked up to an over-look platform and shouted out for all to hear.

"Hey, you drunken bearded blockheads, look up here," yelled Maddlynn.

136

The whole room came to a halt, everyone looking at each other like something was wrong. Maddlynn burst out laughing and the entire room started to laugh.

"Ok clan Gearhead today His High King Thureos came all the way to say hi so look sharp and try to get the oil out ya dang beards and come on up and say hi. Oh... and his grandson, this young scrawny Prince Arthus has joined us as well. The High King says Prince Arthus will be staying this whole year, so we do have to be sure we show him the Dwarvens ways of getting rid of scrawny and puttin on some serious muscles by workin the way that the Ultimate Great Creator intends that we should be workin, the Dwarvens way and the Ultimate Great Creator's way as well," said Maddlynn with a wide grin.

The crowd roared and cheered, as they all started almost running towards the over-look area where Maddlynn had led the High King, Prince Arthus and Zeck.

"BREAK OUT A KEG OR TWO OF DRINK! Shouted some Dwarvens.

"BREAK OUT THE GOOD SMOKES! Shouted some other Dwarvens.

There was a long bench along the inside railing of the over-look. Arthus took one look at that and even though it looked dirty with soot, he still sat down and began to rub his tired legs.

Arthus was surprised just how many of these bearded folk wanted to look at him, and each one commented on how small he was and how it was a shame his beard hadn't started to grow yet and such. Arthus began laughing out loud. A Dwarven handed him a mug of something that smelled like oil. But just as he smelled it, the High King grabbed his shoulder and gripped his shoulder tightly.

High King Thureos spun Arthus with his hand towards him quick, gave him a very stern look, then leaned real close to Arthus face and looked him right in the eyes, and said, "You better not even think to drink that! And, then as quickly spun Arthus back around to face the Dwarven who had given him the mug.

Arthus then handed the Dwarven back the mug with a sheepish smile and a shrug. The Dwarven shrugged and then handed the same mug to the High King Thureos.

Soon everyone had said their greetings and were back to work though Arthus could have sworn at least half of the Dwarvens were actually drunk.

High King Thureos still holding the full mug that was handed to him sat down next to Arthus.

"Well, these are the Dwarvens; a very lively bunch. They love what they do, and none are better at it than them. They are mighty hunters and even mightier warriors, with extraordinary creative minds. Please get to know them well, my grandson. You will spend many of a day working side-by-side with many of them. In order to gain their trust, love, and support, you do have to show them your willingness to stay and work until you literally drop. Now let's go. We better head back, I still have to meet up with Northern Guard before it gets too late tonight. They have a door leading into their area located on that platform where our pallet was laid down. They do have a pretty nice barracks located behind Maddlynn's workshop and home. We will sleep in their barracks with them tonight. And, tomorrow morning we will head out to the Yelin village, said Thureos. Having said that, the High King winced with his face in a way which let Arthus know he really did not like what was inside the mug, but he drank the mug filled drink without stopping, that he had earlier told Arthus not to drink. He then burped a burp like only a High King could burp. He wiped his bearded face and got up.

Maddlynn remained on the over-look when the High King, Arthus and Zeck all headed back to Maddlynn's workshop and home. The High King led them over to the Pallet, quickly went through his own belongings and found the rest of the items he had brought for Arthus. He opened Arthus' backpack and placed some of the items into the backpack. Grabbing out a different big carrier bag, he placed the other items into it.

"I have three of these minus fifty degree all-in-one sleeping bag tents that I brought with me from the palace, which are perfect for the extreme cold of this tundra. They have a synthetic material in them that is made from some of the bio-fuel from the bio-fuel plant which Clan Arial operates. That bio-fuel plant was designed by the Dwarven engineering team here. Clan Gearhead truly is helping us properly use, protect and preserve our planets resources." He handed one to Arthus to tie onto his backpack. He handed one to Zeck and said, "Be sure you tie this onto your backpack as it is much better than the down versions that everyone has been using for several years. When the down ones got wet, whomever was in those froze to death. These have proven never to absorb any type of moisture. They are also much warmer to sleep in than the old down versions. Also, Zeck here is a box of special chem-pack foot and hand warmers to pack in your backpack too. Each hand warmer last about four hours. I already put a box in Arthus' backpack. Arthus, you have your dagger. Zeck, do you have a dagger? Asked High King Thureos.

"No, my High King. I'm sorry, but I don't have a dagger. But, I do have a pair of throwing Tomahawks that I made myself and I can throw and stick those like no body's business! In fact, I just made two more sets of those, which are hanging right over there on that rack over there. Let me get those and bring you both each a set of those. They are very fine throwing weapons, though they do take a bit of practice to get really good at hitting your target with them."

Zach jumps down from the platform where he had been sitting waiting on the High King and Arthus to finish packing. He runs over, grabs the two sets of tomahawks that he had finished making just the other day. He brings them over and gives one set to Arthus and one set to the High King.

"Here you go. You both keep those and learn to use them. They are great for many uses. As you can see, I designed these so that there is a piece of flint tucked into each of the handles. And, there is super strong climbing cord already wrapped around each of the handles too. That way they can be used to help start a fire, or the climbing cord can be used for helping to tie up a tarp, or a tent. The axe heads are really sharp, so my mom made me these great axe head coverings out of heavy leather. The back sides of the axe heads act as a hammer too. If you look here you can see I drilled a special hole through the steel here and here where they can be tied easily to any backpack from both ends, which keeps them secure so that they don't bounce against your body as you walk. I made some other sets that did not have that feature, but I sent those back to the smelter, as they didn't function like I wanted them to. These are my latest design. I kept tweaking and trying different features to make this better and better. There are two long leather straps on each handle too so that you can tie them right up to your backpacks easy."

"Wow Zeck, these are really cool looking, said Arthus.

"That is a true statement, Arthus. Zeck, these are fantastic. I will certainly treasure this gift from you for many years. And, now, allow me to gift you a very special dagger, which is often worn by the Silver Thorns. I have a strong feeling that you will appreciate this. In fact, I will task you with finding a way to improve on its design. I know you can do that."

"Oh, wow, thank you very much my High King. I will certainly treasure this gift and I will honor your words by accepting your challenge. Hopefully by next year you will see several design features that I come up with. Perhaps in the future, the Silver Thorns will all be wearing and using one of my designed daggers."

"Well, you keep working on these tomahawks too. A few slight changes and all of our Silver Thorns will want to carry those too," said High King Thureos. He added, "Have you thought of adding a sawing feature into the handle, so that it can be used as a way to cut wooden poles?

"Wow! That is a great idea to consider to add to what I already have here. I will work on that to see how best to design that into the upper handle area. I thought about taking the bottom tip of the handle drilling it out and putting in a small fish tackle kit into the inside, but I had trouble with that screw cap end breaking off when I threw it. Perhaps I should design that feature into the handle of the dagger, and design the saw feature into the handle of the tomahawk," said Zeck.

"That is a great idea to start with, Zeck, said High King Thureos." But, now it is getting late and we must start out early in the morning right after breakfast. Zeck, you know where the northern guard barracks is, correct?

"Yes, said Zeck.

"Good, tomorrow morning bring Arthus directly there after breakfast. Now head home and be sure to lead Arthus again, just to be sure he knows his way," said High King Thureos.

Soon Zeck and Arthus were heading back out of the tunnels towards the outside where it is extremely cold above ground. Drake met them a little ways from the outside, about the same location that they were when they took their coats off due to the heat. Arthus had not yet felt like he needed to put on his overcoat and gloves. He did not feel nearly as cold as he thought he would. Then he thought to himself, "The warm tunnels were so hot and closed in that I am actually happy to be going out here in the cold air for a bit. Drake, Zeck and Arthus all headed to the house.

Inside the house, Zeck, Crystal and Drake all picked up some small smooth stones and were then using a unique tool to cut or burn symbols into the smooth stones. Arthus turned to Drake.

"What are you all doing," asked Arthus?

"We are making Ruins. Come I show you," smiled Drake. Arthus grabbed a seat next to Zeck, who gave him a strange glance.

"Here," said Chrystal as she was handing him one of the small stones.

When Arthus touched the stone, it felt warm, and not just because someone had it in their hands, or because it was inside the house in the warm air of the house. It had a warmth all of its own. Arthus actually could sense the Life-energy in it. The stone felt like it was filled with Life-energy.

"Where are these stones found," asked Arthus?

"Good question, Prince Arthus, said Drake. They are found right next to the First God's Tree. As you know that is located where the palace is located in the center of God's Forest. The River of Life that goes past the massive garden where First God's Tree is located is a very special river. The Alda gather these special stones from the bottom of the river and trade them to the Clan Arkwright trade department that is in Harmony City. Then these are transported by Golden Griffon flocks to the docks in Clan Arial. Then they go by cart to the Cargo Shuttles. And from there they come here where we carefully craft them into different Ruins. Each Ruin symbol has a different meanings or words written in the ancient words of Heaven's Golden City. We use them for all kinds

141

of things, from lighting the forges to helping make heavy objects feel as light as air," said Drake.

"Wow, that is amazing," said Arthus.

"But for tonight, we need to get some rest. Why don't you all go take a shower and then head up to bed? You and Zeck got a long hike tomorrow," said Crystal.

Arthus nodded; he was quite tired, so he quickly went up to the room they gave him. They already made his bed, and his clothing was already put away in a beautiful cedar lined multi-drawer chest, that he had not seen earlier when he was up here. Arthus grabbed a towel and a rag that had been laid out for him. He noticed that they had also laid out a bath robe and a set of very warm looking woolen pajamas. He carried these down the stairs to the bathroom and quickly removed his outer clothing took a hot shower. Arthus wondered how the water was being heated inside the house, but realizing he could ask later, he quickly scrubbed his body clean, washed his hair, brushed his teeth, dried off, put on his clean pajamas, which were incredibly soft and comfortable, put on his bathrobe, checked to be sure that the shower and sink were as clean as he had found them, and then left the bathroom and climbed back up into his attic bedroom. There he crawled into bed under a super thick warm wool and down filled blanket. He looked at the leather bracers. Then he smiled, thinking of how much Jade would love to see all this, and quickly fell asleep.

Chapter 9
The Northern Mountains

"Arthus, I do believe you said not to treat you any differently from others, so get your scrawny butt out of bed this instant! Yelled Zeck into Arthus' ear.

Arthus immediately opened his eyes and sat up, and said, "Yes, exactly right. Thank you Zeck.

"Mornings come early, as a day's work is always long and tough here. You be sure to get and set yourself an alarm as I am not going to act like your personal alarm clock!" Declared Zeck, who then said, "Breakfast is waiting and you are dawdling!"

Arthus thought to himself, "Wow, this morning came way faster than I would like." Getting up and dressing quickly in clean underwear and then putting on the same clothing he had worn the day before. He then quickly headed to the bathroom, wet and combed his hair back and tied it as he had been taught to do by Nessie, his very first childcare nanny, who worked at the time for his dad, the Prince from a time when he was very young. He brushed his teeth and washed his face and hands. Then he took his toothbrush back up to his room quickly, and then almost ran down the flights of stairs. At the table were Drake, Chrystal and Zeck, waiting for him to have prayer together before they ate. Arthus bowed his head to them, sits down in front of a bowl of porridge and then put his hands together quickly. Drake led them all in the same prayer that he had learned at the Clan Arial farming village with Grag,

Shelly and Jade. He ate about half of the bowl, when a loud knocking came from the front door.

Drake arose from the table and opened his front door. Arthus grandfather, the High King, Thureos was here.

"He had not been willing to wait at the barracks for Zeck and I to come meet him. Instead, here he is. Always seeming to be in such a hurry," thought Arthus quietly to himself.

"Ready? You two grab all your gear that we prepared together last night. Be sure to have your daggers and tomahawks, and Arthus grab your long sword too as you actually might need it," said High King Thureos from outside the front door.

Arthus ran back upstairs and grabbed his backpack, and strapped on his dagger and his long sword to his heavy utility belt. On the back of his backpack he had already tied the tomahawks that Zeck had given him the night before. The bottom of his backpack he had strapped on the all-in-one tent that his grandfather had given to him. He came back down the stairs and quickly put on his boots, gloves and heavy fur overcoat. Then putting on his backpack he headed outside. He immediately noticed that Zeck was already there waiting with the High King. In Zeck's right hand he is holding long halberd-type weapon, which is a spear, but below the long spear tip has two wide double curved axe blades.

The High King Thureos waved goodbye to Drake and Chrystal and said, "Drake and Chrystal, I promise to do my very best to keep Zeck safe."

The three of them all headed towards the east end of that very long street. At the far end of the street on the northern side of the street a huge gate was attached to the rock face of the mountain, which had a fairly large tunnel cut into the mountain behind it. Heading inside the tunnel opening they immediately turned west and there behind another metal gate, was a stable.

Arthus appeared shocked as there were several enormous white bears inside the stable. Arthus knew about them only from what he had read in his-holo books. They are called, *Ice Bears*.

Clan Urial Northern Patrol Guard was already waiting there at the stables. They were made up of Cundo and Dwarvens, all having long beards and wearing a strong, but very thin layer of chain mail sewn between layers of leather, fur, synth-blend, and thick wool. Four others joined them. One was an older Cundo, who wore a bearskin fur wrapped around his synth-blended with chain mail, leather and thick wool armor. The head of the bear went over and was permanently mounted to his heavily lined helmet, while the claws of the bear were strapped onto his bear fur mitten gloved hands. The neck of the bear draped down to form a hood, which wrapped up under the chin of his head. That Cundo man quickly knelt before the High King.

"Our High King, we of Clan Urial Northern Patrol Guard welcome you once again. He carried a spear, a longsword and a shield. Behind him was a Cundo woman who had a bow and on her side, two axes, and wore light leather style armor. She also wore a rather large white bear fur poncho-style cloak as an overcoat. Arthus guessed she was a scout. Beside her was another Cundo male, who also had on light leather armor and a white bear fur poncho-style cloak as an overcoat. Arthus guessed that he too was a scout, but noticed that neatly strapped into his poncho were several small anti-personnel mines. He carried a long bow with a rather large quiver of arrows. There were several different kinds of tips on his arrows, including double and triple razor tips, and some that actually explode on impact. There on his right shoulder, riding as if it is completely tame, is a live white owl. The owl's black round eyes were giving Arthus a strange stare. Then there was an Old Dwarven, who wore very dark brown heavy fur and had a crossbow strapped low on his back. High up on his back and with the handle going diagonally down across his back, with a strap coming around and across his chest, he carried an oversized two-handed Axe. He was pulling four huge Ice Bears out from the stable by their tethers. The last Dwarven was using a long handled pole like thing that obviously had a spear head attached at the top, but just below the spear there appeared an inner bladed crook like looking thing. He was pulling three huge Ice Bears of the stables by their tethers.

Arthus thought to himself, "I wonder what that weapon is called?

"We will each take an ice bear and ride it to the Yelin village. We should arrive in about four hours as long as no storm hits us, and as long as there aren't any attacks by the wild tundra Ice Wolves," said the leader with the bear head on his helmet.

Arthus looked at the four; they were far different than any of the Clan Urial members he met before, who were the primary military Clan of Malon. Clan Urial made up most of the guards and knights all across Malon. Their job was to patrol and make sure travelers stayed safe from dangerous animals and such.

"Why the confused face, my young Prince," asked the Northern Guard Leader.

"Sorry, I have met many from Clan Urial, but none of them appeared to look like you all do right now," Arthus stated.

"Ha, ha, I see. Well you probably don't yet know much of our Great Northern Tundra Lands, or of this Northern Peak Mountain Range. Well, this unit of guards that we have here are mostly born around here, and some of us are from the northern tribes. We wear a blend of some very modern synth-blend armor that is made from materials produced in the bio-fuel plant down south near the Clan Arial farming village and the rest of our outfits are in honor of the ancient style armors of our people. For thousands of years our people have served as the protectors of all of the northern tundra and Northern Peaks Mountain Range. Creating the Clan Urial Northern Patrol Guard was an agreement between all of our various peoples groups and your grandfather, High King Thureos. Before he helped us understand the importance of working together as one cohesive unit, we were always fighting back and forth as separate warrior tribes. He has proven over and over again the value of training with all the various tribes and clans on Malon, and through all that training we learned it really was best to be fighting side-by-side against the common enemies of God our Great Creator. We really do a much better job at protecting travelers and tradesman that come here from all of the clans. We are especially proud of how all of the various northern tribe peoples are working together on common goals and objectives. Our people are much better fed, better clothed, and have some better living conditions that we did all those years ago. These accomplishments is why we remain so faithful to our High King."

Arthus knew of some northern tribes, like the Yelin, though he had never yet met a Yelin, but he did not know that even some Cundo peoples had actual tribes up here in the north, who lived out in the wild tundra. He knew that some Cundo people have chosen on their own to move away from the cities and villages, to live completely off by themselves, becoming almost wild like. High King Thureos had no problem with people choosing that lifestyle as long as they didn't start any kind of aggression, thieving, or other illegal activities. Like the Yelin tribe, many Harmony City folk thought that people who decided to live wild like that were like beasts or barbarians. However, looking at these Cundos, Arthus could see they were all well-disciplined and battle-hardened.

"Young Prince, have you ever ridden an animal before," Asked a Dwarven?

"Yes, I rode the Yaule on the Arial Plains," said Arthus.

"Ah, good! Ice Bears ain't much different than Yaule, so put your boot in this here stirrup, climb right up and sit down in the saddle, and grab onto their saddle handles here and here. Put your other foot on the other side into the stirrup over there. Then just hold on tight. Ice Bears are not as fast as them Yaule, but they are strong enough to plow through all this deep snow quickly enough. If you're not holding on with all of your might, the deep snow they plow through will knock you right off. And, you don't want to get trampled by the Ice Bears plowing quickly behind you. Many a times people have died that way, said the Dwarven.

Arthus climbed up as instructed. Sensing a bit of irritation in the bear, he leans forward and scratched it right behind its ears. The bear let out a small growl of approval. Arthus then grabbed onto the two side handles exactly as instructed and made sure his boots were securely in the stirrups. Before climbing up on his own bear the High King Thureos stopped alongside of Arthus' bear, takes a thick, but short tie down strap with snapping swivel hooks on both ends. Wraps the tie down around Arthus' waist, ties it one time and then hooks the ends of the strap also into the handles that Arthus was holding onto.

147

The High King Thureos says, "No need pretending your muscles are ready and get yourself killed. With this strap though, you are more ready to ride an ice bear for the first time! And, I am sure by the end of this year, you won't actually need this safety strap!"

Soon as everyone was mounted and ready. The knight with the owl let it fly out ahead of them, and they were off. The Journey was slower than what a Yaule can cover, but no way could any Yaule ever get through all this deep snow. At some points, the bear even disappears with their riders under the deep soft snow, a little farther forward it would raise up again from the deep snow, and then shake its head and body quite rapidly to get the snow off.

The owl screeched, flying over ahead, spying for trouble.

A couple of hours of riding, the owl came down quick, landed on the forearm of the knight and started making a fuss, flapping and screeching.

The Leader of the four came back to where Arthus and Thureos were.

"High King Thureos, there seems to be a bad storm coming in; a small blizzard may take a couple of hours to pass. There is a cave not far from where we are that we should take shelter in. Just up the way, we should hurry it be an hour, and it will hit us," said the Leader.

"I trust in you and your men; if you think its best, then lead the way. Come Arthus and Zeck stay close. We may have to spend the night there instead of at the Yelin camp if this storm takes a while to pass.

"A blizzard isn't anything to laugh at; many Predators love to use them as a mask for their attacks," said Zeck.

"Yes, you are right in that Zeck. It is obvious you have been living here, and have learned about the dangers that blizzards can become, said High King Thureos.

The group pushed their mounts to hurry towards the shelter. But suddenly the female scout yelled a command and turned her bear and came riding back with her bear from far out in their front.

"Sir, Ice Wolves have taken over the cave, and definitely there is an Alpha, at least one that we spotted," she reported.

"Curses, it seems like they might have been sensing the storm, headed there for cover, or possibly sensed both the storm and had spotted us and then tried to setup an ambush for us when we came in for cover," said the Leader.

Arthus looked confused. "How are Ice Wolves planning an Ambush? Aren't they just wild animals," asked Arthus?

"Well, that be the Alpha Ice Wolf's doing," said the Leader.

"Arthus, you read about Ice Wolves, but what the books fail to mention is every so often, a large pack picks a pack alpha, the strongest of the pack. This causes almost a mutation in the pack where the pack becomes like a single-minded unit. Once the Alpha has mastered controlling the pack like that, then the Alpha has control of the combined minds of many Ice Wolves. Hence, an Alpha actually becomes smarter through practice. Similar to a military commander is able to think and plan. The more subordinate Ice Wolves join up into its pack, the smarter it becomes. An Alpha Ice Wolf has been known to be able to stand up on two legs. We have seen where an Alpha Ice Wolf actually figured out how to wear armor. We are sure they can use telepathy to control the pack. This is why they're so dang deadly. They are among the top predators of the Great Northern Tundra, and the enemy of the Yelin," said Thureos.

"Following a slightly wider path that we followed, I have half a dozen other men, as flank guards, three to each side, besides us four. He turns to the female scout, you go to the west and inform the flank guard there, I will go to the east and inform the flank guard there. If we are careful, working as a unit together we might be able to take out that Alpha, or at least make it retreat. We need to take that cave before the storm hits. And, we don't have much time maybe ten minutes or so until the storm hits," said the Guard Leader.

The High King Thureos smiled a wide smile and said, "Don't forget I am here also, and my body aches for a really good fight," He then jumps down from his bear mount and starts pulling his fabled weapon from its sheath, it was a golden tube, but soon it turned into a mighty spear of gold hue that pulsated by life energy.

"Angel Wing! That is the special gift Michael the Archangel handed down to High King Thureos" said the Guard Leader in amazement. And, then turns his bear to warn the east guard what they are getting into. The

Guard Leader came back on his bear in about two minutes and reported, "The eastern flank is ready."

The female scout came back about the same time as the Guard Leader and reported, "The western flank is ready."

"Alright, let's not allow our High King to do this all on his own. Let us prove what we have trained and learned through other such battles. There is a reason we are called the pride of the North and Clan Urial. The unit moved into action thoroughly trained and disciplined in their craft; they moved forward without fear. The male scout and female scout took up oversight positions and took fire. Two Ice Wolves dropped dead. They knew that act would in fact alert the Alpha, who was inside of the cave of the danger, as it could actually sense the loss of two of its ice-wolves minds. There was a loud howl from the cave, and eighteen Ice Wolves burst forth from the cave mouth, followed by an enormous wolf, which actually had on a chainmail covering over its chest. That chainmail covering was familiar to the Great Northern Guard as being off of one of their dead comrades. The Alpha wolf stood up on two legs, scanned the warriors in front of it, and howled then looked to the wolves to its right and nodded then to its left and nodded. The Ice Wolf underlings all started to move left and right to attempt to circle the Guard Leader, the two Dwarvens, the east and west flanks of the Northern Guard who had joined him and the High King.

"Arthus, you and Zeck stay back by the Ice Bears. Have your weapons drawn and be at ready. Pay attention now or you won't be here to pay attention later, commanded High King Thureos. Really, if you don't, you could die here," said High King Thureos.

Arthus and Zeck stayed back with the Ice Bears, who were getting very restless.

Zeck says to Arthus, "Your sword might be good to have out right now, since you haven't had time to practice with your new tomahawks. Ice Wolves are deadly, but one good swipe of an ice bear paw can take an Ice Wolf head clean off. However, if these Ice Bears go into a frenzy, not much would be left in their way, so it is probably better to keep them out of this fight. Put your hand over and rub behind their ears like I am with mine. That might calm them down enough to keep us from getting trampled by them." Zeck sticks his spear butt side down into the snow and unleashes his two tomahawks from his backpack. He hooks one over the saddle horn. The other one he pulls the leather covering off of its axe blade. Then lays it by his feet and grabs the other one back and pulls the leather off its axe blade. Then he lays it by his feet and picks up his spear again with one hand. The second hand he picks up one tomahawk and stands ready to throw it.

Arthus pulls the sword from its sheath. He also pulls out his dagger, but thinks twice and puts them both back. Then says to Zeck, "I will ready my Tomahawks too. Once you throw your two, you can then throw mine too. That way you will have four chances to kill Ice Wolves with them." Arthus reaches around and unsnapped his two Tomahawks and tossed them over to Zeck. Zeck quickly unsnapped the leather covers off of their axe heads too and laid them in close reach.

"Great plan," says Zeck who spots an Ice Wolf sneaking around a tree and with perfect aim sinks his first Tomahawk into the Ice Wolf's skull dropping it dead.

The blizzard came on then fast and furious in a way which even trying to see your hand in front of your face became almost impossible. Then they heard a loud bang. The earth shook, and in the center was Thureos, who had slammed his Angel ing into the ground, and a huge blue circle like wall of fire burst forth blowing all the wind and snow away from around them in all directions. All the loose snow from where they stood out to about four meters around the group was gone. The blizzard couldn't penetrate the fire bearer. This also prevented any sneak attack by the wolves. But the half-starved wolves showed little fear and jumped forth one after another. But the warriors of Clan Urial and the Northern Guard were no newbies to these creatures and cut them down without any trouble. Then one of the knights was slammed hard by the Alpha, then lifted and thrown into a nearby creek, where the waters were freezing. This would spell his death if they didn't get into shelter fast. Another knight attacked, but the Alpha reached out; its clawed hand grabbed the knight and, with a swift movement, slammed him down into the ground and bit down into the man's neck blood spurted out, covering its maw. It stood and howled in victory, but short-lived next

151

caught everyone by surprise. A Blazing spear hit the Alpha in its upper shoulder, taking it clear off its hind feet and slamming into the cliff's side by the cave. The Alpha howled out in pain and anger, but as the blazing spear had cut all the way through its shoulder it couldn't move. Thureos ran over and stood before it. Thureos no longer even looked normal; his body glowed a golden hue. His body had actually doubled its size; he had removed his upper armor allowing the wind to bite his bare chest and allowed his beard to flow behind him in the wind. He raised his hand and his Angel Wing spear shot up and through and back out of the Alpha shoulder. But, Thureos had already pulled out his glowing dagger and using that in one motion pined the Alpha to the rock wall next to the cave mouth. Angel Wing instantly floating back and returning into to his hand, Thureos slammed the spear once again into the ground. Hanging pinned by Thureos' glowing dagger the Alpha howled, and one of its Ice Wolves came at Thureos left side, but without even looking, Thureos caught the that Ice Wolf by the throat with his outstretched left arm and hand. Without looking away drove the panicked wolf into the snow then speared it dead using Angel Wing in one fluid movement. The Alpha looked on in horror; it knew it messed up big time. Whatever it faced was far beyond anything it could ever dream of fighting. It howled in pain.

Hearing a roar, Arthus noticed that a couple of Ice Wolves had attempted to sneak behind the group of Ice Bears. When they charged the Ice Bears all it did was cause the Ice Bears to go off rampaging fleeing away from Arthus and Zeck into the blizzard. Arthus having seen the wolves, started to try to grab his sword and dagger...

Zeck had noticed that there were actually three of the Ice Wolves, and one of them was coming up a little hill that Arthus' ice bear was. Still sitting in the saddle is Arthus with the tie strap still around him. Arthus' ice bear decided suddenly not to stay to see the end of the fight. It took off into the blinding blizzard with Arthus still strapped into his saddle.

Arthus was able as the bear took off under him to grab onto the strap that held him onto the bear. The bear was frantic and scared and just kept running at its full speed into the blizzard. Arthus's face was growing numb from the stiff sheer wind but couldn't get himself lose, and three of the Ice Wolves were chasing them. One of those looked like it might be an Alpha.

"Dang, I bet in the confusion of the bears an Alpha slipped away from the fight with grandfather and is chasing down what this wolf believed was a much easier meal," said Arthus. All he had was his sword, and his dagger. He knew he was no match for an Alpha as scrawny as he was. They were running full on for what seemed like forever. One Ice Wolf caught up and slashed the back of the bear's legs sending it toppling over and twisting. At the same moment the backwards aimed swivel hooks came loose of the saddle, throwing Arthus free of his saddle. Arthus quickly got to his feet, pulled his sword and his dagger quickly out of their sheaths. Then the Alpha wolf and the bear squared off with each other. The smallest Ice Wolf that had been chasing the bear along with the Alpha came at Arthus, but Arthus slashed at it with his sword. Again the smaller wolf attempted to attack. But, this time Arthus jumped back and to the side and then jumped forward, running his blade into the creature's side just left of its shoulder joint. The edge of the blade went through into its heart. The smaller wolf yelped then dropped dead. A third wolf arrived right then and growled a low growl, but something that looked like a large spear five times bigger than anything he had seen before screeched past him and stuck the last wolf in the chest, killing it and pinning the dead wolf to the spot. Arthus froze, because whatever it was that could throw that sized spear was no ordinary person. He turned to see a creature that had white fur all over its body similar to an ice bear, but this creature stood almost as tall as a two story house. Its head was as big as the whole ice bear's body. Its face looked incredibly fierce, with tusks coming out of its lower jaws and curly ram's horns sticking out each side of its head. It had two arms and two legs and walked upright like a human. The creature had now grabbed and was holding onto the Alpha Ice Wolf with one outstretched arm, and then grabbed it with its other arm, and with a mighty twist, it broke that Alpha Ice Wolf's neck, then tossed it aside like it was a throw toy. Arthus was happy that this once strong Alpha was lying dead on the ground in a heap.

Arthus immediately put away his sword and his dagger. Then he stood head bowed and tried using the same sign with his hands that he had been taught to use with the Aldus for this giant beast creature. Turning his palms up, not looking at the giant beast creature directly into the face. Suddenly Arthus noticed movement to a different side and quickly glanced that direction. There were other such creatures all around him. He remained where he was and kept his head down with his hands palm up.

"You're a bit smallish to wonder out in the Great Northern Tundra, young-ling," said one of the giant beast creatures with a deep voice.

Arthus's jaw dropped, and he was dumbfounded.

"Whose young-ling are you? What Tribe do you belong? Come on child," said another one of those giant beast creatures.

Arthus was too scared and shaking to speak. Suddenly a loud thud next to him spooked him. He looked and staring him right in the eyes after having knelt down onto one knee was the creature that had killed the Alpha Ice Wolf. The creature had one hand close to Arthus, which he had laid down on the ground. The creature then turned his hand in an upright position right in front of Arthus, like Arthus had been doing with his hands.

Arthus saw that motion with the creature's and, and noticing a kind smile on the creature's face. He saw this creature's giant, but very kind looking eyes.

The giant beast creature allowed his Life-energy senses to flow out from him.

Suddenly Arthus' Life-energy senses were enhanced. He instantly sensed the Life-energy inside of these creatures and realized they were not going to harm him. That feeling immediately calmed his mind and body, where he was no longer shaking and no longer afraid.

"I apologize. I have never seen one such as you. My name is Arthus of Clan Arkwright, Prince of Malon and grandson to High King Thureos," Arthus said with a bow.

"Ah, you are the one our High King spoke of, but why are you here alone young-ling and with such company," said the large creature.

Arthus quickly explained what had happened.

"I see," said the large creature. It pointed to one of the other giant creatures, who had picked up, carried and laid Arthus' ice bear mount next to Arthus.

Arthus bent down over his dead ice bear, gently rubbed it behind the bears ears and said, "I thank you in the name of God and in my own name for trying your best to escape with me, and even though you were afraid, you faced that Alpha Ice Wolf and protected me until your death. You are highly honored!" Arthus laid his hand over where the heart of the ice bear is located. He then allowed his own life energy to pass through the dead ice bear and out into the ground surrounding it, and said, "May God bless Malon with your sacrifice!"

The ice bear had died from what looks like a large bite wound from the Alpha Ice Wolf to its throat. The Alpha had bitten into the Ice Bears throat and tore it out with its teeth, killing the ice bear outright.

Arthus then reached out and closed the ice bear's eyes. "This was such a beautiful animal and it is a tragedy to see its brutal end."

"You truly are your grandfather's child. Not many of your kind would show kindness or even sorrow to one of their rented mounts," the giant creature said. It turned to the others of its group and commanded, "Light one of our exploding green smoke signal arrows and shoot it up into the sky towards the south in order to signal that we have located someone here." He then turns his head back towards Arthus and said, "That exploding green smoke signal in the sky will hopefully be noticed by your grandfather and the other members of the Northern Tundra Guard that accompanies him. If they hear that explosion and can see the green smoke from where they are located, they will soon come here to join you. Now come along with us as our village isn't far now. We must get you out of this storm and by our fire," said the giant creature.

After saying that, the giant creature stood back up and turned and began to head off. The other creatures all followed him. Arthus followed him too.

Arthus observed that this giant creature, who had killed the Alpha Ice Wolf and that first spoke to him, was a little bit larger than the other similar giant creatures that were following him. He also carried a huge log sized club weapon, too big for any Cundo to lift, but which easily fit perfect into this giant creature's hand. The giant creatures came into an area that had been encircled with giant boulders, which were stacked upon one another forming a thick and tall barrier wall. They went through a very tall and even much taller and wider metal gate that was built into the wall. This gate's had horizontal and vertical cross bars that formed giant squares. Each of the metal bars making up the edges of the squares were fairly thick. Arthus could see it was built specifically to be opened and shut only by the hands of one of these giant creatures. Upon entering the enclosure space, Arthus saw that there were several massive mammoths, and these giant creatures were mounting up onto one of them each. Suddenly, the giant creature with the club leaned down and put out his giant hand for Arthus to climb up onto his hand. Once Arthus climbed onto his giant hand, he lifted him up onto the mammoth's back and placed him onto a Cundo sized saddle which was tacked onto the mammoth closer to its head. The giant creatures had a much larger saddles that were tacked back a little bit and up on the hump of the mammoths. Arthus noticed that one of the mammoths in the enclosure had a massive hathi howdah tacked up on its back. Other mammoths had massive cargo carriers tacked up onto their backs.

The giant creature behind Arthus said to Arthus, "Cover your ears, tightly young-ling." As soon as Arthus covered his ears tightly, then the creature put his two giant hands up by his own mouth and yelled out some kind of deep and extremely loud bellowing sound, which ended in a very high pitch. That bellowing sound actually lifted high up into the air and completely surrounded the whole area, reaching out for several kilometers in all directions.

The other giant creatures immediately joined in, each yelling out one of those incredible bellowing sounds. Joined all together, the bellowing sound then actually seemed to bounce off of the ozone layer of Malon and echo back down towards the Great Northern Tundra.

By the time the bellowing sound came echoing back down to again bounce against the tundra Arthus could feel that the bellowing sound had gained in Life energy. The bounce of the sound against the tundra caused the winds of the blizzard to stop blowing for a few moments. As the bellowing sound disappeared the winds of the blizzard again instantly returned. Then all of the giant creatures on their massive mammoth mounts headed out of the enclosure and started slowly walking towards the southeast.

"Your people... they are the ones we call Yelin, am I right? Asked Arthus to the giant creature riding behind him on the massive mammoth.

This bigger giant creature laughed a deep-sounding chuckle and says, "Yes! That is what many peoples groups on Malon call us. That name they give to we snow folk seems to relate to our Great Life Yell, which you just witnessed. Since the dawn of all creation, we have lived in this tundra, herding our rams, goats, and our mammoths. The Great Creator and Sustainer of all things, the One your kind call God, has blessed us with our Great Life Yell, and we do go Yelin out that bellowing sound in His honor fairly regularly."

"Young-ling Arthus, you have shown true bravery and kindness. I will tell our High King about your actions. Someone as young and as scrawny as you fell an Ice Wolf and even headed back into the battle towards a bigger Ice Wolf without panicking. I knew that bigger Ice Wolf would surely kill you and so I quickly threw one of my Life-energy filled spears killing it, before it could kill you. That is when you saw me come and grab up that evil Demon-Bonded Alpha Ice Wolf. I also noticed how you stood your ground to attempt to face off against it. I knew I had to kill it too, that is why I grabbed it and twisted it neck. You saw me do that and saw how big I was. But you didn't attempt to attack me with your sword, or your daggers instead you immediately sheathed them. You did not try to flee after seeing me do that. You only stood quietly, and honored me with the same sign of respect that is given towards the Alda, with your hands turned right side up, keeping your head bowed and not looking me direct in the eyes. All of this tells us you are mighty strong in spirit and heart. You will always be welcome with we Snow Folk," said the giant Yelin.

Arthus smiled and said, "You greatly honor me with your kind words as no one has ever said that to me before. Truth is, everything happened so fast. I don't know if my brain or emotions was even able to handle all of it. I just reacted," said Arthus.

The Yelin smiled brightly and said, "Of course you reacted, but you reacted with bravery and it was that sign of bravery that helped you to survive. I have witnessed so many much better trained, and much older clan warriors who failed to act bravely. Instead they fled from the battle and died needlessly while running away. You bravely pulled your sword and dagger and faced your enemy! My words to you are true. Having seen you in action, we are highly honored to have you as our Prince of Malon! You have truly gained our respect! You are a fine young-ling, who will always bring great honor to Clan Arkwright, to your father the Prince, and to your grandfather, the High King.

Soon Arthus could hear the growl of some Ice Bears arriving. He looked in their direction and the members of the Northern Tundra Guard were double riding on their backs. High King Thureos was riding one of the Ice Bears, and laying over the ice bear behind him was the dead guard's body. Tied behind the Ice Bears being dragged on the ground were twelve dead Ice Wolves and among them Arthus could see the dead Alpha Ice Wolf that High King Thureos had earlier pinned into the rock wall next to the cave. When Arthus saw this he instantly realized that the Ice Wolf pack had more than one Alpha.

"I am sorry, my grandson. I realize that I was a little too excited to join in the battle. Perhaps I shouldn't have been showing off a bit for the troops. Instead of killing this Alpha right away, I left it pinned up alive into the rock cliff, while I continued to fight with all of its subordinate Ice Wolves. If I had just killed it instead, they would have lost their singular mind and may not have had other members of their pack come after you. Because of my error, I almost lost you," confessed High King Thureos.

"Thank You, Elder One, for finding my grandson," said High King Thureos.

"In truth High King, Your Grandson almost ran into us on our way back from a fishing trip. We heard the Ice Bear let out a cry in pain and watched as it did a twisting flip throwing your young-ling Arthus off of its saddle. Then I witnessed with my own eyes the bravery of your young-ling grandson, Prince Arthus. Instead of running from the battle in fear he quickly pulled out his sword and dagger and took on the slightly smallest of the three Ice Wolves and killed it. Then he immediately started moving right at a bigger Ice Wolf. I knew that one was way too big for him so I threw my Life-energy filled spear and killed it for him. I saw how the ice bear had died from the Demon-Bonded Alpha Ice Wolf and it was then coming back towards Prince Arthus. That young warrior ran straight at that Demon-Bonded Alpha Ice Wolf too, but I quickly grabbed that Demon-Bonded Alpha Ice Wolf and then with a twist broke its neck. Your young-ling Prince Arthus did not know what or who we were. He did not try to engage us in battle, nor did he attempt to run away from us. He sheathed his sword and his dagger, then standing there bravely with his hands upturned and his head bowed, not looking us directly in the eyes. He only honored us greatly by using the same honored greeting used with the Aldas. Your young-ling and very scrawny grandson has proven himself worthy of his position as our Prince of Malon. He is a fine representative of Clan Arkwright, his father the Prince, and to you his grandfather, our High King Thureos. He was ready to fight on to the very end. After the battle he showed deep kindness and remorse for his fallen Ice Bear. He honored the dead Ice Bear with his prayer and with his Life-energy push. I witnessed this with my own eyes and life energy senses. We brought his Ice Bear here; if you give permission, we will perform the passing ceremony for the Mighty Ice Bear," said the Elder one.

Thureos bowed his head to the Elder one and said, "Your words honor us greatly, Elder one. We would be pleased to participate with you in the passing ceremony for the Mighty Ice Bear. You mentioned that there was a second Alpha Ice Wolf that killed this Ice Bear, which you dispatched. That means that this Ice Wolf's pack had two Alfa Ice Wolves. Did your snow folk bring the Ice Wolves that were killed here too?

"No, we left the three of them dead on the battle field a little bit northwest of our mammoth enclosure, said the Elder one.

Hearing that, the High King motioned to his two scouts and said, "Go to the northwest of the mammoth enclosure and drag those other three Ice Wolves to the stone altars of the God's Tree Seedling Circle outside of the Yelin village. Prince Arthus killed the slightly smaller one and this Yelin Elder one killed the second Alpha and the other larger Ice Wolf. The rest of the Great Northern Guard will continue on with us to that God's Tree Seedling Circle, where we will lay all of these dead Ice Wolves including this oldest Alpha which I dispatched with my Angle Wing weapon. We will offer these Ice Wolves on the altars as part of a Great Gifting Ceremony after we join the Yelin for the passing ceremony for the Mighty Ice Bear this evening."

Soon the traveling group of Clan Arkwright, Clan Urial and the Yelin arrived at the Yelin village. To get into their village, the group rode down through a path leading down a steep canyon. The path led between two extremely high cliffs and emptied into a large box canyon area where here and there some large cave entrances were hiding. The extremely high ridges of the cliffs surrounding the box canyon sufficiently blocked the cold winds. Most of the wind really couldn't reach all the way down in the box canyon. It wasn't nearly as cold as it was outside of this box canyon area up on the main tundra. Several very large circular yurt houses made from huge wood poles and treated mammoth skin furs were located in the box canyon. The yurt houses seemed quite massive to Arthus, but to the Yelin, they were just right. A sizeable longhouse was in the center of the box canyon floor. Going inside of one end of this longhouse, Arthus notices that there is a large round ring, similar to a fire ring, but was much bigger. It had been beautifully crafted from shiny metal. Its grating appeared incredibly ornamental as it was made from handcrafted metals. It had a large variety of leaves, grape clusters, pomegranates, chestnuts, various flowers, intertwining vining and branches. It also had a variety of birds and smaller animals. All of its ornamentation had been handcrafted from metal and blended perfectly into the grating of the large shiny metal ring. Inside of the ring, Arthus could see was filled with blue and red glow stones. It was giving off heat like crazy, so much so that the whole longhouse was very warm inside. In the very center of the far end of the longhouse sits a Yelin sized wooden throne. Again, the wood on this throne had been beautifully carved with ram horn style circles at the ends of the arm rests, On one outside side of the throne was carved a ram, on the other outside side was carved a mammoth. Mammoth tusk ivory was also used in the beautiful inlaid ornamentation surrounding the carvings. The various color ivory inlays surrounding the carving of First God's Tree were made to look like Cundos, Ignoles, Dwarvens and Yelin. The back facing the room had been beautifully carved to represent First God's Tree inside of a circle of inlaid ivory from the tusks of the mammoth and from ram's horns. The carvings were also inlaid with ivory made from ram's horns and tusks of the mammoth. Behind the throne was a beautifully embroidered tapestry. The various threads used within the embroidery work were gold, silver, blue, red, pink, purple, white, yellow and brown. The background of the tapestry is a tightly weaved black wool rug made from the wool of the longhaired black goats that the Yelin raise. The tapestry is representing the entire history of the Yelin, from God's creation of Malon up through the lineages of the Yelin. Also included, was a section showing the High King meeting for the first time with the Yelin and shows a scene with the High King is being given one of Michael the Archangel's molted Angel Wings by the Archangel, and another section shows Arthus father, the Prince, first meeting with the Yelin. That seen shows Arthus' father when he was a little older than Arthus, here in front of this same throne.

The Elder one went right up to the throne and sat down on it, and motioned for High King Thureos and Arthus to come and join him. Two Yelin came in from a side entrance carrying Cundo and Ignole sized thrones that were also beautifully ornate with hand carvings and inlaid ivory. They sat them down beside the Elder one's throne on the left side, side-by-side. High King Thureos and Prince Arthus sat down beside the Elder one.

The other Great Northern Guards from Clan Urial with their Ice Bears dragged the dead Ice Wolves and the dead Alpha Ice Wolf over to their God's Tree Seedling Circle as they had been instructed. One of the Yelen *Snow Folk* went with them to help lift and lay the dead Ice Wolves on the altars as these natural stone altars were much larger and taller than the ones that are in any of the Cundo and Ignole and Dwarven cities and villages. Soon the two scouts came dragging the other two Ice Wolves and the other Alpha Ice Wolf, also to the God's Tree Seedling Circle. The Yelin again helped to lift those also up onto these Yelin *Snow Folk* sized natural stone altars. But, before they laid the Alphas upon the altars, the Yelin had removed the chain mail armor from the two Alphas as these had been removed from dead Clan Urial Great Northern Guards after Ice Wolves had killed and ravaged their bodies.

The Yelin handed the two scouts these two chain mail armors and said, "Your fellow honored fallen in the Great Northern Tundra deserve to be honored by bringing to their families this armor that they bravely wore into battle when they died. These evil Demon-Bonded Alphas never should have dishonored them! Their evil is broken now as their life blood has been given back to Malon. We trust that the Great Creator and Sustainer of all things will prevent the spread of their evil as their bodies are given in the Great Gifting Ceremony to be held later this evening."

Then the two scouts and the other members of the Great Northern Guard all followed the Yelin down through the canyon into their box canyon village. Then they dismounted again, led their ice bear mounts into one of the box canyon's hidden cave entrances where there was another gated stable for the Ice Bear Mounts. They began to inspect their Ice Bear Mounts for any possible wounds. Not seeing any, they began brushing their mounts white fur. The Yelin that went along with them on his mammoth mount, took his mammoth into a much larger cave entrance, where there was an underground stable for their mammoths. The other mammoths were already inside the stable there and they began trumpeting a welcome to their fellow mammoth and greeting each other with their trunks.

Behind the Ice Bear stables was a Clan Urial Great Northern Guard Barracks and attached to that was an infirmary. The wounded guards were treated in the infirmary. Behind the infirmary there is a morgue. Their dead guard comrade is laying naked on a metal table in that morgue, where he is being treated with a washing from water taken from the River of Life near the First God's Tree in God's Forest. This special River of Life water washing is done as last rights from a specially anointed priest before dressing him again into a special set of burial armor. A beautiful laser cut stone and metal casket lay nearby; ready for his internment.

"Thank you for coming to my home, High King Thureos. Soon my Snow Folk shaman will prepare the Mighty Ice Bear for the passing. Until then let us talk about recent events and warm your grandson here," smiling the Elder said.

"Thank you as always, Elder, and thank you for what you had done for my grandson after I realized his Ice Bear mount had taken off with him still tied in his saddle. I had not noticed this happening while we were in the throng of battle. I was distraught even more so when I discovered three Ice Wolf track sets in the snow following after Arthus' ice bear mount. Thinking about what might have happened never does the heart good! I do thank God, the Great Creator and Sustainer of all things, that Ice Bear carried Arthus directly towards your location. I feel certain now that actually was all in God's divine plan," declared High King Thureos.

"Arthus, you should know that Zeck killed four Ice Wolves, two with his own Tomahawks and two with the ones you had tossed back to him before you were dragged off by your Ice Bear. He related that you had witnessed his perfect aim with his first throw of his Tomahawk. I do believe those weapons are mighty important to practice with as they seem to be capable of instantly bringing down the Ice Wolves from a good distance before they can reach you. Anyway, he was fighting another really big one with his long spear axe contraption when a Dwarven crossbow bolt ended that Ice Wolf's fight. Other than a few deep scratches, he seems to be doing alright. He is in the infirmary behind the Clan Urial Great Northern Guard Barracks. The field medic there will have him all stitched and plastered up with a bandage by now," related High King Thureos.

"So it seems you've shown the Yelin your best side! That is great! I was hoping they would take a liking to you. Even though the Yelin *Snow Folk* were there when Michael the Archangel gave me this Angel Wing, it still took me several years to gain their favor. Then in turn it took your father the Prince, back when he was a little older than you, several years also to gain their favor. You however, have seemed to gain their favor from seeing you in this first battle. You are turning into a fine prince! I am not worried at all, seeing how you will continue to grow even more in favor with God the Great Creator and Sustainer of all things, and with all you meet here on Malon. We will participate in the Yelin *Snow Folk* ice bear's passing ceremony and then in the Great Giving Ceremony tonight at the God's Tree Seedling Circle located just up by the entrance to this canyon. Then we will spend the night in the Urial Great Northern Guard Barracks. I am sure by then this blizzard will die down. Be patient and quiet now, while I talk about other business issues with the Elder one. Once I return to the Palace, I will make sure Prince Benroy hears of your bravery, accomplishments and growth," said High King Thureos.

Several Yelin *Snow Folk* carried their gifts of their ram skins, ram horns, whole dead rams, goat skins, whole dead goats, woven woolen tapestries, woolen clothing, blankets, and of the furs and tusks of fallen mammoths up and laid them out on the natural stone altars surround God's Tree Seedling in their God's Tree Seedling Circle located up and out from the canyon in the tundra, but fairly near to the canyon entrance. Then they headed back down and into their village.

A few hours of business talk and the Elder one spotted his shaman enter and stand at the far end of the longhouse. Seeing that, the Elder rose up off his throne and motioned for the High King and Prince Arthus to follow him. They exited the longhouse following the shaman.

Elder one said to Arthus, "We are heading to our Shaman's Oracle Chamber."

Going across the entire box canyon to the very far end and entered what appeared to be a natural cave opening in the rock face of the cliffs. Lined up in lines in front of this cave opening there were various strange looking mobiles made from various things. Some of the mobiles were made from small and medium sized bones. The tops of the mobiles with the bones had black crows and black ravens that had been turned into taxidermies so that they appeared to continue to fly, even though they were dead and stuffed and had twine running through them. There were also several strange looking ornately painted totem poles which were lined up in between the various mobiles. The tops of the totem poles each had a small ring hole in them and the twine was tied between all of the poles from which all the various mobiles hung. Some of the mobiles looked like various shaped wooden ring like frames, each with patterns of strings crisscrossing over them like a spider web of sorts. Those also had large feathers and beads tied to them. Embedded into the various eyes of the totem poles were various colored Life-crystals. The huge natural cave opening was a little bit bigger than the tallest of the Yelin *Snow Folk*. Going inside of the natural cave, it opened into a much larger and perfectly circular cavern. Arthus believed this cavern had to have been carved out in this perfect circle because caves and caverns don't usually form in perfect circles. All over the walls of the inside of the cavern and all over the ceiling there were strangely painted animals of every variety. But it appeared that the paint that was used for painting the animals was actual blood mixed with the juices of wild berries from various plants. Arthus noticed there was a very strange looking natural stacked boulder rock circular altar which had the Dead Mighty Ice Bear laying on top of it. Hanging here and there around the circular cavern ceiling were very heavy twines. And, there were various sized antler horns hanging from those twines. Also hanging onto many of the twines were bones of various sizes. Here and there also hanging from the heavy twines there were many varieties of medicine bags, which contain various objects and spices and such. Embedded here and there into the walls and ceiling surrounding the room were glow stones which were all dimly lit. At the very bottom and round the outside edge of the natural boulder stone circular altar there was a huge natural stone table, which the very edge had been carved out to form a kind of donut shaped pool that went all the way around the natural boulder altar sitting above it. Arthus could see that the Mighty Ice Bear had been completely drained of his life's blood and that pool appeared to have been filled with water and with the blood of the Mighty Ice Bear. All around this pool were several fur pelts which had been sewed together and were covering the rest of the entire floor of the natural cavern. Straight up from this boulder altar above the Ice Bear in the ceiling of the natural cavern there was a single drilled hole that went up through the ceiling and completely up and out of the ground on the Tundra above where this cave in the box canyon was located. There was a hint of natural light which Arthus could see shining down through that onto the Mighty Ice Bear.

Elder one said, "All of our non-*Snow Folk* in the room, you will need to cover their ears as my Snow Folk Shaman, will be calling all those who live in our village to come here now with a Life-Yell. The High King, Arthus, Zeck, all of the Urial Great Northern Guard in the room quickly covered their ears.

Then the Yelin *Snow Folk* Shaman stepped back outside and with his two hands and yelled from his mouth the same bellowing sound that Arthus had heard earlier.

Immediately the entire village of Yelin *Snow Folk* all joined in the bellowing. The sound of their yell filled the box canyon area quickly and shot clear up to the ozone layer surrounding Malon and bounced off of the ozone layer and echoed back down against the ground being filled with Life-energy, which caused the blizzard surrounding the box canyon on the tundra to be pushed back in every direction for around fifty kilometers, as the unique shape of the box canyon acted much like a musical box resonator, but much more profound. As the sound of the bellowing dissipated the blizzard did not even seem to have any more power to start up again.

The Yelin shaman came back into his Oracle Chamber followed by every member of the Yelin *Snow Folk*. They came in and sat down on the fur pets that surrounded the donut shaped pool of blood and water and the natural boulder altar where the Mighty Ice Bear had been laid. The Snow Folk filled up a good portion of the circular Oracle Chamber. High King Thureos, Prince Arthus, Zeck and the entire Urial Great Northern Guard squad were sitting cross legged on the fur pelts closest to the pool of water and the natural boulder stone altar. Arthus noticed that even the Clan Urial Priest had come in following the Yelin *Snow Folk*. He came around and sat cross legged beside the other squad members. Several healers followed the priest and also sat cross legged alongside of the priest and the guard squad.

The Yelin shaman said, "For those of you who have never experienced this ceremony, let me tell you that we will provide you a set of welding blinders and a set of cushioned earplugs that fit into the ear canals of your ear, but all you non-Snow Folks must also put their fingers in their ears over those earplugs and push tight, when I tell you to do that, and do put your blinders on when I tell you to do that. Otherwise, you will never hear or see again in your life, and none of us want to be responsible for causing that level of discomfort."

With that said, some young Snow Folk came up passing out the welding blinders and the ear plugs. These young Snow Folk were dressed with bone and teeth necklaces around their necks and bone and teeth bracelets around their wrists and bone and teeth bracelets around their ankles, exactly like the Snow Folk Shaman was wearing. However, they did not have the strange headdress made from a stuffed black raven and what looked something like a strangely shaped birds nest made out of sticks and clay like mud and many different kinds of bird feathers and such that the Snow Folk Shaman had on his head.

Soon, all non-Snow Folk in the Shaman's Oracle Chamber had a set of welding blinders and a set of cushioned ear plugs.

Then the Snow Folk shaman shouted, "Great Sky Father!"

Then the Shaman and the young Snow Folk dressed similar to him began to dance and make various noises with their mouths and hands all around the donut shaped pool and huge natural stacked boulder altar that the Mighty Ice Bear was laid dead on. After several minutes of doing this dancing going around the center area and making the various noises, they stopped.

Then Elder one shouted, "Great Sky Father!"

Once again the Shaman and the young Snow Folk dressed similar to him began to dance and make the same kind of various noises with their mouths and hands all around the same area again. They danced all around, but this time they were going in the opposite direction as the first time they had done this.

Then Elder one stood up and said a few words in an ancient language of the Golden City. Then the Snow Folk Shaman began to dip the tip of a huge feather into the pool of blood and water. He took that huge feather and wrote Ruin letters on the various huge natural boulders of the altar under the Mighty Ice Bear. After he finished doing this the Ruin letters all glowed. Then Elder one sat back down.

Then the Snow Folk Shaman says, "Great Sky Father take honor in the sacrifice of this Mighty Ice Bear, who gave his life in battle against Your enemy, that evil Demon led and infused Alpha Ice Wolf and his subordinate minions. We know that these Northern Tundra Ice Wolves who have been Demon-bonded have been cursed by You our Great Sky Father for having willingly bonded themselves with one or more of the fallen Demon Angels who are also forever cursed. As their blood was spilt out upon the Great Northern Tundra of Malon in the battlefield, may You oh God the Great Creator prevent their Demon-bonded spirit from traveling the Great Northern Tundra. Instead, chain them down in the Pits of Your Lake of Fire and Brimstone, where they cannot ever bond again to any other of Your creation."

Then the Snow Folk Shaman said, "Prince Arthus, give honor to this Mighty Ice Bear."

The Yelin Shaman, handed Arthus a rather large stone bowl filled with water and said, "This is the water from the River of Life that flows by the First God's Tree in God's Forest. Prince Arthus, pour out this water upon the head of the Mighty Ice Bear.

Prince Arthus obeyed.

He noticed that the Mighty Ice Bear had already been thoroughly washed Snow Folk Shaman in the waters of donut shaped pool area that surrounded the base of this huge boulder altar that the Mighty Ice Bear had been laid upon.

"Now Prince Arthus, do you witness, that our Great Sky Father had in His divine plan to have this Mighty Ice Bear carry you away from the battle, to then become hurt by one of the minions of the Alpha Ice Wolf and only then when doing battle with the Alpha Ice Wolf lost his life bravely...Prince Arthus, you lay your hand on the head of this mighty ice bear and say, *I Do Witness!*"

Prince Arthus, repeated, "I Do Witness!" Then Arthus added, "I honor you Mighty Ice Bear, in the fact that you had the great responsibility for protecting me, and when you run with me on your back away from the field of battle and directly towards these here highly honored Snow Folk, which the many clan peoples on Malon call *Yelin*. You instinctually obeyed the divine plan of our Great Sky Father, who is the Creator and Sustainer of all things I also honor you in the name of my grandfather, the High King of Malon, Thureos, in the name of my father, Prince Benroy, and in my own name, Prince Arthus Arkwright of Clan Arkwright. You fought bravely and sacrificed yourself while facing off with that Alpha Ice Wolf. I honor your obedience in all of your hard working life of being a mount for the Great Northern Tundra people, and I fully honor your death."

Once again, Arthus closed his eyes laid his hand down on the head of the Mighty Ice Bear and pushing out with his Life-energy into and through the bear, through the huge boulder stones, through the blood and water mix in the donut shaped pool surrounding the base of the altar and out through the Oracle Chamber floors and walls and ceiling, into and through the legs and bodies of all those seated cross legged on the fur pelts on the floors until he could sense all of the Life-energy flooding through them and back from them into himself.

Feeling the Life-energy flowing from Arthus, the Yelin *Snow Folk* Shaman smiled at Prince Arthus and said, "Thou art highly honored by our Great Sky Father." Then he motioned to Arthus to follow him back away from the huge natural boulder altar and to sit back down cross legged on the fur pelt by the High King. The Snow Folk Shaman and the young Snow Folk, who were all dressed somewhat similar to the Snow Folk Shaman all took their places cross legged on the fur pelts.

Then the Snow Folk Shaman said, "All our non-Snow Folks, now put on your welding blinders and put those earplugs in your ears and then hold your fingers over the flaps of your ears real tight.

All of the non Yelin *Snow Folk* peoples groups in the room put on their welding blinders and pushed the cushioned earplugs into their ear canals then with their fingers pushed against those natural ear flaps with their fingers to thoroughly muffle sound.

The Yelin *Snow Folk* Shaman then placed his hands up by his mouth and yelled out a bellowing call like nothing Arthus had heard before. The High King had only once experienced it. The entire congregation of Yelin *Snow Folk* joined in and their bellowing call melded together, echoing louder and louder and louder and continuing on and on and on and on, bouncing off of all the Shaman's Oracle Chamber walls, ceiling and floor. The bellowing call pushed its way out through the entry of the cave into the boxed canyon and from there into the sky towards the ozone layer surrounding Malon. The bellowing call also pushed its way up past the Might Ice Bear and up through the drilled hole that went from ceiling above the natural boulder up through the rock of the cliff and shot towards the sky. The bellowing sound shot skyward up through that to the ozone layer of Malon. As the Yelin continued their bellowing sound traveling and building higher and higher in pitch. Up at the ozone layer surrounding Malon the ongoing bellowing sound filled with Life-energy, so much so that the sound gathered together like a whirlwind up near the ozone. Suddenly a very bright and fairly wide single beam of light like a giant laser beam came from the whirlwind filled Life-energy of the bellowing sound which shot straight back down from the ozone layer through that large and deep drilled hole above the natural boulder altar. That giant laser beam of light completely incinerated the Mighty Ice Bear and even dried up all the water and blood in the donut shaped pool surrounding the altar. Once the Yelin saw the beam of light they stopped bellowing. The sound slowly stopped reverberating off of the walls of the chapel. The beam of light dissipated into a rather hot steam which all of the congregation could feel.

After that incredible experience, the non Yelin *Snow Folk* took off their welding blinders and pulled out their earplugs, happy to have been given them to protect their eyes and ears. The young Snow Folks dressed similar to their Shaman quickly gathered up the welding blinders and ear plugs. Then the entire congregation and the Yelin *Snow Folk* Shaman left the Shaman's Oracle Chamber and walked through the entire length and width of the boxed canyon, gathering to themselves their weapons. Everyone then headed up and out of their canyon to where God's Tree Seedling Circle is located. By that time it was almost night.

It did not take long after arriving at God's Tree Seedling Circle when eleven Aldas showed up.

The Elder one, the Yelin Shaman, the Priest, the High King and Prince Arthus all stood forward and greeted the tallest and oldest of these Alda, with their heads bowed slightly and their arms held forward a little bit from their bodies and their hands turned upwards. The High

King then goes up to the Alda elder and says something quietly to the eldest of the Alda. Then he turns and motions for all the crowd to bow. Everyone bows deeply including High King Thureos in the direction of First God's Tree.

King Thureos says, "We thank you God our Great Creator and Sustainer of all things in Your creation for your bountiful gifts to all of us on Malon. We pray your grace and mercy will keep us all together at peace with each other. We pray we keep helping each other as we have been doing these past many years. And, now we honor You and all that You give to us by giving back to You of Your blessings to us. We also give these dead Alpha Ice Wolves and their mind-controlled minions and ask that you would please make a way to prevent the fallen from having any farther Darkness influences on Malon."

The High King once again turns towards the eldest and tallest of the Alda. And holds his hands out in an upward direction, while everyone else remained bowed deeply towards First God's Tree. The ten younger Aldas quickly go gather all of the Great Gifting tithe and all of the dead Ice Wolves including the two dead Alpha Ice Wolves, and then gathered once again behind the eldest and tallest of the Aldas.

The eldest and tallest of the Aldas then appeared that it slightly bowed its upper trunk where its eyes, ears and mouth were located, and then reached up and forward with its two largest branch arms, twists its branches so that all of the leaves of the tiny branches attached to the two largest branch arms are turned upside down and towards the sky. These leaves immediately turn golden brown and fall off of this Alda elder onto the ground. He then lowers his arms, raises back up straight, turns around on its roots and then leads all the other ten Aldas back to the south in the direction of God's Forest. It did not take long for them to disappear as the night sky was getting late.

Everyone headed quickly back to the canyon entrance of their village and quickly headed down into the canyon and back out into the box canyon where the village was located.

The High King says to Arthus and Zeck, "You two head to the guard barracks and get to bed. I still have business to discuss with Elder one."

Then he turns and walks back into the longhouse where he goes and sits down again.

The Elder one goes to Elder two and says, "Gather the Snow Folk Council." He then heads back into the longhouse.

Soon the longhouse was filled with the Snow Folk Council, where they met and discussed many things late into the night.

That night Arthus didn't get much sleep. The Alpha Ice Wolf was appearing before him again and again in his restless dreams. Zeck was snoring inside his all-in-one bedroll tent not far from where Arthus and High King Thureos had laid their tents in the barracks.

One of the Urial Great Northern Tundra Guards woke Zeck from his snoring. "Grab your bedroll tent and pillow roll and follow me," commanded the guard. Zeck obeyed. The guard led him around the back of the barracks, past the infirmary and past the morgue, and a bit further back into the dark cave. "This is where we put any of them that do any snoring in their sleep, said the guard while pointing with his glow-stick to flat rock area on the cave floor.

Arthus awoke again when he heard his grandfather High King Thureos come into the barracks and then entered the main office of the Urial leader of the Yelin outpost of the Clan Urial Great Northern Guard and began to talk to him about many important things. Arthus was still completely exhausted from the long day. He thought to himself, "Grandfather is always so busy with so many responsibilities. I worry that he never truly rests or relaxes. I know that tomorrow we will all head back to Northern Peak City, and then grandfather will quickly leave again, without me getting a chance to really speak heart-to-heart with him, or even get any chance to spend time with him." While hearing the muffled sound of his grandfather's voice, finally, he drifted off to sleep with no more thoughts of the Alpha Ice Wolf plaguing his dreams.

Chapter 10

Working in the Mines and in the Halls of Flames

In the morning Arthus and the High King and Zeck were in the longhouse of the Yelin Snow Folk Village. While waiting on the Yelin *Snow Folk* Council to gather again, Arthus recalled how the night before, the Yelin *Snow Folk* did that beautiful and powerful ceremony for the Mighty Ice Bear, where their Life-energy yell, that was given to them by God, the Great Creator, was used to completely incinerate the bear and the water surrounding the bear. Then Aldas coming and receiving the Great Gifting.

Elder one was seated on his throne. He motioned to Elder two. And Elder two opened some large metal clad wooden chests that were laying there in the longhouse. Elder one gifted Arthus with three Ice Bear pelts.

The Elder one had said, "One was for you Prince Arthus, to remind you forever of the Mighty Ice Bear that honorably gave his life. And, one is to be given by you to your hosts, Drake and Chrystal. One is to be sent by you back to the Arial Village to Jade's parents, to thank them for also having hosted you."

Elder one then turned to Zeck and said, an Ice Bear pelt is also gifted to you Zeck, but Zeck I also have a special gift for you as I understand you dispatched four of them Ice Wolf underlings. Some of our Snow Folk have found a den of Ice Wolves a little while back and successfully dispatched all of parents and other Ice Wolves. They captured all of the newborn pups before they could even suck from their mother's teats. Our Snow Folk Shaman has been raising them on the waters of the River of Life since they were captured. They are all exactly eight weeks old. The Clan Urial Great Northern Guard has prepared a kennel specifically for these Ice Wolf pups, and their Clan Priest assures me that he can continually provide them with the water from the River of Life for the rest of their natural lives, which is usually only 15-19 years. The gifting that I am offering you comes with a deep responsibility, which I am absolutely certain you are ready to provide. You are to care for these pups, help raise and help train them, every single day for the next 15-19 years, and that is in addition to the duties you already committed to provide to our High King for improving the Silver Thorn Daggers and improving on the tomahawk that you already created for the Silver Thorn Patrols and Guards. And, besides any duties required of you in the mines and with Maddlynn in her forge workshop. I am aware you have many more years before you will attend the academy. Every morning you are to work closely with the Urial Great Northern Guard in order to acclimate the Ice Bears to these Ice Wolf pups as they grow older. I am sure this will improve the Ice Bear mount's behaviors when they encounter wild Ice Wolves out on the Tundra. The Ice Wolves you help raise might even become a great help to fight alongside of the Clan Urial Guard, with the Ice Bears against any Demon-Bonded Ice Wolves. My hope and prayer is they may even break the cycle that the Demon underworld has over the Ice Wolves, and can end our need to destroy entire wild packs. If we can do that, the Ice Wolves will go back under the full authority of God our Great Creator and Sustainer of all things in His creation."

The elder one then turned again to Arthus and said, "Arthus I am gifting you with a fallen mammoth skin, which has been beautifully lined with incredibly soft cashmere wool from the goats and rams that we raise. The elder one said, "This is to help keep your scrawny body warm as you use it for a blanket up in the attic bedroom at Drake's and Chrystal's home." The elder one said, "Arthus I am gifting you with six ram's skins and six goat's skins with their wool still attached. One ram's skin and one goat's skin is for you. Two ram's skins and two goat's skins are for your hosts, Drake and Chrystal. One ram's skin and one goat's skin are for you to send to your friend Jade. Two ram's skins and two goat's skins are for you to send to Grag and Shelly. Besides those Arthus, here are two matching beautifully hand carved fallen mammoth tusks, and said, "One is for you for you to keep forever in your bedroom on a shelf high above the head of your bed. Whenever you move from place to place bring this along, always place it up high upon a shelf above the head of your bed. Once you return to the palace, again place it high on a shelf above the head of your royal bed. Hidden in its carving is a Life-energy infused prayer that will bless your sleep and your dreams. There is a second Life-energy infused prayer specifically for someday, as you pass your seed into your wife, your own child or children will be conceived in full honor of God the Great Creator. The second matching mammoth tusk is for you to send to your friend Jade. That one too has a special hidden life-energy prayer that will bless her sleep and her dreams. Again there is a second special hidden life-energy prayer that God the Great Creator will honor on her behalf and on behalf of her child/children someday. Tell her in your letter, you send along with it, that I said she must set it up high on a shelf above the head of her bed, and when she marries someday she is to place it again high up on a shelf above the head of her marriage bed."

The Elder one, then said, "Arthus I am also gifting to you and to your friend Jade matching ram's horns that had been hollowed out and turned into shofars, which when blown through make the sound of our life bellowing yell, but on a level much-much quieter then the snow folk yell. The elder one showed Arthus how to blow through one to make the sound. The elder said, "One is for you and one is for your friend Jade. In your letter to Jade, also share with her all of what you heard and seen and experienced when you heard the sound of our Great Creator gifted Life Yell. Explain to her that the sound these ram's horns makes brings honor to the Name of God the Great Creator. As it is God the Great Creator and Sustainer of all things, that breathed into all living things, the breath of life, and they became a living soul. The very sound of loud breathing which comes out of these shofars when blown truly is correctly sounding out the unpronounceable Name of God the Great Creator."

Next Elder one then gifted Arthus with two goat's horns, which had been hollowed out. To the thinnest ends are locking push in caps, which when removed are then able to be filled up and then emptied again from those thin ends. To each locking mechanism there was a small strap which was attached to a metal ring that surrounded the horns on their thinnest ends. To the widest end there was attached tightened ram skin leather coverings, which were permanently attached using metal rings that surrounded the wider ends of the goat's horns. Long leather shoulder straps with swivel snap rings and clasps were also attached to the two metal rings at both ends. The thinner ring also had a belt clip permanently welded to it, so that it could also be worn on a utility belt without the over the shoulder strap if needed.

When he gave these two matching horns to Arthus he said, "These are very special spirit horns, with special Ruin carvings in ancient words from the Golden City in honor of our Great Sky Father, the Creator of all things. You must only fill these with water from the River of Life. Never taint these with any other waters or drinks. One is for you to carry everywhere you go. Never leave it empty. Again, keep it always filled with water from the River of Life. A drink from these will help heal from near death wounds. One is for you to give to your friend Jade. Explain to her exactly what her special spirit horn is for. Warn her also never taint her horn with any other waters or drinks. Let me warn you, if for any reason one of these horns ever gets filled with any other waters or drinks, other than from the River of Life, a drink from this after that brings instant death. I have witnessed this with my own eyes. Someone did not obey and filled one with another water or drink and then took a drink. They instantly died, dried up into a mummy, then into a skeleton, and then disintegrated into dust and were carried away by the winds, all within seconds before my eyes. They are just that dangerous to use in any other way. My Snow Folk shaman is here with a large bowl filled with water from the River of Life. Take these now and fill them both with this water. Then push their caps on them and carry both of them on your body. Once you get back to your hosts house you can prepare to send one to your friend Jade with your letter written exactly as I instructed."

Zeck was standing next to Arthus attentively listening to ever word said by the Elder one. The elder one turned to Zeck and said, "I am gifting you too Zeck with two ram's horns, made into shofars and two special spirit horns of the goat like I gave to Arthus. One of each is for you and one of each is for your future wife. I am fully aware you have not met her yet, but when you go to the Malon Academy, after your One Hundred Years Day Celebration, I am certain you will meet the woman you are to marry there. Arthus will carry your two ram's horns and your two goat's horns along with the other items I am gifting to you with him in my own hathi howdah back to Northern Peaks City as I know you will be riding your Ice Bear mount. Also, Zeck, if you faithfully raise and train the pups with the deep responsibility that I have gifted to you, the next time we have a fallen mammoth with tusks, I will have those tusks made similar to the ones I gifted to Arthus and to his friend Jade. They will be carved for you and for your future bride, whomever she may be as well.

Arthus and Zeck, I have one more gifting to send to Drake and Chrystal. In those two giant shiny steel crates is ram's meat and goat meat. In this third giant shiny steel crate filled with Ice Bear meat.

Turning to the High King the Elder one said, "my High King Thureos, to honor you for helping to dispatch that Alpha Ice Wolf and his minions who all have been such an evil scourge that has been so long terrorizing many travelers here in the Great Northern Tundra, I am dispatching several of my snow folk and several of my village mammoths to accompany you and your fellows all back to Northern Peaks City. You shall ride in my hathi howdah with Prince Arthus and Elder two. Elders three and four and the other snow folk will all help to guide and secure the cargo platform mounted mammoths that I am also sending along with you. The Urial Great Northern Guard has suffered a loss, which I am certain his family and friends and comrades back in Northern Peaks City will feel for a long time to come. His casket will ride up on one of my village's cargo mammoths also with some of the trade cargo that I am sending with you. Your two more severely wounded Urial Great Northern Guards will remain here in the infirmary for some time until their wounds have completely healed. The rest of your guards and scouts and Zeck can each ride their Ice Bears along with my village's mammoths. I will also send the Urial Great Northern Guard leader in Northern Peaks Village several Ice Bear cubs that have been weaned in the spring. They can raise and train these weaned cubs to become part of their patrols."

Elder one, motioned to the High King that he had a more personal issue to discuss. The two walked away for a private conversation. "My High King, I had a vision during the night in which I was told to tell you this: 'You are the High King of Malon, but our Great Sky Father has also entrusted you with a family. You are always so crazy busy with the affairs of Malon, that you are often neglecting the needs of yourself and of your family, especially true when it comes to your grandson Arthus, who desperately wants you to take some one-on-one time only with and for him. Arthus worries about the fact that you are always in a hurry to go to the next important meeting, that you are not truly resting and relaxing ever, that you never once truly focus your attention of him. He has many questions that he silently says to himself in his mind. Questions about various things that he observes around him on a daily basis. Questions that you already know the answers to, but are not allowing any time in your rush to slow down so that they can be answered. Arthus has an eager observant mind. He sees problems and visualizes incredibly accurate and often complex solutions, but his grandfather is not there to offer a listening ear. In fact throughout his life there has been no one there to listen to him long enough so see the incredible value his mind already is conceiving and all of that is a great gift from our Great Sky Father, Who is constantly downloading into Arthus concepts and solutions to various problems. Therefore, my High King, please postpone for just two days your plans to rush off to meet the next clan or the next village. Take Arthus and walk around just the two of you through Northern Peaks City. Sleep a full eight hours. Meditate for two and a half hours by reading the ancient canonical book which our Great Sky Father has passed down to all of us. Pray together, sing together, and teach Arthus how to play the ancient game called, *Go,* which you loved to play when you were one of the trainers in the Academy. Give Arthus two days, before you leave him again for the rest of this year. Don't just trust other people to help you raise your grandson.'"

Then the Elder one laid his hand on the High King's shoulder and allowed his own life-energy to force push out from himself into the High

King. Instantly the High King was drawn in his senses the moment that Elder one received the vision from the night before. He saw in his mind Gabriel the Archangel take the WORD vision from the hand of God and bring it to Elder one commanding him to share this WORD with the High King.

The High King pondered the WORD vision in his heart. He knew he had a meeting scheduled that would take his immediate attention. He decided in his heart that he would fulfill this WORD vision as soon as Arthus finished this year and had traveled with him again. He decided he wouldn't just leave Arthus for a third or fourth year somewhere else. He would bring him back to the Palace and become Arthus' personal trainer himself.

Arriving back at Zeck's house Arthus and Zeck carefully cleaned off their boots and stepped into the mud room of the house. Removing there boots and gloves and overcoats and laying down their backpacks, they then walked into the house. Drake and Chrystal were there working again on Ruins.

"Hello everyone, I am back, and I brought gifts, Chrystal and Drake," said Arthus as he motions them to come to the front door. Outside is the Northern Peaks Welcoming Guard holding a pallet filled with the gifts that were gifted to Arthus, Zeck, Chrystal, Drake and Jade.

Arthus pokes his head out the door, says to the guard, "put down the pallet and two of you start carefully handing the items on the pallet to Drake and Zeck and I to carry inside.

Chrystal interjects in her very kind voice, "I can help carry as well, I'm stronger than I look."

At hearing this, the guard put down the pallet and they lined up between the pallet and the front door to the house. They carefully passed along to each other each of the crates filled with meats to one to Zeck, and one to Drake. Arthus and Chrystal carried one together each holding an end the rest the way into the living room space. The four of them quickly returned to the front door as various packages of items were handed to them. They went back and forth fairly quickly, but carefully moving the stuff into their house. The last items were the carefully wrapped mammoth tusks. Arthus brought them in and carefully laid them on some large pillows alongside of the ram's horns that were given by the elder one.

"I have one more, but this one I send as a gift to Jane, a friend of mine in Arial valley," said Arthus.

"A great friend," rolling his eyes, Zeck says to Arthus, "If you are truly honest with your feelings you will know that Jade is way more than a great friend to you. More like a girlfriend."

"No, I am really not ready for a girlfriend, she's just a great friend of mine that I really care a lot about. But, if I was ready for a girlfriend, she would be a great girlfriend," replied Arthus.

"Well, if she is cute, and if your just friends, then I can make a move. But only if she's cute," teased Zeck.

Arthus just shook his head no, smiled and said, "Not gonna happen Zeck!"

Arthus thought to himself silently, "Jade and Zeck, ya... no, he knew her too well. She never fall for him.

Going through the list of items gifted in his mind, Arthus says, "First things last, last things first." Then says to Chrystal and Drake the three very large metal crates are filled, one with ram meat, one with goat meat, and one with Ice Bear meat. This was gifted to you all as my host family, by the Elder one of them called Yelin by most people's groups on the planet, while they call themselves "Snow Folk."

"There are two ram's skins, and two goat's skins, for Drake and Chrystal for hosting me in your house for this year. Each are still covered with the wooly hair. They too were gifted by the Elder one of snow folk."

"There are two ram's horn shofars that are Zeck's. And, there are two spirit horns, for only the waters of the River of Life, which are Zeck's. These were gifted by the Elder one of the Snow Folk and Zeck was there, heard the words of warning, the purpose for them and all. Zeck. Why don't you run those two shofars and two spirit goat horns of yours up to your room right now? You can explain to your parents all of the words related to those after we finish unpacking and sorting this out."

"There is an Ice Bear skin that is Zeck's, and one for you both here too."

"Drake, the Elder one gave me several items which I need to send to Jade, and her parents, Grag and Shelly. Some items are extremely fragile and very beautiful and have great significance. Besides these items he gave me many items too. Some of those items are extremely fragile and beautiful. One item in particular I am going to need both yours and Chrystal's permission to help me take care of. He said that I must place the beautiful ornamental fallen mammoth tusk on a shelf high above the head of my bed."

Immediately Drake and Chrystal looked at each other kind of sweet like, drew in a deep breath, and both said, "Ah..." at the same time. "The Elder one gifted Arthus with a peaceful dreams and marriage and fertility prayer mammoth tusk."

Drake then said, "Of course you have our permission to have it on a shelf high above your bed. I will install a shelf there first thing tomorrow for you."

Chrystal elbowed her husband, Drake lovingly. "I know at least one matching item the Elder one gave Arthus to send to Jade..."

Arthus noticed how the two of them were giggling while continuing to work together putting away the meat from the three very large metal crates, and said to them, "The Elder one of the Snow Folk gifted me a matching peaceful dreams and marriage and fertility prayer mammoth tusk for Jade. He also gifted me, as well, a matching ram's horn shofar and a matching horn made from goat horn also for Jade. He also gifted me wooly ram's skins one for Jade, one for Grag, and one for Shelly. He also gifted me wooly goat's skins, one for Jade, one for Grag, and one for Shelly."

After saying that, Arthus began to carry his and Jades more precious items up to his room, where he carefully laid them on his bed. Zeck came down and carried the last of his own items up to his room. Arthus was in his room carefully laying the two mammoth tusks on his bed. He then came back down and carried his two matching shofars up to his room, laid those carefully on his bed. He then came back down and carried the two horns made from the goat up to his room. He then came back down and carried the 4 wooly rams skins up to his room and laid them by his foot locker. He then came back down and then carried the 4 wooly goat skins up to his room. He then came back down and carried his giant fallen wooly mammoth fur bedspread up to his room. He then came down and picked up his backpack from the mudroom and carried it up to his room. He then came down and carried his Ice Bear fur skin up to his room. And then fairly exhausted from climbing up and down the stairs over and over and over and over again, he sits down and begins to unwrap the packaged Ice Bear skin.

Hearing someone climbing his stairs to the attic he says, "Come on in."

Zeck says, "Thanks."

In Zeck's hands are the two tomahawks that he had tossed down on the ground by Zeck right before the Ice Bear he was riding took off going crazy like, being chased by the second Alpha and two underlings.

Zeck says, "I never had a chance to say thank you for tossing these tomahawks back down to me. I know that what you did in that moment saved my life. I will never forget that for as long as I live. That said though, I am not going to stop being tough on you, because I do have to make sure that you turn your scrawny muscles into muscles at least as big as mine by this time next year. But, if you ever need someone to talk to, or if you have questions in your mind that need answered about anything I might already know, or if you need a friend, I am here for you. And, don't worry, I won't try to steal Jade's heart out from under you no matter how beautiful she might be. I was just teasing about that. And, by the way, I did clean the blood back off of these and sharpened them again."

"Thanks Zeck. I really do appreciate having you here with me. I really do want to be your friend. I still don't have an alarm clock yet, do you know where I can get one?" Asks Arthus.

"I will wake you up tomorrow morning and after breakfast take you over to the Clock Smith Shop. I recommend you get two if you never had one before. Get one with a really loud ringing bell and then get one that chirps and whistles. Between the two, they should wake you up. If not, I will setup you up with a special contraption, where a synth-blend bounce hammer comes down after the second alarm and starts banging you in the head until you get up," laughs Zeck, who then said, "I've got a long – long day tomorrow, so I am going to take my shower and head to bed. Hope you have fun unpacking all these gifted items. Tomorrow, we have to figure out how to carefully pack the more fragile items to send to your sweetheart down in the Arial farming village." After saying that, Zeck leaves Arthus' attic room and heads down the steep step ladder.

Arthus went down and talked with Chrystal about turning the extra Ice Bear Pelt into a hood and shoulder cap for Jade. Then went back up to his room to write Jade a holo-mail.

The next morning he discovered that Chrystal had already finished making the smaller Ice Bear pelt into a hood and shoulder cap for Jade. She said it did not take her long as it was a smaller Ice Bear pelt. Arthus had everything already packed that Elder one wanted him to send along for Jade and Grag and Shelly.

"Time to begin. I must spend a few minutes each day before my regular duties at the Urial Great Northern Guard Kennel to ensure that those Ice Wolf pups have plenty of food and River of Life water to meet their needs. And then head down into the mines to work for today. You will get to do some serious mining today, so come on," said Zeck. Arthus jumped up, threw on his pull over shirt as he had noticed that was appropriate wear down in the mines. Then he put on his overcoat, boots, and gloves and picked up his pickax, and headed out the door following Zeck.

The leader of the Urial Great Northern Guard said, "Zeck the kennel is all ready, and the Ice Wolf pups are in a big rock hewn tunnel area that they can grow into over this next year. Each morning come here quick and then go into their kennel. You must do that for this Ice Wolf pack. My guard is not real keen on this whole idea by Elder one. If it works we may have a way to break the evil hold over the Ice Wolves, but if it doesn't it will be your responsibility to dispatch each and every one of these Ice Wolves with no mercy! Is that understood?"

"Yes, and your absolutely right. If your guardsman or I see any sign that these Ice Wolves will become evil Alphas or join with evil Alphas, I will dispatch them immediately! No mercy! I really do hope it works though because it would be great to have a pack of Ice Wolves working for us instead of against us," Said Zeck.

"That is true said the commander. No go in and get them fed and give them the River of Life water of the river of life that the priest has put in the keg barrels back there. I will assign one of my guard to each pup to raise personally once we are certain that this is a great idea."

Zeck went in and the pups all acted like normal puppy dogs, coming up to him, licking him and letting him pet and play with them. After a few minutes he had fed them and watered them. Then petting each behind the ears he left the tunnel area and out of the Kennel.

Arthus asked the Clan Urial Guard Captain for a special favor, "Would you mind if one of your Clan Urial Guard patrol would accompany my packages to the Clan Arial Valley and ensure that they make it safely to Grag, Shelly and Jade's family house. Elder one gifted these to me and some of the items are very beautiful and incredibly fragile and it would be a shame if anything were to happen to them, like getting broken or damaged. I know your patrol guards are always so busy, I hate to ask, but please." Arthus noticed the very surprised look on the Clan Urial Captain's face, then said, "Well thank you for making this happen for me. I do appreciate it." Then Arthus left the packages with the Clan Urial Captain quickly, and without giving him a chance to verbally respond. Arthus departed to join Zeck.

Soon Zeck and Arthus arrived in one of the deepest parts of the mines. Maddlynn was waiting for them to arrive.

"Ah, good, you are here. I wanted to show you what me Dwarvens and some of the hardier of ya'alls Cundos mine here, Arthus," said Maddlynn.

Zeck interrupted, and said"Maddlynn, I need to inform you of what Elder one and High King Thureos has each assigned for me to do, before we head down into the mines. That way you will be able to help me advocate with the Dwarven Foreman so that he understands why I will be coming there about 30 minutes later than I usually have done each morning. I don't want any misunderstandings! Ok?"

"Anyway, Maddlynn, Elder one has assigned me the responsibility to attempt to bond with and help raise a pack of Ice Wolf pups that were taken from their mom and dad before ever even sucking on their mom's teats. For the past eight weeks the Yelin Shaman has been giving the pups only River of Life water taken directly from the River of Life by the First Life Tree along with their goat meat and rice. They say it seems to be working and from what I saw today just a few moments ago before we came in here to meet with you, they might be right. Anyway I am the only one allowed to feed and water and play with them. The Urial Great Northern Guard Commander will only assign one guard per pup to train with if they are certain this is working. At any time the guards or I even get any since that the pups might be turning evil, or turning into Alphas, or being used by evil, it is solely my responsibility to dispatch them without mercy. The other responsibility that was assigned to me by High King Thureos is to continue to improve on my tomahawk design, which I will need to work with your engineers to do sometime soon. Then the High King also gave me the task of improving on the design of this here Silver Thorns Dagger. Remember how I tried putting the fishing tackle kit and cap into the handle of my throwing tomahawks only to discover how they just broke off too easy due to the pounding they receive when throwing. Well these Daggers are not throwing knives, so, we are going to figure out a way to work that idea into the handles of these. We also need to improve on the back section of the knife here to allow the Silver Thorns to use the back to remove fish scales. A kind of saw tooth section there should do the trick, and if we ensure the saw teeth are sharpened in one direction but not the other, that too can be used to saw small sticks or possibly cut through steel wires. I've now explained my idea about that to you and will leave this dagger here with you to talk that over with your engineering team about. Ok. Well that's it. We can head down to the mines now."

"Well, now haven't you suddenly grew up all responsible, to be given such from Elder one and the High King! So proud of you Zeck. Now, we are getting late dawdling here, best come on with me then," said Maddlynn. They went into another area of the tunnels that led down into the mountains. This area was rich with ore. The mine almost glowed. The soil and minerals were rich with Life energy. She pointed towards the ceiling; there was a massive root going from one side into the other wall.

"Those roots belong to First God's Tree, as well as one or more of the God's Tree Seedlings. They be a running all throughout Malon. They fill this world with Life energy even deep down here and in the depths of great oceans and even into the deepest lava rivers. These roots grow right through it. They make all life on Malon grow to the extreme," said Maddlynn. She then pulled a piece of ore out of a mine cart.

"This is what we call Life ore. We turn Life ore into many things from armor, weapons, tools to well everything. The only difference is how we melt it down, blend it together as there are many kinds of metal ore types. Some is super shiny and almost never rusts. Others make almost unbreakable swords and knives. But each ore type gets blended with Life ore when it is smelted and or forged into what we need. We also are cautious not to over mine this mineral. So we open new mines and close old ones so that the First God's Tree roots have time to rebuild and replenish the Life ore. There are many more and more minerals which grow over time, and then we reopen old mines and discover once again they be as rich as they were before they were ever mined before, then the cycle continues. As all life on Malon, we are one massive circle. We trade with each clan, and we help one another expand to grow and improve. With that lesson, I leave you to work," said Maddlynn. She waved, and a scruffy Dwarven walked in and frowned.

"Zeck, you bring in the village shorty to help you mine ha his arms fall off before an hour," said the Dwarven.

"Ya, I told him this wasn't his area; he be better spending his days hiding in a library," said Zeck smiling."

Arthus grinned real big as he knew they were just messing with him.

"We shall see how long I last, and I will make you eat your words," said Arthus.

"Alright, young Prince, that is the spirit. Now get to work. We got a lot to mine today, and if you follow through and keep working until the last whistle, I'll buy ya yer drinks," said the Dwarven with a laugh. Then he said, "You can call me Foreman. The mines are mine to run, so mind your business and no horseplay. This can be dangerous work, so if you have any questions, don't be afraid to ask your friend Zeck here. Zeck has been here many times and knows what he's doing. Zeck, you watch out for the newbie. Let's just see if you can give a hard days work then go in and drink our fill," said the Foreman. Hours went by, and a whistle blew.

"Alright, you bearded sons of trolls, time to go home or better to drink and party," laughed the Foreman.

A cheer roared from all the miners, and everyone headed back up out of the mine.

Arthus, could barely stand up straight. He slowly clipped the strap from his belt to his pickaxe. He then began to walk out very slowly, actually dragging his pickaxe by the strap behind him as he had no energy left to lift it. His shoulders throbbed, and his arms burned. His pull over shirt and undershorts were both completely soaked in sweat. He felt as if he was ready to drop to the ground and pass out.

The Dwarven Forman from earlier came up, glancing at Arthus, immediately burst out in laughter, and said, "Well, young Prince of Malon, I may have to shave my beard. You lasted all day! Not bad for a young man."

Zeck smiled and said, "He also looks like he was going to pass out any second." Then Zeck looked at Arthus and said, "Arthus... you really look so tired, while I have enough energy to go even longer."

The Dwarven Foreman looked at Zeck and laughed even harder. Then he said, "Well now, let's be honest young Zeck. You usually stop mining around noon. However, I see you perhaps found a good friend and a rival for which to help push each other to keep on working. As I watched you today, I swore I would buy you both some drinks if you made it to the last whistle. So now that you actually did make it to the last whistle, and if you actually do have energy left in your bodies, then let's go join everyone in the great tavern and drink, sing and dance the way only Dwarvens can.

Zeck smiled at Arthus and said, "Yes! Let's go get a drink. I do think we earned it today."

Arthus nodded only because he desperately wanted to sit down.

Being a bit ornery, Zeck says, "Ok Arthus, here we drink like we work. Don't make me think you are too wimpy for drinking."

Reluctantly accepting the challenge, Arthus swigs down a shot. It burned as it went down, but it wasn't too bad tasting.

Zeck then swigs down a shot. And then waved for another.

Arthus seeing Zeck waving, also waves for another. Again swigs down a shot. Not counting shots, but thinking it was only a few drinks later, Arthus in an obviously intoxicated voice, says to Zeck, "I don't feel sore anymore. Gosh, I don't... I don't even feel anything. These here drinks...these here drinks must knocked the pain right out of me." Then Arthus stood up and tapped Zeck and put his finger up to his lips and said, "Shh! Don't you be telling the High King about me coming in here with you. I know he don't want me drinking this kind of thing. Then Arthus starts stumble walking towards the door and went out into the cold night air.

Zeck, who thought he had drank a few more shots than Arthus had, pushes himself up from the table and says to the Dwarven Foreman, "Thanks for this hospitality! His majesty the most honorable Prince of Malon has already left the building." He then bowed jokingly and said, "I bid you all goodnight!" Zeck then stumble walks to the door and out into the cold of the night to discover Arthus is leaning against the outer wall of the building.

Arthus says, "I don't even feel cold right now."

"Come on Arthus. Time to go to home," says Zeck as he takes a hold of Arthus' upper arm and pulls him slowly along the street. As they approached Zeck's house Arthus' stomach wretches and he leans forward pukes out onto the ground in the middle of the road that they were walking on. Zeck slaps lightly on Arthus' upper back with his hand and says, "Best you did that here instead of inside my house."

Arthus says, "Sorry, I'm a bit warm and a bit light headed. Sorry. I can't even get my thoughts straight."

Stopping at the porch to scrape his boots, Zeck points down at Arthus boots, and says, best clean those off before you step in the house."

When they finally removed their boots, gloves and overcoats and put away in the mud room, and then entered the living room, Drake and Chrystal were not very amused.

"I see you two worked and played hard today. I have to talk with the Foreman about encouraging our young ones to drink hard drinks," said Chrystal.

Arthus just sat down on the floor smiling. "I feel great. My arms are killing me mam, but no, I feel great," said Arthus mumbling.

Chrystal shook her head and helped Zeck get up the stairs and into his room.

Drake helped Arthus start a steaming hot bath and added some unique salts into the water.

"These salts will help your body recover faster along with a good night's sleep," said Drake.

Drake left Arthus, who then, still not capable of thinking clearly at all, climbed into the bath still fully dressed. The healing waters washed over his body. He awoke to a massive headache, still in the tub, which had turned very cold. He noticed that there was a really weird taste was in his mouth.

"Eww, what is this taste? Oh my head? A knock on the door sent pain into his brain. Sorry I am getting out," said Arthus. Arthus removed his wet close even though his head was pounding. He brushed his teeth, tongue and cheeks and dried off with a towel. Then put his dry pajamas on. He placed his soaking wet clothes in the dirty clothes hamper and then opened the door. "Sorry. I took too long."

Zeck was standing outside the bathroom, also looking like he was in pain.

They both just grunted at each other. Arthus walked to the closet and climbed the stairs to his attic bedroom. Seeing that it was already time to get up, Arthus took a clean set of clothing out of his foot locker and changed clothes again. Then he walked down the stairs and out into the living room. Drake and Chrystal were already hard at work on their Ruins that laid across the table. Drake smiled; knowing how Arthus felt, he slid him a strange, smelly green-colored drink.

"Drink that, Arthus. It will help get rid of your hangover headache," said Drake. Arthus groaned and downed the foul-tasting drink.

"Gosh that's nasty," said Arthus.

Zeck entered the living room, downed the smelly green-colored drink that Drake handed him. Then Zeck said to Arthus, "Nasty it is, but it really does kick a hangover headache!" Then he placed his empty glass on the table, gathered his lunch, and lifted his pickaxe.

"You ready, Arthus. We must get to the kennels and then down into the mines. We are late already and the Foreman won't like us being late."

Arthus nodded, and quickly grabbed his lunch and his pickaxe and headed for the front of the house.

Zeck and Arthus quickly readied themselves and left the house, moving as fast as their legs could handle it. Zeck spent 30 minutes with the pups, playing with them feeding and watering them with the water from the River of Life. When they walked into the mine, a group of the Dwarvens all clapped and cheered and the Foreman laughed.

"Welcome your royal highness to what we are all certain is your first day ever in your life working with a pounding hangover headache. Three cheers for Prince Arthus and Zeck!

Again, the Dwarvens cheered and clapped loudly, which Arthus and Zeck knew they did just to mess with them.

"Glad to see you both are still among the living. You both drank so much last night even we Dwarvens were worried you'd never wake again," said the Foreman.

"Wait, how much did we drink?" asked Arthus.

"Ha, enough to make an old Dwarven proud you two wouldn't allow the other to have the last drink, so you two just kept going until we had to cut you off. So be proud of the pain in your heads and get to work! I hope you are good and ready," smiled the Dwarven Foreman.

Several days later, Arthus got a message from Jade it read.

"Got the hood and shoulder cap and other items you sent to me and my family. The ornamental mammoth tusk is so beautiful on that high shelf above my bed. I have an idea for my shofar and your shofar, which I will share with you next time we see each other. I read the warning you sent about the spirit goat horns. I will talk with my father and mother about getting a keg barrel of the water from the River of Life for which to refill that with. Now, I heard you killed an Ice Wolf, so cool wish I could have been with you. It sounds scary and yet fun, and I think it would be a great place to learn to hunt. But, as you know we are always crazy busy here on the Farm. Also, Fang decided to join the family and stay with me at our house. He is really a bit too big for my small bedroom, but I know that is where he wants to be when I am home. He follows me everywhere.

I know that I can actually hear his thoughts. Well, I talk with you later, as fathers telling me that it is time to start my daily stuff. Stay safe city boy," wrote Jade.

Arthus smiled and closed his eyes. He mumbled, "It has been a long couple of days."

Days turned to weeks, and weeks turned to months of Zeck dealing with the pups each morning, and then Arthus mining every day all day long and Zeck mining for five straight days all day long and working with the Urial Guards training the Ice Wolves one day and in the Forge the other day. Arthus only agreeing one day a week to do any drinking with Zeck and their Dwarven friends. Arthus limited himself to two shots even then, because he did not like the feeling of being out of control of his senses. It took a good six months before Arthus was feeling less and less tired. Once he noticed that he seemed less tired then after each long day, and before he sent his daily holo-mail message off to Jade, he looked at himself in the mirror and could see his body was getting much stronger.

One day at breakfast, Zeck says to Arthus, "Maddlynn is scheduled to meet with you today to show you how to operate the forges. We are not going to be mining day in and out now. Now we must begin to focus on processing all of the ore we were mining and start smelting and forging with it into whatever we will be assigned to make. So head upstairs and get your leather bag that the High King prepared for your days in the forge."

In his room Arthus picked up his standard gear but this time opened his chest and took out a leather bag. This held an assortment of hammers, claw-looking things and other tools used by metalsmiths to forge items. He tied on a thick leather apron and strapped leather gloves to his hands. Then took out the goggles he wear to protect his eyes from the heat and metal. Zeck was already waiting outside for him, then they set out towards the Maddlynn's workshop and house. While Zeck did detour to complete his daily 30 minute routine in the Ice Wolf kennels.

"Good of you to come time to learn how to craft a bit of metalwork. Let me I show you how to work the heated minerals into whatever object or gear needed today," said Maddlynn when they arrived in the main cave chamber.

"Follow," said Maddlynn. As they came to the area where the forgers were, a massive explosion rocked the entire cavern.

"What was that?" asked Arthus. Maddlynn frowned.

"Oh, I am sure I know," said Maddlynn. She ran off towards a big open room built into the far wall where the smoke and fire as being put out. A Dwarven came out covered in soot and oil, wearing brown pants, soot covered white tunic, leather apron, and some strange looking goggles. He coughed a bit and took off his goggles to wipe them clean.

"Blast it, Emon. How many times did I tell you to ask for permission before you do any more of your experiments?" Said Maddlynn.

Arthus and Zeck ran up.

"Ah Emon, ya, I figured. He is trying to make a special weapon to help him get a recommendation into the Silver Thorn Knights, so he tries different combos of chemicals, powders, and such. Some crazy combinations will explode," said Zeck grinning.

Arthus closely observed the Dwarven. He had dark-colored hair that was long and neatly braided, as was his beard, long and also neatly braided.

"Ah, come on, Maddy, you know I need to be making new bombs, and I have another idea how to use a small amount of that exploding power to create a special projectile style weapon," said Emon.

"I know your one of my brightest, but you really could end up blowing up the entire cave. Now go clean up and help Arthus learn how to use a forge and start on something small as he is new," said Maddlynn pointing towards Arthus. Then she says, "Zeck, you are not new, but follow along, help Arthus and while you are at it you might learn something new.

"Fine, Maddy, I get it. Hey, you two come here," said Emon. The two of them walked over.

"Ah Zeck, and who's your friend?" asked Emon.

Arthus begin to fold his hands and bow. "I am," began Arthus. But was cut off by Zeck.

"Hey, better be careful he's the High King grandson," laughed Zeck.

"Ah, right, I almost forgot Maddy mentioned you would be coming around here soon.

"Whelp, let's be gettin ya to it," said Emon. He walked back into his lab with Arthus and Zeck following and turned on the big exhaust fan. "Now that will help get this place's air cleaned out," he said. Then he showed them to another smaller room that held his smelters and a large forge. Emon spent the rest of the day showing Arthus and Zeck how to load the smelter in order to melt the ore down to a hot liquid state and then how they use special molds that shape the liquid as it cooled into pretty much any shape you needed. Once these cooled, some things are reheat it up but not to liquid, then pounded on in anvil with special tools to help finish shaping the item which you wanted to craft.

For the next couple of months, Arthus and Zeck came down to Emon's lab, workshop and home to help him create many different things from the ore.

Zeck continually worked to improve his tomahawk design, and even came up with several different tool styles, each with unique additional uses. One had only added the saw blade teeth into the handle. Which was perfectly weighted and stuck exactly how Zeck's one he killed the four Ice Wolves with. One had the axe head turned into a smaller flat digger pick on one side and a spike pick on the other, like they use in the mines, but which was the same smaller size as his tomahawk. Above the flat and pointed pick where normal picks end, he added a short dagger like tip. This small pick tool also had the saw blade teeth in the handle. The thought there was that this could be used out in the field while hunting or camping, wherever needed, in order to dig, pick, saw or even stab with. Another one with the engineers help, they redesigned the gripping area of the handle. It still had the hard and virtually unbreakable metal, but added a strong, but much softer handle covering that used synthetic materials made from bio-fuels. This style too he added in the saw teeth handle. That one took a few tries before the engineers and Zeck had a perfectly weighted one just like his one he killed the four Ice Wolves with. After they perfected that one, Zeck told the engineers to improve the pick-digger style one with the same synthetic material bonded into the grip of the handle, making this much more comfortable on the hands during picking and digging as the handle seemed to bounce just a little. Once they perfected that and found that it worked as Zeck had wanted it to, then he then told the engineers to modify the larger pick-axes that they use regularly in all the mines with the same kind of soft grip handles. Once those new pick-axes were handed out to the miners, this greatly improved their issues of arm fatigue and increased production during digging Life ore as well as other metal ore.

The last tool he redesigned was a folding camp shovel. He designed that with a double folding hollow handle that screws apart, filled the center handle with first-aid supplies, fishing tackle, and a folding straight razor. The hand end section had kind of a triangle like contraption, where the hand grip is covered in the synthetic soft handle material like the hand grips on the tomahawk and pick/diggers. The shovel itself had saw teeth in one side. The shovel head can be turned on the handle and locked into place and either folded completely 3 times, or folded once for forming a sort of picking shovel, or used completely straight as a short shovel. When folded one time, it also makes a great one leg seat for when someone needs the need to take a poop in the field; allowing for a bit of added comfort when someone has to go. When the camp shovel is folded up three times there is a leather snap covering with hardened synth-blend material bonded to the outside of the leather making it waterproof, which the shovel fits in. This also has utility belt clips attached into the camp shovel covering so that it could be worn securely on the heavy webbed utility belt.

The dagger that was given to him by High King Thureos, with the engineering team, hollowed out the handle and added in a very small first aid kit, a small fishing kit with line and hooks, had a specially designed flint which pulled out with the cap, and a steel inlay life-energy bonded into a section of the back of the blade, and also had the fish scaler saw teeth in the back along a thicker part of its blade, back close to the cross piece of the handle. Then outside the actual handle grip Zeck had the engineers add the same comfortable synthetic material bonded to the metal.

Zeck sent a few of each of his finished designed tools to both Prince Benroy and High King Thureos for field testing before the engineers would put them into full production.

Zeck also worked with both Arthus and Emon to completely redesign the halberd-type weapon that he had carried into battle with the fifth Ice Wolf. He knew it would have killed him if that Dwarven crossbow bolt had not killed it first. He wanted his halberd-type weapon to also be able to send out a projectile from its front end. And so, this new design had the entire staff hollowed out from the top spear point down to about where someone standing holds their hand out naturally to grip the staff, while the butt of the spear shaft rests on the ground. They designed it so that the long blade spear tip can be screwed onto the top end of the staff or removed. The double wide blade axe remains where they are. However between them is located a front sight that is slightly adjustable to the right or left of center. Down on the handle there is a trigger mechanism that has been inserted into it about where the hollow section ends, but also into where the solid section of the lower handle is. The opposite side of the handle from the trigger and yet a little bit more up the pole, there is a flip up rear sight where someone can look down the length of the handle from that sight to see the front sight to be sure that it is aiming correctly. The person bearing this long staff weapon does not have to look down the sights, if they can learn to aim from their hip?

Then they made a special bolt, similar to the crossbow bolt, but which the rear of the bolt had been hollowed and filled with the special packing and explosive materials that Emon had figured out how to make. That bolt was also made thicker though, so that it perfectly fit inside the hollow of the handle of this new halberd-type projectile shooting weapon. Also, the inside of the hollow part of the handle had been bored so that when the projecting bolt came out the front end of the weapon it would be spinning in the air making it aim more true until it hit its target. There was a pull-back cocking mechanism on the opposite side of the trigger, which when pulled back caused a firing pin to pull back against a pressure creating spring, which kept tension on the firing pin. When the trigger was pulled back it released the firing pin with a force that caused it to hit the back end of the bolt, which then caused the packing material to ignite and then explode with enough force that it would send the bolt out of the long staff weapon about 400 meters and still be able to hit its target. The first designs of this weapon where quite crude, but they found that projectile bolt would shoot out and travel almost perfectly straight for about 400 yards.

Zeck, Emon and Arthus sent their crude designs to the engineering team to farther improve the handle portion of the weapon. But, only after testing several ways to improve the exploding bolt, as some of the very early models successfully exploded causing the entire staff weapons staff to also explode. Luckily Zeck and Arthus had convinced Emon to test that outside away from people and buildings and use kind of crude makeshift vice to hold the weapon and then they used a long thin wire to pull the trigger.

Emon used their early design explosion experiences to design a shrapnel creating exploding handled grenade with a 6 second delay in the fuse allowing it to be successfully thrown and explode from a safe distance away. His shrapnel grenade pipe throwing weapon won him a recommendation for Silver Thorn Knights.

Emon celebrated by spending several of their lunchbreaks for a week showing them how to craft various glass artwork pieces using a large glass burning oven. That oven can help make a large variety of finished glass objects, not just blown glass bowls and glasses.

The work in smelting and forging was incredibly brutal, even more so than mining day after day, week after week. Arthus and Zeck stood in the hot, humid rooms dressed only in brown pants, and leather aprons, sleeveless cotton t-shirts and with big leather gloves with cuffs that reached up to the elbows to protect from the extreme heat. Months blended; they awaken and split up only for Zeck's thirty minute morning routines with the Ice Wolves, and the one day each week that Zeck is training the Ice Wolves with the Urial Guardsman. Otherwise they start their day pounding metal until it became dark and the last whistle sounded. Everyday Arthus was smelting or pounding all day. Every night to head back to Zeck's home to soak and recover, then head back the next day.

In his room trying to think about what he was going to write in the holo-mail to Jade, Arthus writes, "Only a month is left, until my grandfather will come for me, and I wonder, where will he send me next? There are the fishing villages by the sea, even a large settlement in the desert far to the south, or maybe sent to stay with an Ignole village inside Gods Forest."

A knock on the door brought him back to his senses. He walked over and opened the door. It was the Captain, who was the commander of Clan Urial Great Northern Guard.

"Well, have a look at you, my Prince. You have grown more muscular over the last several months. Your muscles have grown strong. I can tell all the mining, smelting and forging has doubled your muscle size and tone," said the Commander. Then he added, "It's a remarkable thing from nowhere," and he handed him wrapped package and said, "This is the newly designed guard's uniform you are to wear for the next month. Starting tomorrow morning at O-Dark-Thirty you are reporting to our guard station and learning with us all about the open tundra and how we, Clan Urial Great Northern Guard, work. And, starting tomorrow, you be staying at the barracks near the gate, where the Ice Bear and Ice Wolf kennels are located. You are going to be assigned the daily chores of brushing the Ice Bears, cleaning kennels, standing guard, doing combat training, and going on patrols. I hope you're ready for a month of hard work and little sleep. You might see a lot of this old Cundo." Laughing the Captain and local commander bowed, and turned around and walked out.

Arthus took the uniform out of its wrappings and talks to himself, "It is a newly designed uniform. There is the standard tunic made of wool. There is a hooded Ice bear cap that the hood was the shape of an ice bear's head. Ah, the synth-blend material bonded into chainmail is the new design. This is worn over a standard wool shirt as armor. The old design was not good for the tundra. This is the standard wool shirt. These are standard large boots where the pant legs would strap over the boots to keep snow from soaking into his wool socks. This is seven pairs of wool socks. This is seven pairs of cotton t-shirts. This is seven pairs of cotton underwear shorts. These are the standard large leather gloves with wool glove inserts. In all, this gear will be warm but a bit heavy."

Arthus goes back to his holo-mail to be sure he finished what he was saying, and adds, "Just discovered that I will be playing the roll of Great Northern Guardsman starting at 4:30 in the morning. I still wear the leather bracers you made me every night while I sleep, as its impossible to wear during the days here. It is too precious of a gift from you to me. Hope to see you and at least spend a little time with you after this month."

Arthus pretty much packed everything he owned, with the exception of the fragile shofar and the incredibly ornate mammoth tusk, as those cannot be brought to the barracks. He knows there is no private spaces to put those kind of precious things in there. The rolling trunk foot locker that his grandfather gave him is a normal standard for military guard barracks. That, his backpack and his tele-mask. He hauled the rolling trunk foot locker down the stairs with Zeck's help using straps like he had seen the Dwarvens do when he arrived. He brought his backpack and Tele-mask. Everything was just outside on their front porch. It was 4:00 AM. He knew he had 30 minutes to be in formation at the barracks. He thanked Zeck's parents for all they had done for him, including safeguarding his shofar and his mammoth tusk until he was ready to pick those up too, before his grandfather came for him and took him on to the next location. Zeck was also outside with a bag waiting.

"Whelp time for us to go join the guard," said Zeck smiling.

"Zeck, why you aren't you going you live here? You don't need to join me, do you?" Asked Arthus

"Of course I am going. I am old enough now, and my name came up," said Zeck laughing.

"Your turn," asked Arthus?

"Ah yes, everyone when they are a certain age, are put into a list to do rotations in the guard to help do our part. My friends say it is mostly cleaning and standing guard. But according to the Captain and local commander you and I get to help the patrol also, so this be sweet," said Zeck.

"I didn't know you all switched back and forth," said Arthus.

"Ya, we do it, so no one gets complacent and it gives some guards a break for a bit to rest up. But let's get going. The Commander said, 'Be in formation at O-Dark-Thirty, which is 4:30 in the morning' And for military guard, being late means extra drills. Let's go now, said Zeck. Soon Arthus and Zeck had picked out a bunks in the barracks, placed there gear down, dressed into their uniforms and ran to formation.

Arthus was surprised at how light all of his gear really was. He thinks to himself "It really must have been all the back-breaking work we have been doing over this last year. The gear he wore almost a year ago had been so heavy, but now it wasn't even bothering him, even the height and cold that once made it hard to breathe. He didn't even notice for a while now.

The commander showed up, and someone yelled, "Attention!"

Then the commander walked in and informed them of where to and how to store all of what they brought with them. "Prince Arthus, we have a special locking area where any non-regulation items are to be stored. Most of what you brought with you is non-regulation, so you will know what to do about the rest. Is that understood?

"Yes Sir! Said Arthus.

Inspection in two hours. Another guard member came over and handed each of them some sheets that showed how exactly each of their items goes into their locker spaces. Then said, two hours Boots, get moving.

The first guard inspection went fine. Then the Captain, local commander came in inspected their area and their gear.

"Alright, not bad for new Boots. You have a long way to go, but for today you go to the stables and help the others clean up the place, including the Ice Bears, brush their fur, and make sure they have plenty to eat, and water to drink. Boot Arthus, you will shovel the stables poop out into the bins and wash it down with that huge hose out there," commanded the commander.

"Boot sir, what's that mean," asked Arthus? The commander eyed Arthus.

"It means your nothing but something to step on, now get going," commanded the commander.

"Yes, sir," they both yelled. They were running for the door. The rest of the day, they spent at the stables. That night they ate with the rest of the Urial Guards. Four men were off to the side just laughing and drinking. The commander walked over after a bit.

"Ok, Zeck, Arthus, and you four, you're on guard for the first six hours. Then you can get some rest when relieved now get going," said the commander. Arthus and Zeck were to patrol the walls walking back and forth on the battlements. They had a special Night-vision mask they wore. It also helps keep the wind off their bare face; the eye slots had small scanners. It would scan back and forth for any heat signs. The hours drug on as they kept walking up and down. Suddenly Zeck waved Arthus over.

"Look," said Zeck. He pointed about a mile out there scanner picked up a couple of Yelin walking up and one Mammoth. What was weird is the heat sensor kept seeing small hot spots trailing behind the group, then it hit Arthus's blood. Arthus rushed over to a bell and started the alarm. The commander rushed up to where they were carrying a scanner.

"Sir looks like a group of Yelin, and if I am right there bleeding badly and there are Ice Wolves trailing after them," reported Arthus. The commander took a look and nodded.

"Your right, men, be on guard. We got wounded friendlies, and incoming enemies, grab the healer and let's head out," yelled the Captain.

In mere minutes an entire patrol was mounted and rushing to help the wounded. In less than ten minutes, they had helped the group get to shelter behind the walls, and the healer and his team were busy helping keep the Yelin alive. One of them that was not as severely wounded told them they were not far from here and were ambushed by three Alphas working together with over fifty Ice Wolves. Ten Yelin had died in the fight, and only one Alpha had died.

"This isn't good. Alphas used to rarely team-up, which means we must have a Chief Alpha on our hands," said the commander.

"A Chief Alpha," asked Arthus? "I never heard of anything like that," said Arthus.

The commander nodded and said, "Most people have not, because it is so very rare. It has only happened, I believe, only twice in all of history. A rare wolf is born that has the ability to make all other Alphas obey its will. Last time this happened it took the High King and well over a hundred of his best Knights to deal with it. We need to kill it before it enslaves any more Alphas, or it could be a major threat to all of us here on the Tundra and even perhaps all of Malon. Send an emergency alert holo-message to the Clan leaders and to our High King: We need every available man standing ready! Emergency Alert Muster all Northern Guard Reservists and tell them be here in full battle armor, weapons ready by O-Dark-Thirty, *which means, 04:30 hours.* And, get all active Clan Urial Great Northern Guard back here immediately," commanded the Captain.

A couple of scouts ran off in different directions. Within two hours every active locally stationed guard member was in full battle armor with various weapons up on the city walls and up on the mountain range battle towers above the city defending their northern, and east and west flanks. By the next morning there were over one thousand, men women, and Dwarvens all in full battle armor with various weapons ready. Half of them were marching to the Yelin village in order to help defend them. The others were to stay and guard the walls, and all of the mountain's north, east and west flanks. One reserve guard member was positioned every five meters all around their perimeters. There were four platoons of twenty-five each which were double-timing in full battle armor and weapons ready in circles over and over and over around the entire perimeter of the city.

The emergency alert holo-message had arrived in the middle of last night to the Palace. As soon as the Clan Chiefs and the High King received the alert, they immediately in turn sent out emergency alert musters to all the cities, villages, and clans on Malon. Within a few hours every military post and outpost on Malon had their entire active and reserve guards in full battle armor and weapons ready.

The High King was taking no chances. He sent an order to all his military commanders, "All military airships on Malon were to be loaded and ready for combat orders within four hours." He sent an order to all his Knights and Silver Thorns, "As soon as each of the local airships are loaded with weapons and guards, they are to head to Northern Peaks City and to all Great Northern Tundra outposts and also to provide support to Clan Arial farming village, and to the various trade routes surrounding the entire Tundra and Great Northern Mountain Range from all points on Malon."

By 10:00 in the morning several military airships arrived and landed in front of the main gates to the Northern Peaks City. High King Thureos and Prince Benroy, Arthus' father, arrived by military airship with several Silver Thorn Commanders along with around three-thousand Knights.

The Clan Urial Great Northern Guard Captain, who is the local commander, commanded, "Prince Arthus, you and Boot Zeck will join me in welcoming your grandfather the High King and your father the Prince to Northern Peaks City. Now come along double time!"

Several squads in full battle dress armor were in formation at attention in front of the gates where the airships had landed. As the High King and Prince Benroy disembarked from their military airship the commander motioned to Prince Arthus standing next to him to give them greeting.

"Welcome High King Thureos and Welcome Prince Benroy, to Northern Peaks City," said Prince Arthus as he bowed.

Bowing more deeply, Captain Urial, Commander of the Clan Urial Great Northern Guard said, "At your orders High King Thureos and Prince Benroy."

The High King Thureos waved. Prince Benroy kept his face stern looking, but nodded at Arthus.

The High King spoke, "Thank you for this honor Captain Urial, Commander of the Clan Urial Great Northern Guard. I only wish these were peaceful circumstances which had brought us to meet with you! Prince Arthus will need to join with us at the Combat Command Tent."

A huge combat command tent had been setup in the field right behind where all the airships had landed. Surrounding the command tent on three sides there were multiple rows of extremely long and very sharp spike metal barricades that had been placed there earlier by the guard while the huge command tent was being erected. In between all the spikes was stretched out razor wire. At the four outer corners there were four rather tall metal framed battle towers erected and each of those towers had Dwarvens with crossbows. At the base of each of those erected towers were stacks of sandbags on all sides. At the center of each of the tower platforms, where the Dwarvens stood guard, were hundreds of extra crossbow bolts in steel ammo boxes stacked up. Along the left and right of the path leading up to entrance to the command tent there were more of those extremely long and very sharp spike metal barricades. And again the razor wire had been stretched out and placed into those. There were two more of the towers placed beside the pathway entrance to the left and to the right, which were setup exactly like the ones at the outer four corners. There was a squad of Dwarven Guards carrying battle axes and crossbows running circles around and around the outer perimeter of all of that over and over.

Upon entering the large command tent Arthus noticed that there were a couple of the clan leaders who were already inside waiting for the High King and the Prince Benroy to arrive. Grag was there and when he spotted Arthus he smiled brightly and nodded to him. Arthus put his hands together like in a prayer like fashion and bowed his head to Grag. Grag in turn did the same to Arthus. The High King and Prince Benroy both had folded their hands in a prayer like fashion and bowed their heads over and over as they silently greeted the various clan leaders while heading up the center isle to the platform at the far end of the command tent. As they were doing this each of the clan leaders also did this.

Prince Arthus motioned to Zeck, "We must respectfully stand back here near the entrance and allow High King Thureos and Prince Benroy to conduct the War Council."

Overhearing Prince Arthus speaking to Zeck, the commander quickly said, "Yes boots, stand at parade rest here at the left and right of the inside entrance to the command tent and no more talking. Just listen and learn!" The commander then went up and took his proper place inside the command tent.

The Elder one of the Yelin *Snow Folk*, Silver Thorns, Silver Knights, Silver Scouts, and various clan leaders all gathered around a large holo-table that had a 4D map of all of the Great Northern Tundra and Great Northern Mountain Ranges projected above it to begin to make battle plans. They hoped to discover where the Chief Alpha hid his headquarters and kill him before he grew any more powerful. They hoped to kill him before he became a threat to the entire Great Northern Tundra and Great Northern Mountain Range.

Suddenly a male Cundo Urial Scout burst into the tent. He ran directly up to the High King to make his report. "My High King, King, and highly honored clan and village leaders, we scouts followed many of the Ice Wolves into the far Northern Mountain Peaks." The scout then points to a location on the 4D holo-projection above the holo-table. The holo-map projection, suddenly appeared to expand that exact location. A very clear satellite view of the area could be seen by all. "Right here there is a maze of caves and caverns in this area." The scout again pointed to the holo-map. Suddenly the holo-map appeared to become a view of the ground penetrating radar from the satellite. And, there were hundreds of underground tunnels and caverns that appeared. These tunnels and caverns were filled with red heat images. "The Ice Wolves have turned all of this area into a natural and unnatural fortress. The worst part is we actually saw at least six Alpha Ice Wolves with hundreds of Ice Wolf underlings appearing almost as if they had formed a large military style encampment surrounding this area. The sheer size of the encampment area alone could easily hold at least two thousand Ice Wolf underlings. We also believe there are far deeper tunnels than what our ground penetrating radar can observe from the Archangel built satellite in space hiding around and under this area. The ground penetrating radar already shows these obviously unnatural tunnels leading into larger caverns from the natural caves located here. If the Ice Wolves have the level of technological skill to build these tunnels, then perhaps they have created a much deeper and wider maze of underground areas. Perhaps an entire city-like societal structure is there. With that many Alpha, and that is only the ones we saw outside the cave entrance, and with the amount of heat signatures that we are reading from the Archangel built space satellite, we might be looking at perhaps thousands or even tens of thousands of Ice Wolves," reported the Scout.

Hearing and seeing this, High King Thureos says, "Then perhaps we are too late. They have grown stronger than I had hoped. I will have to bring in at least twenty thousand more of our trained military guard from around Malon. I will also call in at least two thousand more of the Silver Nights and bring all of my Silver Thorns here." Turning to Prince Benroy, he asked, "Do you have a report yet of how many airships and military troops stand ready?

Looking at his holo-reader Prince Benroy replied, "We have five hundred and fifty airships standing ready, and we have one hundred thousand army troops standing ready at airship fields around Malon. There are at least another million and a half reservists, who were called up by the emergency alert muster system, who have already checked in to their posts and outposts all around Malon. That is besides all of the Silver Nights and Silver Thorns all around Malon who also stand ready."

"Ok. Send the following message to the Silver Nights and Silver Thorns and Clan Urial Guard: By order of High King Thureos and Prince Benroy, all the fully loaded five hundred and fifty airships are to head to this location immediately. Two thousand of the Silver Nights and all Silver Thorns are to report to this location within the next twenty four hours. Twenty thousand of the regular army troops, meaning several battalions with their battalion commanders from major military bases, are to head to Clan Arial Valley. Twenty thousand of the regular army troops are to report to the other villages on the far side of the Northern Peaks Mountain Range to take up positons to support those villages. Forty Thousand Reservists are to fill the empty battalion locations within the major cities at the major military basis, where we pull the regular army troops. Besides this I want twenty thousand of the best and smartest Reservists to head directly here. They are all to leave when the airships arrive at their locations to bring them here. Within two days at O-Dark-Thirty they are expected to be in Battle Formations at all of their assigned locations."

Then the High King says to the Captain Urial, the local Commander, "Double the guard on the walls and have the ones at the Yelin village pack up to pull back to the city."

Then the High King says to Elder One, "It is far safer for all your Snow Folk to come here. I will send many to help ensure your safety. Also, all the other mountain and tundra tribes need to come behind our city walls."

A bright light portal appeared instantly and Michael the Archangel stepped through it and into the tent. He was taller than all others. He wore a silver-gold armor. A pure white cloak made from his own Angel feathers covered some of his armor. A golden halo floated above his head. The Archangel Michael who is forbearer to High King Thureos and to all Cundo is an impressive sight to see today as always. Arthus had seen Michael many times; he often came to the Palace and worked with the Silver Knights and Silver Thorn to train them and to advise the High King. His skin was fair, almost shinny. He didn't have the Cundo or Ignole pointy ears; instead had round ears and short golden hair and short blond beard. He had a scar that went up the left side of his cheek across his left eye, stopping at the hairline.

Michael the Archangel says, "My apologies, High King. I went to check out the Ice Wolves for myself. It is far worse than any of your scouts have seen and far worse than what can be seen in your 4D holo-map even with the enhancements available to you from our space satellites. This Chief Alpha has truly become a warlord. He has pure black fur and wears leather and bone armor. In fact he has several chief-level Alphas following him. But I also made a discovery when I was there, one which you must see and hear for yourself," Michael raised his arm in the air; a bright light portal appeared before them like the one used by all of the Angels to travel from world-to-world throughout the Myriasphere of universes, and then two hooded figures step through. Michael nodded, and the two hooded figures removed the hoods. The whole room went silent. Two Ice Wolves stood before them. One was a regular blue and silver fur. The other had light brown fur and blue eyes. The light brown fur and blue eyed Ice Wolf carried in one hand a large staff that was made from a tree branch. This type of tree branch was not one many had seen before. Both Ice Wolves immediately kneeled before High King Thureos very deeply to a point that they were prostrate on the ground and used their front paws to cover their face just below their eyes.

High King Thureos took a deep breath, allowed his Life-energy to push through his body down through his feet into the ground and out towards and into the two Ice Wolves, who he could clearly sense had no thoughts of hatred and no hearts filled with evil. In fact they were filled with the LIGHT and TRUTH and GRACE that only creatures who honor God the Great Creator and Sustainer of all things can possess. Sensing this, the High King raised his hand and said, "I welcome you in the Name of God and my own name. Please stand now and state your purpose."

The two Ice Wolves stood up. Michael the Archangel walked towards the High King and then came around and stood behind High King Thureos.

The Ice Wolf with the wooden staff said, "Thank you, Michael the Archangel, for allowing myself and my friend to come through your Angel light portal, with one of your invisible Angels. And, thank you High King Thureos, who is highly favored of God the Great Creator and Sustainer of all things. My name is Goran, and this is my right-hand Dorgan. He is also my bodyguard. I am the son of my father, Black Fang, but I am not of what has become of my father, the Demon-Legion-Bonded Chief Alpha who has become the War Chief Alpha over all the Chief Alphas, Alphas and underling Ice Wolves," said Goran.

"Over all the Chief Alphas, Alphas and underling Ice Wolves? Wow, this is far worse than we ever thought," interrupted Maddlynn.

High King Thureos motioned Maddlynn to be quiet and said, "Please have respect and hold all comments until our guest has finished explaining his purpose for coming in peace here before this war council!" Then High King Thureos said, "Please continue."

"Yes, well, because my father has bonded himself to the Demon horde, who calls himself, *Legion, for they are many,* my father has grown very powerful and argent and is filled with Darkness. In his twisted

Darkness, my father is filled with greed and believes he now has enough Ice Wolves to take all of the North," said Goran.

Arthus' thoughts interrupted silently, "No! If he moves to war, we will all be destroyed."

"Many of the Chief Alphas, Alphas and Ice Wolves are not at all Demon-Bonded and do not want war. Some are Demon-Bonded. The Demon-Bonded Chief Alphas and the Demon-Bonded Alphas want war. There are some of the non-Demon-Bonded that have agreed to go to war, because they believe if they win, no more will we go hungry, or have to deal with the freezing weather, and other nonsense that those who have not strived for learning and seeking TRUTH will never understand.

I am the first of the Ice Wolf Druids, a group of Ice Wolves who discovered how to tap into this world's Life-energies. Most of us Druids only use our power to heal and bring a little life to the frozen areas that we can find. Dorgan here is a part of a monk pack that trains their bodies and minds into a weapon, but they also have made a vow to follow peace unless for self-defense. This had angered my father, and most of his monk pack were killed. I was able to save him and only a few others. They came to serve the Druids to protect us, since our power is mainly used to heal and grow things," said Goran.

"I see. Now that you have introduced us to you and let us know a bit about your background, why have you asked to come before us today," asked Thureos.

"I want to ask for your help to stop my Demon-Legion-Bonded father and then destroy all the various pathways on Malon which allow the Demons to become bonded with Ice Wolves and with any other beings on Malon. I also ask you to please not kill all of the Ice Wolves, but only kill those that have been Demon-Bonded, once my father falls. I know the God given Life-energy power of the High King and the power of the entire military forces of Malon. After we kill my Demon-Legion-Bonded father, and also destroy the various pathways in which the Demons can be bonded with Ice Wolves and any other beings on Malon, and destroy all the Demon-Bonded Chief Alphas and Demon-Bonded Alphas, I need your help to build the rest of the Ice

208

Wolves into a God honoring clan, like all the other peace seeking and God honoring clans on Malon, which then can join the High Council and serve all of Malon. I know that only doing this will bring true peace in the Great Northern Tundra and the rest of Malon," said Goran.

Dorgan just nodded.

"I see, and is there anything else you need to tell us, which will help us?" High King Thureos said?

"We will help your war council members here to any strategic information that they need, said Goran.

The High King sat down on a chair at the head of the large 4D holo-map projection table. He then closed his eyes and again reached out through his Life-energy senses into everything and through everyone in the entire room. He then started sitting back in deep thought.

Then the Elder one of the Yelin *Snow Folk* stood up from where he had been sitting on the ground and said, "If we Snow Folk that you all call, *Yelin* have any say in the matters being discussed here in this here war council, then we demand no peace to these dark spirits!"

Michael the Archangel immediately said, "Please sit back down, Elder one. Know this as TRUTH, the majority of the Ice Wolves are no evil beings. In TRUTH, they are very much like yourself and all of the Snow Folk. They too are God created beasts, that were born and live and have evolved here on Malon by the same God given Life-energy as all the living and thinking beings of Malon." Michael the Archangel had a look in his eyes, which commanded respect. His words were filled with Life-energy, strength and peace.

The Elder glared back at Michael the Archangel, but when Michael finished speaking to him he sat back down.

Michael the Archangel then said, "If true evil were in this place, myself and the other Angels that came with me through the portal would destroy them without mercy. Let me make my point even clearer so that everyone here understands. Not even this Black Ice is wholly a creature of Darkness. What I mean by that is he was not born in Darkness. He was born in the same Life-energy, just like all of you were born, with the exception of High King Thureos here as he was created from one of my feathers. He may have been deceived into this Demon-legion-bonding, as you are claiming him to be, due to his anger, hatred, and greed. All of those are a powerful tool of the King of Darkness, but until he draws his last breath there is always a chance that the King of Darkness and this Legions of Demons can lose their hold over him. He can repent of the path into Darkness that he is on and he can seek mercy and forgiveness from the God the Great Creator and Sustainer of all things. This is why we Angels will not lift a hand to help either side. Our job is to build this world, but what happens here domestic between different physical beings we have no involvement with."

"Thank you, Michael," said High King Thureos getting up onto his feet and walking over to Elder one, he sat down on the floor in front of him. "Elder one. Not long ago, much of Malon also thought of your Snow Folk as evil-beast-monsters that needed to be completely destroyed. Then I came up here to the Great Northern Tundra and Great Northern Mountain Range and met with you. And then I helped all the peoples of the north to know you as a God honoring people's group, yes different in size and in appearance then all the other people's groups, but a sentient being, that thinks and herds and hunts and gathers and has incredible creative abilities. And there is that Life Yell that all you Snow Folk go around Yelin. We honor you and the incredible Yelin gift God gave to you by calling you, *Yelin*. However, if your people's group would prefer, I can decree that everyone on Malon stop calling you, *Yelin* and call your people only by the name which you call yourself, *Snow Folk?* And you do know that you have my respect and honor and friendship, right? You also know how I had to do a ton of negotiating with a sword and a ton more negotiating with words and deeds to convince all the people's groups on the planet that you are not at all evil-beast-monsters. You have earned your seat on this war council and on the High Council. And so, my friend, do these Ice Wolf people also not deserve to have the same chance as we gave to your people?" Asked High King Thureos.

The High King then stood up and walked back up to the table in front of his chair and in front of Michael the Archangel and addressed everyone.

"As High King, my job is to unite and bring as much peace as possible, so if your father, Black Fang, wishes to come and sit down in peace talks, I will hear what he wishes," said High King Thureos.

"Thank you, my High King. I will ensure my father hears of your desire to have peace talks with him, and I do hope reason will bring us all together. However, if he will not listen to reason, then Michael and/or his unseen Angels will need to please create a light portal for me and Doran again to come here and help you devise the best strategies to help defeat what has become of my father." said Goran.

Michael waves a hand, and the light portal opened once again. The two wolves walked through, and the portal closed.

"Alright, everyone, our command still stands and reinforcements are on their way here and to their posts as we have ordered. Being prepared for war and providing an overwhelming show of force may bring peace a chance. If not, it will bring us into a war that will not be easy or quick. Let us still bring the Yelin Snow Folk here and the other village peoples too. We must also ensure that Northern Tundra City is fully supplied and reinforced. Grag, please open the war supply barns that are located by Clan Arial farm village and be sure to get those supplies to here and to all of our troops, at the locations which have been sent to your holo-reader. Now, let us end here for the day and get some rest, then we meet tomorrow at O-Dark-Thirty in battle formation. After formation we will come in here to finish our planning," said High King Thureos.

All nodded, got up, and left talking to one another. High King Thureos smiled and nodded to Michael, who nodded back and left the war council tent. High King Thureos sat down and was deep in thought.

Prince Benroy took Michael, Prince Arthus, and Zeck and went over to the kennels.

"What do you two young men think of your first war council meeting," asked Prince Benroy?

"I don't know, to be honest, the Ice Wolves showing up changed everything, not sure what to think, say, or do," said Prince Arthus.

"I really don't trust them, and the north would be so much safer if we simply wiped them all out," said Zeck.

"I see now, you see a bit of what is going through your High Kings mind. Anything he decides will cost so many lost lives. No matter what he decides many Ice Wolves will die, as well as how many peoples who serve as soldiers in this war, and how many innocent bystanders will get caught in the fight even though they don't lift a weapon in offence or defense. Too many will be returned to their families dead, or left to rot on the fields of battle. All of this is just a huge burden your grandfather, the High King has to bear on his shoulders. As the Prince of Malon, I will also bear this burden, even though the decisions rest on your High King's shoulders. Arthus, also as Prince of Malon, you also will bear the results of the High King's decisions. Remember this, Arthus, war is never a good answer unless given no other viable choices."

Prince Benroy turned and spoke to Zeck, "I hear good things about you, Zeck! How you have used your creative mind and skills to develop some new weapons and tools. I also hear how you have been helping to raise and train a litter of Ice Wolf pups. I would like you to show me your pups and allow me to witness with my own eyes the progress of their training."

Zeck brought Prince Benroy and Arthus and Michael right into the kennel with the Ice Wolf pups. All of them were very well behaved and followed every command that Zeck gave them.

Prince Benroy said, "I do see the possibility for great things in the future having spent this time observing with my own eyes and Life-energy senses. I must now go as I have to be available to meet with the commanders of the troops as they arrive. I know that I will get no sleep this night. However, I want both of you to arrive wide awake for the O-Dark-Thirty formation, so you two are ordered to get some sleep."

Prince Benroy and Michael walked away. Arthus and Zeck then headed back to the barracks where they are sleeping that night. However, surprisingly Michael was waiting for them outside the door of the barracks.

Chapter 11
Archangel, Alda Matriarch and the Quest

"Young Prince, sorry to interrupt, but, may I have a private word with you," asked Michael the Archangel?

"Umm, ok," said Arthus, a little shocked that the Archangel wished to talk with him.

Arthus turned to Zeck, "You need to go on into the barracks, while I go and visit with Michael. I shall join you soon."

Zeck quickly entered the barracks and closed the door behind him. Arthus walked a short distance away, where Michael and he could speak privately.

"Your grandfather told me that you been had been having nightmares back while living in the palace. He said something about a dark throne room place, which had a dark being, with black flames for eyes and with abilities to shapeshift his body into a blend of a large man and a multi-hooded snake shadow. Please, as this is very important. You must tell me exactly what you have seen in your dreams in detail."

Arthus closes his eyes, takes in a deep breath, and pushes out with his Life-energy senses to help him calm his mind, his spirit and his body.

While Arthus explained the dream in detail to Michael, he closed his eyes.

"What you saw is a vision, which the King of Darkness intends to make happen. It is not an absolute future, as everything he spouts is coming out from the Dark and twisted reality that only he sees in his own mind. He has fully denied TRUTH and therefore everything he thinks and speaks are lies, but which are blended in with his twisted view of LIGHT, which he only can see through his own Darkness. In the real

LIGHT of TRUTH, it is only what the future might hold for you and all of the physical realms, if he can convince more Angels, and people's groups and other creatures, all created by God, and for God's Glory, to bond themselves with his Demon followers and then follow him into his greedy Darkness," said Michael.

"Furthermore, what you saw in your dream was the Throne-room of the Hellcore void. The being who sits on the Throne of Darkness that you saw in your dream-vision, was once a brother to myself. He was the Light Bearer Angel, who through the Life-energy infused within music and with his skills in music could bend, prism and refract light. Over time and with much practice perfecting his skills, he even learned to turn light into portals in the Myriasphere, which contains all of the universes, which he then taught all Angels to do. That light portal skill allows any Angel and few other beings to step through and move instantly from one world into another anywhere in any of the universes within the Myriasphere. And, whatever we Angels or the other specially gifted beings are touching can also be moved from one world to another instantly. With God's permission, we can use the portals to allow various people's groups and animal creatures to migrate from one world to another, like we have done for all the Dwarvens and many of the Yaule, which as you know that your grandfather brought with my help from one of Malon's moons, Creed, here to Malon. Anyway, my once brother, instead of choosing to use his musical and light bearer abilities for the good of all universes, he set his heart and eyes upon taking over the Throne of God the Creator and Sustainer of all things. It was his crazy greed that caused his fall into Darkness, and along with him all those that followed his greedy ambitions. He has been turned into the King of Darkness. Instead of remaining a God honoring light bearer, he used his abilities to bend, prism and refract Darkness. And again through time and with much practice learned to shapeshift his own self into the Serpent King, also known in various cultures throughout the Myriasphere as Quetzalcoatl, Hydra, Nagas, and a Dragon. He has appeared throughout history as a flying serpent, a dragon, a multi-headed and hooded snake, an Angel bearing false light, and a man.

He is capable of shapeshifting the Darkness inside of him at whim into a blend of any of those."

"The King of Darkness, having transformed himself into the Serpent King, and in direct disobedience to God's commands for all His Angels, has joined himself to an evil subservient female fallen Angel, Leviathan, who he has also trained. She has learned from him and has become a Naki, Queen of the Nagas. This evil joining as the Serpent King and Naki, together, they have born many evil spawned children and have spread their evil children through Dark portals in the Myriasphere to many worlds throughout all the universes. What you saw and experienced in your dream was his blend between his Serpent King form and his darkness filled Angel man form and his ability to shape shift the Darkness into dark shadows that shape shift around and through him. The flaming Darkness within him has consumed him with greed and hatred." said Michael.

"The Alda matriarch has also told me of yours and Jade's encounter with one of the four meter long evil Nagas children, while you were together in your bi-annual hunt, and how you bravely faced the evil Nagas child stabbing it with your dagger. That cut with your dagger turned the Nagas child into a dual-headed Hydra, which is an evil transformation towards becoming an even more powerful Nagas. The young Alda you met in that battle had sensed this evil transformation and immediately came to destroy the Nagas-Hydra hybrid, before you with your dagger continued in that battle to help it complete its transformation into a full-fledged multi-headed Hydra. Once a Nagas gains five heads it completes its transformation into a Hydra, where it can then begin to train and transform into a Naga King, called Quetzalcoatl. If that had happened and it then joined itself to a female Nagas child and then trained her into becoming another Naki, then entire world of Malon would have been taken over by their fully evil spawned Nagas children. That young Alda truly saved you and all of Malon by helping you and killing that Nagas-Hydra hybrid."

"I also heard from the Alda matriarch that you and Jade cooked and ate the Nagas-Hydra hybrid. They realized that you both did that, because you each gifted some of your Nagas-Hydra Hybrid jerky in the

Great Gifting at the God's Tree Seedling Circle in the Clan Arial farm village." I need you to know that by eating the Nagas-Hydra hybrid, you and Jade and even Fang and his Yaule tribe and any other wild animals that discovered its remains and have eaten it, have each successfully overthrown the Dark powers of that Nagas child. Meaning that you have greatly hindered the King of Darkness's plans against you and your world. You also have given the King of Darkness a real reason to want to kill you and Jade and Fang and all of Fang's pack, and every other creature that found and ate any of the Nagas-Hydra hybrid. This may also be why so quickly this Dark Fang has also become the Chief warlord Alpha and in his Dark ambition and greed has taken authority over all of the Chief Alphas and Alphas and Ice Wolf underlings. I am certain, the King of Darkness is desperately trying to find another way to destroy Malon." said Michael.

"Now Arthus, I will take you to meet the Alda Matriarch for she has a quest for you. Archangel Michael opened a light portal and took Arthus' arm and stepped through the light portal. They stepped out in a meadow deep in the swamplands east of harmony city. There in the meadow were many Aldas and the Alda Matriarch. The Alda Matriarch glowed like the reflection from the light of the moon. Behind the Alda Matriarch is what looks very much like a large stone doorway that leads nowhere as it had two huge natural upright stones and another huge natural stone that was laid over the top forming a doorway.

Arthus quickly bowed slightly in the direction of the Alda Matriarch and raised his arms out a little bit in front of him and turned his palms up towards the sky. Arthus kept his head bowed and did not look directly in the eyes of the Alda Matriarch.

The Alda spoke in a voice that sounded like the crackling of wood and the bristling of the leaves, "Arthus, come with me through my door."

Suddenly a glowing root like branch came out from the side of the Alda Matriarch and wrapped gently around one of Arthus' forearms. Then the Alda Matriarch turned and with her to larger branch like arms brushed her leaves up against the two sides of the huge stone doorway. Instantly Ruins from the ancient language of the Golden City appeared as if from nowhere and they were glowing. Arthus could hear a humming sound coming from the stones and then a light portal appeared inside the doorway. The Alda Matriarch easily walked through the light portal while pulling Arthus through with her.

Stepping out of the light portal into a deep underground cavern that has a river flowing very fast coming from somewhere and going to somewhere, but where it comes from and where it goes to Arthus couldn't tell. Surrounding the entire walls and ceiling of the cavern were huge Life-crystals. There were many tiny glowing flying ferries flitting about in the cavern. The moonlike glow from the Alda Matriarch caused the various Life-crystals to prism the light in the cavern into many beautiful colors.

The Alda Matriarch says in her crackling of wood and bristling of leaves voice, "Kneel to be anointed for I have a quest for you. For here on my altar by the source of the waterfall which pours into the River of Life are several horns which glow. They are filled with the original source of this River of Life back when the Creator originally made this world planet and all that is in it. Only those anointed by my special oil can join in on this quest to carry and use one of my horns which glow. You will use the water that is within these horns which glow, waters which never runs dry, to help cleanse all the tainted waters on Malon and then into many of the waters on other world planets in the Myriasphere. No matter how much you pour out of these waters in these horns, there will always be more to pour. The children of the Serpent King and Naki, Queen of the Nagas have swam in and defecated into many waters, opening a way which those who swim in or drink from those tainted waters to begin to learn Dark Magic and begin to join their hearts and minds to the Darkness."

Arthus kneels down onto the cavern floor and again bows his head and reaches his arms out slightly and turns the palms of his hands up towards the ceiling of the cavern.

Suddenly a Redwood tree nymph appears next to Arthus and the nymph reached up into the branches of the Alda Matriarch and from deep within her branches he retrieves another glowing goat horn. The Redwood tree nymph then takes the glowing goat horn and pours a glowing oil from it onto Arthus' head. Then the Redwood tree nymph puts the glowing horn back up and deeply into the Alda Matriarch branches. Then the Redwood tree nymph goes over and gets one of the horns which glow from the Alda Matriarch's Altar, beside the underground source of the waterfall, which comes out of the mountain and drops into the River of Life across the river from the base of First God's Tree in Harmony City. He then places the strappings of the glowing horn over Arthus' body. And then goes and kneels beside Arthus and puts his own arms up and turns his palms up towards the ceiling in the cavern.

Then suddenly a bright light comes down from one of the Life-crystals in the ceiling and Arthus is back in the meadow where the stone doorway is located, except the Alda Matriarch did not come back here with him and the huge stone doorway is covered in vines and briar branches and it is almost impossible to see that they are even there.

Arthus thinks to himself, "If I had not known where those stones were in this meadow, I would never had noticed them even if I walked by them several times. The jungle overgrowth truly hides them well."

The Archangel Michael says, "It is time to get you back." And, he opens a light portal and takes Arthus back to the guard barracks.

"You are truly blessed and honored with your quest, said Michael the Archangel.

Michael then said to him, "That glowing holy horn you now carry, needs to go under your garments as your quest is to remain a secret, which only few know of."

Then instantly, a light portal appeared, Michael the Archangel stepped through it and disappeared along with the light portal.

Arthus quickly opened his uniform tunic and took one arm out and put the horn that glows under his arm and then covered it back up with his uniform tunic. He suddenly felt very tired. He walked over to the barracks door, opened the door, went inside, showered, dressed in his pajamas, and brushed his teeth. Then he laid down on one of the barrack's bedroll cots. He turned and punched his pillow roll so that it became more comfortable for his neck and laid his neck and head back into it. Pulling up his blanket over his chest, laying his arms over the blanket. He folded his hands and closing his eyes he said out loud, "I do thank you God for your grace and mercy and for entrusting me with this quest which the Alda Matriarch has anointed me to do. I do pray that your hand will continually guide me. That you will fill me with wisdom in order that I can faithfully fulfill any task that you give for me to do." Arthus then took a deep breath, allowing his Life-energy to flow out from him and into all of the guards in the room that lay sleeping and allowed his mind to quiet his thoughts. Soon he drifted off to sleep a dreamless peaceful sleep.

Chapter 12
The Quest of Cleansing of the Waters

"Arise Sir Arthus, anointed of the Alda Matriarch," commanded a Redwood tree nymph telepathically who appeared at Arthus' bed at 2:00 in the morning.

Arthus opened his eyes and sat up on the side of his bed. There by his bed stood a Redwood tree nymph.

"I have been sent to guide you to the waters," said the Redwood tree nymph telepathically.

Arthus stood up and said out loud to the Redwood tree nymph, who he remembers seeing before down in the cavern with the Alda Matriarch, "And, what is your name."

"My name is Timothy and I am a guiding Redwood tree nymph, who has been assigned to serve as your guide as you are to go about your quest. I am also to help guide you in wisdom as you had asked the Creator for this. Now eat this very small cake of Life-minerals and take a drink from your horn which glows, as these will build your Life-energy, said the Redwood tree nymph Timothy telepathically into Arthus' mind.

Arthus says the thoughts telepathically, "Can you hear my thoughts as I am thinking these words to you, Timothy, or is the telepathic communication only a one way channel?"

Timothy said telepathically, "I can read your thoughts, or hear you when you speak out loud. And, I can speak out loud too. But, I think it best not to talk out loud when others around you are sleeping."

Arthus immediately put the very small cake of Life-minerals into his mouth and quickly realized that it really tasted a lot like a mix of mud and grass, and so he swallowed the very small cake rather than chewed it as he drank a little bit of water from his horn which glows. Instantly his body was filled with Life-energy and he was no longer tired. He quickly grabbed the glowing horn and hung it over his neck and shoulder then put his uniform tunic on over it. Arthus just finished getting his boots on his feet and the Redwood tree nymph Timothy waved his hand and a light portal opened. Holding onto Arthus's forearm the Redwood tree nymph Timothy and Arthus stepped through the light portal into the kennel where Zeck had his pups.

"Add a drop of water to these pup's water barrels, said Redwood tree nymph Timothy.

Arthus obeyed. Then the Redwood tree nymph Timothy waved his hand again and another light portal opened. Again taking Arthus' forearm the Redwood tree nymph Timothy and Arthus stepped through the portal.

They stepped through the portal and instantly were standing beside one of those special Priest wagons that has a huge Life-ore metal tank on it, which carries water from the River of Life that flows by the First God's Tree all over Malon to various clans and villages. This one was brought here to Northern Peaks City because of the possibility of a war.

The Redwood tree nymph Timothy pointed to the top cover of the water wagon and said, "Cleanse the waters in that wagon too."

Arthus climbed up to the top of the large water tank on the wagon. He poured a little water from his glowing holy horn. He noticed that instantly the waters inside this wagon glowed with Life energy. He climbed down and put his arm out for Redwood tree nymph Timothy to lead him through another portal.

They stepped out of the portal onto the top platform above the tall water tower which supplied all the waters into the Northern Peaks City. There on the platform was a metal covering with a circular metal handle that spins open in order to then lift the lid of the covering, swinging it upwards and then laying it back on hinges.

The Redwood tree nymph Timothy pointed at the lid of the covering and said, "Open that and pour into it."

Arthus obeyed, and then closed the lid again. As he spun locked the lid and stood up, the Redwood tree nymph Timothy opened another light portal and took Arthus' forearm and again stepped through the portal.

This time they stepped out onto the water tower platform which fed Great Northern Tundra village. Arthus recognized the same kind of lid and quickly opened it and poured into it and closed it and locked it and stood up again to see another portal, and then put his forearm out for the Redwood tree nymph Timothy, who nodded approval and took his arm and stepped through the portal.

This time when they came out of the portal they stood deep underground in a natural cave somewhere under the Great Northern Mountain Range.

The Redwood tree nymph Timothy said, "The underground river at your feet feeds many of the rivers and streams and springs throughout the Great Northern Mountain Range."

Arthus understood what that meant and quickly poured into the underground river. Then he again extended his forearm and the Redwood tree nymph Timothy took him through another light portal.

This time when they stepped out of the portal they were standing deep underground again, but this was no ordinary cave. It appeared as if this large space had been hewn out of the rock of the mountain and there was a large pool of water located in it.

The Redwood tree nymph Timothy said, "The Ice Wolves have enslaved some captured Dwarvens to build this pool of water for them. The Seer who is using Dark Magic and Dark Ice the War Chief of the Alphas have defecated into these waters and poured the blood of murdered Alphas and others into it and then through Dark Magic they are forcing the Ice Wolves to swim and drink from these waters, which turns their Life energy pack-mind into a tool of enslavement. Cleanse these waters and in the future these waters will not be able to enslave the Ice Wolves."

Arthus pours water from his glowing holy horn into the pool. The brackish waters in the pool glow and the glow quickly spreads out and fills the pool with its glow. Then Arthus extends his arm for the Redwood tree nymph Timothy to lead him through another light portal.

This same process was repeated over and over and over into various lakes, streams, rivers and ponds all over the Northern Tundra and even into waters surrounding the entire northern regions for what seemed like many hours.

"It is time to be back for formation," said Redwood tree nymph Timothy grabbing Arthus' forearm and leading him through another portal.

Arriving again at the barracks, Arthus discovers that only two hours had passed while he had been cleansing the waters with the Redwood tree nymph Timothy.

The Redwood tree nymph says, "As your guide, I will be with you as I have been commanded to be, but invisible to most other's eyes. You too will see me mostly only when I guide you to the waters of Malon, which we must do in secret. There may come a time where you will need me to become visible for others to see, but we must be very careful. If that happens, I will come in a disguise which should sufficiently hide what I am. Only Michael the Archangel, the High King, myself, you, the Creator, and of course the Alda Matriarch, who gave you this quest know of your duty of cleansing. Each morning I will appear to awaken you from your sleep and give you a tiny cake of minerals to eat, and with it you shall drink from your horn which glows. And each morning we will continue to go to cleanse the many waters on Malon. The tiny cake of minerals and the waters from your horn which glows will empower your Life energy and strengthen you as if you slept throughout the night. And each day we will be back before your formation. I am hiding myself from your view now, but I am not gone away."

Suddenly the Redwood tree nymph Timothy, walked over beside the wall by Arthus' bed and became almost invisible. When you look directly at him it appears that you are looking at some kind pattern of a Redwood tree that looks as if it is part of the wall itself. Arthus saw a little bit of movement in the pattern and then felt a single pinch on his forearm.

Timothy says telepathically, "Do not stare at me, or others might begin to pay too much attention."

Chapter 13
War of the North

"Zeck, it is now 4:05 in the morning and we must be in formation at 4:30, so get out of bed and get dressed quick," said Arthus smiling.

Zeck quickly rolled out of bed and stood to his feet, and seeing Arthus fully dressed in his battle dress and armor, said, "Wow, I am truly impressed! You actually awoke before me and are already ready for the day." Then Zeck quickly put on his battle armor and boots and made his bunk up perfectly tight with the four corners creased like they had been taught. He took out a small metal plug and bounced it upon his bed to be sure it would pass inspection.

Arthus meanwhile also ensured that his own bed and locker space would pass inspection. Satisfied with the results, he and Zeck headed out to the battle formation area arriving with only two minutes to spare. The battle formation began and ended within a short amount of time.

As soon as the formation ended Zeck headed to the kennels to take care of his pups. He quickly fed and watered them and rubbed behind their ears. As they were drinking their water, each of the pups were filled with Life energy. One by one they came over in front of Zeck and knelt down on the ground in front of him and put their paws up over their noses and below their eyes. Zeck was very surprised by this action. He stepped back and then sat up one of the big water barrels to further observe his Ice Wolf pups.

"What is going on with you pups today," said Zeck

At the same time all of the pups replied, "We have been given water from the River of Life, which has broken the curses which our parents were subjected to. We are now free Ice Wolves. The Great Spirit has freed us from our bondage. And, in our freedom we gladly choose to serve Him and High King Thureos and will follow your orders Zeck, even to the death if needed."

Hearing the pups speak and say that to him in unison, shocked and amazed Zeck. Zeck said, "If that is true which you have said, I want you each to stand up on your hind legs and spin around three times and then sit back down and again bow like you did before."

At the exact same time all the pups stood to their hind feet and legs, spun around in the same direction three times, and then sat back down, and then bowed themselves down upon the floor as they had done before.

Seeing that the pups all obeyed exactly what he had said, Zeck commanded: "Stay!" Then he left the kennel, locked the gate behind him and ran to find the Captain, Commander of the Clan Urial Great Northern Guard to tell him and bring him to see what is happed to the Ice Wolf pups.

Soon the commander and all of the Clan Urial guardsman that had been working and training the pups met at the kennel with Zeck. They followed Zeck into the kennel to discover that all the pups had remained bowed down on the floor exactly where Zeck had told them to stay.

Going back over and sitting down onto the water barrel, Zeck said, "You may rise."

All the Ice Wolf pups stood up. Then Zeck said, "Turn around and face the commander." And instantly, all the Ice Wolf pups turned around and faced the commander. Zeck said, "Bow down to the commander and to each of your trainers." The Ice Wolf pups all immediately bowed down and put their paws back up over their noses and below their eyes. Then Zeck said, "Now sit up and repeat what you said to me word for word." All of the ice dogs sat up and again in unison repeated word for word what they had earlier said to Zeck.

After they finished speaking Zeck says, "Now, each of you go up to your respective trainers and address your trainers by their names and then walk in circles around them, then bow again before them. And await their command to rise."

All the Ice Wolf pups immediately did exactly what Zeck had said.

The commander and all of the pup's trainers were very impressed by what they seen and heard. The commander said, "I must go inform the High King what has happened to these Ice Wolf pups. Follow me Zeck. I will send you all a holo-message to bring each of your Ice Wolf pups to the war council tent if the High King so desires." Zeck then followed the commander over to the war council tent.

Arthus was already in the war council tent with all the other council members, but again standing at the back like he had the day before when the commander and Zeck entered. "Wait there Boot," said the commander pointing to the opposite side of the entrance at the back. Then the commander went up to the High King and said, "High King Thureos Zeck has discovered a miracle has taken place with the Ice Wolf pups that he and the Urial guard have been raising and training. It is something that I think you and all of these fine War Council Members should see and hear for yourselves."

The High King already aware of what the Redwood tree nymph Timothy and Prince Arthus had been doing, said, "Yes commander, I do believe everyone here in this war council tent needs to see and hear for themselves what Zeck has discovered with the Ice Wolf pups. Have your men bring them here and introduce them officially as we have spoken about before."

When the Ice Wolf pups and their trainers entered the war council tent, the commander yells, "Introducing the first Clan Urial Great Northern Guard Ice Wolf Patrol!"

From the back of the war tent, Arthus observed a very shocked look on most of the council members. He heard many deep breaths coming from almost everyone. The Ice Wolf patrol came up the middle isle and approached the 4D holo-table, which the High King was sitting behind. All of the Ice Wolf pups in unison bowed deeply before the king, laying in a sitting position on the ground, with their front paws placed up above their nose and below their eyes.

The High King motioned to them and said, "You may rise and address this War Council."

In unison all the Ice Wolf pups sat up. Then they all stood up on their back two legs and spoke in perfect unison. "We thank you our High King and honored war council members in the by the power of the Great Spirit, Who in His WISDOM has given unto us great mercy and destroyed all the influences of the Chief Alphas. His great mercy also has filled our minds, hearts, bodies and souls with Life-energy. This Life-energy has enabled us to speak in your common language. We now pledge ourselves into your service our High King and promise to serve and protect all who the Great Spirit with our lives. If you must go to war with the Ice Wolves, we will gladly fight and die if we must, honorably by our Urial guard trainers."

The High King looked at the young Ice Wolves and said, "You are much too young yet to go into battle against the other Ice Wolves. Continue to train your bodies, minds, spirits and souls for the rest of this first year of your lives. After you complete your training you will then be better prepared and much stronger in body. Return to your Kennel along with your trainers. Continue to serve them faithfully and in the future when you are ready then you will join them at their sides as they patrol the Great Northern Tundra and Great Northern Peaks Mountain Range."

The High King said to the commander, "It is time to break down this war tent and bring most of our armies to the front. Ensure also that we leave enough leaders and guards here to protect Northern Peaks City and all who take refuge behind these city walls. Be ready to march in two hours."

Many soldiers were filling their personal canteens from the Great Northern Peaks water supplies, which Arthus had cleansed the previous night. The Cundo Priest came out of the city gate with a special water carrier wagon filled with waters from the River of Life which flows by the First God's Tree where the palace is also located. This is the same wagon, which Arthus had cleansed the night before.

A massive army marched through the Great Northern Tundra along-side a large portion of the Great Northern Peaks Mountain Range. Then they turned and began the arduous march into the Great Northern Peaks Mountain Range towards Tzevaot Peak, the largest and tallest of all the mountains in the Great Northern Peaks Mountain Range. This mountain is nowhere near the outside areas of the mountain range. However, it was up under Tzevaot Peak and its surroundings where Black Ice had his headquarters. Tzevaot Peak Mountain was a massive natural fortress on its outsides. Throughout many thousands of years the Ice Wolves had slowly and meticulously built this area into multiple underground cities. Since taking power, the War Chief Alpha had captured, enslaved and forced many captured Dwarvens and other people's groups into making a lot of military type improvements around the entrances to the underground cities, and even within and around the underground cities. Outside surrounding any natural cave entrances there were several mazes made from messily put-together stone walls and there were also multiple metal gates that served to slow down any military trying to do ground warfare.

Whenever Dwarvens from both reserve guards and regular guards were approaching this area and saw how badly put together the rock wall mazes were, they began to laugh. It looked like it had been intentionally sloppily put together, unlike what Dwarvens normally would do with their joining in on the worship of God in creating anything.

Arthus could see many Alpha Ice Wolves, who had armor and weapons were here and there all over Tzevaot Peak Mountain, and it appeared that each of them had at least a battalion of Ice Wolf underlings that they were commanding. The underlings normally only use their claws and fangs to tear into their enemies, where Alphas can use weapons too. Thousands upon thousands of Ice Wolves could be seen on the sloops of Tzevaot Peak Mountain and upon the slopes of many surrounding mountains just waiting for the command to attack.

Black Ice was supposed to arrive and sit with the war council to talk peace. That was the hope, at least. A guard ran in and announced that a massive black armored Ice Wolf with several other armored Ice Wolves had arrived. Thureos nodded, and then he and the other council member walked out to meet this War Chief Alpha.

Outside stood a giant black Ice Wolf. He was in iron and heavy black leather armor. A small Yelin Skull that had been engraved with evil symbols was adorned on one of his shoulders. He growled and moved

228

with his head. Two of his armored wolves tossed Goran and Dorgan to the ground. They were barely alive as they had been beaten badly and had cuts all over them.

"What is this?" Demanded High King Thureos.

"This is my answer for these traitors and weaklings who wanted me to come and make some kind of a peace deal with you. I am the greatest of all the Ice Wolves on Malon. I will not bow to you or to your armies that came here today! However, you will bow before me, as I remove your head. I will boil your head and place your skull across my armor as a groin protector, so-called High King as I curse you and your God." said Black Ice with a mocking growl.

"You truly want war, so be it," said High King Thureos. Then he motioned to the commander. "Take these two Ice Wolf friends to our healers as I have made a promise to Goran that I will not kill all the Ice Wolves once this war has ended with Black Ice's demise." Looking again at Black Ice, "You have now made your threat clear, now be gone, back into to this mountain fortress and hide yourself behind your Chief Alphas and your Alphas and underlings. Do not worry as it won't be long and I will soon see you and then in the Name of God the Creator and Sustainer of all things your head will be removed from your shoulders. You and any of your Chief Alphas and Alphas who may have been Demon-bonded will soon be dead." said High King Thureos.

Two Clan Urial guards grabbed the two wounded Ice Wolves and took them away to the healers. Black Ice laughed a laugh that sounded like a very weird and Darkness filled twisted growl. He turned and left with his guards. Once he was heading up the path to the mountains, he howled and was joined by a large group of his Chief Alpha Ice Wolves. This group then entered into one of the natural cave entrances through the makeshift maze. It wasn't too long and many war battle howls could be heard.

The war cry howl signaled that the war had begun. Soon whole battalions of Ice Wolf underlings sprang down, heading for the front lines of the Clan Urial lines. Arthus couldn't believe that this so-called War Chief sent his underling wolves to their deaths without even the slightest care. The front lines of Dwarvens moved instantly and used their shields, locking them into an interconnected wall of Life-ore steel. The attacking wolves could not even budge the sturdy Dwarven warriors an inch. Behind them spear-wielding warriors lunched their spears up and over this shield wall and also pushed more spears through each of the small gap holes designed specifically into each of the shields for this very purpose. The entire front line of Ice Wolf underlings were sacrificed in order that the next wave of Ice Wolves might be able to climb up over their bodies and over the Dwarven shield wall.

High King Thureos came out of the war council tent in his full Silver Gold armor wielding Angel Wing. He raised Angel Wing in the air with one hand while he blew his shofar with the other. He was instantly transformed at least double his normal size. "Forward, push them back," commanded High King Thureos.

The Dwarvens, pulled their spears out and then with a very powerful push, threw the dead Ice Wolves back off their shield wall. The Dwarvens stepped up onto the piles of dead Ice Wolves and immediately poked their spears out again from all the gaps in the shield wall like they had previously. More spears were thrown up and over the shield wall and thousands of arrows were shot into the air over the wall and up onto the mountain sides, where the majority of them hit and so many Ice Wolves. The Dwarvens continued pulling spears back, raising their shield wall plowing forward, and then pushing spears again through the gaps. All the while, spearmen and archers hitting their marks. The Dwarvens walked up and over the corpses of dead Ice Wolves without stopping. The snow on the ground was turning red with the blood of so many dead Ice Wolves, and yet so far not even one single man on their side of the shield wall was even wounded. Soon they came up to several small cave openings. The second row of Dwarvens shield carriers came forward. The others broke and moved up the slopes beside each of the cave openings. Soon as Ice Wolves underlings and Alpha Ice Wolves tried coming out from their caves they were met with the impenetrable wall of metal shield and spears blocking their way. These Dwarvens waited, then would move in unison left and right, allowing several Alpha Ice Wolves and Ice Wolf underlings through into the trap, which the Dwarvens and Cundos had setup for them. As soon as they came through the opening, then the Dwarvens behind the two sections of shield would close the gap in the shield wall behind them. The Alphas and their underling Ice Wolves only stumbled directly into several armed Dwarvens and Cundos, who quickly killed them with a single move. An Alpha Ice Wolf had a Dwarven smash into its hind knees with a Dwarven war hammer. As soon as it dropped, another Dwarven with a two-handed battle axe brought it down, cleaving in two through its Alpha wolf skull down into its chest. While other Ice Wolves took spears to all of their sides and chest.

On the mountain sides not near the cave openings, Dwarvens continued pushing forward. There were now clearly three distinct walls of shields, each one following the other up the mountain slopes. Any Ice Wolf Alphas or their underling Ice Wolves that happened to climb over the first shield wall were only met with multiple spears, battle hammers and battle axes. Once the group was killed, the shield welders moved again over and over the bodies of the enemy as they were piling up.

Arthus looked up the mountain from the top of a Dwarven made metal tower that been brought to the battlefield and assembled within minutes after their arrival. The tower was located right by the war council tent. He thought to himself, "So many Ice Wolves lay dead. This wasn't even a real battle, just total slaughter. These Ice Wolves are very strong creatures, but they didn't stand a chance against the well-trained Clan Urial and Clan Arkwright. Suddenly Arthus hears a very loud seemingly twisted howl. He looked up to where the howl came from. The War Chief Alpha, Black Ice was standing out on the very edge of a ridge high up above the first Dwarven shield wall. Five massive Chief Alphas came up next to him and stood right beside him at the very edge of that ridge. All of the Chief Alphas were wearing heavily clad leather armor. Their armor appeared that it was mixed from multiple types of armor and bone pieces. Arthus guessed that those armor and bone pieces were from various victims these Chief Alphas had probably killed. Suddenly, the five Chief Alphas leaped down off of that high ledge and over the first shield wall line and then charged the main forces where High King Thureos and Prince Benroy were standing at the forefront. The five Chief Alphas charged forward, then at least ten Alphas also leaped down from the same ledge following their Chief Alphas. Prince Benroy raised his two-handed sword and charged at one of the Chief Alphas. Behind him several of the Arkwright elite charged in. Prince Benroy sort of dropped and slid under the oncoming Chief Alpha, who had leaped arms and claws outstretched. As Prince Benroy slid under, he slashed his sword, cutting off both of that Chief's hind legs. Instantly King Benroy was back up and moving on to face another Chief Alpha. One of the Arkwright elite soldier's was already bringing his broad sword across the wounded Chief Alphas neck, whose head rolled from its shoulders and dropped onto the snow. Meanwhile a couple of front line soldiers had fallen by some of the Alphas that had followed their chiefs. And, one soldier was killed when a Chief Alpha bit his head clean off.

High King Thureos was facing off three of the Chief Alphas that stood before him in his Clan Armor of Silver and Gold and his helmet with a griffon figure with its wings outstretched. He stood before the three giant Chief Alpha Ice Wolves without fear. He had Angel Wing in his right hand, the Golden spear turned into a long sword, and then another sword appeared in his left hand. Both golden blades seemed to shine in the sun, which shared its light, but not its heat this far north. Thureos moved at speed Arthus never seen. He almost disappeared then was between the three chiefs. One swayed and fell; its head was slashed clean from its shoulders without it even realizing it happened. The swords became a halberd and were with a quick movement Thureos spun Angel Wing around his body, and into the second Chief's side, cutting deeply into its side as the force of the blow seemed to pick up and throw the second Chief far off. It then lay helpless bleeding out on the snow. The third Chief came forward, but Thureos stopped it with an outstretched arm. He had caught the wolf by its mouth, forcing the jaw closed. His hand then picked up the wolf like it was a rag and slammed it back down into the snow holding it fast. The Chief attempted to slash at the High King with the claws of his four paws, which did come scrapping against his armor, but none even left a mark. High King Thureos brought up his spear with one movement and plunged it down through the heart of the wolf, pinning it to the ice. It only yelped, then sort of jerked its legs and died. As each Chief Alpha died their own Alphas seemed to pause momentarily and gave a short howl. When they paused any underlings that they had which remained alive also paused momentarily and gave a short howl. The elite Urial and Arkwright guardsman took advantage of that moment to advance on the Alphas closest to them. Many Alphas were killed during that pause and howl.

Arthus continued to observe and mentally absorb the battle scenes that happened in front of him. Only minutes had went by, but to Arthus this battle seemed to last very long. A howl burst out from the left and below him. He spun to discover that Goran had emerged from the healing tent. He stood in leather and cloth armor, his staff at his side; the battle came to a standstill. He had been given a drink of the water that comes from the River of Life that flows beside the First God's Tree. It was also from the same wagon that Arthus had cleansed the night before. Goran seemed full of Life-energy. He walked, now fully healed, onto the battle field. He pointed his clawed paw finger towards Black Ice.

"Is this enough for you, father? How many of our people already lay here in pools of their blood. If you still wish to fight, then I have no choice but to directly challenge you myself and hopefully save what lives of our people that I can," said Goran.

Black Ice growled then leaped down. As the massive black Ice Wolf walked onto the battlefield, no one stood in his way as the two meet.

"You welp dare challenge your War Chief," growled Black Ice.

"Yes, to save our people from your blood lust, I do challenge you," said Goran.

"Fine then, I have no son," snarled Black Ice.

Black Ice pulled a chain from his back. One side had a clawed blade. The other was a one-handed ax. He whipped the chain around with a mastery that surprised even Arthus. The chain whipped forward, but Goran knew his father and stepped far out of the way. He brought up his staff. His eye glowing with Life-energy the color emerald green. Suddenly roots shoot forward from the Tzevaot Peak Mountain. Black Ice slashed one of the roots with his ax, but another one wrapped around his chain arm and locking it to the ground. Black Ice growled as another root grabbed and lifted his ax out of his hands before he could hack at it. Another root shoot forth, piercing Black Ice in the side. The massive wolf howled out in pain and slashed down with the other clawed paw, successfully cutting the root that was deep in his side and gripping and ripping it back out of himself. He limped backward, trying to hold the blood from spilling out of the wound. But Black Ice wasn't done. He bound forward faster than Goran expected and slammed the hilt of his ax into the back of Goran's head with such strength that it sent him flying and landing in the snow several feet away. Goran didn't move. His body laid face down in the snow. Black Ice howled as he began heading toward Goran to finish his kill. Before he took two steps High King Thureos stepped between him and Goran.

"Goran, I hope you survive, but for now as High King, I must face all threats to my world and its people," said High King Thureos. Thureos lifted up Angel Wing and pointed the now spear towards Dark Ice. "I gave you every chance for peace and to evolve past your basic nature, but you even are willing to murder your flesh and blood for your blood lust and power, then you have no place on Malon," shouted High King Thureos. Angel Wing glowed brightly and more brightly. The sky turned dark and clouds swirled around, and the wind started to blow. High King Thureos body grew two more times in size than Arthus had ever seen before. He began to glow brightly. Angel Wing glowed an even bright golden, almost as if was alive. Thureos walked forward. The ground shook; his eyes were filled with a golden color. Then with one slight movement, his legs bulged and sprang, and he launched himself covering the three meter distance between himself and Black Ice in a twinkling of an eye. He grabbed Black Ice's massive Ice Wolf face with one hand and with a face up open palm on the other he Life-energy launched them both up in the sky many meters above the giant trees. And then grabbing the Black Ice by the tail with the open hand. From the still up in the air, he throws the War Chief Ice Wolf back down to the ground slamming the great wolf headfirst into the ground. Not even waiting for his body to bounce, High King Thureos flies back down and kicks the Ice Wolf in the chest. The blow shattered bone and sent the Black Ice flying back into the side of the cliff face. Before Black Ice's body could even fall from there, High King Thureos threw Angle Wing which flew and pierced through the wolf's stomach and pinning him upside down from the rock faced cliff a meter below the high ridge where he had been earlier. Black Ice howled out in pain, and blood poured from its mouth and the hole in his stomach. All the Ice Wolves, and all of the Urial and Arkwright forces stood in amazement and shock. Black Ice growled but couldn't get himself free.

"I will never accept you as my Alpha; you and your people will be crushed under our claws and fangs," cursed and growled out Black Ice.

"No, father," said Goran. He was limping over be held up by Dorgan.

"You have failed. The High King has shown you how powerful the immortal king is and the difference in your Dark powers compared to the powers of Life, which only the Great Spirit provides. You are no longer the Ice Wolves' War Chief Alpha as the High King has beaten you in single combat. He has broken you and your hold over the Ice Wolves," said Goran.

"No! I will not be stopped. My people will break forth from this frozen hell, and we will tear all others to sunder, then I will rule over this world. That is my destiny," said Black Ice.

"I am sorry, father, but for the sake of our people, that future you want can never happen," said Goran. He eyes glowed brightly with Life-energy and he pointed his staff. Several roots shot forth from the cracks in the rock cliff behind Black Ice, piercing through his body. One shoot forth wrapped around his massive black Ice Wolf neck and tightened until there was a snap as the roots completely severed Black Ice's head from his body. The mighty beast was no more. Goren closed his eyes and howled. Tears flowing from his eyes. "I loved what you once were father before you bonded with the Demon horde called, *Legion, for they are many,* and then began your greedy quest for Darkness, power and death. Forgive me, father. I wish you could have seen reason and followed a more peaceful path," said Goran.

High King Thureos allowed his own Life-energy power to disperse, shrank back down to normal size, and then turned to go meet Goran and Dorgan.

"Goran, what you have done shows me your resolve, and if your people stand down and come to the peace table, I am willing to hear you out. But first, your people must decide who is your new ruler," said

High King Thureos. He turned and walked back, raised his hand, and Angel Wing shot forth from the cliff out of Black Ice's body returning to its master's hand. Thureos returned to the front lines and had the forces pull back but kept up their defenses. The day had been long. Twenty of Clan Urial had fallen, but over a thousand Ice Wolves lay out in the snow there blood turned a good mile of mountainside red. There were many more wounded Ice Wolves that had been shot with arrows or met a spear. Thureos entered the tent, removed his helmet, and sat on a throne style chair in the command tent. Arthus walked over to bring him a glass of wine and a platter with bread and salted meats.

"Ah Arthus, thank you. Come... sit in front of me, and tell me what you have observed from seeing war for the first time. Do not hold back. I want to know what you really think from this experience?" asked Thureos

"I feel sad for the Ice Wolves that died because of Black Ice's greed. I think deep down, before he bonded with the Demon horde called, *Legion, for they are many,* he only wanted to bring his people prosperity and a chance to live in places that are not so frozen and barren. I have heard that this area has very little food or even little wild life for which to hunt, so his people were probably starving. I am sure that the Demon horde had deceived him, making him think that by bonding with them he could then have all the power he needed to force enslavement upon other people's groups. Black Ice thought if he could win against us and bring his people out of the frozen north, they have plenty of game and land. But his lust for war and power over others became his undoing," said Arthus.

"Yes, my grandson. Never forget this: War is never a good choice if given any other means. The lives that are sacrificed are never worth it. Also know this: Power through blood always ends in more blood, and then it crumbles due to one's fears of losing that power. Now we must wait, pray and hope that Goran can bring the other Ice Wolves under his banner. If he can do this, then we can sit down with other Chief Alphas and see if this can end with Black Ice's death and these senseless deaths of so many Ice Wolf underlings that you witnessed on the battlefield today. Peace can find a better way for us all. Perhaps, the battle is done for today, or maybe there will be some skirmishes for several more days. Go now and get some sleep. I too am so exhausted after witnessing all of the senseless deaths. I will call for your father and for you if and when any message is sent from the Ice Wolves," said High King Thureos.

Arthus rose, bowed, and went out to find his tent where he quickly laid down. He stared at his leather bracers thinking of Jade and all that he needed to write to her about. Arthus quickly realized Zeck was already asleep, but his tent was not quite far enough away from Arthus' tent as he was snoring away. Arthus got up and motioned to one of the night watchman.

"Go over to the infirmary tent and ask the priest to give Zeck a drink of the healing water that the priest brought with him. Perhaps that water can heal Zeck of his snoring," commanded Prince Arthus.

Arthus then went back into his tent, laid down inside his bedroll, and closed his eyes, hoping the next day bring peace and less bloodshed. He was disturbed a little by the conversation that took place with the night watchman, the priest, and Zeck.

Zeck practically yelled, "Water, how is River of Life water going to stop my snoring, and who gave the order?"

Arthus laughed out loud and yelled, "Just drink it Zeck and go back to sleep! Maybe it will heal you and we all can get some sleep tonight."

Hearing Arthus's voice, Zeck laughed out loud and said, "Oh of course your Majesty, Prince of Malon needs his beauty sleep. Just give it here and we shall see if this is a good prescription for snoring. Zeck swigs down the cup of water and instantly is filled with Life-energy. More than he ever felt in his life before. He then turns and goes back into his tent and lays down and sleeps a dreamless sleep without snoring.

"Arise Sir Arthus, Anointed of the Alda Matriarch," commanded the Redwood tree nymph Timothy who appeared at Arthus' tent at 2:00 in the morning. Arthus opened his eyes and quickly climbed out of his tent, expecting to see the Redwood tree nymph Timothy. Timothy remained invisible this time because there were night watchmen and other guards marching and keeping guard. He grabbed Arthus forearm handed him the very small cake of minerals and said "Eat this and take a drink of the waters from your horn which glows." In the dark of the night with only border torches lighting up the night, Arthus felt the very small cake more with his hand then he could even see it. He raised it to his mouth and quickly swigged it down. Timothy led Arthus around to the back of a large wagon, then opened the light portal and they both stepped through. They stepped out to have Arthus pour water from his glowing horn into several supply barrels filled with water that was located high up on the mountain. "These barrels were taken from water sources before they had been cleansed," said the Redwood tree nymph Timothy. There are many like this in the caves surrounding this area. Timothy touched Arthus' glowing horn and it glowed slightly brighter, just enough for Arthus to see as he worked quickly and quietly. Then they continued to step into and out of portal after portal after portal as Arthus poured the water from the horn which glows into various watering troughs, watering bowls, and many, many barrels. They also stepped out of portals at various ponds hidden within natural caves and caverns all over the mountain range. Some were home to wild Ice Bears and wild brown bears and wild black bears. There were even hidden hot springs that needed Arthus to cleanse their waters. They continued to do this also all throughout the underground Ice Wolf city for what to Arthus seemed like hours, but again at exactly 4:00 in the morning Arthus was back in front of his tent.

Three days later, Goran and Dorgan, and several other Alphas in armor came down the Mountain with a White flag showing their surrender and wish to talk peace. Goran meet with all the Clan leaders, including High King Thureos and Prince Benroy, all sat around the holo-table to hear what the Ice Wolves wanted to ask. Arthus and Zeck also were in the tent to observe the talks and learn how the leaders try and reach a way to move forward in peace.

"We welcome you in the Name of God and in our names, Goran, and Dorgan once again to this war council meeting. I understand you have become High Chief of your Ice Wolf people, so congrats to you, and I hope that this will help bring our people to a quick and peaceful resolution," said High King Thureos.

"Thank you. I come before you all today in total surrender. All Chief Alphas and Alphas and their various Ice Wolf packs will follow my command. I am so terribly sorry for my father, who in his pride and greed and hunger for power has brought on this tragic war and has caused so many to die needlessly. I have decided that I cannot and will not demand or ask for anything, but for you to fulfill your promise to spare the remaining of my people, with the exception of any who seemed to be Dark in their Hearts and Minds from getting involved in Dark Magic. There are several Chief Alphas and Alphas who had been using the Pack Mind in a corrupt way. Those that yet remain alive, due to their great crimes we have locked in a prison cell. Now, we throw ourselves at your mercy and pray to the Great Spirit, Who you call God the Great Creator and Sustainer of all things, that you will allow us to earn your trust and over time to make amends," said Goran who then kneeled down deeply onto the ground and placed his front paws up above his nose and under his eyes.

Dorgan then nodded and kneeled deeply placing his front paws above his nose and under his eyes before High King Thureos, Prince Benroy and the other clan leaders.

"Please stand, young High Chief Ice Wolf. And, you too Dorgan," said High King Thureos. Then addressing Goran the High King says, "You have shown me your desire to end the bloodshed. I understand your people have been starving here in this far Great Northern Tundra and Great Northern Peaks Mountain Range, so if the other chiefs are willing, we love to help bring your people help in the form of relief with emergency food supplies, and livestock. Along with the livestock I will assign trainers to come and help train your peoples how to raise their own livestock. We have some technologies that have shown real promise in development of sustainable underground farming. The farming technicians that are showing progress with this, will come and help you setup your own underground sustainable systems. That way in a short amount of time your underground cities will be able to provide enough food sources to sustain your livestock and your Ice Wolf people too. I do however expect that if your father or any of his Chief Alphas, have any slaves, that those are brought here and freed from their slavery. We are aware that in the past there have been enslaved Dwarvens that have been forced to dig tunnels and such for your Ice Wolf peoples. In the future if you are in need of the help of the Dwarvens to expand your underground cities, it is important that you and your peoples end the practice of capturing and enslaving people to do forced work. We will all gladly help each other on this planet to ensure everyone has what is needed without needing to force anyone into slavery. Does this make sense to you Goran?"

"Yes our High King. I will ensure that your wishes in this regard are immediately handled, said Goran.

"Have our priest come into the war council tent and offer a cup of water from the River of Life to each of our new friends," commanded High King Thureos.

The Cundo high priest came into the war council tent carrying a couple of large mugs filled with water from the wagon which he had brought with him from the River of Life and handed one to each of the Ice Wolves, who nodded and drank them quickly. Their eyes immediately glowed with Life-energy.

The High King then said, make sure if you have any wounded Ice Wolf underlings that they also get treatment in our healing tent and that they too get a drink of this water that comes from the River of Life that flows near the First God's Tree.

"Thank you again kindly our High King. This River of Life water is certainly a gift from the Great Spirit, which brings Life-energy to all who drink it," said Goran.

"Now seeing how these Ice Wolves have surrendered, I think we should agree to give peace a chance here," said High King Thureos.

Most of the chiefs agreed except the Yelin Elder, who snarled at the thought.

"I still think we should wipe them all out while we have them at our mercy," stated the Eder Yelin.

"No, I will not murder a race of living beings because of your old blood feud," said Thureos.

"I think we have all suffered over the years by the Ice Wolves. Many of my kin and those of the tribes have long hated the Ice Wolves and their raids. But, if High Chief Goran can bring a true peace for us all and end once and for all the death on both sides. We Dwarvens of the Great Northern City welcome the Ice Wolves as friends," said Maddlynn.

High King Thureos rose up from the table.

"If your Ice Wolf people are up to the task and truly want to discard their basic instincts to kill, steal, and enslave, and ready to evolve and join us to work together for all the good of Malon, becoming Clan Ice Wolves of Malon, then we will all help you in any way that we can," stated High King Thureos for all to hear.

"Yes, thank you, my High King. To help bring my people as a whole, they need to know they are not starving for one, and we do want to be able to grow here in this specific Northern Peak Mountain. My people have asked if I could rename this mountain from Tzevaot Peak to Red Fang. This is due to my people's blood spilled in this senseless war. We never want to forget that greed and violence will only get us more blood. We would like the help of the Dwarves to build Red Fang into a true home-like their city. I will ensure all slaves are freed as you have said."

The High King said, Tzevaot Peak, means *God's Armies, or Hosts of God's People.* And, sense the armies of the Black Ice, were so needlessly sent to their deaths because of his greed and killed by the Armies of Malon, who are all part of God's Shield, turning the white snow covered ground red with blood on the sides of this mountain, it seems fitting that the name may be a changed into combination of these meanings and your Ice Wolf Clan will also carry this name: Great Spirit's Red Fang Army Mountain. Your Clan will be known as the Great Spirit's Great Red Fang Clan. Does this sound appropriate to you Goran?"

"Yes! Oh Yes! That is a highly honored name! It will help all of our Ice Wolf peoples to realize that we are under the rulership of the Great Spirit and remind of the cost of failing to follow His guidance in our lives. Thank you High King Thureos."

Then Goran went over and deeply bowed before Elder one of the Snow Folk, *Yelin*. He said, "I beg you to forgive the Ice Wolves and help me to end the blood feud between my people and your people. I beg you to please show us their ways of cuddling and how to raise livestock."

Not waiting for a response, he quickly got up and again stood over in front of the High King. We also know there a path nearby that leads

241

to a gully near the sea. It's usually a bit icy and dangerous, but fishing can help a great deal in bringing in food, but we are not natural fishermen, so we need training in many areas. My proposal is that you will allow me to send two Alphas, ones that I completely trust to work with your clan. I hope to do that for other clans as well, because as the Alphas travel around and learn from different clans, the Great Spirit's given abilities with our Life-empowered Pack Mind will allow me and others to learn and share what we learn. As my people grow in knowledge and skills that will help my people to advance far faster and help us catch up with the rest of Malon. I will gladly provide wolves to train with your Urial and Arkwright Guard. They will become a great help guarding and patrolling some of the most dangerous areas. They will answer to whomever the High King decides. As you get to know them and see their abilities, you will see that they will be great troops in your armies. If we can help in any other ways, just let me know," said Goran.

"I see, Goran, you can go. I will talk this over with the clans to get their vote, then we shall tell you our decision," said Thureos. Goran and Dorgan both bowed and left the tent, and went to meet up with their guards.

"So we heard that the Ice Wolves want and need us and we all heard what is needed to help them become equal active members of Malon. So now, what is each of your thoughts? Asked High King Thureos.

"I, the head of Clan Gearhead, would love to help. This will bring the Ice Wolves as allies and would secure much of the north. If they truly help the guards patrol and guard the trade routes, that would be a big boon," said Maddlynn.

"I do not trust them right now, and neither will I nor my Snow Folk any time soon, but I do trust in you my High King. If you really do believe that these Ice Wolves want only peace and a positive common good future for their people and ours, then we will trust in your judgment. If all they wish is to learn how to herd goats, or some other such hardy northern livestock, then with utmost caution, I and my Snow Folk will help teach them. They must agree to remain where they are assigned and agree to remain under the strictest guard. It will be a long time before we see that any of their kind can be trusted to come anywhere near our village. If ever either of the two Alphas that shows up to learn from us harms any of my people, then they will be put to death without mercy," said Yelin Elder one.

"I know you spoke about some new underground sustainable technologies for growing foods. I don't know much about that yet, though it sounds quite promising, if we can work together somehow with the scientists and engineers to make that kind of thing actually work for them. I do know that it is way too baron and much too cold of a climate to grow any real crops up above the ground here. I am aware that clan Gearhead has had some success with raising livestock underground, but that comes with all sorts of health issues to resolve. Like closed loop biofuel plants, air filtration systems, water purification systems, and feed. I am happy to provide trainers that can talk them through many things. Also, you know that I always need more hands working out in the fields, and there is always need for more patrolling and scouting the forest roads. I am sure that Ice Wolves once well trained and trusted can be very helpful, so if you my High King believe they can be trusted, we welcome a couple to the Arial Valley," said Grag.

"I trust in you, High King. If you believe these Ice Wolves can become disciplined warriors and scouts, then Clan Urial will agree," said Jacob Clan Urial Weapons Master and leader. Arthus had only met Jacob a few times. It was said he trained all warriors in combat and weapons in the Academy.

"I follow my father and High King so that Clan Arkwright will like always follow," said Prince Benroy. Then another stood, Arthus didn't recognize her. She was a tall and slender, Ignole woman. She had long very white – white hair.

"I, Eden of Clan Raphial agree this be a great opportunity to study the Ice Wolves and this Life-energy pack mind first hand, and to see if these beast-people can become truly a productive force for us all. So Clan Raphial will follow the High King," said Eden.

A final hand shot up holding onto a mug. "Cheers! Clan Raziel will always follow our High King. He's never run us astray before, and I doubt he will now. So I say we love to have the furry beast learn to fish. We need Clan Gearhead's Engineers to help us design and build

243

some boats that can work with the icebergs an all up here in the frozen waters," said Decor. Decor was the head of the clan who mostly lived on islands out in the Great Ocean. They were made up of hardy, strong Cundo who fished and crafted boats and even with help from Archangels had created vessels that could dive deep down into the sea, where they could avoid the surface storms, and often catch sight of many giant, and sometimes more dangerous creatures. The Great Ocean was a massive body of water that covered most of Malon. On Malon, there was only one enormous continent. The rest of the planet was made up of huge seas, which actually did touch each other, but where they touched it was amazing how the waters did not just mix together, but turned again towards its own sea area. There were many small Islands here and there, but the sea was no picnic, and it was said there were creatures that swam deep in the seas large enough to swallow hundreds of ships in one bite. Arthus shuttered at the thought. Arthus wasn't sure if those stories of those large creatures were tall tales told by fisherman, or if there was truly creatures that enormous living under the ocean.

"Alright then, I take it we are ready to vote then," said Thureos. He then placed a box down on the table, wrote on a piece of paper then put it in the box. Then the rest followed; after a couple of minutes Thureos rose took the documents and counted them out of the six clans, and Yelin the Yelin was the only one who voted no.

"Then we have an agreement, so be it. Guard bring in Goran," said Thureos. A couple minutes later guard came in, followed by Goran.

"We have talked it over, and a majority voted to accept you and your people. We will be sending a group of Cundo, Ignole, and Dwarvens to help build up your mountain home. Also, we are taking two Alphas under guard to each of the clans to learn how to help improve your lives through fishing and trade, herding, and whatever they can. We will also take several Alphas and their pack to learn to become scouts and warriors in Clan Urial. But know that your people compared to most of Malon, have a far shorter life span, so I am not sure you Goran will live to see your people become a true part of our world, but you help start it. That is itself a great thing which you do, and I will make sure your name is well known as the one who saved his people," said High King Thureos.

"Thank you all. You have no idea what this means to me, and those who are like me wanted to stop all the bloodshed. This day will be far remembered! In the distant past many of my people only lived for around fifteen to nineteen years. But with the help of gaining in Life-energy and with proper diet and exercise some of our people have actually lived as much as a hundred years. Which still must seem almost sad in comparison to your lifespans reaching thousands upon thousands of years. But I can be sure to make the dream continue on from generation to generation. One day my people will stand shoulder to shoulder with all of Malon," said Goran.

"So be it now you may return in five days we will come to take away those who wish to go and learn, and we will bring the ones who will help build up your home here. Everyone seems like all has been taken care of. The ships are waiting to take you all back to your clans. So go with my blessing and tell your clans what has been decided and help them see this is best for all of Malon. Thank you all," said High King Thureos. He bowed, and the Clan Elders bowed some talking amongst themselves left to head back to their clans.

"Prince Arthus, come on up here and sit down with your father and I and tell us what you think of today's meeting," said High King Thureos?

"I hope it all works out. I saw the bloodshed, and I hope that will be last time we have to needlessly kill that many Ice Wolves, or ever go to war with any other on Malon," said Arthus.

"I am glad you see the wisdom in our decision. I would like you to stay here with Goran and learn a bit from them for the rest of your month, which should be just over three weeks. Then you can stay one night again with Drake and Chrystal just so you have a chance to say your goodbyes and gather your belongings that you have been safekeeping there in your attic bedroom. Then I take you to see both the Desert folk and those who live on the sea, but you won't be staying there. I have decided it's time for me to take a far more personal training and teaching role until you come of age to attend the Academy on Elemental Island. So after we see both the desert and sea tribes, you be back in the palace under my personal training regiment, so prepare yourself for it will be far more than anything you have done so far," said High King Thureos.

Arthus bowed, then left to find High Chief Goran and let him know he was to join him.

"High Chief Goran, there you are," called Arthus.

"Ah, young Prince, how can I help you," asked Goran? Arthus explained what his grandfather had told him.

"I see; well, once you gather your things, I will be outside the gate waiting with my guards. I was already told several miners, and Dwarven crafters are ready to join with us too. I understand that their equipment will be shipped in before tomorrow. If it's true about the effectiveness of the Dwarvens as builders, we should have most of this Mountain built and turned into our true home," said Goran. Arthus nodded, then ran off.

Arthus wanted to see Zeck and grab his things. Soon as he reached his and Zeck's tent, it had already been packed, and Zeck was standing smiling.

"Welp, yes... guess this is it, my friend. Been glad to have you, and I'll make sure my parents know you're returning only for one night in three weeks, but don't worry about them, or your good dreams and marriage tusk, we'll be sure to keep that safe for you." said Zeck smiling. He reached out and grabbed Arthus's arm just behind the elbow.

Arthus grabbed ahold of Zeck's arm just behind the elbow smiling broadly and said, "Thank you, my friend. Please do tell Drake and Chrystal thank you for me from the bottom of my heart, and I do plan to see you all in three weeks. Before we know it, since we both are about the same age, we will attending the Academy together, so let's plan to also meet up there," said Arthus. They both unclasped from each other's arm. Arthus grabbed his tent and gear and departed, heading to talk with the commander.

"Captain Urial," said Arthus.

"Yes Boot! Well, it appears I shouldn't really call you Boot, though it is a term of endearment to all my young lads, like yourself, who have come to work and train with me and Clan Urial Great Northern Guard. I heard you have been reassigned to go with Goran for the next three weeks. So, without you needing to ask, I will send your personal belongings that you have locked in our storage back at our barracks area over to Zeck's parent's house, so that you can pick that up all from there when you get back. I know that I did not get much time to get to know you Boot... I mean Prince Arthus, but you do seem like a fine young man that takes orders and does not cause trouble. The High King wants you to spend some time with High Chief Goran. And, the High Kings command is always ours to obey. It is obvious that the High King trusts your intuition, wisdom and judgement. I will assign my two very best scouts to be your personal guard for the next three weeks. I know that they will carefully watch your back while you are at the Ice Wolf's underground city. They will bring their night vision equipment with them too. Now...is that your reason to come see me, or was there something else you needed?

"Yes Sir, that was it commander. I do thank you for not treating me any different than your other boots in the short amount of time I spent with your guards. And, I will return this here Great Northern Guard uniform all cleaned up for your next boot to use when I get back in three weeks to Northern Peaks City, said Arthus.

Chapter 14
Ice Wolf Underground City

High Chief Goran was waiting for him and the others to help guide his new allies deep into their underground fortress city. They went through the makeshift maze area which then led to a path. They continued climbing up along the steep pathway that led up the mountain cliffs. Soon he was standing on the edge of the cliff ledge area that earlier during the battle the Chief Alphas and Black Ice had leaped from. Looking down from this vantage point one could see just how much of battle field below was littered with dead Ice Wolves and how the snow was splattered with so much blood. There were soldiers carrying stretchers with any living wounded into both the infirmary tent and into the war council tent, which was converted into a make-shift infirmary for the many - many wounded. A large amount of the forces of Malon were departing, while many still remained. Goran stood looking out over the vast Tundra with tears in his eyes as he took in the scene.

"Let us go. I will show you my people's home," said Goran as he wiped the tears from his eyes.

Arthus and at least a hundred Dwarvens and Cundo followed Goran as he entered a natural cave opening, which had a main tunnel carved deep into the mountain. Arthus observed as they walked deeper and deeper into the mountain that there were several makeshift barriers made from piles of rocks that they had to climb over. Then all along the sides of the tunnel here and there were small piles of glow stones, which helped to light the way. They continued deeper into the mountain until the tunnel emptied into a vast cavern. All around the outside walls of the cavern there were Ice Wolf dens carved into the rock faced walls. In front of several of the Ice Wolf dens were spikes with large Ice Wolf skulls stuck onto them.

Arthus asked Goran, "What do those spikes with the Ice Wolf skulls represent? I see they are not in front of every Ice Wolf den in here."

Goran replied, "Prince Arthus, those spikes with skulls represent the fact that the one who lives, or lived in that wolf den is, or was a Demon-bonded Alpha. Part of the rights of passage into becoming a Demon-bonded Alpha was to challenge and kill an Alpha Ice Wolf, and then take their head, boil it, engrave upon its skull and then spike its skull for display in front of their den. There are dens that you will see later on today where the Demon-bonded Chief Alphas have racks and stacks of Alpha Ice Wolf skulls in front of their dens. We know part of why they did this was to instill fear in other ice Alphas and other Ice Wolves. However, I have ordered that all such displays be moved into the hall of memories. It would be inappropriate to completely destroy these as they are a real part of our history. However gruesome or evil these items may seem, we must never forget the depths of depravity and Darkness that Demon-Bonding causes. I never want my people to repeat this kind of evil. If I just destroy them, then future generations of Ice Wolves would not have any concrete way to observe and remember and learn from the mistakes of our past leaders.

Goran led them further into the mountain down a very long tunnel. This tunnel opened up into another vast natural cavern. In the center of this cavern was a large highly polished stone raised circle area with a huge natural stone altar built up onto its center.

"What you are seeing here, is my own meditation circle," said Goran. He continued, "I come here daily to pray and meditate and seek the Great Spirit for wisdom and guidance. The Great Spirit, Who I believe your people call God, and Who other peoples of Malon refer to as the Great Creator, or the Great Creator and Sustainer of all things, or the Ultimate Creator, first communed with me here and led me down a path of righteousness for the sake of my people. I have tried to honor the Great Spirit and so I built this large altar area here. You will notice that the natural stone altar has been fashioned much like the natural stone altars that are in front of God's Tree Seedlings in the God's Tree Seedling Circle near the Snow Folk's box canyon entrance to their village and near other Clan villages all around Malon. Anyway, I polished the surface of the floor here in order to reflect the roots of First God's Tree, and/or the roots from God's Tree Seedlings that are sticking down from the ceiling of this cavern high above our heads. I place a stone bowl upon that altar there to catch the melting snow or rain water that seeps in from the mountain above following all those God's Tree roots along down to where they finally drip down and land inside of the bowl. I was a rather young Ice Wolf when I first discovered the dripping water coming down into here. I used that same stone bowl way back then to catch the water. And, when it was almost full I took a drink from the water. Because that water had been touching the roots of God's Tree, I was instantly filled with Life-energy and began to recognize the Great Spirit's desire to commune with me. I began to share from this bowl of water to several of my friends. Dorgan's pack was among the first that I had secretly shared with. There are several Alphas and a few Chief Alphas that I had secretly shared this water with as well. None of those that I have shared this water with have become Dark in their hearts or minds. In fact I noticed that none of them was ever even really controlled by one of the Dark Magic of the Seers. I believe there is something special about this water that helps to prevent blind obedience to any Dark influences, but I cannot be certain without conducting some good scientific research, but I chose on the side of caution. I have already ordered all the Dark Alphas and Dark Chief Alphas to be placed in the prison pit and I have securely locked them down in that. I am awaiting the High Kings orders to see if we will have to kill them. I will show you later where that is."

When Arthus was alone finally with his two Urial Guard Scouts he ordered them, "Go back out of the mountain the way you came and bring to my quarters several barrels of the water from the wagon that the high priest had brought from Northern Peaks City. As you know, that water has been taken from the River of Life that flows by the First God's Tree where the palace is located in God's Forest. I want those here to see if we can help Goran."

Arthus did not tell them that this water had been farther cleansed by him using his glowing horn. Arthus did not even try to explain why he actually wanted those barrels of water for Goran.

The Urial Guard Scouts correctly guessed, "Oh, Prince Arthus... are you planning to give these barrels of water to Dark Ice's Alphas and Dark Ice's Chief Alphas, who were involved in the Dark Magic mind-control twisting of the Pack Mind, and who are now being held in the prison pit? Do you really think that is a good idea? That water fills anyone who drinks it with Life-energy. Those Dark Alphas and Dark Chief Alphas would gain a lot of strength from that water and might be able to break out of their prison pit, overthrow the security guards and possibly worse."

Arthus, just smiled and said, "Just do as I have commanded you to do. I will make sure that all additional security measures are in place before we send those barrels with River of Life water down to the prisoners.

When the barrels of River of Life water came Arthus and Goran and several hundred heavily armed security took the barrels and lowered them into the prison pit. The prison pit did not have any other sources of water, so sooner or later each of these Dark Alphas and Dark Chief Alphas, who had swam in the Nagas infected waters and then learned about Dark Magic would be forced to take a drink from those. Arthus knew the moment that they took a drink their ability to use mind control over any other Ice Wolf would end. Now it is just a matter of waiting until their thirst forced them to drink.

Two and a half days went by before the youngest and smallest of the Dark Alphas took a drink from the River of Life water. Instantly he was filled with Life-energy and in the next instant his ability to use Dark Magic mind-control over the other Ice Wolves ended. The Life energy gave him a great amount of strength, which he could feel in his body. In his new found strength he foolishly attacked one of the oldest Dark Chief Alphas, who was much older, and way better trained than the Young Dark Alpha was. The oldest Dark Chief Alpha quickly leaped to the side and then lunged back at the younger Dark Alpha ripping its throat out with one swift bite. The ordeal with the younger Dark Alpha seemed to weary the older Dark Chief Alpha.

"The fool! Why did he throw his life away here in this prison pit by attacking me? We really need to be working together if we are ever to escape from here and enact revenge." As he walked away shaking his head, he goes over and takes a drink from the water barrel. As soon as he had taken a drink he was instantly filled with Life-energy. An instant later his ability to use Dark Magic mind-control over other Ice Wolves was taken away. He did not know that this had happened to him though. The Life-energy replenished his strength and began to quickly heal his body from the long day.

Over the next three days each of the Dark Ice Wolves had taken a drink of the River of Life water and had lost their ability to use mind control over other Ice Wolves, while being filled with Life-energy. As they felt a great boost to their energy and strength, they enjoyed that feeling. They drank over and over and over again until they were all very full of the River of Life water. The barrels were starting to run dry. The Dark Chief Alphas started blaming the younger Dark Alphas for drinking too much of the water and not conserving it. A huge fight broke out amongst the Dark Alphas and Dark Chief Alphas and they all killed each other.

Within a few weeks the Clan Gearhead engineers and scientists and Clan Arial had worked together and setup an underground hydroponic and aquaponics and aeroponics system that incorporated glow stones for the plant lighting, fresh water circulating through pipes and automated drip systems into various types of planters and rectangular baths lined with synth-blend liners. There was a large circular pool cut out into the rock floor and lined with a synth-blend liner. Inside of this was a rather large sump pump. Several other giant pools were also cut out of the rock floor. These also had been each lined with the synth-blend liner. Everything was filled with fresh water from a mountain spring. When no one was looking Arthus poured a little of his glowing horn water into the circulating water of this system. After twenty four hours live fresh water fish were added to the large pools of water where they went. A spongy like rock and wool mixture was added to some of the rectangular plant baths and various plants that were high in proteins and vitamins for food staples were added. Several baths had various lettuces, kales, and cabbages floating on trays above the circulating water. There was a huge swirl filter coming off from the giant fish pools and a huge bio-filtration system added into the system right before the water would go back into the sump pump tank. There were many, many vertical towers of plant starts. The underground air space was heated to a steady temperature of 75°-79° F, and the water temperatures flowing throughout the system were kept at 69° F. The fish tanks were large enough that the water actually cooled in those to about 60-65° F.

The Dwarvens had mined out a huge other underground circular space and in that space a giant rabbitry was designed in order to house about ten thousand domesticated giant rabbits. The giant rabbits were shipped in from other areas on Malon.

Arthus's three weeks were up very quickly and he headed with his two scouts back to Northern Peaks City to stay one last night with Drake and Chrystal and Zeck. Before he went to their house he grabbed a large metal pallet and brought it over with him and sat it outside. After a delicious dinner of ram stew and dumplings he headed up to his room and organized and packed up all of his belongings.

Arthus was extremely careful to wrap and package his mammoth tusk and his shofar in a way where these would not get broken. He also packaged his goat horn from the Yelin Snow Folk. As he carefully put these things into a well-designed crates for shipping, he recalled how he had carefully wrapped and packaged and shipped their matching pieces to Jade. He had been so worried that they might get broke in transit that he had requested Captain Urial the local Clan Urial Guard commander to "Please assign a patrol guard to accompany the packages and hand them personally to Jade, Grag and Shelly on his behalf." He recalled the shocked reaction of the commander at that encounter and later thought perhaps his assignment to clean the poop out of the kennels was directly related to having made that request before.

Arthus mumbled to himself, "After having seen the guards and patrolmen out there on the battlefield fighting for their lives in that senseless war, I feel ashamed for ever having made that request."

The next morning Maddlynn's Welcoming Guard were already standing holding the pallet up with their straps when Arthus came out with his belongings from Zeck's, Drake's and Chrystal's house. Zeck followed Arthus out of the house and said, "Goodbye Arthus. See you at the Academy if not sooner."

"Goodbye Zeck. You have been a good friend! I am sure we will get together soon," said Arthus. Turning to Drake and Chrystal, he folded his hands like in a prayer and said, "Thank you again in the Name of God and in my name for your incredible hospitality you have shown to me. I will appreciate you and honor you for the rest of my life."

Arthus first headed to Captain Urial, the commander of the local Clan Urial Guard. When he arrived he handed him his loaned uniform, which Arthus had cleaned while packing. Then he said to Captain Urial, "I want to apologize to you and your men. After seeing your men fighting on the battlefield with their lives at risk, I realized how utterly foolish I was for ever having made the request to you a year back when I asked you to send one of your patrol to Clan Arial Valley to personally hand my packages to Grag, Shelly and Jade. It really was a foolish and inappropriate request that I made of you. Please forgive me for having done that.

Captain Urial smiled, "Well yes it was foolish, and yes it was inappropriate, but I knew you was our young Prince, who probably did not know any better. I obeyed your request and I informed the High King of your request. He told me to make sure to have you clean the poop out of the kennels to humble you a bit. I can see you are humbled, and I truly appreciate that you came to apologize to me and to my men. That battle scene really must have helped you grow a little wiser. I trust you learned something very valuable from all your learning here and you will continue to grow in favor with God and all of the people's on Malon. Now get out of here and head to Clan Arial Valley.

Arthus then headed to the cargo shuttle loading area to catch his shuttle going southbound towards the Clan Arial transfer platforms. He was soon in his cargo shuttle and on his way.

Over the next several months the Ice Wolves' mountain was really getting an upgrade. The Dwarvens mined out another huge area and built an underground goat farm complete with air filtration systems that went clear out to the outer cliff face of the mountain. One powered filtration tunnel was bringing fresh air in and one tunnel was pushing dirty air through multiple layers of filtration, which would need to be replaced from time to time. The floor of the goat area was raised up and gapped so that the goat's feet could stay dry. Under the floor was a large enough space that a full grown Ice Wolf could easily walk around in it on two hind legs without bumping their head on the beams that held the floor up. The rock walls in the goat area had drinking troughs carved into them. These were made so that the water could be easily changed out daily.

The Dwarvens mined out an area up near the top of the mountain for a huge underground water reservoir. Then they piped the water from a natural hidden spring up into that and provided a way for this to overflow naturally back down to the same place where the natural spring had fed a short creek and a waterfall. The water was only diverted away for a short amount of time each day so that they did not destroy the natural ecosystems of the water flowing downstream.

As more and more of the Ice Wolves drank of the cleansed waters they were filled with Life energy and empowered against any Ice Wolf using mind control over them. The cleansed waters did not remove their ability to mentally work together in unison and unity, rather this enhanced their Life-energy pack mind abilities. The Life-energy also helped them to have no desire to be trying to learn Dark Magic, to become Seers and such.

Chapter 15
Blood Sands

The wind started to get warmer on Arthus's face as they rode in the High King's hathi howdah on the back of the Golden Griffon. They observed the scenery below as they flew up and over the Great Southern Mountain Range and were headed now into the Red Sand Sea, or as many people referred to it as the Blood Sands. Arthus remembered reading in the Library of Holos that this place was named after the blood-red colored sands of this desert.

Arthus says to his grandfather, High King Thureos, "This Red Sand Sea below us seems like it goes on and on forever."

High King Thureos smiled and replied, "Much of the region south of the Great Southern Mountain Range of Malon's giant continent is a vast desert. However, before the continent's southernmost edge the desert ends abruptly. Then there is a fairly wide band of land filled with tropical rainforest jungle trees and plants. Many species of animals and even some peoples choose to live out their lives in that tropical rainforest. The rainforest and mangrove swamplands are highly dangerous places, just like the swamplands east of Harmony City, but they also contain great benefits for all the peoples of Malon, like peat moss farming that can only take place within the swamplands. There are many various wild healing herbs, as well as many wild spices that can only be found hidden deep in the rainforest. Right along the edge of the oceans in many places the jungle turns into a fairly large mangrove swamp area which has many large and small reptilian creatures, as well as a variety of fish and birds."

The High King raised his hand and motioned to the Captain who was leading the Golden Griffon flock that they are to turn a bit to the west now. They have been flying on their Golden Griffons all night.

Arthus started thinking back over their very rushed day as he had left Zeck's, and boarded the cargo shuttle and then transferred his belongings to the large cart and rode on the Yaule to get to the Clan Arial village, where Jade was waiting for him at the Golden Griffon platform. He felt he barely had time to take a short walk with Jade over to her house where he ate lunch with Grag and Shelly and Jade. Jade made sure she showed him where she had placed her ornate mammoth tusk high above the head of her bed. And she gave him a gift of a tough leather covered carrying case which she had made with her own hands. The case was built specifically to hold and protect his shofar, as it really is supposed to be carried on a person and not kept as an ornamental piece in one's bedroom. The inside of the leather case was lined with very soft cashmere wool. Arthus knew that his shofar will fit perfectly into this case. On each end of the ram horn shaped case were metal swivel bucklers. A finely crafted leather shoulder belt was attached to those bucklers. Jade put it over Arthus' shoulders and adjusted the shoulder belt. She also showed him that she had made one for herself that matched the one she gave him, with the exception that hers was shaped in the opposite direction as their shofars were made out of a matching pair of rams horns from the same ram. She then showed him her goat horn that she had been wearing every day since it had arrived. Arthus quickly poured a drop from his glowing horn with the water which was given to him by the Alda Matriarch into Jade's goat horn. As he knew this would farther cleanse the water that was inside of Jade's goat horn. As soon as he did that Jade's goat horn glowed for a moment. Jade had actually not noticed that her horn had glowed for that moment.

"What did you do that for?" Asked Jade.

Arthus smiled and said, "I just needed to add a little more River of Life water into your goat horn." Arthus did not explain farther.

After lunch Arthus headed out to the small family sized shower room and quickly took off his heavy clothing that was making him sweat in the heat of the Clan Arial's farming valley. He took a quick shower and then put on his regular work clothing and tunic and came back outside to find that Jade was waiting there for him to come out.

Jade walked with him back to the platform and before he could walk up the steps she grabbed him by the arm turned him towards her and quickly kissed him. It was more like a peck kiss, but it did land on his lips. Then her face blushed bright red. Arthus' face blushed red too.

Jade quickly said, "I really wanted to thank you for writing to me almost every day. I missed you so much, and I looked forward to reading each of your holo-messages, and..."

Before she could finish her thoughts Arthus grabbed, hugged and kissed Jade on the lips and he did not stop with just a quick kiss. Jade then wrapped her arms around Arthus and then without thinking, slightly lifted up her right lower leg. Jade's slip on shoe on that right foot fell off her foot onto the ground behind her.

Jade's father, Grag and the High King Thureos were standing up on the platform and witnessed the kiss.

"Alright you too young love birds. It is time for Arthus and I to go," said High King Thureos while raising his eyebrows and having a chuckle in his voice. He added, "We have a long trip ahead of us."

Grag said as Arthus passed by him, "I already warned you if you stole her heart, then you will have to do right by her. Now obviously, the one is true, so in the future I expect you to make the other true too!"

Arthus with a huge smile on his blushing face, bowed his head to Grag and then kept walking towards the High King's Golden Griffon.

Arthus, the High King, and Cundo assistants quickly packed up two additional Golden Griffons besides the one that had the High Kings hathi howdah on it. A Captain of one of the many Urial Guard Units was also on a Golden Griffon and he was in the front of the flock. Two additional Urial Guards on their own Golden Griffon's flanked them, one on each side. The flock flew towards the Great Southern Mountain Range, with its beautiful silver peaks that divided the entire Clan Arial valley from the desert. Trade routes snaked their way through the many small valley gaps between the taller silver peaked top mountains and along-side of river cut canyons and creeks that meandered all through these mountains. By following the trade routes they didn't have to fly up into any of the colder parts of the mountain range. Arthus was glad to pass low enough he could see the traveling traders who use Hondargs as pack animals to carry their goods from the sands to the valley and so forth. Hondargs were big animals with a prominent horn that came out of their face and looked like rigid armor plates along their back that came to four large spikes on their tails. These creatures were raised out in the Red Sands Sea and were a great way to pack huge loads of trade goods due to their incredible size and strength.

Many deadly creatures made the Red Sands Sea, also called *Blood Sands*, and the rainforest and mangroves their home. This is why Clan Urial had a significant presence in the desert sands. Many members of Clan Urial are regularly used as private bodyguards for the traders. That was besides all their members who served in the military and constantly patrolled the various trade routes on Malon. There was always a need for them to help keep the more deadly animals away.

Arthus observed many groups of Clan Urial riding in both directions on Valkers, which are large flightless birds. These Valkers have red-colored feathers and could run up to about seventy five kilometers an hour. They have two very powerful legs and their feet have four frontal toes and two back toes that each have very deadly claws. The top of their heads have a natural heavy external bone armoring that they often use as a ramming type weapon. Their extremely sharp and powerful beaks were also nothing to joke about. These giant flightless birds were often found in wild flocks all over Malon in different regions. However, each region's flocks seems to have its own distinctive colored feather features. They are very dangerous when raised completely in the wild, however when they are found and collected up while still in their eggs and then hatched, the babies as they open their eyes, visually bond with and can safely be raised by trainers as domestic ground mounts. They do make great ground mounts to run back and forth between Red Sands Sea, *Blood Sands* and Arial Valley through the mountain passes. They are used like this in many other trade routes too, but not on the Northern Tundra or in the Great Northern Peaks Mountain Range as it is much too cold there for them. Clan Urial even add additional armor to some of their domesticated flocks and then use them to help fight in some combat situations.

Arthus spotted a massive skeleton in an area that they flew through. He pointed to it and asked his grandfather, "What is that massive skeleton?"

High King Thureos said, "That skeleton is from a long-dead Wenbe. Wenbe are massive vertebrate worms. They are among the most deadly of all the wild creatures that can be found in the ground and often above ground here in Malon. Clan Urial with Clan Arkwright often hunt them to make sure none could grow to full size as that one had obviously grown to before it died. If allowed to grow after just a couple of hundred years, they could swallow entire towns in their massive grinder-like mouths. A Wenbe mouth housed rows upon rows of opposite spinning dagger-like teeth. The Dwarvens often use the baby ones to help quickly carve out new tunnels but then kill them when they start growing too big. The largest one I have ever heard of was one found by Dwarvens deep under the Great Northern Peaks Mountain Range. That Wenbe was around a hundred feet long and forty feet around. Luckily the thing was sleeping when they happened upon it. The Dwarvens filled the natural cavern around where it was sleeping with explosives and blew it up before the thing could wake up to become a huge problem for their mining operations."

After a long while of flying west over the Red Sand Sea, *Blood Sands* they turned south again. In the southernmost distance that he could see there seemed to be what Arthus thought might again be a mirage. They were flying in that direction for a while and it did not seem to get any bigger. Arthus allowed his mind to wonder again, thinking about the kiss he had with Jade. He touched his leather bracers and smiled.

"Arthus, over there is Alkas City," shouted High King Thureos as he pointed to a large, almost circular area that was a little farther to the south.

Arthus looked and a little before the dessert ended and the rainforest jungle began was a large oasis city built into and around massive sandstone bowl shaped structure. Around the sandstone bowl shaped structure the sand had been mounded up like a sand dune embankment on all sides. And outside of the sand dune embankment there was a donut shaped pond that completely encircled the sand dune embankment and the sandstone bowl shaped structure. Arthus knew from the holo-books he read that long ago, even before Arthus's father was born, the Alkas were a huge and highly dangerous problem for many of the peoples groups on Malon.

The town was coming into view, so Thureos motioned for the captain to lead them down to the landing area. They came into a landing on a road that circled around several meters to the outside of the donut shaped pond waters of the oases. There was a large raised platform there on the opposite side of the road where they landed. On the backside of the raised platform also encircling the road around the pond there are several large stables. Besides stables that had been built for Golden Griffons, there are stables that had been built to house Hondargs, and stables for housing Valkers. Each of the stables were quite large. A few Cundos and Ignoles ran out from a guard shack to begin unloading the two additional Golden Griffons they had brought with them with their cargo carriers fully loaded. The Captain that had led the flock greeted them.

Before they had disembarked from the High King's hathi howdah, the High King used this one-on-one opportunity to give Arthus a quick history lesson. He said, "As you are aware from your holo-readings Arthus, I was forced long ago to bring all of the armies of Clan Urial and Arkwright and completely wipe out the Alkas. You see the Alkas were huge insect creatures that were blood red in color, perfectly matching the color of the red sands. They had massive pincher like teeth and a poisonous spear like tail stinger. Their entire bodies and legs and even their pincher teeth had a very strong exoskeleton armor. Their massive pincher teeth could cut right through metal like it was butter. They were a constant threat to the people living in or around the Red Sand Sea. Their insect armies often swarmed through the Great Southern Mountain Range, killing and eating on their way. The Alkas central nest was discovered hidden down under that giant sandstone bowl shaped structure surrounded by a sand dune embankment. The sandstone which is mostly hiding under the sands had been meticulously carved out by the Alkas. There were many tunnels and cavernous openings and such hiding deep under the sandstone bowl like structure, and hidden deep under the water in the oasis and even out beyond this city hidden under the sands surrounding this whole area. At the base of that outer circular sand dune embankment is a wide donut shaped oasis pool. That oasis pool appears to have been carved out of the sandstone underneath it, and it has a natural spring feeding its waters."

High King Thureos continued, "After the Alkas were exterminated, Clan Urial made the entire underground nest area into their own military base. Soon after that traders came, and then a city grew around the outer ring of the oasis. It became a great location to raise and dry various spices. The blood red sands of the Red Sand Sea are used in glass making and in making various pottery vessels. As the city grew it really became almost a natural trading post, where many spices, other made things, and where various fish and sea creatures caught in the sea could be taken throughout Malon for trade."

High King Thureos continued, "At some time in their history, the Alkas had carved out a large tunnel that led under the sands and under the jungle floor all the way to the sea from within their nest. The rainforest jungle and the mangrove swamps are very difficult and very dangerous to navigate from above ground to reach the sea. The traders prefer that Alkas tunnel much more than trying to deal with all the deadly creatures in the rainforest jungle and those that live in the mangrove swamps. Once the Clan Urial guard had discovered that huge tunnel led out to the sea, they built a massive metal and rock fort out and around the other end of the underground tunnel where the seashore has a beautiful natural bay. Then they built a very long T-shaped sea wall and added multiple boat docks behind the sea wall in the bay. Ships of various sizes could come and go from that sea port. Many fishing ships bring their catch to that port area and then trade their catch for various kinds of foods, and other things needed by all the small fishing islands that doted the Great Sea. That port has really become essential for all of Malon."

"Ok Arthus, now it is high time that we go meet up with Zeel Urial here and get his report about how things in the sands and jungles and mangrove areas are going."

Zeel is the second in command of Clan Urial. Arthus recognized the name, Zeel Urial as being one of the most famous Cundo Warriors of all of Clan Urial. Arthus remembered reading in the Library of Holos holo-books that many years ago, there had been a combat tournament, and Zeel had come in the first place, beating even the best of Clan Arkwright.

High King Thureos walked over to the Guard Shack and spoke to a couple of Clan Urial Guards, who immediately bowed to the High King. Both of the guards pointed in a direction out of the city and apologized to the High King on behalf of the commander. Thureos burst out laughing and said, "Captain Zeel Urial has forgotten we are coming in today and has left on a hunting patrol for a large Wenbe."

Returning to where Arthus was unloading some personal items from behind the High King's hathi howdah, he says, "Well now it appears that we have some free time on our hands Arthus. Why don't we go and check out the markets and see for ourselves how the local people are doing," said High King Thureos.

"Really, alright! I was actually wanting a chance to see the market as I heard so much from various traders in Harmony city about this place, said Arthus."

"Yes, it one of the biggest outdoor Markets on Malon and one that everyone needs to see at least once in their lifetime," said High King Thureos.

A rather old Ignole man who had been standing a ways off to the side started waving and ran up to them.

"My High King and Prince Arthus, my name is Asher Urial. Captain Zeel put me in charge of this landing area here today. So, I just realized that it is my responsibility to welcome you and then be your guide for the time being while Captain Zeel is out with his patrol hunting that oversized Wenbe. Prince Arthus here might be interested to know that I am regularly one of the Malon Academy instructors," said Asher.

"Well, thank you, and glad to meet you, Asher. I think I have heard of your name as one of the most talented Elementalist instructors. And, I think you are not far under Jacob in the Academy if my memory is right," said High King Thureos.

"I am glad you heard of me. Yes, Clan leader Commander Jacob is the Master of Arms of the Academy. I am one of the three Master Elementalists of the Academy. I am the Fire Master Elementalist to get to the point," said Asher

"Thank you again, but, we better get going. I sure do want to have time to quench our thirsts at your local tavern. And, I want to check out and show Arthus around the Open Air Night Market before Captain Zeel returns and we have to get on with doing business," said High King Thureos. He then said, "Oh, and we need to know where we are going to be staying tonight as we need to drop off our personal gear there first. After that, then we can head around enjoying this rare opportunity for some down time."

Asher bowed again and then turned and led them off.

Arthus is carefully observing everything he sees and hears. From up here on top of the platform Arthus looks across the road at the donut shaped oasis and sees that there is one fairly narrow metal and stone foot bridge with two fairly tall heavy metal security towers standing to the left and right of the entrance to the foot bridge. Between the two towers were heavy iron gates that raise up and down for added security. The foot bridge led over the donut shaped pond and up onto the ridge of the giant sandstone bowl like structure. The inside side of the sandstone bowl shaped structure were fairly wide steps that led down into the center of the sandstone bowl. In the very center was the opening that led down into the military base. The opening had a heavy metal spiral staircase leading down into the underground military base.

They left the donut shaped pond road and entered the city by going through the iron gates between two massive sandstone guard towers. Most of the city was made from sandstone and brick. However, some buildings were made out of hardened mud pressed outer walls, which were obviously mixed with the red sands of the desert and some kind of vegetation.

Arthus asked Fire Master Elementalist Asher, "Where did the builders collect the mud and the vegetation from in order to mix with the red sand to build the mud pressed wall houses and buildings? I already noticed that vegetation is very rare in this desert area. Although I did see some big yellow and green spiky plants and a few giant palm and coconut trees located at only one spot along the edge of that entire donut shaped oasis pond."

Asher said, "That is a very good question Prince Arthus. Obviously it had to be brought here from somewhere else. The closest vegetation from this area is to the south in the rainforest jungle and beyond that is the mangrove swamps before reaching the Great Sea. I'm sure if they collected those from either of those locations, doing so was mighty dangerous. It is also possible that dirt and vegetation could have been brought here across the Red Sands Sea from the Great Southern Mountain Range, then mixed with water to turn the dirt and sand and vegetation into the mud pressed houses and buildings. Whichever is the case, it had to be an arduous undertaking?"

Arthus continues with quiet observation: Other than the circular road way that led all around the oasis water filled donut shaped pond, the buildings of the city were located between perfectly straight streets. There were some young Cundos and Ignole children playing out on many of the city roads. Older people could be seen sitting in small groups everywhere any shade could be found. Most of the Cundo and Ignole here appeared as if the sun had made their skin of their faces a much darker shade of color than the Cundos and Ignole from the other side of the Great Southern Mountain Range. Everyone they saw here wore rather thick robes and hoods made from thick wool strand and with some kind of heavier fiber material blended between the thick wool strands. Arthus was surprised that they wore such thick material in this heat. They were covering up as much of their skin as possible. Arthus looked down at his gear. He wore hard leather armor but it had silk inner lining and silk hood. His pants were mainly just made of some cloth and leather. It was very hot out, but his clothing was made in a way that allowed airflow which helped keep his body relaxed.

Arthus was enjoying the city; it was lively but peaceful at the same time. As they walked along he smelled something was being cooked that smelled sweet and spicy. There were many other smells, some good and some that really were not at all pleasant. Arthus guessed that the very bad smell was coming from a sewer line that may have some technical problems. A thought came to his mind about the engineers that had designed and built the biofuel plant which was located a good ways down-wind from the Clan Arial farming village.

Arthus said, "My High King, perhaps we should see if the city here needs help from the engineers that designed and built the biofuel plant a good ways down-wind the Clan Arial farm village."

High King Thureos smiled and said, "I see you are thinking with wisdom from your learning these past two years. I will certainly relay that suggestion to Captain Zeel and to the City leaders here.

They started to hear the shouts of the Market place where people were shouting out about their wares and so many people were walking around and even crowding around some outdoor and some indoor stores. They passed by one side street which led to a secondary tunnel entrance of the former nest where a Majority of the living houses and Clan Urial main base was. Here again along this side street were two very tall heavy metal towers and an iron gate that raises and lowers in between the towers for added security. Arthus could see a security guard was on top of each of the towers and another one was standing in a guard shack behind the gate. Continuing on up the road they soon came to a three-story sandstone building with a sign of a mug on it. Asher led them into the building. This place is called Alkas Inn. Inside the main room was a man sitting behind a desk, then to the right, the space opened up to several round tables filled with people laughing, drinking, and talking about different things. On the far wall was a counter where a Dwarven ran back and forth, giving out drinks and taking orders to a cook in a back room.

"Welcome, Asher. Who do you bring into town with you," asked the man behind the desk?

"High King Thureos and his grandson, Prince Arthus will need your best inn suite for the night," said Asher.

The man almost fell backwards out of his chair. Then jumped to his feet and bowed deeply, "Sorry, my High King, I didn't recognize you. I am the innkeeper here. I will make sure that we get you a two-bedroom suite ready for you as soon as possible," said the Innkeeper.

"Thank you! We want to give your city a good look around before we come back for the night. Can you take care of our gear and get it safely into the room when it is ready?" asked High King Thureos.

"Yes, certainly you can take your gear into my back office area back in there," pointing his thumb behind him. "And I will be sure to keep your belongings perfectly safe, and then have it moved to your rooms once I know that they are ready for you. I do hope you have a great time in our city my High King," said the innkeeper continuing to bow deeply.

High King Thureos smiled and said to the innkeeper, "No need to bow deeply here. A slight head bow is kindly appreciated. It brings less attention, when no attention is desired."

"Of course, of course," said the innkeeper who stood up and then bowed his head slightly over and over. The innkeeper then quickly goes over into the main doorway of the tavern and restaurant area and motions to a big burly Clan Urial Cundo who was standing by the main doorway. "Hey Todd, you must stand guard at my office door to be sure that the High King's and Prince Arthus' gear are kept safe. And then you will need to ensure to guard the door outside of their suite once their gear gets moved into there after I make sure their rooms are ready for them."

The big burly Clan Urial Cundo, Todd came over and stood guard outside of the innkeeper's office door. High King Thureos and Prince Arthus placed their gear into the office and then left the inn and headed back towards the city's open night market. Soon Arthus could smell once again a mixture of different spices and other things from the marketplace. Before he knew it, they were in a fairly crowded Open Air Night Market. Hundreds of square and rectangular tent covered topped booths were setup in a huge sandstone and brick paved area. Each of the booths had people selling everything imaginable. There were booths with beautiful rugs, booths with embroidered tapestries, booths with clothing, booths with pots and pans, booths with various serving and eating utensils and dishes. Some booths had fine jewelry, including gold and silver necklaces, bracelets and finger rings of all sizes. Some booths had various animal furs. There were booths that had different kinds of live animals for sale. Others were filled with different things out for trade, and more than one shop had its doors wide open. He could see shops with fantastic clothing, and some had different statues carved out of bone and metals. One shop that caught his eye was a local blacksmith with armor and weapons out on display. The open areas had food staples, some with freshly cooked meats and other smells that made his mouth water. He could see many elder Cundos and Ignoles and even some Dwarvens sitting around smoking pipes and chatting under any shady place they could find. A couple of buildings had mug signs that marked them as other taverns. But the one he wanted to see was the spice shop. Thureos smiled. Knowing what Arthus was thinking, they walked around to one of the far ends of the market; there was a large building, doors wide open inside was vials of different powders and sacks of salt and other strangely colored powders. A Dwarven with a red beard and no hair was inside.

"Well, if it ain't me High King, come again to see my wares and see how we here have been doin' me guess?" Asked the Dwarven with a grin.

"Hail to you good Fagor Dwarven Master of Spice and Head of the Salt Mines here in blood sands," said Thureos.

"Ya always welcome. It has been a bit since you last came around our fair city. What brings you, and if my guess is right, this fine young muscular lad be Prince Arthus?" asked Fagor

"I am showing Prince Arthus around the Blood Sands, but we are not staying long. We are also heading out to the Great Sea to visit some of the island fishing towns. Then we will take a ship back up and around the western ocean then up the rivers all the way to Harmony city," said High King Thureos.

"I see, well me Prince, what ye think of me humble shop here? I bet your nose never smelled so many wonders anywhere else on Malon is me thinking," said Fagor.

"Yes, the smells coming from your shop was the first thing that hit me when we entered this city. I have never seen so many different kinds of spices in one place. They have spice shops, nice ones in Harmony city, but your shop blows them all away," said Arthus.

"Well, ain't that the nicest thing I heard from anyone but your grandpa, me High King. I got some sample bags for traders to use. Why not take that with you and try some of the different flavors with the food you get around town. Just don't use too much of the red hot chili powder as that can be serious hot spicy stuff even for us Dwarvens," said Fagor.

"The High King said you are the Head of the salt mines? I saw a lot of salt when I worked on the farms of Arial Valley," asked Arthus.

"Ah yes, we trade much salt with them of the valley to help keep meat for many months. One of our biggest export trade products we have here in the blood sands is salt. Salt is rare in most places on the continent, but there are great sums here in blood sands if you know where to look. We Dwarvens know our minerals, and some of us know a great deal about various plant species. Going around where most folks would never go for finding wild rare edible plants that we collect roots and all and then carefully cultivate using the best scientific methods and engineering technologies we Dwarvens have ever created. Then we take care to dry the parts that need drying out to make some of the best spices on Malon. Farming salt is just one of our specialties as you are aware, and like my mining and crafting brothers, what you see around you here is my very best efforts and creations for the Ultimate Great Creator that all Dwarvens pray to as we go about our crafts," said Fagor.

"Yes, I know I spent a year working alongside Clan Gearhead in the Great Northern Peak Mountains. Their abilities to craft and their honest dedication to join in the great music of creating with the Ultimate Great Creator are a beautiful thing to behold. The sheer rhythm of all the processes of creating is incredible. I dream that I too will continue on the path of my destiny and faithfully participant in the creative rhythm of God the Creator and Sustainer of all things. I see excellence in so many things that the Dwarvens do, and I hope that God always sees excellence in me and in what I do, both now and in my future," said Arthus.

"Ah, so you met Maddy and her Dwarvens. Me clan up north there is a very hardy bunch of Dwarvens. That is nice you spent time working there with them. It been far too long since me been up there. Maybe one of these days me must join a trading group to go see how me clan be faring. Me have a couple of kids working up there ya might a met one. Me eldest, Emon as he be loving to tinker with exploding powders and such things," said Fagor.

"Yes, I am great friends with Emon, and yes he's still up to his old tricks and giving Maddy a hard time," said Arthus with a smile. "The first time I met him, he had blew some powders up in the lab. The last time I saw him he had helped my friend Zeck build a new prototype projectile weapon and he figured out a way to make a hand throwing stick shrapnel grenade with a six second delay fuse. The projectile weapon has a lot more engineering work to figure out, but that exploding throwing stick shrapnel grenade weapon won him a recommendation for Silver Thorn Knights. That is one mighty dangerous weapon too. You should be real proud of your eldest son, Emon! That's for sure!" Declared Arthus.

"Well now Arthus, we've been here enjoying our down time and our visit here with Fagor long enough. It is about time to see if Captain Zeel Urial has come back from hunting with his patrol," said Thureos.

"Well, good to have seen ya again me High King Thureos and Me young Prince. Glad to hear me eldest son, Emon doing so well and his working hard and earning a recommendation does this old Dwarvens' heart good! Me glad to hear of me kin. And, make sure you come by soon, me High King Thureos. Next time ya here, me will be taking ya to me salt farming mines to see how things are looking, me make sure," said Fagor.

They both waved and headed back through the market, stopping to grab some cooked meats and other fresh tropical fruits that can only found in the Blood Sands. With the samples of the spices, Arthus tried them on the local foods. Some were great, some not so much. The Dwarven didn't lie about how the red powder was far too spicy. It burned Arthus's tongue so bad he actually dunked his head into a whole bucket of water with his mouth wide open. Seeing Arthus do that in an attempt to wash away the heat of the red powder spice caused High King Thureos to burst out laughing.

They left the market and walked back through the city towards the gate that they had entered when leaving the donut shaped oasis area.

As soon as they arrived at that gate, a tall, dark-skinned Cundo man in rugged leather and silk armor with a hood covering his bald head stood in front of other such dressed Clan Urial Guards.

"Prince Arthus, this is Captain Zeel Urial second in command of Clan Urial," said Thureos as they walked up. The man turned and bowed deeply as he saw them walking up to him.

"It is a pleasure to meet you, young Prince Arthus, and always good to see you, my friend and my High King. How are things going in the north?" asked Zeel.

"The north is getting along so far. The Ice Wolves have shown their willingness to change for the better. I was impressed how many of your clan came to the battlefield up there so quickly. It showed me how well you have been training the Clan Urial while your Commander, Jacob has been busy attending to his other duties at the Academy," said High King Thureos.

"Thank you! My clan has worked hard to be ready for anything, anywhere if called on. I will make sure all the captains of the clan hear your praise, said" Captain Zeel.

Chapter 16
The Wenbe Hunt

Well, I am about to head out one more time; we have a massive Wenbe to hunt. We returned to get re-geared and if you wish to join us, be good for the Prince to see how we on the sands take it down," said Captain Zeel.

"Hum, not a bad idea. I haven't been on a Wenbe hunt in so long. It will be great to see if you have come up with any new techniques with which to bring one down," said High King Thureos.

"Then it's settled. Men grab some extra gear for our High King and for the young Prince here as well. Be sure to get two more Valkers from the stables! We are going on a hunt with our High King and with Prince Arthus," yelled Zeel. A couple of Zeel's men ran off to do as ordered. Soon one of the guards brought Arthus and Thureos a large spear-like weapon tied to a thick metal cord. He handed him two weird-looking gloves and some boots with spikes on the bottom. The gloves had two circular gears sown into the tops, and the cord was fed into the gears, and then a hardness was strapped around Arthus back where the cable went around and into another device that was on his back.

"Now, let me Demonstrate how these work," said Captain Zeel. He pointed the spear-like weapon towards the upper levels of the wall and clicked a button. A high tension spring shot forward and instantly the shaft of the spearhead comes shooting up. The spearhead at the tip of the shaft slams into the wall and pokes itself fairly deep into the upper side of the wall. Just below the spear's head is a metal loop, which had a cord tied into it. That cord ran on down through a heavy metal loop at the back of Captain Zeel's heavily armored gloved hands, down along his arm armor through other loops and into a special high speed spring tension spool device that was strapped onto Captain Zeel's back. Captain Zeel then hit a switch on his hardness, and the gears on his hands spun. The device on his back instantly retracted the extra cord as Captain Zeel was pulled very quickly up to where the spearhead had just entered the wall. With ease, Zeel flipped over, landing one of his feet against the wall and then pulling the spearhead free from the wall. Then landing on top of the upper wall. From on top of the wall he gave a deep bow to Arthus and Thureos.

"Well, I do see clan Urial has come up with some new tricks since last I came this way, said High King Thureos smiling. He then added, "I do think Captain Zeel here really likes playing with his shooting spearhead gear and showing off to his High King and his Prince Arthus. What do you think, Arthus?"

"Ya, that's cool; what are these things," asked Arthus?

"I am glad you like them. These are a new little thing the Dwarvens came up with to help them to climb cave walls very quickly. I witnessed them using them the last time I was up in Great Northern Peaks City. Anyway, I thought if I might modify its use, then it could help us to climb up onto the larger Wenbe with far more speed than how we had been doing it all by hand," said Captain Zeel who had repelled back down from the top of the wall.

"Yes, I really can see how these high speed spear climbers would help you in getting on top of the Wenbe, making for much quicker take downs when you hunt," said High King Thureos.

"Well, we head to an area where you can get a couple of practice using it, then we head to where the patrol is keeping the Wenbe in wait," said Zeel. The guards brought out two large wagons filled with explosive barrels and some unique crossbows with combustible material put onto the bolts. One of the Wagons also had a massive crossbow on it. Both were pulled by Hondargs armored with an extra layer of metal armor. Arthus looked at the Valker he was riding and was excited. He never rode one, but how different would it be from the Yaule or the Griffons, he wondered. The giant bird had a saddle on its back and had a metal faceplate where the rains were tacked into. The faceplate was also being used to protect the bird's eyes and face from kicked-up sand. He placed his foot in one of the saddle's stirrups and kicked his other leg over and into the other stirrup. The bird was used to be ridden and didn't make any protest. His bird was a dark Red with black lines going down its back. He thought the beast was a pretty beautiful creature. Soon everyone was geared up and ready. Arthus pulled part of the turban he was wearing over his face and pinned it like he did when they flew the Griffons over the sands to protect his face from the sun and sands.

"Alright, everyone here we ride," said Captain Zeel. He kicks the side of the Valker, and they were off at a run. Arthus noticed that the Valkers were far faster than the Yaule and the best part far smoother ride. Dune over dune they went. Finally, they hit an area where there were some giant cliffs, and it was here that Captain Zeel had them spend a few hours training with what Captain Zeel called the high speed climbing and repel gun. Once Captain Zeel was satisfied that both Prince Arthus and High King Thureos were very familiar with using it, they rode on. Less than three hours and they came to a group of Clan Urial Patrol Guards. There was a fairly massive Wenbe that was only a couple of miles from the trader road, which is why they had to bring this vertebrate worm down.

The Urial were riding Valkers around and around the beast, making it quite unhappy but making sure it didn't go any closer to where travelers would be. Zeel halted the group getting ready to set up the attack. The patrol had three massive crossbows with large thick metal wire cables which would be drilled at one end into large stones that were also brought with them. These stones would slow the Wenbe even keep it from diving down into the sands. The plan was to have the large stone restrict the Wenbe from behind. One wagon with the explosives would ride out in front, getting the worm to chase them. The others would use the Repel guns to get to the top of the beast and use large spears and other smaller explosives to wound the creature. This would cause the Wenbe to open up its deadly high speed opposing spinning teeth jaw where the more explosives are then dumped into its mouth and set to explode once inside. This would cause devastating damage to the Wenbe, and then they could quickly kill it if it wasn't dead already.

"Not a bad plan. We used to have giant very sharp metal spikes jammed into the cliff walls not too far off the ground, we would dig a ditch to jump and or fall down into right before the sharp tips of the barbed metal spikes. Then we had to get the Wenbe to chase after us towards the sharp barbed metal spikes, we would jump down or fall down into the ditch as the Wenbe would crash itself into the sharp barbed metal spikes. Being pierced upon those barbed metal prevented them from escaping and then we just cut them to pieces. But, that was very dangerous to the team trying to get the Wenbe to chase them," said High King Thureos.

Captain Zeel nodded and said, "And, it still is very dangerous for the ones being chased! Luckily we have learned and we no longer have to jump or fall into a huge ditch or get impaled along with the Wenbe on sharpened barbed metal spikes."

They all went to work. Soon the group was ready, and Arthus was put onto the cart with the explosives. They would be prepared; one of Clan Urial Dwarven Guard Warriors was in charge of making sure the explosives were ready. The only thing Arthus didn't like was the fact that when the worm ate the cart, so would be the Hondarg that was pulling the cart. But, currently that loss couldn't be helped, until they can figure out a better way of dealing with these massive highly dangerous creatures. The two others would repel up around the open mouth just before it bit down. He was a bit nervous at that, but he slapped his face and focused on the job at hand. Soon the group heard the Wenbe coming after the decoys Zeel and Thureos were upon its back, stabbing down into a couple of the things, small eyes or whatever they were. Arthus couldn't tell. It was coming on fast; the Dwarven nodded to Arthus. They got ready Arthus and the others pointed the repel gun to the right upper side of its mouth. It sounded like an avalanche the roar, and he could smell the breath of the massive vertebrate worm. The smell was incredibly putrid and it was like it actually breathed rancid death. It was nauseating.

"Now," said the Dwarven!

They pulled on the triggers of their climbing repelling guns and then instantly Arthus and the Dwarven were both flying up and out and away from the giant mouth of the massive vertebrate worm just a split second before the open maw crashed down onto the cart. The opposing rows of spinning grinding teeth ground everything to the outside of its mouth into splinters and dust. But, the barrels of explosives actually flew perfectly centered down into its gullet without getting near its grinding teeth. As soon as Arthus feet landed onto the back of the Wenbe he ran down its back. Arthus' one arm was stretched out holding his lifeline and allowing the wire to keep spinning quickly pulling him farther and farther down its very long and very huge back. He wanted as much distance as possible from where the explosives would be going off. When he saw the Dwarven shoot his second spear off and into one of the other carts far to the right where the trigger to the explosives was waiting for him, Arthus fired his second spear head hook into a significant spike that covered the remainder of the meters going down the Wenbe's back and landed perfectly piercing into its huge tail. The first cable line he disconnected from, which let go slack. Arthus immediately flew again swinging down and back up near where High King Thureos and the others waited. Most of the Urial Guards were already bracing themselves behind several spikes near its tail end. Others were already repelling down its sides very fast and then jump rolling away as the massive vertebrate worm kept speeding forward. Arthus braced himself behind the significant spikes near High King Thureos. Then Arthus looked over at the Dwarven who had flown over and was now already on the cart. The Dwarven hit the switch to the explosives and there was a huge bang and rumble deep inside the massive vertebrate worm. A ball of fire came shooting out from inside the Wenbe's mouth. With the explosion immediately the Wenbe began thrashing its huge head back and forth. The Wenbe let out a very loud roar sound and then came crashing down with blood pouring from its mouth. It continued twitching for a while, but it was not too long before it laid completely still. It was dead!

Clan Urial let out a loud cheer.

"Not bad for your first worm," said Captain Zeel slapping Prince Arthus on the shoulder not long after they all were sitting around the second cart. All were taking a hiatus to drink while getting their gear ready for the trip back. It did not take very long and everything was packed up in the cart and they were ready to head back.

"Hey...what about the body," asked Arthus?

"Ah, don't worry there. Our traders and another Patrol are already on their way to strip the skin and bones and meat from the Wenbe. Whatever might be left the wild animals around here will enjoy for a very long time," said Captain Zeel.

High King Thureos said, "Let's all just take a rest and enjoy some of this fine refreshment Captain Zeel has so graciously provided!"

Arthus took the cup that his grandfather handed him and immediately took a big swig. He noticed that as he took a drink his grandfather smiled and raised his eyebrows a little. Arthus realized suddenly that his grandfather must have figured out that he had already drank some strong liquor before this moment. Arthus smiled back sheepishly and then shrugged his shoulders as he downed the rest of the cup. He handed the cup back to his grandfather, who filled it again and handed it to him again.

Arthus quickly said to his grandfather, "Just two. I only ever drink two, because I know that I must stay in control of my mind and body!" His grandfather without saying anything only nodded approvingly.

It wasn't long and everyone seemed rested enough. Arthus heard a noise and as Zeel had said, another group came up with several huge carts. Some were loaded with equipment for skinning and cutting large parts off of the Wenbe. Captain Zeel said a few words to the incoming group, before they were off riding again back to the city. Arthus enjoyed the ride. The sun was almost set, and the wind was blowing not hard but more fabulous now, and he loved the quiet ride back and was surprised just how fast the Valkers were. It seemed like it only took half the time getting back as it did going out earlier. As soon as they arrived the Valkers were stabled, watered and fed. The High King and Prince Arthus turned their equipment back over Captain Zeel, who then bowed to them both.

"Twas a good hunt, my High King. I am glad I got the chance to run with you both today, but I am sure you and your grandson, Prince Arthus are tired and ready for some sleep. I know you are planning to head out to the sea docks tomorrow and then soon you'll be sailing off to the Islands.

Let's head over to the inn where you will be staying for some food and conversation," said Captain Zeel. With that, they headed back to the inn, and discovered that their rooms were ready. Captain Zeel and the High King and Arthus ate and talked in a private dining area. After a hearty meal and one drink. Arthus bid Captain Zeel farewell and retired to his room. He pulled out his holo-reader, checked his messages, wrote Jade a quick letter on what he saw that day, and then fell asleep.

"Arise Sir Arthus, Anointed of the Alda Matriarch," commanded the Redwood tree nymph Timothy who appeared at Arthus' bedside at 2:00 in the morning. The Redwood tree nymph Timothy handed a very small cake of minerals to Arthus who quickly swallowed it down with some of the water from his horn that glows. Arthus was led through many portals where he poured water from his glowing horn into many water sources from the Great Southern Mountains, through the blood sands, and all around the rainforest jungle and even into the mangrove swamp. It seemed like it took more than two whole days to accomplish this to Arthus, but again, they were back precisely at 4:00 in the morning of that same day.

Arthus guessing, asked, "Redwood tree nymph Timothy are you somehow capable of manipulating time when using these light portals?"

Redwood tree nymph Timothy responded, "Well, no actually, it is not I that can manipulate the time. No tree nymph can do that. In fact even Archangels or Angels cannot manipulate time as we are all simply created beings. The reason for this time manipulation is that the Creator is LIGHT, and not just any light, but the TRUE LIGHT that actually exists outside of time. The Creator, Who is LIGHT, wanted even more light and said, "Let there be light, and there was light." That created light from His WORDS is itself a sentient thing in full obedience and cooperation with the Creator, Who is LIGHT. Therefore, LIGHT and His created light can and does enter into time and actually has the ability to pick and choose different points in time and space to impact. In a very real sense, LIGHT is guiding the created light portals that we Redwood tree nymphs use and that all the Archangels and Angels are allowed to open and close and use to travel around with. When we step through the created light portals for a brief moment, like the twinkling of an eye, we are literally stepping into the Presence of LIGHT and out of time and space then back out of the Presence of LIGHT and back into time and space."

Chapter 17
The great Sea

When Arthus finished showering he discovered that High King Thureos was already gone, his stuff already packed up. Arthus went over to his bag and pulled out a set of clothes, kind of like the ones he wore when he was working with Clan Arial. Just a heavy white tunic and pair of work pants pulled on his leather boots and picked up his cloak, and went down to eat breakfast. The innkeeper brought out a mug of ale and eggs, and some biscuits with a gravy Arthus never had before. He loved it and ate his fill and drank the ale. Soon High King Thureos came back and went to sit next to him.

"I went to check on our ship, and it's ready whenever we get there. I know the Captain personally, and she is a great Captain, so our voyage should only take a few days to reach the main Island where Some of Clan Arial and Clan Urial had set up fishing ports. But what Arthus knew of these islanders was that they were far different from the clans he met before even Grag, head of Clan Arial, didn't oversee the Islands. They were almost a clan of their own. The leader of these ports was a female Ignole named Coral. They said she was a master of the water elements, but that's all he heard about her. High King Thureos didn't seem too excited to see the woman.

"So grandfather, what is this Coral like," asked Arthus?

"Well, she is a bit rough around the edges. She is a powerful Life-energy user, and yes her specialty is water which helps keep her towns safe from bad storms or floods. The great sea isn't a place for the weak or frail. It's a hard life out there, and to lead them, you need a bit of harshness so that Coral can seem a bit ruthless, but she demand's the very best out of her people, and she doesn't like land-dwellers to get into their business so much," said High King Thureos with a grin.

"I see. Well, I do hope I learn a bit before we head back to the palace," said Arthus. With that, they headed out. They left the inn and headed towards the underground tunnels.

"Under these bigger buildings is the various city business owner's and workers actual living spaces. They are carved out of the sandstone underground surrounding the underground military base. That is where most of the city's people actually live. The buildings above grounds were primarily business type buildings, which mostly have private accesses into their various underground dwellings. The main tunnels serve as a secondary access into their underground dwellings," said High King Thureos.

They came to a stable and got three Valkers. They loaded their bags onto one of the Valkers and climbed on the other two and headed out. The long tunnel from the city, under the rainforest jungle and mangrove swamps to the outer sea shore where the tunnel emptied into the inside of the incredibly huge fort and sea port with the sea docks beyond that, was more than twelve hours if it is walked by foot, but with the Valkers, they could reach it in a few hours. All along the inside of the tunnel there carved out arches and in each arch were glow stones inside of beautiful ornate metal grated cylinders. There were also forced air filtration systems embedded into the ceiling of the tunnels. Arthus noticed along each wall was a deeper drainage ditch and every once in a while there was a sound of water draining away. Arthus could hear the sounds of mechanical pumps similar to the ones he heard in the mines up north. As they neared the Great Ocean, Arthus could hear the sounds of sea birds and waves. The Great Ocean's waves were slapping up against the shoreline. There were a lot of various bird sounds. They came out of the tunnel into the huge fort. Immediately there alongside of the road was another stable. They dismounted and tethered their Valkers to the platform rings. Then gathering the gear, they headed along a wooden dock. The huge metal and rock fort walls seemed incredibly massive in size. They extended from both sides and above the tunnel opening out along the shore for at least five kilometers in each direction.

Then they turned and went out into the sea quite a bit. Arthus guessed this was to keep the wild animals from the rainforest jungles and the mangrove swamps from entering the sea port area. The wind smelt of sea salt and felt great after the underground ride through the tunnel. Arthus could see all the sea docks were very busy with traders and ship workers running all about loading and unloading their cargo. Many ships of all shapes and sizes were anchored in the bay. Mostly along the massive sea walls and docks, with more ships out to sea either heading this way, or that.

Arthus asked his grandfather the High King about the different styles of ships and so High King Thureos used this unique opportunity to give Arthus a chance to learn something.

"You see Arthus all these various styles of ships, some are only for sailing along the shorelines for catching fish. Others can sail way out in the open seas, said High King Thureos.

The High King continued, "Malon has two very large rivers that flow towards the ocean at the far western coast and again towards the far eastern coast of the continent. Both of these very large rivers have their starting point at the massive three sided waterfall. That waterfall, as you are probably aware, is located at the far back side of the palace at Harmony City. The center stream of the waterfall lands into a small third river. The First Gods Tree on Malon is planted at the very center of a massive First God's Tree Circle right up close to the banks of that small centered third river. That small centered river is called, *The River of Life* because it flows directly by the First God's Tree planted on Malon. That First God's Tree has roots which extend first out into the waters of that river, nourishing it and filling it with Life-energy. That is why the waters in that small river and its southern facing waterfall there are often considered holy waters, because they come directly from the underground source, which is continually fed by that small River of Life itself. You are aware that both ends of that small third river disappear into the underground. That underground is continuously Life-energy cycled back up to feed the center waterfall. Though there are many tiny underground tributaries running in almost every direction from that river, due to following along with the First God's Tree roots, the River of Life never runs dry, and no other waters feed into that small river. All of life on Malon has been given various levels of Life-energy because of those waters and because of the extensive roots coming off of the First God's Tree."

"Anyway... the two sided waterfalls are fed from a huge underground rivers from way up high on a mountain behind it. There are also underground rivers flowing around the far back side of that mountain back out into the sea running both east and west. Thanks to the Archangels, who helped instruct the Dwarvens, Ignoles and Cundos, we have built a way for the ships to travel up the rivers towards Harmony City from both the east and west coasts of the continent. Not too far from the mountain with the waterfall the ships must turn north and follow artificial waterways towards the back of the mountain on the east or west side depending on which ocean they came in from. They would go through these special sections of the artificial waterway, which can be raised and lowered in tiers. Alongside of the artificial waterways, but underground where they meet their respective underground rivers, there are port authority docks where the goods from those ships can be unloaded when coming from the ocean, and loaded back up with various trade goods headed towards the ocean. Those tier sections of the artificial waterways, that I mentioned, help to lower the ships down in kind of water steps until they actually go into the underground rivers behind the back side of the mountain. The underground rivers going both east and west were enlarged enough that ships could travel easily through those underground rivers and head all the way back out to the ocean. Here and there across Malon along the underground rivers the Dwarvens have helped us build access tunnels to help traders reach underground shipping ports that are stationed alongside of the two eastward and westward running underground rivers. Near the ocean again the ships would exit the underground rivers in artificial waterways that can be raised and lowered in tier like steps. Thus allowing the ships to come back up and exit back into the Great Ocean at sea level. These rivers and waterways and tunnels are all well-designed, with high powered air-filtration and ventilation systems. Each of Malon's port authority dock areas is fully equipped with trading shops, inns, restaurants, taverns and worship sanctuary centers for meeting all of the weary traveler's needs. Modifying the rivers both above ground and below ground has made trading and traveling to and from the Great Ocean far faster than ever before," instructed High King Thureos.

"Now that you know a little more about the shipping to and from the oceans by rivers, let me help you understand more about the various ships you see out here in the bay around this southernmost ocean port. You see, many style ships and even low flying cargo shuttles are torn apart by the extremely bad storms that come often upon the open sea. With the Archangels helping the Dwarvens and master ship building crafters, they came up with ships that could dive deep under the surf of the waters and then from below drive right through the most extreme ocean storms. You see how these newer diving style ships are rather long in their length, while significantly narrower in their width. The front and rear ends are almost pointed. The underbelly of these ships has a ridgeline that is rather pointed from the front all the way to very near the back end. There is an area on the far back end near the bottom that has a giant step in area running in the opposite direction of the rest of the ship. There is a fairly giant metal rudder sticking down from the center of that step in area. And, there are two giant fan shaped blades also in that area; one sticking out from the back of the ship on each side of the rudder, but a bit away from the left and right motions of the rudder. The sides of the ships along the entire length are somewhat obtruding as they bow outwards, but yet still keeping these ships in very much a rectangular type shape. The top of these ships are rounded for the most part. There is an oval-like tower about in the middle of the top of these ships. Inside the top of those ovals is a reasonably large space that is flat, except for the very outside edges that were walls are built higher to prevent someone from falling off the top. The floor of that oval shaped area has some kind of metal grating material, which allows for non-slipping foot traffic. Huge circular heavy metal air-tight doors are near the very front of those tower floors. The circular door had a round steel wheel in it that spins to lock and unlock from both the inside and the outside of each ship. Those doors when open allowed the personnel inside the ships to exit from above the main control room chamber where the Captain and the first mate and some other higher ranking crew are guiding their ships. That tower area is an area where the Captain and other sailors can go outside to look around. Do you notice that there is a metal stair case spiraling down to a flattened platform on top of the rounded dome of the front of the ship? And, then there is another metal staircase gets lowered at the edge of that large flat platform down to the side of the ship. That staircase when lowered is placed on top of a port authority ramp which extends from a shipping dock. Thus allowing the ship's crew members to enter or exit the ship. All the cargo that gets carried by those ships has to be packed in such a way where it can be lifted up and fit down through the large circular watertight access doors at the top of those towers. Each package is weighed at no more than sixty kilograms, which is about 120 pounds. And they are always packaged and measured precisely. When those round air-tight doors are closed, the entire ship becomes air-tight and can then dive underwater to escape any bad storms on the surface of the seas. There are specially designed air/water baffle tanks that are used for making the ships to dive or to come up to the surface. There is just enough room in these ships that could hold a score of workers and at least fifty tons of cargo. There are very few luxuries on those types of ships. The Captain and First Mate each have private quarters, but all the rest of the crew sleep in very tightly built bunks that are only meant for sleeping. They have a small ship's galley, where the chef prepares the meals. They carry a few kegs of ale. They do have a weapon's room. They do have a latrine and showers. They each also have a very small-scale biofuel/fertilizer plant, which processes all excreta and food scraps. Every port authority shipping dock area is equipped with a way to capture one hundred percent of the biofuel sludge, greenhouse gasses and fertilizer," said High King Thureos. Who then added, "That reminds me that you mentioned we should send a request to the head biofuel engineer to go to Alkas' City and solve that horrible smelling sewage problem that they have."

"Just so you know Arthus, we are not traveling this time on one of the newer diving ships. You see out there at the far end of the sea wall to the east. The giant beautiful old wooden sailing ship called, *Torn* is the one we will be riding on. Torn was once the flagship of the entire fleet of sea ships. As you can see, these kinds of older ships use three giant masts and smaller mast that is pointed at an angle towards the very front. All of those giant sails catch the winds and push and pull those ship along the sea in a zig-zag fashion. They have been upgraded with the same powerful engine as the other newer ships with the giant fans spinning under the water. The newer engine, however is only used when the wind is not blowing" said High King Thureos.

Arthus stood on the dock in front of the ship called, *Torn* and said to his grandfather, "It really is a big beautiful ship!"

"That she is! That she is!" said Captain Coral who had spotted them from her ship, climbed over the edge ropes, jumped down onto the long ramp, then running down to the bottom, leaped and then came to a quick stop on the wooden dock at the far end of the seawall right behind Prince Arthus.

Prince Arthus quickly turned around to see who had said that. Arthus observed Captain Coral's sudden appearance. She wore a beautiful sea captain's uniform. It had a ruffled collar and front and ruffled cuff shirt, like the one's worn for special occasions in the palace and at various clan festivals. The cashmere wool tunic was a maroon color with six fancy gold colored braid loops which went over the oblong leather buttons. Her tunic's front was shorter, meeting at her waist in a Λ-like pattern, just above her fancy belt buckle. The back of the tunic had two longer tails that reached down almost to her ankles. The shoulders of her tunic had fine gold braided epaulets attached to them. The epaulets also were rounded out above each of her shoulders and gold braided tassels were hanging all around the outside of gold braided round pads. Her pants matched her tunic, but ended with a big button cuff just below her knees. There all along the outer seam of the pants is a gold braid trim. Her super highly shined black square toed boots also had gold braids for their laces. She wore a leather whip on her left hip and a curved sword with a big back hand guard on her right hip. She wore a very fancy triangular shaped hat that included a giant maroon colored feather hanging gracefully down her back.

Captain Coral quickly took her fancy feathered hat into her right hand; outstretched and curtsied politely. And, then she said, "Welcome to come aboard my High King and Prince Arthus." Then she stood up and gave them a very firm look and said sternly, "Just mind you now. Stay out of my way and out of all my crew's way, or I will gladly throw you both over board!"

Arthus started to laugh, but High King Thureos tapped his arm, gave him a stern look and said, "She is not joking!"

It was two days since they left the sea wall dock area. The smell of salt air, the sounds of the sea, and the slow rocking of the boat were intoxicatingly relaxing. Arthus found it very difficult to stay awake. He wondered why High King Thureos wasn't going to make him stay a year at both Blood Sands, and on the islands to really get to know this kind of work and to have a chance to get to know the locals like he had with both Clan Arial and Clan Gearhead. But, all his grandfather would tell him was he would see once they both returned to the palace. It had also been over two years since he last walked the streets of Harmony City, or sat in the Great Library reading about the world around him. He knew he was seeing and experiencing for himself so much in the last two years. He had felt a bit homesick, but he also felt strangely sad that he was returning to the palace. He glanced north to see if he could see the First God's Tree from where they were in the Great Ocean. Noticing that the skies way off in the northern distance are cloud covered. He sat his back firmly up against a lower side railing of the ship and allowed his thoughts to wander in kind of a day-dream like state. He thought about how Harmony City was so carefully built into God's Forest. He recalled how he had explored all of the sections of the city, even the parts that were built around and even inside of the southwestern side of the giant three sided waterfall. Almost all of the city was meticulously constructed, and though it was made beautifully from a variety of materials from all over Malon, he realized how it had always felt so artificial to him. He had learned from a child how with the help of Archangels and the Dwarvens, the people of Malon built these huge highly ornate metal platforms that went in five levels around the outside of the southwestern facing waterfall. Then inside of the mountain over and all around the southwestern section of the underground river that fed that section of the waterfall had been beautifully carved into deep tunnels and cavernous underground dwellings. The underground river that fed the center southern facing waterfall was intentionally left natural. The Archangels had told the Dwarvens not to carve into that underground river section. Only the western side of the mountain and western side of the western underground river that fed the southwestern facing waterfall was allowed to be carved into.

The city was called Harmony City because it was built into God's forest where no tree was ever cut down or harmed. The people's houses and businesses that were above ground were carefully built around all of the trees within the sprawling city areas south of the River of Life. Every builder always left a wide section around each tree base for beautifully planted gardens. Many times there were narrow meandering curving hallways leading between and around the trees and garden built into a single house or building. Many of the houses bedrooms and living spaces were often separated by being lifted up very high up above the leaves and branches of any nearby trees on ornate columns. To get into one of these high and lifted bedrooms or living spaces one had to climb ornate spiral staircases that exited from one of many meandering hallways. The plumbing for these houses was always a carefully planned out operation as they could not dig into any of the main tree root systems. Arthus remembered seeing a Dwarven working on installing plumbing and he was using very soft bristle brushes and tiny tools to carefully dig in order to not harm any main root systems. Arthus thought about the people living in the high up bedrooms, when they needed to use the latrine during the night hours and having to climb down from their bedrooms wander through how many meandering hallways just to go pee. When he was much younger that thought always made him laugh quietly to himself. Each of the homes and businesses were a marvel to look at and wander through, but nothing in Harmony City compared to the ornate palace.

Some upper halls of the ornate palace led onto beautiful garden lined walkways that led up and over some of the lower First God's Tree branches and then continued on over the River of Life. Those walkways led into the other parts of the city that surrounded the huge three sided waterfall. Arthus had heard since he was a child how the First God's Tree was so big that on clear days from some areas on the Great Ocean its top could be seen in the distance. It was much taller than the mountain behind it with the huge three sided waterfall and its trunk is almost as wide as the length of the small River of Life. Some people said that it was taller than all of the mountains on Malon. In fact First God's Tree was actually taller than the planets stratosphere and even reached into the protective ozone layer surrounding the planet. First God's tree had grown in the middle of the continent beside the small River of Life with the southern facing section of waterfall that dropped from the mountain on the opposite side of the River of Life. The Eastern facing waterfall went into the huge river going east, but as it went it led through a wide swath of swamplands. Those swamplands were deemed far too dangerous for any people to travel. Only the Aldas ever seemed to go into those actual swamplands. The people who traveled by ships on that section of river stayed safely inside of their ship. God's forest surrounds all of Harmony City and the massive life-giving tree.

Noticing some movement nearby Arthus looks and Captain Coral had just sat down not too far from him.

Arthus said, "Captain Coral, mam, I have heard from a child the First God's Tree could be seen on clear sky days from some of the places in the Great Oceans. Have you ever seen the First God's Tree from your ship?"

Captain Coral replied, "Oh yes, many, many times I look up towards the north from around here, or to the east when I am sailing up the eastern side of the Great Ocean, or to the west when I am sailing up the western side of the Great Ocean to see the First God's Tree. On a clear day we use that instead of a compass. On a clear night the stars in the sky be part of our guide. One of the brightest stars seems to always hang up in the night sky above that First God's Tree. Another thing you might be interested to know is how some of the deepest diving ships with them special viewing window ports have spotted the First God's Tree's massive roots going so far down into the ocean that no one knows where they ever end under the ocean."

Suddenly, a massive splash and water came lapping up over the side of the ship where Arthus was sitting. It startled Arthus. He quickly grabbed onto a side rope that hung next to him along the railings and looked around. A massive fish-snake-like creature had surfaced just off the starboard side, which Captain Coral had said the first day on the ship, meant the right side of the ship. It was right behind Arthus. A loud whistle blared from up high in the ship's bird's nest lookout. Everyone but Arthus scrambled to gather up their weapons, just in case if the creature attacked. Arthus had been too shocked by the sheer size of the creature that was just outside the ship next to him. It was four to perhaps five times the size of the Wenbe that they had hunted and killed in Blood Sands. The creature quickly sank back down into the waters and swam away.

Captain Coral walked laughing back over to where Arthus was sitting with his hands wrapped securely into the rope and said, "First time seeing a Sea Serpent, my young Prince? O don't worry yourself. Them not usually wanting a fight, but we fight no other if we had run into a Sea-drag. It's a good thing they're such a rare sight to see on the surface, as they prefer the deep black of the sea."

"Sea-drag? What on Malon are those?" Asked Arthus.

"Ah, they are large half-fish half-lizard. They are very long almost snake like and have two large fins that work a lot like wings. They have massive teeth in their giant mouth. At the very end of their very long tail there is a super sharp very large spike, which it can fire off like a spear. Their hides are hard like armor. Coming out from below their mouths and then hanging out in front of their mouths they have kind of an antenna like thing with a light on the end that they can turn on. They actually do that in order to attract various other sea life to where they will then quickly eat those. There are many deadly creatures in this here ocean. If you don't know what you're doing out here, you'll end up food. Remember my words," said Captain Coral. She walked off, while continuing to laugh.

Arthus quickly decided he had enough of the main deck and went down below deck to where a room had been set up for him and High King Thureos, who he discovered was already in there sleeping deeply. Arthus laid down and rested for the last stretch of the voyage.

They reached the main Island before dark that day. The whole island appeared to be about as large as the Alkas' City. There was a significant bay area which again had been built onto with huge boulder sea walls and the top was covered with heavy timbers.

Arthus questioned High King Thureos, "Where had all the heavy timbers been cut from, because from what I understand almost all trees on Malon are not something anyone is allowed to cut down for any reason?"

"All cut timbers come from off world. There is a special farming planet that raises and harvests trees responsibly. We have successfully traded with them many times throughout the years. Many years ago some of the wilder places around Malon had harvested some of the forest's trees. It took a lot of negotiating with a sword to get them to stop harming our own planet in that way. Once we finally earned peace then we showed them where the other planet is that responsibly farms and harvests trees. The Yelin Snow Folk have greatly appreciated the ability to trade for the timbers that they needed, rather than seeing more of the Great Northern Tundra and Great Northern Peaks become a complete wasteland. A recent negotiated trade with that planet will allow the Yelin Snow Folk and other wilder tribe locations to begin a reforestation project here on Malon" replied High King Thureos.

The dock was busy with traders, and again all the port markets were selling different size fish and other sea life. Many people were out and about.

Captain Coral said, "There is a really good inn that I will show you both too, where you can spend the night at. After we drop off your things and get them secured, then I will take my High King over to the main naval base where we can meet with the naval base's commander, Captain Chuck. I know that we do need to talk over how things were going out there and if they are needed any specific supplies. I want to keep on doing my best to ensure that what they need is properly ordered and on its way."

Turning away from Captain Coral and looking at Arthus, the High King said, "It won't be much longer until you head to the Malon Academy."

Arthus asked, "Will I need to travel back out here to reach the Academy?"

"Yes, well close. The Malon Academy is actually on another huge island in the Great Ocean created by the Archangels for all of Malon to go and train and learn of their place in the world," said High King Thureos.

"How far is it from here," asked Arthus?

"If you head directly there from Alkas sea port on one of the newer diving style ships, it takes three days. But if you come by this type of ship from here, you have to add about one day more, so at least four days from here." said High King Thureos.

"I see...so going directly there is better, or that just depends on whether I will need to come through this way again before heading to the Malon Academy. Anyhow, I know that I can hardly wait to see it. But, I know that I must wait until it is actually my time to head there," said Arthus.

"Yes, you are almost to your fifty-third life year. When you reach your one hundredth life year, you will travel to the Malon Academy to study there for nine hundred years. Once you graduate in your first thousandth year, you will be given the choice of what clan that you wish to serve under and what you wish to do with your life," said High King Thureos.

"I already know I wish to stay with Clan Arkwright and become a Silver Thorn like my father and become one of the top warriors who protect our home from any threat that might come," said Arthus.

"I see. Well, time and training will bring much more clarity and peace in your mind and heart over every decision you will need to make," said High King Thureos.

"Wow, nine hundred years of studying and training on the same island! I am so glad you allowed me to have these past two years seeing and working and learning in other places on Malon. I truly loved it, even on the toughest days. Nine hundred years! That almost just sounds like forever. I know it's really not forever, but nine hundred years? By that time I can probably memorize every book that has ever been written!" Exclaimed Arthus.

"Anyway once we return to the palace from your fifty-third year life day celebration and until you celebrate your one-hundredth year life day, I will be personally training you to prepare for the Malon Academy. And, don't believe it will be anything like what you experienced before at the palace, where you had a lot of free time. You will be training with me in the wee morning hours from O-Dark-Thirty, then from 8:00 in the morning until supper time you will be studying with a friend of mine. During supper times you will sit by my side, during which, from time to time, I will teach you to play the ancient game called *Go*. You will find that game will teach you how to strategically think. After I have taught you the basics of that game, we will each begin to make one move per day. That will seem like a lot of time between moves, but it will give you time to think and contemplate on the various strategies of play. After supper time each evening and into the evening you will stand by my side and see how a King works during his days with helping to keep the peace throughout all of Malon. You will sit in when the heads of all the clans meet and when I meet with anyone who wishes to see me personally. Two hours before bed, we will train a bit more. Then we will go to heal our bodies and minds in the hot springs that I had built into the room beside your new room off of the training platform in the palace. Then before sleep we both go down to the base of First God's Tree, where we will spend at least twenty minutes reading from the ancient canonical book and then 10 minutes meditating on what we have just read. When we return to our bedrooms, we breathe in the Life-energy and do our daily Life-energy push out into the world around us. Then we sleep. This kind of schedule will repeat itself day after day after day. Throughout the next forty-seven life years, your body will slowly come into its adult form. I want to make absolutely sure you are ready for the academy. I know you already possess a special gift of wisdom and insight into things that most people don't seem to grasp at any age. You also have a youthful curiosity, which can and has caused you to face some trials. Stay observant. Stay wise. Train like your life depends on it, because it really does. You must be at your very best and fully prepared for the various trials that will lay before you," said High King Thureos.

"As you wish, grandfather, I will do my very best not to let you or my father down," said Arthus.

Arthus thought of what this next phase of his life and training will be like, and was a bit nervous. He knew that his grandfather seemed always in a rush to get to his next important meeting. He also heard from others how his grandfather was not any kind of easy-going trainer. The palace guards who often sparred with the High King had said he never goes easy on anyone. Several of them even needed a couple of days with healers and priests to heal their wounds and emotions. Arthus was also excited to get this kind of challenge. He would get much more one-on-one time with his grandfather, which he truly longed for. Before, when he lived in the palace, he was mainly was taken care of by Sylla, mostly because Arthus's father was always gone with the Silver Thorns. After all, he was their commander. Arthus knew it was actually much harder for his father to be around him, since his mother died for his sake. This always pained Arthus's heart when he thought of it. His father had always been very distant and even cold towards Arthus. High King Thureos had noticed this, and then took Arthus to live with him, but Sylla was the one who was a constant presence since she was a caretaker in the palace. She helped take care of Arthus almost like his mother, Laella would have if she was alive. Thureos is the High King, and as such he couldn't always be there for Arthus. The main reason Arthus dreamed of becoming a Silver Thorn was so that his father would have to acknowledge him, and he hoped, even longed for a breakthrough into his father's heart. After seeing his grandfather in the fight against Black Ice, he wanted to become much more vital standing side-by-side with his grandfather and father; shoulder-to-shoulder no matter what threat befell their people.

"Alright, Arthus, I am off to talk with Captain Coral. You can walk around by yourself if you like, or go get some rest if you like. I will see you a bit later," said High King Thureos. He left Arthus in their room.

Arthus decided to head down, get a bite to eat and a mug of ale, and then see what was around the island city. Arthus sat down at a table outside of the Inn and watched people going about their business. He had a bowl of rice, salted fish and some other sea creatures and an excellent cold ale. The fish was good, a little bit too dry, but it tasted good. The other seafood was actually great tasting. Some he did find a bit tough to chew through, but he definitely enjoyed both his meal and his drink. He noticed a couple of small children running up and down the dock, which brought a smile to Arthus's face. He enjoyed watching kids enjoy life, and he hoped they would live a long peaceful but challenging work-life like all of Malon. He thought back when he was a small kid running around the streets of Harmony and watching ships and griffons flying in and out. He got up and walked around, enjoying the sounds and smells of the sea. He saw several Fishermen all crowded around one smaller ship that had hauled in a massive sized fish with rows of Razor teeth. They were all congratulating him on his catch. The fisherman was explaining his hard fight to bring in what they called a Razor-fin. Arthus walked off the end of the docks and down onto a very clean sandy beach and found a nice quiet spot under a tropical shade tree to sit down in the sand. Arthus pulled his boots and socks off and was putting his feet deeply into the nice warm sand. He pulled off his tunic and bound it up as a pillow and laid back, basking in the warm late-afternoon sun. He started to drift off between the cool sea breeze and warm sand and the lapping waves. Arthus fell into a deep sleep. Arthus woke up to being half-buried into the sand. A couple of kids laughed near buy. The kids figured the sleeping young man would be more comfortable if only his head weren't under the sand.

"Well, look at me; what am I going to do now," said Arthus to the kids.

"Well, you looked cold in the setting sun, so we thought you like a blanket of sand," laughed one of the kids.

Arthus asked, "So who might you all be?"

"I am Tom, he be Cald, and she named Sapphire," said Tom.

Arthus smiled and brought himself up out of the sand to stand against the tree. It took him a few minutes to shake the majority of the sand off and out of his clothes and skin.

"I am Arthus Arkwright," said Arthus with a bow.

"O my, he's the Prince," said Sapphire while giving Tom a sock in the arm.

"O crap, sir, I hope you're not mad about the sand," said Cald.

"No, no, you are okay! So, is this the normal of what you three do for fun around these parts? I am only here for the night and I would like to see all that I can, said Arthus.

"Ya, we have some secrete hideouts here and there," said Tom.

"We should bring him to the hidden grotto," said Sapphire.

"Shh, Hey, don't spill our secret place, dummy," said Tom.

"O come on Tom, he loves it," said Cald.

"Fine," said Tom crossing his arms.

"Follow us; we show you something cool," said Sapphire.

Arthus followed Tom, Sapphire and Cald along the beach and then away from the beach into some more rocky area. Fairly quickly they came to a small gap between a rocky cliff and the ground, just enough to squeeze through. When Arthus finally managed to get through the hole, he was shocked. The cave was significant. At the back was a large opening with water coming in. The sunlight hit the water and bounced to the nearby Life crystals that adorned the place, making colorful prism lights filling the cave. Colors of blue, green, and some others danced across the walls and ceiling. The kids smiled and ran through the other opening to a large grotto cut off on both sides by the cliffs where the water lapped in, and Arthus could see some fish jumping out over the small wall that cut off the grotto from the sea. They were large fish blueish-purple in color with a long nose and big eyes. They made a clicking sound and were what Arthus thought playing by jumping over the far wall back and forth. Kids smiled and ran through the water and over to the fish, which seemed to make very happy sounds, and began to play with the kids. Kids took out a small ball and threw it over the small wall, and the fish went after it to slap it back with their tail. Arthus smiled and looked around. There were many shell creatures and some smaller sea life in the small pool. He soon bent down, pulling up a small round Crystal ball-shaped.

"It's so beautiful," said Arthus staring into the crystal as the light of the sun-filled it.

"They're called Sea stones," said Sapphire.

"Ya, they sometimes wash up here. We like to gather and trade them with the local traders for different things. Those are very popular with the Dwarven crafters we were told," said Tom.

"Well, I can see why. Here, Sapphire, I let you hold onto this one for me," said Arthus handing the small girl the crystal. The girl's eyes went wide.

"Thank you, Prince Arthus. I make sure I hold onto it," said Sapphire.

"Just Arthus, please. None of you have to call me Prince, except when adults are around, Ok?" said Arthus smiling.

The girl named Sapphire just smiled and nodded. After a couple of hours of playing with the kids and the fish, it was getting dark, so Arthus took the kids back to the docks where a Cundo woman stood by, not looking too happy with the three kiddos.

Arthus quickly put his hands together in a prayer like fashion and said to the kid's caretaker, "I am Prince Arthus Arkwright. And, I do apologize for my not having received permission from you first, when I requested of these three children to please take me on a unique island adventure. These young children have all been exceptionally well behaved and provided me with quite a good time."

"Oh, Prince Arthus, please forgive my stern reaction earlier. It is just sometimes frustrating to try to keep up with these three. You see they lost their parents from shipwrecks. The caretaker thanked Arthus for watching the kids and then took them back to the local orphanage.

Fairly soon, Arthus was sitting back in the Inn waiting for Thureos to return, who did not take too long after Arthus had finished off a third mug of ale. Usually I only drink two, but this ale is really good.

"So you have a good day," asked Thureos?

"I did, but I like to ask you and Captain Coral about the orphans I met today," said Arthus.

"I see yes life here, and other places that have a dangerous living condition such is life on the sea, sands, and in the wild tundra, in the mountains, and yes even in God's forest you have known and even seen at many times how life can end suddenly. Sometimes when that happens, loved ones are left behind. But, you should not worry for such kids, for when some adults lose their lives and leave behind children, their clan always steps up. A clan always protects the clan as a whole for better, or for worse. They certainly will help raise the kids, and I also make sure they are always provided for. One of my main reasons for travelling each year is to check up on any orphaned children and how are the security and safety of the regions and clans. The city head leaders make me aware of any special needs that may require some level of intervention. A true King should never sit on some thrown barking orders. Therefore, I must get out among my people to see how life is for them. That way, I can see for myself and not just be told that things are well. You never know if a clan might not tell you the whole truth to try not to worry you. Once a close friend had a major problem, when that happened they figured they could solve it themselves and not burden me with the issue. In the end, he failed to stop the issue and it was not an issue that ever should have been hidden. It caused great destruction to not just himself. His entire life has suffered since then. From that time, I learned never to trust even my closest allies and friends with everything. I intentionally show up in person at multiple times and often even in some inconvenient times. I have learned that showing up among people helps show them their High King has a face and isn't some far away overpowering force. This is also why I divide the power between myself and the clan leaders, all elected by their clan, and no clan leader ever lives higher than that of their people. Even though I live in the palace, I know the palace's atmosphere surrounding the High King and King and Prince must never be seen as a party hardy or lazy style of life. We must lead by example. That includes what we fill the inside of the palace with. It is not just filled up with fancy things. There is some fancy things, but not too much. That is why the Great Library was built inside the palace and not stuck out somewhere else in the city. The palace has always been a place open to the people, and much more than just where I live. Clan Arkwright has many who live within our walls, and clan leaders come and go. A true leader always makes sure his people come before himself," said High King Thureos.

"I see," said Arthus. He thought hard about what his grandfather had told him. He knew that the palace was mostly very hard wood. Even High King Thureos throne was made of very hard wood, and though there were some pillow throws, he knew that even these were not made to sit with any comfort in mind. He remembered as a kid he asked High King Thureos why his big chair hurt his butt. His grandfather explained that a king shouldn't get too relaxed sitting on his butt when work is needing to be done. Arthus smiled at that and started to fall asleep. He could already hear the loud snores of his grandfather in the bed next to his.

Precisely at 2:00 in the morning the Redwood tree nymph Timothy arrived to find Arthus already on his feet, dressed and ready. Arthus quickly ate the manna loaf and they were off through the light portals. They stepped out of the first portal onto the water tower that supplied fresh water to the island that Arthus was already on. He could see the old flagship Torn in the bay. He quickly unlocked and poured the water from the glowing horn into the island cities water tower access portal. Then the Redwood tree nymph Timothy opened another portal, took Arthus forearm and stepped through. They came out of the portals on one island after another pouring the water into ground waters, city water supplies, and military base water supplies. And, there were many times they stepped out into inner ship storage rooms, where there were stacks of water barrels. Some of the ships had huge fresh water storage tanks, which he added a little of the water too. There were three places where Arthus was actually being held up by the Redwood tree nymph Timothy over the Great Ocean. From those specific three places all the ocean currents in that part of the ocean flowed out and around from. To Arthus it seemed like he kept going for several days in and out of portals, all around the Great Ocean on the east and west and south. And just when Arthus felt like he was ready to pass out they stepped through a portal again back to the inn where the High King still lay snoring. The Redwood tree nymph Timothy said, "Add some water to the High Kings water flask." Arthus obeyed. The time was now 4:00 in the morning and suddenly Arthus felt completely refreshed, like he had slept all night. The Redwood tree nymph Timothy opened a portal and left. Arthus went into the shower room, took off his clothes, showered and then changed his clothes again. When he came out the High King had just woke up.

"Good morning Arthus. Today is the day we head back to Harmony City," said High King Thureos.

Captain Coral met them in the lobby at the inn to eat breakfast together with both the High King and Prince Arthus. He brought with him the caretaker and the three orphaned children that Arthus had met the night before as a surprise. The children each had a glow stone in their left hands from the grotto to give to Arthus and in their right hands to give to the High King.

Arthus hugged each of the kids and told them, "When you get old enough, you each need to make sure to meet up together with me at the Malon Academy. I will be there for nine hundred years, so there has to be some time where our paths will surely cross. Thank you all so much for giving me a wonderful adventure last night. And thank you for these beautiful glow stones. I will treasure them."

High King Thureos said to the kid's caretaker and to the kids, "I hope you all are really hungry this morning." He then motioned to the Innkeeper to come over to the breakfast table. As soon as the Innkeeper arrived at the table, the High King said, "Order the cook to make whatever these children here and their caretaker want to eat and put it on my tab!"

The kids all cheered as they climbed up into the chairs beside Prince Arthus.

After breakfast, Captain Coral bid them both good luck and let them go on their way. He thanked the caretaker for bringing the kids back over and assured her if there were any needs that the kids might have the clan would step-up to help her.

High King Thureos and Arthus stood on the deck of one of the new ships sailed by the massive fans under the ship. They had packed and boarded. It took just moments and they felt like they were speeding through the water. By the time the galley chef announced it was lunchtime they were already over halfway towards the far western sea. By the time of the dinner announcement they had just rounded the Southwestern corner of the continent and started heading north. Just as sun went down and the two moons were brightly showing in the night sky, they had reached the mouth of the western river. The Captain blew his whistle and said, weigh anchors. Arthus could hear huge chains being lowered into the ocean. The crew of the ship were relaxing and getting settled down. Arthus and the High King both went down and entered the cabin area where they were to sleep for the night. The High King quickly fell asleep and Arthus noticed he was not snoring. He smiled at the thought of the High King taking a drink of water, having his Life energy boosted and even the little things like snoring were being healed. Arthus drifted off to sleep.

At precisely 2:00 in the morning, "Arise Sir Arthus, Anointed of the Alda Matriarch," came the voice of the Redwood tree nymph Timothy. Arthus quickly sat up and ate the manna loaf that the Redwood tree nymph Timothy handed him. Again the Angel took Arthus forearm opened a portal and stepped through. They arrived back after Arthus had poured the water from his glowing horn into what Arthus thought were about a thousand or more locations all around the western ocean islands and coastal areas. Some of the locations were right where very dangerous beasts were within a few feet of them. The Redwood tree nymph Timothy simply lifted his hand and the wild beasts seemed to instantly fall asleep even while standing. Arthus poured into the waters as instructed. Redwood tree nymph Timothy lowered his hand, then opened the light portal and exited. The wild beasts woke up a few seconds after the portal had already closed. This moving through portals and pouring continued on like this for what seemed like many hours. Then the Redwood tree nymph Timothy opened a portal and they once again were back in the cabin where the High King was sleeping peacefully and still not snoring. Arthus smiled again about this.

At sunrise the Captain blew his whistle again and yelled raise the anchors. Within minutes the ship had turned and headed into the first of the series of artificial waterway tiers that raised the ship in steps up over the river's mouth and into the main stream of the river. The going up the river towards Harmony City was a little slow and steady as they were having to move against the currents of the river. Arthus wondered what life will be like back in Harmony City. He had been away a long time and had seen so much of their world, and he really didn't want this wandering adventure to end. He lifted his holo device and sent a message to Jade with some pictures of the sea. He missed her. She had become someone so special to his heart; more than a friend, but yes a great friend too. Then there is his two good friends Zeck, and Emon, three people he hoped to see again.

"Arthus, come here while we are on our way up the river. I am going to train you on the way to meditate to help you heal both your body and mind," said High King Thureos. Soon Arthus sat cross-legged next to his grandfather.

"Now, clear your mind and focus on yourself because as you know inside all of us is the Life-energy. I want you to try and feel it. And when you do then grab hold of it and spread it through your whole body like the water below this very ship. Let the Life-energy flow through from your toes to fingers to the top of your head," said High King Thureos.

Arthus quickly felt his Life-energy; an almost electrifying feeling deep inside his body. He focused his mind and let his Life-energy grow. Soon he could feel the Life-energy flow up from his chest through his arms and head, it was clearly flowing throughout his body, but he couldn't keep a hold of it to keep it inside his body, which was what his grandfather wanted to help him to learn. Instead, it flowed out from him and into the surrounding ship and even out to other people's bodies. Arthus' own Life-energy seemed to drain away from him, as if it was gone. Arthus knew it wasn't really gone, but the intenseness of trying to focus it, had quickly wore Arthus' out. Arthus knew how to send out his Life-energy and even when touching a living object like a tree or other living being he could actually draw back from the Life-energy flowing out from them. But, Arthus was only touching the deck of this metal ship. Arthus opened his eyes and sighed. He had sweat dripping from his face.

"Yes, before you master this, it will always take a toll on you, but once you master holding onto the Life-energy and not letting it escape from your body, that will help to heal your wounds and calm the many stresses that are always working against your mind," said High King Thureos.

They were already inside a portion of the river's faster flowing currents. There were large mountain cliffs on both sides, and here the river currents were so fast. The ship slowly and surely continued up stream against even these fast currents. Arthus could tell that the speed of the propeller fans had been increased significantly. If not they would never had been able to keep going up against these currents.

Arthus said out loud, "There is no way anyone could possibly ever swim in this area of the river, unless you are part fish."

They continued working their way upstream slowly and steadily. It wasn't long and the river stream currents had slowed down. When Arthus noticed that the ship seemed to pick up speed he looked around. The river had opened up through a little corner of Arial Valley. Arthus looked out across that open area and immediately noticed that there on the shoreline were several people waving at the ship they were on. He recognized that one of the people waving was Grag. With him were several members of Clan Arial. Arthus spotted at the end of the group's line there was a fairly large Yaule and a standing next to the Yaule is a beautiful young red haired woman waving Arthus' way. He smiled and waved back as they passed by. It was Jade, of course; she had grown too in the year and month that he had been away. Arthus' mind wondered back to the month before when they kissed. He wished that the ship would stop here and allow him time to hold and kiss her again, yet Arthus knew unfortunately, that the ship wouldn't or couldn't stop right here in the river to allow them even to stop and say hi. The ship continued moving along. Then it took a fairly big bend in the river and then headed in a slight southerly direction. The river turned another bend directly towards the south and Arthus recognized that they were now just entering the far northwestern end of God's forest. Arthus went back to his meditation training. Arthus was meditating intensively when the river turned to the east and then turned again to the north beside the mountain.

"Arthus, it is time now to gather our things as we will be heading out of this ship as soon as it is going through the artificial tier waterways which will bring it down to its port fairly quickly. Once we are on the western port docks we will be taking one of the Golden Griffons back to the Palace," said High King Thureos.

"Ya... I'll get my gear," said Arthus. Soon he watched as the ship entered a large bowl area with metal walls all around filled with water then more quickly, a large metal wall lifted behind the boat, inclosing it then water under the ship was splayed out down into the river . The water and the ship dropped down a level. Then another wall opened up in front of them. The ship pulled forward into the next artificial tier. The wall closed behind them again. Again, the water under the ship splayed out down into the river, which caused the ship to lower even more. By going through the fourth of these artificial waterway tiers, the ship had gone completely down to a level that led into a huge underground tunnel. Before them is a large underground port. Other ships are already docked further into the underground tunnel alongside of the port. As soon as the ship was docked Arthus and the High King took their gear over to the local stables, which were located just outside the tunnel and up above the ground. Arthus and High King Thureos gathered several Golden Griffons, one of which had a hathi howdah tacked onto its back. All the others had cargo platforms tacked onto their backs. The port authority had several strong Cundo men quickly unloading all of the ship's cargo that was headed to Harmony City. It wasn't long and the entire flock of Golden Griffons were all loaded, and the loads all had strong strapping and netting tying their loads down to their cargo platforms. One of the Clan Urial Guard Silver Thorn Scout members and six other Clan Urial Guard members were all coming along on their own Golden Griffons as security. The Silver Thorn Scout took up a position to the front. The six guards took up their positions each alongside the outer edges of the flock; three on each side. Arthus and the High King were in the hathi howdah on their Golden Griffon at the very center of the flock. The entire flock took off quickly. The flight was like the first night out of the palace. They rose high up into the sky and within an hour they were flying over Harmony city with its five platforms. Arthus could see the people working, kids playing on playgrounds, and the ornate palace with its Great Library. Before them was the First God's Tree. So, so big around and so, so high it went up into the atmosphere.. Arthus knew he would fall from his mount back if he tried to lean out of the hathi howdah to try to look up at the canopy. Breaking away from the main flock, they were flying around the massive trunk of the First God's Tree. They continued flying in ever increasingly higher circles around and around and around the First God's Tree until higher up in its branches built along its sides, but much more naturally grown into the tree itself there was a large naturally grown platform. Up on that large naturally grown platform,

Arthus knew well were the Palace stables, the same stables that he had hung around as a child, and the same one his grandfather and him flew out from that day a couple of years ago. They climbed out of their hathi howdah and hopped over to the naturally grown raised platform. The Stable Master was there taking their mounts.

Chapter 18
Back in the Palace

Sylla had arrived on the Golden Griffon Stable's Platform before they arrived and was waiting. She bowed to them and said, "Welcome home, Prince Arthus. My... you have grown taller and much stronger over the last couple of years! I almost can't recognize you. I do hope your travels were very educational," said Sylla.

"Thank you, Sylla. Good to see you as well, and yes, seeing so much of our world has shown me a lot. It has shown me what it means to everyone living on Malon, and much more about what the responsibility of being Prince of our world means," said Arthus.

"Then the past two years away has been well worth your time young man, and I am very glad you are back. I have missed you," said Sylla.

"Now go take your stuff. Sylla knows what room you be staying in. I made sure your new room was close to mine," said High King Thureos. After saying that, High King Thureos left to take care of business.

Arthus followed Sylla up to one of the highest floors of the palace and to a room beside his grandfather's. It is a bit bigger than the one where he lived in the palace before. It is a large naturally grown wooden floor and also had naturally grown wooden walls. Arthus could tell that the floor and walls were actually called forth by Druids from First God's Tree. The ceiling was also wooden, though arched and appeared to be made from other wood, unlike the walls and floors of the room. Inside the room there is an extra-long single bed with a hardwood frame under its mattress, a single long shelf is hanging high up on the wall, made from other wood, but this shelf is somehow embedded into the wall by the Druids, above the head of the bed. On his floor are a couple of big metal clad wooden chests. There was a reasonably large multi-drawer clothing dresser attached to a hanging closet which had several sets of thick training tunics and training pants. Hanging in the closet Arthus recognized that there were also two complete sets of brand new official royal Arkwright uniforms. Along with the royal pants and tunics were the fancy frill collar and fronted shirts, with the frill also around the cuffs. A door at the back end of the room led out onto a wooden deck that was walled in, but had no ceiling. The deck was lined with wooden weapons from one-handed swords, wooden poles, even several different style spears. Some of the long poles had a long wooden curved blade attached to their ends. Arthus recognized all of these were various combat training weapons, which were built to look like the real combat weapons. When someone gets hit by these combat training weapons, they really do hurt as they are quite dangerous, but they normally are not intended to kill during training practice drills. Arthus is aware that these training weapons still can actually kill. The deck was actually three times more in size than the Arthus' bedroom inside. A second door from the deck led into his grandfather's bedroom. And, a third door from the deck led into the artificial hot springs tub, shower and latrine room. It hit Arthus that this is a training area, and that his grandfather intentionally never lives in comfort, but in his own training area. The entire center floor of the deck had soft synth-blend mattes built slightly down into it. The top of the entire deck was still flat.

Arthus opened up and entered into the artificial hot spring tub, shower and latrine room that had been built-into a third natural grown hardwood room next to Arthus's bedroom. He looked around, then exited it again. They have their training area and a place to heal up after each long day. Knowing his grandfather, he knew he will need the healing from the artificial hot springs tub. He also knew for the next forty-seven more years there wouldn't be many days away from using this training deck.

Sylla came back into Arthus' room and said, "I have been told to give you a schedule you'll be keeping from now on. Your grandfather wanted me to bring it to you. It looks like every morning, starting at 4:30, you have a workout training routine you have to go through. Then

307

you shower and change at 6:45. You will eat breakfast at 7:15. You are to meet up with your instructor down in the Great Library at 8:00. You eat lunch at 12:30. Again, at 13:00 you will be with your instructor in the Great Library. At 16:00 you will be with your grandfather, High King Thureos from that point each day while he deals with clan meetings, and any personal appointments with the king, including eating dinner and doing something called *Go* around 18:00. At 20:00 each evening, you will train with High King Thureos here again for one hour. At 21:00 each evening you will use the hot-springs spa located in the room next to your bedroom to help you heal from your day. At 21:40 you be down at the sanctuary at the base of First God's Tree, where you will begin reading from the ancient canonical book. At 22:00 you will spend 10 minutes in meditation about what you have read. At 22:30 you will back up here and in bed with your lights out, which means rest, because your day starts again at 04:05 every morning. If there are ever any changes to this routine, I will inform you." Sylla then posted the schedule on the inside of Arthus' bedroom door with four tiny sharp needles with rounded heads. Sylla then says, "You see here is a thin cork material covering the whole inside of your door and all tiny push pins stuck in it there. You will find all paper messages or letters you might receive will get posted up on here."

"Thank you! So... what am I to do today until my grandfather is done with all his daily things," asked Arthus?

"Well, today you actually do have the rest of the day off to do as you want. If you need anything, please don't hesitate to ask," said Sylla. She bowed her head and left.

Arthus looked around. He decided to walk down and around the palace then head to the western portion of the city across the platforms to see if anything changed since last time he walked the streets. He quickly realized that the work-life in Harmony City continued on like normal. He returned to the palace ate dinner, drank two glasses of ale, then headed to his room to unpack the rest of his belongings.

In his bedroom he carefully unpacked the ornate marriage prayer and good dreams mammoth tusk that was gifted to him by Elder one. He carefully laid this up on the shelf on the wall above the head of his bed. He unpacked his shofar with its heavy leather and wool lined shoulder holder that Jade had made for him; looking carefully at the leather craftsmanship that she had created with her own hands. He closed his eyes and thought of how beautiful she looked as she was waving at him as they sailed by that morning. Then he thought again about their kiss, and a happy tear rolled down his cheek. He really misses her. He reached out and hung the shofar on a hook that was on the right side of his bed. He unpacked the goat horn gifted to him by Elder one. He hung that on a second hook beside the one holding the shofar. He placed the glowing horn under his bed pillow. And then quickly unpacked the remaining gear that he had brought along with him. One of the large metal glad wooden trunks had the ice bear skin. He did not want that left inside the trunk, but he did not want it on his bed, because it was much too warm for their weather. He also did not want it on the floor to be used as a bear skin rug. The other trunk held the heavy ram skins with their thick wool still attached. Arthus left the room and found Sylla.

"Can you get me a large much thicker piece of that cork material attached to the wall above my dresser? I would like to hang this ice bear pelt that I received from Elder one up on that wall."

"Oh, that is a wonderful idea. I will get right on that for you," said Sylla, who then added, "Is there anything else I can help you with?"

"Actually yes. I would like to have a medium sized keg barrel filled with water from the River of Life and a big dipping drinking ladle placed on a stand on the training porch. I am certain that I will be needing its Life-energy healing powers to help me while I am training. Can you make sure that is there by tomorrow mornings training session?"

"Yes, I can have the high priest bring that right up tonight," said Sylla.

"Ok. Thank you again Sylla for everything you always do for me. I probably never told you this, but you have always been much more like a replacement mother to me. You mean way more to me than any servant, or friend in this world ever could. I love you just that much, said Arthus with tears in his eyes."

Hearing that Sylla started crying too. She went up to Arthus and gave him a big hug, and then said, "You don't know how happy you saying that makes this old woman feel. And, I love you too very much Prince Arthus."

It was 21:10 so Arthus quickly went down to the sanctuary at the base of First God's Tree. There all around the massive trunk of the tree were huge natural stone altars. The holiness table sitting right up against the base of the trunk had a giant ancient canonical book laying open. Next to each of the stone altars Arthus there are smaller copies of the same ancient canonical book. Arthus knelt down on his knees on the ground as he knew no one was ever allowed to sit, climb, or play on any of the natural stone altars. Anything that is ever placed upon them is permanently given in the Great Gifting. Arthus arrived just a little early and so as he began reading from the smaller copy of the ancient canonical book, many other people came over and they too knelt down and began reading. At 22:00 all of the books were closed and everyone then sat cross-legged on the ground where they had been kneeling. Everyone there began meditating on the words that they had just read. Arthus could feel the Life-energy flowing all around and through them as he sat meditating on what he had read. At 22:10 Arthus stood up from the ground and went back up to his bedroom, entered the healing room area and took a quick shower, dried off, climbed into his pajamas and brushed his teeth. Then he laid down in his bed and pushed the Life-energy out from his body into the rooms around him and down through the palace. He could feel the Life-energy flowing back from the First God Tree and from everyone in the palace. He breathed out allowing all of the thoughts in his mind to disappear. Then he closed his eyes and quickly fell asleep.

"Arise Sir Arthus, Anointed of the Alda Matriarch," came the Redwood tree nymph Timothy's voice at precisely 2:00 in the morning. "Take and eat," said the Redwood tree nymph Timothy as he handed Arthus the very small cake of minerals.

Arthus quickly downed the mineral cake with water from his horn that glows and put out his arm for the Redwood tree nymph Timothy to again follow their routine of cleansing the waters. The first stop was the main water tower that supplied fresh water to all of Harmony City. The second stop was from a location deep in the swampy area east of the huge three sided waterfalls. The third stop was the southwestern waterfall, then the southern waterfall, then the eastern waterfall. Arthus noticed how the waters in the southern facing waterfall and the River of Life at its base glowed very brightly when he had poured water from the horn that glowed into it. That glow did not dissipate for many days. The Redwood tree nymph Timothy continued to lead Arthus through many, many portals all over God's Forest making sure every body of water had been cleansed. One of the locations Arthus recognized was where Jade and he had fought with the Nagas-Hydra Hybrid. As Arthus poured water from his horn that glowed the muddy and blackened waters of that creek began to glow incredibly intensely bright. Almost as bright as the glow that Arthus noticed in the River of Life.

The next stop was where Arthus and Jade had found the small Nagas skin. Again as Arthus poured out water from his horn that glows into the little pond by the natural spring waterfall the waters glowed like the other water had, very brightly.

Arthus looked around into the moonlight and starlight lit night sky and noticed here and there at the edge of the clearing in the woods around him he saw that there were several Alda that were bowing in the direction of the First God's Tree. Then there came a great rustling sound being made by the branches of the Alda. One of the Alda spoke in a voice that sounded like cracking wood and rustling of the leaves, "We have found and killed the young female Nagas. She is no longer a threat to Malon!"

The Redwood tree nymph Timothy opened another light portal and Arthus and he stepped through. This portal led them to the underground river at the end of the port platform to the east. Arthus poured from his horn that glowed into its waters and realized this underground river led towards the east to the eastern coastline. The Redwood tree nymph Timothy again opened a portal and they stepped through.

This time the portal opened on the end of the platform on the underground river that ran west towards the western coastline. Arthus quickly poured from his horn that glowed.

Then the Redwood tree nymph Timothy opened another portal and the Redwood tree nymph Timothy and Arthus stepped back into Arthus' bedroom.

"There are still many waters on Malon that need cleansed. There remains countless water barrels also which all need to be cleansed. Even though I know this, I will do my best though not to try to cover so much in each of our early morning portals, I realized a few times, where I took you past your point of exhaustion. In doing that I would be hindering your ability to train properly and be attentive to all of your other responsibilities. I know that you start your combat training in thirty minutes. I also know that there will be nights where your body is hurting so much that it must just rest and heal. On those nights too you are to take a drink from the horn that glows. You will find after drinking that, along with then entering into a deeper rest, while sleeping, it will help you to heal your body and mind and spirit. Arthus, whenever I see that you need that, I know that even God our Heavenly Father rested. Before I go, let me help you learn to focus your own Life-energy so that it can also help you heal," said the Redwood tree nymph Timothy. "I will place my finger here on your forehead. I want you to draw all your Life-energy up towards my finger. But, in your mind see a locked door and place that locked door between where my finger is and where your body is. Do not allow your Life-energy to go out of that locked door. Now try it!"

Arthus took a deep breath and focused on creating a locked door on his forehead. Then he drew up his Life-energy from deep within himself and pushed it all throughout his body. He sensed that the Life energy wanted to leave his body, but he focused his mind on the locked door that he had created in his mind. The Life-energy was pounding itself against the locked door and then circling back into his body and running around throughout his body. Suddenly there was an incredible surge of his Life-energy like nothing he had ever felt before. It was like his entire body was on fire with Life-energy and every painful thought, every sore muscle, every scrape or bruise was melted away.

The Redwood tree nymph Timothy took his finger off of Arthus' forehead. "You have done very well, Arthus. Now I must go take care of another assignment until tomorrow morning. However, as I am assigned to be your personal guide, if you need me just call on my name. If there is ever need of more than I can do alone, blow on your shofar, and the loud breathing sound of God's Holy Name will bring many Angels." And, with that, he lifted his hand and a light portal appeared and he stepped through and was gone.

Arthus quickly exited his bedroom and entered the room with the artificial hot springs bath, shower and latrine area. He showered and then quickly dressed in the white padded training gear. Then he exited and went out into the center of the training deck, sat down cross legged and meditated on what the Redwood tree nymph Timothy had him doing Arthus realized that was the second time he ever heard any voice of the Alda. He had heard they normally communicated telepathically. High King Thureos walked out onto the deck dressed in the same type of gear as Arthus.

High King Thureos asked, "Have you practiced the meditation technique that I have taught to you?"

"Yes. And, the Redwood tree nymph Timothy showed me a trick that helped me to actually use it already this morning, before he left."

"Oh, good. I am sure you will need to use that many, many times each day as we train over the next forty-seven years," said High King Thureos.

"We start your long journey of combat training right now today. This will prepare your body for many of the physical trials you will face at Malon Academy. Your daily studies in the library with your tutor, and your nightly reading and meditation on the ancient canonical book at the sanctuary at the base of the Life Tree will help you learn so much as well as build you up spiritually too. So, stand up now as I begin to train you in different weapons and martial maneuvers. I will also train your body and mind to know how to take hits and how to avoid a hit. Now shall we begin," said High King Thureos.

Then High King Thureos went over, picked up one of the wooden poles, and motioned for Arthus to do the same. Arthus lifted one of the poles and only thought he was prepared for what was to come.

"Now I will start by teaching you a few fighting stances, so let's begin," said Thureos. With that, the training began.

Chapter 19
Elemental Island

Arthus stood on the wooden deck outside his room; bare-chested sweat covered his body and dripped from his hair. He felt the morning summer breeze flow upon and around his face and chest. The moment felt like an eternity. He fell into the wind; it felt as if he was free-flying through the air. He raised both arms stretched. He just finished his daily weapon training routine. Soon, High King Thureos would again stop by, and they spar a bit which met Arthus would probably have a couple new bruises. He winced at the thought for the last forty-seven years. He had been on a constant routine training day in and day out. He looked over to the stand of weapons, everything from staves, swords, axes, and everything in between he had to train with. Even with all the intense training, he was very glad he had all the opportunity to spend so much more time with his grandfather than he had ever had in his life before his two years away. His father had even stopped by every so often to see how his training was going. He realized how his father always made a degrading comments like "Is that all you have learned? I expect much more," which always seemed to sting Arthus. But, that was his father's way. He was the Silver Thorn Knights Commander. All he knew about his father, is that his father was like that with everyone since the death of his mother, Laella.

Everyone Arthus knew that ever worked with his father said, "Don't expect Prince Benroy to ever be given out praises or offering anyone any slack!"

Arthus took in a deep breath and used his Life-energy to dismiss all the thoughts in his head about his father. He focused his energy allowing it to heal his own stresses and brought his thoughts completely under his control. He went over to a pillow he had placed a couple of feet from one of the deck edges. He sat down, crossed his legs, and felt himself fall into himself. Focusing on the training and lessons he had learned, he focused on the wind blowing strongly around him. Arthus realized that he could actually sense the molecules in the wind around him. He practiced moving those in circles creating small vortexes in the wind and inside the vortexes electrical energy released small bolts of lightning. Arthus intentionally allowed those small storms to dissipate, but he sensed that what had happened to him when he was fighting with the Nagas-Hydra Hybrid was some greater level of these small storms that he allowed himself to start and stop with Life-energy. He knew it would take much more practice to learn to control this ability that he had discovered within himself. Several hours must have passed by when Arthus brought himself out of his meditation. His grandfather sat not far from him, also in a meditative state.

"So I see you have been working on your internal elemental healing and recovery and mental training that I taught you so long ago, and that you also have discovered in a small way how to begin to control your own external elemental abilities. Do not get overly excited about that as all of the peoples of Malon have some level of external elemental abilities. I see you practicing and that is good. It is better to practice like you are, then discover you need to use your elemental ability in a dangerous situation and never having practiced it. Releasing too much elemental ability can quickly drain you and can actually harm you as much as any enemies you face if you have not learned how to master it. For a while, rather than creating small storms or possibly larger uncontrollable storms, and then allowing them to dissipate, begin by concentrating on holding onto single molecules of the air." Also, continue to practice the internal element of healing and calmness. Both your external and your internal elements need to always be equally in balance." smiled Thureos.

"Yes, grandfather, I figured you might want to do some more training, and I wanted to recover from my morning exercise and go over your lessons while my body recovered," said Arthus.

"Well then, stand, and we shall see if you have truly put my teachings to heart, for this will be our final spar for today. Later today, you will celebrate your first One Hundred Years Life Day in my throne room. So you will be preparing soon to leave here for the Malon Academy, and we must make this one last sparring session fast for we both have a person waiting for us to arrive," said High King Thureos as he also stood up.

Thureos went over, lifted a large wooden staff, and Arthus went over picking up his latest study two wooden swords. These blades were lighter than long swords and a bit shorter also. He twirled the blades around and around and moved his neck back and forth to loosen up in order that his hands and mind were in balance, a lesson his grandfather had also taught him to make sure your body and mind are always at one with the weapons that one is holding. He has to feel as if they were as much a part of his body as his arms or legs. Arthus went up on his toes then rocked back and forth from toes to balls of his feet to loosen and stretch his legs, for they had grown stiff during his meditation. His grandfather nodded and threw his tunic off, and charged. The staff went out in a stabbing thrust towards Arthus. Still, knowing his grandfather, Arthus backed out of range. Then jumped left, for Arthus had grown to know his grandfather's move a bit, and a starting thrust was mainly just a way to throw off his opponents. With that, Thureos front foot spun on his heal bringing him in a full circle staff along his right arm in a sweeping horizontal attack that made his original stab to bring Thureos closer to Arthus. Seeing that coming, Arthus had rolled under to the left and getting his left arm and blade across. Still, Thureos was faster and leaped over Arthus's sword sweep and landed with his staff to catch Arthus's Right sword horizontal attack. But Arthus spun back to bring his left sword in fast, clipping Thureos on the back of his left thighs which by the wince on Thureos face meant it was a good hit. Arthus didn't stop but allowed his spin to bring him out and around to meet his grandfather, who had recovered from the blow and spun the staff around his back and then out faster than Arthus could get out of the way from. Thureos' staff hit Arthus completely in the stomach. Arthus felt the blast and his air explode from his lungs. He was thrown back a bit and tried to keep his balance, but he was trying to catch his breath. He felt that he had definitely received a real good bruise, if not possibly even broke, a couple ribs, but his grandfather stood back up and smiled.

"That's good enough for this morning. Go see the healer about your ribs and take a hot springs bath. I will have all the stuff you will need at the Malon Academy packed up and ready for you before you're done," said High King Thureos, who then laughed and said, "Let me say you rarely hit me, and that really was a good blow. I got a nice welt just under my rear end, which will make sitting on that throne of mine only the more torturous. But, then, ha, ha, I made sure you felt just a little bit of my pain. Now get going. I have the healer outside in the hallway all ready to take care of us. Make sure you recover fast and be quick also about getting ready in your official royal formal attire. Our guests won't like having to wait all day. Arthus nodded and went into his room, changed out of his training clothing. With his shirt still off, he then opened the door to his bedroom that led out into the hallway. A healer walked in began placing Healing Ruins on Arthus's sore ribs. Then the healer was praying in an ancient language from the Golden City and spent a few minutes sending Life-energy pulses into Arthus ribs to heal the cracked bone and all the blood vessels around the purple blueish color that was clearly visible. Arthus also focused his own Life-energy, placed the locked door in his mind over his forehead, and then pushed his Life-energy directly at the wounded area on his ribs. He actually felt the bone straighten and watched as bruising disappeared. The bone was fixed as if it never happened. The healer left quickly out the door into the hallway and Arthus closed the door behind him, while thanking him for helping him.

Arthus then took a drink of the water in the barrel on his porch, which he had also cleansed from his horn which glowed. Then he went into the healing room area and climbed into the hot springs tub, where he spent about 30 minutes soaking in hot River of Life water that had been also mixed with healing salts. His sore body relaxed. He then took a quick shower and went back to his room, grabbed up his fancy official royal uniform. The blue tunic with all the fancy trim, the fancy ruffled shirt and black trousers with the outer seam trim. He dressed quickly, hiding his horn that glowed under his tunic. He then put on his highly polished shiny black boots. He grabbed up his shofar and his goat horn that Elder one. Then he put on his leather bracers that Jade had made him. He left his bedroom, locking the door behind him. Then he headed to the throne room where this guest and High King Thureos would be already waiting. He walked up to the great wooden doors. They were massive in size and carved from a long fallen God's Tree Seedling that had grown on another planet elsewhere. It was brought here from wherever that had been by the Archangels. There were carvings on the door of Michael standing before Thureos, who was just created from one of his feathers by God. They both kneeled before what was only carved as light and a quote etched into the door.

"Rise my anointed and faithful warrior, for you are to be fruitful and to make the world and the people Of Malon my shield to defend against the coming Darkness. I place them into your and your brother and sister Archangel's hands to raise them and train them well. For you, Thureos, from a feather of Michael the Archangel, created from that, like all the first families of Cundos on Malon, I found you more faithful and humbly willing to stand in the gap. Therefore, I have gifted you with an almost infinite life-span. You will seem immortal to others of your long-living kind, so that you will lead all the peoples of Malon as High King under me to guild your people and honor me. When the Darkness comes, they need a strong and just servant-leader to show them the way," First words from God.

Arthus loved to stand back and look upon the carving, and the written words scribed into the door. Arthus knew that his grandfather, High King Thureos, was created from a feather of Michael the Archangel's wing. He also knew that his grandmother, Amethyst, the High Queen was also created from one of Archangel Michael's feathers as were all the first generation of Cundos. The Ignole race like the first High Priest and High Priestess, all their first generation was created from the feathers of Archangel Raphael. All Cundo and Ignole from then on naturally born children. Prince Benroy, Arthus' father is the son of High King Thureos. Arthus' mother Laella, was the firstborn daughter of the first Ignole High Priest and High Priestess family. High King Thureos has a very real frustration with Prince Benroy's crazy infatuation with royal blood verses non-royal blood. Since all Cundo and all Ignole come from the feathers of these two Archangels, the very notion of any Cundo or Ignole not having the same blood running through them is simply a crazy twisted thought as they are all in a very real sense truly Archangel feather's born. The key difference between all the first generation of Cundos and Ignoles was that God found something very special within Thureos, that he was more honorable, and more faithful, and more intentionally humble. He was found willing to be a servant-leader, training himself and others, and standing in the gap to fight the Dark influences. God picked Thureos to become High King for those reasons alone. Thureos was anointed as High King with the Holy Oil from the Alter of God's Throne Room and then brought into the Throne Room of God and there God the Heavenly Father sent a LIGHT beam filling him and gifting him with almost infinite life-span, and the ability to grow to many times his normal size at will when in battle.

One of the two guards, after a minute, nodded to Arthus, and the door opened. Arthus walked into the throne room. It was a very large space. There were eight very large guards, four on each side of the room. All had blue caps, the sign of the royal guard across one shoulder down their backs. And, they all had very large *great shields* and spears. They all saluted Arthus as he walked by them. At the far end of the throne room sat three thrones. One massive throne made from Life ore, Silver, and gold with a vast Life Crystal where the head would rest. The throne was massive, thirty feet in height and at least fifteen in width. No one ever sat in that throne for who be so huge to fill that. Beside it to its right sat a smaller throne but still far too large for anyone. It was decorated exactly the same as the largest throne. Before the two larger thrones sat a much smaller wooden vines looking throne as if was grown by Druids completely naturally by tree roots. The small throne seemed almost sad compared to the beautiful thrones behind it. Sitting very uncomfortably upon that smaller rooted throne is High King Thureos, for this was his highly uncomfortable throne. The High Kings place from where he served all of Malon. Arthus, when he was little, asked why his grandfather's throne was so sad-looking. His grandfather stated that he was only a high king and was far lower than God, the Heavenly Father who the largest throne was represented as, and the other was for the King of Kings. His throne was intentionally uncomfortable to remind anyone who sat there that served all people should never be in a place of comfort, for becoming too comfortable with one's position, especially if concerned with rulership, power, or authority, instead of service, would welcome corruption and selfishness. It was a symbol to humble High King Thureos and to remind him always his place isn't as an all-powerful ruler but a servant to his people. Thureos stood and waved to Arthus to come forward. Before him stood an older Ignole Woman. Arthus knew her face but couldn't remember her name or place where he knew her from.

"Ah, Welcome, Prince Arthus. I glad you came to join us. This guest here is Katelynn Raphael Clan, leader of Clan Raphael and Headmistress of the Malon Academy. She has come to personally bring you to the Malon Academy and to help answer many of your questions," said High King Thureos.

Katelynn bowed at the High King and then walked over in front of Prince Arthus and looked him over, walking around him nodding.

"You have grown into a fine man, my Prince, and it is an honor. I have looked forward to bring you to the Malon Academy since the day you were born. I saw great things from your father as I helped see him through his Academy years. And, I expect to see great things from you too. However, I do believe all of that can wait as today is your one hundredth year life day celebration. I won't waste your time tonight. I will let the high King have you until you are ready to head out. I will be waiting by the transport when you are ready," said Katelynn. Then she turns and bows again to the High King and says, "Thank you, High King, always glad to sit and drink tea and talk about things with you as always." Then she turned and walked out of the room.

Arthus sighed as he declared to himself, "Great things!" In his head he thought, "What great things is she referring to." Arthus turned to see High King Thureos smiling.

Then Prince Benroy walked out from behind one of the giant thrones, sighed and said, "Finally, she left. I never thought she'd leave. Don't get me wrong, Prince Arthus, Katelynn is a powerful Ignole, and really a nice woman, but she likes to treat people like a grandmother. She is here all day scolding me for this and that, and I just don't have the time, but congrats on your life day. I also expect great things as son and heir to the Royal Bloodline. You have a lot to prove and have to show all why we of Clan Arkwright rule. Do not embarrass your clan or me," said Prince Benroy. With that, he walked out a side door and was gone.

Arthus suddenly couldn't help himself and just let out a laugh.

High King Thureos laughed out loud and said, "My grandson, don't worry, yes the Malon Academy will be challenging, and no it won't be easy, but I trained with you myself these last forty-seven years, and I talked with all those clan leaders who you lived with for the two years I sent you to live and work with them. Everyone has told me nothing but how you treated them with respect and always showed that you would work hard and never use your clan or title to gain any kind of privilege over others, with the exception of that one incident where you did make a special request of the Great Northern Guard Captain to have one of his patrol guards personally hand deliver your packages safely to your girlfriend's house. I told him to make you clean up the poop from the kennels to teach you to humble yourself from that one. And, I know how you humbled yourself, and I also know you wised up a whole lot! I have seen how you handled yourself with the Yelin Snow Folk, with the Urial Guards, with Clan Arial, and how each and every time you carefully observe and listen before you ever open your mouth to speak. That makes me proud! I am so dang proud of you! You are the one true Prince of this world! Your father often forgets that it is not we who rule, but we who serve all others. God rules, we serve! Unfortunately, your father thinks more highly of specific blood ties and is so focused on all the clan rankings, than he ever does about the needs of all those he is supposed to be serving. I have never once witnessed, or ever even heard of him serving anyone, that includes me and you and everyone else in his entire life. This lack of servant heartedness is why God will never will allow me to pass on any burden of my throne over to him. By being firstborn, and only by being firstborn, he is considered a royal prince, but with his dang foolish pride and arrogance, he will never be a True Prince of Malon. His viperous words make me want to officially remove his birthrights to the title Prince, and believe me, I have considered. Yet, I keep praying and hoping for him to change. I hope in my heart that he has accepted that he will never sit on any throne! However, only given commandership over the silver thorns, your father has found his own little niche place within the world where he feels he truly belongs. Even though he never once verbally expresses his pleasure about that, I have reached out with my Life-energy and have sensed how truly happy he really is with doing only that one thing. Apart from his haughtiness, and his deep bitterness and anger, which he never seems to break away from, he is doing that one thing in the best way he knows how."

"As I have watched and observed how you have grown in wisdom and favor with God and all the other people's groups on Malon, I often wonder if you will become the one God sees as the worthy person to take my burden, But, that is not for now, don't worry about that. Today is your One-Hundredth Year Life Day Celebration. Therefore, I do have some surprises planned for you," said High King Thureos as he motioned to his doorkeepers.

With that, the huge doors opened, and Michael the Archangel walked in. He nodded to High King Thureos and walked straight over to Prince Arthus. Michael was dressed in a shining white robe, his wings were not showing right now, but he still glowed with a golden light. In this form he appeared as a rather strong looking man, short golden hair and a short golden beard. Arthus had seen him at other times. One time he appeared as a giant man of over at least four meters tall. Arthus believed that his height changed each time he appeared to them. Just being in the presence of this Archangel, you could feel the enormous Life-energy and a great power beyond that of all the Archangels and regular Heavenly Angels combined flowing all around and through and within him.

"Yes, you have grown into a fine young man. You just now, in fact today, are hitting manhood for your Ignole and Cundo peoples, and so as long as you stay alive, and are not killed in a battle, and only God, our Heavenly Father knows your natural life ends from your natural life beginnings, you should pretty much stay looking like what you look like right now until you are nine hundred ninety nine thousand years old. You will then start to significantly age like all the others of your peoples for your last thousand years. Immediately after celebrating your one hundred thousand year life day, you will pass from the physical realm into a completely spiritual one, because no one that serves God truly dies," said Michael the Archangel.

Arthus is now about two hundred centimeters in height, which is a little over six foot six inches. He is quite strong, not ample, but his muscles are tight and corded from all his year's training with High King Thureos. His skin was still a tad greenish pale, and his ears, like all of his race, were pointy. His long pure white hair is braided in a single long ponytail tied together by his mother Laella's unique bark leather strap as custom with most Ignole families. Arthus wasn't pure Ignole nor pure Cundo, he was half of each.

"Yes, I do also see great things from you, young man! You remind me so much of a much younger Thureos," Michael the Archangel smiled, "but you are not pure Cundo nor pure Ignole. I normally witness hybrids of both usually not surviving past birth, and yes, I do know of your birth and of the intentional sacrifice made by your dear mother, Laella, who had prayed every single day of her pregnancy that God would anoint you and watch over you and guide you and give you great wisdom. She was truly a close friend of mine and very wise woman! I see all of her wisdom and kindness in you. And, I see your servant's heart for all the living things and beings on Malon. I see that you have the same kind of strength and fortitude of your grandfather. And, I don't really see any of the emotional pain and anger, or especially any greed for power and authority that I know your father has in his heart and mind, which is really, really good. Be careful to never allow any of your father's bitter words to take root in your heart, and you will do great things," said Michael the Archangel.

Turning towards High King Thureos, Michael the Archangel raised his hand out and said, "In answer to all your thoughts and prayers and questions about Prince Arthus' destiny in helping you take some of your burden, yes, High King Thureos, I do think it will gladly take to Prince Arthus as it will be wielded with great care and understanding," said Michael. After saying that Michael the Archangel lifted up his other hand towards Arthus, then turned and moved his other hand beside the one he extended towards Arthus. Suddenly there was a small light that appeared above his two outstretched hands. And, then a silver tube appeared in Michael's hands.

"This is Angel Wing like the one your grandfather wields. This is its twin for what Angel only has one wing. But I warn you, this weapon is a weapon forged in heaven for myself and not meant for just anyone, so you will have to master it. Your grandfather took almost half the normal life of one of your people to master his, but I believe that with the proper guidance you can master it before your Academy time is over. This Angel Wing, like your grandfather's, is a special weapon that becomes whatever the wielder needs it become at any given moment. You have witnessed this happening when you were on the battlefield with the Ice Wolves, when your grandfather used his Angel Wing. This isn't an easy weapon to control. First you must master your mind and your own Life-energy during every battle. Any slip in controlling your own mind or your own Life-energy the weapon will change to something else or back to its original form, this small silver tube. That was High King Thureos biggest struggle to make sure to keep a part of his mind trained to focus always on his weapon to make sure it stayed whatever form he needed it to be at all times while also keeping his mind in the fight. From my own observations of you, and from the observations of the Redwood tree nymph Timothy, and from the other unseen Angels that are always around, we believe you have great potential to learn to master this technique quickly as well," continued Michael.

"Now, I must also warn you and your grandfather that no matter what happens in battle or in life, never under any circumstances, ever grab ahold of both Angel Wings at once. For it is a sentient weapon. I had these made specifically for me. If anyone other than an Archangel tries to grab ahold of both of the Angel Wing weapons, it can read in the Life-energy that they are not an Archangel and then destroys the wielder with an excruciating death," said Michael the Archangel.

Michael the Archangel then asked, "Do you think you have what it takes young Arkwright, who is already highly honored and even anointed of the Alda Matriarch, to learn to master this weapon and use it only for the good of all your people, and that of all living beings?"

"Yes, I won't let you down or your belief in me. I will wield Angel Wing with the utmost respect for all the people and living beings on Malon, or wherever else God leads me to go. Thank you for your trust in me," said Prince Arthus.

Michael nodded and bowed, and handed Angel Wing to Prince Arthus. Then waved his hand and portal of light opened up, and Michael walked through and was gone. Arthus looked down at the silver tube in his hand and couldn't believe what just happened. Michael the Archangel of War in the Heavens had given him one of the most powerful of heavens weapons.

"Yes, it is a powerful thing and a huge responsibility to wield one of the Angel Wings. I trained you and have seen what you have already become and what you can become. I do know this, for it was I who told Michael the Archangel of your potential to wield the other Angel Wing. I trust you can and will learn it far quicker than I ever did. Now put that away in here, in the holy anointed trunk with which you will store this weapon. Yes here, that you see by at my feet. I do have a few more surprises for you," said High King Thureos.

Arthus quickly obeyed. The High King waved his hand towards the door keepers, and the doors opened again. In walked three, all smiling, and Arthus jaw dropped open. For before him, was Jade, Zeck, and Emon.

"Well ya, young man. You going to greet us or just stand there dumbfounded," laughed Emon. Jade just ran up and hugged him, for he was indeed in shock. First the weapon, and now his three best friends he had come to know during his travels, were all here on this celebration day. It only took Arthus a second to recover. He smiled broadly at them and even had a tear running down his cheek. He had stayed in touch with all of them through the holo-messaging system. Which was a device most used to talk with friends and family, or for receiving or sending reports, or other news, or whatever needed saying all around Malon. He used it mainly to record messages, pictures or videos to send to these three.

Arthus looked very observantly at Jade as she smiled. She too was now a fully grown woman. She had long red hair braided so beautifully laid down one of her shoulders and tied at the end with a green color bow that perfectly matched her beautiful bright green eyes. He started looking down at her shape and yes, she had definitely grown into her womanhood. Arthus face went bright red. He knew she was just under six feet, and she was very strong from all her years growing up on the farms and forest. She very gracefully wore a green colored shirt that also matched her eyes. Over the shirt she wore a brown suede leather vest. She also wore sued leather half pants that buckled just below the knee. Her outfit fit her body shape perfectly. She also wore brand new heavy leather tie up boots that had a rather high legged top reaching up to just below her knees. The tie strings on the boot matched the color of her shirt and her ribbon and her eyes. Arthus could tell that this outfit was meant for working around the farm. The leathers weren't that much different than what they wore on their hunt, but now definitely much better fitting to her beautiful womanly figure. Her smile and her eyes and her shape suddenly made Arthus knees just give out from underneath him. He just fell to his butt in front of the three.

A little embarrassed, Arthus looked at Zeck, who was now taller than Arthus by at least two whole feet; he was huge! Zeck's black hair was short, and he sported a short black beard that was neatly trimmed. He had a minor scar across his nose, and Arthus could tell all the years mining and forging alongside the Dwarvens had made him into a powerfully strong man. His arms and legs literally bulged with powerful muscles. He wore a grey tunic and black trousers and black boots.

Then Arthus looked to Emon, who seemed the same as he had when they first met, well almost. He was just a little older. He had a large black beard and shaved head. He wore a pack on his back full of his strange devices, Arthus figured. A sizeable two-handed hammer laid across his left shoulder. It looked as odd as the Dwarven, as along its handle had several gears and switches. Emon wore a chain mail shirt and large boots with metal tips on their top. On his head were a set goggles. Arthus smiled at the three and got back to his feet.

"I had no idea you would all be here, and to see you all after so long, well, it was a true shock. I knew I would see you at the Malon Academy, but this here is a true surprise," said Arthus.

"The High King told us that today was a special day for you, and well we all are the same age, just born at different times of the same year. He thought it would be nice for all three of us to go together to where we will all spend the next nine hundred years training right beside each other. In truth, I was incredibly excited when my father Grag received word of High King Thureos, your grandfather's wishes. I have received and treasured all your messages ever since forty-eight years ago, when you left the Arial valley to go up to Great Northern Peaks City. And, then when you came back through for that few hours we were able to spend together, forty-seven years ago. Then all I could do was wave at you on the ship as you came here a few weeks later. I truly couldn't wait to see what kind of man our Prince and great friend had grown into," said Jade. As she said that, she looked Arthus up and down. Arthus didn't get to recognize the reaction that her face had shown, because right then Zeck slapped him on the shoulder and he took his eyes off her for a minute. If he hadn't, he would have seen that her face turn bright red.

A growl from the huge double doors brought the whole room to look over. The eight giant sized royal guards quickly reacted to the sound with their swords drawn. However, the sound that was heard was Fang.

Arthus, seeing Fang, immediately said, "Guards sheath your swords, there is no danger here!" Fang quickly ran over to stand beside Jade.

Fang had been blessed by the Archangel Arial, Arthus knew from Jade messages, that Fang had become her life-bound companion. Because of that blessing, Fang would live as long as Jade did and keep his robust youth as long as Jade did, for they had now become at some kind of spiritual level and Life-energy sense the same being, even though they both kept their own bodies, souls and minds. This Life-bond blessing was a scarce thing; almost unheard of at all throughout Malon. There were few others that had ever been Life-bonded like this. One was High King Thureos to the Mother Matriarch of all the Yaule, who High King Thureos had met when Michael the Archangel had allowed him to portal the first time to their moon, Creed. Creed is the forest moon of Malon, and is the same moon where the Dwarvens were also discovered. All the Dwarvens and many Yaules were then brought by the Angels from Creed to Malon for their own well-being, and they have all truly benefited from choosing to make that move. The Matriarch of the Dwarvens, though greatly saddened by leaving her home and old fortress, understood the importance of making this move to Malon with all of her Dwarvens. The Mother Matriarch of Yaule and many of her Yaule children had decided to remain on the moon. Since that happened Malon regularly sends supplies and resources up to Creed to improve the lives of those that chose to remain there. At least that is the story, as he had learned it. Anyway the Life-bonded always share a telepathic link in order that they are always in contact with one another. If Fang happened to be killed, Jade would immediately feel it. However, that wouldn't cause her to die. There was one such instance, the person that remained alive became so overly depressed by the death of their Life-bonded Yaule, that they ended up killing themselves, rather than seeking anyone's help with their depression issues. After that incident, the practice of Life-bonding has rarely been done. Whatever the Archangel Arial saw in Fang and Jade made him realize that they deserved to have this Life-bond blessing. Arthus was very aware of what that Life-bond meant and knew he could trust Fang as Fang would have the same feelings for Arthus that Jade would have. He walked over and hugged the massive cat. Fang had truly become a gigantic Yaule. Fang was almost twice the size he had been when he saw him forty-seven years before. Arthus pushed his own Life energy into Fang as he hugged him. He instantly could sense the enormous Life-energy and power of the Life-bond that both Fang and Jade enjoyed. Arthus then reached up and gave Fang a scratching pet behind his ears. Fang then kneeled down on all four of his legs until his body lay sort of in a crouched position on the ground.

Arthus then walked around the other side of Jade and said, "Congratulations for being blessed by the Archangel Arial with the Life-bond with Fang. You both truly deserve that kind of spiritual Life-energy bonding experience.

"Oh, Arthus, one more thing before the four of you have to go. There are three young people who have already patiently waited forty-seven years to get to see you again. And, I decided rather than make them wait until they reached their own One Hundred Year's Life Day before getting any chance to see you again, that they also come here for your One Hundred Year's Life Day Celebration," said High King Thureos, who then waved his hands and the huge doors opened up again.

Two fairly young men and a fairly young woman came into the throne room. They were each dressed in fine new Clan uniforms, which Arthus recognized as coming from the island which he and the High King had visited. They came in and deeply bowed down to the High King and to Prince Arthus. Then they each folded their hands in a prayer like fashion and in unison said, "We thank you High King Thureos and Prince Arthus in the name of God, in the name of our clan, and in our own names for inviting us to visit the palace and participate in Prince Arthus' One Hundred Years Life Day Celebration."

"Tom, Sapphire, and Cald! You three get over here and give me a big bear hug! I can't believe how much you all have grown, exclaimed Arthus excitedly. Then he said, "Hey, everyone come meet the three young people that I wrote you all about."

The three came and gave Prince Arthus a hug. Then shook hands with Jade, Zeck and Emon.

High King Thureos said, "Tom, Sapphire and Cald, Captain Coral and the Naval Base Commander have given me regular reports on your living situation and on all your educational and recreational pursuits. You are all the same age now that Prince Arthus was when he went to stay at the Clan Arial Valley and then at the Great Northern Peaks City. Now, Jade's father and mother have asked if I could perhaps get three fine young people to come to help them now that Jade is leaving for the Malon Academy. Anyway, your clan head has given me permission to send you all to live and work with Grag and Shelly and the Clan Arial on in their farm valley. And, just as good of an experience as it was for Prince Arthus, I trust it will also be for you three for the next year. Then after one year there you three will also go up to the Great Northern Peaks City to live and work just like Arthus had done, though Sapphire will mostly work regularly with the Urial Guard up there, rather than in the mines and forge. What do you each think about that?"

Sapphire said, "Oh wow, yes that will be so awesome. I do love animals so much. Farms do have lots of animals to take care of right?"

Tom said, "As long as there is good food to eat and some great adventuring to do I am game."

Cald said, "I love learning about various machines and how they work and taking them apart and putting them back together again. And, I know there are machines that are used on the farm, so yes, please. Getting to work the second year with Clan Gearhead actually learning how various things are made from scratch too. Wow this is going to be so great! I am sure it will be really hard work, but that is better than getting sea sick on a boat any day!"

Sapphire and Tom said in unison, "Oh ya, Cald gets terrible sea sick!"

"Alright then, it is settled. Sylla will come in here quickly and take you to where you will be sleeping tonight and tomorrow morning I will be heading with you three to the Clan Arial Valley to meet Jade's parents, Grag and Shelly."

"Now that you all have greeted one another, I know that there is a frustrated woman waiting for you at the Golden Griffon Platform. The four of you and Fang will be heading their pretty quick. Arthus everything you will be taking to the Academy is already packed and loaded on the Golden Griffon Platform. I even made sure that they carefully wrapped your ornate Mammoth wedding prayer and peaceful dreams prayer tusk. I trust that Jade and Emon already came from their homes ready to move to the Malon Academy too. Your clan should have made sure you had everything you were to bring with you. I trust Jade came with her mammoth tusk and her shofar and her goat's horn too. Zeck and Emon, I trust you brought the loads of weapons that I ordered from you for the Academy too. The Silver Thorns are all enjoying the ones they received. Seeing how you're all shaking your heads yes as I have been talking to you, Katelynn Raphael Clan, leader of Clan Raphael and Headmistress of the Malon Academy, with all her gifts isn't one to make waiting forever, so get a move on. Arthus don't forget to take this holy anointed trunk and what's inside with you." said High King Thureos smiling at the group.

As they were leaving the throne room Sylla came in to say goodbye and to usher the three young friends to the rooms that they were staying in for the night. Arthus gave Sylla a hug as he was leaving.

Soon the four of them were walking out to the same platform where Arthus so many years ago left on a griffon to his first adventure. But this time, a flying multi-segmented transport shuttle was waiting for them and all their gear.

Katelynn was already seated inside the open shuttle door waiting for them.

"Good, you're all here now. Grab your gear and secure it down really good on the pallets in the back section of the shuttle transport, Jade, your giant Yaule named Fang, will he be ok with riding back with the gear by himself, or do you think he would be more relaxed only if you strapped yourself in one of the pull down seats in the baggage area and stayed there with him? I'll leave that decision up to you and him. Everyone else for sure come back up and strap yourselves into these here seats. Hurry now, we need to head to the Elemental Island where the Malon Academy is located. If any of you have any questions for me as we head over, I will be glad to answer them," said Katelynn.

They quickly packed all their gear on the four pallets that were in the baggage compartment and used the tie down nets and the heavy strapping to secure them all down good so they wouldn't move around during the flight.

Jade spoke gently to Fang and was brushing Fang's hair. She knew he had never experienced a flight through the air before. Fang had brought her on his back from the Arial Valley through the God's Forest. Her gear was sent ahead of her by Golden Griffon and was already waiting on the platform for them to arrive. She had him really relaxed sitting in the baggage compartment. But, they hadn't flown up into the air yet, so she wasn't absolutely sure what to expect from him. Jade left him there for a minute and went and spoke with Katelynn saying, "I think Fang will be ok, but this is the very first time he will experience flying. Can we do a short test run to see what his reaction might be?"

Katelynn said, "Yes, I think that is best that we try a very short test run up into the air and back down again with Fang being alone in the baggage compartment. Then if everything seems ok with him, then you can ride up here with us so we can get to know each other better. If not, then we will set an appointment where you and I will meet for tea and get to know each other better there."

Jade went back to where Fang was still crouched down between the pallets of baggage. He still seemed to be very calm. Arthus came over to Fang and held onto Jades hand. Then used his Life-energy push into both Jade and Fang sending a wave of emotional calming and healing through both of their bodies. Jade smiled and squeezed Arthus hand.

"I have truly missed being with you Arthus, and Fang here knows that too," said Jade.

Everyone climbed up into their seats in the main cabin area of the transport and strapped themselves in with the strapping bucklers.

The pilot of the transport shuttle lifted the shuttle up into the air and took a quick run around the First God's Tree and came right back to the platform. Jade unstrapped herself, went back to check on Fang who had laid down and started to sleep. She then came back assured that Fang would be fine by himself while they flew on their way, and strapped herself back into the seat buckler.

"Fang will be just fine back there by himself," said Jade to Katelynn.

"Ok, then Pilot, we are ready to go" said Katelynn and the shuttle took off into the air towards Elemental Island.

"Elemental Island, why is it called that," asked Emon?

"Ah, glad you asked. The island is a massive artificially created island. It was created by the Archangels who know how to blend and manipulate all the various elements found in many places in the universe, including here on Malon. They also built the Malon Academy facilities that you will see in just a few hours. The island is also named the elemental island because it is made to house every type of environment in different sections. The Malon Academy itself is in the very center of all four distinct land environments. Each is walled off from one another. Think of it as a thing in the center which is the Academy with various wall intervals, which all together make up the main academy grounds and then there are passage ways which link into the four outer land environment parts. The whole island kind of is cut with a giant X, except in the center where the Academy is located. In the north part is the mountain regain, south is the desert, west is jungle, and east is a swamp. Each of these areas is teaming with its own dangers and each have special training grounds. The Academy itself is a really nice place. The main buildings are cafes, main lecture halls, offices, and living quarters where the academy staff all live. There are two large dorm buildings, one is for the men, and one for the women. There is a variety of weapon grounds and a stadium. There is a botany dome. Every one of you will have mandatory combat training, whether you plan to become a regular fighter or not. The warrior training grounds and master Jacob who is weapon master is where you be spending a lot of time. The Botany dome is where you will learn all the different types of plants and animals and what can be used for eating, healing and such. There are also many different types of academy lab spaces. Which reminds me, please, Emon, do not blow up our labs, there are plenty of outdoor training places. Some are specifically designed where you can practice all of your fun exploding stuff."

Emon laugh out loud.

Katelynn cut him off quickly, and said, "The first time you blow up something in the wrong area, you will be cleaning out sewage lines and toilets and cleaning all the excrement in the kennels for the next one hundred years. Do I make myself clear?"

Emon said, "Yes mam!"

Katelynn smiled and continued, "In the main lecture halls and library, you will learn math, history, science, and so, so many other things. You might wish to set up your own class schedules based on your own likes, and dislikes. We learned a long time ago, that everything is important for everyone to learn at least something about. There really is a process to the rigorous schedules of learning, so you might as well trust right from the start is all designed for everyone's best interest. There are healing spaces with large hot spring baths and showers that I guarantee you will need to use every single evening. Those spaces are also clearly divided male and female. Over time as you are learning you will be evaluated and coached especially when we see any area which you need improvement, or when we see you excelling in an area, we can help you design some of your later years trainings with those focus areas where you truly show strengths. A few goals that we have in mind is that everyone learns to get along with each other. Keep the combat training competitions in the combat training competitions, and don't ever try to become rival enemies of other Academy Cadets. You will be learning alongside of many different clans and some of them are mixed beast-man evolved. Recognize upfront that they will have distinct cultures and ways of thinking and working that are often quite a bit different then the Cundos, the Ignoles and the Dwarvens. The Yelin Snow Folk, and the Ice Wolves are prime examples of what I am talking about. Their histories still effect how they think about each other, but they are learning to get along, and here we will ensure that their new processes of getting along continue. Everyone will need to learn about the history and culture of everyone else so that we all can learn from each other. And do remember that you will be all living here for the next nine hundred years. Each of the nine hundred years there will be those who are graduating and those who are just coming in. After nine hundred years then you will graduate and join whatever clan you wish to join. The different zones will be used for special training as well as helping you all master your inherit elemental life ability's and each of the elemental masters will be there to help guild you," said Katelynn.

"Wait, what inherit elemental abilities," asked Jade. Before all the others could ask.

"Yes, most don't know what their elemental alignment is if any before they come here for when this place was created by the Archangels they infused each area with high amounts of Life-energy from God. This way it helps those training under whatever element you inherit will come to the forefront and will be easier to learn to control whatever it is you can do. Ignole have the inherited ability to control their external elemental surroundings while Cundo masters their internal elemental inheritance. Why Arthus, you and the very few like you who actually are born of Cundo and Ignole are so special. To see if you become a master of both the external elements and internal elemental, or whether you might be limited in one or the other or both is a test I like to see with you, I admit I am very interested to know. However, that really is something you must find out for yourself during your time here. Alright now all of us should get some rest as we still have a long flight before we arrive," said Katelynn. With that, Arthus pondered what he would see in the coming years and what pathways he might take. He thought about what the High King had said to him, and what Michael the Archangel had said to him. What really is his destiny? He clearly understood that his grandfather and Michael the Archangel had much bigger plans for him than simply becoming a Silver Thorn Knight, like he thought he wanted to be to try to please his father. They both obviously believed in him, for much, much more. With that, Arthus laid his head back and shut his eyes. He reached out with his Life energy throughout the entire transport shuttle touching each and every living being. He sensed in the flow that Jade was playing telepathic games with Fang, who had woke up in the baggage compartment. He knew Zeck had already fell asleep. He could hear Emon's voice as he was looking over some of his books and talking with Katelynn about the biosphere. The pilot of the transport shuttle was very alert to everything happening both on and off the shuttle in the skies surrounding the shuttle. Arthus reached out farther with his life-energy senses and began to actually feel the Life-energies even in the air molecules both inside and outside of the ship. He breathed deeply absorbing the Life-energies into his body allowing his mind to concentrate on helping to bring a calming and healing sensation into all of the air molecules. He pushed the air molecules that were slightly in front of the transport out farther ahead of the transport shuttle and in his mind locked a point in the jet stream barrier a little bit farther out then the nose of the transport shuttle. The actual transport shuttle ride became a bit calmer as it was no longer bucking the wind sheers. Arthus practiced holding onto that thought barrier, while he also pushed a greater healing calmness into all of the passengers on the transport shuttle. In his mind he created a second open door for allowing the healing to flow out, while the first locked door was holding the molecules in the air out in front of the shuttle. Arthus then placed a third open door in his mind where his life-energy was embracing and filling Jade. Arthus was able to hold all three of those Life energy actions happening simultaneously. Arthus could feel Life-energy being pushed back into himself and checked in his three focuses from where that might be coming from. It wasn't coming from the locked molecule out in front of the transport shuttle and he sensed that it wasn't coming from Jade, though he could sense that both she and Fang knew he was embracing her with his Life-energy. The life energy was coming back through the open door that he had created to push healing into all the other passengers on the ship. He reached back through that open door and touched each of the passengers one by one to see if he could sense which person was sending the push back at him. It wasn't Fang. It wasn't Zeck. It wasn't Emon. It wasn't the Pilot. He reached out for Katelynn and found her easily, but it wasn't her either. He pushed again through the baggage compartment onto the pallets of baggage. He immediately could feel the Life-energy push coming from the Angel Wing in the holy anointed trunk he had on his pallet. He remembered what Michael the Archangel had said and placed a locked doorway in his mind between the Angel Wing and himself so that it would not somehow activate and cause a disaster. However, Arthus continued holding onto all four doors now, two locked and two open.

Zeck tapped Arthus on the shoulder as he continued to meditate on the four doors in his mind. Zeck pointed without saying anything out one of the transport portals. Far below was the island they flew over a deep and dense swampland. The island had large cliffs around the outside, so getting there by boat wouldn't be easy, and massive walls surrounded the far end of the swamp they could already see.

"All get ready; we shall be landing soon," said the co-Pilot.

Soon they were over the wall, and before them was the Academy, a massive building shaped like a pyramid but didn't come up to a point; instead, the top was a large flat area where ships landed and took off. This building was the middle of two large buildings that seemed shaped like a strange Mushroom. In the center was a large silo, while every so often, the tower would have a big circular area that went around the middle. There seemed to be at least twenty or so of these before it stopped. Arthus guessed these were the housing, then out to the side was a large oval building. It had no roof in the middle and a large sandy floor they could see the floor stopped. Some walls went up to stands where what look like a thousand or so could sit and watch. In the very center of the floor was a large stone block. Arthus could see several people inside training but could not actually see what they were doing since they all seemed like small insects from the height. On the opposite side of the pyramid was a large dome made mostly of glass and looked like it was filled with plants and such. Each wall had a platform along its top where people could gather, and it looked like lifts took you up or down each side into the different areas. They started their descent and landed on the flat room of the center building.

Even while looking around and observing Arthus continued to focus this way until the shuttle landed in the Malon Academy on Elemental Island. Once the shuttle landed Arthus released the molecules of air he had held out in front of the shuttle. When he did that everyone could literally feel those as they slammed into the nose of the shuttle. There was a slight jolt that the pilot had not caused. Arthus closed the door in his mind and then released it to completely disappear that was sending the calming and healing to everyone on the shuttle. Arthus unlocked the door in his mind to the Angel Wing and found that it had settled itself down, but he had a real sense that it was always ready for him to call it into his hand. Arthus left the door open where he was embracing Jade and he did a double push into Jade with his Life-energy, trying to help her literally feel the love in his heart. Immediately Fang responded to that Life-energy push from the baggage compartment. Fang had clearly felt Arthus' Life-energy push through Jade, which was meant to make her feel his love. Fang let out a low growl.

In his mind Arthus clearly heard Fang telepathically say to him, "Be patient. She loves you."

Arthus smiled and tried to send back a telepathic message into Fang. "I'm trying, but I want to hold and kiss her so much. Fang, Fang, are you there Fang?

Arthus could not hear Fang answer his thoughts so he thought, "Maybe it is just a one way connection right now."

"Or, maybe I am ignoring you, lover boy!" Arthus clearly heard Fang telepathically say into his thoughts.

Arthus laughed.

Fang Growled.

"I wonder if Jade can telepathically hear me too? Thought Arthus as he pushed his thoughts with Life-Energy."

"Don't push your luck, lover boy! I can still rip your throat out anytime I want to with my paw! Besides, telepathically intruding into someone's mind comes with grave responsibilities and consequences. I could feel you pushing with your Life energy filled with love emotions, and some of that felt just a little too fast for someone who had not kissed his girlfriend in over forty-seven years. That is why I opened this telepathic pathway into your mind. And, my ability to communicate this way was a huge gift blessing from Archangel Arial. I know that I should never just use it without permission. But, in your case I had to do something to slow you down! You've only kissed her once and that was over forty-seven years ago. We will all be here for the next nine hundred years. Give her some space and time to get to know you again. That's my advice. Now I am turning off this pathway, so that I can concentrate on what I need to be doing with her. If you really want to communicate with me again in the future, you need permission to start telepathically looking around in my thoughts. Just know that I know the difference between pushing Life-energy for healing and mental calmness and pushing your love emotions through your Life-energy."

"Got it. Thank you," thought Arthus back towards Fang. Then Arthus literally could feel in his Life-energy that Fang slammed the telepathic door shut towards him and locked it."

Chapter 20
Elemental Island

"Welcome to Elemental Island and the Academy. We are in the building that I told you held the cafe and meeting halls and all offices and living space for myself and the other teachers and workers who live here. Men, your dorm is the tall building on the right, and Jade, you will be on the left side. If I recall, your rooms should be around the fifth floor. In the center of each building, a lift will take you to one of the floors. Each floor holds five apartment size rooms. Two will live together in each room. Follow me, and we get you all registered and find your rooms. Many others start today, so after you settle your things in about two hours or so, your welcome ceremony is held in meeting hall three. Now let us get you all taken care of," said Katelynn.

It wasn't long and they were in a sizeable office-like room where other people were getting paperwork and key cards, and such. As soon as they received their assigned rooms and keycards, then Arthus and the rest stood outside the main building.

"OK, it looks like Zeck and I will be sharing a room on the fifth floor, and Emon, your roommate, will be a person named Asher. Jade, you be on floor six of your building, and your roommate will be someone named Zoey. Let us all get our gear and rooms settled, then meet up here in one hour, then we can figure out what to do before the first meeting starts," said Arthus. They all agreed and headed to the dorms. There arrival at their dorms did not take any length of time, and the ID cards on the lanyards that they all were issued allowed them to enter the lift and took them directly to their respective floors. Emon's room was right next to

Arthus' and Zeck's room. They were in room five hundred and two, and Emon was five hundred and three.

When they entered their room, the living room was the first room. They saw a large room with two hard wood couches that lined the outer wall. There was a three foot high table. Arthus had seen tables like these before with Zeck in their home in the Great Northern Peaks City. There were eight chairs that fit around the table. There were two rooms off to one side. One held two large lockers for weapons and gear, and the other had a workstation with areas to work with alchemy and a station for mending equipment and working with your weapons. There was a kitchen, with a fridge, some cupboard spaces with pots and pans and dishes, and drawers which had eating, cooking and serving utensils in them. Arthus opened the fridge and inside was a keg of ale with a tap. Some variety of juices, fruits and vegetables were in the bottom drawer, and a cold cut meats and cheeses were in the top drawer. The very bottom of the fridge had a second slide out area, which was a freezer. Arthus saw that it was stocked with a variety of frozen meats. The kitchen also had a counter with a flat two burner cook top embedded into the counter. There were two built-in blower ovens next to the fridge. There was a hall that went around to a latrine, which included a large shower, a toilet, and a sink. Two doors to either side of the hallway just before the latrine were the two small bedrooms. The bedrooms were not large. Each room had a single very long bed made from hardwood and metal connectors. There was a fairly thick synth-blend mattress on each bed that fit the entire inner frame and platform of the bed. Then there was a four large drawer with two smaller drawers on top dresser. On the flat top of the dresser was a glow-lamp. Attached to one end of the dresser was a tall clothes hanging closet, with a swinging door that closed to help keep the clothes clean inside. At the foot of each bed was a big metal clad wooden chest. The beds weren't at all huge, but plenty long and wide enough for Zeck's big body to lay on. Above the head of each bed was a shelf attached to the wall, fairly high up the wall. Each bedroom also has a writing desk and a chair meant for study.

Arthus put his gear away and dressed in the Academy uniform, which was black boots, Black trousers, a white tunic that had the symbol of the Academy that was tucked into a black belt. Still, Arthus didn't use that one he took out a belt that was given to him by Thureos it held an area for some vile, and on the back where the belt would meet the small of ones back held an area that Arthus could keep Angel Wing in its basic tube form and latch it on one side. Arthus' horn that glowed was tucked under his left armpit inside his tunic. He intentionally put the goat horn over the outside of his tunic in the same place to help hide the bulge under his tunic.

Zeck had changed and was sitting on rather flat floor pillows before the table with the chairs in the living room center. A device was built into the table that projected a halo that could be changed to different channels: local events, a map, and a channel where you could check your messages. Zeck was looking at the map, trying to get the layout of the grounds fully. They could see other buildings, one to the North that held some large open bays. The map identified them as engineering labs. There was a large barn also on the map, next to it was a Yaule training area. Arthus guessed that Fang would be living in the large barn and primarily training in that area, except when they went out beyond the walls of the Academy into the four element environments.

"Well, Zeck looks like we are roommates for nine hundred years, and it's not a bad space if I say so. If you are ready, let's head down and meet with Jade and Emon," said Arthus with a grin.

"Ya nine hundred years it kinda blows my mind we lived a hundred years but to think of nine times that time just here learning studying and training seems over kill, but ya lets head out," said Zeck. Emon was out of his room waiting on them when they walked out of their room.

"So you all get settled they be nice rooms, and me roommate is a fun-looking Dwarven like myself. I introduce ya. His name is Asher," said Emon. They went into Emon's room. A stocky red-haired and bearded Dwarven stood looking around.

"Ah, Emon here. I thought you had left to the ceremony thing. I was wrapping up, making sure all my gear is put away. O, and who are your friends here," asked Asher?

"These be me friends, and they live next door to us. He is Zeck, who worked more than half his life in the mines and in the Forge. And

Prince Arthus be right here. He came to work one year with Zeck and even spent some time working with both me and Zeck on some pretty cool weapons. And friends, this be me new roommate Asher," said Emon. Asher was dressed like them all in the Academy's uniform, but he had a massive hammer, unlike Emon's. It looked like many other blacksmith hammers, but this one was covered in Ruins and had a life crystal built into the bottom of the grip. Asher was a built Dwarven. His red beard was braided and tucked into a brown belt he had strapped around his waist and behind him was a staff leaning on the wall, one of metal at the top a symbol of the Anvil with Ruins also carved into it sat. Arthus thought he recognized the mark, but it was Zeck who looked on in awe.

"You're a Craftier-Caster or training to be one," said Zeck.

"Ah, you know of me order. Yes, me was born of one of the high craftsmen of clan Gearhead," said Asher. Craftsmen be like religious order for Dwarvens since God to them is the Ultimate Creator their priest were some of the top-level craftsmen of Gearhead including Maddlynn, Arthus remembered so this Asher was born to one of the more famous ones.

"Me father's father was the first to reach the level of Priesthood by his famous blacksmith skills, and he was a great Druid of Gearhead named Master Dorgor Gearhead. He taught all he knew to me dad, who me been training under since me was a babe just old enough to hold me hammer. So like them before, me a blacksmith and work with metals to craft beautiful weapons and armor and have a bit of my granddad's Druidism powers of healing and warding. It was Zeck's Pa here who helped me craft me hammer me named Earth-breaker here and my staff over there leanin' 'genst this wall," said Asher.

"Well, they look impressive, and I can't wait to see your skills in action, you craftier-caster," said Arthus. Soon they all were heading down to meet up with Jade and then hit the ceremony. Jade and another female waited for them outside the main building.

"Hey guys, I see you got a new friend too, this is my new roommate Zoelynn. However, she likes Zoey just fine. The rooms are awesome. When I got up there I realized they even made sure that I had a space in there for Fang. He was so happy he did not have to live out in the barn with the other Yaules. He is curled on a giant fat fur covered synth-blend mat in the room," said Jade.

"Welcome, Zoey. Well, these guys are Zeck, Emon, Asher and I am Arthus; we glad to meet you," said Arthus. They all gave her a nod, and she is Ignole from what Arthus could tell. "That name Zoey, I do remember a good while back I knew a much younger rascal of a girl named Zoey. And that young girl Zoey, she would hang around the palace, sometimes getting into a bit of trouble. I saw that younger girl Zoey a couple of times. You remind me of her, but you don't exactly want to be known to resemble that kind of rascal that I saw at the palace, now do you," snickered Arthus.

"Thanks, and I do know you silly. Sure we met many times at the Palace. Where else would I hang out and get into trouble, for my name is Zoey Raphael of clan Raphael, and my mother is Eden our clan leader. I spent a lot of time in both the palace and the Great Library. And, I do remember a few times where it was you that might have been getting in a wee bit of trouble," said Zoey with a smile.

"Right... ha, ha, I thought, you looked very familiar. Yes, how is Lady Eden," said Arthus.

"She is fine still head of the Great Library and researchers of clan Raphael," said Zoey.

Arthus mind instantly recalled, Clan Raphael was the clan put in charge of study and history. Mostly the clan is made up of Ignole who devote themselves to studying everything, and they chronicle everything in the Great Library in Harmony City. Then Arthus' mind observed, Zoey was around five foot five, and she had long black hair and dark blue skin like her mother. She had light blue cat eyes and wore the same academy uniform as everyone else. Zoey was a beautiful girl, for Zeck maybe. Arthus could see, but he still only had eyes for Jade. Arthus observed, but he kept his observation secret.

Arthus looked to the others and said, "We all better get into the ceremony before we are counted late on our first day. I'm sure Katelynn wouldn't enjoy a start like that," said Arthus.

Chapter 21
Ceremony of the Elements

The group entered a large circular chamber. The room was set up so that all seats faced the center stage. There were three levels of the seats. This room alone could hold around a thousand peoples from various clans and races easily. Arthus kept looking the room over; observing everyone as they were coming in and everything, using all of his senses, including Life-energy senses. He focused his Life-energy and opened up one door in his mind that focused part of his mental attention immediately on what was happening down on the center stage. He opened a second door in his mind that reached out with his Life-energy touching through the molecules in the atmosphere into every living thing in the room and then out into the rest of the Academy grounds. He immediately pushed out a calming peace into everyone in the room and to those in the Academy that were still on their way to the ceremony. He could feel almost instantly a wave of stress was being released by everyone. He then pushed out very strong and powerful Life-energy mental acuity healing, which he could feel was being absorbed by many.

At the center of the stage, sat a large device like the one in their bedroom suites on the table but far larger and more complex. Arthus motioned and pointed for all his companions that there is a six to a row set of seats directly parallel to the stage, which seemed to be some of the best viewing spots. They made their way quickly to that section and each took a seat. It wasn't long before the circular chamber had gathered up all the new students. Arthus recognized that there were around four hundred new students of Cundos, Ignoles and Dwarvens based on the empty seats in comparison to the filled seats. All of these new students were joining the Malon Academy at the same time as they were. Above the stage, the ceiling opened, and a fairly large circular platform with an attached ramp descended down onto the center stage. On that disk was Katelynn, then two other trainer staff also started descending down the ramp onto the circular disk platform and then stepping out from there onto the stage. In all, there were three. Arthus recognized all three, one being Katelynn, and the other two were Jacob and Elmont. Jacob, of course, was the head of clan Urial, but he mostly stayed here training all students in weapons. Elmont though Arthus only meet once at the palace, was one of the Master Monk Order here at the Academy. This Master Monk Order included only Masters of Life-Elemental-Energy's and Elmont even though a Cundo figured out ways to master the elemental of the wind. He had witnessed High King Thureos sparring with Elmont, and what a sight it had been. Elmont had High King Thureos truly pushing himself in that fight. Elmont is a tall Cundo, who is wearing padded robes. He has a completely bald face and head, deep brown eyes, and unique tattoos in dark green in different designs covering what Arthus could see of his arms and chest. He wore no boots, just bare feet. In one hand he held a bladed staff weapon made of Life-steel; both ends have a flat blade that looks a lot like fan blades.

Jacob was apposing. He wore ceremonial armor of Clan Urial. He carried his two curved swords sheathed at his sides. He had his redcap clipped to his shoulders.

Katelynn was dressed in a rather ordinary dress, which had the school dark blue and white trimmed colors. The entire room immediately silenced at the three standing before them on the stage.

"Welcome all new students. You have all reached, or are quickly about to reach your first one hundredth year life day, and we are proud to welcome you all where you will be spending a big portion of your life training, learning, and figuring out where you truly wish to belong here in our world of Malon. No matter what Clan you come from, after your nine hundred years here, you will know what Clan in your heart you belong to and where you can best serve to the very best of your ability and talents. Now I have a great joy to begin this ceremony and welcome three others. You will all be surprised that have come to witness this day and to give you all your first lesson," said Katelynn. She then bowed her head and turned, and then all three knelt on one knee as a bright light portal opened before them. Stepping out of the portal came Michael, Urial, and Raphael. Three of the Archangels.

The room went up in a loud cheer then quickly silenced when Michael the Archangel raised a hand. Out of the portal behind them, a large crystallite was brought forth.

"Welcome to the Malon Academy, all you young higher functioning sentient beings of Malon. I am proud to see another group come of age and now work to find their place in this world. We come before you to test your elemental affinity and also to give you a kind of history lesson in a way. This crystallite will change inside as you lay your hands, or paws upon it. The inner chamber of this crystallite will change into different elemental properties, like 'an array of atoms or molecules possessing a long range order and arranged in a pattern, which is periodic in three or more dimensions.' Basically that means whatever inherent element that person is more aligned to. Now my brother Raphael will explain more to you all," said Michael.

"Thank you, brother; as Michael has said, welcome to this unique island that we three have built for this purpose. Here you will learn to master both your body and mind and the Life-energy elemental forces that are within every one of you. For you all, the children of Malon, were created and born closer to God's Life-energy than any other beings of all creation. As you are aware, there are two primary races which are of Archangel wing feather born. The Ignole and Cundo, and as most know, Ignole born of one of my wing feathers, can affect the external elemental realm. In contrast, Cundo, born of Michael's wing feather, can master the internal elemental forces. We clearly must acknowledge the race of hardy Dwarvens that now call both Creed and Malon home as they have greatly blessed so many worlds with their joining in with God's ultimate creative processes. As many of you know the Dwarvens have been gifted with many of the internal and external elemental abilities too, but which are related to all of their under-earth gifts. Then there are races on Malon, which have evolved beyond their beast form through the Life-energy given by God through the First God's Tree and the River of Life which

346

flows by the First God's Tree. A prime example of this are the Yelin Snow Folk, who almost instantaneously after the dawn of the creation of Malon, evolved beyond their beast created form. Besides their Life Yell, the Yelin Snow Folk have various elemental abilities. Some are stronger in external elements and others in internal elements. More recently, in these past one hundred years, the Ice Wolves have evolved beyond their created beast-form. Several of their kind have shown elemental abilities as Druids and some have shown other elemental affinities. The absolute most recent addition to this Life-energy evolution is our Yaule friend, named Fang. Fang, come on in here and take your place over by Jade."

A light portal opened, and Fang stepped through it onto the stage and let out a low growl. A surprised gasp came from everywhere in the room. Even Jade was surprised by this development.

"Fang has shown us that some of the Yaule who live here on Malon have evolved even beyond their evolved form that they already possessed on Creed, and so he will join this student body right alongside of Jade. He is the first non-humanoid to begin training at the Academy. We already know that he has strong Life-energy elemental abilities, and he has telepathic abilities. He won't stay here as long as the rest of you, because he has a responsibility to build up Clan Yaule Fang. His descendants will continue to increase and follow in his footsteps both in their length of life expectancy and in joining with us here at the Malon Academy, though they will stay much longer than Fang himself will," said Raphael. He then added, We Archangels built this facility primarily for Cundos, Ignoles and Dwarvens, and as such it really is not setup for Yelin Snow Folks, Ice Wolves or Yaule, but we do have a plan for building three smaller Elemental Islands specifically for training Yelin Snow Folks, Ice Wolves and the Yaule, as each of their life expectancy differences will mean a great difference in their training schedules and such for each of their peoples. And, we are still quite uncertain as to how that will need to work for their kinds."

Raphael continued, "As you might be aware, there are a very few who can master elements beyond their own race boundaries. A prime example of this is Master Elmont here on the stage. He has trained himself to go beyond one's race boundary. For a Cundo who masters his elemental if he can't create the wind or fire out of thin air, can find other ways to help them bring their element to the forefront. Master Elmont, please demonstrate."

Elmont bowed, then took up his staff and went into a well-practiced dance. His weapon with those deadly fan blades swirling around and around the air around the Master began to thicken and spin around him. He finished with a massive horizontal sweep, and the built-up wind blew out. It felt as if they would all be blown out of their seats. Then it was gone. Elmont stood again, bowed and walked back to his position on the stage.

"As you can see, there are ways to help those who may think themselves disadvantaged rise above any challenge. But let me ask, why is your world called Malon? And, why have all your people been given this gift of this Academy, where you have ones of our stations in Heaven teach you and raise you to do everything that you can possibly know? Prince Arthus, I know you are among this group this time, has High King Thureos, chosen and anointed by God, told you of the reason for all of this?" asked Raphael.

Arthus looked shocked when everyone turned to look at him. He breathed in bringing a powerful calm into his mind, keeping both the door in his mind to the stage open and the door in his mind to the audience open. Then he stood up and said, "What I have learned is Malon in heaven means shield. What that means is we will all be God's shield whenever and wherever the Darkness comes," said Arthus.

"Not bad, yes to both and more. Yes, Malon in Heaven means Shield, but to phrase it properly, *One Who Shields Others*. I now will teach the truth of what was, what is, and from our limited understanding of what's to come. Before all creation, there was, is, and always will be God. He is Pure LIGHT and in Him there is no sentient Darkness, which is pure evil, at all. In Him there is not even a shadow of turning. He, Who is Pure LIGHT and lives presently in perfect harmony throughout all eternity, past, present and future at the same time. He is always in perfect harmony with himself. In His harmony with that perfect One relationship, desired to create more light and more harmonic creative relationships. However, God also wanted to give absolute free choice to all sentient beings that he wanted to create. God knew the only way to give absolute free choice was to first create sentient Darkness. But God did not want Sentient Darkness to have free reign to do whatever it wants, because Sentient Darkness is pure evil, which is polar opposite to God's light which creates life, health, and is wholly good. So God at the same time as He created Sentient Darkness also created an eternal prison where He plans to send Sentient Darkness, when it is the right time. That eternal prison God called Outer Darkness. So then after creating Sentient Darkness and Outer Darkness, God did not want either of those to be right up next to him. It was immediately after that is when God said, 'Let there be Light and there was Light.' Instantly BOOM! God's created Light exploded out by the power of His WORD! And that light pushed itself in every direction that God chose it to go. And that light continues to grow in every direction as God chooses. Everything in the natural and supernatural that ever was made, was made by Him and/ or for Him and always only for His GLORY! The sentient Darkness, which is pure evil, was pushed by the light to the very farthest edges of the inside of Myriasphere. The Myriasphere is the natural existence where created natural sentient beings live and exist. The Myriasphere makes up the multitude of universes, with all their galaxies, planets, stars, and moons. And, the eternal prison called Outer Darkness, which is located within the nothingness was pushed even farther out beyond the Myriasphere, where it will be used someday for the prison for Sentient Darkness and for all who choose to join themselves with the evil of Sentient Darkness. Then there is the heavenly realms that exists outside of Myriasphere up where God has his Golden City, and where His supernatural beings, the Archangels and Angels, and all the souls and spirits of those who are found faithful among the sentient beings go to live for eternity when their natural bodies cease to live.

The supernatural beings that live in the heavenly realms can enter and exit the Myriasphere, causing various creative impacts that are always supposed to be in accordance with God's perfect ordered plan for various worlds throughout the multitude of universes. All who are either created natural sentient, or supernatural sentient as beings were created by God as creative beings. We cannot create exactly like God creates, making something from nothing. However, God allows all sentient to manipulate that which is already created, making it into something else. Similar to when the Dwarvens take Life-ore and other ores and chemicals and mix them together in the smelting processes, and then forge them into many varieties of things.

You should also know only God is at all points in time and space and outside of time and space at the same time. Everything created by Him only exists in one place in time and space, or in the heavenly realm in one place outside of time and space. Created beings can move around, but we are never in more than one place at a time. However, as sentient, our influence on others and on things continues to impact even while we are moving around from place to place. Our influence is similar to when the Dwarvens have made something which is being used by someone else. The reason I made that point is so that you understand that the fallen Archangels, fallen Angels, and even Sentient Darkness, cannot be everywhere at the same time. No, they are in that galaxy past the Dead Zone, which also includes the Hellcore void and the Dead Star, with Satan's throne room. They are there, but their influence is not just there! We must always be diligent to battle their influences that so easily attach themselves to people's hearts and minds.

I hope you are all fully comprehend and understanding, in your minds, in your Life-energy senses, and in your spirits, everything that I am telling you.

Sentient Darkness is quite different from the night sky, which though it might appear dark is truly filled with light, but a various refraction of light which allows night to be. The separation of light and dark that is day and night is not the same meaning as the separation of Pure LIGHT, which is Pure GOOD, and pure Sentient Darkness, which is pure evil. And, Sentient Darkness, which is pure evil, is not in any way equal to God's Power and Glory. It never was and it never will be! There is absolutely nothing that is equal to God in absolute Power and Glory. Everything else, which, or who exists, is not God, but was created. Sentient Darkness is a created entity, which many believe is equal only to created Sentient Light. Sentient Light naturally helps bring life, health, growth and all the good things that are in accordance with God's will.

While Sentient Darkness naturally brings death, sickness, and other very bad things. Sentient Darkness's influences, are always sneaking around in the shadows between the light of day and the dark of night. Those influences always seems to prefer the shadows, pushing on all the grey areas between pure right and pure wrong. Sentient Darkness seems to easily latch onto those that try their best to push the grey areas, so be very careful about your decisions whenever you are facing the grey areas in your life. Sentient Darkness truly believes it is at least equal to God's Pure LIGHT. Even worse, in its twisted thinking it believes it can completely conquer God's Pure LIGHT and then force God into its Darkness. And, you really should understand that Sentient Darkness is truly more powerful than all the Angels and Archangels, but it is not more powerful than God, as God is all powerful. We have all been warned not to touch the Hellcore void, because any created thing which tries touching the pure evil of Sentient Darkness, just touching it is enough to become twisted and enslaved by it. I want you to understand that this Sentient Darkness, which is pure evil, also creates. It creates all evil thoughts, all diseases, all sicknesses, and it created death itself and it created the whole Dark concept of the grave. All the greedy, murderous, thieving, adulterous, and idolatrous thoughts are wholly born from Sentient Darkness.

God in His Grace and Mercy gives every sentient being in his creation the right to choose to follow God, or to choose to follow any of the three greedy paths that lead into enslavement by Sentient Darkness: 'The lust of the eye, the lust of the flesh, and the pride of life.' Choosing any one of those paths during your lifetime only causes you to become joined in with the fallen and Sentient Darkness. So, do not allow yourselves to follow any path into greed. Do not breed any desire for ultimate authority! Do not breed a desire to rule and control others! Do not breed hatred in your minds and hearts for any race of sentient beings! Rather, serve each other in the very best possible ways that you can, continued Raphael.

Eden was the first of God's handcrafted worlds in the Myriasphere, a once beautiful world God called his garden. There are many non-world planets in the Myriasphere, which God's LIGHT created naturally. The

351

world planets, however God did much handcrafting on and none of them are exactly the same as the others; in fact each is very unique. Yours is the final world in the Myriasphere that God handcrafted since His first creation. Not all handcrafted worlds have stayed true to Gods plans as the sentient beings on them have chosen to follow after the example of the King of Darkness and the fallen, allowing themselves to become utterly consumed in the influences of Sentient Darkness. Someday God will send Sentient Darkness and all who choose to follow Sentient Darkness into that eternal prison called Outer Darkness. And, God will do that, when He chooses to do that! Until then Sentient Darkness continues to plaque the Myriasphere. It cannot dwell in the true LIGHT of God's heavenly realms, as true LIGHT dispels Sentient Darkness. However, Sentient Darkness continues to create more Darkness here in the Myriasphere of God's creation, with its false light twisting, its false religions spreading, always working to try to manipulate more sentient beings against what God created for His Good Pleasure. Working against God's Life-energy gifts, which are meant to help bring life and health, well-being and Goodness, through murder, suicide, infanticide, genocide, mass destruction and war sentient Darkness gains Death-energy, which it uses to spread its Dark fog-like and Dark smoke-like oily tentacles out from the Hellcore into nearby planets and its influence into the minds and hearts of those who harbor bitterness, hate, greed, malice, lust and envy. Sentient Darkness, and all who are deceived by it, fully despises all of God's created life. Sentient Darkness has only one true want, and that is to become an ultimate ruler who casts down God from His Throne, and set his own throne up then sending everything into never-ending Darkness, continued Raphael.

And, just like God foresaw the war coming in the heavenly realms and empowered our brother Michael the Archangel with a TRUE LIGHT WORD GIFT, and the sentient Angel Wings, which Michael used to throw down and cast out our fallen brother, Lucifer and all the Angels who chose to follow his path into Darkness, God also foresees the coming war of Darkness here in the Myriasphere. Which is why He has created the two Archangel-feather born races, and has planted the First God's Tree on Malon to fill all sentient beings on Malon with His

Life-energy. All of you, Life-energy filled sentient beings on Malon are part of God's Shield against all the influences of sentient Darkness in the Myriasphere, and not just here on Malon," continued Raphael.

"God foresees a point in time where the physical realm of the Myriasphere and the Heavenly supernatural and spiritual realm of my people will not always be perfectly connected together as one. The physical realm of the Myriasphere will need those who have recognized their Life-energy given elemental powers, trained themselves to use perfectly all the knowledge and skills that we will all try our best to teach you. But, it is you who must desire to fight for all of God's physical creation. This is why the first of your peoples were created from our feathers, and that is why we Archangels have carefully designed and built this Elemental Island training facility and grounds. Here you will be educated, raised up, weapon up, skilled up and in every possible way trained by us. There is coming a point in the future, where we can no longer stand together as your protectors with you. You will have to rise up and take your rightful place as God's Shield protecting all others of God's creation. You will truly need to fight with God for all of the created life in the physical realms of the Myriasphere, exclaimed Raphael.

So now that you know more of the history and the truth of things. I hope this gives you a fire burning within you all to train as hard as you can, for one day you be called to stand and will need the wisdom and fortitude to face the evil nightmares that the sentient Darkness spews forth. For it is you who must choose to train into the very best you can possibly be. You must choose to fight to protect all that God has created. If that is your choice, then now stand to your feet and be counted, exclaimed Raphael.

Everyone within the large circular chamber stood to their feet.

"Now it is time to begin," said Raphael. He nodded to Katelynn, who stood and turned to the students.

"Now, we will call you one by one. After your elemental test, you are free to head out and back to your dorms to finish settling in or whatever you decide," said Katelynn.

It wasn't long before Zeck was called first of his group. Zeck walked up and before the large crystal, and when placed his hand, the crystal turned blue, but the heat was intense for a hot blue flame appeared within the crystal.

"Fire a good element to master, young one. Yes, I believe you show a lot of promise; come by the stadium when you're done so we can fit you for a weapon," said Jacob to Zeck. Zeck nodded, then left, waving to them. Then finally, Jade went up. She touched the large crystal, and the crystal turned a light blue.

"I see you are blessed by the wind like Elmont here," said Katelynn. Jade nodded and left. She waved at Arthus and pointed that she would be waiting in the back for him.

Next was his turn. Arthus slowly walked to the crystal. He placed his hand on the crystal turned bright blue as Jades, but inside the crystal at the top, it looked as if a massive wind and lightning storm was brewing. While near the bottom of the inside of the crystal there was a real sense of calmness and earth-healing. All the room gasped, including the three teachers.

"Well, look at that you are definitely both Cundo and Ignole, isn't that right, Arthus," asked Raphael?

"Yes, Archangel, My mother, Laella was Ignole, and my father is Cundo," said Arthus.

"Yes, now I remember your father Prince Benroy married by the Yelin shaman an Ignole, and one of no small power if I recall. So, as you all know, and I have told you the differences between Cundo and Ignole, a child born of both is very rare, and most don't survive. Still, it seems you were truly blessed for the elements of your parents are perfectly in balance and sync, for you have two external elemental forces, that I can see in here, and I can see you also have been blessed with two internal elemental forces, the ability to bring a calming peace and healing to body, mind and spirit. We have seen whenever there are two completely opposing elements, one would usually tear the other apart, but your external elements are both wind and lightning, which work together in making a perfect storm. And, it seems like you have almost mastered your internal elements which will help keep you calm in the midst of battle and help you to heal yourself when you are wounded. All of these have successfully combined in you, and I cannot wait to see how you master both your internal elemental powers and your external elemental powers to their fullest potential. That won't be an easy thing to master, and with that weapon you have strapped to your back, you will have to train extremely hard. Yes, I can't wait to see how this young grandson of Thureos becomes in the years here," said Raphael. Arthus bowed and went to where Zeck and Jade waited. Soon the whole group was outside. Emon and Asher were Dwarvens, so like all Dwarvens, they were under-earth elemental. Zoey, as pure-bred Ignole, she has some much stronger Druid elemental powers, and also external Healer elemental skills.

"Whelp, Jacob wanted me to come by his stadium for some reason. Why don't we all head over and check it out and the other buildings," said Zeck? They all nodded and headed out. Soon they were at the Stadium, and it was massive. A room just inside the main gate held many weapons and armors. And a large desk.

"This must be Jacobs office look at all these weapons; he must have every kind, and I bet he's mastered every one of them," said Zeck looking in awe.

"Indeed, I have mastered them all over my long years teaching others how to master their chosen weapons. For I be a poor weapons master if I couldn't know a weapon before trying to teach others on its use," said Jacob, who walked in just then.

"Well, good to have you all looking in ah, and Zeck I'm glad you stopped by and with our young Prince in tow. Glad to see you once again Prince Arthus. Well, Zeck, you have the elemental power of fire, and being Cundo, you are like me. I am also born under the fire, and as Cundo, we cannot get just conjurer fire out of thin air, like Ignoles can do. I also know you are Drakes boy, so I have something I think will suit you well as a weapon," said Jacob. Then walked over to another door and opened it went in, then soon came back a Halberd in hand.

"You're a large and strong man, I can tell, and I think with this it will make you truly dangerous that or a large two-handed ax. Let me see the rest of you. Hmm, Jade was it. You a wind like Arthus, while Arthus also has lightning. So you will want a fast weapon or range. And Arthus, let me see you have Angel Wing. I have been told, so we have a problem there since I never wielded Angel Wing, and the only one I know is your grandfather, who could understand that weapon, so I will speak with Michael and Katelynn on how we can best serve your needs. And, I see you two Dwarvens have your weapons already picked and nice ones, I can tell. I will be looking forward to seeing what you two can do with those. Last looks like you Zoey you have the power of over-earth, like most Ignole with that particular elemental, most become Druids, Healers, or Priests, or a combination. You will mostly be using your elemental power as your main weapon, so you best find a great staff or mace like that of Eden your mother, as one of those would be the best to help you," said Jacob.

After leaving the stadium, they all decided to look over the rest of the Academy grounds. Arthus left the others and walked to one of the lifts that take him to the top of the wall and a platform that overlooked the mountain range. He walked out and could feel the wind blowing powerfully around him. So, I really do have the external elemental abilities like other Ignoles from my mother Laella to help control both wind currents and lightning, I thought this was true because of my abilities to seemingly create small storms and release those small storms with my mind during my meditation at the palace. This always felt right. He remembered all the times in the hot sands and back while he worked his fingers to blisters in the fields of Arial valley how the wind had always been a thing he loved to fall into to feel its cooling kiss and how it always made him feel at one. His thoughts went back to the fight with the Nagas-Hydra Hybrid in the river during the great hunt and how he felt electricity build up in him to throw back the giant snake. So what will it feel like when I master these elements, I wonder?

"I like this view as well," said a voice from behind. Arthus spun around; a man who wore a white robe. Tied around his waist was a simple rope, and he was barefooted. He had what appeared to be an almost natural tanned light brown skin, a slightly larger rounded nose, long brown hair and a clean brown beard. But his eyes were like looking at the sky, but much bluer than even the sky.

"I am sorry, I didn't mean to startle you, young Prince. I was asked to come to see you as it will be I who trains you in how to master Angel Wing," said the man.

"You are going to train me on how to wield Michael the Archangels weapon," asked Arthus?

"Yes, I owed Michael a favor, and he doesn't have the time as of now, so I let him know I would be happy to help you in that aspect. Ah, you can call me hmm, Son, yes Son. That is a good name I think while I am here. So when it is time for your weapons training, you meet me here instead of Jacobs training grounds. Yes, this will be a fine place to start," said Son.

"I am sorry, but who are you? I never heard of anyone named Son before, and I don't believe I have ever seen you at the palace or even at the ceremony," said Prince Arthus.

"Well, I Am, Who I Am, and I Am more than what Michael the Archangel is, and I know your grandfather, High King Thureos very well. But, you are correct, I haven't been around Malon very much. I have other duties that normally require my time. But, Father has given me leave to come and help you since Michael will be doing other tasks as of now. I am glad to have met you this day and look forward to getting to know you young Prince," said Son. With that, Son was just gone. Arthus looked around, but the strange man was gone. It was already getting late, and he had classes starting the very next day. It was time to head back to his room.

Chapter 22
Training at the Malon Academy

Years flew by as Arthus, and his friends studied everything from wildlife to combat tactics and everything in between. Arthus spent almost all his free time training with Son on mastering himself. Hundreds of years had already passed, and Arthus was growing a bit frustrated. Zeck and Jade were becoming true masters of their combat arms, and Arthus had barely handled Angel Wing. Son had kept him focusing on mental training and working with different weapons. In a way, becoming great at everything but master of none. However, Arthus really enjoyed all his time with Son, and the man was a great teacher and wise as any he ever met before. However, Arthus often found it quite frustrating as when he would ask Son a question, usually Son would begin to tell a story, rather than giving him any straight answers. Son's stories would always have hidden meanings and it would give him hints that he would have to spend hours or sometimes even days meditating on to figure out the answers to the questions Arthus had asked. Arthus thought it would just save time if Son would just give him straight answers. Whenever he said something about that to Son, Son never lost patience with him.

Son would just smile, and say, "Arthus, think on it."

Son had taught him a lot about himself and his failures, how he felt about his father, and how he was usually worried about failing as a son and as a Prince. Son helped Arthus come to terms with that he may never gain his father's approval and that he had an immense responsibility to put his people first, not be worried about his father's failures.

Arthus learned how to use his mind to control his body farther than ever before. He knew how to push his body to its limits and beyond by willpower alone. Son had him do mental meditation a lot like his grandfather did. Then he spent three hours of switching between five different weapons, then he spend an hour in the mountain field hanging off cliffs, or free climbing. Son always makes everything look easy, and no matter how hard Arthus works, he can never catch up with Son. Son never even breaks a sweat, or breathes hard, and never ever shows an ounce of fatigue. Some days he is taken to the jungle forest areas and then running races with Son through the forest from tree to tree. Which would push Arthus' reflexes running at full speed from tree to tree. You have only split seconds to dodge a branch or a full-on trunk, and Arthus learned the hard way many times how it felt to run full speed into a low branch or a solid tree trunk. But, then as he watched Son doing it, it literally appeared like Son could run right through the trunks of the trees, like they were not even there.

There was one event that dumfounded Arthus completely. They were doing what they often do go free climbing up in the mountain cliff faces, and this time it was a huge and very high mountain cliff face. Arthus was well over halfway up the cliff face is completely covered in sweat, with his hands and toes are really hurting under the strain of the great height and fatigue. And now no matter how hard he tried he couldn't find even the tiniest of handholds, yet Son was right there near him and just a little bit in front of him, not straining at all. He seems like he can easily stick to the cliff walls no matter if where he is climbing is smooth or rough. He notices Son is having no problems even when he is hanging on at times with just one finger.

Arthus became completely frustrated and says, "This is damn hard, when I am not finding anywhere to stick my hands!"

Son just laughs, then stands up sideways and walks around on the side of the cliff, just like someone could that is walking on level ground. Son begins whistling a tune and begins to walk circles around Arthus, right while Arthus is hanging there on the side of the cliff. Then Son says, "Yes, yes, I can see your point about this being hard on you. I guess I really can help you out with that." Then Son takes his finger and starts

359

flicking his finger to create little ledges and then poking his finger into the solid rock cliff creating finger sized grip holes here and there right into the solid rock cliff from right above where Arthus was hanging from on up the cliff wall and then on up to the very top of the cliff. Then Son just walks back down sideways to where Arthus was hanging, and truly aching under the strain, and then he gets back into a climbing position, which is looking like he is free hand climbing, using his hands just like Arthus is doing, and acting like nothing ever happened. Seeing Son do that, leaves Arthus in shock and completely dumfounded, he even almost lost his grip he was so shocked. He regained his sense and started climbing up again following Son up and to the top.

Once at the top, Arthus said, "Son, how did you do that?"

Son just sat there and laughed. Then Son says, "Arthus, how did I do what?" He acted like he did not know what Arthus was talking about.

Arthus says, "You know what I am talking about. How did you walk on the side of that cliff, just like as if you were walking on level ground? And, how did you just push your fingers into the cliff wall and create all those grips?"

Son laughed again, then says, "Arthus think about it!"

Now Arthus was sitting under a waterfall, allowing the cool water to flow over his body. After another morning, he lifted his hands and squeezed the pain out of them, focusing on tightening and releasing the tightness. He noticed how tougher his skin had become. It almost felt as rough as leather. He closed his eyes and fell into himself, allowing his sore muscles to release all the built-up lactic acid and put them into a more relaxed state. He then went into his special training allowing every muscular system to flex and release over and over. Soon Arthus's entire body vibrated. He did this after every training section to help flex even parts of his body that he usually didn't use. Arthus opened his eyes and started to stand. The pressure of the waterfall was intense, but Arthus almost didn't notice it. He smiled, because when he first started this part of his training, the waterfall would practically force him face down. He could barely take a few minutes before having to leave, but now he could spend all day under the powerful cooling water.

"Good, so glad you are doing better. I am glad that our time has been spent so well. Now, I believe it's time for you to start wielding Angel Wing," said Son.

"Thank you, Son, you have not just taught me how to master myself, but you taught me so much about life and so much more. I do believe I am ready to become one with Angel Wing," said Arthus.

Not long, Son stood bare-chested across an open field they used for combat training. Son wielded a staff. Arthus took out his silver tube that was Angel Wing in its natural state. Arthus fell into himself, allowing his training and instinct to lead his mind and body became one he also felt himself become far more aware of his surroundings. Angel Wing also became a staff, Arthus allowed his mind to focus on Son and charge. The two clashed together, staff slapping against the team over and over as the two spun around each other. Son came around, turning his staff behind him, then, with an overhead chop, brought the weapon down, but Arthus meet it with the middle of his then Angel Wing became two swords in both his hands. Arthus went into a dance flowing his left sword horizontally across, then with his right came and deflected Son's staff from another strike. Son jumped back and lowered his body and stuck out with the team's point, but Arthus turned Angel Wing into a large shield in front of him, with Angel Wing taking the whole blow that way. A second later, Arthus dropped and spun, allowing Angel Wing to become a staff once again, but Son had leaped over and back.

"Good, good you have done well so far, but it's time for you to head back. Your classes will begin soon, and I hate to get another ear full from Katelynn about how I am selfish taking all your time," smiled Son.

"Yes, of course, and I hate to get another lecture also, said Arthus. They both laughed. Arthus let Angel Wing return to its inactive state and placed it into a holder on his gear. Arthus dressed and then bowed to Son and ran off to get back to the main Academy grounds. Jade was waiting for him just inside the forest gate.

"Well, I was about to go looking for you, Arthus were going to be late again," said Jade with a smile.

"Yes, yes, I know, but I was actually training with Angel Wing finally. I might have lost track of time," said Arthus. They ran on towards the main building.

Soon Arthus and his friends sat in the main auditorium, which filled quickly. Soon everyone was sitting around nervously. They heard they have an introductory class this day, and almost all of the Academy had come. Soon a gate opened and out walked Michael and with him was Son.

"Welcome all. Today you will be the first class where we delve into the nightmare that is those ether born of Darkness or have been twisted by its evil. This is Son he will be telling you more of a historical tale, a tale of one that breaks all of us of Heaven's heart and will make you start to understand what it is that you and what we have been facing since the beginning of all things," said Michael.

"Thank you, Michael, Yes you can call me, Son. And, I know many of you may never have heard clearly about me. I Am, Who I Am, more than Michael and the other Archangels of Heaven. I am I have been watching from afar mostly and helping your Prince here master himself. But today, I have a story to tell of the Bard of Heaven and his fall into the King of Darkness," said Son. Son walked over and sat down cross-legged before them all. Michael went above and started up a program into the holo device. A map of the Myriasphere came forth, universes and stars, and galaxies and planets were all before and around them throughout the room.

"This is a holo-map you see here represents all of the Myriasphere or all physical life, all the many universes, their galaxies with all the stars and all the planets and moons and all of the space debris is seen before you," said Son.

Arthus heart felt like it stopped. His breath was taken aback. Even the holo-map, on such a small scale was so vast it barely fit in their massive room. So much was out there that made Arthus feel small indeed, and all his world was just like a speck of sand on a beach that stretched farther than Arthus ever dreamed of.

"Seeing it mapped out in this scale like this it is breathtaking, is it not? Realize that the tiny specks of dust sized planets and stars and galaxies and universes that you are observing on this tiny scale map that are tightly woven together, in reality are quite huge. The vastness of one galaxy is huge. And each universe has at least hundreds of thousands of galaxies, and some of them have millions of galaxies and there are many, many universes, all together which make up the whole of the Myriasphere," said Son.

Son continued, "Our true story starts at the very birth of all you see before you. We must go back to the very creation," said Son. The holo changed to a massive explosion of light followed by a wave of energy flowing from one point in a huge Sea of light. Then they watched as stars took shape planets, then galaxies, universes, and then all of the Myriasphere once again was before them. You see the bright LIGHT space which is way up at the top there and that sits outside of the Myriasphere? That bright LIGHT space represents the Heavenly Realm, and inside that Heavenly Realm there is a Golden City."

Son spoke loudly and said, "Going back a little in this story to show you more about the Bard of Heaven..."

Then before them was a city of gold and silver, of many precious jewels and had a warmth and such a bright LIGHT. It was a place all in the room knew that was not a part of their physical plane. Then they heard it. A music that flowed around them and before them stood an Archangel. He turned and faced the Giant White Throne that was filled with an almost blinding bright LIGHT. There is a River of Life pouring out from under the Throne. As with all the Archangels he had six massive white wings and he was dressed unlike any of the other Archangels in a fine leather tunic, leather pants with leather boots and a tall pointy leather hat that on one side held a white feather. He was standing before a choir of Angels and an orchestra of many other Angel musicians. Lucifer picked up his own musical instrument off of its stand. His instrument he picked up was a very beautiful violin. He held the violin to his chin with one hand on the frets and strings he was plucking and pushing various strings down to change the sounds as he used his other hand to hold a beautiful bow with very tight hairs, which he his hand and arm moved in different contortions as it slid back and forth across the strings causing an absolutely beautiful piece of music to flow from the violin.

363

As he played the other musicians in the Angel band played supportive layering music with other various stringed and wood wind musical instruments. Then the Angel choir behind him sang, "The Son was filled with Life and Power." The music and the Angel choir went on and sang of worlds and people beginning to grow. All while the music and song is happening the light surrounding the throne prismed from a great many of various colored Life-crystals into multiple colors. The sight and song had brought tears to Arthus's eyes. He looked around, and saw that everyone in the room openly wept. Then the music came to a close, the light prism colors disappeared and the Archangel laid his instrument down on a pedestal then as he faced the throne he bowed deeply.

The Archangel stood back up, "For your glory My God, our Heavenly Father, my Heavenly King of Kings, and to Your Great Spirit. To all my Archangel brothers and sisters and to all my Angel brothers and sisters, I do hope the music and prism light show which I have come back to share with all of you has truly moved and blessed you all. I have traveled so much of the Myriasphere and have met with so much beauty of Your creation, my God and our Heavenly Father," said the singer.

"You have outdone yourself truly, Lucifer. You have been away for a while, but now with your return, all of Heaven awaits your beautiful words, your music, and your beautiful prism light show of so many colors. How long do you plan of staying this time Lucifer bearer of light, and so highly gifted in music, song, and light?" Asked a voice that sounded like the voice of many waters, which none could see He who spoke, but all in the room knew it had to be God Himself talking.

"My God and our Heavenly Father, your praise always is worth my travels, but please, I will not stay long. I have so much more to see, for it is your word filled with Life-energy power that brings what once was nothing to life, and with such fullness it inspires my music, my practice, my ever improving skills, which blend Your gifts of music, and light into such glorious prisms, and with the light portals which come from perfected music blended with your perfect LIGHT, I am not one to stay in one place long. When I go, I will be heading farther than I have ever gone before and can't wait to see what new wonders are out there among all of your worlds and stars," said Lucifer.

"I see, then may your journey be filled with wonder, go with my blessing as always," said God.

With a final bow, Lucifer left, heading down to the gates of Heaven.

Son continued sitting cross-legged on the platform. "Did you all enjoy the performance of the one nicknamed the *Bard of Heaven*? His created Archangel name was Lucifer, which literally means *Light Bearer*. The Bard of Heaven had been gifted above the normal Angels, like all Archangels, with incredible creative abilities. Originally, he was greatly gifted in his abilities with music and in his abilities with light, so much so that he led all the heavenly musician Angels. He was so gifted in music that over time he had so perfected his talents in music, which he learned could refract and shape light into multiple prisms of color like you all just enjoyed. He taught all the other Angels in heaven to also be able to do that. He even figured out how create light portals, where he could step through and move from planet to planet throughout all of the Myriasphere. Again, he taught all of the Angels in heaven to be able to do that."

Son continued, "The Bard of Heaven hated staying in one place long. He almost never was in the golden city as he truly enjoyed going out and seeing all the various world planets and the incredible life which God created. He was always going from one world planet to another world planet. He had been gifted also with the power of illusion. His voice could tame the vilest of beast with ease. He truly had a way of amazing even the most stubborn of people. He would go and change his appearance to fit in with whatever the prominent sentient race was on any given planet. He did this in order that he could watch and learn and truly get to know the population of each world. And, it seemed that each new world he visited would give him great inspiration for completely new musical performances. He truly loved playing the harp and lute, but he easily mastered every type of instrument that he could find, and some which he even created from various objects. After visiting each world for a reasonable amount of time, he would return to heaven in order that he could take the time to teach what he created to the other Angels in Heavens orchestra. Once they all learned their parts then they all put on a concert for all of heaven and God. Usually he wouldn't spend more than five decades in any one place or in heaven, and about five decades had passed and Lucifer had just completed another performance similar to what you just saw, but different, as the people he had been with and the worlds he had seen way out by the edge of the Myriasphere were very beautiful, but that world planet was so near the edge of the Myriasphere one way they looked at night was towards nothing and the other way was towards the entire myriasphere in front of them. This contrast of the two sides of that planet gave the people that lived there a very unique perspective, which Lucifer had used in his final concert. And that concert was incredibly interesting how he weaved the perspectives of those that were seeing nothing with those that were seeing everything. Of course after that concert concluded, Lucifer was getting restless once again so he was off dressing in his traveling gear which was mostly a traveling tunic some pants and leather boots and a large hat with a feather in it he would pack his lute and harp and maybe a flute also and then he be off.

This time was different. When he walked through the portal to the world he had last visited, a whole lot had changed. He saw that the planets had been pushed way back and into different orbits. He saw that the sun in that galaxy had turned dark and it felt completely wrong. Then when he looked around for the people on the planet, he noticed how most of them were changed and twisted into absolutely horrid creatures, some who still resembled any kind of humanoid sentient appeared undead, but at least half dead as they walked around. Lucifer flew up out of the planet's atmosphere and that is when he saw some kind of massive black fog and charcoal black smoke like humongous thing, which had some kind strange oily like tentacles made of the same black fog and charcoal black smoke, slowly consuming the world planet. As it was reaching out its oily tentacles and spreading itself over the surface of the planet, everything caught in it either died horribly and instantly, or was turned into a hideous undead but half-dead creature.

The holo 4D projector changes again. Lucifer is back in God's Throne Room.

Lucifer is frantic and says, "I just watched some kind of evil darkness thing destroy a world that I had just visited about five decades ago. It was the world planet, which I had used as my inspiration for the music and song in my last concert, where the people's perspectives were so different as one side of the planet faced the nothingness beyond Your Myriasphere and the other side of the planet faced everything. That is in one of Your very beautiful galaxies by the farthest edge of Your Myriasphere. I absolutely sure that Darkness thing is something that is pure evil and the sun in that galaxy is now dark and it truly felt very wrong! Last time I was there everything was perfect and beautiful, but now that pure evil Darkness thing is either killing everything it touches or turning everything it touches into some undead more than half-dead horrendous creature. After seeing what it just did, I know that Darkness is only pure evil and needs to be destroyed! Please send out all of your LIGHT and your heavenly armies and kill that thing before it can harm anything more.

In a voice that sounds like many waters, God our Heavenly Father said, "No! I will not destroy the Sentient Darkness and no you are not authorized to go to war with the Sentient Darkness. Fear not! I know exactly what Sentient Darkness is and everything that it is capable of doing. From the beginning of creation I have already set up a perfect plan in action, which will take a while to become fully ready. Lucifer, you and all my other Archangels and Angels are to stay far away from the farthest edges of my Myriasphere creation until My plan is fully ready to execute. Do not go anywhere near that Sentient Darkness. I know you care deeply about the life and all the beauty of those world planets, but you just must just trust in Me, and in My plan."

Son continued, "Many years went by and Lucifer continued to watch from a reasonable distance that galaxy. Slowly world planet after beautiful world planet falls to the pure evil Dark oily tentacle like finger clutches of Sentient Darkness. It had consumed six out of the seven world planets in that galaxy, and as yet, Lucifer had not seen God doing anything to stop the Sentient Darkness. As he watched, Lucifer allowed the root of bitterness to get planted into his heart. That bitterness turned into Lucifer becoming very angry at God, because those worlds were once incredibly beautiful and all of that life and beauty that was once there has become terribly twisted and destroyed. The more worlds he saw being destroyed, the angrier he became. By the time the sixth planet fell he had conceived in his own heart to take matters into his own hands. Lucifer then decided to convince other Archangels and Angels to follow him into a war against the sentient Darkness. Then Lucifer went in secret and told all of the Archangels of the threat. When the Archangels learned of the threat, seven Archangels besides Lucifer decided he was right and wanted to act. Once again Lucifer and his seven who agreed went before God trying to convince God.

God said, "No! Even though six of the world planets in that galaxy that were full of life and beauty had already fallen, and the seventh planet is being attacked, No! I already told Lucifer that from the very beginning of creation, I have already set in motion a plan. You must all just trust in Me and in My plan!"

Lucifer had already convinced all seven of these other Archangels that if God says, No again, even knowing that Sentient Darkness has already taken six planets, and is attacking the seventh planet in that galaxy, then we must gather together Heavens Angels and convince as many as possible to go with us to war anyway. So, when God said, "No," they immediately left and secretly gathered all the Angels. One third of Heavens regular angels agreed that they would follow Lucifer and so they formed a fighting force and betrayed Gods command, and went to war anyway. They opened a light portal to the seventh world and stepped onto it as it was being consumed. They fought with all they had against the Sentient Darkness and its minions and soon were driving it back but not without great loss. They had drove it back off the seventh planet, and off the sixth planet, and off the fifth planet, and of the fourth planet, and off the third planet, and off the second planet and were actually driving it back to where Lucifer first saw the Sentient Darkness. However, by now most of the regular Angels had been consumed and then twisted into Sentient Darkness' own minions. Even Lucifer and the other seven Archangels were starting to become twisted things. Lucifer was no longer his beautiful radiant self and was actually beginning to panic. That is when they decided to retreat. Lucifer and his seven Archangels and all the remaining only partially mangled angels fled back to heaven. Michael the Archangel who had all the while refused to join them, even calling them all mad for trying to go against God and His plans and wishes, now drags the broken and twisted Lucifer and the others before God.

Lucifer begs God to heal him and all the others that had followed him and restore them to their former beauty.

God was beyond angry that they had disobeyed and betrayed Him. He turns His back towards them. God says, "Now because of your foolish actions one third of My heavenly forces are gone. All you have accomplished was temporarily pushing Sentient Darkness back several worlds. While at the same time with all of My heavenly Angels that have been consumed and completely twisted by Sentient Darkness, you have only helped it to gain far more power than it ever had before. For your betrayal I have decided that I won't heal any of you of your twisted states. What I will do is this: I am pouring My Pure LIGHT into Michael the Archangel and gifting him to grow many – many times larger than he is normally, and gifting him with strength and with power, more than all the other Archangels and Angels of Heaven combined." As God spoke, the thing which He spoke came to be. Michael the Archangel was huge and filled with strength and power. Then God said, "Michael, throw all of these who had disobeyed and betrayed Me out of Heaven. They are banished, never to return!

Michael instantly took on all the surviving twisted and damaged Archangels and Angels who had disobeyed and betrayed God, and grabbed them and threw them all out of heaven and down into the Myriasphere.

Lucifer opened a portal back to the world and they stood before the massive darkness that once again was starting to return. He was beyond anger and now was falling into despair he felt that what he done was right and God was a fool. As he stood there, he heard a voice in his head. It was a deep powerful voice but cold and had a wrong feeling, but the voice showed him visions of what the darkness was and that God was lying to them all. Then it showed him power like he never saw before and how he could not only regain his full self but how to gain true power like no one ever had before. All he had to do was allow the darkness in and become one with it. Lucifer looked down at his

369

hands one had become a twisted gray colored and his nails had become more like claws and was starting to look as if the skin would fall off. His face was twisted so much. Half his mouth had become tusk, and now he had three eyes on one side of his face, and his hair was falling out. So he looked up and in his mind accepted the darkness deal. Out of the air a black portal opened and a black oily tentacle thing poured forth flowing around Lucifer and then became a circular massive ball of complete Darkness. The other Archangels tried to attack it, but nothing could break its surface. Soon the Darkness pulsed and cracked like an egg. Black fog, smoke, and oil spewed forth. Out stepped Lucifer, but he was different. He was naked, and his hair was like it once was, but now it had turned a white grey color, his body had grown a very pale colored hue. Then he looked there way and smiled. His eyes had changed. The iris of his eyes had a greenish glow; an unholy glow. But, the rest of his eyes, where the whites of his eyes should be was pure black. When he spoke to them his voice sounded like before, only now it has a Dark power behind it. Hearing his voice it leaves one only with a cold Dark feeling now. He raised a hand, and before they could move the Sentient Darkness shot forth and consumed all the Archangels. The other Angels attacked, or tried to, but Lucifer easily took them all down. Soon the Sentient Darkness finished with the other Archangels, who one by one they rose and followed him through the Dark portal into its heart where a black metal throne covered in demonic symbols and skulls Lucifer walked over and sat down the throne which glowed with an unholy light and the Sentient Darkness covered Lucifer once again. This time when it left, black metal scale armor covered his body a black metal skull helmet now rested over his head. Where his eyes were, now only black flames. The other seven Archangels all now turned into his six Princes and one Princess of darkness, who all kneeled before there new lord. Lucifer stood, waved a hand, and Dark portal opened were they could look into the golden city. In the city a massive Dark portal opened, where all in heaven could see that Lucifer was standing before a black throne.

Lucifer spoke then, "God of LIGHT and Life know now that I once known as Lucifer now I am reborn as Satan, and I am the god of Darkness and Death. I will make it my mission to devour all You hold dear, and I will push you of your high and mighty throne and make You one day kneel before me.

God, now very angry rose up and forced the portal closed. Then God sat back in sadness for He was angry at Lucifer, but He loved all his children. However, now Lucifer was gone and Satan had now given the darkness a true devoted mission. God decided He would have to speed up His plans. God took His finger of Pure LIGHT and then pushed a long thin circular balloon like bubble out from the edge of the Myriasphere, but still did not pop a hole in the edge of Myriasphere. Then God grabbed the entire galaxy that the Hellcore void is in and pushed it into that balloon like bubble commanding the planets to align in order like they are. And then God created the dead zone between the Galaxy that Sentient Darkness and Satan and all the Demon Princes and Demon Princes are in. Then God commanded Michael the Archangel and all His Archangels and Angels to keep Sentient Darkness from gaining any more space past that dead-zone and then God began to create Malon.

Son continued, "Only God knows all that has happened in the time since that King of Darkness has setup his throne on the Dead Star inside the void space where no life exists. Hellcore is the void and the Dead Star that Sentient Darkness continues to survive in. The Galaxy where Hellcore is located has seven world planets, which are also now completely consumed by the Darkness and its hordes of Demons. The seven Archangels who followed Lucifer have all been twisted and turned into the most dangerous of our enemy's pawns. They are the Six Demon Princes and one Demon Princess. Hellcore literally appears like a place within their universe and within the Myriasphere which is completely void of light. Those planets next to Hellcore also have become void of light. And, here on this side of that pushed out galaxy, which now almost appears as if it is a black hole at the edge of the Myriasphere, but it is not, as it actually leads into a pushed out galaxy. One might think of it like a long skinny balloon with its mouth on this end where the Dead Zone is located and way near the other end is the Hellcore Void and the Dead Star inside the Hellcore Void. That Dark almost perfectly circular Dark area of space is actually fairly wide. Wide enough to easily fit each of the world planets and their atmospheres and ozone layers and beyond almost perfectly circular space as God's Light pushed that galaxy into that stretched out balloon like finger of space. Again, the Dead Zone is the space between that galaxy and all of the rest of this universe. Malon and your two moons are sitting directly in line on the outside of that Dead Zone and that galaxy. That is why God chose to build Malon here as His shield."

Son continued, "Now, We will explain to you the Demons and their armies and what we know of them to date. The weakest of all the Demon Princes is Belphegor, who once was the Archangel Belpre. He is now the Gluttonous Demon prince of the world now called Sloth, for he causes those who fall into his clutches to be doing very little as he the feeds on their wills and on their ambition, draining it from their hearts and minds and spirits. And, the world planet he is in control of is the first world planet into that galaxy beyond the Dead Zone."

Son continued, "Azazel rules over the second world. He is the father of most of the lower Demons; He is the Demon Prince of the world now called Wrath. He is the one who is the general over most of the militant forces of the galaxy surrounding Hellcore. He sends forth his Demons and his Demon-bonded in waves that we the Angels have stopped from getting past the dead zone, which as I explained before surrounds the outer edge of the galaxy. The world planet he is in control of is the second world planet from the Dead Zone."

Son continued, "The third Demon Prince is Mammon, who is the Prince of world now called Greed. He gets his strength and energy from all who seek only after wealth and increase without any desire to put their wealth and increase into the common good of all." His world is littered with vaults filled with the ill-gotten wealth of his followers. The world planet he is in control of is the third world planet from the Dead Zone.

Next is the very twisted wife and lover of what has become of Lucifer, Levith. Now, she is the incredibly twisted monster known as Leviathan. She was trained under the King of Darkness in the abilities to shapeshift herself like he does from almost human-like form, a large carp fish form, a dragon-like form, and into a flying snake-like form. That is why she is also known as the Naki, Queen of the Nagas. She is the Princess of the world called Envy, and her world is a black ocean of difficult things. Satan in his Serpent King form and Leviathan in her Naki form had joined together in a forbidden joining, which then she has birthed all the Nagas male children, who while growing and by going through trial of combat, can become Hydra. Once they gain five or more heads they are no more simply Nagas, or even just Nagas-Hydra Hybrids, for then as full-fledged Hydra they can begin to train to become Quetzalcoatl. Quetzalcoatl are by far the worst of these spawns as they have turned into murderous and mind-controlling Kings of the Nagas. She also birthed female Nagas, who through joining with a Quetzalcoatl, becomes a Naki Queen of the Nagas. Somehow since their joining they have used someone with Dark Magic to open Dark portals to send at least one male and one female Nagas child into many world planets where living beings are to be found. These children of the Serpent King, also known as King of Darkness, or Satan, and the Leviathan, Naki, Queen of the Nagas, enter their new world's rivers, lakes, creeks, and most other bodies of water to swim and defecate into the waters, as this is what all snakes do. By doing this they help deceive the sentient beings who may drink from or swim in these waters to become involved in Dark Magic, murder, do mind-control and other evils. You all remember what happened to Black Ice, the War Chief Alpha, who had threatened a Seer who had swam in the waters and had drank from the tainted waters of the Nagas and started practicing Dark Magic. Dark Ice used the Dark Magic casting Seer to twist the Life-energy Pack Mind into a mind-slave pack mind. And, those he could not control through the Pack Mind he threatened by intimidation. Several of his Chief Alphas and Alphas though had been made to swim in the waters that both Dark Ice and the Seer had defecated into. Then they used some Dwarven slaves to build a large underground pool, and filled it with tainted waters, then used that Dark Magic influenced water to force many Ice Wolves into mental-bonding slavery and then to their deaths, using their God given Life-energy capabilities for their own evil purposes."

Son continued, "By now you all know that the Ice Wolves who were under these evil influences are no more, and through God's grace the waters of the Great Northern Tundra and Great Northern Peak's mountains, and many other places on Malon have been cleansed from the Nagas' influences. Many years ago a younger Alda helped Prince Arthus and Jade kill the large male Nagas on Malon, and that cleansing process is still almost daily ongoing throughout Malon. I understand that the Aldas have successfully killed the younger female Nagas too. Whenever a Nagas, Hydra, or Quetzalcoatl is found on a sentient world anywhere in the Myriasphere, God has declared that they are to be killed without mercy. While Leviathan herself is in control of the fourth planet in from the Dead Zone.

Son continued, "Next we have JezeBeelz, now known as Jezebel-Beelzebub who also goes by Beelzebub-Jezebel, no longer having any resemblance to an Archangel, this totally twisted it has turned itself into a transvestite She/He, or He/She, abomination creature and is now the Prince/Princess, or Princess/Prince of the world now called Lust. Lust is filled completely with unnatural sexual liberty. This abomination creature is both the mother and the father to all its self-birthed Succubus, and its world is one of torture and pleasure, for it feeds off of both. Its children and their subatomic Succubus worms deceived the population of the world planet into believing all the lies of all its sexual perversions. Its perversions deceive the minds of its victims into believing that God is not right in how they were created and tricks them into causing self-mutilation of their bodies and especially that of their sexual organs. Its goal is to end the possibility of natural procreation of the various sentient species. Its subatomic Succubus worms digs their way into the brains of the deceived and eat away all possibility of receiving Truth, and cursing them towards ever increasing and ever more self-destructive perversions. We know that at least some of these Succubus and their subatomic worms have been sent by Dark portals and by someone other than the Demon Prince/Princes with Dark Magic abilities to control Dark to other world planets in the Myriasphere too. Jezebel-Beelzebub is in control of the fifth world planet in from the Dead Zone."

Son continued, "Then there is Zobald, once known as Zobal, is now the Prince of the world known as Death. He is one truly to fear, for he was once the Archangel who presided over death, as the Death Angel, but he now enjoys manipulating people's minds and bodies into murderous and suicidal thoughts and actions and feeds off their hatred, their wars, their murdering, their suicide, and all of the crazy emotions tied to all of those. His world is a vast wastelands of death. It is said that the very ground is covered deeply in the bones of all the souls that the Sentient Darkness has consumed as it has taken over Hellcore. Death is the sixth world planet in from the Dead Zone.

Son Continued, "Sephtis is the name of the sixth Demon Prince. His world is now called decay, where the undead only think that they find somewhere to sleep during the day, but then the Darkness forces them to come back awake every night, where they relive their last night over and over and over again not able to fully die, though their bodies are full of septic sores and worms from flies eat their septic sores. Decay is the Seventh world planet in from the Dead Zone."

Son continued, "Lucifer is by far the saddest of all the Demonic Devils, for he who was so greatly gifted in both light and music arts, and truly loved life and all of life-energy creativity so much, in that one decision to disobey God, then go and try to take matters into his own hands, took on something only God, Himself has the power and authority to defeat. That single decision to disobey God the father, caused his fall and he then as he continued to fall farther and farther into the darkness became completely twisted in his greed for the power, and then in his pride and arrogance towards God, he has turned himself into Satan, King of Darkness. Instead of humbly possessing his proper position in Heaven, he has only become possessed himself by the very Sentient Darkness he went to fight against. All his love has turned into hatred. His entire purposes now is to destroy all life. Satan has even tried to leave the Hellcore throne Room, but his attempts are futile. He regularly sends messages declaring war on God and bragging about how he and all his fallen have deceived and twisted others into choosing to follow him into the clutches of Sentient Darkness. However, they remain in their own destructively transformed galaxy that surrounds Hellcore, where they only in their forever twisted thinking, think they rule over their domain. However, every so often they continue to try to send out their armies through spaceships and through dark portals to spread Darkness farther and farther through the Myriasphere. Satan, who declared himself as the King of Darkness, sits on his throne in the room on the Dead Star inside the heart of the Hellcore Void."

So now you know the true history and the leaders of the very thing that one day will threaten your very doors," said Son.

Son continued, "I pray to God on your behalves that you will heed my warnings, that you will dig deeply into all of your studies, your meditations, and your various trainings and seek Him for guidance and wisdom far beyond yourselves. For only He is the Giver of all good gifts and abilities!"

The moment Son had finished speaking, He then instantly disappeared, right while they were all looking right at him.

Soon after, they were all dismissed. Arthus knew he had a lot to think about, but he went with his friends to get some food and then to meditation and then to get some sleep.

Arthus meditated a lot on what Son had said.

Chapter 23
The Grand Tournament Announced

Arthus stood on the wall that led to the Forest zone just outside the Academy. He watched as the sun rose over the horizon. He was wearing his standard training gear, but he had added some weights and a heavy pack during his morning routine. He smiled; he had been at this Academy for so long he wondered how life was going back on the mainland. Jade had returned home for a bit to take Fang back to his pack, for most Yaule don't live nearly as long as the primary races. Fang had been studying and training also at the Academy, when he realized he must be obedient and intentionally pass on his genetics to other Yaule in order to father cubs that could become then members of Clan Yaule Fang as Michael the Archangel had charged him with on the first day of his Academy Training. Only his newly gifted genetics would allow the Yaule to live as long as the primary races, and only those gifted genetics could become part of Clan Yaule Fang. He and Jade discussed this issue at length on many occasions since Michael the Archangel had brought him through the portal from Jade's and his room into the first ceremony assembly. After Son had given his talk, Fang truly understood that he had a great responsibility to all the Myriasphere to build a strong and capable clan that could spread out into many worlds in the Myriasphere and work with any higher functioning sentient beings as they must prepare for the war against darkness that is coming. Fang's pack of female felines in God's Forest had actually been greatly neglected by his long absence from them. Several generations of Yaules had come and gone since he became Life-Bonded to Jade and since he came to the Academy. After Son's talk tonight, Michael the Archangel agreed that Fang should quickly return and procreate with all the healthy females of the Yaules as possible, while they were still capable of carrying cubs. Michael said that Raphael would go there to meet with him and them when he arrived. Arthus remembered what it was like when he first met the cub long ago. He had finally grown close to the big guy, and now he will be gone for many years as he begins to build the Clan Yaule Fang on Malon. Arthus realized how important that role for Fang really was and how important the Clan Yaule Fang would be for Malon and all of the worlds in the Myriasphere his clan would be able to help in the future. He knew the life-bond that Fang and Jade had with each other and this bond would not go away just because they were half way around their world from each other. Still, he hoped Jade was doing alright. He knew she would return in a few days. A call coming in brought Arthus out of his thoughts. Looking down, it was Katelynn calling.

"Hello, Arthus. I hope I am not bothering you, but I need to speak with you and your friends as soon as you can get them all together at my office. I already messaged Asher, Zoey, Zeck and Emon. I know Jade won't be back here for a bit, but I have something that you'll all be excited about. So please get with me as soon as you are able," said Katelynn.

"Alright, I'll go change my gear quick, grab all my friends and meet you at your office as soon as I can," said Arthus.

"Thank you," said Katelynn. She hung up. So, then Arthus lifted his pack back up and started to run back towards his room. Soon Arthus had changed his gear, and then gathered all his friends outside Katelynn's office.

"Come on in," said Katelynn. They all went into surprise, for Katelynn wasn't alone, for Jacob and Maddy were both waiting for them.

"Welcome, everyone, come in and sit down. Everyone, Maddy here has something she wanted to give you, and Zeck, Jacob has made a request to Maddy to help yourself," said Katelynn.

"Yes, sorry, Zeck, I would have told you but I really wanted to run this idea by Maddy before I brought this idea before you," said Jacob. Everyone looked a bit lost.

"I am sorry, let us explain a bit Prince Arthus, your grandfather, High King Thureos has asked me to make you a very special custom armor set to get ready for the Grand Tournament. So I come to ask if your friends would also like custom armor crafted for them as well. Now, I usually don't do this, but I decided it really is a lot of fun to craft new armor types. But Jacob here has asked me to help Zeck craft a new weapon that best suits him also. And, Jacob's idea for Zeck's weapon seems like it might be an amusing item to make. He would like to make a Halberd but with a custom Long Axe blade on one side that comes down to the middle of the spear handle and is imbued with fire ruins to make it go ablaze when wielded, and yet also needs to be upgraded with a shooting spear head type javelin mechanism that uses the exploding wadding trigger systems that Emon and the weapon's engineers had been designing over the last many years, and only recently perfected, in the upper end of the spear, and with the trigger mechanism built down where they won't interfere with the normal use of the weapon. The spearhead shoots out and has a cable that goes through the length of the inside of the spear staff and through those crazy climbing and repelling gloves, and then has the speeding spool pack system on Zeck's back. That way it becomes kind of an all-in-one fighting and escaping weapon/tool," said Maddy.

"That really does sound like a weapon I would love," said Zeck. He nodded over to Jacob, who nodded his head in return.

"So I need to have you all come for a couple of days back to Great Northern Peaks City, where Jade will also meet us there for a couple of days to gather together everything I will need for all your new armor and gear and to make sure we build your armor so that it fits each of you perfectly and to ensure that crazy back spooling systems strappings are perfectly sized for Zeck's big body" said Maddy.

"I have also approved this temporary leave for each of you as it goes alongside of the planned break for everyone to prepare their teams for the Grand Tournament, which will begin in only a month's time. I will be announcing all the Grand Tournament information later today in the meeting for everyone. So, right after the final announcements in the meeting, you all need to have enough gear for your couple of extreme cold to extreme hot days and meet at the transportation shuttle dock to head out with Maddy at that point. You may go in a couple of hours. I see you at the auditorium," said Katelynn.

With that, they all left headed back to get ready. Zeck was super excited to get to see the weapon Jacob and Maddy have in mind. Arthus thought about what kind of armor he wanted. He thought of the plate armor his grandfather and father wore, but He wanted something a bit different. Arthus contacted Jade before he went to the meeting and told her about the upcoming Tournament. When they met up in Great Northern Peak's City, he let her know what it was all about and found out that Fang had returned to his pack and Raphael met him there. Together with the Archangel's approval found several lovely lady Yaules to start a large family with. The Archangel needed to test each of the female's Life-energy and elemental abilities before he could bless their unions, and extend their lifespans to better align with Fang's life-bonding with Jade, as he would most likely live on for almost nine thousand more years. Arthus smiled, thinking of Fang running wild with all his new wives fighting over his attention, and what it would mean becoming a father multiple times over fairly quickly. Arthus realized that Fang would sire a whole lot of children over his nearly nine thousand nine hundred year extended lifespan. Every pregnancy of Yaules produces anywhere from five to eight cubs, and they can get pregnant at least twice each year, Arthus wondered about the Yaules that remained on Creed and if any of them had evolved enough to perhaps boost Clan Yaule Fang even quicker.

Later, Arthus and the others were sitting back in the auditorium like always, waiting for the big announcement. Before long, Katelynn stood on stage. This time Jacob was the only other one with her.

"Thank you all for coming. Some of you hear already know or have been a part of this great event before. As you might have been wondering, the Grand Tournament that we hold each year is about to arrive. Now only the students who have been in training for their first four hundred fifty years and only the students completing their last four hundred fifty years participate each year. Every other student remains an observer only. For those who are observers only, this is still highly important as you will get to witness and learn by watching from both the students that are halfway through their training and from the students which are about to graduate. We here at the Academy hold these grand Tournaments to test your skills to show yourself and the teachers how you have grown over your time here. For those who second time in this Tournament, this is your graduation test to see if you are ready to truly leave us and return as a full-fledged member of any clan. For the first time, you will start with a written exam. Then you will get with teams of two where you will have to show off your combat skills in a grand arena before everyone here. Some honored guests will also be attending, like High King Thureos and Prince Benroy and some of the Silver Knights Captains and also some of Clan Urial leaders to see if any of you show promise to join their ranks someday. Other clan leaders are also here as many of them also want the chance to see for themselves your various skills. Some are more interested in seeing your internal or external elemental skills mastery than they are just your combat skills. It is very important that you do incorporate throughout your competition the best of your elemental abilities and your combat skills." said Katelynn. She motioned, and Jacob steps forward.

"Thank you all for coming. Yes, you will get with teams of two. I suggest you pick people you know complement your fighting style. And ones you know have your back. This is no game; this will show all how you have improved your skills and talents as warriors and even as Life-energy elemental wielders. The fights will happen in my Arena, where you will have free reign to use any tactics or weapons you wish to fight with. We have master-level healers who will be on standby to make sure no deaths acquire but absolutely do not hold back. For your opponents will not be showing any mercy. Remember, there will be leaders of both my clan and the Silver Knights watching you see if you are worthy of our clans. Suppose it is your goal one day to enter our clans. You better not hold back. I have seen many show some amazing talents over the years, so I am looking forward to this year's Tournament. Also to the winner will get to stand before High King Thureos and ask a favor if, within the High King's power, he will grant it to the best of his ability. Also, you have one week to send any request to have any custom gear or weapons crafted by the Dwarvens, so make sure you get in your request forms. Trust me, and you do not want to miss out on that. As stated before, any weapon or Life-energy elemental power is allowed, so get with those you wish to team up and figure out a good strategy. I can't wait to see you all in the Arena," said Jacob.

With that, they were dismissed. Arthus and Zeck returned to their room.

"Well, Zeck, who you want to team up with," asked Arthus?

"Well, I was thinking you at first, but no, I want to ask Zoey or Emon that it would be better to improve strategy since we both are way more up close combat. I think a long-range or good life caster would be best to balance the team," said Zeck.

"Ya, I agree, and the truth is I rather face you one on one. You're my best friend and my rival, and I love to see who can better the other in full out. Plus, I think I will ask Jade to join my team," said Arthus.

"Yes, to face off one on one in an epic showdown that would be the show of a lifetime, wouldn't it," said Zeck smiling. They both laughed out loud and gathered their gear. Soon Arthus, Zeck, Emon, Zoey, and Asher were at the dock at the roof over the main building waiting for Maddy to show up so they could board then leave. Arthus wondered if the cold north city had changed much in the last, what it is now... almost five hundred years almost since he had been up to there? Soon Maddy arrived carrying a lot of parchments, and they all climbed in to head out.

"This be my first time to the Great Northern Peak's City. I heard it's so cold up there, said Zoey with a frown.

"Yes, it is cold, but I miss my home and love to see my family and all the others once again," said Zeck.

"Yes, and to get a good Ale, the stuff at this Island is far too bland, and no were near the greatness of the Dwarvens," said Emon with a deep laugh. Arthus smiled. He also couldn't wait to drink and sing along with the bearded folk. Before they knew it, they were landing. Jade was already there sitting by a fire in a hut nearby, drinking some warm coffee, and was happy to see them. She smiled at Arthus and gave him a large bag she had brought with her.

"I brought that with me, as my father said you were asking about them long ago, and when he got his hands on one, he made sure I bring it for you," said Jade. Arthus looked inside and smiled. Inside was a significant rolled Yaule skin that could be turned into clothing or whatever that could change its color still to match its surroundings.

"Alright, this is great. I can have Maddy add this to the armor she is making," said Arthus.

"What is it? Hand it here. Oh my, yes, I can come up with a great way to add this to armor. Yes, I have an idea forming right now. Yes, now let's hurry. I have work to do and many forgers and crafters to gather," said Maddy. They all ran on Zeck's left to say hi to his family. He would meet them later on. Soon they moved down into the Dwarvens caverns below the mountain. Jade and Zoey looked on in amazement for it was their first time ever seeing the Dwarvens homes. Arthus missed the smell and the constant music all around him. It brought him back when he had been there before, working day in and day out, mining and sometimes drinking with the hardy folk. Soon they came to Maddy's office, and she took out her parchments and had already started drawing designs of different armor pieces.

"Alright, I am going to have you one by one come into the back room where you will strip down, and I get your measurements for the armor. Then you can go about your business. If you think of any good ideas you like added to your armor, don't wait long to tell me, for once I start, I won't want to stop my work, or go back to pulling something apart to change it. Soon they were all done and went out to explore. Arthus went with Emon and Jade to the local tavern there. The old Foreman and his crew were just then arriving after a long day.

"Well, shave my beard Arthus my good prince, have you grown, and is this your lady? She is a mighty beautiful one, I should say my good boy has it been as long as to have you grown into a good looking lad," said the Foreman. Arthus blushed, and so did Jade.

"Well, meet again, you old slave driver. I come here to drink with you and to show Jade here the hospitality of you good folk," said Arthus.

"Ah, good, come, lets us talk and drink and sing. I love to know all that you been up to since you left us those many years ago," said the Foreman. Soon Jade and Arthus drank and watched the Dwarvens dance and sing the night away before retiring to a room that had been set out for the group. Emon, Zeck, and Asher had returned to their families, and Zoey had retired early that day. Arthus had been meditating and dreaming of the armor he wanted, and had a clear vision of what he wanted coming forth. Arthus sat up, drew it out on a parchment nearby, and ran off towards Maddy's office, forgetting to put his shirt on. Arthus smiled, for this would make even Maddy smile.

Chapter 24
The Northern Ice Drake

Arthus smiled after he left Maddy. He could still hear her laughing in glee at what Arthus had brought her. He couldn't wait to see what she would do with the ideas he showed her. He left up the tunnels. It would be day soon, and he would see what was in store. Soon, all had awakened and joined Arthus, who was eating a hardy breakfast of chicken eggs, biscuits, sausage, and warm gravy at the town guardhouse. He had talked with some of the northern guards he had spent time with when he was up here all those years ago. He found out a squad was about to head over to the Ice Wolf new village up where they had first started it at the far Northern peek, so Arthus talked the others into joining the patrol to see how things had changed over the years. He also wished to visit the Yelin village on their way back and what he heard made him think things have improved much between the Ice Wolves and the Yelin clans, and he was glad for he didn't wish to see another bloody fight again any time soon.

Zeck, Jade, and Asher decided to join him. Emon would stay behind. He wanted to do more work before it was time to return to the Academy. So the four of them borrowed some thick coats and winter gear from the town guard and joined the patrol. It was fantastic to ride the mighty Snow Bears across the open tundra.

"You didn't lie, Arthus, when you told me how bright and cold it was up here when you wrote to me all those times after you left the Valley," said Jade. He could barely hear her voice muffled behind the mask she wore to protect her face from the biting winds and sheer coldness of a constant assailant.

"Don't worry, we reach the Ice Wolf village soon," said one of the guards. Within an hour, the guard was right. They had reached the Northern Mountain in an hour, and the gate that led to the village built around and inside the massive Mountain. Arthus led them inside the place was far different than he remembered all those years ago. The town was more than that now. It was about the size of the Northern City; many Yelin and Ice Wolves walked together going about their daily lives. Arthus could tell that part of the city had Yelin yurts set up. A full port was built with many big ships anchored at its bay. Each vessel had a plate of Life steel made into the front base going out like a spear. Arthus figured what it was for right away to help the ship plow through the ice on the waters. He also saw many he knew were part of the Fishing villages of the great sea moving around the docks. Soon they walked around and into the Mountain itself. Inside was built a lot like the undercity of the Dwarvens but designed in the Ice Wolf style. Many side dens where the Ice Wolves lived and talked and an area where the most of the normal Ice Wolves, which were caged up. Not all Ice Wolves had evolved past their primal created nature, and for the safety of everyone else, Clan Red Fang felt it was important that they were caged and fed River of Life water with their food until either they began to show that the Life-energy in the River of Life water had helped them evolve, or if not, they would just allow them to remain caged. Soon they came upon a great Iron door with Markings of the fight between Black Fang High King and their first Druid king depicted on it. They walked in, and in the center of the room was a Throne where a large White Wolf sat. He wore simple clothing like most of the Ice Wolf Druids did.

"Well, if it isn't the Prince Arthus once again to step foot in a place he helped my people build into our home, I sure much had changed since my grandfather sat on this throne. Sad day it was when he and my Father passed, but we have kept the peace and grown since you last stepped foot here," said the great wolf with a bow.

"Thank you! I don't know your name, but I am truly at awe at how much has changed and improved over the years, and was truly sorry to hear of your father's and grandfather's passing. I knew your grandfather to be a very wise and powerful druid and leader of his people and glad to see his line has kept his dedication to growth and peace," said Arthus returning the bow.

"Ah yes, sorry I haven't introduced myself. I am called Whitefang, High Chief of Clan Red Fang. Named such since, unlike the Black fur of my great grandfather, I have pure white fur, as you can see. But what brings you to our far reaches of the north? I hope all is well with my High King Thureos," said Whitefang.

"Do not worry for my grandfather as ancient as the old man is, he is healthy as always. I came with the patrol from Great Northern Peak's City to see for myself just how your home has changed and to allow my friends here to meet you all. Zeck, you know of, and these are my other friends, Jade, and Asher. Jade is from Arial valley and like Zeck, Asher is from the Dwarvens city, but both have never seen the home of the Ice Wolves," said Arthus.

"I see... well then, welcome to you all. I have heard much of the warm and open plains of Arial Valley. I need to go there one day to see it for myself. But I am glad you have come. I'm about to send some of my Wolves with myself to investigate roomer of an Ice Drake making territory not far from here actually it be on the way back to Northern Peek city if you mind to join us I sure you all are formable now that you been training in combat I can tell by looking that you have grown into a strong warrior and be glad of the help," said Whitefang.

"Ice Drake, ya if one has shown up, it's not good! They are a powerful beast and deadly. It said that one blast of their icy breath could turn one's blood to ice," said Zeck.

"We will be glad to join you and your warriors, and I'm sure the patrol from Great North Peak's City would also wish to join in, but we need better protection from this creature," said Arthus.

"Do not worry, for I have druid powers to help shield you all from most cold attacks, and I have better pelts for your friends can wear to help keep more of the cold from your bones. Besides, this won't be the first Ice Drake my people have faced with the help of north Peak's guards. We have dealt with them many times over the years. They are rare but not unknown to us up here. Ice Drakes can grow very large; they have fairly large wings, thick, scaly hides and fangs and claws made of frozen glass-like diamonds, but their breath is the most dangerous, as Zeck said, it can freeze even one like us to our very blood. We know of ways to prevent them from such an attack, and we have specially crafted fire weapons created by Dwarvens to break through the Drakes tough hide. So if you allow myself and my pack to go in first and trap the Ice Drake's mouth closed with our special weapon, then come in and help us bring the beast down, we will be most appreciative," said Whitefang. Arthus looked to the others all nodded their approval.

"Alright, Whitefang looks like you have four more warriors to join you in this fight," said Arthus. Soon they were all geared up with warm pelts made from naturally fallen Northern Mammoths and the patrol with Whitefang and several of his druids and warriors and headed towards where the Ice Drake had been spotted near a smaller mountain that had a large cave known to be there. The cave is where they had guessed the beast had turned into its home. The patrol from North Peak wasn't surprised at all to hear of the Ice Drake, for they had patrols that had fought beast like that before not many returned after a fight with a fully grown one, but the accounts suggested that this wasn't a fully grown one yet they all hoped. So they soon came to an open area just before the cave entrance, and they found a boneyard of all kinds of remains of Mammoths, Snow bears, and even many dead Dwarvens and Ice Wolf remains around the cave. Arthus allowed Whitefang and his pack to move in first to scout out the Ice Drakes size and if it was inside the cave at all. They had hoped to find the beast sleeping to use their powers to trap the beast down for an easy win, but the cave was empty at that time, and worse by the evidence of what was left, it was a fully grown female for several of her eggs were found inside, which meant that this Drake would fight like Hellcore if they were discovered here.

"Well, this could be far more than what we can handle. We might want to get lost soon and come back with a much larger fighting force to deal with this Drake," said Whitefang.

"We are outside our expertise, so I shall follow your lead, Whitefang. So if you think we should go, we better get out of here. Leave the eggs, for now. If the mother comes back to a bunch of destroyed eggs, she could go into a rage and target one of the city's that won't be ready for an attack. Best to go without it knowing we been here," said Arthus.

"Yes, you are right, let's go," said Whitefang, but before he could finish, they heard a loud sound of beating wings and a sign something had landed just outside the large cave. They all froze because they all knew the mother had returned. An ear-piercing roar burst forth, for the mother could smell the intruders they all figured. Whitefang and his men ran forth. The Drake burst into the cave with such force that it almost collapsed. The great Ice Drake came to a halt in the center of the large cave. The Ice Drake thrashed and turned in all directions, staring at those who dared come to its nest.

Arthus could see that no one was hurt from when the Drake forced entrance so far. It was time to act. But Whitefang and his pack and the patrol from the city were already on the move. Whitefang and his druids were already bringing forth large roots to entangle the Ice Drake's feet and trying to pull the giant beast to the ground, but the Drake was tearing them out just as fast. Zeck brought forth his large new Halberd. He ran his hands down one of its sides, and the blade burst into bright red flames. Zeck raced in with the Northern patrol to surround the thing, always trying to keep away from the deadly mouth.

Arthus was shocked at how fast the large man moved. He watched Zeck leap over the Drake, landing on one foot then jumping once again before the Drake could snap around, slamming his burning Halberd Ax head deep into the back of the Drake just below its left wing. The Drake roared in pain as the Fire burst forth, burning, and when Zeck jumped back, the Drake left-wing hung down, now completely useless.

Arthus smiled and said, "Good! That hit keeps the Ice Drake from flying out of the cave, or to take to the air. Arthus looked to Jade, who already had her bow out and an arrow flying right into the Drakes right eye as its head spun toward them. The fast growing and grabbing Druid roots were finally starting to pull the beast off balance that and the warriors sticking hits around like seeing a giant bug being devoured by tiny ants is what Arthus was picturing. But it wasn't down yet, and its head spun on three of the member of the patrol, two dwarves and a Cundo female, and breathed all three were instantly frozen solid; dead before they could even try to get out of the way. Zeck struck home again, then slashed across the back left hind leg, taking it cleanly off and leaving behind the Fire to burn at what was left. Blood pouring out of the Ice Drake which roared and turned again. As Arthus stood by Whitefang and Jade, it looked Arthus's way, and he knew they were in trouble for it breathed. Arthus could feel the Ice cold wind come straight towards him and the other two. Wait, Wind, it had lived Wind at him. Arthus fell into himself, brought up his hands, and commanded the Wind in that breath to halt. All in the room came to a standstill, and then all were in awe as the Drake breathed and Arthus stood in its path, arms and hands outstretched, but the Wind stopped and flowed around the three.

Arthus felt all the years he spent trying to master the elements had come to good use. He could feel the Wind dancing around them. He could feel his mind-controlling the path of that deadly cold Wind. He allowed the breath to disperse around the walls cave. The temperature definitely dropped but nothing fatal as receiving the complete breath would have been. The Ice Drake eyed Arthus with a deadly glare. It roared but then two large root shots beneath its maw and rapped it bring the head down, pinning its head and mouth closed.

"Don't let them kill my babies," begged the Ice Drake speaking telepathically into Arthus' mind.

Whitefang knelt out of breath. Sorry, it took too long to get the thing to shut its mouth. Now we can end its suffering. Zeck immediately jumped on the beast's neck, bringing his large Halberd above his head, summing all his physical strength enhanced by his Cundo blood and Life-energy bringing the flaming Ax blade down, and easily severing the Ice Drake's head from its body. The Ice Drake's eyes clouded over. It was definitely dead!

Arthus stood quietly meditating and pushing with his Life-energy into the Ice Drake's eggs. He could sense the fact that they were clearly already sentient and sent a calming and healing Life-energy push into them.

Whitefang commanded to his druids, "Deal with any of the injured group. They took the bodies of those who had fallen out to be brought back to the city to be buried with full honors. Arthus made sure of that. Zeck wrapped a chain around the Ice Drakes head.

"This thing will make a fine trophy back home. I wonder whether I am now Zeck Ice Drake Slayer," said Zeck with a smirk.

"Well, my Friend, you have shown me I have to fight with everything I have if I am going to win the upcoming tournament," smiled Arthus.

"You have all done great things for our people, Arthus. I owe you my life. I was in shock seeing you stop a full-on breath like that; I have never seen a wind user be able to control something that powerful before so fully," said Whitefang.

"Yes, I could feel the Wind in the breath. In truth, my fingers got a bit frostbit, but I'm glad I was able to stop the breath for not just you, but my life and that of my dearest, wouldn't be here if I weren't able to turn that breath away," said Arthus. He looked to Jade, who smiled at him and blinked and nodded her thanks. Whitefang and Asher started moving over to the Ice Drake's nest to destroy the remaining eggs.

Suddenly Arthus yelled, "Stop! Don't destroy those eggs!"

Whitefang, Zeck and Asher all said in unison, "Wait, what?"

Arthus quickly explained, "Whitefang, it was not that long ago that your Ice Wolf peoples evolved past your beast created natures. These Ice Drakes, though they are so incredibly dangerous, also have the right to evolve past their beast created natures. I sensed a very strong feeling in my Life-energy while we were fighting with this Ice Drake mother that she really did not desire to harm any of us, but that it was us who had intruded on her den of eggs. She then clearly recognized my use of elemental wind to stop her breath from harming Jade and I. She pushed in her own Life-energy at me in that moment right before Zeck jumped on her and killed her, she knew she was going to die, and in my mind, I clearly telepathically heard her say, 'Don't let them kill my babies!' In past years many thousands of years ago, High King Thureos led his armies and exterminated an entire species of giant bug creatures that were constantly attacking and killing the Cundos and Ignoles and many other species in the Blood Sands. I understand why he did that for that situation, in that time, but I have learned that we higher functioning sentient beings are placed here as God's shield to protect all living things,

391

especially those that have evolved with Life-energy filled sentient gifts. Telepathy is absolutely an evolved Life-energy sentient gift. And, whether we like it or not, this evolved creature's use of their Life-energy filled elemental ice breath, in order to protect her nest of eggs is proof that they have evolved beyond their created beast natures, or are extremely close to that stage in their development. Just like your Ice Wolf grandfather, who believed in peace and harmony with all of sentient life on Malon, these Ice Drake babies deserve the chance to prove they too can live in peace and harmony with all the rest of sentient life on Malon. Therefore I plan to ask the Archangel Raphael and my grandfather, High King Thureos to help find a way to provide a safe haven for these Ice Drakes. Perhaps they are somewhat like the Valkers, which when they are born and raise in the wild, are quite dangerous, but when born and raised in a carefully controlled environment can be guided into a harmonious existence with all sentient beings.

Whitefang shook his head in agreement and said, I sure hope what you are saying can come true for these Ice Drakes like it has for us.

Hearing what Arthus was saying, Jade smiled brightly and went out and took a big fur blanket off of one of the Ice Bear mounts that they were riding, and came back into the cave and started carefully picking up the Ice Drake eggs and wrapped them each up in the fur blanket. Then she used a good sized rope cord to carefully tie them so that the blanket had enveloped each of the eggs where they wouldn't bounce up against each other. Then carried them back out to her Ice Bear mount and tied them onto the back behind her saddle. Then she came back in smiling and grabbed one of Arthus's hand in both of her hands and then stood there staring at him lovingly.

After hearing and seeing all of that, Zeck walked over and set the remaining nest ablaze with the Fire from Halberd.

"Zeck, I got to say that weapon is truly something," said Arthus.

"Glad you like it. Maddy just got it finished before we left. It seems Jacob had sent her a letter asking her to make sure it was made even before we got here. I got to say I am truly in love with this Halberd, Ax, and spear Javelin hybrid fits me well. I even had my father help me inscribe the thing in Ruins three: Once, for weight to make the weapon lighter, Fire to make the blade of the weapon burst into flame when I run my hand over it, the third is to make the blade edge always sharp and to never go dull," said Zeck.

"Well then, Zeck, it definitely fits you," said Arthus. The weapon was indeed a masterwork. It was as long as a Spear even came to a sharp spear-like end which wasn't a spear but a Javelin with a cable that ran through the entire length of the handle. One side had a massive blade half like an ax, but the blade curved down the lower back to about halfway down the shaft. On the other side was an enormous spike. From the look, Zeck could either use it as a two-handed ax, or a thrusting spear or shoot the Javelin end from a good distance into almost any surface and then be whisked up by the cable and that spool contraption, to wherever that Javelin head had imbedded itself. The lower part of the handle had the trigger mechanism for the Javelin feature. The whole weapon was only a little over four feet long, so almost half the man's height. It was made of Life steel and was indeed a beautiful weapon to behold. The weapon fit the large muscular man to a tee. Zeck now was eight feet in height, towering over Arthus, and his muscles were just plain massively bulky. He had grown a nice trimmed beard and short black hair. Arthus marveled at his best friend, for no other could truly challenge Arthus as Zeck could for them over the years had a rivalry going, always trying to outdo the other. Arthus took out Angel Wing and smiled as much as Zeck boasted at his weapon. Arthus knew in his heart he already had his true partner as Angel Wing was so much more than just anyone weapon and more than even he could imagine.

"Whelp, we better head out before it gets dark. It takes a couple of hours to get to Great North Peak's City," said Arthus.

"I wish to go and inform the head of the deaths about the fall of the Ice Drake mother and to make sure that these guard patrol bodies are properly returned to their families," said Whitefang.

"Thank you, but please, leave the bodies to myself. I will gladly make sure they are given the best, and that their families are taken care of," said Arthus.

"Thank you anyway, my Prince, but as a fellow leader up here in the north, I need to make sure I also do my part honorably. And, this role

393

is squarely on my shoulders to bear. Now please, let us head out," said Whitefang.

Before the night got dark, the group had entered the city. Arthus and Whitefang went to see the city guard captain and Maddy, who was saddened to hear of the losses and even more surprised when they handed the head of the Ice Drake to them as proof of the bravery of their dead. Arthus and Whitefang meet with the dead families explaining their final stand and how they fell. Arthus gives his word that they have the full support of the royal family and be buried with full honors.

Jade meanwhile, had talked with the Clan Urial Guard Captain, who provided what she would need. Then she took the Ice Drake eggs and placed them, fur blanket and all carefully into a fairly large metal clad wooden trunk, which she had added extra fur blanket padding under and around. Then she and Zeck, Zoey and Asher all waited for Arthus and Whitefang to return.

When Arthus and Whitefang returned to the Urial Guard area, Arthus quickly sent a holo-message to his grandfather, High King Thureos about the whole Ice Drake ordeal and asked him to get a message to the Archangel Raphael and try to figure out how they could make some kind of a Safe Haven for the Ice Drake eggs, where they possibly might hatch out like the Valkers and then be given a reasonable chance by talking to them through their telecommunication abilities to choose to live in harmony with all sentient beings on Malon. When he had finished sending that message Arthus spoke with the Urial Guard Captain and asked, "Can you please help ensure that these Ice Drake eggs get safely to wherever the High King and Archangel Raphael want them to be?

"Yes, of course! That would be exactly what needs done, said the Captain.

After that, they all headed to the mead halls of the Dwarvens pubs, and there was a party like none Arthus had ever seen. Zeck stood on a table telling the story of how they fought the great Ice Drake, and the Dwarvens drank and cheered and danced for their dead and to the death of actual danger to all of the north. The head of the Ice Drake was mounted above the hearth of the excellent pub for all to see when they came there below a plaque was put with the names of all who died.

All the party kept yelling, "Zeck Ice Drake Slayer," and then pounding twice with both hands on their tables, over and over and over again. They would stop only to down another mug of ale.

Maddy had told Arthus to come by before they retired for the night. So after Arthus' third mug of ale, he stands up and says, "Sorry my Dwarven friends and brothers, but Maddy is already waiting for us! But, you just keep on drinking and celebrating on behalf of my good friend Zeck here, who will gladly ensure your tabs get paid for the night!" Then Arthus punched Zeck in his big muscled arm and said, "Isn't that right, Zeck Ice Drake Slayer?"

Zeck said, "Yes that's right! Drink hardy me hard working Dwarven buddies!"

A loud cheer went up all around the room and at every table the Dwarvens all chanted, "Zeck Ice Drake Slayer! Pound. Pound. Zeck Ice Drake Slayer! Pound. Pound."

At that the group left to head over to Maddy's workshop. Most had more than three mugs of ale and were probably half-drunk, but still had enough of their wits about them to be amazed when they entered Maddy's place. There before them, on full display, is each of their armor sets. All their faces brightened as one for Maddy and all her Dwarvens craftsman had done such outstanding work. Arthus had meditated about and even dreamed of his armor set, but what he saw in that moment was even better than he had imagined.

"Well, what you think, me and me boys worked through the night and day to finish ya's new equipment. Their all master level work as it keeps ya warm in the cold and cool in the heat, and all be custom fitted to each one of ya'all bodies. So, be making sure you all take top spots in the upcoming Tournament to show off our skills," said Maddy.

"We will do that for sure! I have never seen such beautiful work before! It's even more than what I ever dreamed of, and we all thank you, for now, I truly believe we are all ready to return and take the Tournament by a storm," said Arthus.

"Ah, Jade, I have something for you," said Maddy. She took out a longbow like none had ever seen before. It was Silver in color but made of wood.

"This longbow be made out of a fallen branch from the First God's Tree itself. The Alda Matriarch gifted it to ya, by way of me, as she said ya be needing this longbow crafted by our very best bower along with an Aldar. Then there be this quiver filled with arrows. It be made from some of me best leather hides I had kept in stock, and then it too be embedded with these Ruins that instantly replenish each the arrows after they be shot. Also, as ya pull forth each arrow they be filled with different elemental properties of ya choosing. These and the Hybrid Halberd-Javelin Tool me helped make for Zeck is some of me very finest work. Now come let me show ya'all the armor," said Maddy.

"Arthus, your armor be what ya wanted. The boots be having three life steel plates running the length from your toes to just below ya knee. The pants be created from the hair of the Hondarg, a tough but flexible cloth that be dyed black. There be a good sized pouch along the left thigh to hold whatever ya wish. The belt be also made from Hondarg leather. The tunic be the same, as the chest plate and back plate cover from your navel to your chest. The plates are held together by leather straps. I will show you later how to remove the outer armor. Next be your gloves along the outside hands are life steel that forms around your knuckles up to your wrist. They have forearm coverings too, but that part be slightly different from what you might have been thinking about as I added some unique features there. Ya notice how the both be fingerless and sport a holo-display built into them. One of my latest designs has many functions like terrain map display and has built-in communication and can control your mask which me be gettin' to. Now to the outer coat, I used the Yaule skin ya brought to me to be craften a special hooded trench coat for ya. It goes down to the back of ya knees. The outer side be changin' color as the Yaule do. Ya can bring up the hood, or not, whatever you wish. The inside be laced with a specially made Life-steel where ya won't even feel it. They now be makin' the Life-steel into a fine string that be coated in a durable synth-blend material. The High King be already havin' many shirts fitted, making it light but durable. The inside of ya coat be made from the fur of Dreg, so it be soft and warm. Now to the mask, which also becomes a full-face helmet when needed. The mask itself be built into your tunic. Let me show ya see how the top of the tunic wraps around ya neck here. Ok, then now with the wrist devise hit that button for half mask," said Maddy. Arthus did, and a black mask like the tele-mask Arthus used before, formed over the nose and mouth of the manikin before Arthus eyes.

"What, How," Arthus stared dumbfounded.

"Yes, it is a new thing me just created. Me haven't come up with a name, but pretty much. Me developed a way of using Life-steel and some new-fangled technology to make these tiny micro see-through machines that I can program to do different things here. I have them come out of mini storage areas along ya armor to form around ya face and then become an air filtration system, so in the most poisonous places, ya should be able to breathe easy, and even in low air, or no air environments, these little guys will make fresh air for you. Now hit full mask," said Maddy. Arthus did without question. And the mask went over the head of the manikin, completely turning into a solid glass-like face smooth but for the air filter part of the mask.

"In full mode, me minis spread over ya entire head. This be allowing for full head protection and be as strong as any full plate helmet be. It also be the same functions but be addin' a bit of fun for one. Ya can change the sight of the mask. If ya be wanting to see in the dark, can do, or for heat-signature seeing, it be working the same way. It also has an inbuilt mic and hearing devices so ya can stay in touch with whoever ya set up ya communicating with in the holo-display on your wrist devise. All of you have these full head masks and wrist things built into your armors. It's something High king asked me to be coming up with years ago, and only now me have finally finished it. You be the first ones we try it out on," said Maddy beaming with joy.

Arthus put his hand on the chest of his armor. This was his. It was beyond anything he dreamed of. He asked, "Are we allowed to put them on now?"

"Yes, I want all of ya to dress. I have changing rooms ready for each of ya. I come by and make sure all is working, and all fits. Now get!

Me explain all to each of ya as me be helping ya dress. Me mean it now, get going," said Maddy as she began pushing them to move towards the changing room booths.

Arthus felt a bit embarrassed as he was naked getting his gear on when Maddy burst into his changing room booth. She didn't even seem to notice, but he could tell he wasn't the first she just burst into without caring that they were naked. Arthus quickly put on his new Life-steel threaded and coated in synth-blend briefs, and then his pants, slipping his foot into the boots and pulling the special boots on over his pants, then strapping them into place. Then Arthus put on his special armor's under tunic. Next, with Maddy's help, he took the front and back plates each had two leather straps that fit over the shoulders, then two straps that came around the side that could be adjusted to fit as tight as Arthus wanted, then he pulled on his coat and gloves the inside was warm and soft. There was a place just under his back steel plate with a pouch that could store Angel Wing under his coat which he liked. On the left side tucked under his armpit there was a special secret locking and unlocking latch door that went to hidden pouch under his armor that was made specifically for his horn that glowed. That way his armor would fully protect it from getting destroyed during a fight. Maddy assured him not even a lightning bolt or explosion would get through that special armor. The Yaule fur coat changed to a dark stony color to match the room around him. He smiled. The coat sleeves came down just to his elbows, but the gloves came up to cover his wrist and forearms. Everything looked in place. Maddy helped Arthus understand his new wrist holographic device. He activated half mask, and as he saw the mask formed up over his mouth and nose, he had no trouble breathing, and it also didn't feel like it was tight like the normal tele-mask. This one felt like it was just a part of him. He could quickly turn his head, and the mask stayed snug to his face. He was even shocked as hard as he could twist and turn his head, there was no seem leakages, or any uncomfortable feeling. So he activated the entire mask. He felt the micro tiny see-through machines flow over his head like putting his head underwater for a second and then he opened his eyes. The mask showed him every detail of the room in front of him. It even enhanced the various lights and shadows of the room. He looked down to his wrist device, then switched sights to heat vision, and he couldn't see much since the caverns they were in were pretty warm already, so he switched to night vision and since it was already light in the room he kind of had X-ray vision, as he could see through Maddy's clothes and body to her strong but short Dwarven bone structure. He changed it back to regular vision. He was so blown away by the skill of the design and craftsmanship. Maddy and her engineers and her crafters truly outdid every imagination in making these. He was worried about his long hair he had might get in the way, but no, the mask perfectly wrapped around his head and even allowed his hair to flow out without breaking the seal. Whatever micro minis those little machines were, they were capable of wrapping themselves around every one of his hair follicles, and even without pulling on them when he moved around. They flowed with his movements perfectly. He pulled up the hood and then walked over and looked into a mirror, and he felt a real sense of pride in knowing all the hard creative work that the Dwarvens honored God the Ultimate Creator with their joining in on that process. This outfit certainly was a sure sign that they were intricately connected to the Creator! Soon he walked out, now fully equipped with his new gear.

Jade was already dressed in her armor and waiting there for him. As soon as he saw her he actually gasped, for her armor was much like Arthus gear, but fit for her beautiful body so perfectly along every one of her womanly curves. Her armor made her look even more stunningly beautiful. She also had a Coat like Arthus. The most significant difference was the incredibly beautiful longbow and quiver she had strapped to the middle of her back with the bow strung over her shoulder. She looked Arthus over and smiled and nodded, and he smiled back and gave her a low bow.

"Well Jade, I have to say I never thought anything could make you more beautiful, but Maddy has truly outdone herself this time," said Arthus. Then his face reddened, for he couldn't believe he just told Jade she was beautiful to her face.

"Thank you, and I have to say Arthus, you don't look half bad for a Prince," said Jade teasing him. Her face was a slight shade of red also.

It didn't take long and Zeck walked out of his dressing area. His armor was far different than theirs. His was far heavier looking too. He has full plate armor from head to feet. He isn't wearing a coat. Instead, around his shoulders and down his sides he wears a pelt of a sizeable Black Ice Wolf. The head of which was fixed up on one of his shoulders. His armor otherwise looked a lot like the ones a Silver Thorn Knight wear. It was all White with silver trimming. His gloves were not similar to the ones of the rest of his friends were wearing, because his right arm is completely wrapped from wrist to shoulder. The elbow obviously bends easily, but along the entire back of the right arm there are the retracting and repelling javelin cable loop eyelets made from some special life ore and other metal ore. The back of his armor has the cable spool on special strap connectors, which is removable from the rest of his armor if he is not planning to use it at any given time. His back armor plates were carefully designed to allow that pack to be quickly connected or disconnected and each of the eyelet loops going down his arm has a pinching spot on them where the cable can be easily inserted or removed from his special arm repelling glove system. His left arm glove is made to look similar to the right arm glove, but this one has the holo-display like all of his friends have. The mask on Zeck's armor looks a lot different from theirs as it forms around his face and head making Zeck look truly menacing. This has a glowing red line running from bottom to top in the middle down the center of Zeck's face.

Emon and Asher had similar-looking armor to the ones before, but Asher had more cloth than the armor plate. Zoey had a tiny armor plate and a lot of robes. Maddy had told her it was like Arthus tunic light but strong so she could move far more manageable than the others, but also couldn't be stained, which for a healer working around wounded people a lot, she is glad of.

Each was given a beautiful metal clad wooden trunk to store their armor in. They all quickly went back into their changing rooms and changed back into their normal clothes. They stored their gear in their trunks. Maddy's Great Northern Peak's Welcoming Guard each grabbed up and carried one of the trunks for them and followed them out to where they were staying. The each truly needed some rest as it had been a very long day, and from what Maddy told them, Katelynn was set to arrive earlier the next day to take them back to the Academy.

"Arise Sir Arthus, Anointed of the Alda Matriarch," said the Redwood tree nymph Timothy at exactly 2:00 in the morning. Arthus sat up quickly and swallowed the very small mineral cake down with a little of the water from his horn that glowed like every day since this water cleansing quest had been given to him. And, just like every time before, his body was instantly filled with Life-energy and fully awake.

Arthus said while throwing on his clothes and grabbing his horn that glowed, "Timothy, I sent a holo-message to Archangel Raphael about the Ice Drake eggs. I do hope that he and my grandfather can find a way to provide a safe-haven for them, so that they have a real chance to come into harmony with all of the sentient beings on Malon."

"That will be their responsibility and concern now. It is good that you recognized how you are the Creator's shield to protect all life. Now however, you have your quest to focus on, as there are still many waters on Malon to cleanse," said the Redwood tree nymph Timothy.

Arthus asked, "Where will we go after cleansing all the waters on Malon?"

"Don't concern yourself with exactly where the light portals take us, as they all are assigned according to LIGHT's great plan. During these early morning vigils, focus your mind on what you have been assigned to do, why you have been assigned to do it, and on who assigned you to do it. Do all things in honor of LIGHT! Never again concern yourself with where you are ever assigned to go. Always serve in absolute humble obedience, because, that is the key to follow according to LIGHT's great plan," said Redwood tree nymph Timothy.

"Ah... great advice, which I receive!" And, with that Arthus held out his arm for Timothy to lead on according to LIGHT's great plan.

Chapter 25
Tournament Explained

It seemed like a dream. Before they knew it, they were back at the Elemental Island and with only a month away from the tournament. Today, he knew when they gave them the general rules and the match. Every so often, the tournament would be changed up so no one who knew about a previous contest would know what was in store. Arthus was excited. He wanted to show everyone that he wasn't some pampered prince. Arthus decided that he would simply honor God the Heavenly Father and do his very best. After spending so long under Son's mentoring he knew he should not be concerned which place he took in the Tournament. And, because of what both Son and the Redwood tree nymph Timothy said, he had settled in his mind that he should not concern himself with where his place should be, or about earning a specific place, based on his own pride. He settled the stressful issues in his mind of how much work he had put into his training and study all these years. He tried his best to settle in his heart that his father may never truly acknowledge him and may always look down on him as some failure not worthy of his time. He realized that God, his Heavenly Father had already chosen and anointed him and is using him according to His good pleasure. He will do his best and he will be in complete obedience to whatever assignments God assigns to Him. Arthus laid down upon the cool rock he had been meditating on since earlier that morning and just looked up at the clouds and opened his heart and mind to the will of God, his Heavenly Father.

"I see you are taking a break already, a young one, and something is bothering you. I can read it on your face, so come and tell me what has you so distracted today," said Son.

As soon as he heard Son's voice tell him that, Arthus slipped off of the rock and went to his knees, and said, "Son, I am glad to see you as always, but more than that, I want to acknowledge You, for I know Who You Are! My heart leaped within me, when I had realized that You are not just someone called Son, but,.."

Son, raised his hand and cut him off and said, "Yes, Arthus, well... not everyone acknowledges and accepts that right now, but thank you for acknowledging and accepting that! Now come up and sit. And tell me the one real thing that has you distracted,"

"It's should be nothing. But, I know that you already know it really is something! I was thinking of the tournament and my father. In truth, I know that you have trained me to push things like this out of my mind, for it can only hold me back, and for a brief moment I had thought if I could win the tournament, would my father finally see me as a worthy son and Prince, or would he still see me as a failure and not worthy of his time and attention" said Arthus.

"I see so that's what on your mind, and yes I trained you that such thoughts will only hurt you and hold you back. But I understand, and I have known your father for many years; he was such a great man at one time. The Angels had such high hopes for him when he was your age. But, you must understand that God, never chose him to replace your grandfather, and then he allowed the excuse of the death of your mother, Laella to turn him into this bitter, prideful, angry man, which you know," said Son

"Why wasn't my father chosen to replace my grandfather? He is a strong warrior and has always shown he is devoted to the protection of our lands and the lives of the people," asked Arthus?

"Well, as I said at one point, he was a good candidate as the Archangels and Angels had thought, but when they brought the subject to God, who can see far more into the minds and hearts of people, as well as able to see past, present and future all at the same time. He saw the wrong kind of pride and he saw a real greed for power and rulership which your father kept pondering in his heart. Your father puts stock in the royal bloodline, far more than he should, for in a real way, he's always seen himself above all others. The Angels couldn't see his heart, so they didn't know. Anyway, these ways of thinking and pondering over and over again, can and often do turn towards Darkness if not accepted by the person as truly inappropriate to consider. God sees that Malon would be suffering in his hands if he was ever made a King or especially if he were to become High King. Your mother, Laella truly always kept him in check, and it was she who brought the best out of him. It was a very sad day for him, when she chose to give up her life in order that you could be born, for she knew the whole time she carried you in her womb, it was either her life or your life. Laella prayed everyday throughout her pregnancy that God would fill you with wisdom and continually be your guide! She chose your life over her own out of pure love, and that is the greatest gift any mother can give to her child. She literally and figuratively entrusted your life over to God for His good pleasure. And, she was right when she did that. For when the time came and God gave you an anointing and an assignment, you fully accepted it and then humbly prayed, 'I do thank you God for your grace and mercy and for entrusting me with this task. I pray that your hand will continually guide me. That you will fill me with wisdom in order that I can faithfully fulfill the task that you have given to me.' The Redwood tree nymph Timothy and myself are both a direct answer to your prayers and hers," said Son.

"You knew my mother, Laella well. Can you tell me more about her? My grandfather only told me some, but my father won't even talk about her," asked Arthus?

"Alright, I tell you what I know and what I thought of her. Laella was a mighty Ignole. She was a true master of wind and water. They called her the Ice Queen of the field, for she used her powers over the elements to turn water with the wind into freezing ice and snow. But it was her tactics that truly won her so many fights. She was also a kind and gentle soul. Laella had the bloodline of the first Ignole High Priest and High Priestess. So like your father, who remains only by bloodline a prince, she was, in a way, a princess. She had long silver-white hair and silver eyes like yours. Laella was a truly lovely woman that could make even the Angels blush. She loved to tease your father. I remember them well here at this school. Your father was always serious and full of Royal Pride. Everywhere he walked, he did so like he was marching. Oh, it was funny when Laella would run up and pull pranks on him. At first, your father couldn't stand her, but after she completely stomped your father in the tournament, he saw her in a new light, and soon they became good friends. Then before long, it was love. Everyone had warned them that though Ignole's and Cundo's love was never forbidden at all, because of your genetic differences, a pregnancy and a child was a dangerous thing for them. As you know, very few children from those live, and most who do live are born with several disadvantages. Your father did worry, of course, even after they wed, he told her that he had asked about ways to keep himself from having kids from her. But, your mother Laella wouldn't hear of it. She wanted a child more than anything, and soon she did become pregnant with you. Let me tell you that day was the happiest day for your mother, Laella. She was beaming with joy, but your father went into a panic. He spent all his time in the Great Library or asking around trying to find any way to make it far safer for her when the time came for your birthing, but found nothing to solve this problem. Finally, your mother, Laella forced him to accept it, and she did do her best to help get rid of his panic, which did happen soon after he finally accepted. He was just as happy as your mother. He helped her pick out everything for your room, and though your mother, Laella originally wanted to name you Ace, your father came up with the name Arthus, and your mother also agreed, and so together decided on that instead. Then the day came of your birth, and she gave all her power and strength to make sure you be born with no issues. We knew that the birth wasn't going well, and so did she, but she didn't care. Laella was determined to make you come into this world, and when it was all over, she held you before your father with a big smile on her face. I remember what she said that day 'This is our son, the future of both our people. I'm sorry I can't help you raise him into the man I know he will be, but don't lose faith, and don't lose yourself in your grief for I will always watch over you both.' Then her head laid back, and she passed from this life and joined all the other souls in the Golden City. Don't worry, I've seen your mother,

405

Laella many times there in the Golden City, and she couldn't be more proud of you, Arthus, and I know if she could, she would give your father an ear full over what he has become," said Son.

Arthus trying as he might, couldn't stop the tears from running down his face.

"I wish I could have known her, and thank you, Son, for this. I think I am ready now," said Arthus. He stood up wiped the final tears from his eyes and said, "If I am going to win this tournament, I have decided I am not even going to try to win this tournament, for sake of my father. However, I will try and win this tournament for my grandfather, for Malon, for myself, for my mother, Laella, who I know is watching over me, for you Son, and especially, all for the glory of God, my Heavenly Father."

"Though you might think it would help you if I could bring her here to see you face to face, those who passed from this life into the Heavenly Realm, cannot return. It breaks many of God's tenets to ever bring a living person into the Golden city, unless God has specifically requested them to come. He is the only one that ever allows that to happen, and that is into His throne room, like you have been before as He requested. Never to meet your loved ones. But, when it's your turn, if you continue to choose God as your ruler, as you have said you do, and allow Him to be the forever Guide for your life, then you will always desire to live a good and honorable life, and you will seek forgiveness for failing to be able to perfectly live perfect, then by the Grace and Mercy of God, He will allow you at your time to come into the Heavenly City and rest," said Son with a smile, and then Son said, "It is time for you to go!"

"Ya, I better go quickly! We will find out all the information on the tournament, and I'm sure it is starting soon," said Arthus. He gathered up his shirt and Jacket and ran off towards the meeting hall.

Soon Arthus met up with the others and again was sitting in the grand auditorium. But this time, Katelynn never showed up, but High King Thureos, Prince Benroy, and Jacob came to stand before them all.

"Welcome all. Today, we three will tell you how the tournament will be held, how to advance, what happens if you lose, and what you are fighting for. As you know for the last what now four hundred and fifty years for some of you and others this is their last tournament for one is held around this time. For those who first time in a tournament welcome, and for those going, I say good luck. We will be looking forward to you displaying your skills, which will prove how hard you have been training. There will be two rounds for this tournament. Prince Benroy if you please," said High King Thureos.

"Yes, in the first round, you will be in a team of four. Each of your teams will be assigned one of the four elemental regions to fight in. Your job in round one will be to use all that you learned to survive for one week, while battling other teams within your zone. There will be around one hundred teams this year, so that puts about twenty-five teams into each zone. After the week is done, whatever team reaches back here and in one piece will be allowed to continue to the second round, which will be a two on two fight between all those left standing until only two are left," said Prince Benroy.

"Now for those of you, whose final tournament this is, before your graduation, you have a third round, which is a paper test that takes place the day after this first two round tournament is over. That paper test covers all that you have taught over the entire nine hundred years. After all of you have completed that test, those are then graded and reviewed while you wait patiently in your dorms. And believe me when I say that it will be graded and reviewed carefully by all the clan leaders, as that process takes time, so please do be patient. Only after that process is finished, then will you each be given your own lists of different clans that are wanting you to join their ranks. From that list that you are given, and only from that list that you are given, you must then carefully pick the one you think best suits you, and what it is you want to do the rest of your lives as full members and citizens of Malon," said Jacob.

"Thank you all and good luck to you all. I can hardly wait to see who will come out on top and where you all will go after this is all over. Now you are all dismissed for teaming up into four pairs. You have one week to decide what your teams will be and submit them to Jacob. We have a process then amongst us leaders to figure out which teams will be sent into which of the four quadrants. That is all. Have a great week," said

Thureos. With that, the three left, and the room erupted with chatter people running to others already setting up their teams for the matches.

"Too bad it's only four per team," said Arthus loudly to of all his friends, Jade, Zeck, Asher, Emon, Zoey, and himself. There are six, which means two of his friends wouldn't be able to team up with him.

"Arthus, don't worry too much. I won't be teaming up with you because I want to face off against you in the final match, so don't lose before then," said Zeck holding out his hand.

Arthus smiled and grabbed his friend's hand. "Ya you too my friend pick a team well for I want to face you also in the final match," replied Arthus.

"Well, I can't leave the blockhead to do it on his own, so I join his and make sure he makes it to the final round," smiled Zoey.

"You sure Zoey," asked Arthus?

"Ya, it's fine. I want to face off against Jade. You two are not the only rivals among us all," said Zoey.

"True, I hope to see you at the end also," said Jade. With that, Zeck and Zoey ran off to seek their other two teammates.

"Well, if no one else wishes to go, then it is Jade, Asher, Emon, and myself as a team. Everyone fine with that," asked Arthus.

"You have no problem here! I will be glad to fight by your side. And, our friend Asher here is a hell of a fighter and priest, so he takes care of any wounds. I have my bombs and my new weapon I will show you all later. Both will come in great handy," said Emon.

"I looking forward to trying out the new armor, and I know that the new bow that Maddy had crafted for me will hold up, so I ready whenever you are," said Jade with a wink.

"Alright, sounds good. I'll go turn in our names and find out what they want us to do for the rest of the week," said Arthus. He left them to meet up later at the cafeteria and went over to where Katelynn was waiting by a table where the team sign-up sheets were being taken and turned in. Zeck was already at table two other besides Zoey was there. One Arthus didn't know looked to be one of the senior students, and the other he knew a fellow student named Jake. Jake was a dark-skinned Cundo from around the Blood Sands, a member of Clan Urial and a student Arthus didn't really care for much, as he was in a lot of the classes that he and Zeck were in, and seemed to act like Arthus was his rival. He was very popular with a lot of the other students. He was seen as being one of the best in their class. Arthus thought the guy could be too competitive, and he caught the guy looking at Jade a lot, and that made him not too happy with the man. Zeck smiled and nodded to Arthus as they went by, and Arthus nodded back and turned in his paperwork.

"So it is you, Jade, Emon, and Asher. Not a bad team well-rounded, But, I was kinda surprised when I saw Zeck without you," said Katelynn.

"Ya, we are best friends but also rivals who want to face each other at the end, so we decided to get with different teams. I also want to ask what do we do for the next two weeks while you pick what teams go where and so on," asked Arthus?

"Well, you free to stay here and work with your team on strategies, or you're free to take a shuttle to wherever as long as your back the day before the tournament begins, that be when we post where what team will go where," said Katelynn.

"Thanks, that's what I hoped for. I'll see you when it's time," said Arthus. He ran off to meet up with the others. He had a perfect idea he wanted to do if the others wanted. Soon he found them hanging out at a table. He joined them.

"Ok, we are all turned in and ready I think we should meet up tonight to have a strategy meeting, then we are free for almost two whole weeks to do whatever, so I was thinking, why not have you all come to my home in Harmony city at the Palace for a week or so to blow off some steam we can hang out in Harmony city and relax a bit before we should come back.

"I'd love to. I barely even seen harmony city, and I want to see the Palace more," said Jade.

"I have to come a bit later. As I want to return to Great Northern Peak City and finish up the last touches on my new weapon? I'll tell you about it tonight," said Emon with a grin.

"Then I go with Emon, as I know he will need a great crafter by his side, both for fixing up his weapon perfect and for drinking and dancing at the Dwarvens Pub. Then we will meet you in Harmony City in a few days," said Asher.

"Alright, then that's the plan. I can't wait to show you all around. Been so long since I been home, I hope not much has changed in the last four hundred years," said Arthus. With that, they broke for the day. Arthus went back to his room to pack his stuff and give Sylla a call to let her know Jade and he would be coming in tomorrow and that others would join them later. When he reached the room, Zeck was already there with Zoey.

"Well, what you two planning on doing for the next week or so," asked Arthus.

"What you mean, I guess not much, since we have almost two full weeks off," said Zoey.

"Well, Jade and I are heading to Harmony city to take a break from everything. Why don't you two also come? It'll be good not to overwork yourself, or to stress out too much before the tournament begins," said Arthus?

"Not a bad idea when you plan on going," asked Zeck.

"Probably head out early tomorrow. Emon and Asher will come a couple of days later after they take care of things up in Northern Peak City," said Arthus.

"Then I guess we join you two. Be good to see the city you grew up in. Never been there myself, but I heard how cool it is," said Zeck.

"Yes, it's been a while since I been home also," said Zoey.

"Ya, that's right, you are also from Harmony City. I almost let that slip my mind," said Arthus. Arthus then went into his room to pack and called up Sylla, who was happy to have them, but told him the palace was too busy for them to stay in. Instead Arthus could take his friends to stay at his father's building, in the apartments his father used to live in within the city itself. She would go and make sure it was ready. His father's and mother's former attendants still lived there, and she was sure that they wouldn't mind as the place is enormous. She told him the guy's name was is Beldor, and then also is Nessie, who attended his mom and then became Arthus' first caretaker when he was a baby. She said she would call them, make sure it was alright, and get back to Arthus when it was all set up. Before the meeting, she called him back and informed him that she and Mr. Beldor would greet them on their arrival. Arthus had thanked her and went to meet up with the others. Emon had set up the meeting in his room. He wanted to keep his new toy a secret from everyone until the last minute. Before long, they were all sitting and waiting on the silly Dwarven to show them what he and Maddy had come up with.

"Here it is. It looks a bit weird to you, but I promise this thing is going to be soon a new way of fighting for many," said Emon. He had pulled open a large case and inside was a significant thing Arthus wasn't sure how to explain it. It was about two feet long. One end had a circular hole, then along one side, it had a piece of metal that stoked up almost half an inch and went back into a weirdly shaped arch. It had a handle and a trigger locking mechanism on the other side. On the side of the device is a tiny life crystal and a switch that had three settings that read, *safe, stun, and deadly.*

"What is this thing," asked Arthus?

"Well, I don't have a name for it just yet, but it's something myself and Maddy have been working on for years. I came up with the idea, but she helped me improve on it greatly not yet fully worked out as it gets dang hot after a couple of fires, which I want to work out with her before I see you in harmony city. Now watch what this baby can do," said Emon. He pointed to a big manikin dummy that Asher had pulled out. It had several scorch marks in it already. Emon lifted the device and put the slightly arched end against his shoulder. His chin went into another arch along the side of the device, his eye looking down the length of one of its sides through a back sight and through its front sight. His hand switched the device to stun and put his hand palm open against the handle, and put one of his fingers onto the trigger. He gripped the handle tight, pulled the weapon back into his shoulder, focused it on the target, and then pulled the trigger. The device glowed a bit from where the crystal was, and then a quick flash of blush light shot forth, not a long beam but a short burst that slammed into the target, blasting the dummy manikin off its feet, leaving behind a black mark.

"What was that?" Asked both Arthus and Jade at the same time.

"Ya both like me new weapon, me see. It needs a name, but if we can fix out all the bugs, it is something! What ya think? Tell me true," said Emon.

"I like my bow better, but I can see why you and Maddy are so happy about this new toy of yours. It can fire well whatever that was a lot faster than most can move, and if that's a stun, I hate to see what kill is," Jade said, laughing.

"Came to me when I saw Maddy working with the cannon people about trying to turn life crystal energy into a weapon using the canon idea. At first, the device was as huge as a canon and had a devastating effect but trying to pull a large cannon around was not the best idea, so we decided after many failures to make it much smaller and easier to handle. With this and my hammer and my other tricks, I think we do well in the upcoming tournament," said Emon.

"It is powerful, but let's not rely too heavily on this new toy of yours, Emon. We don't know all its defaults yet," said Asher.

"Right now, let's come up with a plan," said Arthus. Soon they had come up with a plan for each of the four elemental areas. They didn't know what one they were to be thrown into, but they wanted to ensure they had everything they needed no matter what terrain they had to face. With that, they ended their meeting and went back to their rooms to pack and get ready for their trip.

Chapter 26
Harmony City

Soon Arthus and the other four were heading towards Harmony city. First, they took a shuttle to a port just outside one of the fishing villages Arthus had been to before on his travels. Still, they didn't stay long. They were welcomed to join the next ship out and sail to Harmony city like before I take a whole day almost and the ocean between the islands and the main continent was a bit of easy travel luck was on their side no storms or sea creatures attacked them. The wind was strong thanks to Arthus with his ability. He kept the ship moving as fast as the Captain would allow. Soon they were already flowing down the river entrance, and large mountains on either side loomed. Arthus remembered the last time he and Thureos traveled this same route. He saw how his friends look on in wonderment. Jade stood at the bow of the ship, leaning over and watching the waves as the ship glided by her red hair with the blue of the water made Arthus's heart skip a beat. She was gorgeous, and more and more, it was hard not to stare at her. They had become closer than ever since joining the academy. They were both now seen as young adults still, but he wished he could walk over and wrap his hands around her and hold her, but he didn't, he held himself back. It seemed like forever as they traveled up the river. Finally, the Captain yelled for Arthus to stop the wind; they were almost to the other side of the mountains, and just like that, the mountains fell away, and they sailed down the western river past Arial Valley and into the God's forest. Clan Urial guards who traveled with boats picked up weapons in case of a beast attack. There was one large Gorga, which is a large ape-like creature who did jump on board. Some like him do attack travelers and steal whatever food they can when the jump on board, but the Urial Guards were well trained and instantly killed the creature without any trouble. An hour after the Gorga incident, they could hear way off in the distance the roar of the great falls. Where Harmony city also was. Arthus could see the excitement on Jade's face. She had come to the Palace before, but by shuttle, so she didn't get to see much of the City. Soon came to the end of where the natural river continued on towards the great falls, and where they had to turn north along the side of the mountain into the tiered canal that Arthus and his grandfather had taken before.

Arthus explained what they were seeing, "Ships really couldn't go all the way west into the southwestern falls, and really this river is too narrow for any two way travel. That is why the special tiered water elevator canal was built to take them down to the underground port, which then led to the underground river and back out to western side of the continent where it again met the ocean. Anyway we will quickly make it into the port, and the platform, where we could take Golden Griffons to the platform at the Palace and then go by foot into the city. However, if you all are up for it there is a separate platform at the port where we can take a carriage and go direct to my father's building bypassing the entire palace, which is the way I think we should go, because as Sylla said, the palace is crazy busy. Best not go there at all."

Arthus explained, "On the southwestern side of the base of the falls, water flows first into a fairly wide open area, and that though it was big it wasn't really deep. At the outer southern and western edge of that large space a fairly substantial wall with vents allowing the water to keep going west into the river. Some of those vent holes for water were channeled through huge pipes into the tiered canal that they are now in. That water then allows the ships to go through the tiers as water was raised and then spewed out back into the river and lowered. It was built so ships could go down to the underground port, which is a very short distance really on the northwestern area of the mountain that has the huge three sided water fall. The whole system was built to improve the process of shipping from the western side of the ocean. On the eastern side of the mountain another similar channel does the same thing, but taking people to the northeastern underground port, that take ships from the eastern side of the continent to Harmony City and back again underground and out to the ocean that way. However, most travelers and ships don't prefer the eastern side as the swamplands they run through are much more dangerous."

Arthus continued, "Before the Dwarvens helped build the canals, there used to be a giant platform right here that basically went from here all the way to the base of the waterfalls and only one ship at a time could ever come up this river and then they had to take it all the way back out into the ocean before the next ship could come through this river. This whole new system is much better as ships can all follow each other through the big U on each side. Meaning much more cargo moves much quicker. A long time ago in this port were heading into there was just a dock and that wasn't much. Well that old dock has been improved much as this whole port was built. Back then it was just several large storage buildings, a barracks for guards that protected the port, and another lift that would take travelers up to the City."

Arthus continued, "The old lift has been upgraded, and that is the way we are headed. Grab your gear now and follow me."

They left their ship down onto the platform and followed the long platform past the Golden Griffon area. Then a little farther they saw the lift. They entered the lift and it now ended inside a really large building. An Urial Guard was there and he welcomed them into the City. Across the building by a huge door was a carriage and they walked over to it. The four wheeled carriage was pulled by a Hondarg and there was an Urial Guard in the upper front holding the reigns. They climbed in and Arthus told the guard where to take them. The carriage took them around and into the tunnel that led through the underground of the western side of the mountain towards Harmony City. It soon brought them to Arthus father's building. They entered his father's building where Sylla and Mr. Beldor were waiting to greet them.

Arthus explains what they had been seeing, "The City itself is a massive technological marvel. The City was based on several levels of platforms that were built into the sides of the waterfall and upward to the upper level, which was the same level as the God's forest across the great falls was First God's Tree its roots massive in size grew out here and there of the other falls and some of them were used as walkways. The City was built so that it didn't disturb the natural Forest. Buildings were usually built at the treetop level of some of the larger trees of God's Forest, and each of the platforms were quite massive, each having about 300 square miles around. There were five of the platforms scattered around the south and southwestern sides of the falls. Each one had a purpose. The Great Library platform, which was located by the south waterfall between God's tree and extending over the River of Life, which is also part of the palace, where labs and scientific researchers lived around and worked. Mostly Clan Raphael lived there and worked there, as Zoey could easily guide you through all of that, as that is where she lived. Then one had a recreational area, rides, and parks, where people could go and blow off stress and enjoy their day. One held the markets where stores were held to trade food, and whatever you can find; inns and such for traveling merchants were also there. All one had to do was show the city market guild what they wished to trade, and they were given an area to trade. There was one platform where Clan Urial was stationed and trained. But the upmost platform was mostly housing, and one of the most interesting buildings was Prince Benroy's house. Arthus father rarely lived there. He spent most of his time in Clan Arkwright Silver Thorns' training grounds, since he was the head of that order. Prince Benroy's house was a bit into the Forest. It was a large tall building. In the middle of the four winged building was a round area. Inside the round area were four lifts, each which opened in one of the four wings. And, went up or down to each of the levels. Each level of each wing was its own large apartment. The building was basically empty at the time, with the exception of the private quarters for the caretaker, Mr. Beldor, and also for the private quarters of Nessie. One of the wings where Prince Benroy's apartment was in on the top is the wing where they would be staying. Each of them got a floor apartment to themselves, because Zoey had decided she stay at home with her mother and her family. Arthus took the top floor, which was his father's apartment, where he had his own private bedroom suite. Jade took the middle floor apartment, and Zeck took the bottom floor apartment. All three in the same wing. The other wing apartments were all left empty and were rarely used by Prince

Benroy, and then only for entertaining various clan dignitaries when he was required to do so.

Sylla and Nessie both led each of them all into their own apartments. As they did so, they greeted and talked with each of Arthus's three friends, especially Jade.

"Well, I hope you can all get settled in. Let me know if you need anything or wish to go anywhere. I happily help make sure you know how to get around," said Sylla as she left each of them at their apartment space.

"Thanks, but I think I get some rest and then I go check out market tonight," said Zeck.

With that, Zeck nodded to the rest and left them going into his apartment. Jade also went in and settled down, then Sylla and Nessie, after helping Jade, took Arthus to the top floor, which is Prince Benroy's actual quarters, whenever he stays in the city. Sylla then gave him a hug and headed back to the palace to attend to her duties.

The apartment suite was very large. It had Prince Benroy's private bedroom, a bathroom with shower, and living space with a table and sitting pillows. It also had a smaller private bedroom, where Arthus would be staying. The bedroom had been redecorated after Arthus grew out of childhood, but it was still considerably small for an adult's bedroom as this had at one time been his nursery room. There even is an outer deck where Arthus could go out and lookout. The sight outside on this deck was beautiful. God's Forest was all around them, and animals and smells brought Arthus back in time where; he loved to spend time exploring the City and part of the Forest that the City also was built into. Arthus looking around the apartment realized that it must have been years since Prince Benroy had been here; many years. Arthus continued to look around and on a shelf he found a picture of his father Benroy and mother Laella when she was alive and he was younger.

Nessie, Prince Arthus's first caregiver, before Sylla, came in and smiled sadly.

"I knew your mother, Laella. She was a very close friend of mine. Some even saw us as sisters when we were younger. Laella loved your father, and it is why I became your first caregiver. In the end after she

417

passed, your father turned for the worse. He couldn't or wouldn't even try to take care of you, and yet I knew your mother, Laella would want someone to look out for you, so I took it on myself to become your first caregiver. And just look at you now; you have grown into a proper Prince that she'd be mighty proud of. At least that's what High Kings thinks when he talks to me about how you're doing, said Nessie.

"Thank you. How have you been? I have been away. I hope you are not too bored around the Palace, without having to chase down my little butt all the time," said Arthus with a laugh.

Sally replied, "I have been keeping busy. The Palace would fall apart without mine and Sylla's guiding hands. How would that make your grandfather look? But tell me about this Jade girl. I can see she is a very beautiful woman, and I've seen the way you look at her. So tell me are you seeing her yet?"

"What... well, no, we are not really together, together, just friends, but yes, I really do care a lot for her. Since I first met her long ago when I first went to Arial Valley. I know way back then we did share one kiss, and it was great, but I was so young way back then. We hadn't seen each other in 47 years after that, and then seeing her at the Academy already four hundred and fifty years, where she and I have such a beautiful close friendship. I'm not sure how she feels, and I don't want to hurt the friendship we have, by trying to push it, so I haven't told her all of my feelings," said Arthus.

"I see. Well, you better figure out soon if she's worth the risk, or you might lose her to someone else. Finding a girl as good as she is, and as lovely as she is, that likely only comes around once. Now show your friends around the City and enjoy your time off. I am here on the bottom floor of the wing directly opposite of the lift to the right if you need me," said Nessie.

With that, she left Arthus to grab a snack and sat out on the balcony listening to the wind blow through the trees and the sounds of nature mixed with the City. Arthus heard a noise, and on the terrace below his, Jade was sitting enjoying some hot drink and looking out at the City. Arthus smiled.

"Jade, would you like to join me in a walk around the City? It's such a nice breezy evening, and I think it is a perfect time to walk around," said Arthus. Jade looked up and smiled.

"Of course, I love to walk around with you. Let me finish my drink, and I get ready. I'll meet you out front," said Jade.

With that, Arthus changed his clothes to a casual tunic, pants, and boots. He brushed teeth and his long hair now, which reached the bottom of his shoulders, then tied it up with the leather bark strap passed down to him by his mother, Laella. He put on his leather bracers Jade had given him all those years ago. And he carried the shofar with the cover she had made for him. The horn that glowed was on him, but under, as that was always kept under his tunic. The other goat horn he put over his shoulder in plain view. On his back he had his Angel Wing, in its original form. He looked in the mirror, then nodded to himself, and left to wait for Jade. Soon Jade came down. She wore a summer tunic-like she had while on the farm with some shorts and ankle-high boots. Her flaming red hair was tied up behind her. She smiled at Arthus.

"Wow, you look ready for anything," said Jade.

Arthus asked, "So what would you like to see first? As he was intentionally rubbing the bracers she had made for him all those years ago."

"I see you still have the bracers, and the shofar cover I made for you, and I do know we are not the kids we were way back then, but the heart that I gave to you Arthus, that heart has never changed. I know we are great friends, and I do intend to keep that great friendship with you. But hey you, my heart it wants more! So, as this here is the city where you lived a good portion of your life, and we will get this night and maybe just a little bit of tomorrow to be alone together, I expect you will know how to make this girl, who gave you her heart, have a beautiful time together, where hopefully Arthus, you will be able to fill up more of what my heart wants from this..." And then she touched his hand with her finger and said, "Whatever this is. And, maybe you could show me a little bit more how Arthus used to live and be. Because I know you have changed and I have changed too. Oh... I really do hope you get what I am trying to say to you Arthus," said Jade.

419

"Alright... first we head to the market, then down to the Library. Then it is around dinner, so we can stop at one of my favorite places to eat. It didn't take long and they were walking together along the Market filled streets. Jade was in shock. She had never seen so many different stalls or shops open, trading everything from fish to spices to armor and weapons. Not only that, but Dwarvens, Ice Wolves, and even every so often, an Alda would walk by. Everyone would make sure they moved out of the walking tree path. Jade was in a shock to see so much in one place. Arthus smiled to himself. Knowing how Jade felt, he remembered the first time his grandfather took him into the city as a small child. Soon they came to the Great Library of Malon. The building was a massive tower. It had to be around fifty stories tall, all had many levels within lifts, which would take you to whatever floor you liked and on every floor, there was a clan Raphael scholar to help if you need any help. There were around thirty floors in all sectioned off to one another, and each section dealing with different subjects was all studied and updated as newly discovered.

"So what would you like to look over, or would you like to just walk around a bit," asked Arthus?

"I don't even know where to begin. This place is beyond everything I ever imagined," said Jade.

"Well, I know how much you love animal life. Why don't we head there and find some books on some rare animal life, or we can check out History of whatever? Or we can call it and head to my favorite food place," said Arthus.

"Ya, I think we should just come back. I am hungry, and I would like to see more of the City, and at least a little more of your heart, before I get lost in books," said Jade.

"Alright, good idea I could spend days lost in here," said Arthus.

Soon they were heading through some side streets. After around twenty minutes or so, Jade started to think Arthus had gotten them lost. Arthus then turned the corner, and before them was a small building with blankets covering the doorway. Arthus smiled, walked up, pulled one of the blankets aside, and motioned for Jade to enter.

"Hey Chef Stonebeard, you old grump! Are you still alive, and making your slop?" yelled Arthus towards a back room.

The building was small. A bar and two tables fit into the small area, and a door was covered by another sheet where some clanging and sounds of pans hitting the floor and some other curses yelled by some deep-voiced man.

"Hey, I don't know who thinks they are to come into my home and call my masterpiece slop. Ye better be ready to fight to ye last breath, you damn hooligan," said a man's voice coming from the back.

Soon a Dwarven came stomping out. He was built like a master fighter. Bald, but a large brown and gray beard was tucked into his belt. He wore a chef hat on his head and, in one hand, had a substantial cleaver. He had significant bushy eyebrows, but as soon as he came out and saw Arthus, he threw the cleaver and stuck it into the floor. Then he ran up, and crushed Arthus in a massive hug. Arthus's face was bright red.

"Well, if it isn't me young Prince, my Creator. My, have you grown since me last saw ye. So, come in, find a table. Give me a minute. Me got to finish up this last thing, and me come to sit with you a bit. And your lass here is a beauty. Mighty good for you!" Chef Stonebeard punched Arthus in the shoulder and ran back pulling his cleaver out of the wooden floor on his way into the back before either could say a word.

Arthus laughed out loud when he could finally breathe again and walked over, pulled a chair out for Jade to sit, and when she took a seat, he sat down next to her. Not long, Chef Stonebeard came back out with two folded papers and sat down across from them.

"So me heard you went to the Academy, so me take it you got a break, and you came to see ye old friend to get a full belly here. Take these me sweet beauty, cause Arthus already knows me menu here, but me sure you like to look over my specialties. And if ya wish me can make you the daily special. Me make sure it makes ya never want to eat anything anywhere else, but me cooking," said Stonebeard.

"I like my usual, and you know how I like it," said Arthus with a smile.

Jade looked over the menu, and she was shocked. She looked around. It seemed like a small, not well-known place, but the menu was on a vast level, from delicate seafood to things she had never even heard of. She decided to let Arthus help her choose.

"Arthus, what are you getting? I can't decide everything sounds wonderful," said Jade.

"She would want one of your Seafood specials. And tell your brothers back there I said hello. Also, Maddy wanted me to say hi to you and to tell you to come home one day soon and see how everyone is doing," said Arthus.

"Ah, me forgot you been to North Peak's City. Oh heavens, it has been a long time since me have seen me sister. Yes, me have to go home soon and see her and all me friends. Hey Boys, we got two top specials, one be Prince Arthus' favorite and one be me seafood special," said Stonebeard. He got up and said, "Now Prince, if ya don't steal this here beauty's heart and keep it forever, you're as big a fool as they ever come! Am I not right lass? He gave her and Arthus a wink, and walked away. Three other Dwarvens popped their heads out, waved, and hurried back into the back room. Soon more people showed up. One was an Ice Wolf with a Dwarven who sat at the bar chatting about their goods and how trade was going up North. Soon some smoke wafted out over their heads and went out of the blanket sheets. The smell was terrific; Arthus could see Jade's face go into a smile, and their mouth was drooling a bit, which she quickly wiped away, embarrassed. Soon the food was done and sat on the table before them.

"Whelp you two enjoy and me beauty, I know ya won't ever forget to want to come back here after eating that. I guarantee! I better get back to work," said Stonebeard.

He went off and started to talk with the two at the bar. Arthus smiled at Jade. They both looked to their food. There was oven-baked bread sitting in the middle. Jade had a fillet of fish called a Sharp-fin. That is a rather large fish caught up near the colder seas and are one of the best-tasting fish on all of Malon. Sharp-fin was baked to a brownish hue and coated with a special breading that Stonebeard will never tell anyone how he makes it. She had a giant rice bowl with a salted liquid that helped make the rice taste great. Also were several raw cut fish mixed with rice, and some strange colored items? She looked down with puzzlement but picked it up looked at Arthus. He smiled and nodded. So she ate it, and her eyes widened, and she smiled and kept eating. Arthus plate was his favorite a Piglos steak grilled to medium-rare, steamed veggies, and a vast boiled giant crab. Soon both sat there, leaned back full, and Stonebeard came back dropped off two large foaming beers, which Arthus knew from his time up North and laughed out loud for it was one of the Dwarvens more potent drinks. The next hour or so, Arthus and Jade laughed and drank with Stonebeard and the other customers of the small dinner. But It was time to head back. Jade was really too drunk to walk, so Arthus let her ride piggyback and walked her back to the house. She was laughing and talking gibberish most of the time. Arthus smiled, for the woman he loved was so close to him he could feel her breath on his cheek and neck.

"Arthus, thank you for today, best time I had in a long time, and I am glad I got to spend it with you, for you don't know, but I always wanted to be closer to you. I wish I dared to tell you maybe one day I will be able to tell you that my heart longs to be closer to you. And, Arthus when are you ever going to kiss me again. It been like five hundred years since the last time," said Jade, who then asked, "When are you going ever tell me you love me?" Shocked, Arthus looked back and saw that Jade was talking in her sleep. She had passed out drunk. He smiled and rested his head back against hers.

"Yes, my love, my heart longs for you too since the day I laid my eyes on you. Now it's almost too much to handle, but one day I will hold you in my arms and tell you before all that you Jade are my one and only," said Arthus. Soon Arthus arrived back at the house and helped Jade get into her room. Lucky Zoey was also there. Zoey let Arthus know that she would look after her and helped her get into bed. So Arthus went up and got himself into bed. As he lay there, he hoped Jade meant what she had said that she didn't say something by mistake because of the drink. Maybe that is what she was talking about before they went anywhere tonight. She did tell me her heart wanted more, of whatever this is as she touched my hand... I really do hope she loves me tomorrow when she has a hangover. Soon he dropped off to sleep, but quickly woke up, needing to go throw up several times into the latrine. "That dang Dwarven drink is a bit too strong for anyone else but Dwarvens," he said laughing.

"Arise Arthus, Anointed of the Alda Matriarch," said Timothy at precisely 2:00 in the morning. He then said, "Arthus, Arthus, Arthus, 'Strong drink is raging, and them that are deceived thereby are not wise.' Alright this very tiny mineral cake won't fix that. I'll see you tomorrow," he then opened a light portal and stepped through to the base of First God's Tree, where he then turned himself into a Redwood Tree.

The next morning Jade felt horrible. Whatever was in that drink had kicked her butt! As she took a shower and started feeling more sensible she closed her eyes to try to get a clear picture in her mind of what she had done from the moment they left that Dwarvens' place. She remembered the food tasted incredible. The Dwarven gave Arthus the biggest possible straight talk that she hoped he would listen to. She got the mug of Dwarven beer. Maybe several. Then she was Drunk and Arthus had to carry her because she couldn't walk. She remembered telling him she wanted to be closer to him, yes. And, I know I clearly told him I had given him my heart before we left, so did he say anything about wanting her? Jade Yelled, "OH I CAN"T STAND IT ANY MORE, IT HAS BEEN ALMOST FIVE HUNDRED YEARS! AND I WANT HIM SO BAD TO KISS ME AGAIN AND TELL ME HE LOVES ME!" Then she held her hand to her head and says, quietly "Oh I have a terrible hangover!"

Zoey walked in and laughed and said, "That be the Dwarven Beer you drank. That stuff will kick your Cundo butt! Dwarvens love it though! I'll see if I can get you something to kick that hangover! I do see how he looks at you. I know he is sweet on you. I cannot understand why he won't just make a move, girl!"

Nessie brought some of the same nasty green stuff to both Arthus and Jade. Arthus immediately knew what it was and swigged it down. "That is just as nasty now as the first time I ever tasted it."

Nessie said, "Then why would you ever be needing to have to taste it again? You know better!"

"Yes mam, I do. And, I am sorry that I ever forgot what that Dwarven Beer could do to my brain."

Nessie said, "I am taking some of this to Jade too. And I swear I heard her yell as I was walking up here to bring this to you, that you haven't kissed her in over five hundred years and when are you ever going to tell her you love her. Arthus that woman is in love with you, and you are as dumb as a rock if you don't figure out how to get over your stupid shyness and let her know how you really feel about her!"

"You're probably right about that! And, I know someone else too, much more important than me or anyone else in this world that I really need to apologize for getting drunk last night! I missed a mandatory assignment early this morning, that I know I had no business missing! I have to go pray as soon as this Dwarven caused headache feels a little better!"

Nessie said, "Well a mandatory assignment which you missed that makes you know you need to go pray is no small matter. Go right now down to that sanctuary in front of God's First Life Tree, and apologize to God quick! He is waiting on you now, and God is mighty busy! You better get! And, then come back up here and kiss your girl by tonight, or you'll be needing an appointment with God after I take to whipping your butt like I did when you was little, but this time I won't be holding back!" Then she laughed and walked away shaken her head.

Arthus sprinted out of his father's room down into the lift, and when it opened, ran all the way to the sanctuary at the base of the First God's Tree. He immediately went to his knees, closed his eyes, and prayed: "God, My Heavenly Father, In the Name of Son, and in my own name, I beg Your forgiveness for allowing myself to get drunk on that Dwarven Beer, and then missing my assignment time. I pray that in Your Grace and in Your Mercy, You overlook my lack of... how did Son put it? Oh, yes, my 'lack of perfectly being perfect.' I ask you to continue to overlook any of my failures, and continue to guide me and fill me with the wisdom that I need to fulfill this assignment and any future assignment that You ever choose to appoint to me. I hope it is ok to ask You to tell Your Redwood tree nymph Timothy, that I am sorry too, if not, I will be sure to tell him myself tomorrow morning. Is it possible to ask You for Your Grace to provide me one day off here and there, when I might be doing something so foolish in the future? Because, there really are times, I do want to just relax and have fun with my friends, like I had fun with Jade last night. And, please get me over my silly shyness, so that I will have the boldness to tell Jade how I really feel about her. And, if it is in Your will, and in Your plans for my life, that she is to become my wife, I would greatly, greatly appreciate that! Thank You!"

Arthus opened his eyes to discover that Son was standing patiently in front of him, waiting for him to finish.

"Arthus, let's go take a walk together as we talk," said Son.

Arthus stood up and walked alongside of Son.

Son said, "Arthus. Your prayers have been received and answered. You are forgiven for not being perfectly perfect. And, yes, from time to time you can have a day of rest and relaxation where you can let your hair down and have fun with your friends. Even God rested and celebrated on the seventh day after He started creating the Myriasphere, with all of its universes and their galaxies and their stars and their planets and their garden worlds where he made plants to grow and placed all of the creatures and birds and fish and animals and peoples. As He rested and celebrated, He enjoyed it so much that He told everything He had made that they too were to take a rest and celebrate. He expects you to do that from time to time, while at the same time, He wants you to use wisdom and not allow your mental acuity to be completely harmed by what you might drink. You are God's Shield, and there is a responsibility in that even on your days which you might choose to rest and relax and celebrate. You are aware that more than two mugs of Dwarven Beers or more than two short glasses of any other strong drink impacts your mental acuity. So, while you relax and celebrate, just don't allow yourself to get drunk, wherein is excess. And, in answer to your third point, about Jade, God knows your ends from your beginnings all at the same time. He created time and so He stands outside of it, meaning He is literally at all points in time at the same time, plus He is equally presently in eternity past and eternity future all together. That is why He is all knowing, more than any other. He is the same for Jade as He is for you! He has highly honored and anointed you. And, because He knows both of your hearts and futures, way better than you could ever know them, He appointed various circumstances in your past where you both would realize that you were blessed from the very beginning of your life in your union to be together. He has blessed your union together and 'what God has joined together, let no one put asunder!' Elder one of the Yelin Snow Folk was obedient to fulfill his assignment in having the matching naturally fallen Mammoth tusks turned into your marriage prayer and sweet dreams prayer. The prayers written on those were perfectly aligned with God's blessing of your union together. The matching shofars taken from the horns of a ram, when they are blown, actually makes the loud breathing sound of the unspeakable Name of God. Whenever either or both of you blow into that, you honor Him and call on His Name! You are to carry those to call on His Name before you ever go into battle. I am not sure that was clearly told to you before, so I am telling you now. From now on before you or Jade, ever go into a battlefield with anything, or anyone, blow on your shofars, and then recognize and honor God, Who battles with you and for you! The matching horns of the goat that you both often carry. These are symbols of your call to service to others. In battle, those are used to help heal those that are wounded. Now regarding your shyness. Shyness is actually a gift that God places in you and in others to help slow you all down until the time and place is right for you to be joined together in Holy Marriage. The fact that you prayed to get over your shyness is a sign that you are truly getting ready for sharing your hearts together. But, before you join together, you must also go honor her mother and father, who are awaiting you to come ask them for their permission for your joining. And, you must ask your grandfather, even though he already knows that your union together is blessed by God. Your father also knows this, but you do not need his acknowledgement, and he will not give it. He must just learn to accept it, because he knows God has already blessed it, and again, 'what God has joined together, let no one put asunder!' Now, Arthus, are you ready to go ask Grag and Shelly for their permission for you to date their daughter in preparation for your future marriage? I am ready to take you to them if you are."

Arthus replied, "What? Oh, yes, yes I am ready."

Instantly, Son and Arthus were outside of Jade's family home in the Clan Arial Farm Village. Arthus was a little shocked, but he quickly recovered and knocked on Grag and Shelly's door. Shelly answered her door with a bright smile.

"Oh Son, what a pleasant surprise. And, my you have brought Prince Arthus with you. Look how you have grown into a fine handsome man. My Jade must be turning completely red faced every time she looks at you. Anyway, let me send for Grag and then the four of us can visit together. I am sure it must be important enough for Son to have brought you here, and from the looks of it without Jade. Oh, my. Let me hurry now. Just have a seat in the kitchen while I go get Grag."

Shelly turns goes out to the porch, pulls her slippers off and puts her boots on and then runs to one of the barns nearby. Soon, Grag and Shelly both returned and were outside on the porch pulling their boots off before entering the house.

"As I said, honey. Son and Prince Arthus came alone and they are waiting to talk with us. So let's get inside and make them feel welcome," said Shelly.

As Grag and Shelly entered the house, Grag says, "Welcome again to our humble home, Son. And, you too Prince Arthus. My, my, my. You have grown into a fine man. I hear you came alone together, so I hope this is good news that you bring to us."

"Son says, Yes, this is very good news that we have come to you with. Arthus here is finally ready to make the steps forward into his blessed union, with Jade. Now I am going to be quiet and let Arthus speak for himself."

Arthus says a bit red faced and shyly, "Son brought me here in order that I can ask both of your permissions to officially begin dating your daughter Jade, who I plan to marry someday if she will have me."

Both Grag and Shelly said in unison, "Well its about time! And, Yes!"

"Jade has been pouring her heart out in so many messages over these past five hundred years, just waiting for you to tell her you loved her. It is good you wanted to wait for both of you to grow up a lot more. And, we know that you have another four hundred fifty years before you both graduate from the Academy before you can get married. We also know how crazy busy you both must be with all your studies and all

428

your trainings. Again, yes, yes, yes. You have our permission to date our daughter! Isn't that right Grag," She said, as she elbowed him.

"Oh, yes! Yes that's right. I am very glad to hear you intend to fulfill your responsibility for stealing my daughter's heart all those years ago. And, I too am glad that you have had the wisdom to be mighty, mighty patient as you were growing up. I also appreciate you giving us at least another four hundred and fifty years to plan your wedding celebration! And, what a wedding that will be if I have anything to say about it," said Grag.

Shelly said, "Do you both have time to stay for lunch?"

Son said, "No we've got to get back. Arthus has others waiting on him."

"Ok. Well... You know you are welcome to come anytime Son, and next time please plan to stay and eat some of my fine cooking, ok? And, Arthus I do hope you and Jade and all your friends will come and visit us here sometime soon. I hear so many good things about all of you."

Son, smiled and nodded.

"We will. Bye for now, said Arthus.

Son and Arthus vanished from Grag's and Shelly's kitchen and instantly appeared in the throne room of High King Thureos.

"Well, well, what a pleasure seeing you again, Son. And, I see you have brought Arthus. How are you doing grandson? It has been mighty crazy busy these past few days here in the palace," said High King Thureos.

Arthus said, "Son has just taken me to get permission from Grag and Shelly to date their daughter Jade, over the next four hundred and fifty years in preparation for a wedding that I know won't take place until after we graduate. And now, Son has brought me here to get your permission as well. Do I have your permission, my High King and grandfather?"

"Well of course you have my permission. I've known you too lovebirds have been sweet on each other for over five hundred years now. I am glad you have had wisdom to grow up a whole lot more since you gave her that kiss back in Arial Valley about five hundred years ago. And, I trust you will have enough wisdom to continue to honor her and absolutely wait for your marriage before actually joining together with her, in the way that produces children. You do want that joining to be fully blessed by everyone, including God, my Heavenly Father, and by Son? Isn't that right, Son?

Son said, "Yes, that is right! And, I do appreciate all of your wise words."

"Well Arthus, your friends are waiting for you to join them and the High King Thureos, your grandfather, is as he said crazy busy. You head to your friends and I will go do what I am assigned to do next," said Son, who then disappeared leaving him in the High King's throne room.

"I know your busy, grandfather, so I will get going quickly to meet my friends. You do look a bit weary, so I hope you get a chance to rest and relax between all of your busy schedules. I do love you, and yes you can trust me to keep both myself and Jade for after our wedding."

"That is very good to hear. I will inform your father. Here in my pocket is a ring, which you will give to Jade immediately now that you have her parents and my permission. Take it now, and get going, because I have a lot of work to do," said, High King Thureos.

Arthus took the ring and bowed and turned and headed for the huge double doors which were opened just enough to let him out the door. The hallways outside the throne room were completely crowded with many people waiting to go in and meet the High King. Arthus squeezed through the crowd. He finally made it past the crowd and entered the lift and rode it down and then left the palace. He then sprinted back to his father's building where his friends were all gathered and were just sitting down for lunch.

Arthus said, "Hi everyone. I am glad to find you are all gathered together here. And, Jade, may I take your hand for a moment?"

"Um... sure, said Jade."

As Arthus held her hand, he then got down on one knee and held the ring up for Jade and the others to see and said, "Jade, I have just met with your parents, Grag and Shelly, and then I met with my grandfather, High King Thureos. I have received their permission and blessing to tell you this: I am in love with you and I know you love me too. I am asking for your hand now as my officially engaged, to date you, and to kiss you, and to let everyone on Malon to know that I intend to marry you after we graduate from the Malon Academy. That is, if you will have me?"

"Finally! Oh my, yes, yes, yes! Of course," said Jade excitedly almost screaming as she took the ring and let Arthus put it on her finger.

As soon as Arthus stood back up she grabbed him and kissed him very quickly, then pulled away and said, it has been over five hundred years..."

Arthus cut her words off by kissing her back and not stopping. All their friends let out a huge cheer.

Zoey exclaimed loudly, "Finally he wised up and made his move! Then said, alright everyone, this calls for a mighty Dwarven style celebration! I know were not Dwarvens, but we can have fun like them. Let's all go eat and drink and dance! When are Emon and Ashur joining us?"

Arthus responded, "They will join us as soon as Emon fixes the overheating bug issue that his new faser beam blaster, or is it laser blaster, weapon contraption has after it gets fired. He said the thing gets too hot and he doesn't want it blowing up in his hand, or worse. They need figure out a way to heat shield it for his own hands, and in a way where the heat dissipates, and isn't always sent through the blast. He is wanting it to effectively stun someone, like giving them an electric shock which knocks them out, but doesn't just burn a hole right through them, when on stun. While in the kill setting, he does want to burn a significant hole right through whatever he is aiming at. Right now it burns a tiny hole in stun setting and probably a significant hole in kill setting. Even that tiny hole if it was made in the wrong spot on someone's body would kill them. He doesn't want it to do that. Hopefully they can figure it out quickly and come join us as we party together."

Chapter 27
The Grand Tournament Begins

The two weeks passed by faster than they could believe, too soon. They had all had to return to the Academy and now waited fully geared and standing before the central pyrimidine for the final announcement to begin. Arthus team includes himself, Jade, Emon, and Asher. Stood ready, Zeck was not far from him, and Zoey and they had teamed up with two others. One was named Jake. He was one of the top ten students, and one Arthus knew Prince Benroy, his father wanted to recruit into the Silver thorns. The other he didn't know.

"Welcome, today begins the Grand Tournament. I hope you all prepared. All of you passed your initial written exams the other day, and now you are ready for the practical combat test. You have all picked your teams, and now we will tell you what regions you will fight in. The first part will whittle down teams until there are four teams left, one from each area. Then last four teams will come to the grand arena, where they will face off each other until only one team is left. Team Leaders head to the tables before me there you will be told what region your team will be heading," Said Katelynn. With that, Arthus nodded and walked up. Zeck joined him.

"Here, hope that we get different areas so the finals can be me vs. you, right Arthus," asked Zeck.

"Yes, my friend let's hope our fight is the final match and lets everyone see what we can do, said Arthus.

They both shook hands and walked over to the table. Zeck team was given the mountains, while the Arthus team got the swamplands.

"Good luck to you. Make sure you make it," said Zeck. Arthus nodded and walked back to his team.

"So, what are we going," asked Jade?

"The Swampland's," said Arthus.

"Hmm, whelp, that's going to be a troubling area. There are a lot of trees, but in some places the water can get rather deep and muddy, that and the wildlife are something we have to worry about. Plus, the farther we go out, the deeper the water gets. We Dwarven aren't the greatest of swimmers, and my powder, if it gets wet, it will become useless," said Emon.

"Yes, my thought has been the same. Jade, have you been into the Swampland many times? I haven't spent much time there," asked Arthus?

"Ya, I been there many times with Zoey to help her collect materials for her study's I know of some smaller packed trees that kinda form an island of sorts. I suppose we should make it there as it will be one of the best places to hold up and defend. We will especially need to watch out for the Anacondas and the Lizard Beast, who enjoy hiding underwater and ambushing people. Arthus and I had faced one of those big Nagas before and barely survived, but that's when we were little. Anacondas are not quite as dangerous as really big Nagas are, but they are a giant snake too, and if they get you they will squeeze you to death and eat you, death is still death. There are some smaller venomous snakes and some venomous spiders that seem to call the swamps their home. Some plants are poisonous. If you don't know and touch them wrong or especially eat their berries, which are pretty serious. Just be glad they don't have all the wildlife here that can be found in the great Wetlands around in God's Forest or along most of the southern coast of the Great Ocean. We will need a load of fresh water to drink, as we cannot drink at all from the brackish swamp water. Some of the areas of swamp waters have toxic gases and other toxins in them. Therefore, we must get antidotes for toxins, and poisons, and for venom. And, we'll need bring along a lot of water proof bags. Besides our own equipment, Asher and I will collect the right Antidotes we will need, while you and Emon get the extra equipment. Like lots of rope and lots of waterproof materials. Also grab some of those small inflatable rafts from the equipment area, as our smaller Dwarven friends need those for sure." said Jade.

"Don't forget you will need your tele-mask. Oh ya, all our Armor has the new tele-mask and helmets built right in them. There are many pockets of poison gas around, so we might really be needing to wear those full on to keep the gas out. Still... bring your carry pack tele-masks as backups, as these new helmets she made are being tested on us first. We don't want to find out they are not working in a pocket of toxic gas with no backup. Keep them complete when we get into the deeper parts," said Arthus.

It didn't take too much time to gather what they needed and pack it up very good. Then they were all gathered in front of the gate where they were to enter the swamplands.

Several hundred people were gathered in each area. They knew that around a hundred teams would dwindled to one group each over the next three days. They were given half a day each before the actual wargames began. That way, all teams could find their specific place that they wanted to make as their base and start planning how to secure their area. Above each of the four quadrants a ship was flown that had a hologram of the time left and how many were still in each zone. A load buzzer and the gates opened, and off they went.

Their team was a bit slower than some. Having two Dwarvens in a place like this definitely made them work to make it to the spot they picked. They took time to inflate the rafts and flow them out into the deeper parts of the swamp where the mangroves were. This is an area where water was deep, but there were a lot of thick trees growing together enough to make some small hidden islands. Soon they came to where Jade had pointed out on the map they still had an hour before the wargame tests began, so they quickly set up their camp. Arthus had brought a small hologram map. He gave Jade several scanners. These were small devices that could stick to any surface, creating a grid around their camp. Anyone who crossed that grid would alert the map showing how many and what locations.

Jade was the fastest in areas like this, plus she was a master of bow and stealth. Jade had been champion of the Biannual Hunt every hunt after Arthus had left, and he couldn't be more proud to see how fast she could move her beautiful body from tree to tree. It took her less than ten minutes to set up a large grid area. Emon and Asher got their gear ready. Asher was speaking in an ancient language that suddenly caused Ruins to appear on many of the trees surrounding their camp. He also dropped Ruin rocks all around in the brackish waters of the Mangrove swamp. If some dangerous wildlife got past their grid these Ruins should make them want to leave. Emon had made up several waterproof bags filled with his special powders and then wrapped them all up again in larger waterproof bags to hopefully protect them. Asher picked up each of them that Emon had made and drew a Ruin on them, instantly the outsides of the bags stayed dry. Arthus was on watch. He used the built in tele-mask and helmet in full on mode, which were built into his armor to watch the area in a thermal vision. He also tested the air and water for any toxins or poisons. So far, they were clear and ready. When no one was looking his direction he popped open the secret compartment under his left armpit and pulled out the horn that glowed and poured a little of the water, from the River of God, into the brackish waters surrounding the camp. For a little bit the water where he had poured into glowed just a little bit. He quickly put that back into its secret compartment.

Arthus asked, "Asher, have you trained much in the Druid ways, as I have heard you speaking in an ancient language, and watched how Ruins have appeared from thin air?"

"Well, yes and no," said Asher. He then added, "Druids and Craftier – Casters do have a lot of things that cross over onto each other. The Druids can use their Life-energy and elemental abilities to bring the roots as well as branches and such from trees and plants up out of the ground or directly out of the trees and do all sorts of things with them, even building completely natural platforms and such like those you've seen on the First God's Tree. They help make life grow. Where we Crafter – Casters use our Life-energy and elemental abilities to speak various protections of the things that are as well as craft amazing things."

Soon, the flying ship made a loud sound, and the timer started.

"Jade, Emon, and Asher, get some sleep. I will stand first watch. We will change out every four hours for the first day. Then we will send out two at a time to scout a little father out as we move back toward the gate," said Arthus. They all agreed. Arthus watched as the night became morning. The numbers of combatants started to slowly go down as teams were taken out left and right. About eighteen hours after they made base, three groups fighting came into their grid. Arthus held his team back until all three were so engaged they had no idea the four of them had spread out around the three groups now with about two members left in each team. Arthus gave the signal and in a split second they attacked. Jade fell two with one shot each her arrows bedding themselves into their opponent's shoulders dropping them down into the water below. Emon tossed one of his lit powders at the feet of two others, and the explosion also sent them flying off into the water. Asher landed next to one and took the guy in the knee with his hammer, and that was all from that one. Knowing they had been outplayed, the last one stood to face Arthus. Arthus smiled and bowed his head, one hand against his heart and other outstretched in an apology and lifted he had allowed his internal electrical current to flow down his arms and into his fingers let it go a bolt of blue crackling lighting struck the man full in the chest sending him into the water below.

"Alright, everyone let's help out our fallen friends heal their wounds and get them out of the water to safety," said Arthus. Soon they had all three teams out of the water and were helping them dress any wounds and sent up a signal flare for a ship to come to pick them up. As they waited, a massive eruption of water and a gigantic Anaconda rose to smell the blood it had come to feed. Jade and Arthus were already on the move. Jade ran up one of the limbs and jumped. Flipping over the massive snake, fired two shots at once down into the eyes of the serpent. It roared out in pain.

"Everyone, make sure you're not touching the water," Arthus yelled.

Arthus ran down and slammed his hands into the murky water releasing a torrent of lighting into the water, which rose the Anaconda. It grew its tong flailing out of its mouth where Jade's arrows were burst into flames. Smoke rose from the massive snake' mouth, and then it fell into the water where it lay dead. Arthus rose braced himself against the tree for letting go so much energy at once, which took a toll on him. He had

436

mastered the wind, but lightning still had a limit to which he could use it. He has to work on that, he noted but smiled to himself. Long ago, he and Jade had met a huge Nagas, and the young Alda, that day, had saved their lives.

Jade was suddenly there with her hand out to him. She smiled down at him and was thinking the same now that they were so much more than they once were.

After the ship took the other teams away, Arthus said, "I think this location will have attracted a lot of attention. I think we should move out now and begin to hunt the other groups."

By the third day, Arthus and his team had made a secure area near the gate and had taken down ten other teams. There were only five remaining teams out of the hundred teams. Directly in front of the entrance, the five teams had gathered for their showdown. Arthus and his team was one of the first to arrive, so they had a really great place with the wall next to the gate to protect their backs. All the other teams had to come against them from only one direction. Emon used the last of his powder bags to weaken two teams. Jade was in the back, taking shots as she was able. Asher was in the center, using his cleric powers to boost the group's physical strength and keep them from getting fatigued. Arthus was amazed by Emon, who had picked out a massive two-handed hammer. Emon crafted the thing. Its hilt held different gears, and when he twisted a part of the hilt, electricity was bursting from the hammer's head. When one of the enemy team came a bit too close, they felt the power of a Dwarven and that mighty hammer, for when he hit someone with it, the jolt threw anyone far from the mighty Dwarven. One hit and they were usually done! Arthus smiled, then focused. He allowed the wind to flow around the group, turning up the waters and dirt, then he went into the now misty windblown battlefield. He allowed Angel Wing to become twin-long swords. He came upon three who were trying to get back to back with the area now hard to see in, unlike Arthus, who used his Life-energy to feel his way through all the molecules of air in the wind. This allowed him to feel also exactly where his rival team members all were. As enemy's charged into arm's length before they knew he was there. He slid under the fist, rolled forward and using the sides of both his swords he slammed them into the face of one, as the fighter fell back Arthus used him to run up and over the soldier behind twisting around slashed down taking the second fighter down by the shoulders, Angel Wing instantly switching to shield form and blocked the attack from the first fighter. Then Arthus spun turning Angel Wing into a spear using the back of the spear he took out the legs of the first fighter then slammed the butt of the spear into the second fighter's shoulders who then fell back, laying out cold. Then Arthus hit the first soldier as he tried to get back up on the head and laid him out cold. Arthus then ran back. He knew from the molecules in the wind that only two remained. One was fighting Emon, and the other was going after Jade. But when he got there, both were down. Emon was standing on the one he had knocked out, and Jade, who carried two long daggers, had forced her fighter to try flee. As he tried running away along the wall, she pulled her longbow and pinned him to the wall clean through his one shoulder with an arrow. Arthus called the wind to disperse, instantly the wind stopped the dust and water dropped and the battlefield was clear to see through. His team were the only ones left standing. A few moments later, the gate opened. Katelynn was standing just inside the entrance.

"Congrats to you, Arthus, Jade, Emon, and Asher, for you are the first team to finish the first stage. You are free to go and get some rest and clean up and make any repairs you need before the final fights tomorrow," said Katelynn.

"Ya, I think I speak for us all; we stink and really need a shower," smiled Arthus. Soon his team was outside the dorms.

Arthus said, "Alright, you all did a great job out there, but the hard fight is about to begin, especially if we need any repairs. I know Asher and Emon can fix our gear up very fast. Everything that needs washed, I'll gladly run it to the cleaners after my shower, leave what you wish with me in ten or so minutes after we all get showered, and as I take what I can to get cleaned, Asher and Emon you both will want to also get all of our gear carefully looked at by our Dwarven friends. Then we can all go eat dinner and get some rest. Does that sound like a good plan to everyone?"

They all nodded and headed to their dorm rooms to shower. They quickly came back down and the team had gathered up all their armor and gear. The Dwarven went to work looking over the armor and equipment for any damages while Arthus and Jade took their clothing and other gear to be washed and cleaned for swamp water smelled mighty foul indeed. When their work was done, they all sat together, ate a hearty meal, and then they drank to their victory. Arthus smiled.

"Just so you all know. I have committed to Son, that I will only drink two of any type of hard liquors or Dwarven Beers, as I have come to realize that I am God's Shield and must keep my mental acuity at all times! That means I will not get drunk with you! Now, I will gladly have fun and dance and make those two drinks last as long as our party keeps going! And, I won't hold it against you if you choose to get far wasted, But, please never try to push me to drink more," said Arthus.

Soon other teams arrived. Zeck and Zoey were among them. They looked a bit run down, but Zeck smiled and walked over.

"I see you have won your first round as well. Good, I expect nothing less from my friend and rival. Now, are you ready to face me, Arthus? I won't hold back, and I hope you show me everything you worked for these last four hundred and fifty years," said Zeck.

"Of course, and you look like your worn out, like you spent a few days in Maddy's halls of flames, instead of enjoying all the cool mountain elements where you were out there, my good friend. I was surprised when your team wasn't waiting for us when we got out," said Arthus with a grin.

"Yes, well, the mountains are not some easy soupy, messy slop. We had to climb by hand up to many high peaks and battle across many cliffs before the end, and I must say, it was a fun fight! I did get to test out my javelin climbing feature on my halberd weapon several times. It works really sweet. One team pushed us greatly, but in the end, we won the day," said Zeck.

Then Zoey yelled, "Hey Zeck, we gotta go. We must get our gear and clothing taken care of."

"Ya, I hear ya," replied Zeck as he swigged a drink of Dwarven Beer from one of the mugs that were on the table. He then raised it above his head and said, "May we have a fight that will shock and awe even your father, Arthus until then keep your arm strong and your mug full!"

Zeck then quickly walked off to follow Zoey.

Emon and Asher cheered for the Dwarven toast and then started to sing a Dwarven fighting song: "Raise your mugs, me brothers, for today we drink, and tomorrow we fight, For what more can be asked of those who live among the cold, the wolves, and the stone..."

The song went on for several minutes.

Jade smiled, stood up, grabbed onto Arthus' hand, jerked him quickly up off of his chair, and let out a really loud cheer. Then she pulled Arthus up close to her and kissed him right there in front of a room full, well of everyone that was there. Then she pushes him back a little and lifted her head up and yelled, "Woohooweeee!" She then left to go get her rest.

Arthus' face was bright red as he stood there staring at her as she walked away. It wasn't long and Arthus left as well to go get him some rest.

Chapter 28
The Colosseum

"Welcome all to the final match. I am the Weapons Master of the Academy and Master of this here Colosseum Jacob. The four teams before you are this year's finalists showed great strength or resourcefulness to become the top team out of one hundred who went into the zones. Many of you sitting here today know of their power and cunning. Those of you watching from the holograms all over Malon, thank you for watching the next generation of warriors, some of whom are in their final years, and some still have a long way to go. We watch this fight every year as our four hundred and fifty year students and our 900 year graduating students each have a chance to prove what they learned. The rest of the student body gets the opportunity to learn from their own observations each year and it challenges them to continue improving their own skills at a much greater level. The clan leaders as well as the High King and Prince Benroy are also here to observe and evaluate and hopefully to see how the next generation is growing and let them show who they are in the ring. This will always be a two on two teams match, then the last two teams standing will face-off, and the last team standing will be the academy grand champion team. Then after that, the two graduating finalists will be put into the grand final dual to see who actually the Academy's graduate strongest warrior is. Now the grand final dual is always only for those whose final year this is, and they will be graduating with high honors. This year we have two eyes to join the Silver Thorns. Their names are Garth and Elisabeth. They are the final top two graduates who both have shown the most growth over their nine hundred years here. Now for the four-team leaders, come and bring your teams so all can see. Team blue includes team leader Arthus Arkwright Prince of Malon, Jade Ariel Daughter of Clan leader Grag of Clan Ariel, Emon of Clan Gearhead brother to the one and only Maddlynn Clan Gearheads clan leader, and final member of team blue is Asher of clan Gearhead from one of the High Craftier-Caster family's. Now for team red, with team leader Zeck of clan Gearhead, Zoey, daughter of Eden the Clan leader of Clan Raphael, Elgeuor of Clan Gearhead, and Jake of Clan Urial. Then he read off the last two teams of clan gold and black," said Jacob. Elgeuor was a dark-haired, scarred Dwarven who carried two large axes across his back. Jake was a dark-skinned Cundo, from the Blood Sands desert area like Zeel. He had a small shield and a curved sword Arthus knew was called a scimitar.

"That Elgeuor is going to be a tough one. I've seen him around the North. He is a powerful warrior of our clan and known as a promising berserker," said Emon.

Arthus nodded. Arthus also saw Zeel use a scimitar and small shield and knew how deadly that fighter was. Arthus thought to himself, "If Jake, who has always been very competitive and acting like my rival, if he is anything like Zeel, I know that Zeck had picked a rather tough team to beat. The other group was one-off four Dwarvens, and the other was two elemental Ignole and Cundo warriors.

"Now team blue will face team black, and team red will be team gold, then the winners of those two fights will face off with whatever remains of teams are left standing. Arthus looked back at Zeck, but Zeck had run off towards the entrance there. Maddy stood with a large bag and handed it to Zeck, who picked up the Dwarven lady and hugged her, and ran off with the bag. Arthus team was first his team faced the Dwarvens team black. They were well trained as they took their positions opposite of one another. Three of the Dwarvens took up a shield wall while the last one fired crossbow bolts at them. Arthus had Emon take up a shield with Asher and make their shield wall to help keep the nasty bolts from them. The Dwarven marksman was good, but Jade was far better. Team black only opened the wall large enough for the Dwarven to get off a shot, and Jade timed her shot perfectly, and as they opened, she fired, and her shot hit home. Arthus had used his elemental power to give Jade's arrow a bit of a shocking enhancement, so when the arrow flew through the opening it hit the Dwarven in the collar, he went limp and fell over. The three shield Dwarvens stunned, looking back, didn't see Emon and Asher charge them soon the fight was on. Emon slung his shield lifted his mighty two-handed hammer, and slammed it into the back of one of the Dwarvens. Asher was, on the other with his hammer and shield, he battled back the other Dwarven. Arthus ran forward. Arthus pulled Angel Wing from his back and turned it into a long pool. The final Dwarven braced behind his shield, waiting for Arthus to run into him, but Arthus never did. Instead, Arthus used the pool to spring far over the braced Dwarven and landed silently behind. Arthus turned Angel Wing into a spear and stabbed the Dwarven in the back, lifting him, and pinning the now angry Dwarven face down in the sand. Arthus looked over. Jade had helped Asher take down his Dwarven by firing an arrow into the Dwarvens shield shoulder, which caused the Dwarven to be unable to lift his arm to block Asher's next blow, which took the Dwarven in the face knocking him out cold. But Arthus was impressed by the Dwarven facing Emon. He took strike after strike with Emon's shock hammer, and he could see the Dwarven could barely stand being shocked every time he tried to block the attack. But Emon jumped back, surprising the Dwarven, and Emon smiled and pointed at the Dwarvens feet. There was a small bag with a wick that was lit. The Dwarven looked up dumbfounded when his world turned upside down, as the explosive powder took and blasted the Dwarven high up into the air. Halfway on his way back down, Emon's hammer meets the Dwarven square in his chest, and that was that. Jacob ran over.

"That's it, team blue wins and what a fight! What do you all think," said Jacob. The arena exploded with cheers. Arthus stood by his team and waved to the people in the stands. But Arthus did notice one who stood arms crossed with a scowl across his face. Prince Benroy Arthus's father looked not at all impressed. Arthus team walked back to the waiting area. Zeck came out of a backroom now Arthus saw it was shocking. Zeck wore all-new armor. It was like the heavy plate armor the Silver knights wore, but it was different. Arthus could tell it was custom-made just for Zeck. He looked a bit scary. His gloves were spiked at the knuckles, and where the plates didn't cover, Arthus could see a Life-silver chain mail protecting his vital spots. The Helmet he wore was one solid piece with no eye slits, but Arthus knew all too well he could see them and breath with no trouble as much as his armor was like his new weapon. Zeck held an even newer Halberd mixed with an Axe head on one side that came down to half the shaft. But this one was black as night and had rows of carved ruins running down its handle and part of the ax blade. Arthus knew Zeck had Maddy make him a new set and helped him craft that weapon. Arthus could read some of the Ruins carved into the ax for lightness, making the weapon as easy to wield as a stick. The other Ruin said Flame-biter. Across the blade. Zeck looked over to Arthus, and his Helmet retracted into his armor.

"Well, Arthus, what you think this is why I went up North I had an idea, and Maddy made it come to life," said Zeck.

"You look like I going to have a hard time taking champion of our final fight, but I am looking forward to seeing how it holds up looks heavy as hell," said Arthus.

"Not at all look here," said Zeck. He turned and pointed to a spot just below his armpit where ruins were carved into the armor, and it made the gear weigh as much as an everyday shirt. Arthus laughed.

"Good luck out there can't wait to see what you can do," said Arthus grasping Zeck by the arm.

Zeck's team went up, but the three others stepped back and relaxed at the one end of the battlefield. Only Zeck stood before team gold.

"What, does Zeck plan on taking down team gold all alone? I get he has new gear, but he might be allowing it to go to his head," said Arthus.

"Ok, change of plans looks like team red will only be using Zeck to fight, and team Gold has agreed. So if Zeck loses, his team loses. Now let's get this going," said Jacob.

Team Gold looked angry that Zeck would think so lightly of them to face them four on one. But they thought it was a better chance to win this. So the two Cundo warriors attacked with perfect coordinated attacks. Zeck didn't move. He allowed the first two to stick his new armor, and to all those who looked on, the first warrior's weapon just completely shattered against Zeck's shoulder armor. Zeck caught the warrior with one outstretched hand by his neck and, like whipping a rag doll, threw the man across the field into one of the team gold's Ignole Elementalist. Zeck then turned and punched the second warrior in the chest with his spiked fist and lifted the man with one arm and slammed the warrior into the ground at his feet, then turned towards the two others. One of which just got back to his feet. The other one struck the ground with his staff, and large roots shoot forth, but Zeck moved his hand up his axe blade and it instantly flamed to life with a blue-white flame which covered the ax blade and slashed right through the root sources as if they were paper, then he charged faster than any thought the heavily armored warrior could. Arthus knew that Zeck had been mastering his natural Cundo abilities, allowing one to enhance one muscular output by half of whatever body they wish to. So Arthus guessed that Zeck improved his legs and used them to spring himself farther than anyone thought possible. Zeck caught the first Ignole by his face bending the man over backward and slamming his head into the sand. Then, his ax attacked the last in the side, sending the Ignole flying and rolling to a stop some ten feet from him. The whole arena was dead silent.

"Well, I guess that's it then. Team red wins, and will now face off against team blue in the final match," said Jacob. The whole arena burst into cheer. Zeck stood and waved. Arthus noticed even Prince Benroy looked interested. Zeck team rose and joined him, nodding their approval. Emon and Asher whistled behind Arthus.

"Well, now how are we going to take on Zeck wearing that," said Emon.

"We can do it just stay focused on our opponents, and if we take out his team first, then all go after him, we can do it," said Arthus.

Arthus team walked over to their side. Zeck team on the other and Jacob in the middle.

"Alright, are all you ready for the final fight, red team versus blue team. Now we shall see who should be called champion," said Jacob.

"Jade, you take Jake to keep back as much as you can, and be extremely careful as that scimitar is nothing to scoff at. Emon can you handle Elgeuor, and Asher keeps Zoey from entangling us with her earth elemental powers, said Arthus. They all nodded, and the fight began. Jade was the first to fire her arrows flew past in a blurred one-hit Jake in a thigh, but with the small shield, he deflected most. The dark-skinned Cundo warrior charged Jade, but she was much faster than he and outpaced the man, all the while taking shots at any opening she could find. Emon and the Dwarven Berserker smashed into one another. At the same time, Asher used his earth elemental powers to keep Zoey from using hers, so Zoey pulled out her spear and rushed the Dwarven priest, who had his staff of pure steel with the shape of an anvil at its head. Arthus and Zeck stood apart as the fighting around them crashed about.

"Well, my friend, I waited for this chance since we arrived here. When we were young and stood guard, we spared many times, and we never got to see who truly the better warrior is. So now is our chance to show everyone how far we have grown together," said Zeck. Then the man knelt before Arthus.

"My Prince, allow me the honor of fighting you with everything we have," said Zeck. Arthus smiled and knelt before Zeck.

"Of course, my friend, let show all of Malon our fight," said Arthus. They rose and took up a fighting stance. But they didn't move as the fighting around them kept getting more and more intense. Both, just stood there unmoving.

Thureos sitting high above watched them both closely.

"I see what they're doing, he said to his son, Prince Benroy who stood beside them looking on. They are fighting in their mind's eye both Arthus and Zeck are planning out their moves as the other counters them. It's been a long while since I have seen two fighters, who know each other so well that they can actually read the other's movements before they even move. This will be one crazy fight for Arthus. This Zeck is a true Cundo warrior. He will be a great addition to the Silver thorns," said High King Thureos.

Prince Benroy nodded and said with a scowl, "Yes, this Zeck does have potential to be a great warrior, but he's still not royal blood, so Arthus better not embarrass me by losing!"

High King Thureos looked to his son with a bit of sadness in his eyes and some anger. High King Thureos thought to himself, "That was the problem with Benroy. That is why God the Heavenly Father, and why the Archangels would never pick him to be the next High King. Prince Benroy puts far too much stock into bloodlines and is just has too much dang pride and arrogance." The High king sighed, then looked down.

To the fight again. Emon and Elgeuor were exchanging blows one after another, but Emon had the upper hand. His hammer was giving Emon the upper hand. Emon slipped off one of his powders, but before he could throw it, Elgeuor slammed into him, holding him tight.

"If you're going to let one of those off, going to have to take your explosion with me," said Elgeuor.

Emon smiled and lit the fuse. The explosion sent them both crashing into the walls of the arena. After a bit, Emon climbed to his feet, but Elgeuor didn't.

"Blaw ha, ha, I have taken many of my explosions to the face. How ya think I made these blasted things," said Emon smiling. But the fight was over for him, and he knew it. Emon walked over to Elgeuor, sat next to the knocked-out Dwarven, and pulled a flask from his belt. Jake and Jade still fought on. She ran out of arrows, so she took up her twin swords and went at the warrior. They both were equally matched, though Jade faster, but Jake was far more trained with the blade, and soon both stood away panting. Then with one final attack, Jade rushed in. She slipped by Jake's blade slash and slashed both the back ends of her swords into the man's shoulders, dropping him to his knees, but he slammed the hilt of his blade into her stomach, and both fell to the ground. Jade was knocked out, and yet Jake too was unable to continue the fight. Asher and Zoey stood to the side, both drenched in sweat and panting hard. They both expended their ability for the day, and both realized they couldn't beat the other, so they broke off their fight calling it a draw, and went to use what powers they had left to attend to their wounded companions.

Now the battlefield was empty but the two warriors who stood in the unmoving middle sizing the other up then as the arena fell to silence, they moved both so fast it was almost hard to see and shocked the entire stadium by the suddenness of their attacks.

Prince Arthus was far faster and could carry a lot easier than his bulky friend, but Zeck was well protected and powerful. Arthus knew he would be in trouble if he got hit full-on by Zeck. Arthus turned Angel Wing into his favorite form and most trained with the spear and spun around Zeck, slamming the side of the spear into the armpit of Zecks raised arms, for Zeck came at him with a large overhead chop. Zeck grunted but tried to close his arm and catch the weapon, but Angel Wing shrunk and slipped quickly out of Zeck's grab. Arthus spun again, trying to keep to Zeck's back and sides. And slammed Angel Wing into Zeck's legs and arms as he ran. But Zeck turned on Arthus faster than he thought he could and punched out.

Angel Wing became a shield, but Zeck's punch was powerful, sending Arthus flying backward. Most of the blow was absorbed by Angel Wing. Arthus rolled and leaped back to his feet. Zeck was already charging, so Arthus turned Angel Wing into a sizeable two-handed sword and allowed the elemental of electricity to flow up his arms and up the blade. Zeck's ax flared up in the white-blue flame, and Arthus Angel Wing clashed. Zeck did well to hold the mighty warrior, but Zeck was pure Cundo, so Arthus was being pushed back, but the metal on metal made Zeck take a good load of shock from Arthus. Zeck, however didn't retreat from the electrical shocks. Instead he pushed on. Arthus fell to one knee holding Zeck's ax blade only inches from his face.

Then Zeck released the pressure and brought a knee up into Arthus's chin. Arthus felt like all the teeth in his head just shattered. Such force did Zeck bring up with that knee. Arthus stumbled back, keeping his vision steady blood poured from his mouth. His eyes started to darken, and he felt as if the world was spinning. Then he felt an exploding pain slam him in the chest, sending him spiraling to the ground, and Arthus laid on the ground, pain racking his entire body. Arthus soon felt a warm pulse spread through his body, and when he opened his eye, the only one he could open at the time since one was swollen shut. Zoey and Asher and a couple of other healers stood above him, healing his wounds. Zeck sat not far from Arthus.

"Welcome back to the living, my friend. They are about to announce my victory, and I didn't want you to miss it," smiled Zeck.

Arthus said weakly, "Ya, I did lose, but man, was it a fun fight. Though I think you broke out all my teeth. Did you really need to knee me in the jaw?" Arthus sat up. He could feel most of his body now. The healing helped a lot.

"Now that you have awoken, I like to announce the winner," said Jacob, who walked back to the center of the arena.

"Today, we saw a fight worthy of two legends, and we have a champion come here, team red. Team red and warrior of flame and Axe Zeck Gearhead, Dwarven berserker, Elgeuor of Clan Gearhead, Zoey Raphael healer and master of the earth, and their final warrior of the desert sands Jake of Clan Urial. But what a fight we saw between these warriors. Let's hear it for team red and team blue who fought to the final man and shown what it means to be true warriors of Malon," said Jacob.

The crowd cheered. Thureos walked over to the stage, followed slowly by Prince Benroy. Zeck and team red, you have shown me and all here a great fight. I will be watching your growth with interest. I am sure Prince Benroy would love a warrior as yourselves in the Silver thorns or whatever clan you wish to join," said High King Thureos. Prince Benroy nodded in agreement.

People started to leave as the last fight between the two graduates wasn't to be told until later that day, so most went to eat or recover. Arthus waited now, mostly healed except for his jaw, which slightly ached. He was waiting to see his grandfather and father. Zeck had left with the rest of his friends. Prince Benroy walked over, scowling at Arthus.

"So why are you here, son? Are you waiting to be praised for your fight with Zeck, because you get no praise from me! You are a disgrace to our family and me out there today! To think one of Royal Blood would so easily fall to a Gearhead, and not even a clan leader child, but a low-born warrior like that. I can't even look at you! Be gone from my sight until you can make up for your disgrace," said Prince Benroy. Then Prince Benroy walked off. Arthus fell against the wall and slid down, putting his head in his knees and closing his eyes.

"What's wrong, my grandson? Why do you look like you failed at something," asked High King Thureos?

"I'm sorry, grandfather, but father said, I have disgraced myself and our family for losing, and said that I am unworthy of the royal bloodline," said Arthus. Thureos looked surprised.

"Arthus, what does he mean disgraced us? Did you not face Zeck with all you had and fight him without holding back, or did you flee from the battle knowing how strong your friend was? No, you stood and fought with all of your heart and soul! So, how possibly could you have disgraced our family," said Thureos.

High King Thureos looked around saw that Prince Benroy was just starting to leave the arena. He gritted his teeth and yelled very loud.

"Hey you, boy of mine! You need to get rid of this stupid idea of royal blood being worth more than others. If you don't get your dang prideful, bitter, and hate filled heart and head out of your buttocks, it will be your own downfall. Your stupid pride blinds you!"

The High King smiled as he turned his head back to Arthus and said, "No! In fact you completely surprised me with how well you fought. I watched how you showed true leadership during all the phases." Then his face turned sterner as he said, "And you, Arthus, need to stop wanting your fathers approval. You are a grown man, so stand up, and next time he tells you, 'you are a disgrace,' you stand right up to him and knock his head off. Now get up. A Prince sitting here sulking is much more of a disgrace than one who fought with everything in him win or lose. Now find your friends and celebrate Zeck's win. I can't wait to see how much you grow before your graduation." At that the High King grabbed Arthus by the hand.

Arthus smiled and nodded, grabbed his grandfather's hand tighter, pulled and stood up, brushed himself off, and ran off to see his friends. They celebrated almost the entire night, and Arthus barely made it back to his room and passed out.

"Arise Sir Arthus, anointed of the Alda Matriarch. Oh, wow Arthus you have gotten beat up pretty bad. Ok, then, I suggest you pour yourself a glass full of that water from your horn that glows and drink it down. That will greatly improve your own bodies healing abilities. Then you sleep tonight and tomorrow I will come check on you again," said the Redwood tree nymph, Timothy.

"I should complete my assignment faithfully no matter how much pain I am in," said Arthus.

"Your father is filled with hate and bitterness. He is nothing like our Creator, Who is full of love! No, Arthus, you need to rest even as our Creator has also rested! Now, take and drink from the horn that glows. Then allow your mind to fully focus on your Life-energy healing elements that you have inside you. Use the locked door method as you have been taught, in your mind to force the Life-energy to heal both your body and your mind and your emotions. Use that also to heal you of any bitterness and anger you might have inside you towards your earthly father. Instead of feeling inadequate and worthless. Instead, meditate and focus on what Son has talked with you many times about your life. Allow no words of that your father spoken in bitterness and anger, to steal your joy, or the hope within you! Allow no root of bitterness to plant itself in your heart and mind, for it is that very thing that has bankrupted your father's whole life! Because of his continual poisonous thoughts and lies that pour out of his mouth, even the one position of authority he has will be being taken away from him, and another will take his place. I will be here tomorrow as I am today, said the Redwood tree nymph, Timothy who became almost invisible as his Redwood tree pattern was once again barely visible as it appeared only to be part of the wall.

Chapter 29
Final Competition

The Years flew by. Arthus and Zeck once weekly took to the field to put their skills over and over at one another. Jacob oversaw each of their fights to make sure they didn't overdo it. Jacob had explained to them that their rivalry would make them truly strong. Though every time Arthus either tied or lost to Zeck, never could he overcome the sheer strength and Life-energy power that Zeck possessed and constantly worked to perfect. Over the years, they became indeed closer, more brothers than friends. Besides his regular training with Son, Arthus also trained with the two masters, Izzie and Elmont, to improve his elemental control. And, before they all really realized it, the final four hundred and fifty years had flown by them. Now the final test had come once again. And, like all the top warriors from every graduating class of the Academy, Arthus and Zeck are selected to compete in the coliseum for the final battle.

This time Arthus was tied with Zeck in a fight that lasted several hours of both going far beyond anything the crowd had ever seen. But they both successfully knocked each other out in the end, and the fight was called a draw.

They had all made it through the nine hundred years that they had spent growing and learning, and becoming closer and closer as friends. Each mastering his own body and mind and spirit. That final battle was over and all their tests were complete and now they were just coming up and standing up on the center platform where they knew they were to be acknowledged by the High King.

Everyone who was there was filled with joy, with the sole exception of Arthus's father, Prince Benroy, who once again showed his seething anger at Arthus for not becoming number one. Prince Benroy immediately went down from where he was seated right after the fight. He went down into the arena and climbed up on the stage where Arthus was standing. He was literally foaming out evil lying words, which were intended only to belittle Arthus, right there on the stage in front of the entire crowd.

Suddenly, to everyone's shock, High King Thureos had enough of his son's pride and arrogance and hate and total disrespect. The High King rose up from where he was seated on the platform, in front of the arena and confronted his son.

"Benroy, you still are so lost in your grief, and anger, and loss, and stupid pride that you have become an utter fool. I've been silent for too long. I have stood by and watched you spew your lying evil hate filled words, which only belittle your son, and hurt all of our people. You are fool for thinking that you being of my blood makes you better than everyone else around you. I tell you now that this is why God and all the Angels have forbidden you from ever taking the crown from my head. You have become far too prideful and arrogant and you are filled with your bitterness and hate. You are so foolish. If you cannot forgive yourself and Arthus for the loss of your wife, then you never find happiness, and I think it's about time you go and figure out what you truly believe and want in life. So as of now, you are removed as head of the Silver Thorns, and I am telling you to leave, now. Go on a personal faith-walk journey to rediscover the truth. If you have a problem with my order, then draw your blade and try and show me that it is I who is wrong," said High King Thureos as he walked down from the stage into the arena.

In a foaming rage, Benroy drew his blade and jumped down from the stage and attacked. Even Arthus, he could see his father was completely lost to his anger and rage, and in a state like that, really in no way, could anyone face-off with Thureos. Thureos didn't even draw his weapon. He sidestepped Benroy and caught his sword arm with strength beyond anything Arthus had ever seen. Thureos twisted Benroy arm, forcing the sword to drop from his hand, then lifted and slammed Benroy into the arena's stone floor. The High King backed up as Benroy tried to rise, but instantly Thureos kicked him in the side with all his power. There was a very loud cracking sound, and Benroy flew across the arena into the far wall with such force it actually cracked the stone wall where he hit. From there, Benroy fell to the ground and laid without movement.

"Guards, remove Benroy from my sight. He is stripped of his command and banished from all military benefits. He will live out his days on small and very Remote Island, where he will remain under a constant guard. His guards will give me regular reports, to prove he has obeyed my command and remained there, not in any way commanding over, or ruling over the guards that watch him, but instead he will humbly be serving them as a servant of the very guards who guard him. To all hear my command, Benroy is no longer a Prince of Malon. Perhaps someday, he will repent and the Angels of Heaven will come to tell me that my son is once again worthy to return to my side," said Thureos. The High King immediately turned and walked away, leaving the arena with Zeck and Arthus and the crowd in shock.

Healers and the guards took Benroy whose body looked broken and bloody.

Never has Arthus, ever seen High King Thureos treat anyone with such anger.

William, the right hand of Benroy in the Silver Thorns, took command. William was a strong and kind commander, who all respected and followed. High King Thureos officially promoted him into Commander of the Silver Thorn Knights and gave him the title, Paladin of Silver. This rank and title were rarely bestowed on anyone, but William had earned it.

Arthus immediately recalled the words that the Redwood tree nymph Timothy had told him four hundred and fifty years earlier, how his father Benroy would have the one thing in which he had authority over taken away from him and given to another. And, he knew that God had foreseen this very day happening because of his bitterness, and hatred and lies which filled his bankrupt life and mouth.

Chapter 30
Graduation Ceremony

Arthus and his friends in their final days at the Academy, appropriately celebrated. Then came the announcement that they had all been accepted into the Silver Thorns Knights Training. They also learned that their training started immediately after graduation, without any real break-time in between. Arthus knew that this meant he and Jade would have to wait to have their wedding until after they could graduate from Silver Thorns.

Their graduation ceremony was a solemn occasion, with all the graduating students wearing special and very dignified gowns and caps. There trainers and academy leaders and all the clan heads were there. High King Thureos took this occasion to express his appreciation for all the trainers and leaders and all of the graduating students. He also called Zeck and Arthus forward.

Then High King Thureos said, "I offer you both and all who observed my own angry reaction towards Benroy, my sincere apology. For I know, though I was right to deal with my son, to remove him from his position, to strip him of all his rights as a prince of Malon, to banish him until he comes to his senses, I was still wrong to allow myself to become so angry and in front of everyone I used my anger to abuse him. And abuse...well, all abuse is wrong! I was wrong to allow my anger mixed with my strength to abuse my son. Please forgive me for that abusive display of my anger."

Now, Zeck and Arthus, as is tradition, you both can ask me for one thing that is within my power to give.

Zeck spoke first and said, "I have already received the one thing that I dreamed most of and that was to be accepted into the Silver Thorn Knights training. The second thing I appreciate most in this life has to become like a brother to Prince Arthus.

The High King said to Arthus, "I sense that you too feel like Zeck is your brother."

"Bring me the Golden Bowl from over behind the podium," said High King Thureos.

An attendant quickly brought the Golden Bowl.

"Now, kneel and put out your right hand Zeck. Kneel and put out your right hand Arthus," said High King Thureos.

They both did as the High King commanded.

The High King took his dagger from his sheath and said, "I cannot make you actual birth brothers, but I can make you blood-brothers." And, then he cut a small slice into each of their palms of their hands and said, hold your cut hands together over this Golden Bowl."

They both obeyed smiling brightly, grabbed onto each other's cut hands over the Golden Bowl.

Then High King Thureos used his own goat horn and poured waters from the River of Life that flows by the First God's Tree, waters that had been farther cleansed from Arthus' horn that glowed, over their two hands, and declared, "I High King Thureos do now declare that Zeck and Arthus are now and forever more, Blood-Brothers.

"Arise Sir Zeck, now to be known of both the Clans Gearhead and Arkwright," said High King Thureos.

"Arise Sir Arthus Arkwright, Prince of Malon," said, High King Thureos.

Then High King Thureos said, Prince Arthus, is there something you want to ask of me, which is in my power to give?

"I wish to have the Priest send my father, Benroy regular barrels of water from the River of Life, which flow beside the First God's Tree, as I know those waters can help to heal his body, his mind and his spirit. And before each of those barrels are sent, you know that I wish to add a little extra something, which you and I are aware will also help him. Perhaps those waters will make it possible to break away from the influences of

Darkness that have been plaguing his mind and heart for these many years," said Prince Arthus.

"We can definitely make that happen, and yes, let us hope and pray that he will receive the healing from those waters that God wants for him."

At that the High King turned and addressed the entire room of graduating students. "We are so very proud of each of you who have spent these past nine hundred years of your lives preparing to become not just a part of the clans that you have chosen, but also warriors who are all part of God's great shield to all others. Enjoy this last night together with all of your graduating classmates at the official party which we have prepared for you. After the sky turns night, you will all get to enjoy the fireworks show that our Dwarven friends have prepared for you. Now, you each will have only two days to report to your new clans. After the fireworks display ends, head to your dorms and get packed up and ready for each of your departure shuttles that will start loading up at O-Dark-Thirty tomorrow morning. Make sure you get on the shuttle headed to your respective homes and then meet with your current clan leader to ensure you have what you need to move to your new clan. For those who are going from graduation to Silver Thorn Knights Training, Paladin of Silver, Commander William will expect you to be in your formation at O-Dark-Thirty the day after tomorrow at the Front-Line Disembarkation Port at the Silver Thorns Training Grounds between the southern sands and the great swamplands. You have all been given the exact coordinates.

At 04:30 the next morning Arthus caught his shuttle home with High King Thureos. Both of them spent the majority of their ride home in deep meditation.

Before leaving the shuttle, Arthus turned to his grandfather, High King Thureos and said, "The Redwood tree nymph Timothy had told me four hundred and fifty years ago that my father would have his one position of authority taken away from him and given to another because of his pride, arrogance and continual hate filled lying mouth. The moment you stripped my father of his position as the Silver Thorn Commander and removed him from his title as prince, the words that the Redwood tree nymph Timothy said to me back then, instantly came back into my mind. You were only fulfilling those prophetic words, when you said what you said. And, yes, you were not perfectly perfect when you allowed your anger to get you so worked up to kick my father, the way that you did. And, I really do understand how and why that happened. But know this, I love you and I completely forgive you for that as I know he had it coming for a long, long time. Know this also, I am really angry at my father for always talking like that to me, like I am worthless and such, but Son told me never allow any of my anger to be rooted as bitterness in my heart. Son helped me realize that I must forgive my father, whether he ever changes or not, and not just for his sake. Son said, 'Holding a grudge only means you are digging two graves in your heart and soul. One of the graves is the hate and anger and bitterness aimed at the other person, but the other grave is your own.' Son helped me know that I needed to intentionally choose to forgive my father. And, that is no easy thing to do, because he really is so damn hardheaded! But, I don't want to be like him allowing anger and bitterness to take ahold of my mind, my heart and my soul. And, I ask that you to forgive my father too, whether or not he ever changes, for the same reason. Please hug me now, so that I know, that you know, that me and you grandfather are really ok and really good! I have missed you beyond what you can imagine during most of these nine hundred years. I really love you!

High King Thureos and Prince Arthus hugged and cried for a little while.

Then the High King said, "I ordered a large supply of keg barrels to be taken from the River of Life. They are in a storage room ready for you to take your horn that and pour a little into each of those barrels. We will send those by shuttle to the remote island, where I banished your father. It will be the only water he will be allowed to drink and cook with." Then High King left the shuttle and headed off towards his throne room as he had to attend to other business issues.

Sylla met Arthus in the hallway outside of his bedroom doors. They hugged quickly, and then Arthus entered his bedroom. Inside his room were stacks of various gear and supplies that High King Thureos had already ordered for him. Arthus quickly sorted through and gathered up the gear for his next trip to the headquarters of the Silver Thorn Knights and to the Front-Line Disembarkation Port. Once he was sure that everything he needed was sorted and ready, then he left his room and immediately headed over to eat dinner at his favorite Dwarven restaurant.

Chapter 31
The Silver Thorns

The Silver Thorn training base was unlike any other. They did have a much smaller one on Malon, but this one, their main one is on the Dead Moon. For Malon had two moons, Creed the larger forest moon and the Dead Moon, which primarily was just a large rocky moon. On this Dead Moon, however, there is a massive dome fortress that was built by the Archangels. This dome fortress was named Front-line Base. It was the main base where Silver Thorn knights are trained and where they live.

The other base was between the southern sands and the Great swamplands to the east on Malon, where they patrolled the different areas with Clan Urial. There is a specific coordinates on that base, which is Disembarking location for traveling to and from Front-Line Base.

Silver Thorn Trainees are always stationed for their initial training on the Dead Moon within the Front-Line Base. Here they all had individual rooms for this military base was built in a way in which it completely filled and even surrounded the dead moon's largest moon crater. It also went way down into the ground of the moon almost reaching the dead moon's core.

Every day, there mornings started at exactly 04:30 in the morning in formation and ended at exactly 19:30 again in formation. Their schedule for the first year was exactly the same every single day. At 4:05 in the morning the huge alarm bell and flashing lights would wake everyone up. Then from 4:05 to 4:25 everyone made their bunks up in military style, faced their lockers to ensure they could pass inspection, and then spent time polishing their boots, ironing their uniforms, cleaning their rooms, and cleaning the main hallways and latrine areas. At 4:30-4:45 they were in formation while their rooms and common areas like hallways and latrines were getting inspected. They each were assigned to individual squads and each week different squads were assigned different common areas to clean. Once a month everyone did a deeper cleaning of their own rooms, the hallways and latrines and spent time on their hands and knees cleaning all of the parade and exercise areas for at least one whole day. If anyone's personal area or their squad's common areas failed inspection their entire squad spent an extra day detail cleaning some of the many base common areas. And, those inspectors used white gloves to see if one speck of dust or dirt or grease was found. After formation each day they all went to the exercise grounds and did military style exercise routines that touched on every major muscle group of each person's body, no matter what body type you were. They all did that for two hours. Then they all hit the showers and changed from out of their first exercise uniforms. In exactly fifteen minutes they were down again in formation and they all double timed over to the chow hall where they ate breakfast. Every breakfast there were choices for main dishes, Pilgos bacon or Sausage, eggs, toast, a toast that had been dipped in a batter of eggs, milk, cinnamon spice and vanilla spice, whole wheat pancakes, a kind of soupy rice, hot oatmeal cereal, fresh and sundried fruits, and Pilgos Milk, fruit juices, and River of Life water. Though there was a large selection, they were each given exactly ten minutes to eat and no one was allowed to carry anything out of the chow hall to snack on later. Also, there was never any talking allowed in the chow hall. As soon as their ten minutes were up they had to stand up go to the trash bin, scrape any remaining food off of their trays, then put their trays and tableware on the dirty dish cart in the tubs assigned for those. Then head immediately headed back outside and back into formation, where they waited for the last person in their original formation line to come back out and join the formation. Usually that last person was the main drill leader, who was always the first to also go inside the chow hall. If anyone came out after the drill leader, they did one hundred pushups, or one hundred squat-thrusts, or one hundred sit ups, depending completely on the mood of the drill leader at the given moment. Leaving the chow hall they double timed over to the combat drill area and for the next two hours they did drills with various weapons using martial arts drills. Then they double timed over to the classroom building where they spent until 12:00 studying and memorizing all the various military regulations, military rank and structure, taking apart and putting back together various types of weapons, learning various combat strategies that the Angels as well as the silver thorns had learned through many actual combat situations. Then again they ate lunch at the chow hall exactly like they had for breakfast, only other food items were being offered. Every lunch meal there were at least four selections of main dishes, salads, soups, a variety of fresh fruits, a variety of deserts, Pilgos milk, a variety of juices, and River of Life water. Then they spent their afternoons doing one-on-one combat with someone that could push them to do their very best. Zeck and Arthus and Jake and one other very competent Cundo always seemed to always get put together as rivals. Several times Arthus and Jake would be put against each other, and several times Zeck and Jake would be put against each other and several times Arthus and Zeck would be put against each other. Actually over the five years Jake and Arthus started to become friends. As Jake had learned that Arthus and Jade were engaged, he put his eyes onto another beautiful girl in the Silver Thorns, and that easily helped remove any problems Arthus had with him from early on in the Academy. Dinnertime like breakfast and lunch again at the chow hall. After dinner they did meditation routines, and more one on one combat drills. Then they showered for five minutes each and then soaked in a hot springs tub filled with River of Life water and special salts for 15 minutes. They rinsed off in the shower again and then dressed in comfortable wool/cotton/synth-blend and sweat pants and sweat shirts. Everyone always wore exactly the same looking clothes at the exact same times throughout the whole first year. At 19:30 they were in formation and then released for their evening to take their clothes to the laundry, go to the markets, or do whatever. Then at exactly 21:00 they read from their copies of the ancient canonical books for exactly 20 minutes. Then spent 10 minutes meditating on what they had read. Then they headed back to their respective rooms as lights out was exactly at 21:45.

The second year, third year, fourth year and fifth year pretty much was like the first year except they had a lot of one week long to one month long trainings in the forests and jungles on Creed.

The Angels had built this entire place as their own training base and used it as the frontline against the area of space which they called the dead-zone. The dead-zone is an area of deep space between this galaxy and the galaxy that contains Hellcore. Here the Angels watch for any enemy attempts to either escape from there or where they might try enlarging the Hellcore Darkness filled void itself. Every so often the Demon Prince General sends an armada of space ships filled with Demon-bonded and mind controlled towards this galaxy through the dead-zone. Arthus had seen many Angels in full armor take off from Front-Line, and some because they went too far, unfortunately did not return.

Angels have been the protectors of all galaxies and universes within the Myriasphere to make sure the armies of Darkness never made it past this point. If it be true, that sometime soon the responsibilities will be placed squarely on their shoulders to make sure the armies of Darkness never make it past the Dead-zone, then not only Malon needs to be equipped and trained and on patrol, but every planet that housed life in all the other galaxies in this universe, and then all the other universes within the Myriasphere are also needing to be equipped and trained and on patrol. If any ignore the threat, they are all very much in danger of being twisted and turned into more bloodthirsty Demon-bonded and/or Demon-mind controlled

No one alive on Malon, other than the Angels had ever even seen one of the Demon Princes. Arthus hoped they really never would. However, many on Malon have seen the Demon-bonded, and those Demon-Bonded had physically and spiritually joined themselves somehow to the actual Demons who either had actually been on Malon and did the Demon-Bonding on Malon, and arrived there by Dark Portals, or whether these creatures and people had been somehow tricked and then led through dark portals to Hellcore, where they then received their joining which made them become Demon-Bonded and then sent back through Dark Portals to Malon to Demon-Mind-Enslave others. Arthus believes God truly knows exactly how this took place. And, of course the Demons that did the Demon-Bonding also know how they did this. Arthus realizes it is always possible that there are actual Demons hidden somewhere on Malon. Arthus recalled Black Ice and how he was Demon-Horde-bonded. And, Arthus recalled the huge Nagas-Hydra Hybrid, child of the King of Darkness and Naki, Queen of the Nagas. Arthus knows that Son mentioned they were sent by Satan, the King of Darkness as he has become the Serpent King, and Leviathan, as she is also Naki, Queen of the Nagas through Dark Portals to Malon and to all the other worlds where sentient beings live. That means all of those worlds need to have all their waters cleansed, just like Malon. Arthus realizes that as big as the Myriasphere is, this really is a huge task that the Alda Matriarch has given to him to do.

The Front-Line base was not all just training grounds. It housed many buildings and a market, even some areas for recreation, but here the Angel's favorite thing to do was sing and dance. Music was truly the Angel's major pastime activity. When they were not fighting, they were singing, dancing, or sitting near one of the Angel bards, while they sang all different things from strange worlds, old wars, or fallen friends. Arthus knew of bards, and he found himself wanting to learn a bit of the music and the singing. There was a Life-energy power to it which he saw in action, when a bard sang over a wounded warrior, and it brought peace and even helped his body heal right before his eyes. Music to the Angels has such incredible power. He even saw a group of Angels in training all take up harps. As they played, other Angels threw explosive fireballs and other energy weapons, but the combined music created a perfect life-energy shield and protected the warriors who stood below it. Arthus recognized the incredible power in music and wished he could learn to play. One of the Angel bards smiled at Arthus. His name was Gabriel. Gabriel thought Arthus showed potential as a warrior bard and gave him a lute made from a special wood and with hairs of an animal only found in heaven. He then gave Arthus a violin made like the Lute. He also showed Arthus the basics about reading music from a book he gave to him, and showed him some basic fingering. Arthus was a better warrior than a bard, but he practiced whenever he could, and is slowly

464

getting better. At least Zeck stopped throwing things at him whenever he started to play. Jade loved the music also and loved to sit by and watch Arthus practice.

The forest moon, Creed was also used as training grounds for mock battles and other training courses. Creed was almost twice the size of the dead moon, with a massive Jungle and Forest that almost covered its entire surface. Creed also has one incredibly huge mountain. That mountain is where the High King had been introduced by Michael the Archangel to the Dwarven race. And, the forests of the moon is also where the Yaule are from. The one incredibly huge mountain on Creed is where the Dwarvens had built their first home before their mining resources became so depleted. Their survival and their ability to join in with ultimate creator's creative work, became much harder and harder. The majority of Dwarvens had moved to Malon. Their massive Dwarven fortress that had been built into the entirety of the mountain, truly became a relic of days gone by. Though it served as a great location for holding mock training battles.

At the main gates to the Dwarvens fortress home stood two massive statues built out of pure black steel. Emon told Arthus they were the first two kings of the Dwarvens people above the gates was a massive anvil the statues looked as if they were making something on the anvil. One was holding a pair of large clasps. The other statue had one arm raised in its hands was a hammer raised to stick whatever they were making. Emon explained to Arthus it symbolized the Dwarven worship to the Ultimate Creator. They had come to the forest moon a few times during their training to do combat training in the forests and in the jungles. And they had seen the fortress from afar during a few of those combat training exercises.

Arthus and his team had been training hard to pass the written and combat tests to become full Silver Thorn Knights. There on Creed, it has been already almost five years since they graduated from the Academy and are now actually trained to be full Silver Thorn Knights, except for this final mock battle that they were about to engage in.

Arthus prepared his team to do their final training mission, a mock battle. One team was defending the large Dwarven fortress, and his team was to attack and steal a flag from deep within and bring it back out to an evacuation point where they were to be picked up by transport. The mission would be a three-day test. If they pass, they are welcomed as full Silver Thorn Knights. Arthus team comprised all his friends from Zeck, Jade, Emon, Asher, and Zoey. The team they went against was the Jake and Garth team. Both were strong and had made the finals in the last Academy battle. They had around ten warriors to help them protect the fortress, so it was not in Arthus's team's favor, but Arthus knew his team, and knew they could do what needed done. Tomorrow they are flown to the moon by shuttle then dropped off about a day's hike from the fortress, giving them two days to attack and take the flag. Arthus had already explained his plan to the others, and now all were preparing their gear for the mission.

Arthus mind wondered a bit. He thought about his father and how many Silver Thorn Knights that his father had trained and then brought to this very point in their training, where they too had gone through this very mock combat exercise. Arthus thought about his father being in exile as Benroy remained in exile, and though Arthus hoped his father would figure what truly had driven him to that bankrupt state and even he prayed that his father would find his way back from the deep despair that had claimed his heart, he had already forgiven his father completely, no matter whether he changes and gets restored, or never changes and stays forever in exile. Arthus had completely focused on the WORDS Son had spoken over his own life, and over what the Redwood tree nymph Timothy had said. Arthus had made up his mind and heart to trust what God saw about himself and never allow any root of bitterness to plant itself into his heart!

Arthus realized his mind was wondering and that he was staring off into space and then mentally returned to the task at hand.

The mission he had created sounded like a good plan, he thought, and the others agreed. They would land then, after they had gotten closer to the mountain, they would spread out and scout the area in a ten-mile radius from the mountain itself. On the side where the door was had a long open valley that would make a sneak attack impossible. But the Jungle around was also very thick and wouldn't be easily traversed. A

466

large river on the west side went around to the front gates under a large stone bridge just before the gate. He figured that Jake would put many men just above the gate and on the large stone bridge with arrows or other projectile weapons if his team tried to attack anywhere from the front trying to use the river to get close. Three large chimneys led down into the Dwarven forges below the upper levels of the mountain. But these were a risk for if Jake had trapped them or had people waiting, it was a long way up in the open, for which to climb to get to the chimney openings. And, then only small chimney openings to try and climb down the inside of. Attempting to make it to the top of the chimney would probably make them easy targets. So Arthus had decided to have his team break up into three teams. He and Zeck would go around to the west and try to get there by the river. Jade and Zoey would go in from the east through the Jungle. Their two Dwarvens would go up into the Mountain and attempt to sneak up from the north way to where they could get a good view of the chimneys and the roof areas. Everyone is stay in communication through their built in armor holo-display, head mics and the tiny ear speakers. When done scouting how their enemy might be set up they were to go back again five miles and meet up in a small clearing just south through the tree line from the wide open valley area. Once they all gathered back together then they would decide which be better to go in through the main gate or by the chimneys. But thanks to Emon, they also knew another way just under the west side where the river touched the mountain was an area where underwater sewage exited, and if lucky, wasn't barred up. They could try swimming up and into the lower areas of the fort, and since the fort was abandoned hundreds of thousands of years ago, the sewage wouldn't be a nasty thing, especially being that whenever it flooded, that was an area where water flowed into the fort and washing it out fairly clean into the river. For now, though his gear was ready and it was late, so he went and climbed into his cot and fell asleep.

Chapter 32
Creed Moon of Malon

The shuttle flew over the valley and deeper into the jungles fairly far south of the Mountain. The Jungle was thick and dense. Soon the shuttle hovered over a small clearing. It was already getting late, so this clearing would be where Arthus and his team would spend the night. So they got together, made camp, and talked about the mission and what they thought Jake's defense would be. But not long, they sat together laughing and drinking a little, for they knew they had a long walk, but they were not technically on mission until the following day. Creed had its dangers, but most of this area appeared well used as they spotted many smaller animal tracks as they were setting up their camp. Arthus took out his lute and played a song that he had been practicing. He didn't put words to it, just let the music drift into the night air. The others laughed and drank, especially the Dwarvens, and Jade sat by Arthus slowly sipping on her mead, looking at him, and then looking up at the stars, and then looking at Malon in all its glory from there. The planet they had lived on their whole life looked way more significant with its blue and green colors. Malon was so much larger than the moon, and looking up and seeing their home was breathtaking. Zeck was cleaning his gear and sharping his halberd ax, but as Zeck did this, with his foot, he tapped to the music. So Arthus upped the beat of the music, and the others quickly danced along.

Suddenly the sky lit up as flying object that looked like a flaming falling star, or flaming meteor flew past overhead and had even broke the sound barrier as it came in. Everyone dropped down as the thing was heading from south to north straight towards the Mountain. Arthus immediately feared for Jake and his team. He ran over and grabbed up the radio and called Front-line.

"Hey, Front-line come in, please we may have an emergency on hand," said Arthus.

"This is Front-line. What is the issue," said the radio operator.

"We just saw a large meteor or some kind of flaming flying object flying from outer space that broke the sound barrier as it came in. It is headed directly towards the Mountain. Please get in touch with Jake's team and have them to get prepared for impact," said Arthus.

"Roger, thank you. We are getting Jake's team online now," said the operator.

A few seconds later the radio squawked, "Thank you for the warning. Jake's team saw it in-coming and already took cover and waiting for impact to let you know if the mission is still a go or not," said the operator.

A couple of minutes later, there was a huge explosion, and the ground below them shook, knocking Arthus and his team right off their feet.

It was minutes before the Front-line operator came back online. The voice said, "Jake and his team remain unharmed and the mission is still a go. The meteor hit the side of the Mountain and crashed through several levels of the Dwarvens old underground fort, but all of Jake's team were alive and unharmed. It appears the damage won't get in the way of your mission. Jakes team said they were going to do a quick inspection. If we hear anything else we will let you know. Font-line out."

So they returned to enjoying the night air, and soon all went to bed.

The next day was hot and humid as working in the Dwarvens Forge, mixed with the hot springs steam bath house put together, but the group went on their way. They broke camp earlier and were already to the spot where they would split up. Jade trained Zoey to travel more swiftly through trees and brush, and none were better than Jade. She had become a true master of scouting through thick forests or Jungles. So she and Zoey were off in a flash. But Emon and Asher, on the other hand, were going to take a lot longer. They just got out their ax and started to cut their way straight north through the Jungle. Arthus knew those two could be heard for miles singing and slashing their way towards the meeting place. He smiled, knowing anything or anyone who tried to take on the loud Dwarvens would not enjoy the experience. So Zeck and he ran on, following the river bank heading a more western route. The Jungle to their left was thick, and the rains had started not a cold shower, but one that was hot and mixed with the sweat dripping down Arthus face making their travel all the more painful, but soon they came to the bend where the river went back off to the North.

"We better slow down. Jake may have sent out scouts to try and figure out which way we are approaching from and then learning that, try set up an ambush for us. So why don't we go just inside the Jungle border? We get better shelter from this rain and some shade. We also need to take a break soon before we drop dead from this heat," said Zeck.

"Ya, your right lets head in and take a break. My clothes feel almost twenty pounds heavier than before, and a cool drink will feel great," said Arthus.

They traveled a bit in and climbed up onto a large Jungle tree and took out their water held in a container that kept the contents either warm or cold, depending on what they set the temperature control on the bottle. Arthus took a long cold drink. The water was so cold it hurt his teeth a bit. But soon, he felt refreshed and ready to move on.

"Everyone check-in. How is your progress going," said Arthus?

"This is Jade, Zoey and I have reached the eastern side of the Mountain so far, no sign of any of Jake's team, and I can't see any sign of Jake's team guarding the main valley or bridge or the large gate," reported Jade.

"Same here on our end, not one sign of rivals," said Emon.

"Alright, everyone, Jake had to post some guards; weirdly, he wouldn't have anyone outside the fort. Zeck and I are almost to our scouting point. Keep in contact if find anything out of place, watching for traps also," said Arthus. With that, they packed up and continued their way. Arthus was trying to figure out what Jake had in mind. If none were outside the fort, Jake had fortified the entire defense inside. This was going to be a hard fight. As they got, closer something foul was in the air.

"What is that smell its just horrid," said Zeck

"I smell it, so let's find out, smells like something dead been left out to rot," said Arthus.

Soon they came upon several Yaule cats that been cut to shreds and the ground was soaked in their blood. The bodies of these cats were just left out in the sun to rot and decay.

"What creature could kill and leave their prey like this, I never seen anything that butchers this way," said Zeck.

"Yes, I hate to find out what did this. Let's keep sharp. This was done sometime during the night, is my guess. Hey everyone, check in. We found several dead Yaule, and they don't look like any animal could have done this that I know," said Arthus.

"This is Jade, no signs of anything like that where we are," said Jade.

"Ya, we see lots of torn-up trees and such some have wicked claw marks but no signs of whatever did it," said Emon.

"Alright, keep alert. We need to figure out what could have done this and where it went," said Arthus.

Arthus and Zeck looked for hours and found no other sign of whatever butchered the Yaule. So they went and met up with the others at the small clearing they used as their base before attacking the fort. With the strange events, no drinking or singing happened that night. They ate quietly and made a plan for their two hour watch routines. Zeck and Zoey had the first two hours, Emon and Asher had the second two hours, then Arthus and Jade had the last two hours until daylight. Arthus didn't sleep well. He tossed and turned. He dreamed of being alone in the Jungle. A large female Yaule came before him out of the dark Jungle. She glowed a silvery light.

"Young Prince, why do you sleep while blood is fresh on the wind. I found my children cut and murdered. Do you know who could have done such a deed? Please do not fret, for I know you and your people would never do such a horrific thing. Long have I been friends with the High King. I even allowed my children to go and live on Malon, free to live how they wish, but to find so many cut down has me saddened. The day is breaking. I hope you awaken soon and find whatever killed my children, and may I be able to sink my teeth and claws into them," said a large Yaule, one of pure white and silver. Arthus awoke with a jolt. He was covered in sweat and jumped to his feet, pulling forth Angel's Wing.

"You ok, lad? We just about to wake ye, but you seem plenty awake, don't worry, get dressed, we get Jade up," said Emon. Arthus nodded and rose, dressed, and went to question the Dwarvens if they saw anything weird.

"Emon, did you two notice anything weird during your watch? I had a weird dream of a massive Yaule of pure white and silver. This Yaule called all others her children and was asking me things in my dreams," said Arthus.

"Yes, I had the same dream or was close to it," said Jade. The Dwarvens looked at one another then nodded.

"You speak of the Mother of Yaule, and we call her Martin. She is immortal like Thureos, and the only ones who have seen her are our first kings and your grandfather, High King Thureos. It is said she glides through Creed Jungles and can ever speak through your mind. She is mighty but kind to all who respect nature and leave her children at peace. There must be trouble if she been seen in your dreams, and with the butchered Yaule you found, she sure to be out hunting those who are responsible," said Asher.

Arthus thanked the Dwarvens, and they went off to bed. Arthus and Jade kept watching it be several hours until light, and Arthus felt that something was very wrong. A cold chill ran down his spine. He focused his Life-energy and began to seek through the molecules in the air out as far as they could go. He did not sense anything directly, but it still felt like something is wrong. He motioned to Jade. Let us prayed to God our Heavenly Father that nothing will go wrong. Whatever this very wrong feeling that I am having, may be part of His warning.

472

Chapter 33
Darkest Night

After the dawn, Arthus and his team set out for the valley south of the main gate to the fort. When they arrived, Arthus had Zoey and Asher stay at the far side of the valley and set up an area for medical needs in case something really was wrong. For once again, Jake's team was no were in sight. Arthus didn't know why but he felt something was very bad. There should be at most minor signs of their enemies in the last couple of days, but the last time they heard anything from their opponents was the night the meteor had fallen. So Arthus and Zeck took up the lead while Emon and Jade took up the rear. They moved slowly, checking out for traps or anything that might explain why Jake had not placed anyone outside. When they reached the bridge that led to the gate, they were surprised to find the gate wide open, no sign of light within the darkness of the fort, so they took an hour to cover the south side of the mountain to see if there was any sign anyone. But still nothing.

"Something isn't right. I have a terrible feeling," said Zeck.

"I know, I have the same feeling as I see where that meteor had hit," said Arthus pointing to a large hole inside of the fort. They went over, but the impact had broken through the fort walls and went more profound than they could see.

"I bet me beard that this hole goes as far as the throne room, which is very far down, we best just go by the gate and see what Jake has in store for us," said Emon.

"Your right let's get this over; I don't think my nerves can take much more of this," said Arthus.

They went over to the gate. Zeck willed his halberd to blaze with fire and led the way in. Emon took up next to help guide Zeck into and through the massive fort. Jade went in next, and Arthus took up the rear guard. Inside the enormous gate was a long bridge that, far below, a river of lava flowed. The bridge went about two miles into the mountain and then came to the second inner gate. They moved slowly, watching the far walls encase there were areas where archers could hide but by the time they reached the second gate, still no sign. The second gate wasn't fully open but was open enough to place a large metal bar and force it to open farther, and soon they were in the first chamber. There were sizeable empty cave buildings built into the walls around the place.

"This is the Dwarven market here. In old times we Dwarvens would trade and sell things, and they're used to be bakeries and other food stalls that would be around. At least that's what I been told," said Emon. They went slowly clearing each abandoned building, and still nothing they came to large stairs one led up other down.

"Well, if I am Jake, I put the flag down in the throne room that is about four floors down," said Emon.

"I agree. Let's head down and watch for anything," said Arthus. It took a couple of minutes, but they arrived on the second floor. Here was the fort armory and guard housing. The stairs were always on the opposite side of each floor, so one had to work their way slowly and couldn't just rush down to whatever floor they wished. They had to travel across each floor until they reached their destination. So like above, they took their time searching each room. This time they found signs of movement. Several weapon stands were emptied of their weapons, or some had been kicked to the floor altogether, almost like there had been a fight in several of the buildings. For at least a full day, if not two, several cold fires had been used. So the team gathered at the stairs and continued going down. The third floor was the forges. This room was hot today, and lava was channeled through the space by large metal pipes into massive forges. Arthus almost could imagine what it must look like hundreds of Dwarvens would be running back and forth making armor and weapons and tools and so much more. Emon had to stop and stand in silence for a bit, honoring his ancestors. After searching and finding old signs of life again, they continued to descend. It had to be five hours since they came into the fort if not already half the day. The fourth floor was massive. At one end was an enormous door with runes carved onto the door. But before that was the main housing of the Dwarven people. Many buildings were built right into the sides of the mountain, and many were made on top of other houses. This reminded Arthus of the Dwarvens new home in the Great Northern Peak's City. He had his team spread out and search. There had to be someone around somewhere.

Emon and Zeck went to the left side, and Jade searched the right. Arthus felt in his Life-energy the pull to check out the main throne chamber. He soon reached the massive doors. It was sealed shut. Then Arthus heard Zeck and Emon shouting. Arthus ran over with Jade hot on his tail. Zeck had pulled someone out of an armor locker. He looked terrible, his armor covered in blood. After looking over the man, Arthus recognized him, it was Jake. He was pale and unconvinced. One of his arms was missing like something had ripped it off him, for the wound was not clean in any way and shreds. He was also covered in scratches. Emon ran over. He had brought some healing items and started to tend to the man.

Zeck asked, "What in Hellcore could have done this to him? And, where are the rest of his party?"

"Not sure, but you and Jade better go search the other buildings fast, but stay together and stay very alert, for whatever did this might still be in here somewhere," said Arthus. They agreed and ran off to look for anyone else. Arthus watched Emon bind the man's arm and work on healing his cuts. Arthus looked over to the Throne room and started walking towards it again. He pulled Angel Wing from his belt and pushed the gate slowly open to where Arthus could enter. Just as Arthus entered the gate, Jake's eyes flew open. He grabbed Emon's shirt. His eyes were crazed and full of pure fear.

"Have you seen the shadows, there everywhere, beware the Darkness is here. They killed everyone. I, I hid and heard them being slaughtered I don't know what they were, but they came from the shadows and, and," said Jake. Then he fell back. It took Emon a moment to gather himself and yell for the others. Arthus didn't hear Emon or Jake's words. He had entered the throne room, and it took only a moment for the stench to reach his nose. He doubled over and threw up, the room was a sight of pure horror. The dead body's laid everywhere, some half-eaten and one at the far end just before the throne was a woman body spiked into the ground by a large metal rode had been driven through her open mouth, and the way through pinning her as if she was standing her clothing had been torn away. Her front had been partly eaten away. There was another spear with a severed head put on it and one body pinned that had no head whatsoever. Angel Wing was burning white light. Arthus almost couldn't recognize or realize as it was such carnage Arthus that had never seen before. At the far end, the light was shining down a massive hole. There at its base, was a crater. Arthus walked over and looked down. A gigantic black ball about eight feet around it was completely black, and it had a glossy shine to it. Arthus looked down to Angel Wing. It was almost blinding the way it was glowing.

"Arthus, Jake awoke for a sec. You need to come here," said Zeck, Arthus turned. Zeck had just walked in and was having the same reaction by the look on his friend's face.

"Arthus what, we need to go whatever can do this I don't know what to say we need to get Jake to a healer and report what we found here," said Zeck.

"Your right. Sorry I have never seen anything so evil in my life. I want to tend to the dead, but your right Jake comes first, and we need every Silver Thorn Knight here figuring out what could have killed all these people," said Arthus.

"Front-line, this is Arthus. Can you read me," said Arthus. But only static and someone tried to reach back, but they were too far down.

"Zoey, can you read me," asked Arthus.

"I can, but you're coming in broken," said Zoey.

"Contact Front-line let them know we need e-vac and to bring as many Silver Thorn Warriors and even alert the Angels. As many as possible get here. One man is in serious condition, and the others here have all been killed. Let them know we need back up immediately. Let them know we found some unknown pure black metal object where the meteor had crashed," reported Arthus.

"All are dead; I mean, yes, of course, I relay the message," said Zoey.

"Zeck can you carry Jake, the rest of us let's move it. We need to get to the valley and hope we get out before whatever attacked Jake's team realizes we are here," said Arthus. The others pointed to Angel Wing.

"Has it ever done that before," asked Jade?

"No, but it feels like it's warning me of something very evil nearby. We need to go and fast," said Arthus. He looked back at the throne room and noticed that the light was fading over the hole above the black object. Then he heard a loud hissing sound, and fog of pure darkness flowed out of the crater and out stepped a creature Arthus had never seen. One from the deepest darkest nightmares. It was tall and lengthy. It had one large red and yellow eye on top of its pointy head, a largemouth of pointed teeth, and large clawed hands behind it whipped a tail like a scorpion with a significant spike at its end. The creature looked Arthus way and almost looked like it smiled. It tossed a severed head through the open door towards them, and an evil crackling hissing noise sounded from the thing. Then it faded into pure black smoke. The fog shoots forth like something living, spreading towards the empty throne door.

"Run all. Run as fast as you can go, Zeck, you in the lead go," yelled Arthus. He lifted Angel Wing, which light forced the fog like black smoke to back off some, and they ran faster than they had ever run before. A creature's face appeared out of the mist, and Jade shot an arrow into its eye. The beast screamed an ear-piercing cry and faded back. They kept running past the forges. At this point, Arthus wished Dwarvens didn't make their fort so darn hard to go up floors. But in less than thirty minutes, they reached the inner gate and ran through. Arthus and Emon, slammed the gate closed, and bolted back following their friend's fog rose from the sides of the bridge and the red glow below from the lava faded. The darkness spread forth all around the friends. One creature came along and slashed its long deadly claws towards Zeck, who yelled out in pain as it cut the big man across his shoulder opposite of where he held Jake. Zeck spun and brought his halberd across, taking the creature's head clean off. Then Zeck kept running. Blood was pouring from the cut across his shoulder, but the big guy refused to stop and was first through the gate into the light of day.

477

Emon followed through, tossing one of his larger explosives towards the bridge behind Arthus. Which went off, and Arthus, who was only feet away, was thrown to his stomach, but Arthus was fast. He rolled over and got to his knees fast. An arrow flew right past the right side of his face and took another of the creatures in its eye. But before Arthus could fully get back to running, another beast, one larger than most, leaped up over Arthus. Its arms spread wide, its many fanged jaws spread to bite Arthus head off. But Arthus brought Angel Wing up in spear form and drove the divine weapon through the creature's chest. The beast looked shocked and screamed and exploded in a white light, which caused the darkness all around them to be pushed back. Creatures stopped attacking and stepped back. Fear could be seen in their face.

"Come on," yelled Jade, who was standing at the entrance. She fired a few more arrows and ran out Arthus. Right on her heels. They didn't stop there. They ran on towards the area where Zoey and Asher waited. Zeck had already reached them and was being treated by Zoey while Asher was trying to heal Jake. Behind them, the darkness shot forth, spreading out then up across the face of the mountain. Then it started to spread out over the bridge. Soon the black fog faded, and hundreds of the black creatures were now visible across the bridge and over the side of the mountain. They had stopped their advance at the end of the bridge. They gathered like a wave of death before Arthus and his friends.

"Zoey tell me you reached someone on Front-line," asked Arthus?

"Yes, they said to hold on. They are sending in everyone free and able," said Zoey.

"Good, I hope they get here soon," said Arthus. Unlike the others, a massive creature, this one large red-skinned giant, appeared out of the fog and marched forth toward the front line of the beasts. This giant black-armored creature was twenty feet tall, had back-rigged spiked armor, and carried a massive spiked mace. The beast came to the front of the line and lifted his enormous mace and roared the wave came forth.

"Be ready. Here they come. Zeck, Emon, and I take front jade, get back into a tree, and use the height to try and take out as many as you can. Jade and Asher, you have healing and our flanks," commanded Arthus. Emon grabbed up his shield and hammer, and Arthus turned

Angel Wing into a long sword and shield. Both, glowed with a burning white light. Zeck took up just behind Arthus and willed his large halberd to flames. The darkness hit, but the friends stood firm, Arthus and Emon keeping the front safe with their shields and Zeck hacking and killing creatures with every slash. Any creature who hit Arthus's shield was repulsed several feet then shot dead with a well-placed arrow. Vines shoot forth, catching and spearing creatures all around Zoey's side of the group. The friends fought with everything they had, and what felt like hours were only minutes of the growling, eternal fight. Then there was a roar like none had heard yet, and a massive silver Yaule and several other smaller ones came running through the Jungle. The large one leaped far over the party and headlong into the giant. One slash from its large clawed paw took the face and head of the giant. The other Yaule crashed into the creature's claws on both sides, raking. But with even this large group of Yaule, Arthus knew thousands outnumbered them. Then he heard the sizeable Yaule voice once again in his thoughts.

"I sorry young prince, if I had known so many Demons had gotten onto Creed, I would have warned you and sent word to Thureos. But don't be afraid. These Demons feed on fear and suffering," said Matron.

But as the night wore on, even the large, powerful Yaule mother was pushed back and showed signs of fatigue. It was almost night now. The sun was already falling fast, and in the darkness of the night, Arthus knew these Demons would have far more advantage. Another large red giant appeared and brought its mace down over Zeck, but Zeck was no small thing, yes, the giants were big, but the thing was surprised when Zeck enhanced his strength matched the power of the blow with an upraised arm. Zeck then slammed his halberd into the giant's left knee to bring the thing down, and with one final slash, he split the large Demon head in two. They fought on Demon bodies lay all around the group by the hundreds. But still no sign of ending. They were losing hope, but a white light exploded into the air above the valley. Demons died by the hundreds where ever the light touched, and before them in full armor hovering just over the battlefield was Archangel Michael. His six white wings spread out and his golden-white armor shining in the dark. Next to him, Thureos in full armor stood as he flew towards the group.

479

"Well fought all, sorry it took us so long. We just got word from Front-line that something terrible happened on Creed and that's when Michael felt the evil of these Demons on Malon. We quickly informed the Front-line to allow us to deal with this threat. So here we are, anyone hurt," said Thureos. Before Arthus could answer, Michael raised a hand, and above them, all, a ball of such pure light appeared this caused all the darkness in a ten-mile radius to burn away. All Demons inside that range were turned to ash.

"Jake here has lost an arm and probably his mind for what he's been through. Sorry to say all of his team was killed in the fort. The rest of us are tired and bruised but no serious injuries, However the Yaule have suffered here greatly." reported Arthus.

"You all done well to stay alive for so long, and I am proud of you, Arthus today you have seen things beyond evil, and I know it pained your heart dearly, but your all safe. We shall leave this fight to Michael for his duty is to slay Demons, so you get a rare sight and see Michael at his full glory and power," said Thureos. They all stood and watched, and Michael surveyed the battlefield then pulled forth a sword, and with one swipe of the blade, a line of pure white light shot forth across the mountain face, and all the Demons on it were destroyed. They turned to ash, and the entire mountain face was just gone.

"Do not fret! Arthus did you see the Dark craft," asked Michael?

"It's at the fourth floor down in the throne room. At that side of the mountain there a big hole where the thing landed," said Arthus pointing towards an area on the mountain.

"Thank you. After I destroy their Dark vessel, they should not be able to spawn more of their evil kin," said Michael, then flew off towards the mountain and just flew into the hole. Soon, a massive light poured out of every hole and gate in the mountain, and the ground shook then silence. A couple of minutes later, Michael came through the gate and flew towards them. I have destroyed the Demon ship and put all the bodies left by their evil deeds to rest. Then I cleared all Demons from the fort. As far as I can tell, that is all of them. I am genuinely sorry for what you had to see. If my warriors didn't fail you a couple of nights ago and destroyed that ship long before it came here, you would never had to witness such evil. Now it is time I take you all back to Front-line where you can rest, and my healers will tend to Jake here. I hope we can heal the man's mind and soul after surviving such horrors. My healers will help Zeck too. Gather your things; we leave as soon as able," said Michael and walked over to the edge of the valley and looked on in sadness. Soon as they gathered their gear and Jake's team gear that was found, they all gathered. Michael opened a portal, and soon the group walked from the battlefield to a large room on Front-line.

Back on Creed on the top of the mountain, hidden behind some giant boulders, a Dark figure stepped out of its hiding place. Unlike the Demons before, this man was a large man, dressed all in black armor. And, he wore a cape and cowl covering his head. "So... Michael stepped in. That's too bad. I thought my Demons had a chance this time to make a good stronghold outside our galaxy, but it seems like we have more than just the Angels to worry about. It appears like God has created a powerful foe for us to fight. If I mistook, that one held Angel Wing, a divine weapon and one of Michael's favorite, so not only are they powerful, they can wield weapons that can utterly destroy our Demons. My master Belphegor would be interested indeed. The man walked over to the side of the mountain on a large stone wall, and with a one-pointed armored finger, started to carve out symbols that glowed a dark green, and soon a portal of pure Darkness opened, and the man walked through.

Arthus stood before William, Thureos, Michael, and other Archangels. He told them of all that happened on Creed. The Archangels apologized for failing to stop the ship before it reached the moon and for the loss of so many. Michael then stood and walked before all.

"I'm sorry to relate this to you after such a tragedy, but in under a decade from now, we, the Angels of heaven, will no longer be around to help guide and fight with you. For God has decided after the betrayal of several of my kin on a world far from here called Eden. That it's time to separate the physical and spiritual realms once and for all, let me explain what has happened to Eden. Eden is God's garden or was supposed to be. He created a race of beings God called, man or Humans. This race fell and was moved to another world planet called earth. Even though they fell, they still had promise. But, over time they have betrayed God repeatedly. Now the world has fallen to worshiping some of my kin who fell to evil desires. These Angels went to this world and joined with some of their female humans creating half Angel half-humans they call themselves Nephilim. They are mortal humans but with the powers far beyond them, and some of the stronger ones killed their fallen Angel - Demon fathers and took upon themselves the titles of demagogues and have forced many humans to worship them as if they were gods. I have slain a few of them myself. One called himself Zeus, and another Odin. Like a plague, these half beings have caused God to become enraged at both the fallen Angel - Demons and humans, so God will flood the entire planet in less than ten years, killing all life. Once done, God will use his power to separate the physical plane from the spiritual one once and for all no longer will we Angels be able to stand with the physical realm and help fight against the creatures the Darkness has already turned into the Demons you saw today. Those you saw were mostly shadow Demons creatures born out of Darkness to serve in whatever ways it wishes them to. This is why you were created and raised to become the shield for all life here in the physical realms. You, who have the power of Angels and the wisdom to use it for good, but are still a part of this realm will be charged with building ships. We will show you how to create them before we go, and once built, you will go forth and drive the Darkness and its forces out of every world planet back into the actual Hellcore void, and then keep them from escaping the Hellcore void. You are not to enter into Hellcore void itself. God has even told his faithful Archangels and Angels that they are not to enter the Hellcore void. Before Son warned us of this, several very righteously zealous faithful angels tried to take the fight into the Hellcore viud. None of them returned! There have been times that during the battles between the Dark Forces of Hellcore and the faithful Archangels and faithful Angels that some of God's faithful Angels have went too far and did not strictly adhere to Son's warnings. We have unfortunately lost each of those brothers to the Darkness. Everything that goes into Hellcore void turns Dark and only Darkness tries to escape from Hellcore void. Leave the fight that only God our Heavenly father can fight, to God our Heavenly Father! God is setting in motion a plan to seal the Darkness once and for all behind a powerful barrier. I don't yet have the details of that barrier, but I know once it is built God will fill it with His LIGHT. And then that barrier will last till the end of time itself. Until then, you and your people Thureos will be charged with keeping the Dark armies in the galaxy surrounding the Hellcore void no matter the cost. Between now and when that permanent barrier is set in place, then your people will be needed to go clean up the rest of the world planets from the influences of the Nagas, Hydra, and Quetzalcoatl. Also the world planets where the Succubus have contaminated. Only after the Myriasphere is cleaned and all these spawns of Darkness and their Demons are eliminated, will you all be allowed to go forth into all galaxies to see all worlds and life that you strove so hard to protect. God has said all but the galaxy where Eden and earth are located will be open to you. Eden remains sealed from entry for God has plans for that planet and its people if they ever deem worthy in the end to receive God's forgiveness and mercy, which I don't think they will. But I am not God; I follow my orders and allow him to decide who is worthy and who isn't. The world planet earth is specifically someplace where Son is going to go someday to be the LIGHT to that world. He has said that he won't remain there long, but his WORDS and influence will remain until the end of time. That is all I have for you, Thureos. I know you have questions. Let us go, and I fill you in on what I can also send for Maddy and other crafters, for they will be filled in on how to build the ships you need to transport your armies into the worlds that have been contaminated outside of the Hellcore void." said Michael. With that, they were all dismissed. Arthus walked the station halls lost in thought. He sat down at a bench with the best view of Malon and stared out at his home. He didn't even notice when Jade walked in and sat beside him until she put her head on his shoulder. Her cheeks were wet with tears; she had been crying.

"I'm sorry; they just told us that Jake's arm is forever lost, and his mind is completely broken. They will do all they can to try and help him, but it may have really been a mercy to have allowed him to die back there. I had never seen so much evil, and I heard that the Angels have plans to send us out to fight against armies just like what we just faced. I am scared and not sure we will be ready for that time," said Jade.

"I know, I feel the same way. I have never seen so much evil that we faced down there, but we will be ready for I believe that God will not leave us helpless and because all of life in the physical realms depend on us. They stared out the windows at Malon. Soon Jade put her head on Arthus's shoulder again and grabbed his hand in hers. After several minutes they just sat in the comfort of each other.

"Jade... I don't know what is going to happen in the future, but you know how much I love you. Your parent will have our wedding rea..." said Arthus. Before he could finish, Jade put a finger to his lips then kissed him. They sat there in each other's embrace.

"I was so happy almost four hundred and fifty five years ago, when you finally told me you loved me, and asked me to marry you, and we kissed. Our plans for the wedding were supposed to be after graduation from the Academy, but then we all got into the Silver Thorns Training, And, then yesterday, down there on Creed, I thought if we died down there, I was going to regret not getting the chance to get to our wedding night and enjoy all that it entails. I know I am being a little selfish, when I see and hear everything that Michael said, knowing we will be going off to be God's Shield in the frontlines of the battle, over and over and over again. But, Arthus, I want our wedding night quick! I want to tell my parents the wedding is on. Are you ready for that? I want everything about you at least once before the end," said Jade crying and giggling.

Arthus and Jade did not notice that Zeck and Zoey had quietly walked up to them.

"Well, Arthus...Are you ready for that? Zeck said, while punching him in the arm. You still haven't told me, or Emon, or Asher, who you were making your best man. And Jade, hasn't said who was going to be her Bridesmaid either, am I right, or am I right? Zoey?

Zoey, just raised her eyes and said, "That be me. As I got some great plans for her bridal shower, which includes some strong Dwarven brews and lots of dancin! I know I'm an Ignole, but I truly like them strong Dwarven brews and dancing! But Arthus best quit putting it off. He best bust a move quick! Otherwise, I will call forth some roots and tie him up onto to the back of Fang so he can drag him to the wedding! Both Fang and me are getting mighty tired of hearing Jade saying how she can't keep waiting forever for her wedding night. She wants Arthus something awful!

Jade sat there with a bright red face and a huge smile.

Arthus grabbed her and kissed her again, then he turned to Zeck and said, three best men, and were having a wedding, quick! Well as quick as High King Thureos will allow anyway. And, of course I'll send a message to my grandfather today.

After Arthus sent the message about he and Jade wanting to get married as soon as they graduated from the Silver Thorns to High King Thureos, his grandfather responded with one sentence:

"Patience Arthus and Jade as you are all getting assignments which will take all your attentions for the next five years of your time."

He immediately showed Jade the message, and she said, well what is five more years compared to what we have already waited. But, you best kiss me and hug me every chance you get for this next five years!

Epilogue
What the future holds

Arthus and Jade became closer and closer over the last five years since that horrible night they all graduated to full-blown Silver Knights being trained, and Soon Arthus had become one of the top commanders with Zeck. Jade became head of the Silver Knights scouts, and Emon became head of the Knights Artillery unit, which he helped create with his explosives. They made massive cannons that would fire large projectiles and other devices to help the knights on the battlefield.

Fang was crazy busy building up Clan Yaule Fang, and almost all his children had incredible Life-energy abilities. He did agree to meet with the Yaule queen to discuss helping him to continue to strengthen his Clan and to discuss much stronger mutual help to the Silver Nights. Thanks to avenging her children, the Yaule Queen wanted to have more of her Yaules involved with the Silver Knights too. Many of the young adult Clan Fang Yaules began to train at the Malon Academy. Other Yaules that could not pass certain Life-energy elemental abilities tests, and that were not able to use telepathic abilities either joined the Urial Guard patrols or Clan Arial as regular mounts. Only when they showed certain battle competencies they were also trained to be mounts and companions for the Silver Thorn Knights and Scouts on the battlefield. One young Yaule and one of the Matron's personal daughters, who had exceptional Life-energy elemental abilities and telepathic abilities, became very close friends with Jade. She is named Bella. Because of the influx of more Yaules from Creed and all the added lifespan of the Yaules born from Fang, it wasn't long, when many scouts had a Yaule companion, and then units of Yaule cavalry were born. Some serious armor was crafted to fit the large cats, and they looked and really were terrifying on the battlefield.

Arthus had gone back into training with Thureos to try and master even more of the traits of Angel Wing. He also took private music lessons with one of the Angel bards to try and build his skills within the Life-energy power of music.

Arthus and Jade were soon married. Their ceremony was held at the High Kings Palace in the throne room the entirety of Malon watched on in celebration, for it was a rare occasion for a Prince to marry his true love. Jade's mother and father laughed that their children hid behind their legs so long ago and how Jade had teased Arthus on being such a shut-in. Grag laughed and drank beside High King Thureos. It had been a great night. Arthus awoke that night and walked to the outer patio outside their bedroom, as now Jade has joined him in his room. He enjoyed the training patio, where he spent many of his days being beaten over and over again by his grandfather. From this high up level in and on First God's Tree as he looked out to the south, far in the distance on clear days, he could see the three large spaceships being built following the guidelines of the Archangels. Very quickly his people would be a space-traveling people and that was without having an Angel portal. Arthus thought about how those were always a way faster way to travel. Their mission would begin at first with three massive ships to scout out the galaxy surrounding the Hellcore void and then set up a forward base. Then, a campaign to drive all the darkness back into the Hellcore Void would start in full. Arthus was shirtless, standing just in his night pants, very comfy cotton pants. The wind was blowing a relaxed, warm breeze. It felt good to stand out and enjoy the night air, for they had been trapped on Frontline and Creed far too long.

Suddenly he felt Jade's hands run across his chest. She stood behind him, holding him close. She wore just a silk nightshirt that revealed far more than hiding, and the beauty of her body was beyond anything he had imagined in his life. Her bright green eyes stared into his, and her long red hair blew behind her in the wind. He lifted her in his arms and kissed her, hugging her close. He carried her back to the bedroom, where he would show her a night of love and passion.

The Redwood tree nymph Timothy already knew he was not to come for seven days and seven nights after the wedding.

Far away in the Hellcore void on a Dead Star, upon Throne made of broken bones and black stone sat an unmoving figure. He wore a helmet that looked like a human skull with a black crown on his head. He was enormous and powerful looking. Before him was a long table set. At their places sat the Demon Princes and Princess, all but one. Which made the man on the throne clinch his fist.

"That lazy Belphegor, Prince of Sloth again failed to appear when summoned. A few years ago, I sent a Dark Death Knight, Dark lord Belgor, into work with the Prince of Sloth. Now, I will have the Dark portal of Dark lord Belgor forcibly rerouted to this very Throne Room chamber of Hellcore!" Yelled Satan as he cast a Dark Magic Spell towards an open portal at the end of the long table.

Instantly, The Dark Knight, known as Dark lord Belgor, who really is secretly one of the strongest Dark Knights of the Armies of Darkness under Zobald's control, even though he is working in the employ of Belphegor, stepped through the portal and entered the Dark Hellcore Throne Room. He was once a mighty enemy of Satan and his Hellcore Princes and Princess, and a well beloved hero to his world. But then his world, Mortarion, was conquered by Zobald the Prince of Decay. Zobald brought the death of his world named Mortarion, by using his dark powers to make the entire planet into a massive graveyard filled with nasty creatures, none more terrifying is Belgor, who fell into Darkness' Trap trying to save Mortarion and slay Zobald. He was then told by Zobald that he was being promoted, even though he had failed to save Mortarion. His promotion was also a deception, for he was then Demon-Mind-Bonded and turned into a Dark Death Knight. After much training in the Dark Magic Arts, was then given the diminutive title of Demon lord, though not in fact a Demon. Demon lord Belgor was later given by Satan to Belphegor, Prince of gluttony and sloth.

Satan said, "I only gave Belphegor my Demon lord Belgor, because he is the laziest and weakest of all my Demon Princes, if he can even really call himself that, for this punier Demon lord Belgor has more power and common sense than the fat creature Belphegor, who is so lazy, sitting on his throne, thinking he is too good to come when his Master called."

Upon entering the Hellcore Throne Room and seeing Satan and all the Princes and Princess seated at the table, he went to his knees and bowed deeply.

"How may I serve you my King of Darkness? Asked Belgor.

Satan yelled, "That lazy fool Belphegor has ignored my demand that he come before me and sit as we plan our next strategies. Why? What could possibly have kept his lazy butt in his throne on Sloth?"

Demon lord Belgor said, "I don't know why he is not here, as I took a massive amount of Belphegor's forces and was attempting to set up a forward command at the Forest Moon Creed past the Dead-Zone. Prince Zobald secretly charged me with this mission, because he knew Belphegor was too lazy to even try to train his own Demon warriors and Demon-Bonded Minions, much less take them on any mission past the Dead Zone."

And was that mission successful Demon lord Belgor?" Yelled Prince Zobald, who then asked sternly, "Or, did you fail our King of Darkness again?"

"We had sent your secret asteroid looking ship to crash into the Ancient Dwarven Throne Room and immediately shredded a small group of warriors who were taken completely by surprise. We even spread out and attacked a bunch of giant cat like creatures too. We were preparing to deploy the second phase, when our ship was discovered by another small group of warriors, one of which I know was carrying Angel Wing. But these were no Archangels or Angels, and in fact it was a small force of only six individuals. Two were pure blood Dwarvens, Two were Females, but from what races we do not know. The other two were male warriors, also from what races we do not know. All were quite skilled. The two big men more than the others as the one was quite tall and incredibly strong. The other shorter, and appeared like he might be a half-breed between the two races that the females were. And, it was he that was the one, the shorter half-breed one, who wielded Angel Wing and he was quite skilled in its use. He had killed many of Belphegor's Demons with that Angel Wing. While the others only killed a few.

We finally had them all surrounded when Michael the Archangel and another large man showed up with a force of Heaven's Angels. Michael the Archangel wiped out what was not already killed by the six warriors who fought as one for many hours and just barely survived, but only due to Michael's showing up. There are a lot of those large cat creatures, led by a ghostly looking female of their kind, who jumped into the battle also when Michael showed up. I was stationed way back up on the mountain behind some giant boulders overlooking the battle. They did not see me when they had left the battle scene. That is why I was able to open a Dark portal and escape. I was on my way to Sloth to report the losses of so many to Belphegor, when my Dark Portal was rerouted to your throne room. Though your plan Prince Zobald to create a foothold past the Dead Zone failed, I am sure that this Intelligence Report was well worth my Dark life to bring it back here. As you know, my life is yours to take at any time, my King of Darkness, my Demon Princes, and Demon Princess," said Demon lord Belgor

"Losing a massive force to the Archangel Michael is always a risk, but to discover some new race of beings that have the power to stand toe-tote with my armies worries me greatly," said Satan, King of Darkness, who had made himself a lord over all of the Demon Princes and Demon Princess and all of their fallen Demons. He then commands, "I must find a way to see what was going on, so bring me my Dark Crystal!"

Instantly a Demon-Mind-Bonded minion stood bowing his head and holding the Dark Crystal in front of Satan's Throne.

Dark flames shot of Satan's eyes and instantly incinerated the head off of this Demon-Mind-Bonded minion. As he fell bleeding from his neck, the Dark crystal absorbed what was left of his life-energies and began to glow a dark glow and floated in the air in front of Satan.

What once was Lucifer, now Satan, King of Darkness, Serpent King, Master of Hellcore, whose eyes were set ablaze with a Dark Fire, his real physical body cracked and creaking, for he rarely moved his physical form, cast Dark magic, stared into a giant Dark crystal that floated in front of his throne. His Dark and twisted mind peered through the Dark crystal, he could see through all space. He tried to focus on the world just out side the deadzone but it was looking into the light of a sun he quikly looked away and allowed the dark crystal to go dark. In spite of the pain and anguish he felt by moving his physical form, his anger was boiling, so he stood and turned his face to Belgor and said, "Go and fetch your master, Belphegor. Tell him if he isn't in my presence before this Dark night is out, I will make sure he starves in one of my deep dungeons, do you understand, little lord," said Satan.

"Yes, my King of Darkness, I will inform my Prince right away," said Belgor, who then ran to the Dark portal, stepping through.

"Satan, King of Darkness, and Master of all Hellcore void and the galaxy surrounding it, why do we have to have that waste of space, Belphegor in our presence anyways? He's so lazy, and smelly, and is just a nasty disgusting fat sight. He never brings anything of monetary value to Hellcore," said Mammon.

"Yes, I know, yet he continues to have his vile purposes within my grand plan. We will wait for his reports. I fear God is going to bring new enemies into our realm. God is planning something! Of which, I do not know, but I feel we won't enjoy it if He succeeds," said Satan as he again sat down upon his Dark throne, staring through his floating Dark crystal and waited for his last Prince to arrive. Though knowing Sloth it take the fat worm to reach them he reached down and lifted a large cup made from the scull of some demon who thought it could take his seat from under him. It was filled with a rich red wine he drank from it smiled even if this army is powerful, his armys have been getting restless this would be a grand way to give them some enjoyment at the least. He didn't truly care for any of his demons or well anything but his revenge so no matter how many fell he would just make more as his darkness spread through out all the Myriasphere. He sat back and smiled yes soon very soon.

Author Bio
Main Author
Daniel Cunningham

Daniel Cunningham was born in 1987. He grew up as a pastors kid and a major fan of Fantasy and Scifi. He loved Everything from comic book heroes like Spider-man, and novels such as the Lord of the Rings, to shows like Star gate. He learned much and had a very active mind but was a total geek. When he graduated High School in 2006 he Joined the United States Marine Corps at 19 years of age that same year. He became a Marine Corps grunt, a 0311 Rifleman. He served in the Iraq and Afghanistan wars. After 4 years he left active duty to go to college were he kept switching his major trying to find what best fit him after six years of college Daniel decided enough was enough left and went into the MO southern State University police academy after graduating though and realizing he wouldn't make a good cop he took a Job for a security firm and during that time other creatives inspired him to write his book series after he and others watched as every franchise they once loved betrayed there fan base or was bought out by some corporation then turned against what the original creator wanted. So decided it was time a new franchise to be born one that couldn't be bought or twisted by others and him powerless to do anything but voice his opinions. Now he hopes that all who read and love this new universe that Daniel has put together for most of his life and now is shared with you all and hopes it brings joy like so many fantasy books and story's had brought him over the years. Now Daniel runs his small YouTube channel called The Myriasphere Origins while working on his book series and takes care of his five kids who he hopes will also love his story's and hopes one day to help bring other small creators to the forefront to inspire more and more story's that will also bring joy to people and a chance to escape all life problems and dive into worlds of wonder and amazement.

Editor's

Nathan Cunningham
Chuck Cunningham
Cover Artist
the talented
Vladyslava Ostapenko
and NyRiam

CPSIA information can be obtained
at www.ICGtesting.com
Printed in the USA
JSHW031439061122
32623JS00001BA/6

9 798885 673662